PENGUIN  CLASSICS

THE STORY OF THE STONE
VOLUME 2

ADVISORY EDITOR: BETTY RADICE

CAO XUEQIN (1715?–63) was born into a family which for three generations held the office of Commissioner of Imperial Textiles in Nanking, a
family so wealthy that they were able to entertain the Emperor Kangxi
four times. But calamity overtook them and their property was confis-
cated. Cao Xueqin was living in poverty near Peking when he wrote his
famous novel *The Story of the Stone* (also known as *The Dream of the Red
Chamber*), of which this is the second volume. The four other volumes,
The Golden Days, *The Warning Voice*, *The Debt of Tears* and *The Dreamer
Wakes*, are also published in the Penguin Classics.

DAVID HAWKES was Professor of Chinese at Oxford University from
1959 to 1971 and a Research Fellow of All Souls College, from 1973 to
1983. He now lives in retirement in Wales.

THE STORY
OF THE STONE

A CHINESE NOVEL BY
CAO XUEQIN
IN FIVE VOLUMES

*

VOLUME 2
'THE CRAB-FLOWER CLUB'

*

TRANSLATED BY
DAVID HAWKES

PENGUIN BOOKS

PENGUIN BOOKS

Published by the Penguin Group
Penguin Books Ltd, 80 Strand, London WC2R 0RL, England
Penguin Group (USA) Inc., 375 Hudson Street, New York, New York 10014, USA
Penguin Group (Canada), 90 Eglinton Avenue East, Suite 700, Toronto, Ontario, Canada M4P 2Y3
(a division of Pearson Penguin Canada Inc.)
Penguin Ireland, 25 St Stephen's Green, Dublin 2, Ireland
(a division of Penguin Books Ltd)
Penguin Group (Australia), 250 Camberwell Road,
Camberwell, Victoria 3124, Australia (a division of Pearson Australia Group Pty Ltd)
Penguin Books India Pvt Ltd, 11 Community Centre,
Panchsheel Park, New Delhi – 110 017, India
Penguin Group (NZ), cnr Airborne and Rosedale Roads, Albany,
Auckland 1310, New Zealand (a division of Pearson New Zealand Ltd)
Penguin Books (South Africa) (Pty) Ltd, 24 Sturdee Avenue,
Rosebank, Johannesburg 2196, South Africa

Penguin Books Ltd, Registered Offices: 80 Strand, London WC2R 0RL, England

www.penguin.com

This translation first published 1977
27

Copyright © David Hawkes, 1977
All rights reserved

Printed in Great Britain by Antony Rowe Ltd, Chippenham, Wiltshire

ISBN: 978-0-14-044326-4

IN MEMORIAM

R. C. Z.

CONTENTS

8 CONTENTS

NOTE ON SPELLING

CHINESE proper names in this book are spelled in accordance with a system invented by the Chinese and used internationally, which is known by its Chinese name of *Pinyin*. A full explanation of this system will be found overleaf, but for the benefit of readers who find systems of spelling and pronunciation tedious and hard to follow a short list is given below of those letters whose Pinyin values are quite different from the sounds they normally represent in English, together with their approximate English equivalents. Mastery of this short list should ensure that names, even if mispronounced, are no longer unpronounceable.

$$c = ts$$
$$q = ch$$
$$x = sh$$
$$z = dz$$
$$zh = j$$

CHINESE SYLLABLES

The syllables of Chinese are made up of one or more of the following elements:

   1. an initial consonant (b.c.ch.d.f.g.h.j.k.l.n.m.p.q.r.s.sh.t.w.x.y. z.zh)

   2. a semivowel (i or u)

   3. an open vowel (a.e.i.o.u.ü), *or*

a closed vowel (an.ang.en.eng.in.ing.ong.un), *or*

a diphthong (ai.ao.ei.ou)

The combinations found are:

   3 on its own (e.g. *e, an, ai*)

   1 + 3 (e.g. *ba, xing, hao*)

   1 + 2 + 3 (e.g. *xue, qiang, biao*)

INITIAL CONSONANTS

Apart from c = *ts* and z = *dz* and r, which is the Southern English *r* with a slight buzz added, the only initial consonants likely to give an English speaker much trouble are the two groups

        j q x   and   zh ch sh

Both groups sound somewhat like English *j ch sh*; but whereas j q x are articulated much farther *forward* in the mouth than our *j ch sh*, the sounds zh ch sh are made in a 'retroflexed' position much farther *back*. This means that to our ears j sounds halfway between our *j* and *dz*, q halfway between our *ch* and *ts*, and x halfway between our *sh* and *s*; whilst zh ch sh sound somewhat as *jr, chr, shr* would do if all three combinations and not only the last one were found in English.

SEMIVOWELS

The semivowel i 'palatalizes' the preceding consonant: i.e. it makes a *y* sound after it like the *i* in *onion* (e.g. Jia Lian)

The semivowel u 'labializes' the preceding consonant: i.e. it makes a *w* sound after it, like the *u* in *assuages* (e.g. Ning-guo)

VOWELS AND DIPHTHONGS

i. Open Vowels

a   is a long *ah* like *a* in *father* (e.g. Jia)

e   on its own or after any consonant other than y is like the sound in French *œuf* or the *er, ir, ur* sound of Southern English (e.g. Gao E, Jia She)

e   after y or a semivowel is like the *e* of *egg* (e.g. Qin Bang-ye, Xue Pan)

i   after b.d.j.l.m.n.p.q.t.x.y is the long Italian *i* or English *ee* as in *see* (e.g. Nannie Li)

i   after zh.ch.sh.z.c.s.r. is a strangled sound somewhere between the *u* of *suppose* and a vocalized *r* (e.g. Shi-yin)

i   after semivowel u is pronounced like *ay* in *sway* (e.g. Li Gui)

o   is the *au* of *author* (e.g. Duo)

u   after semivowel i and all consonants except j.q.x.y is pronounced like Italian *u* or English *oo* in *too* (e.g. Bu Gu-xiu)

u   after j.q.x.y and ü after l or n is the narrow French *u* or German *ü*, for which there is no English equivalent (e.g. Bao-yu, Nü-wa)

ii. Closed Vowels

an   after semivowel u or any consonant other than y is like *an* in German *Mann* or *un* in Southern English *fun* (e.g. Yuan-chun, Shan Ping-pen)

an   after y or semivowel i is like *en* in *hen* (e.g. Zhi-yan-zhai, Jia Lian)

ang   whatever it follows, invariably has the long *a* of *father* (e.g. Jia Qiang)

en, eng   the e in these combinations is always a short, neutral sound like *a* in *ago* or the first *e* in *believe* (e.g. Cousin Zhen, Xi-feng)

in, ing   short *i* as in *sin, sing* (e.g. Shi-yin, Lady Xing)

ong   the o is like the short *oo* of Southern English *book* (e.g. Jia Cong)

un   the rule for the closed u is similar to the rule for the open one: after j.q.x.y it is the narrow French *u* of *rue*; after anything else it resembles the short *oo* of *book* (e.g. Jia Yun, Ying-chun)

iii. Diphthongs

ai   like the sound in English *lie, high, mine* (e.g. Dai-yu)

ao   like the sound in *how* or *bough* (e.g. Bao-yu)

ei   like the sound in *day* or *mate* (e.g. Bei-jing)
ou   like the sound in *old* or *bowl* (e.g. Gou-er)

The syllable er is a sound on its own which does not fit into any of the above categories. It sounds somewhat like the word *err* pronounced with a strong English West Country accent, (e.g. Bao Er).

PREFACE

THE twenty-seven chapters of this second volume of *The Story of the Stone* cover a period of less than nine months – 257 days, to be precise – from the twenty-fifth of the fourth month of the year in which Bao-yu and Wang Xi-feng nearly died from the effects of black magic, to the night of the Lantern Festival on the fifteenth of the first month of the following year – a year to the day after the Imperial Concubine's 'visitation' which was described at some length in chapter 18 of the first volume.

Although this second volume is not without its excitements – two suicides and three incapacitating beatings in a matter of months seems a fairly eventful record even for a great Manchu household of the early eighteenth century – it is a picture of the daily routines in the life of this great household that emerges most vividly from its pages. No more, in this volume, are the supernatural overtones which reverberated through volume 1 to be heard: no Fairy Disenchantment here, no Magic Mirror, not even a glimpse of that disreputable but mysterious pair, the mad monk and the crippled Taoist. The narrative of this second volume is firmly grounded in the affairs of this world, and the author himself seems to share the indefatigable preoccupation of his characters with *things*: never have clothes and furnishings and objets d'art been described with such meticulous and loving care as they are in the pages of this volume.

Apart from this interest – in their case aesthetic rather than acquisitive – in material possessions, the preoccupations of the younger characters in this novel are mainly literary ones, and the text abounds in passages containing references to books, plays and poems which to the Western reader, lacking the literary background that Cao Xueqin was able to take for granted in his Chinese contemporaries, might often seem puzzling or incomprehensible. I make no apology for having occasionally amplified the text a little in order to make such passages intelligible. The alternative would have been to explain them in footnotes; and though footnotes are all very well in their place, reading a heavily annotated novel would seem to me rather like trying to play tennis in chains.

But these occasional small amplifications are not the only departures I have made from the available texts. For the benefit of the learned reader I ought perhaps to explain that this translation in effect represents a new edition of my own. For reasons which I shall endeavour to make clear, I do not think it is possible for a modern translator to follow any of the existing versions without deviating from it occasionally.

Owing to the unfinished state in which Cao Xueqin left it, *The Story of the Stone* contains a number of obviously unintentional discrepancies: for example, the fact that the Duke of Rong-guo's name is given as 'Jia Yuan' in chapter 2 but as 'Jia Fa' in chapter 53. A careful examination of the existing texts suggests that much of Gao E's editorial activity was aimed at removing inconsistencies of this sort. Unfortunately his alterations are sometimes misguided and not infrequently have the effect of making the text actually worse. Observing the number of cases in which his editing is demonstrably wrong, well-wishers are apt to advise the translator that he should forget about Gao E altogether and stick to the text of the manuscripts. But since it was in many cases the unsatisfactory state of the manuscripts that prompted Gao E's editorial intervention in the first place, to follow this advice would simply mean abandoning one set of problems for another. Experience has taught me that it is best to treat any divergence of Gao E's text from the manuscripts as a signal to begin looking for the difficulty that prompted the alteration and, having identified it, endeavour, where necessary, to find a solution of one's own.

Let me illustrate this with an example.

There is a passage towards the end of chapter 28 in which Bao-yu calls for a maid to take some things to Dai-yu. The text of this in Gao E's printed edition is as follows:

> Calling Nightingale to him, he said: 'Take these things to your mistress.'

'How strange!' we think when we read this. 'Why should he go to the trouble of calling over Dai-yu's maid Nightingale when he is surrounded by maids of his own? And how rude, to summon her without a by-your-leave to her mistress!'

Now if we turn from the printed text of Gao E's edition to the photographic facsimile of Gao E's manuscript draft which was published in Peking in 1963 we find:

> Calling Nightingale to him, he said: 'Take these
>   your mistress
> things to   ~~Miss Lin~~ .'

'Miss Lin' has been crossed out and 'your mistress' substituted.

Turning now from Gao E's draft to the photographic facsimile of the 'Geng-chen' Red Inkstone manuscript (Peking 1955) we find:

>   Zi-juan
> Calling ~~Zi-xiao~~ to him, he said: 'Take these
> things to Miss Lin.'

'Zi-xiao' has been corrected to 'Zi-juan' (Nightingale) by the alteration of the single character 'xiao', and someone, perhaps the person who made the correction having second thoughts, has later crossed out the 'juan' but put nothing else in its place.

Zi-xiao makes only one other appearance in the 'Geng-chen' text, in a list of maids' names in chapter 27. There, too, the 'xiao' has been crossed out and she has been turned into Nightingale by the substitution of 'juan' for 'xiao'. This time there have been no second thoughts – though, curiously enough, 'Nightingale' in this case is quite *certainly* wrong, because the narrative makes it clear that Nightingale could not at that moment have been in the company of the other maids listed. In Gao E's printed text we find her place in the list taken by the name of one of Bao-yu's maids, Ripple.

If, in the passage at the end of chapter 28, it is in fact Nightingale that Bao-yu is talking to, 'your mistress' rather than 'Miss Lin' would be the way in which he would refer to Dai-yu. In that case Gao E's alteration would be an improvement.

But though correct in his suspicion that something was wrong with the text, Gao E was incorrect in his diagnosis of what it was. In the text(s) he was editing it was 'Nightingale' that was wrong, not 'Miss Lin'. So in altering 'Miss Lin' and leaving 'Nightingale', though acting with the best intentions, he only succeeded in making matters worse.

The mysterious 'Zi-xiao' must belong to a stage in the novel's development in which Cao Xueqin had still not finally settled on the names of some of the maids. Obviously the person intended in both the passages where her name occurs is one of Bao-yu's senior maids: Skybright, Emerald, Musk or Ripple. In translating the passage in chapter 28 I have in fact put 'Ripple'.

If making emendations of this kind is felt to be outside the proper scope of a mere translator, I can only plead my concern for the Western reader, who is surely sufficiently burdened already with the task of trying to remember the novel's hundreds of impossible-sounding names, without being subjected to these vagaries of an unfinished and imperfectly edited text.

There are some discrepancies which no amount of editing could remove and with which it would be dangerous to tamper: for example, Bao-yu's and Bao-chai's repeated assertions in the opening chapters of volume 2, that he and Dai-yu grew up together from infancy and that Bao-chai was a comparative late-comer, clash with the narrative in chapters 3 and 4, in which Bao-chai is shown arriving only days or at the most weeks after Dai-yu.

Admittedly the decision where to draw the line between what may and what may not be emended is a somewhat arbitrary one, and to a textual critic the subjective arguments and rule-of-thumb methods of the translator-editor may seem arrogant and unscientific. But a translator has divided loyalties. He has a duty to his author, a duty to his reader and a duty to the text. The three are by no means identical and are often hard to reconcile.

Perhaps I should not dwell too long on these problems arising from blemishes in the text of the original, when it is all too probable that my translation will be found to contain a large number of blemishes of my own. I must entreat those Chinese friends who honoured my first volume with their attention to point them out to me so that they may be amended in some future edition.

*

In preparing this second instalment of my translation I have been helped by a number of friends, both English and Chinese, with books, information or advice. I am particularly indebted to Dr Glen Dudbridge for a copy of the 1963 photolithographic facsimile of the manuscript which I elsewhere refer to as 'Gao E's draft'. But for his generosity it is unlikely that this invaluable tool would ever have come into my possession.

*

The late Professor Zaehner, to whom this volume is dedicated, said after reading volume 1 that he 'preferred *homo lacrimans* to *homo ridens*'. It is true that a great many tears are shed in this novel, but I hope that those who read this volume will find some laughter in it as well.

DAVID HAWKES

CHAPTER 27

Beauty Perspiring sports with butterflies
by the Raindrop Pavilion
And Beauty Suspiring weeps for fallen blossoms
by the Flowers' Grave

TO CONTINUE OUR STORY,

As Dai-yu stood there weeping, there was a sudden creak of
the courtyard gate and Bao-chai walked out, accompanied by
Bao-yu with Aroma and a bevy of other maids who had come
out to see her off. Dai-yu was on the point of stepping forward
to question Bao-yu, but shrank from embarrassing him in
front of so many people. Instead she slipped back into the
shadows to let Bao-chai pass, emerging only when Bao-yu
and the rest were back inside and the gate was once more
barred. She stood for a while facing it, and shed a few silent
tears; then, realizing that it was pointless to remain standing
there, she turned and went back to her room and began, in a
listless, mechanical manner, to take off her ornaments and prepare herself for the night.

Nightingale and Snowgoose had long since become habitu-
ated to Dai-yu's moody temperament; they were used to her
unaccountable fits of depression, when she would sit, the picture of misery, in gloomy silence broken only by an occasional
gusty sigh, and to her mysterious, perpetual weeping, that was
occasioned by no observable cause. At first they had tried to
reason with her, or, imagining that she must be grieving for
her parents or that she was feeling homesick or had been upset
by some unkindness, they would do their best to comfort
her. But as the months lengthened into years and she still
continued exactly the same as before, they gradually became
accustomed and no longer sought reasons for her behaviour.
That was why they ignored her on this occasion and left her
alone to her misery, remaining where they were in the outer

room and continuing to occupy themselves with their own affairs.

She sat, motionless as a statue, leaning against the back of the bed, her hands clasped about her knees, her eyes full of tears. It had already been dark for some hours when she finally lay down to sleep.

Our story passes over the rest of that night in silence.

*

Next day was the twenty-sixth of the fourth month, the day on which, this year, the festival of Grain in Ear was due to fall. To be precise, the festival's official commencement was on the twenty-sixth day of the fourth month at two o'clock in the afternoon. It has been the custom from time immemorial to make offerings to the flower fairies on this day. For Grain in Ear marks the beginning of summer; it is about this time that the blossom begins to fall; and tradition has it that the flower-spirits, their work now completed, go away on this day and do not return until the following year. The offerings are therefore thought of as a sort of farewell party for the flowers.

This charming custom of 'speeding the fairies' is a special favourite with the fair sex, and in Prospect Garden all the girls were up betimes on this day making little coaches and palanquins out of willow-twigs and flowers and little banners and pennants from scraps of brocade and any other pretty material they could find, which they fastened with threads of coloured silk to the tops of flowering trees and shrubs. Soon every plant and tree was decorated and the whole garden had become a shimmering sea of nodding blossoms and fluttering coloured streamers. Moving about in the midst of it all, the girls in their brilliant summer dresses, beside which the most vivid hues of plant and plumage became faint with envy, added the final touch of brightness to a scene of indescribable gaiety and colour.

All the young people – Bao-chai, Ying-chun, Tan-chun, Xi-chun, Li Wan, Xi-feng and her little girl and Caltrop, and all the maids from all the different apartments – were outside in the Garden enjoying themselves – all, that is, except Dai-yu, whose absence, beginning to be noticed, was first commented on by Ying-chun:

'What's happened to Cousin Lin? Lazy girl! Surely she can't *still* be in bed at this hour?'

Bao-chai volunteered to go and fetch her:

'The rest of you wait here; I'll go and rout her out for you,' she said; and breaking away from the others, she made off in the direction of the Naiad's House.

While she was on her way, she caught sight of Élégante and the eleven other little actresses, evidently on their way to join in the fun. They came up and greeted her, and for a while she stood and chatted with them. As she was leaving them, she turned back and pointed in the direction from which she had just come:

'You'll find the others somewhere over there,' she said. 'I'm on my way to get Miss Lin. I'll join the rest of you presently.'

She continued, by the circuitous route that the garden's contours obliged her to take, on her way to the Naiad's House. Raising her eyes as she approached it, she suddenly became aware that the figure ahead of her just disappearing inside it was Bao-yu. She stopped and lowered her eyes pensively again to the ground.

'Bao-yu and Dai-yu have known each other since they were little,' she reflected. 'They are used to behaving uninhibitedly when they are alone together. They don't seem to care what they say to one another; and one is never quite sure what sort of mood one is going to find them in. And Dai-yu, at the best of times, is always so touchy and suspicious. If I go in now after him, *he* is sure to feel embarrassed and *she* is sure to start imagining things. It would be better to go back without seeing her.'

Her mind made up, she turned round and began to retrace her steps, intending to go back to the other girls; but just at that moment she noticed two enormous turquoise-coloured butterflies a little way ahead of her, each as large as a child's fan, fluttering and dancing on the breeze. She watched them fascinated and thought she would like to play a game with them. Taking a fan from inside her sleeve and holding it outspread in front of her, she followed them off the path and into the grass.

To and fro fluttered the pair of butterflies, sometimes alighting for a moment, but always flying off again before she could reach them. Once they seemed on the point of flying across the little river that flowed through the midst of the garden and Bao-chai had to stalk them with bated breath for fear of startling them out on to the water. By the time she had reached the Raindrop Pavilion she was perspiring freely and her interest in the butterflies was beginning to evaporate. She was about to turn back when she became aware of a low murmur of voices coming from inside the pavilion.

Raindrop Pavilion was built in such a way that it projected into the middle of the pool into which the little watercourse widened out at this point, so that on three of its sides it looked out on to the water. It was surrounded by a verandah, whose railing followed the many angles formed by the bays and projections of the base. In each of its wooden walls there was a large paper-covered casement of elegantly patterned latticework.

Hearing voices inside the pavilion, Bao-chai halted and inclined her ear to listen.

'Are you *sure* this is your handkerchief?' one of the voices was saying. 'If it is, take it; but if it isn't, I must return it to Mr Yun.'

'Of course it's mine,' said the second voice. 'Come on, let me have it!'

'Are you going to give me a reward? I hope I haven't taken all this trouble for nothing.'

'I promised you I would give you a reward, and so I shall. Surely you don't think I was deceiving you?'

'All right, I get a reward for bringing it to you. But what about the person who picked it up? Doesn't *he* get anything?'

'Don't talk nonsense,' said the second voice. 'He's one of the masters. A master picking up something belonging to one of us should give it back as a matter of course. How can there be any question of *rewarding* him?'

'If you don't intend to reward him, what am I supposed to

tell him when I see him? He was most insistent that I wasn't
to give you the handkerchief unless you gave him a reward.'

There was a long pause, after which the second voice replied:

'Oh, all right. Let him have this other handkerchief of mine
then. That will have to do as his reward – But you must swear
a solemn oath not to tell anyone else about this.'

'May my mouth rot and may I die a horrible death if I ever
tell anyone else about this, amen!' said the first voice.

'Goodness!' said the second voice again. 'Here we are talking away, and all the time someone could be creeping up outside and listening to every word we say. We had better open
these casements; then even if anyone outside sees us, they'll
think we are having an ordinary conversation; and *we* shall be
able to see *them* and know in time when to stop.'

Bao-chai, listening outside, gave a start.

'No wonder they say "venery and thievery sharpen the
wits",' she thought. 'If they open those windows and see me
here, they are going to feel terribly embarrassed. And one of
those voices sounds like that proud, peculiar girl Crimson
who works in Bao-yu's room. If a girl like that knows that I
have overheard her doing something she shouldn't be doing,
it will be a case of "the desperate dog will jump a wall, the
desperate man will hazard all": there'll be a great deal of
trouble and *I* shall be involved in it. There isn't time to hide.
I shall have to do as the cicada does when he jumps out of his
skin: give them something to put them off the scent –'

There was a loud creak as the casement yielded. Bao-chai
advanced with deliberately noisy tread.

'Frowner!' she called out gaily. '*I* know where you're hiding.'

Inside the pavilion Crimson and Trinket, who heard her say
this and saw her advancing towards them just as they were
opening the casement, were speechless with amazement; but
Bao-chai ignored their confusion and addressed them genially:

'Have you two got Miss Lin hidden away in there?'

'I haven't *seen* Miss Lin,' said Trinket.

'I saw her just now from the river-bank,' said Bao-chai. 'She was squatting down over here playing with something in the water. I was going to creep up and surprise her, but she spotted me before I could get up to her and disappeared round this corner. Are you *sure* she's not hiding in there?'

She made a point of going inside the pavilion and searching; then, coming out again, she said in a voice loud enough for them to hear:

'If she's not in the pavilion, she must have crept into that grotto. Oh well, if she's not afraid of being bitten by a snake – !'

As she walked away she laughed inwardly at the ease with which she had extricated herself from a difficult situation.

'I think I'm fairly safely out of *that* one,' she thought. 'I wonder what those two will make of it.'

What indeed! Crimson believed every word that Bao-chai had said, and as soon as the latter was at a distance, she seized hold of Trinket in alarm:

'Oh, how terrible! If Miss Lin was squatting there, she must have heard what we said before she went away.'

Her companion was silent.

'Oh dear! What do you think she'll *do*?' said Crimson.

'Well, suppose she *did* hear,' said Trinket, 'it's not *her* back-ache. If we mind our business and she minds hers, there's no reason why anything should come of it.'

'If it were Miss Bao that had heard us, I don't suppose anything *would*,' said Crimson; 'but Miss Lin is so critical and so intolerant. If *she* heard it and it gets about – oh dear!'

But just at that moment Caltrop, Advent, Chess and Scribe were seen approaching the pavilion, and Crimson and Trinket had to drop the subject in a hurry and join in a general conversation. Crimson noticed Xi-feng standing half-way up the rockery above the little grotto, beckoning. Breaking away from the others, she bounded up to her with a smiling face:

'What can I do for you, madam?'

Xi-feng ran an appraising eye over her. A neat, pretty, pleasantly-spoken girl, she decided, and smiled at her graciously:

'I have come here without my maids and need someone to

take a message back to my apartment. I wonder if you are
clever enough to get it right.'

'Tell me the message, madam. If I don't get it right and
make a mess of it, it will be up to you to punish me.'

'Which of the young ladies do you work for?' said Xi-feng.
'I'd better know, so that I can explain to her if she asks for you
while you are doing my errand.'

'I work for Master Bao,' said Crimson.

Xi-feng laughed.

'Ah ha! You work for Master Bao. No wonder. Very well,
then, if he asks for you while you are away, I shall explain. I
want you to go to my apartment and tell Patience that there is
a roll of money under the stand of the Ru-ware dish on the
table in the outside room. There are a hundred and twenty
taels of silver in it to pay the embroiderers with. Tell her that
when Zhang Cai's wife comes for it, she is to weigh it out in
front of her before handing it over. And there's one other
thing. There's a little purse at the head of the bed in my inside
room. I want you to bring it to me.'

'Yes madam,' said Crimson, and hurried off.

Returning shortly afterwards, she found that Xi-feng was
no longer on the rockery; but Chess had just emerged from
the little grotto beneath it and was standing there doing up
her sash. Crimson ran down to speak to her:

'Excuse me, did you see where Mrs Lian went to?'

' 'Fraid I didn't notice,' said Chess.

Crimson looked around her. Bao-chai and Tan-chun were
standing at the edge of the pool looking at the fish. She went
up to them:

'Excuse me, does either of you young ladies happen to
know where Mrs Lian went to just now, please?'

'Try Mrs Zhu's place,' said Tan-chun.

Crimson hurried off in the direction of Sweet-rice Village.
On her way she ran head-on into a party of maids consisting
of Skybright, Mackerel, Emerald, Ripple, Musk, Scribe, Picture and Oriole.

'Here, what are you gadding about like this for?' said Skybright as soon as she saw who it was. 'The flowers want

watering; the birds need feeding; the stove for the tea-water needs seeing to. You've no business to go wandering around outside!'

'Master Bao gave orders yesterday that the flowers were only to be watered every other day,' said Crimson. 'I fed the birds when you were still fast asleep in bed.'

'What about the stove?' said Emerald.

'It isn't my day for the stove,' said Crimson. 'The tea-water today has nothing to do with me.'

'Listen to Miss Pert!' said Mackerel. 'I wouldn't bother about her, if I were you – just leave her to wander about as she pleases.'

'I'm *not* "wandering about", if you really want to know,' said Crimson. 'If you really want to know, Mrs Lian sent me outside to take a message and to fetch something for her.'

She held up the purse for them to see; at which they were silent. But when they had passed each other, Skybright laughed sneeringly:

'You can see why she's so uppity. She's on the climb again. Look at her – all cock-a-hoop because someone's given her a little message to carry! And she probably doesn't even know who it's about. Well, one little message isn't going to get her very far. It's what happens in the long run that counts. Now if she were clever enough to climb her way right out of this Garden and stay there, that would be really something!'

These words were spoken for Crimson to hear, but in such a way that she was unable to answer them. She had to swallow her anger and hurry on to look for Xi-feng.

Xi-feng was in Li Wan's room, as Tan-chun had predicted, and Crimson found the two of them in conversation. She went up to Xi-feng and delivered her message:

'Patience says that she found the silver just after you had gone and took care of it; and she says that when Zhang Cai's wife came for it she did weigh it out in front of her before giving it to her to take away.'

Crimson now produced the purse and handed it to Xi-feng. Then she added:

'Patience told me to tell you that Brightie has just been in to inquire what your instructions were for his visit, and she said that she gave him a message to take based on the things she thought you would want him to say.'

'Oh?' said Xi-feng, amused. 'And what *was* this message "based on the things she thought I would want him to say"?'

'She said he was to tell them: "Our lady hopes your lady is well and she says that the Master is away at present and may not be back for another day or two, but your lady is not to worry; and when the lady from West Lane is better, our lady will come with their lady to see your lady. And our lady says that the lady from West Lane sent someone the other day with a message from the *elder* Lady Wang saying that she hopes our lady is well and will she please see if *our* Lady Wang can let her have a few of her Golden Myriad Macrobiotic Pills; and if she can, will our lady please send someone with them to *her*, because someone will be going from there to the *elder* Lady Wang's in a few days' time and they will be able to take them for her – " '

Crimson was still in full spate when Li Wan interrupted her with a laugh:

'What an extraordinary number of "ladies"! I hope you can understand what it's all about, Feng. I'm sure *I* can't!'

'I'm not surprised,' said Xi-feng. 'There are four or five different households involved in that message.' She smiled graciously at Crimson. 'You're a clever girl, my dear, to have got it all right – not like the simpering little ninnies I usually have to put up with. You have no idea, cousin,' she said, turning to Li Wan again. 'Apart from the one or two girls and one or two older women that I always keep about me, I just dread talking to servants nowadays. They take such an *interminable* time to tell you anything – *so* long-winded! And the airs and graces they give themselves! and the simpering! and the um-ing and ah-ing! If they only knew how it makes me *fume*! Our Patience used to be like that when she first came to me. I used to say to her, "Do you think it makes you seem glamorous, all that affected humming? – like a little gnat!" I had to talk to her several times about it before she would mend her ways.'

Li Wan laughed.

'I suppose if they were all peppercorns like you, it would be all right.'

'This girl's all right,' said Xi-feng. 'Those two messages she gave me just now may not have been very long ones, but you could see how clear-cut her delivery of them was.'

She smiled at Crimson again.

'How would you like to come and work for me and be my god-daughter? With a little grooming from me you could go far.'

Crimson suppressed a giggle.

'Why do you laugh?' said Xi-feng. 'I suppose you think I'm too young to be your god-mother. You're very silly if you think that. You just ask around a bit: there are plenty much older than you who'd give their ears to be my god-daughter. What I'm offering you is a very special favour.'

Crimson smiled.

'I wasn't laughing because of that, madam. I was laughing because you had got the generation wrong. My mother is your god-daughter already. If you made me your god-daughter too, I should be my own mother's sister!'

'Who *is* your mother?' said Xi-feng.

'Do you mean to say that you don't know who this girl is that you've been talking to all this time?' said Li Wan. 'This is Lin Zhi-xiao's daughter.'

Xi-feng registered surprise:

'You mean to tell me that this is the *Lins'* daughter?' She laughed. '*That* couple of old sticks? I can never get a peep out of either of them. I've always maintained that Lin Zhi-xiao and his wife were the perfect match: one *hears* nothing and the other *says* nothing. Well! To think they should have produced a bright little thing like this between them! – How old are you?' she asked Crimson.

'Sixteen.'

'And what's your name?'

' "Crimson", madam. I used to be called "Jade", but they made me change it on account of Master Bao.'

Xi-feng looked away with a frown of displeasure.

'I should think so too,' she muttered. 'Odious people! One can hear them saying it: "We've got a 'Jade' in our family the same as you", or some such impertinence.'

She turned to Li Wan again:

'I don't think you know, Wan, but I told this girl's mother that as Lai Da's wife is so busy nowadays that she doesn't even know who half the girls in the household *are* any longer, I wanted *her* to pick out a couple of likely-looking girls to work under me. Now she promised that she would do this; but you see, not only has she not done so, but she's actually gone and sent her own daughter to work for someone else. Do you suppose she *really* thinks her girl would have had such a terrible time with me?'

'Don't be so touchy,' said Li Wan. 'Her mother is not to blame. The girl had already started service in the Garden before you ever spoke to her about it.'

'Oh well, in that case,' said Xi-feng, recovering her good humour, 'I'll have a word with Bao-yu about it tomorrow. I'll tell him to find someone else and let me have this girl to work under *me*. Still – ' she turned to Crimson, 'perhaps we ought to ask the party most concerned if she is willing.'

Crimson smiled.

'As to being willing or not, madam, I don't think it's my place to say. But I do know this: that if I was to work for you, I should get to know what's what and all the inside and outside of household management. I'm sure it would be wonderful experience.'

Just then a maid arrived from Lady Wang's asking for Xi-feng, who promptly excused herself to Li Wan and left. Crimson returned to Green Delights – where our story now leaves her.

*

We now return to Dai-yu, who, having slept so little the night before, was very late getting up on the morning of the festival. Hearing that the other girls were all out in the garden 'speeding the fairies' and fearing to be teased by them for her lazy habits, she hurried over her toilet and went out as soon as it was completed. A smiling Bao-yu appeared in the gateway as she was stepping down into the courtyard.

'Well, coz,' he said, 'I hope you *didn't* tell on me yesterday. You had me worrying about it all last night.'

Dai-yu turned back, ignoring him, to address Nightingale inside:

'When you do the room, leave one of the casements open so that the parent swallows can get in. And put the lion doorstop on the bottom of the blind to stop it flapping. And don't forget to put the cover back on the burner after you've lighted the incense.'

She made her way across the courtyard, still ignoring him.

Bao-yu, who knew nothing of the little drama that had taken place outside his gate the night before, assumed that she was still angry about his unfortunate lapse earlier on that same day, when he had offended her susceptibilities with a somewhat risqué quotation from *The Western Chamber*. He offered her now, with energetic bowing and hand-pumping, the apologies that the previous day's emergency had caused him to neglect. But Dai-yu walked straight past him and out of the gate, not deigning so much as a glance in his direction, and stalked off in search of the others.

Bao-yu was nonplussed. He began to suspect that something more than he had first imagined must be wrong.

'Surely it can't only be because of yesterday lunchtime that she's carrying on in this fashion? There must be something else. On the other hand, I didn't get back until late and I didn't see her again last night, so how *could* I have offended her?'

Preoccupied with these reflections, he followed her at some distance behind.

Not far ahead Bao-chai and Tan-chun were watching the ungainly courtship dance of some cranes. When they saw Dai-yu coming, they invited her to join them, and the three girls stood together and chatted. Then Bao-yu arrived. Tan-chun greeted him with sisterly concern:

'How have you been keeping, Bao? It's three whole days since I saw you last.'

Bao-yu smiled back at her.

'How have *you* been keeping, sis? I was asking Cousin Wan about you the day before yesterday.'

'Come over here a minute,' said Tan-chun. 'I want to talk to you.'

He followed her into the shade of a pomegranate tree a little way apart from the other two.

'Has Father asked to see you at all during this last day or two?' Tan-chun began.

'No.'

'I thought I heard someone say yesterday that he had been asking for you.'

'No,' said Bao-yu, smiling at her concern. 'Whoever it was was mistaken. He certainly hasn't asked for *me*.'

Tan-chun smiled and changed the subject.

'During the past few months,' she said, 'I've managed to save up another ten strings or so of cash. I'd like you to take it again like you did last time, and next time you go out, if you see a nice painting or calligraphic scroll or some amusing little thing that would do for my room, I'd like you to buy it for me.'

'Well, I don't know,' said Bao-yu. 'In the trips I make to bazaars and temple fairs, whether it's inside the city or round about, I can't say that I ever see anything *really* nice or out of the ordinary. It's all bronzes and jades and porcelain and that sort of stuff. Apart from that it's mostly dress-making materials and clothes and things to eat.'

'Now what would I want things like that for?' said Tan-chun. 'No, I mean something like that little wickerwork basket you bought me last time, or the little box carved out of bamboo root, or the little clay burner. I thought they were sweet. Unfortunately the others took such a fancy to them that they carried them off as loot and wouldn't give them back to me again.'

'Oh, if *those* are the sort of things you want,' said Bao-yu laughing, 'it's very simple. Just give a few strings of cash to one of the boys and he'll bring you back a whole cartload of them.'

'What do the boys know about it?' said Tan-chun. 'I need someone who can pick out the interesting things and the ones that are in good taste. You get me lots of nice little things, and I'll embroider a pair of slippers for you like the ones I made for you last time – only this time I'll do them more carefully.'

'Talking of those slippers reminds me,' said Bao-yu. 'I happened to run into Father once when I was wearing them. He was Most Displeased. When he asked me who made them, I naturally didn't dare to tell him that *you* had, so I said that Aunt Wang had given them to me as a birthday present a few days before. There wasn't much he could do about it when he heard that they came from Aunt Wang; so after a very long pause he just said, "What a pointless waste of human effort and valuable material, to produce things like that!" I told this to Aroma when I got back, and she said, "Oh, that's nothing! You should have heard your Aunt Zhao complaining about those slippers. She was *furious* when she heard about them: 'Her own natural brother so down at heel he scarcely dares show his face to people, and she spends her time making things like that!' " '

Tan-chun's smile had vanished:

'How *can* she talk such nonsense? Why should *I* be the one to make shoes for him? Huan gets a clothing allowance, doesn't he? He gets his clothing and footwear provided for the same as all the rest of us. And fancy saying a thing like that in front of a roomful of servants! For whose benefit was this remark made, I wonder? I make an occasional pair of slippers just for something to do in my spare time; and if I give a pair to someone I particularly like, that's my own affair. Surely no one else has any business to start telling me who I should give them to? Oh, she's so *petty*!'

Bao-yu shook his head:

'Perhaps you're being a bit hard on her. She's probably got her reasons.'

This made Tan-chun really angry. Her chin went up defiantly:

'Now you're being as stupid as her. Of *course* she's got her reasons; but they are ignorant, stupid reasons. But she can think what she likes: as far as *I* am concerned, Sir Jia is my father and Lady Wang is my mother, and who was born in whose room doesn't interest me – the way I choose my friends inside the family has nothing to do with that. Oh, I know I shouldn't talk about her like this; but she is *so* idiotic about these things. As a matter of fact I can give you an even better example than your story of the slippers. That last time I gave you my savings to get something for me, she saw me a few days afterwards and started telling me how short of money she was and how difficult things were for her. I took no notice, of course. But later, when the maids were out of the room, she began attacking me for giving the money I'd saved to other people instead of giving it to Huan. Really! I didn't know whether to laugh or get angry with her. In the end I just walked out of the room and went round to see Mother.'

There was an amused interruption at this point from Bao-chai, who was still standing where they had left her a few minutes before:

'Do finish your talking and come back soon! It's easy to see that you two are brother and sister. As soon as you see each other, you get into a huddle and start talking about family secrets. Would it *really* be such a disaster if anything you are saying were to be overheard?'

Tan-chun and Bao-yu rejoined her, laughing.

Not seeing Dai-yu, Bao-yu realized that she must have slipped off elsewhere while he was talking.

'Better leave it a day or two,' he told himself on reflection. 'Wait until her anger has calmed down a bit.'

While he was looking downwards and meditating, he noticed that the ground where they were standing was carpeted with a bright profusion of wind-blown flowers – pomegranate and balsam for the most part.

'You can see she's upset,' he thought ruefully. 'She's neglecting her flowers. I'll bury this lot for her and remind her about it next time I see her.'

He became aware that Bao-chai was arranging for him and Tan-chun to go with her outside.

'I'll join you two presently,' he said, and waited until they were a little way off before stooping down to gather the fallen blossoms into the skirt of his gown. It was quite a way from where he was to the place where Dai-yu had buried the peach-blossom on that previous occasion, but he made his way towards it, over rocks and bridges and through plantations of trees and flowers. When he had almost reached his destination and there was only the spur of a miniature 'mountain' between him and the burial-place of the flowers, he heard the sound of a voice, coming from the other side of the rock, whose continuous, gentle chiding was occasionally broken by the most pitiable and heart-rending sobs.

'It must be a maid from one of the apartments,' thought Bao-yu. 'Someone has been ill-treating her, and she has run here to cry on her own.'

He stood still and endeavoured to catch what the weeping girl was saying. She appeared to be reciting something:

> The blossoms fade and falling fill the air,
> Of fragrance and bright hues bereft and bare.
> Floss drifts and flutters round the Maiden's bower,
> Or softly strikes against her curtained door.
>
> The Maid, grieved by these signs of spring's decease,
> Seeking some means her sorrow to express,
> Has rake in hand into the garden gone,
> Before the fallen flowers are trampled on.
>
> Elm-pods and willow-floss are fragrant too;
> Why care, Maid, where the fallen flowers blew?
> Next year, when peach and plum-tree bloom again,
> Which of your sweet companions will remain?
>
> This spring the heartless swallow built his nest
> Beneath the eaves of mud with flowers compressed.
> Next year the flowers will blossom as before,
> But swallow, nest, and Maid will be no more.

Three hundred and three-score the year's full tale:
From swords of frost and from the slaughtering gale
How can the lovely flowers long stay intact,
Or, once loosed, from their drifting fate draw back?

Blooming so steadfast, fallen so hard to find!
Beside the flowers' grave, with sorrowing mind,
The solitary Maid sheds many a tear,
Which on the boughs as bloody drops appear.

At twilight, when the cuckoo sings no more,
The Maiden with her rake goes in at door
And lays her down between the lamplit walls,
While a chill rain against the window falls.

I know not why my heart's so strangely sad,
Half grieving for the spring and yet half glad:
Glad that it came, grieved it so soon was spent.
So soft it came, so silently it went!

Last night, outside, a mournful sound was heard:
The spirits of the flowers and of the bird.
But neither bird nor flowers would long delay,
Bird lacking speech, and flowers too shy to stay.

And then I wished that I had wings to fly
After the drifting flowers across the sky:
Across the sky to the world's farthest end,
The flowers' last fragrant resting-place to find.

But better their remains in silk to lay
And bury underneath the wholesome clay,
Pure substances the pure earth to enrich,
Than leave to soak and stink in some foul ditch.

Can I, that these flowers' obsequies attend,
Divine how soon or late *my* life will end?
Let others laugh flower-burial to see:
Another year who will be burying me?

As petals drop and spring begins to fail,
The bloom of youth, too, sickens and turns pale.
One day, when spring has gone and youth has fled,
The Maiden and the flowers will both be dead.

All this was uttered in a voice half-choked with sobs; for the words recited seemed only to inflame the grief of the reciter – indeed, Bao-yu, listening on the other side of the rock, was so overcome by them that he had already flung himself weeping upon the ground.

But the sequel to this painful scene will be told in the following chapter.

CHAPTER 28

*A crimson cummerbund becomes a pledge of friendship
And a chaplet of medicine-beads becomes a source of
embarrassment*

ON the night before the festival, it may be remembered, Lin
Dai-yu had mistakenly supposed Bao-yu responsible for Skybright's refusal to open the gate for her. The ceremonial farewell to the flowers of the following morning had transformed
her pent-up and still smouldering resentment into a more
generalized and seasonable sorrow. This had finally found its
expression in a violent outburst of grief as she was burying
the latest collection of fallen blossoms in her flower-grave.
Meditation on the fate of flowers had led her to a contemplation of her own sad and orphaned lot; she had burst into tears,
and soon after had begun a recitation of the poem whose
words we recorded in the preceding chapter.

Unknown to her, Bao-yu was listening to this recitation
from the slope of the near-by rockery. At first he merely nodded and sighed sympathetically; but when he heard the words

'Can I, that these flowers' obsequies attend,
Divine how soon or late *my* life will end?'

and, a little later,

'One day when spring has gone and youth has fled,
The Maiden and the flowers will both be dead.'

he flung himself on the ground in a fit of weeping, scattering
the earth all about him with the flowers he had been carrying
in the skirt of his gown.

Lin Dai-yu dead! A world from which that delicate, flower-
like countenance had irrevocably departed! It was unutterable
anguish to think of it. Yet his sensitized imagination *did* now
consider it – went on, indeed, to consider a world from which
the others, too – Bao-chai, Caltrop, Aroma and the rest – had

also irrevocably departed. Where would *he* be then? What would have become of him? And what of the Garden, the rocks, the flowers, the trees? To whom would they belong when he and the girls were no longer there to enjoy them? Passing from loss to loss in his imagination, he plunged deeper and deeper into a grief that seemed inconsolable. As the poet says:

> Flowers in my eyes and bird-song in my ears
> Augment my loss and mock my bitter tears.

Dai-yu, then, as she stood plunged in her own private sorrowing, suddenly heard the sound of another person crying bitterly on the rocks above her.

'The others are always telling me I'm a "case",' she thought. 'Surely there can't be another "case" up there?'

But on looking up she saw that it was Bao-yu.

'Pshaw!' she said crossly to herself. 'I thought it was another girl, but all the time it was that cruel, hate—'

'Hateful' she had been going to say, but clapped her mouth shut before uttering it. She sighed instead and began to walk away.

By the time Bao-yu's weeping was over, Dai-yu was no longer there. He realized that she must have seen him and have gone away in order to avoid him. Feeling suddenly rather foolish, he rose to his feet and brushed the earth from his clothes. Then he descended from the rockery and began to retrace his steps in the direction of Green Delights. Quite by coincidence Dai-yu was walking along the same path a little way ahead.

'Stop a minute!' he cried, hurrying forward to catch up with her. 'I know you are not taking any notice of me, but I only want to ask you one simple question, and then you need never have anything more to do with me.'

Dai-yu had turned back to see who it was. When she saw that it was Bao-yu still, she was going to ignore him again; but hearing him say that he only wanted to ask her one question, she told him that he might do so.

Bao-yu could not resist teasing her a little.

'How about *two* questions? Would you wait for two?'
Dai-yu set her face forwards and began walking on again.
Bao-yu sighed.

'If it has to be like this now,' he said, as if to himself, 'it's a
pity it was ever like it was in the beginning.'

Dai-yu's curiosity got the better of her. She stopped walking and turned once more towards him.

'Like *what* in the beginning?' she asked. 'And like what
now?'

'Oh, the *beginning*!' said Bao-yu. 'In the *beginning*, when you
first came here, I was your faithful companion in all your
games. Anything I had, even the thing most dear to me, was
yours for the asking. If there was something to eat that I
specially liked, I had only to hear that you were fond of it too
and I would religiously hoard it away to share with you when
you got back, not daring even to touch it until you came. We
ate at the same table. We slept in the same bed. I used to think
that because we were so close then, there would be something
special about our relationship when we grew up – that even
if we weren't particularly affectionate, we should at least have
more understanding and forbearance for each other than the
rest. But how wrong I was! Now that you *have* grown up, you
seem only to have grown more touchy. You don't seem to
care about *me* any more at all. You spend all your time brooding about outsiders like Feng and Chai. I haven't got any *real*
brothers and sisters left here now. There are Huan and Tan,
of course; but as you know, they're only my half-brother and
half-sister: they aren't my mother's children. I'm on my own,
like you. I should have thought we had so much in common –
But what's the use? I try and try, but it gets me nowhere; and
nobody knows or cares.'

At this point – in spite of himself – he burst into tears.

The palpable evidence of her own eyes and ears had by now
wrought a considerable softening on Dai-yu's heart. A sym-
pathetic tear stole down her own cheek, and she hung her head
and said nothing. Bao-yu could see that he had moved her.

'I know I'm not much use nowadays,' he continued, 'but
however bad you may think me, I would never wittingly do

anything in your presence to offend you. If I *do* ever slip up in some way, you ought to tell me off about it and warn me not to do it again, or shout at me – hit me, even, if you feel like it; I shouldn't mind. But you don't do that. You just ignore me. You leave me utterly at a loss to know what I'm supposed to have done wrong, so that I'm driven half frantic wondering what I ought to do to make up for it. If I were to die now, I should die with a grievance, and all the masses and exorcisms in the world wouldn't lay my ghost. Only when you explained what your reason was for ignoring me should I cease from haunting you and be reborn into another life.'

Dai-yu's resentment for the gate incident had by now completely evaporated. She merely said:

'Oh well, in that case why did you tell your maids not to let me in when I came to call on you?'

'I honestly don't know what you are referring to,' said Bao-yu in surprise. 'Strike me dead if I ever did any such thing!'

'Hush!' said Dai-yu. 'Talking about death at this time of the morning! You should be more careful what you say. If you did, you did. If you didn't, you didn't. There's no need for these horrible oaths.'

'I really and truly didn't know you had called,' said Bao-yu. 'Cousin Bao came and sat with me a few minutes last night and then went away again. That's the only call I know about.'

Dai-yu reflected for a moment or two, then smiled.

'Yes, it must have been the maids being lazy. Certainly they can be very disagreeable at such times.'

'Yes, I'm sure that's what it was,' said Bao-yu. 'When I get back, I'll find out who it was and give her a good talking-to.'

'I think some of your young ladies could *do* with a good talking-to,' said Dai-yu, ' – though it's not really for me to say so. It's a good job it was only me they were rude to. If Miss Bao or Miss Cow were to call and they behaved like that to *her*, that would be really serious.'

She giggled mischievously. Bao-yu didn't know whether to laugh with her or grind his teeth. But just at that moment a maid came up to ask them both to lunch and the two of them went together out of the Garden and through into the front part of the mansion, calling in at Lady Wang's on the way.

'How did you get on with that medicine of Dr Bao's,' Lady Wang asked Dai-yu as soon as she saw her, '– the Court Physician? Do you think you are any better for it?'

'It didn't seem to make very much difference,' said Dai-yu. 'Grandmother has put me back on Dr Wang's prescription.'

'Cousin Lin has got a naturally weak constitution, Mother,' said Bao-yu. 'She takes cold very easily. These strong decoctions are all very well provided she only takes one or two to dispel the cold. For regular treatment it's probably best if she sticks to pills.'

'The doctor was telling me about some pills for her the other day,' said Lady Wang, 'but I just can't remember the name.'

'I know the names of most of those pills,' said Bao-yu. 'I expect he wanted her to take Ginseng Tonic Pills.'

'No, that wasn't it,' said Lady Wang.

'Eight Gem Motherwort Pills?' said Bao-yu. 'Zhang's Dextrals? Zhang's Sinistrals? If it wasn't any of them, it was probably Dr Cui's Adenophora Kidney Pills.'

'No,' said Lady Wang, 'it was none of those. All I can remember is that there was a "Vajra" in it.'

Bao-yu gave a hoot and clapped his hands:

'I've never heard of "Vajra Pills". If there are "Vajra Pills", I suppose there must be "Buddha Boluses"!'

The others all laughed. Bao-chai looked at him mockingly.

'I should think it was probably "The Deva-king Cardiac Elixir Pills",' she said.

'Yes, yes, that's it!' said Lady Wang. 'Of course! How stupid of me!'

'No, Mother, not stupid,' said Bao-yu. 'It's the strain. All those Vajra-kings and Bodhisattvas have been overworking you!'

'You're a naughty boy to make fun of your poor mother,' said Lady Wang. 'A good whipping from your Pa is what you need.'

'Oh, Father doesn't whip me for that sort of thing now-adays,' said Bao-yu.

'Now that we know the name of the pills, we must get them to buy some for your Cousin Lin,' said Lady Wang.

'None of those things are any good,' said Bao-yu. 'You give me three hundred and sixty taels of silver and I'll make up some pills for Cousin Lin that I guarantee will have her completely cured before she has finished the first boxful.'

'Stuff!' said Lady Wang. 'Whoever heard of a medicine that cost so much?'

'No, honestly!' said Bao-yu. 'This prescription is a very unusual one with very special ingredients. I can't remember all of them, but I know they include

> the caul of a first-born child;
> a ginseng root shaped like a man, with the leaves
>   still on it;
> a turtle-sized polygonum root;

and

> lycoperdon from the stump of a thousand-year-old
>   pine-tree.

– Actually, though, there's nothing so *very* special about those ingredients. They're all in the standard pharmacopoeia. For "sovereign remedies" they use ingredients that would *really* make you jump. I once gave the prescription for one to Cousin Xue. He was more than a year begging me for it before I would give it to him, and it took him another two or three years and nearly a thousand taels of silver to get all the ingredients together. Ask Bao-chai if you don't believe me, Mother.'

'I know nothing about it,' said Bao-chai. 'I've never heard it mentioned. It's no good telling Aunt to ask *me*.'

'You see! Bao-chai is a *good* girl. *She* doesn't tell lies,' said Lady Wang.

Bao-yu was standing in the middle of the floor below the kang. He clapped his hands at this and turned to the others appealingly.

'But it's the *truth* I'm telling you. This is no lie.'

As he turned, he happened to catch sight of Dai-yu, who

was sitting behind Bao-chai, smiling mockingly and stroking her cheek with her finger – which in sign-language means, 'You are a great big liar and you ought to be ashamed of yourself.'

But Xi-feng, who happened to be in the inner room supervising the laying of the table and had overheard the preceding remarks, now emerged into the outer room to corroborate:

'It's quite true, what Bao says. I don't think he *is* making it up,' she said. 'Not so long ago Cousin Xue came to me asking for some pearls, and when I asked him what he wanted them for, he said, "To make medicine with." Then he started grumbling about the trouble he was having in getting the right ingredients and how he had half a mind not to make this medicine up after all. I said, "What medicine?" and he told me that it was a prescription that Cousin Bao had given him and reeled off a lot of ingredients – I can't remember them now. "Of course," he said, "I could easily enough *buy* a few pearls; only these have to be ones that have been worn. That's why I'm asking *you* for them. If you haven't got any loose ones," he said, "a few pearls broken off a bit of jewellery would do. I'd get you something nice to replace it with." He was so insistent that in the end I had to break up two of my ornaments for him. Then he wanted a yard of Imperial red gauze. That was to put over the mortar to pound the pearls through. He said they had to be ground until they were as fine as flour.'

'You see!' 'You see!' Bao-yu kept interjecting throughout this recital.

'Incidentally, Mother,' he said, when it was ended, 'even *that* was only a substitute. According to the prescription, the pearls ought really to have come from an ancient grave. They should really have been pearls taken from jewellery on the corpse of a long-buried noblewoman. But as one can't very well go digging up graves and rifling tombs every time one wants to make this medicine, the prescription allows pearls worn by the living as a second-best.'

'Blessed name of the Lord!' said Lady Wang. 'What a *dreadful* idea! Even if you *did* get them from a grave, I can't believe that a medicine made from pearls that had been come by so wickedly – desecrating people's bones that had been lying peacefully in the ground all those hundreds of years – could possibly do you any good.'

Bao-yu turned to Dai-yu.

'Did you hear what Feng said?' he asked her. 'I hope you're not going to say that *she* was lying.'

Although the remark was addressed to Dai-yu, he winked at Bao-chai as he made it.

Dai-yu clung to Lady Wang.

'Listen to him, Aunt!' she wailed. 'Bao-chai won't be a party to his lies, but he still expects *me* to be.'

'Bao-yu, you are very unkind to your cousin,' said Lady Wang.

Bao-yu only laughed.

'You don't know the reason, Mother. Bao-chai didn't know a half of what Cousin Xue got up to, even when she was living with her mother outside; and now that she's moved into the Garden, she knows even less. When she said she didn't know, she *really* didn't know: she wasn't giving me the lie. What you don't realize is that Cousin Lin was all the time sitting behind her making signs to show that she didn't believe me.'

Just then a maid came from Grandmother Jia's apartment to fetch Bao-yu and Dai-yu to lunch.

Without saying a word to Bao-yu, Dai-yu got up and, taking the maid's hand, began to go. But the maid was reluctant.

'Let's wait for Master Bao and we can go together.'

'He's not eating lunch today,' said Dai-yu. 'Come on, let's go!'

'Whether he's eating lunch or not,' said the maid, 'he'd better come with us, so that he can explain to Her Old Ladyship about it when she asks.'

'All right, you wait for him then,' said Dai-yu. 'I'm going on ahead.'

And off she went.

'I think I'd rather eat with *you* today, Mother,' said Bao-yu.

'No, no, you can't,' said Lady Wang. 'Today is one of my fast-days: I shall only be eating vegetables. You go and have a proper meal with your Grandma.'

'I shall share your vegetables,' said Bao-yu. 'Go on, you can go,' he said, dismissing the maid; and rushing up to the table, he sat himself down at it in readiness.

'You others had better get on with your own lunch,' Lady Wang said to Bao-chai and the girls. 'Let him do as he likes.'

'You really ought to go,' Bao-chai said to Bao-yu. 'Whether you have lunch there or not, you ought to keep Cousin Lin company. She is very upset, you know. Why don't you?'

'Oh, leave her alone!' said Bao-yu. 'She'll be all right presently.'

Soon they had finished eating, and Bao-yu, afraid that Grandmother Jia might be worrying and at the same time anxious to rejoin Dai-yu, hurriedly demanded tea to rinse his mouth with. Tan-chun and Xi-chun were much amused.

'Why are you always in such a hurry, Bao?' they asked him. 'Even your eating and drinking all seems to be done in a rush.'

'You should let him finish quickly, so that he can get back to his Dai-yu,' said Bao-chai blandly. 'Don't make him waste time here with us.'

Bao-yu left as soon as he had drunk his tea, and made straight for the west courtyard where his Grandmother Jia's apartment was. But as he was passing by the gateway of Xi-feng's courtyard, it happened that Xi-feng herself was standing in her doorway with one foot on the threshold, grooming her teeth with an ear-cleaner and keeping a watchful eye on nine or ten pages who were moving potted plants about under her direction.

'Ah, just the person I wanted to see!' she said, as soon as she caught sight of Bao-yu. 'Come inside. I want you to write something down for me.'

Bao-yu was obliged to follow her indoors. Xi-feng called for some paper, an inkstone and a brush, and at once began dictating:

'Crimson lining-damask forty lengths, dragonet figured satin forty lengths, miscellaneous Imperial gauze one hundred lengths, gold necklets four, – '

'Here, what *is* this?' said Bao-yu. 'It isn't an invoice and it isn't a presentation list. How am I supposed to write it?'

'Never you mind about that,' said Xi-feng. 'As long as *I* know what it is, that's all that matters. Just put it down any-how.'

Bao-yu wrote down the four items. As soon as he had done so, Xi-feng took up the paper and folded it away.

'Now,' she said, smiling pleasantly, 'there's something I want to talk to you about. I don't know whether you'll agree to this or not, but there's a girl in your room called "Crimson" whom I'd like to work for me. If I find you someone to re-place her with, will you let me have her?'

'There are so many girls in my room,' said Bao-yu. 'Please take any you have a fancy to. You really don't need to ask me about it.'

'In that case,' said Xi-feng, 'I'll send for her straight away.'

'Please do,' said Bao-yu, and started to go.

'Hey, come back!' said Xi-feng. 'I haven't finished with you yet.'

'I've got to see Grandma now,' said Bao-yu. 'If you've got anything else to say, you can tell me on my way back.'

When he got to Grandmother Jia's apartment, they had all just finished lunch. Grandmother Jia asked him if he had had anything nice to eat with his mother.

'There wasn't anything nice,' he said. 'But I had an extra bowl of rice.'

Then, after the briefest pause:

'Where's Cousin Lin?'

'In the inner room,' said Grandmother Jia.

In the inner room a maid stood below the kang blowing on a flat-iron. Up on the kang two maids were marking some material with a chalked string, while Dai-yu, her head bent low over her work, was engaged in cutting something from it with her shears.

'What are you making?' he asked her. 'You'll give yourself a headache, stooping down like that immediately after your lunch.'

Dai-yu took no notice and went on cutting.

'That corner looks a bit creased still,' said one of the maids. 'It will have to be ironed again.'

'*Leave it alone!*' said Dai-yu, laying down her shears. '*It will be all right presently.*'

Bao-yu found her reply puzzling.

Bao-chai, Tan-chun and the rest had now arrived in the outer room and were talking to Grandmother Jia. Presently Bao-chai drifted inside and asked Dai-yu what she was doing; then, when she saw that she was cutting material, she exclaimed admiringly.

'What a lot of things you can do, Dai! Fancy, even dress-making now!'

Dai-yu smiled malignantly.

'Oh, it's all lies, really. I just do it to fool people.'

'I've got something to tell you that I think will amuse you, Dai,' said Bao-chai pleasantly. 'When our cousin was holding forth about that medicine just now and I said I didn't know about it, I believe actually he was rather wounded.'

'*Oh, leave him alone!*' said Dai-yu. '*He will be all right presently.*'

'Grandma wants someone to play dominoes with,' said Bao-yu to Bao-chai. 'Why don't you go and play dominoes?'

'Oh, is *that* what I came for?' said Bao-chai; but she went, notwithstanding.

'Why don't *you* go?' said Dai-yu. 'There's a tiger in this room. You might get eaten.'

She said this still bending over her cutting, which she continued to work away at without looking up at him.

Finding himself once more ignored, Bao-yu nevertheless attempted to remain jovial.

'Why don't you come out for a bit too? You can do this cutting later.'

Dai-yu continued to take no notice.

Failing to get a response from her, he tried the maids:

'Who told her to do this dress-making?'

'Whoever told her to do it,' said Dai-yu, 'it has nothing whatever to do with Master Bao.'

Bao-yu was about to retort, but just at that moment someone came in to say that he was wanted outside, and he was obliged to hurry off.

Dai-yu leaned forward and shouted after him:
'Holy name! By the time you get back, I shall be dead.'

*

Outside the gateway to the inner quarters Bao-yu found Tea-leaf waiting.

'Mr Feng invites you round to his house,' said Tealeaf.

Bao-yu realized that this must be in connection with the matter Feng Zi-ying had spoken of on the previous day. He told Tealeaf to send for his going-out clothes, and went into his outer study to wait for them.

Tealeaf went back to the west inner gate to wait for some-one who would carry a message inside to the maids. Presently an old woman came out:

'Excuse me, missus,' said Tealeaf. 'Master Bao is waiting in the outer study for his going-out clothes. Could you take a message inside to say that he wants them?'

' — your mother's twat!' said the old woman. 'Master Bao lives in the Garden now. All his maids are in the Garden. What do you want to come running round here for?'

Tealeaf laughed at his own mistake.

'You're quite right. I'm going cuckoo.'

He ran round to the gate of the Garden. As luck would have it, the boys on that gate were playing football in the open space below the terraced walk, and when Tealeaf had explained his errand, one of them ran off inside for him. He returned after a very long wait, carrying a large bundle, which he handed to Tealeaf, and which Tealeaf carried back to the outer study.

While he was changing, Bao-yu asked for his horse to be saddled, and presently set off, taking only Tealeaf, Ploughboy, Two-times and Oldie as his attendants. When they reached Feng Zi-ying's gate, someone ran in to announce his arrival, and Feng Zi-ying came out in person to greet him and led him inside to meet the company.

This comprised Xue Pan, who had evidently been waiting there for some time, a number of boy singers, a female imper-sonator called Jiang Yu-han and a girl called Nuageuse from the Budding Grove, a high-class establishment specializing in female entertainers. When everyone had been introduced, tea was served.

'Now come on!' said Bao-yu, as he picked up the proffered cup of tea. 'What about this "lucky accident" you mentioned yesterday? I've been waiting anxiously to hear about it ever since I saw you. That's why I came so promptly when I got your invitation.'

Feng Zi-ying laughed.

'You and your cousin are such simple souls – I find it rahver touchin'! Afraid it was pure invention, what I said yesterday. I said it to make you come, because I fought that if I asked you outright to come and drink wiv me, you'd make excuses. Anyway, it worked.'

The company joined in his merriment.

Wine was now brought in and everyone sat down in the places assigned to them. Feng Zi-ying first got one of the singing-boys to pour for them; then he called on Nuageuse to drink with each of the guests in turn.

Xue Pan, by the time he had three little cupfuls of wine inside him, was already beginning to be obstreperous. He seized Nuageuse by the hand and drew her towards him:

'If you'd sing me a nice new song – one of your specials, I'd drink a whole jarful for you. How about it, eh?'

Nuageuse had to oblige him by taking up her lute and singing the following song for him to her own accompaniment:

> Two lovely boys
> Are both in love with me
> And I can't get either from my mind.
> Both are so beautiful
> So wonderful
> So marvellous
> To give up either one would be unkind.
> Last night I promised I would go
> To meet one of them in the garden where the roses grow;
> The other came to see what he could find.
> And now that we three are all
> Here in this tribunal,
> There are no words that come into my mind.

'There you are!' she said. 'Now drink your jarful!'

'That one's not worth a jarful,' said Xue Pan. 'Sing us a better one.'

'Now just a minute,' said Bao-yu. 'Just guzzling like this will make us drunk in no time without giving us any real enjoyment. I've got a good new drinking-game for you. Let me first drink the M.C.'s starting-cup, and I'll tell you the rules. After that, anyone who doesn't toe the line will be made to drink ten sconce-cups straight off as a forfeit, give up his seat at the party, and spend the rest of the time pouring out drinks for the rest of us.'

Feng Zi-ying and Jiang Yu-han agreed enthusiastically, and Bao-yu picked up one of the extra large cups that had now been provided and drained its contents at a single draught.

'Now,' he said. 'We're going to take four words – let's say "upset", "glum", "blest" and "content". You have to begin by saying "The girl is—", and then you say one of the four words. That's your first line. The next line has to rhyme with the first line and it has to give the reason why the girl is whatever it says – "upset" or "glum" or "blest" or "content". When you've done all four, you're entitled to drink the wine in front of you. Only, before drinking it, you've first got to sing some new popular song; and *after* you've drunk it, you've got to choose some animal or vegetable object from the things in front of us and recite a line from a well-known poem, or an old couplet, or a quotation from the classics—'

Before he could finish, Xue Pan was on his feet, protesting vigorously:

'You can count *me* out of this. *I'm* taking no part in this. This is just to make a fool of me, isn't it?'

Nuageuse, too, stood up and attempted to push him back into his seat:

'What are you so afraid of, a practised drinker like you? You can't be any worse at this sort of thing than I am, and *I'm* going to have a go when *my* turn comes. If you do it all right, you've got nothing to worry about, and even if you can't, you'll only be made to drink a few cups of wine; whereas if you refuse to follow the rules at the very outset, you'll have to drink ten sconces straight off in a row and then be thrown out of the party and made to pour drinks for the rest of us.'

'Bravo!' cried the others, clapping; and Xue Pan, seeing them united against him, subsided.

Bao-yu now began his own turn:

> 'The girl's upset:
>   The years pass by, but no one's claimed her yet.
> The girl looks glum:
>   Her true-love's gone to follow ambition's drum.
> The girl feels blest:
>   The mirror shows her looks are at their best.
> The girl's content:
>   Long summer days in pleasant pastimes spent.'

The others all applauded, except Xue Pan, who shook his head disapprovingly:

'No good, no good!' he said. 'Pay the forfeit.'

'Why, what's wrong with it?' they asked him.

'I couldn't understand a word of it.'

Nuageuse gave him a pinch:

'Keep quiet and try to think what *you*'re going to say,' she advised him; 'otherwise you'll have nothing ready when your own turn comes and you'll have to pay the forfeit yourself.'

Thereupon she picked up her lute and accompanied Bao-yu as he sang the following song:

> 'Still weeping tears of blood about our separation:
> Little red love-beans of my desolation.
> Still blooming flowers I see outside my window growing.
> Still awake in the dark I hear the wind a-blowing.
> Still oh still I can't forget those old hopes and fears.
> Still can't swallow food and drink, 'cos I'm choked with tears.
> Mirror, mirror on the wall, tell me it's not true:
> Do I look so thin and pale, do I look so blue?
> Mirror, mirror, this long night how shall I get through?
>   Oh – oh – oh!
> Blue as the mist upon the distant mountains,
> Blue as the water in the ever-flowing fountains.'

General applause – except from Xue Pan, who objected that there was 'no rhythm'.

Bao-yu now drank his well-earned cup – the 'pass cup' as they call it – and, picking up a slice of pear from the table, concluded his turn with the following quotation:

> 'Rain whips the pear-tree, shut fast the door.'

Now it was Feng Zi-ying's turn:

> 'The girl's upset:
>   Her husband's ill and she's in debt.
> The girl looks glum:
>   The gale has turned her room into a slum.
> The girl feels blest:
>   She's got twin babies at the breast.
> The girl's content:
>   Waiting a certain pleasurable event.'

Next, holding up his cupful of wine in readiness to drink, he sang this song:

> 'You're so exciting,
>   And so inviting;
>   You're my Mary Contrary;
>   You're a crazy, mad thing.
> You're my goddess, but oh! you're deaf to my praying:
>   Why won't you listen to what I am saying?
> If you don't believe me, make a small investigation:
> You will soon find out the true depth of my admiration.'

Then he drained his bumper and, picking up a piece of chicken from one of the dishes, ended the performance, prior to popping it into his mouth, with a line from Wen Ting-yun:

> 'From moonlit cot the cry of chanticleer.'

Next it was the turn of Nuageuse:

> 'The girl's upset:'

she began,

> 'Not knowing how the future's to be met – '

Xue Pan laughed noisily.

'That's all right, my darling, don't you worry! Your Uncle Xue will take care of you.'

'Shush!' said the others. 'Don't confuse her.'
She continued:

'The girl looks glum:
   Nothing but blows and hard words from her Mum – '

'I saw that Mum of yours the other day,' said Xue Pan, 'and
I particularly told her that she wasn't to beat you.'
   'Another word from you,' said the others, 'and you'll be
made to drink ten cups as a punishment.'
   Xue Pan gave his own face a slap.
   'Sorry! I forgot. Won't do it again.'

'The girl feels blest:'

said Nuageuse,

'Her young man's rich and beautifully dressed.
The girl's content:
   She's been performing in a big event.'

Next Nuageuse sang her song:

'A flower began to open in the month of May.
Along came a honey-bee to sport and play.
He pushed and he squeezed to get inside,
But he couldn't get in however hard he tried.
So on the flower's lip he just hung around,
A-playing the see-saw up and down.
   Oh my honey-sweet,
   Oh my sweets of sin,
   If I don't open up,
   How will you get in?'

After drinking her 'pass cup', she picked up a peach:

'So bonny blooms the peach-tree-o.'

It was now Xue Pan's turn.
   'Ah yes, now, let's see! *I* have to say something now, don't
I?'

'The girl's upset – '

But nothing followed.
   'All right, what's she upset about then?' said Feng Zi-ying
with a laugh. 'Buck up!'

Xue Pan appeared to be engaged in a species of mental effort so frightful that his eyes seemed about to pop out of his head. After glaring fixedly for an unconscionable time, he said:

'The girl's upset – '

He coughed a couple of times. Then at last it came:

'The girl's upset:
She's married to a marmoset.'

The others greeted this with a roar of laughter.

'What are you laughing at?' said Xue Pan. 'That's perfectly reasonable, isn't it? If a girl was expecting a proper husband and he turned out to be one of *them*, she'd have cause to be upset, wouldn't she?'

His audience were by now doubled up.

'That's perfectly true,' they conceded. 'Very good. Now what about the next bit?'

Xue Pan glared a while very concentratedly, then:

'The girl looks glum – '

But after that was silence.

'Come on!' said the others. 'Why was she glum?'

'His dad's a baboon with a big red bum.'

'Ho! Ho! Ho! Pay the forfeit,' they cried. 'The first one was bad enough. We really can't let this one go.'

The more officious of them even began filling the sconce-cups for him. But Bao-yu allowed the line.

'As long as it rhymes,' he said, 'we'll let it pass.'

'There you are!' said Xue Pan. 'The M. C. says it's all right. What are the rest of you making such a fuss about?'

At this the others desisted.

'The next two are even harder,' said Nuageuse. 'Shall I do them for you, dear?'

'Piss off!' said Xue Pan. 'D'you think I haven't got any good lines of my own? Listen to this:

The girl feels blest:
In bridal bower she takes her rest.'

The others stared at him in amazement:
'I say, old chap, that's a bit poetical for you, isn't it?'
Xue Pan continued unconcernedly:

> 'The girl's content:
>   She's got a big prick up her vent.'

The others looked away with expressions of disgust.
'Oh dear, oh dear! Hurry up and get on with the song, then.'

> 'One little gnat went hum hum hum,'

Xue Pan began tunelessly. The others looked at him open-mouthed:
'What sort of song is that?'
Xue Pan droned on, ignoring the question:

> 'Two little flies went bum bum bum,
>   Three little – '

'Stop!' shouted the others.
'Sod you lot!' said Xue Pan. 'This is the very latest new hit. It's called the Hum-bum Song. If you can't be bothered to listen to it, you'll have to let me off the other thing. I'll agree not to sing the rest of the song on that condition.'
'Yes, yes, we'll let you off,' they said. 'Just don't interfere with the rest of us, that's all we ask.'
This meant that it was now Jiang Yu-han's turn to perform. This is what he said:

> 'The girl's upset:
>   Her man's away, she fears he will forget.
> The girl looks glum:
>   So short of cash she can't afford a crumb,
> The girl feels blest:
>   Her lampwick's got a lucky crest.
> The girl's content:
>   She's married to a perfect gent.'

Then he sang this song:

'A mischievous bundle of charm and love,
Or an angel come down from the skies above?
Sweet sixteen
And so very green,
Yet eager to see all there is to be seen.
Aie aie aie
The galaxy's high
In the roof of the sky,
And the drum from the tower
Sounds the midnight hour.
So trim the lamp, love, and come with me
Inside the bed-curtains, and you shall see!'

He raised the pass cup to his lips, but before drinking it, smiled round at his auditors and made this little speech:

'I'm afraid my knowledge of poetry is strictly limited. However, I happened to see a couplet on someone's wall yesterday which has stuck in my mind; and as one line in it is about something I can see here, I shall use it to finish my turn with.'

So saying, he drained the cup and then, picking up a spray of cassia, recited the following line:

'The flowers' aroma breathes of hotter days.'

The others all accepted this as a satisfactory conclusion of the performance. Not so Xue Pan, however, who leaped to his feet and began protesting noisily:

'Terrible! Pay the forfeit. Where's the little doll? I can't see any doll on the table.'

'I didn't say anything about a doll,' said Jiang Yu-han. 'What are you talking about?'

'Come on, don't try to wriggle out of it!' said Xue Pan. 'Say what you said just now again.'

'The flowers' aroma breathes of hotter days.'

'There you are!' said Xue Pan. ' "Aroma". That's the name of a little doll. Ask *him* if you don't believe me.' – He pointed to Bao-yu.

Bao-yu looked embarrassed.

'Cousin Xue, this time I think you *do* have to pay the for-feit.'

'All right, all right!' said Xue Pan. 'I'll drink.'

And he picked up the wine in front of him and drained it at a gulp.

Feng Zi-ying and Jiang Yu-han were still puzzled and asked him what this was all about. But it was Nuageuse who explained. Immediately Jiang Yu-han was on his feet apologizing. The others reassured him.

'It's not your fault. "Ignorance excuses all",' they said.

Shortly after this Bao-yu had to take temporary leave of the company to ease his bladder and Jiang Yu-han followed him outside. As the two of them stood side by side under the eaves, Jiang Yu-han once more offered Bao-yu his apologies. Much taken with the actor's winsome looks and gentleness of manner, Bao-yu impulsively took his hand and gave it a squeeze.

'Do come round to our place some time when you are free,' he said. 'There's something I want to ask you about. You have an actor in your company called "Bijou" whom everyone is talking about lately. I should so much like to meet him, but so far I haven't had an opportunity.'

'That's me!' said Jiang Yu-han. ' "Bijou" is my stage-name.'

Bao-yu stamped with delight.

'But this is wonderful! I must say, you fully deserve your reputation. Oh dear! What am I going to do about a First Meeting present?'

He thought for a bit, then took a fan from his sleeve and broke off its jade pendant.

'Here you are,' he said, handing it to Bijou. 'It's not much of a present, I'm afraid, but it will do to remind you of our meeting.'

Bijou smiled and accepted it ceremoniously:

'I have done nothing to deserve this favour. It is too great an honour. Well, thank you. There's rather an unusual thing I'm wearing – I put it on today for the first time, so it's still fairly new: I wonder if you will allow me to give it to you as a token of my warm feelings towards you?'

He opened up his gown, undid the crimson cummerbund with which his trousers were fastened, and handed it to Bao-yu.

'It comes from the tribute sent by the Queen of the Madder Islands. It's for wearing in summer. It makes you smell nice and it doesn't show perspiration stains. I was given it yesterday by the Prince of Bei-jing, and today is the first time it's ever been worn. I wouldn't give a thing like this to anyone else, but I'd like *you* to have it. Will you take your own sash off, please, so that I can put it on instead?'

Bao-yu received the crimson cummerbund with delight and quickly took off his own viridian-coloured sash to give to Bijou in exchange. They had just finished fastening the sashes on again when Xue Pan jumped out from behind and seized hold of them both.

'What are you two up to, leaving the party and sneaking off like this?' he said. 'Come on, take 'em out again and let's have a look!'

It was useless for them to protest that the situation was not what he imagined. Xue Pan continued to force his unwelcome attentions upon them until Feng Zi-ying came out and rescued them. After that they returned to the party and continued drinking until the evening.

Back in his own apartment in the Garden, Bao-yu took off his outer clothes and relaxed with a cup of tea. While he did so, Aroma noticed that the pendant of his fan was missing and asked him what had become of it. Bao-yu told her that it had come off while he was riding, and she gave the matter no more thought. But later, when he was going to bed, she saw the magnificent blood-red sash round his waist and began to put two and two together.

'Since you've got a better sash now,' she said, 'do you think I could have mine back, please?'

Bao-yu remembered, too late, that the viridian sash had been Aroma's and that he ought never to have given it away. He now very much regretted having done so, but instead of apologizing, attempted to pass it off with a laugh.

'I'll get you another,' he told her lightly.

Aroma shook her head and sighed.

'I knew you still got up to these tricks,' she said, 'but at least you might refrain from giving *my* things to those disgusting creatures. I'm surprised you haven't got more sense.'

She was going to say more, but checked herself for fear of provoking an explosion while he was in his cups. And since there was nothing else she could do, she went to bed.

She awoke at first daylight next morning to find Bao-yu smiling down at her:

'We might have been burgled last night for all you'd have known about it – Look at your trousers!'

Looking down, Aroma saw the sash that Bao-yu had been wearing yesterday tied round her own waist, and knew that he must have exchanged it for hers during the night. She tore it off impatiently.

'*I* don't want the horrible thing. The sooner you take it away the better.'

Bao-yu was anxious that she should keep it, and after a great deal of coaxing she consented, very reluctantly, to tie it on again. But she took it off once and for all as soon as he was out of the room and threw it into an empty chest, having first found another one of her own to put on in its place.

Bao-yu made no comment on the change when they were together again. He merely inquired whether anything had happened the day before, while he was out.

'Mrs Lian sent someone round to fetch Crimson,' said Aroma. 'She wanted to wait for you; but it seemed to me that it wasn't all that important, so I took it on myself to send her off straight away.'

'Quite right,' said Bao-yu. 'I already knew about it. There was no need to wait till I got back.'

Aroma continued:

'Her Grace sent that Mr Xia of the Imperial Bedchamber yesterday with a hundred and twenty taels of silver to pay for a three-day *Pro Viventibus* by the Taoists of the Lunar Queen temple starting on the first of next month. There are to be plays performed as part of the Offering, and Mr Zhen and all the other gentlemen are to go there to burn incense. Oh, and Her Grace's presents for the Double Fifth have arrived.'

She ordered a little maid to get out Bao-yu's share of the things sent. There were two Palace fans of exquisite workmanship, two strings of red musk-scented medicine-beads, two lengths of maidenhair chiffon and a grass-woven 'lotus' mat to lie on in the hot weather.

'Did the others all get the same?' he asked.

'Her Old Ladyship's presents were the same as yours with the addition of a perfume-sceptre and an agate head-rest, and Sir Zheng's, Lady Wang's and Mrs Xue's were the same as Her Old Ladyship's but without the head-rest; Miss Bao's were exactly the same as yours; Miss Lin, Miss Ying-chun, Miss Tan-chun and Miss Xi-chun got only the fans and the beads; and Mrs Zhu and Mrs Lian both got two lengths of gauze, two lengths of chiffon, two perfume sachets and two moulded medicine-cakes.'

'Funny!' said Bao-yu. 'I wonder why Miss Lin didn't get the same as me and why only Miss Bao's and mine were the same. There must have been some mistake, surely?'

'When they unpacked them yesterday, the separate lots were all labelled,' said Aroma. 'I don't see how there could have been any mistake. Your share was in Her Old Ladyship's room and I went round there to get it for you. Her Old Ladyship says she wants you to go to Court at four o'clock tomorrow morning to give thanks.'

'Yes, of course,' said Bao-yu inattentively, and gave Ripple instructions to take his presents round to Dai-yu:

'Tell Miss Lin that I got these things yesterday and that if there's anything there she fancies, I should like her to keep it.'

Ripple went off with the presents. She was back in a very short time, however.

'Miss Lin says she got some yesterday too, and will you please keep these for yourself.'

Bao-yu told her to put them away. As soon as he had washed, he left to pay his morning call on Grandmother Jia; but just as he was going out he saw Dai-yu coming towards him and hurried forward to meet her.

'Why didn't you choose anything from the things I sent you?'

Yesterday's resentments were now quite forgotten; today Dai-yu had fresh matter to occupy her mind.

'I'm not equal to the honour,' she said. 'You forget, I'm not in the gold and jade class like you and your Cousin Bao. I'm only a common little wall-flower!'

The reference to gold and jade immediately aroused Bao-yu's suspicions.

'I don't know what anyone else may have been saying on the subject,' he said, 'but if any such thought ever so much as crossed *my* mind, may Heaven strike me dead, and may I never be reborn as a human being!'

Seeing him genuinely bewildered, Dai-yu smiled in what was meant to be a reassuring manner.

'I wish you wouldn't make these horrible oaths. It's so disagreeable. Who *cares* about your silly old "gold and jade", anyway?'

'It's hard to make you *see* what is in my heart,' said Bao-yu. 'One day perhaps you will know. But I can tell you this. My heart has room for four people only. Grannie and my parents are three of them and Cousin Dai is the fourth. I swear to you there isn't a fifth.'

'There's no need for you to swear,' said Dai-yu. 'I know very well that Cousin Dai has a place in your heart. The trouble is that as soon as Cousin Chai comes along, Cousin Dai gets forgotten.'

'You imagine these things,' said Bao-yu. 'It really isn't as you say.'

'Yesterday when Little Miss Bao wouldn't tell lies for you, why did you turn to *me* and expect *me* to? How would you like it if I did that sort of thing to you?'

Bao-chai happened to come along while they were still talking and the two of them moved aside to avoid her. Bao-chai saw this clearly, but pretended not to notice and hurried by with lowered eyes. She went and sat with Lady Wang for a while and from there went on to Grandmother Jia's. Bao-yu was already at his grandmother's when she got there.

Bao-chai had on more than one occasion heard her mother telling Lady Wang and other people that the golden locket she wore had been given her by a monk, who had insisted that when she grew up the person she married must be someone who had 'a jade to match the gold'. This was one of the reasons why she tended to keep aloof from Bao-yu. The slight embarrassment she always felt as a result of her mother's chatter had yesterday been greatly intensified when Yuan-chun singled her out as the only girl to receive the same selection of presents as Bao-yu. She was relieved to think that Bao-yu, so wrapped up in Dai-yu that his thoughts were only of her, was unaware of her embarrassment.

But now here was Bao-yu smiling at her with sudden interest.

'Cousin Bao, may I have a look at your medicine-beads?'

She happened to be wearing one of the little chaplets on her left wrist and began to pull it off now in obedience to his request. But Bao-chai was inclined to plumpness and perspired easily, and for a moment or two it would not come off. While she was struggling with it, Bao-yu had ample opportunity to observe her snow-white arm, and a feeling rather warmer than admiration was kindled inside him.

'If that arm were growing on Cousin Lin's body,' he speculated, 'I might hope one day to touch it. What a pity it's hers! Now I shall never have that good fortune.'

Suddenly he thought of the curious coincidence of the gold and jade talismans and their matching inscriptions, which Dai-yu's remark had reminded him of. He looked again at Bao-chai –

> that face like the full moon's argent bowl;
> those eyes like sloes;
> those lips whose carmine hue no Art contrived;
> and brows by none but Nature's pencil lined.

This was beauty of quite a different order from Dai-yu's. Fascinated by it, he continued to stare at her with a somewhat dazed expression, so that when she handed him the chaplet, which she had now succeeded in getting off her wrist, he failed to take it from her.

Seeing that he had gone off into one of his trances, Bao-chai threw down the chaplet in embarrassment and turned to go. But Dai-yu was standing on the threshold, biting a corner of her handkerchief, convulsed with silent laughter.

'I thought you were so delicate,' said Bao-chai. 'What are you standing there in the draught for?'

'I've been in the room all the time,' said Dai-yu. 'I just this moment went to have a look outside because I heard the sound of something in the sky. It was a gawping goose.'

'Where?' said Bao-chai. 'Let *me* have a look.'

'Oh,' said Dai-yu, 'as soon as I went outside he flew away with a *whir-r-r—*'

She flicked her long handkerchief as she said this in the direction of Bao-yu's face.

'Ow!' he exclaimed – She had flicked him in the eye.

The extent of the damage will be examined in the following chapter.

CHAPTER 29

*In which the greatly blessed pray for yet greater blessings
And the highly strung rise to new heights of passion*

WE told in the last chapter how, as Bao-yu was standing lost
in one of his trances, Dai-yu flicked her handkerchief at him
and made him jump by inadvertently catching him in the eye
with it.

'Who did that?' he asked.

Dai-yu laughingly shook her head.

'I'm sorry. I didn't mean to. Bao-chai wanted to look at a
gawping goose, and I accidently flicked you while I was showing
her how it went.'

Bao-yu rubbed his eye. He appeared to be about to say
something, but then thought better of it.

And so the matter passed.

*

Shortly after this incident Xi-feng arrived and began talking
about the arrangements that had been made for the purifica-
tion ceremonies, due to begin on the first of next month at
the Taoist temple of the Lunar Goddess. She invited Bao-
chai, Bao-yu and Dai-yu to go with her there to watch the
plays.

'Oh *no*!' said Bao-chai. 'It's too *hot*. Even if they were to do
something we haven't seen before – which isn't likely – I think
I should still not want to go.'

'But it's *cool* there,' said Xi-feng. 'There are upstairs galleries on all three sides that you can watch from in the shade.
And if we go, I shall send someone a day or two in advance to
turn the Taoists out of that part of the temple and make it nice
and clean for us and get them to put up blinds. And I'll ask
them not to let any other visitors in on that day. I've already
told Lady Wang I'm going, so if you others won't come with
me, I shall go by myself. I'm so bored lately. And it's such a

business when we put on our own plays at home, that I can never enjoy them properly.'

'All right then, I'll come,' said Grandmother Jia, who had been listening.

'*You*'ll come, Grannie? Well that's splendid, isn't it! That means it will be just as bad for me as it would be if I were watching here at home.'

'Now look here,' said Grandmother Jia, 'I shan't want you to stand and wait on me. Let me take the gallery facing the stage and you can have one of the side galleries all to yourself; then you can sit down and enjoy yourself in comfort.'

Xi-feng was touched.

'*Do* come!' Grandmother Jia said to Bao-chai. 'I'll see that your mother comes too. The days are so long now, and there's nothing to do at home except go to sleep.'

Bao-chai had to promise that she would go.

Grandmother Jia now sent someone to invite Aunt Xue. The messenger was to call in on the way at Lady Wang's and ask her if the girls might go as well.

Lady Wang had already made it clear that she would not be going herself, partly because she was not feeling very well, and partly because she wanted to be at home in case any further messages arrived from Yuan-chun; but when she learned of Grandmother Jia's enthusiasm, she had word carried into the Garden that not just the girls but anyone else who wanted to might go along with Grandmother Jia's party on the first.

When this exciting news had been transmitted throughout the Garden, the maids – some of whom hardly set foot outside their own courtyards from one year's end to the next – were all dying to go, and those whose mistresses showed a lethargic disinclination to accept employed a hundred different wiles to make sure that they did so. The result was that in the end *all* the Garden's inhabitants said that they would be going. Grandmother Jia was quite elated and at once issued orders for the cleaning and preparation of the temple theatre.

But these are details with which we need not concern ourselves.

On the morning of the first sedans, carriages, horses and

people filled all the roadway outside Rong-guo House. The stewards in charge knew that the occasion of this outing was a *Pro Viventibus* ordered by Her Grace the Imperial Concubine and that Her Old Ladyship was going in person to burn incense – quite apart from the fact that this was the first day of the month and the first day of the Summer Festival; consequently the turnout was as splendid as they could make it and far exceeded anything that had been seen on previous occasions.

Presently Grandmother Jia appeared, seated, in solitary splendour, in a large palanquin carried by eight bearers. Li Wan, Xi-feng and Aunt Xue followed, each in a palanquin with four bearers. After them came Bao-chai and Dai-yu sharing a carriage with a splendid turquoise-coloured canopy trimmed with pearls. The carriage after them, in which Ying-chun, Tan-chun and Xi-chun sat, had vermilion-painted wheels and was shaded with a large embroidered umbrella. After them rode Grandmother Jia's maids, Faithful, Parrot, Amber and Pearl; after them Lin Dai-yu's maids, Nightingale, Snowgoose and Delicate; then Bao-chai's maids, Oriole and Apricot; then Ying-chun's maids, Chess and Tangerine; then Tan-chun's maids, Scribe and Ebony; then Xi-chun's maids, Picture and Landscape; then Aunt Xue's maids, Providence and Prosper, sharing a carriage with Caltrop and Caltrop's own maid, Advent; then Li Wan's maids, Candida and Casta; then Xi-feng's own maids, Patience, Felicity and Crimson, with two of Lady Wang's maids, Golden and Suncloud, whom Xi-feng had agreed to take with her, in the carriage behind. In the carriage after them sat another couple of maids and a nurse holding Xi-feng's little girl. Yet more carriages followed carrying the nannies and old women from the various apartments and the women whose duty it was to act as duennas when the ladies of the household went out of doors. The street was packed with carriages as far as the eye could see in either direction, and Grandmother Jia's palanquin was well on the way to the temple before the last passengers in the rear had finished taking their places. A confused hubbub of laughter and chatter rose from the line of carriages while they were doing so, punctuated by an occasional louder and more distinctly audible protest, such as:

'I'm not sitting next to *you*!'

or,

'You're squashing the Mistress's bundle!'

or,

'Look, you've trodden on my spray!'

or,

'You've ruined my fan, clumsy!'

Zhou Rui's wife walked up and down calling for some order:

'Girls! Girls! You're out in the street now, where people can see you. A little behaviour, *please*!'

She had to do this several times before the clamour subsided somewhat.

The footmen and insignia-bearers at the front of the procession had now reached the temple, and as the files of their column opened out to range themselves on either side of the gateway, the onlookers lining the sides of the street were able to see Bao-yu on a splendidly caparisoned white horse riding at the head of the procession immediately in front of his grandmother's great palanquin with its eight bearers. As Grandmother Jia and her party approached the temple, there was a crash of drums and cymbals from the roadside. It was the Taoists of the temple come out to welcome them, with old Abbot Zhang at their head, resplendent in cope and vestments and with a burning joss-stick in his hand.

The palanquin passed through the gateway and into the first courtyard. From her seat inside it Grandmother Jia could see the terrifying painted images of the temple guardians, one on each side of the inner gate, flanked by that equally ferocious pair, Thousand League Eye with his blue face and Favourable Wind Ear with his green one, and farther on, the benigner forms of the City God and the little Local Gods. She ordered the bearers to halt, and Cousin Zhen at the head of the younger male members of the clan came forward from the inner courtyard to meet her.

Xi-feng, whose palanquin was nearest to Grandmother Jia's, realized that Faithful and the other maids were too far back in the procession to be able to reach the old lady in time to help her out, and hurried forward to perform this service herself. Unfortunately a little eleven- or twelve-year-old acolyte, who had been going round with a pair of snuffers trimming the wicks of the numerous candles that were burning everywhere and whom the arrival of the procession had caught unawares, chose this very moment to attempt a getaway and ran head-on into her. Out flew Xi-feng's hand and dealt him a resounding smack on the face that sent him flying.

'Clumsy brat!' she shouted. 'Look where you're going!'

The little acolyte picked himself up and, leaving his snuffers where they had fallen, darted off in the direction of the gate. But by now Bao-chai and the other young ladies were getting down from their carriages and a phalanx of women-servants clustered all round them, making egress impossible. Seeing a little Taoist running towards them, the women began to scream and shout:

'Catch him! Catch him! Hit him! Hit him!'

'What is it?' asked Grandmother Jia in alarm, hearing this hubbub behind her, and Cousin Zhen went forward to investigate.

'It's one of the young acolytes,' said Xi-feng as she helped the old lady from her conveyance. 'He was snuffing the candles and didn't get away in time and now he's rushing around trying to find a way out.'

'Bring him to me, poor little thing!' said Grandmother Jia. 'And don't frighten him. These children from poorer families have generally been rather spoiled. You can't expect them to stand up to great occasions like this. It would be a shame to frighten the poor little thing out of his wits. Think how upset his mother and father would be. Go on!' she said to Cousin Zhen. 'Go and fetch him yourself.'

Cousin Zhen was obliged to retrieve the little Taoist in person and led him by the hand to Grandmother Jia. The boy knelt down in front of her, the snuffers – now restored to him – clutched in one hand, trembling like a leaf. Grandmother Jia asked Cousin Zhen to raise him to his feet.

'Don't be afraid,' she told the boy. 'How old are you?'

But the little boy's mouth was hurting him too badly to speak.

'*Poor* little thing!' said Grandmother Jia. 'You'd better take him away, Zhen. Give him some money to buy sweeties with and tell the others that they are not to grumble at him.'

Cousin Zhen had to promise, and led the boy away, while the old lady led *her* party inside to begin a systematic tour of the shrines.

The pages in the outer courtyard, who had a moment before witnessed Grandmother Jia and her train trooping through the gateway that led into the inner courtyard, were surprised to see Cousin Zhen now emerging from it again with a little Taoist in tow. They heard him say that the boy was to be taken out and given a few hundred cash and that he was to be treated kindly. A few of them came forward and led the child away in obedience to his instructions.

Still standing at the top of the steps to the inner gate, Cousin Zhen inquired what had become of the stewards.

'Steward! Steward!' shouted the pages in unison, and almost immediately Lin Zhi-xiao came running out from heaven knows where, adjusting his hat with one hand as he ran.

'This is a big place,' said Cousin Zhen when Lin Zhi-xiao was standing in front of him, 'and we weren't expecting so many here today. I want you to take all the people you need and stay here in this courtyard with them. Those you don't need here can wait in the second courtyard. And pick some reliable boys to go on this gate and the two posterns to pass word through to those outside if those inside need anything. Do you understand? All the ladies are here today and I don't want any outsiders to get in. Is that understood?'

'Yessir!' said Lin Zhi-xiao. 'Sir!'

'Well get on with it!' said Cousin Zhen. 'Where's Rong got to?'

The words were scarcely out of his mouth when Jia Rong came bounding out of the bell-tower, buttoning his jacket as he ran.

'Look at him!' said Cousin Zhen irately. 'Enjoying himself in the cool while I am roasting down here! Spit at him, someone.'

Long familiarity with Cousin Zhen's temper had taught the boys that he would brook no opposition when roused. One of them obediently stepped forward and spat in Jia Rong's face; then, as Cousin Zhen continued to glare at him, he rebuked Jia Rong for presuming to be cool while his father was still sweating outside in the sun. Jia Rong was obliged to stand with his arms hanging submissively at his sides throughout this public humiliation, not daring to utter a word.

The other members of Jia Rong's generation who were present – Jia Yun, Jia Ping, Jia Qin and the rest – were greatly alarmed by this outburst; indeed, even the clansmen of Cousin Zhen's own generation – the Jia Bins and Jia Huangs and Jia Qiongs – were to be seen putting their hats on and slinking out, one by one, from the shadow of the walls.

'What are you standing here for?' said Cousin Zhen to Jia Rong. 'Why don't you get on your horse and go back home and tell your mother and that new wife of yours that Her Old Ladyship is here with all the Rong-guo girls. Tell them they must come here at once to wait on her.'

Jia Rong ran outside and began bawling impatiently for his horse. 'What on earth can have got into him that he should suddenly have picked on me like that?' he muttered to himself resentfully; then, as his horse had still not arrived, he shouted angrily at the grooms:

'Come on, bring that horse, damn you! Are your hands tied or something?'

He would have liked to send a boy in his place, but was afraid that if he did, his father would find out when he went back later to report; and so, when the horse arrived, he mounted and rode off home.

Cousin Zhen was about to turn and go in again when he discovered old Abbot Zhang at his elbow, smiling somewhat unnaturally.

'Perhaps I don't come in quite the same category as the

others,' said the old Taoist. 'Perhaps I should be allowed inside to wait on Her Old Ladyship. However. In this inclement
heat, and with so many young ladies about, I shouldn't like
to presume. I will do whatever you say. I *did* just wonder
whether Her Old Ladyship might ask for me, or whether she
might require a guide to take her round the shrines . . . However. Perhaps it would be best if I waited here.'

Cousin Zhen was aware that, though Abbot Zhang had
started life a poor boy and entered the Taoist church as 'proxy
novice' of Grandmother Jia's late husband, a former Emperor
had with his own Imperial lips conferred on him the title
'Doctor Mysticus', and he now held the seals of the Board of
Commissioners of the Taoist Church, had been awarded the
title 'Doctor Serenissimus' by the reigning sovereign, and was
addressed as 'Holiness' by princes, dukes and governors of
provinces. He was therefore not a man to be trifled with.
Moreover he was constantly in and out of the two mansions
and on familiar terms with most of the Jia ladies. Cousin Zhen
at once became affable.

'Oh, *you*'re one of the family, Papa Zhang, so let's have no
more of that kind of talk, or I'll take you by that old beard of
yours and give it a good pull. Come on, follow me!'

Abbot Zhang followed him inside, laughing delightedly.

Having found Grandmother Jia, Cousin Zhen ducked and
smiled deferentially.

'Papa Zhang has come to pay his respects, Grannie.'

'Help him, then!' said Grandmother Jia; and Cousin Zhen
hurried back to where Abbot Zhang was waiting a few yards
behind him and supported him by an elbow into her presence.
The abbot prefaced his greeting with a good deal of jovial
laughter.

'Blessed Buddha of Boundless Life! And how has Your Old
Ladyship been all this while? In rude good health, I trust?
And Their Ladyships, and all the younger ladies? – also
flourishing? It's quite a while since I was at the mansion to
call on Your Old Ladyship, but I declare you look more
blooming than ever!'

'And how are *you*, old Holy One?' Grandmother Jia asked him with a pleased smile.

'Thank Your Old Ladyship for asking. I still keep pretty fit. But never mind about that. What *I* want to know is, how's our young hero been keeping, eh? We were celebrating the blessed Nativity of the Veiled King here on the twenty-sixth. Very select little gathering. Tasteful offerings. I thought our young friend might have enjoyed it; but when I sent round to invite him, they told me he was out.'

'He really *was* out,' said Grandmother Jia, and turned aside to summon the 'young hero'; but Bao-yu had gone to the lavatory. He came hurrying forward presently.

'Hallo, Papa Zhang! How are you?'

The old Taoist embraced him affectionately and returned his greeting.

'He's beginning to fill out,' he said, addressing Grandmother Jia.

'He looks well enough on the outside,' said Grandmother Jia, 'but underneath he's delicate. And his Pa doesn't improve matters by forcing him to study all the time. I'm afraid he'll end up by *making* the child ill.'

'Lately I've been seeing calligraphy and poems of his in all kinds of places,' said Abbot Zhang, '– all quite remarkably good. I really can't understand why Sir Zheng is concerned that the boy doesn't study enough. If you ask me, I think he's all right as he is.' He sighed. 'Of course, you know who this young man reminds me of, don't you? Whether it's his looks or the way he talks or the way he moves, to me he's the spit and image of Old Sir Jia.'

The old man's eyes grew moist, and Grandmother Jia herself showed a disposition to be tearful.

'It's quite true,' she said. 'None of our children or our children's children turned out like him, except my Bao. Only my little Jade Boy is like his grandfather.'

'Of course, your generation wouldn't remember Old Sir Jia,' Abbot Zhang said, turning to Cousin Zhen. 'It's before your time. In fact, I don't suppose even Sir She and Sir Zheng can have a very clear recollection of what their father was like in his prime.'

He brightened as another topic occurred to him and once more quaked with laughter.

'I saw a most attractive young lady when I was out visiting the other day. Fourteen this year. Seeing her put me in mind of our young friend here. It must be about time we started thinking about a match for him, surely? In looks, intelligence, breeding, background this girl was ideally suited. What does Your Old Ladyship feel? I didn't want to rush matters. I thought I'd better first wait and see what Your Old Ladyship thought before saying anything to the family.'

'A monk who once told the boy's fortune said that he was not to marry young,' said Grandmother Jia; 'so I think we had better wait until he is a little older before we arrange anything definite. But do by all means go on inquiring for us. It doesn't matter whether the family is wealthy or not; as long as the girl *looks* all right, you can let me know. Even if it's a poor family, we can always help out over the expenses. Money is no problem. It's looks and character that count.'

'Now come on, Papa Zhang!' said Xi-feng when this exchange had ended. 'Where's that new amulet for my little girl? You had the nerve to send someone round the other day for gosling satin, and of course, as we didn't want to embarrass the old man by refusing, we had to send you some. So now what about that amulet?'

Abbot Zhang once more quaked with laughter.

'Ho! ho! ho! You can tell how bad my eyes are getting; I didn't even see you there, dear lady, or I should have thanked you for the satin. Yes, the amulet has been ready for some time. I was going to send it to you two days ago, but then Her Grace unexpectedly asked us for this *Pro Viventibus* and I stupidly forgot all about it. It's still on the high altar being sanctified. I'll go and get it for you.'

He went off, surprisingly nimbly, to the main hall of the temple and returned after a short while carrying the amulet on a little tea-tray, using a red satin book-wrap as a tray-cloth.

Baby's nurse took the amulet from him, and he was just about to receive the little girl from her arms when he caught sight of Xi-feng laughing at him mockingly.

'Why didn't you bring it in your hand?' she asked him.

'The hands get so sweaty in this weather,' he said. 'I thought a tray would be more hygienic.'

'You gave me quite a fright when I saw you coming in with that tray,' said Xi-feng. 'I thought for one moment you were going to take up a collection!'

There was a loud burst of laughter from the assembled company. Even Cousin Zhen was unable to restrain himself.

'Monkey! Monkey!' said Grandmother Jia. 'Aren't you afraid of going to the Hell of Scoffers when you die and having your tongue cut out?'

'Oh, Papa and I say what we like to each other,' said Xi-feng. *He*'s always telling *me* I must "acquire merit" and threatening me with a short life if I don't pay up quickly. That's right, isn't it Papa?'

'As a matter of fact I *did* have an ulterior motive in bringing this tray,' said Abbot Zhang, laughing, 'but it wasn't in order to make a collection, I assure you. I wanted to ask this young gentleman here if he would be so very kind as to lend me the famous jade for a few minutes. The tray is for carrying it outside on, so that my Taoist friends, some of whom have travelled long distances to be here, and my old students, and *their* students, all of whom are gathered here today, may have the privilege of examining it.'

'My dear good man, in that case let the boy go with it round his neck and show it to them himself!' said Grandmother Jia. 'No need for all this running to and fro with trays – at your age, too!'

'Most kind! Most considerate! – But Your Old Ladyship is deceived,' said the abbot. 'I may look my eighty years, but I'm still hale and hearty. No, the point is that with so many of them here today and the weather so hot, the smell is sure to be somewhat overpowering. Our young friend here is certainly not used to it. We shouldn't want him to be overcome by the – ah – effluvia, should we?'

Hearing this, Grandmother Jia told Bao-yu to take off the Magic Jade and put it on the tray. Abbot Zhang draped the crimson cloth over his hands, grasped the tray between satin-covered thumbs and fingers, and, holding it like a sacred relic at eye level in front of him, conveyed it reverently from the courtyard.

Grandmother Jia and the others now continued their sight-seeing. They had finished with everything at ground level and were about to mount the stairs into the galleries when Cousin Zhen came up to report that Abbot Zhang had returned with the jade. He was followed by the smiling figure of the abbot, holding the tray in the same reverential manner as before.

'Well, they've all seen the jade now,' he said, ' – and very grateful they were. They agreed that it really is a most remarkable object, and they regretted that they had nothing of value to show their appreciation with. Here you are! – this is the best they could do. These are all little Taoist trinkets they happened to have about them. Nothing very special, I'm afraid; but they'd like our young friend to keep them, either to amuse himself with or to give away to his friends.'

Grandmother Jia looked at the tray. It was covered with jewellery. There were golden crescents, jade thumb-rings and a lot of 'motto' jewellery – a tiny sceptre and persimmons with the rebus-meaning 'success in all things', a little quail and a vase with corn-stalks meaning 'peace throughout the years', and many other designs – all in gold- or jade-work, and much of it inlaid with pearls and precious stones. Altogether there must have been about forty pieces.

'What have you been up to, you naughty old man?' she said. 'Those men are all poor priests – they can't afford to give things like *this* away. You really shouldn't have done this. We can't possibly accept them.'

'It was their own idea, I do assure you,' said the abbot. 'There was nothing I could do to stop them. If you refuse to take these things, I am afraid you will destroy my credit with these people. They will say that I cannot really have the connection with your honoured family that I have always claimed to have.'

After this Grandmother Jia could no longer decline. She told one of the servants to receive the tray.

'We obviously can't refuse, Grannie, after what Papa Zhang has just said,' said Bao-yu; 'but I really have no use for this stuff. Why not let one of the boys carry it outside for me and I'll distribute it to the poor?'

'I think that's a very good idea,' said Grandmother Jia.

But Abbot Zhang thought otherwise and hastily intervened:

'I'm sure it does our young friend credit, this charitable impulse. However. Although these things are, as I said, of no especial value, they are – what shall I say – objects of *virtù*, and if you give them to the poor, in the first place the poor won't have much use for them, and in the second place the objects themselves will get spoiled. If you want to give something to the poor, a largesse of money would, I suggest, be far more appropriate.'

'Very well, look after this stuff for me, then,' said Bao-yu to the servant, 'and this evening you will distribute a largesse.'

This being now settled, Abbot Zhang withdrew, and Grandmother Jia and her party went up to the galleries. Grandmother Jia sat with Bao-yu and the girls in the gallery facing the stage and Xi-feng and Li Wan sat in the east gallery. The maids all sat in the west gallery and took it in turns to go off and wait on their mistresses.

Not long after they were all seated, Cousin Zhen came upstairs to say that the gods had now chosen which plays were to be performed – by which was meant, of course, that the names had been shaken from a pot in front of the altar, since this was the only way in which the will of the gods could be known. The first play selected was *The White Serpent*.

'What's the story?' said Grandmother Jia.

Cousin Zhen explained that it was about the emperor Gao-zu, founder of the Han dynasty, who began his rise to greatness by decapitating a monstrous white snake.

The second choice was *A Heap of Honours*, which shows the sixtieth birthday party of the great Tang general Guo Zi-yi, attended by his seven sons and eight sons-in-law, all of whom held high office, the 'heap of honours' of the title being a reference to the table in his reception-hall piled high with their insignia.

'It seems a bit conceited to have this second one played,' said Grandmother Jia. 'Still, if that's what the gods chose, I suppose we'd better have it. What's the third one going to be?'

'*The South Branch*,' said Cousin Zhen.

Grandmother Jia was silent. She knew that *The South Branch* likens the world to an ant-heap and tells a tale of power and glory which turns out in the end to have been a dream.

Hearing no reply, Cousin Zhen went off downstairs again to see about the Offertory Scroll, which had to be ceremonially burnt in front of the holy images along with paper money and paper ingots before the theatrical performance could begin.

Our record omits any description of that ceremony and moves back to Bao-yu, who was sitting in the central gallery beside his grandmother, and who now called for a maid to bring the tray up so that he could put on his Magic Jade again. When he had done so, he began to pick over the other trinkets with which the tray was covered and to hand them one by one to Grandmother Jia for her inspection. Her attention was taken by a little red-gold kylin with kingfisher-feather inlay. She stretched out her hand to take it.

'Now where have I seen something like this before?' she said. 'I feel certain I've seen some girl wearing an ornament like this.'

'Cousin Shi's got one,' said Bao-chai. 'It's the same as this one only a little smaller.'

'Funny!' said Bao-yu. 'All the times she's been to our house, *I* don't remember ever having seen it.'

'Cousin Bao is observant,' said Tan-chun. 'No matter what it is, she remembers everything.'

'Well, perhaps not quite *everything*,' said Dai-yu wryly. 'But she's certainly very observant where things like *this* are concerned.'

Bao-chai turned her head away and pretended not to have heard.

Now that he knew the kylin on the tray was like one that Shi Xiang-yun wore, Bao-yu hurriedly picked it up and thrust it inside his jacket. But no sooner had he done so than it occurred to him that his action might be misconstrued; so instead of dropping it into his inside pocket, he continued to hold it there, at the same time glancing about him furtively to see if he had been observed. None of the others seemed to have noticed except Dai-yu, who was staring at him fixedly and nodding her head in mock approval

Bao-yu felt suddenly embarrassed. Drawing his hand out again with the ornament still in it, he returned her look and laughed sheepishly:

'It's rather nice, isn't it? I thought I'd keep it for you,' he said. 'When we get home we can thread it on a ribbon and you'll be able to wear it.'

Dai-yu tossed her head.

'*I* don't want it!'

'If *you* don't want it, I'll keep it for myself, then,' said Bao-yu, and popped it once more inside his jacket.

He was about to add something, but just at that moment Cousin Zhen's wife, You-shi, and his new daughter-in-law, Hu-shi, arrived and came upstairs to pay their respects to Grandmother Jia.

'Now why have *you* come here? You really shouldn't have bothered,' said Grandmother Jia. 'We only came to amuse ourselves. It isn't a formal visit.'

No sooner had she said this than it was announced that representatives from General Feng's household had arrived. It appeared that Feng Zi-ying's mother, hearing that the Jia ladies were having a *Pro Viventibus* performed at the Taoist temple, had immediately prepared an offering of pork, mutton, incense, tea and cakes and sent it post-haste to the temple with her compliments. Xi-feng, hearing the announcement, came hurrying round to the central gallery. She clapped her hands and laughed.

'Dear oh dear! This is something I hadn't bargained for. My idea was a quiet little outing for us girls; but here is everyone sending offerings and behaving as if we'd come here for a high mass or something. It's all your fault, Grannie! And we haven't even got any vails ready to give to the bearers.'

Even as she said this, two stewardesses from the Feng household were already mounting the stairs. And before *they* had gone, other messengers arrived with offerings from Vice-president Zhao's lady. From then on it was a steady stream: friends, kinsmen, family connections, business associates – all who had heard that the Jia ladies were holding a *Pro Viventibus* sent their representatives along with offerings and complimentary messages. Grandmother Jia began to regret that she had ever come.

'It isn't as if we'd come here for the ceremony,' she grumbled. 'We only wanted to enjoy ourselves. But all we seem to have done is to have stirred up a lot of fuss.'

Consequently, although she stayed and watched the plays for that day, she returned home fairly early in the afternoon and next day professed herself too lacking in energy to go again. Xi-feng reacted differently. 'In for a penny, in for a pound' was her motto. They had already had the fuss; and since the players were there anyway, they might as well go again today and enjoy themselves in peace.

For Bao-yu the whole of the previous day had been spoilt by Abbot Zhang's proposal to Grandmother Jia to arrange a match for him. He came home in a thoroughly bad temper and kept telling everyone that he would 'never see Abbot Zhang again as long as he lived'. Not associating his ill-humour with the abbot's proposal, the others were mystified.

Grandmother Jia's unwillingness was further reinforced by the fact that Dai-yu, since her return home yesterday, had been suffering from mild sunstroke. What with one thing and another, the old lady declined absolutely to go again, and Xi-feng had to make up her own party and go by herself.

But Xi-feng's play-going does not concern us.

*

Bao-yu, believing that Dai-yu's sunstroke was serious and that she might even be in danger of her life, was so worried that he could not eat, and rushed round in the middle of the

lunch-hour to see how she was. He found her neither as ill as
he had feared nor as responsive as he might have hoped.

'Why don't you go and watch your plays?' she asked him.
'What are you mooning about at home for?'

Abbot Zhang's recent attempt at match-making had profoundly distressed Bao-yu and he was shocked by her seeming
indifference.

'I can forgive the others for not understanding what has
upset me,' he thought; 'but that *she* should want to trifle
with me at a time like this . . .!'

The sense that she had failed him made the annoyance he
now felt with her a hundred times greater than it had been on
any previous occasion. Never could any other person have
stirred him to such depths of atrabilious rage. Coming from
other lips, her words would scarcely have touched him. Coming from hers, they put him in a passion. His face darkened.

'It's all along been a mistake, then,' he said. 'You're not
what I took you for.'

Dai-yu gave an unnatural little laugh.

'Not what you took me for? That's hardly surprising, is
it? I haven't got that *little something* which would have made
me worthy of you.'

Bao-yu came right up to her and held his face close to hers:

'You do realize, don't you, that you are deliberately willing
my death?'

Dai-yu could not for the moment understand what he was
talking about.

'I swore an oath to you yesterday,' he went on. 'I said that
I hoped Heaven might strike me dead if this "gold and jade"
business meant anything to me. Since you have now brought
it up again, it's clear to me that you *want* me to die. Though
what you hope to gain by my death I find it hard to imagine.'

Dai-yu now remembered what had passed between them
on the previous day. She knew that she was wrong to have
spoken as she did, and felt both ashamed and a little frightened.
Her shoulders started shaking and she began to cry.

'May Heaven strike *me* dead if I ever willed your death!'
she said. 'But I don't see what you have to get so worked up

about. It's only because of what Abbot Zhang said about arranging a match for you. You're afraid he might interfere with your precious "gold and jade" plans; and because you're angry about that, you have to come along and take it out on me – That's all it is, isn't it?'

Bao-yu had from early childhood manifested a streak of morbid sensibility, which being brought up in close proximity with a nature so closely in harmony with his own had done little to improve. Now that he had reached an age when both his experience and the reading of forbidden books had taught him something about 'worldly matters', he had begun to take a rather more grown-up interest in girls. But although there were plenty of young ladies of outstanding beauty and breeding among the Jia family's numerous acquaintance, none of them, in his view, could remotely compare with Dai-yu. For some time now his feeling for her had been a very special one; but precisely because of this same morbid sensibility, he had shrunk from telling her about it. Instead, whenever he was feeling particularly happy or particularly cross, he would invent all sorts of ways of probing her to find out if this feeling for her was reciprocated. It was unfortunate for him that Dai-yu herself possessed a similar streak of morbid sensibility and disguised her real feelings, as he did his, while attempting to discover what *he* felt about *her*.

Here was a situation, then, in which both parties concealed their real emotions and assumed counterfeit ones in an endeavour to find out what the real feelings of the other party were. And because

When false meets false the truth will oft-times out,

there was the constant possibility that the innumerable little frustrations that were engendered by all this concealment would eventually erupt into a quarrel.

Take the present instance. What Bao-yu was actually thinking at this moment was something like this:

'In my eyes and in my thoughts there is no one else but you. I can forgive the others for not knowing this, but surely *you* ought to realize? If at a time like this you can't share my anxiety – if you can think of nothing better to do than provoke me with that sort of silly talk, it shows that the concern I feel for you every waking minute of the day is wasted: that you just don't care about me at all.'

This was what he *thought*; but of course he didn't *say* it. On her side Dai-yu's thoughts were somewhat as follows:

'I know you must care for me a little bit, and I'm sure you don't take this ridiculous "gold and jade" talk seriously. But if you cared *only* for me and had absolutely no inclination at all in another direction, then every time I mentioned "gold and jade" you would behave quite naturally and let it pass almost as if you hadn't noticed. How is it, then, that when I do refer to it you get so excited? It shows that it must be on your mind. You *pretend* to be upset in order to allay my suspicions.'

Meanwhile a quite different thought was running through Bao-yu's mind:

'I would do anything – absolutely *anything*,' he was thinking, 'if only you would be nice to me. If you would be nice to me, I would gladly die for you this moment. It doesn't really matter whether you know what I feel for you or not. Just be nice to me, then at least we shall be a little closer to each other, instead of so horribly far apart.'

At the same time Dai-yu was thinking:

'Never mind me. Just be your own natural self. If *you* were all right, *I* should be all right too. All these manoeuvrings to try and anticipate my feelings don't bring us any closer together; they merely draw us farther apart.'

The percipient reader will no doubt observe that these two young people were already of one mind, but that the complicated procedures by which they sought to draw together were in fact having precisely the opposite effect. Complacent reader! Permit us to remind you that your correct understanding of the situation is due solely to the fact that we have been revealing to you the secret, innermost thoughts of those two young persons, which neither of them had so far ever felt able to express.

Let us now return from the contemplation of inner thoughts to the recording of outward appearances.

When Dai-yu, far from saying something nice to him, once more made reference to the 'gold and jade', Bao-yu became so choked with rage that for a moment he was quite literally bereft of speech. Frenziedly snatching the 'Magic Jade' from his neck and holding it by the end of its silken cord he gritted his teeth and dashed it against the floor with all the strength in his body.

'*Beastly* thing!' he shouted. 'I'll smash you to pieces and put an end to this once and for all.'

But the jade, being exceptionally hard and resistant, was not the tiniest bit damaged. Seeing that he had not broken it, Bao-yu began to look around for something to smash it with. Dai-yu, still crying, saw what he was going to do.

'Why smash a dumb, lifeless object?' she said. 'If you want to smash something, let it be me.'

The sound of their quarrelling brought Nightingale and Snowgoose hurrying in to keep the peace. They found Bao-yu apparently bent on destroying his jade and tried to wrest it from him. Failing to do so, and sensing that the quarrel was of more than usual dimensions, they went off to fetch Aroma. Aroma came back with them as fast as she could run and eventually succeeded in prising the jade from his hand. He glared at her scornfully.

'It's my own thing I'm smashing,' he said. 'What business is it of yours to interfere?'

Aroma saw that his face was white with anger and his eyes wild and dangerous. Never had she seen him in so terrible a rage. She took him gently by the hand:

'You shouldn't smash the jade just because of a disagreement with your cousin,' she said. 'What do you think she would feel like and what sort of position would it put her in if you really *were* to break it?'

Dai-yu heard these words through her sobs. They struck a responsive chord in her breast, and she wept all the harder to think that even Aroma seemed to understand her better than

Bao-yu did. So much emotion was too much for her weak stomach. Suddenly there was a horrible retching noise and up came the tisane of elsholtzia leaves she had taken only a short while before. Nightingale quickly held out her handkerchief to receive it and, while Snowgoose rubbed and pounded her back, Dai-yu continued to retch up wave upon wave of watery vomit, until the whole handkerchief was soaked with it.

'However cross you may be, Miss, you ought to have more regard for your health,' said Nightingale. 'You'd only just taken that medicine and you were beginning to feel a little bit better for it, and now because of your argument with Master Bao you've gone and brought it all up again. Suppose you were to be *really* ill as a consequence. How do you think Master Bao would feel?'

When Bao-yu heard these words they struck a responsive chord in *his* breast, and he reflected bitterly that even Nightingale seemed to understand him better than Dai-yu. But then he looked again at Dai-yu, who was sobbing and panting by turns, and whose red and swollen face was wet with perspiration and tears, and seeing how pitiably frail and ill she looked, his heart misgave him.

'I shouldn't have taken her up on that "gold and jade" business,' he thought. 'I've got her into this state and now there's no way in which I can relieve her by sharing what she suffers.' As he thought this, he, too, began to cry.

Now that Bao-yu and Dai-yu were both crying, Aroma instinctively drew towards her master to comfort him. A pang of pity for him passed through her and she squeezed his hand sympathetically. It was as cold as ice. She would have liked to tell him not to cry but hesitated, partly from the consideration that he might be suffering from some deep-concealed hurt which crying would do something to relieve, and partly from the fear that to do so in Dai-yu's presence might seem presumptuous. Torn between a desire to speak and fear of the possible consequences of speaking, she did what girls of her type often do when faced with a difficult decision: she avoided the necessity of making one by bursting into tears.

As for Nightingale, who had disposed of the handkerchief of vomited tisane and was now gently fanning her mistress with her fan, seeing the other three all standing there as quiet as mice with the tears streaming down their faces, she was so affected by the sight that she too started crying and was obliged to have recourse to a second handkerchief.

There the four of them stood, then, facing each other; all of them crying; none of them saying a word. It was Aroma who broke the silence with a strained and nervous laugh.

'You ought not to quarrel with Miss Lin,' she said to Bao-yu, 'if only for the sake of this pretty cord she made you.'

At these words Dai-yu, ill as she was, darted forward, grabbed the jade from Aroma's hand, and snatching up a pair of scissors that were lying nearby, began feverishly cutting at its silken cord with them. Before Aroma and Nightingale could stop her, she had already cut it into several pieces.

'It was a waste of time making it,' she sobbed. 'He doesn't really care for it. And there's someone else who'll no doubt make him a better one!'

'What a shame!' said Aroma, retrieving the jade. 'It's all my silly fault. I should have kept my mouth shut.'

'Go on! Cut away!' said Bao-yu. 'I shan't be wearing the wretched thing again anyway, so it doesn't matter.'

Preoccupied with the quarrel, the four of them had failed to notice several old women, who had been drawn by the sound of it to investigate. Apprehensive, when they saw Dai-yu hysterically weeping and vomiting and Bao-yu trying to smash his jade, of the dire consequences to be expected from a scene of such desperate passion, they had hurried off in a body to the front of the mansion to report the matter to Grandmother Jia and Lady Wang, hoping in this way to establish in advance that whatever the consequences might be, *they* were not responsible for them. From their precipitate entry and the grave tone of their announcement Grandmother Jia and Lady Wang assumed that some major catastrophe had befallen and hurried with them into the Garden to find out what it was.

Their arrival filled Aroma with alarm. 'What did Nightingale want to go troubling Their Ladyships for?' she thought crossly, supposing that the talebearer had been sent to them by Nightingale; while Nightingale for her part was angry with Aroma, thinking that the talebearer must have been one of Aroma's minions.

Grandmother Jia and Lady Wang entered the room to find a silent Bao-yu and a silent Dai-yu, neither of whom, when questioned, would admit that anything at all was the matter. They therefore visited their wrath on the heads of the two unfortunate maids, insisting that it was entirely owing to their negligence that matters had got so much out of hand. Unable to defend themselves, the girls were obliged to endure a long and abusive dressing-down, after which Grandmother Jia concluded the affair by carrying Bao-yu off to her own apartment.

Next day, the third of the fifth month, was Xue Pan's birthday and there was a family party with plays, to which the Jias were all invited. Bao-yu, who had still not seen Dai-yu since his outburst – which he now deeply regretted – was feeling far too dispirited to care about seeing plays, and declined to go on the ground that he was feeling unwell.

Dai-yu, though somewhat overcome on the day previous to this by the sultry weather, had by no means been seriously ill. Arguing that if *she* was not ill, it was impossible that *he* should be, she felt sure, when she heard of Bao-yu's excuse, that it must be a false one.

'He usually enjoys drinking and watching plays,' she thought. 'If he's not going, it must be because he is still angry about yesterday; or if it isn't that, it must be because he's heard that I'm not going and doesn't want to go without me. Oh! I should *never* have cut that cord! Now he won't ever wear his jade again – unless I make him another cord to wear it on.'

So she, too, regretted the quarrel.

Grandmother Jia knew that Bao-yu and Dai-yu were angry with each other, but she had been assuming that they would see each other at the Xues' party and make it up there.

When neither of them turned up at it, she became seriously upset.

'I'm a miserable old sinner,' she grumbled. 'It must be my punishment for something I did wrong in a past life to have to live with a pair of such obstinate, addle-headed little geese! I'm sure there isn't a day goes by without their giving me some fresh cause for anxiety. It must be fate. That's what it says in the proverb, after all:

> 'Tis Fate brings foes and lo'es tegither.

I'll be glad when I've drawn my last breath and closed my old eyes for the last time; then the two of them can snap and snarl at each other to their hearts' content, for *I* shan't be there to see it, and "what the eye doesn't see, the heart doesn't grieve". The Lord knows, it's not *my* wish to drag on this wearisome life any longer!'

Amidst these muttered grumblings the old lady began to cry.

In due course her words were transmitted to Bao-yu and Dai-yu. It happened that neither of them had ever heard the saying

> 'Tis Fate brings foes and lo'es tegither,

and its impact on them, hearing it for the first time, was like that of a Zen 'perception': something to be meditated on with bowed head and savoured with a gush of tears. Though they had still not made it up since their quarrel, the difference between them had now vanished completely:

> In Naiad's House one to the wind made moan,
> In Green Delights one to the moon complained,

to parody the well-known lines. Or, in homelier verses:

> Though each was in a different place,
> Their hearts in friendship beat as one.

On the second day after their quarrel Aroma deemed that the time was now ripe for urging a settlement.

'Whatever the rights and wrongs of all this may be,' she said to Bao-yu, '*you* are certainly the one who is *most* to blame. Whenever in the past you've heard about a quarrel between one of the pages and one of the girls, you've always said that the boy was a brute for not understanding the girl's feelings better – yet here you are behaving in exactly the same way yourself! Tomorrow will be the Double Fifth. Her Old Ladyship will be really angry if the two of you are still at daggers drawn on the day of the festival, and that will make life difficult for *all* of us. Why not put your pride in your pocket and go and say you are sorry, so that we can all get back to normal again?'

But as to whether or not Bao-yu followed her advice, or, if he did so, what the effect of following it was – those questions will be dealt with in the following chapter.

CHAPTER 30

Bao-chai speaks of a fan and castigates her deriders
Charmante scratches a 'qiang' and mystifies a beholder

Dai-yu, as we have shown, regretted her quarrel with Bao-yu
almost as soon as it was over; but since there were no conceivable grounds on which she could run after him and tell
him so, she continued, both day and night, in a state of un-
relieved depression that made her feel almost as if a part of her
was lost. Nightingale had a shrewd idea how it was with her
and resolved at last to tackle her:

'I think the day before yesterday you were too hasty, Miss.
We ought to know what things Master Bao is touchy about,
if no one else does. Look at all the quarrels we've had with
him in the past on account of that jade!'

'Poh!' said Dai-yu scornfully. 'You are trying to make out
that it was my fault because you have taken his side against
me. Of course I wasn't too hasty.'

Nightingale gave her a quizzical smile.

'No? Then why did you cut that cord up? If three parts of
the blame was Bao-yu's, I'm sure at least seven parts of it was
yours. From what I've seen of it, he's all right with you when
you allow him to be; it's because you're so prickly with him
and always trying to put him in the wrong that he gets worked
up.'

Dai-yu was about to retort when they heard someone at
the courtyard gate calling to be let in. Nightingale turned to
listen:

'That's Bao-yu's voice,' she said. 'I expect he has come to
apologize.'

'I forbid you to let him in,' said Dai-yu.

'There you go again!' said Nightingale. 'You're going to
keep him standing outside in the blazing sun on a day like
this. Surely *that*'s wrong, if nothing else is?'

She was moving outside, even as she said this, regardless of her mistress's injunction. Sure enough, it *was* Bao-yu. She unfastened the gate and welcomed him in with a friendly smile.

'Master Bao! I was beginning to think you weren't coming to see us any more. I certainly didn't expect to see you here again so soon.'

'Oh, you've been making a mountain out of a molehill,' said Bao-yu, returning her smile. 'Why ever shouldn't I come? Even if I died, my *ghost* would be round here a hundred times a day. How is my cousin? Quite better now?'

'Physically she's better,' said Nightingale, 'but she's still in very poor spirits.'

'Ah yes – I know she's upset.'

This exchange took place as they were crossing the forecourt. He now entered the room. Dai-yu was sitting on the bed crying. She had not been crying to start with, but the bittersweet pang she experienced when she heard his arrival had started the tears rolling. Bao-yu went up to the bed and smiled down at her.

'How are you, coz? Quite better now?'

As Dai-yu seemed to be too busy wiping her eyes to make a reply, he sat down close beside her on the edge of the bed:

'I know you're not *really* angry with me,' he said. 'It's just that if the others noticed I wasn't coming here, they would think we had been quarrelling; and if we waited for them to interfere, we should be allowing other people to come between us. It would be better to hit me and shout at me now and get it over with, if you still bear any hard feelings, than to go on ignoring me. Coz dear! Coz dear! —'

He must have repeated those same two words in the same tone of passionate entreaty upwards of twenty times. Dai-yu had been meaning to ignore him, but what he had just been saying about other people 'coming between' them seemed to prove that he must in *some* way feel closer to her than the rest, and she was unable to maintain her silence.

'You don't have to treat me like a child,' she blurted out tearfully. 'From now on I shall make no further claims on you. You can behave exactly as if I had gone away.'

'Gone away?' said Bao-yu laughingly. 'Where would you go to?'

'Back home.'

'I'd follow you.'

'As if I were dead then.'

'If you died,' he said, 'I should become a monk.'

Dai-yu's face darkened immediately:

'What an utterly idiotic thing to say! Suppose your own sisters were to die? Just how many times can one person become a monk? I think I had better see what the others think about that remark.'

Bao-yu had realized at once that she would be offended; but the words were already out of his mouth before he could stop them. He turned very red and hung his head in silence. It was a good thing that no one else was in the room at that moment to see him. Dai-yu glared at him for some seconds – evidently too enraged to speak, for she made a sound somewhere between a snort and a sigh, but said nothing – then, seeing him almost purple in the face with suppressed emotion, she clenched her teeth, pointed her finger at him, and, with an indignant 'Hmn!', stabbed the air quite savagely a few inches away from his forehead:

'You —!'

But whatever it was she had been going to call him never got said. She merely gave a sigh and began wiping her eyes again with her handkerchief.

Bao-yu had been in a highly emotional state when he came to see Dai-yu and it had further upset him to have inadvertently offended her so soon after his arrival. This angry gesture and the unsuccessful struggle, ending in sighs and tears, to say what she wanted to say now affected him so deeply that he, too, began to weep. In need of a handkerchief but finding that he had come out without one, he wiped his eyes on his sleeve.

Although Dai-yu was crying, the spectacle of Bao-yu using the sleeve of his brand-new lilac-coloured summer gown as a handkerchief had not escaped her, and while continuing to wipe her own eyes with one hand, she leaned over and reached with the other for the square of silk that was draped over the

head-rest at the end of the bed. She lifted it off and threw it at
him – all without uttering a word – then, once more burying
her face in her own handkerchief, resumed her weeping. Bao-
yu picked up the handkerchief she had thrown him and hurriedly wiped his eyes with it. When he had dried them, he
drew up close to her again and took one of her hands in his
own, smiling at her gently.

'I don't know why you go on crying,' he said. 'I feel as if
all my insides were shattered. Come! Let's go and see Grandmother together.'

Dai-yu flung off his hand.

'Take your hands off me! We're not children any more. You
really can't go on mauling me about like this all the time.
Don't you understand *anything* – ?'

'Bravo!'

The shouted interruption startled them both. They spun
round to look just as Xi-feng, full of smiles, came bustling
into the room.

'Grandmother has been grumbling away something *awful*,'
she said. 'She insisted that I should come over and see if you
were both all right. "Oh," I said, "there's no need to go and
look, Grannie; they'll have made it up by now without any
interference from *us*." So she told me I was lazy. Well, here I
am – and of course it's *exactly* as I said it would be. *I* don't
know. I don't understand you two. What is it you find to
argue about? For every three days that you're friends you
must spend at least two days quarrelling. You really are a
couple of babies. And the older you get, the worse you get.
Look at you *now* – holding hands crying! And a couple of
days ago you were glaring at each other like fighting-cocks.
Come on! Come with me to see Grandmother. Let's put the
old lady's mind at rest.'

As she said this, she seized Dai-yu's hand and began marching off with her. Dai-yu turned back and called for her maids,
but there was no response.

'What do you want to call *them* for?' said Xi-feng. 'You've
got *me* to wait on you, haven't you?'

She continued to walk away, still holding Dai-yu by the

hand. Bao-yu followed a little way behind. They went out of the Garden and through into Grandmother Jia's apartment.

'I *told* you they could be left to themselves to make it up and that there was no need for you to worry,' said Xi-feng to Grandmother Jia when they were all in the old lady's presence; 'but you wouldn't believe me, would you? You insisted on my going there to act the peacemaker. Well, I went there; and what did I find? I found the two of them together *apologizing* to each other. It was like the kite and the kestrel holding hands: they were positively *locked in a clinch!* No need of a peacemaker that *I* could see.'

There was a burst of laughter from all present. Bao-chai was among these, but Dai-yu slipped past her without speaking and took a seat next to Grandmother Jia. Bao-yu, rather at a loss for something to say, turned to Bao-chai.

'I'm afraid I wasn't very well on your brother's birthday; so apart from not giving him a present, I couldn't even make him a kotow this year. I'm afraid he may not have realized I was ill and thought that I was merely making excuses. If you can spare a moment next time you see him, I do hope you will explain to him for me.'

Bao-chai looked amused.

'That seems a trifle excessive. I am sure he would have felt uncomfortable about your kotowing to him, even if you had been able to come; so I'm quite sure he wouldn't have wanted you to come when you weren't feeling well. It would be rather unfriendly, surely, if cousins who see each other all the time were to start worrying about trifles like *that*?'

Bao-yu smiled.

'Well, as long as *you* understand, that's all right – But why aren't you watching the players?'

'I can't stand the heat,' said Bao-chai. 'I did watch a couple of acts of something, but it was so hot that I couldn't stay any longer. Unfortunately none of the guests showed any sign of going, so I had to pretend I was ill in order to get away.'

'*Touché!*' thought Bao-yu; but he hid his embarrassment in a stupid laugh.

'No wonder they compare you to Yang Gui-fei, cousin.

You are well-covered like her, and they always say that plump people fear the heat.'

The colour flew into Bao-chai's face. An angry retort was on her lips, but she could hardly make it in front of company. Yet reflection only made her angrier. Eventually, after a scornful sniff or two, she said:

'I may be like Yang Gui-fei in some respects, but I don't think there is much danger of my cousin becoming a Prime Minister.'

It happened that just at that moment a very young maid called 'Prettikins' jokingly accused Bao-chai of having hidden a fan she was looking for.

'I *know* Miss Bao's hidden it,' she said. 'Come on, Miss! *Please* let me have it.'

'You be careful,' said Bao-chai, pointing at the girl angrily and speaking with unwonted stridency. 'When did you last see *me* playing games of this sort with anyone? If there are other young ladies who are in the habit of *romping about* with you, you had better ask *them*.'

Prettikins fled.

Bao-yu realized that he had once again given offence by speaking thoughtlessly; and as this time it was in front of a lot of people, his embarrassment was correspondingly greater. He turned aside in confusion and began talking nervously to someone else.

Bao-yu's rudeness to Bao-chai had given Dai-yu secret satisfaction. When Prettikins came in looking for her fan, she had been on the point of adding some facetiousness of her own at Bao-chai's expense; but Bao-chai's brief explosion caused her to drop the prepared witticism and ask instead what play the two acts were from that Bao-chai said she had just been watching.

Bao-chai had observed the smirk on Dai-yu's face and knew very well that Bao-yu's rudeness must have pleased her. The smiling answer she gave to Dai-yu's question was therefore not without a touch of malice.

'The play I saw was *Li Kui Abuses Song Jiang and Afterwards Has to Say He Is Sorry*.'

Bao-yu laughed.

'What a mouthful! Surely, with all your learning, cousin, you must know the proper name of that play? It's called *The Abject Apology.*'

'*The Abject Apology*?' said Bao-chai. 'Well, no doubt you clever people know all there is to know about abject apology. I'm afraid it's something I wouldn't know about.'

Her words touched Bao-yu and Dai-yu on a sensitive spot, and by the time she had finished, they were both blushing hotly with embarrassment.

Xi-feng was insufficiently educated to have understood all these nuances, but by studying the speakers' expressions she had formed a pretty good idea of what they were talking about.

'Rather hot weather to be eating raw ginger, isn't it?' she asked.

No one present could understand what she meant.

'No one's been eating raw ginger,' they said.

Xi-feng affected great surprise and rubbed her cheek meaningfully with her hand:

'If no one's been eating raw ginger, then why are they looking so hot and bothered?'

At this Bao-yu and Dai-yu felt even more uncomfortable. Bao-chai was about to add something, but seeing the abject look on Bao-yu's face, she laughed and held her tongue. None of the others present had understood what the four of them were talking about and treated these exchanges as a joke.

Shortly after this, when Bao-chai and Xi-feng had gone out of the room, Dai-yu said to Bao-yu.

'You see? There are people even more dangerous to trifle with than I. If I weren't such a tongue-tied, slow-witted creature, you wouldn't get away with it quite so often, my friend.'

Bao-yu was still smarting from Bao-chai's testiness. To be set upon now by Dai-yu as well seemed positively the last straw. But though he wanted to reply, he knew how easily she would take offence and controlled himself with an effort. Feeling in very low spirits, he left the room himself now and went off on his own.

It was the hottest part of the day. Lunch had long been over, and in every apartment mistress and maids alike had succumbed to the lassitude of the hour. As he sauntered slowly by, hands clasped behind his back, everywhere he went was hushed in the breathless silence of noon. From the back of Grandmother Jia's quarters he passed eastwards through the gallery that ended near the wall of Xi-feng's courtyard. He went up to the gate, but it was closed, and remembering that it was her invariable custom when the weather was hot to take two whole hours off in the middle of the day for her siesta, he thought he had better not go in. He continued, instead, through the corner gate that led into his parents' courtyard.

On entering his mother's apartment, he found several maids dozing over their embroidery. Lady Wang herself was lying on a summer-bed in the inner room, apparently fast asleep. Her maid Golden, who was sitting beside her gently pounding her legs, also seemed half asleep, for her head was nodding and her half-closed eyes were blinking drowsily. Bao-yu tiptoed up to her and tweaked an ear-ring. She opened her eyes wide and saw that it was Bao-yu.

He smiled at her and whispered.

'So sleepy?'

Golden pursed her lips up in a smile, motioned to him with her hand to go away, and then closed her eyes again. But Bao-yu lingered, fascinated. Silently craning forward to make sure that Lady Wang's eyes were closed, he took a Fragrant Snow 'quencher' from the embroidered pouch at his waist and popped it between Golden's lips. Golden nibbled it dreamily without opening her eyes.

'Shall I ask Her Ladyship to let me have you, so that we can be together?' he whispered jokingly.

Golden made no reply.

'When she wakes up, I'll talk to her about it,' he said.

Golden opened her eyes wide and gave him a little push.

'What's the hurry?' she said playfully. ' "Yours is yours, wherever it be", as they said to the lady when she dropped her gold comb in the well. Haven't you ever heard that saying? – I'll tell you something to do, if you want a bit of fun.

Go into the little east courtyard and you'll be able to catch
Sunset and Huan together.'

'Who cares about *them*?' said Bao-yu. 'Let's talk about *us*.'

At this point Lady Wang sat bolt upright and dealt Golden
a slap in the face.

'Shameless little harlot!' she cried, pointing at her wrathfully. 'It's you and your like who corrupt our innocent young
boys.'

Bao-yu had slipped silently away as soon as his mother sat
up. Golden, one of whose cheeks was now burning a fiery red,
was left without a word to say. The other maids, hearing that
their mistress was awake, came hurrying into the room.

'Silver!' said Lady Wang. 'Go and fetch your mother. I
want her to take your sister Golden away.'

Golden threw herself, weeping, upon her knees:

'No, Your Ladyship, please! Beat me and revile me as much
as you like, but please, for pity's sake, don't send me away.
I've been with Your Ladyship nigh on ten years now. How
can I ever hold up my head again if you dismiss me?'

Lady Wang was not naturally unkind. On the contrary, she
was an exceptionally lenient mistress. This was, in fact, the
first time in her life that she had ever struck a maid. But the
kind of 'shamelessness' of which – in her view – Golden had
just been guilty was the one thing she had always most
abhorred. It was the uncontrollable anger of the morally outraged that had caused her to strike Golden and call her names;
and though Golden now begged and pleaded, she refused to
retract her dismissal. When Golden's mother, old Mrs Bai, had
eventually been fetched, the wretched girl, utterly crushed by
her shame and humiliation, was led away.

But of her no more.

*

Embarrassed by his mother's awakening, Bao-yu had slipped
hurriedly into the Garden.

The burning sun was now in the height of heaven, the contracted shadows were concentrated darkly beneath the trees,
and the stillness of noon, filled with the harsh trilling of

cicadas, was broken by no human voice; but as he approached the bamboo trellises of the rose-garden, a sound like a suppressed sob seemed to come from inside the pergola. Uncertain what it was that he had heard, he stopped to listen. Undoubtedly there was someone there.

This was the fifth month of the year, when the rambler roses are in fullest bloom. Peeping through the fragrant panicles with which the pergola was smothered, he saw a girl crouching down on the other side of the trellis, scratching at the ground with one of those long, blunt pins that girls use for fastening their back hair with.

'Can this be some silly maid come here to bury flowers like Frowner?' he wondered.

He was reminded of Zhuang-zi's story of the beautiful Xi-shi's ugly neighbour, whose endeavours to imitate the little frown that made Xi-shi captivating produced an aspect so hideous that people ran from her in terror. The recollection of it made him smile.

'This is "imitating the Frowner" with a vengeance,' he thought, ' – if that is really what she is doing. Not merely unoriginal, but downright disgusting!'

'Don't imitate Miss Lin,' he was about to shout; but a glimpse of the girl's face revealed to him just in time that this was no maid, but one of the twelve little actresses from Peartree Court – though which of them, since he had seen them only in their make-up on the stage, he was unable to make out. He stuck out his tongue in a grimace and clapped a hand to his mouth.

'Good job I didn't speak too soon,' he thought. 'I've been in trouble twice already today for doing that, once with Frowner and once with Chai. It only needs me to go and upset these twelve actresses as well and I shall be well and truly in the cart!'

His efforts to identify the girl made him study her more closely. It was curious that he should have thought her an imitator of Dai-yu, for she had much of Dai-yu's ethereal grace in her looks: the same delicate face and frail, slender body; the same

> ... brows like hills in spring,
> And eyes like autumn's limpid pools;

– even the same little frown that had often made him compare
Dai-yu with Xi-shi of the legend.

It was now quite impossible for him to tear himself away.
He watched her fascinated. As he watched, he began to see
that what she was doing with the pin was not scratching a hole
to bury flowers in, but writing. He followed the movements
of her hand, and each vertical and horizontal stroke, each dot
and hook that she made he copied with a finger on the palm of
his hand. Altogether there were eighteen strokes. He thought
for a moment. The character he had just written in his hand
was QIANG. The name of the roses which covered the pergola
contained the same character: 'Qiang-wei'.

'The sight of the roses has inspired her to write a poem,'
he thought. 'Probably she's just thought of a good couplet
and wants to write it down before she forgets it; or perhaps
she has already composed several lines and wants to work on
them a bit. Let's see what she writes next.'

The girl went on writing, and he followed the movements
of her hand as before. It was another QIANG. Again she
wrote, and again he followed, and again it was a QIANG. It
was as though she were under some sort of spell. As soon as
she had finished writing one QIANG she began writing
another.

QIANG QIANG QIANG QIANG QIANG QIANG QIANG . . .

He must have watched her write several dozen QIANG's in
succession. He seemed to be as much affected by the spell on
his side of the pergola as the girl herself was on hers, for his
eyeballs continued to follow her pin long after he had learned
to anticipate its movements.

'This girl must have something on her mind that she cannot
tell anyone about to make her behave in this way,' he thought.
'One can see from her outward behaviour how much she must
be suffering inwardly. And she looks so frail. Too frail for
suffering. I wish I could bear some of it for you, my dear!'

In the stifling dog-days of summer the transition from clear to overcast is often sudden, and a little cloudlet can sometimes be the harbinger of a heavy shower. As Bao-yu watched the girl, a sudden gust of cool wind blew by, followed, within moments, by the hissing downpour of rain. He could see the water running off her head in streams and soaking into her clothes.

'Oh, it's raining! With her delicate constitution she ought not to be outside in a downpour like this.'

In his anxiety he cried out to her involuntarily:

'Don't write any more. Look! You're getting soaked.'

The girl looked up, startled, when she heard the voice. She could see someone amidst the roses saying 'Don't write'; but partly because of Bao-yu's almost girlishly beautiful features, and partly because she could in any case only see about half of his face, everything above and below being hidden by flowers and foliage, she took him for a maid; so instead of rushing from his presence as she would have done if she had known that it was Bao-yu, she smiled up at him gratefully:

'Thank you for reminding me. But what about you? You must be getting wet too, surely?'

'Aiyo!' – her words made him suddenly aware that the whole of his body was icy cold, and when he looked down, he saw that he was soaked.

'Oh lord!'

He rushed off in the direction of Green Delights; but all the time he was worrying about the girl, who had nowhere where she could shelter from the rain.

*

As this was the day before the Double Fifth festival, Élégante and the other little actresses – including the one whom Bao-yu had just been watching – had already started their holiday and had gone into the Garden to amuse themselves. Two of them, Trésor – one of the two members of the company who played Principal Boy parts – and Topaze – one of the company's two soubrettes – happened to be in the House of Green Delights playing with Aroma when the rain started and prevented their leaving. They and the maids amused themselves by blocking up the gutters and letting the water collect in the courtyard. When it was nicely flooded, they rounded up a number of mallards, sheldrakes, mandarin ducks and other waterfowl, tied their wings together, and having first closed the courtyard gate, set them down in the water to swim about. Aroma and the girls were all in the outside gallery enjoying this spectacle when Bao-yu arrived at the gate. Finding it shut, he knocked on it for someone to come and open up for him. But there was little chance of a knock being heard above the excited laughter of the maids. He had to shout for some minutes and pound the gate till it shook before anyone heard him inside.

Aroma was not expecting him back so soon.

'I wonder who it can be at this time,' she said. 'Won't someone go and answer it?'

'It's *me*!' shouted Bao-yu.

'That's Miss Bao's voice,' said Musk.

'Nonsense!' said Skybright. 'What would *she* be doing visiting us at this time of day?'

'Let me just take a peep through the crack,' said Aroma. 'If I think it's all right, I'll let them in. We don't want to turn anyone away in the pouring rain.'

Keeping under cover of the gallery, she made her way round to the gate and peered through the chink between the double doors. The sight of Bao-yu standing there like a bedraggled hen with the water running off him in streamlets was both alarming and – she could not help but feel – very funny. She opened the gate as quickly as she could, then, when she saw him fully, clapped her hands and doubled up with laughter.

'Master Bao! I *never* thought it would be you. What did you want to come running back in the pouring rain for?'

Bao-yu was by now in a thoroughly evil temper and had fully resolved to give whoever opened the gate a few kicks. As soon as it was open, therefore, he lashed out with his foot, not bothering to see who it was – for he assumed that the person answering it would be one of the younger maids – and dealt Aroma a mighty kick in the ribs that caused her to cry out in pain.

'Worthless lot!' he shouted. 'Because I always treat you decently, you think you can get away with *anything*. I'm just your laughing-stock.'

It was not until he looked down and saw Aroma crying that he realized he had kicked the wrong person.

'Aiyo! It's you! Where did I kick you?'

Up to this moment Aroma had never had so much as a harsh word from Bao-yu, and the combination of shame, anger and pain she now felt on being kicked and shouted at by him in front of so many people was well-nigh insupportable. Nevertheless she forced herself to bear it, reflecting that to have made an outcry would be like admitting that it was *her* he had meant to kick, which she knew was almost certainly not the case.

'You didn't; you missed me,' she said. 'Come in and get changed.'

When Bao-yu had gone indoors and was changing his clothes, he said to her jokingly:

'In all these years this is the first time I've ever struck anyone in anger. Too bad that *you* should have been the one to get in the way of the blow!'

In spite of the pain, which it cost her some effort to master, Aroma was helping him with his changing. She smiled when he said this.

'I'm the person you always begin things with,' she said. 'Whether it's big things or little things or pleasant ones or unpleasant ones, it's only natural that you should try them out first on me. Only in this instance I hope that now you've hit me you won't from now on go around hitting other people.'

'I didn't mean to kick *you*, you know,' said Bao-yu.

'Who said you did?' said Aroma. 'It's the younger ones who normally see to the gate; and they've grown so insolent nowadays, it's enough to put *anyone* in a rage. If you'd given one of *them* a few kicks and put the fear of God into them, it would have been a very good thing. No, it was my own silly fault. I should have made *them* open the gate and not gone to open it myself.'

While they were speaking, the rain had stopped and Trésor and Topaze had left. The pain in Aroma's side was such that it was giving her a feeling of nausea and she could eat no dinner. At bedtime, when she took off her clothes, she saw a great black bruise the size of a rice-bowl spreading over the side of her chest. The extent of it frightened her, but she forbore to cry out. Nevertheless even her dreams that night were full of pain and she several times uttered an 'Aiyo' in the midst of her sleep.

Although it was understood that he had not kicked her deliberately, Bao-yu had felt a little uneasy when he saw how sluggish Aroma seemed in her movements; and when, during the night, he heard her groaning in her sleep, he knew that he must have kicked her really hard. Getting out of bed, he picked up a lamp and tiptoed over to have a look. Just as he reached the foot of her bed, he heard her cough a couple of times and spit out a mouthful of something.

'Aiyo!'

She opened her eyes wide and saw Bao-yu. Startled, she asked him what he was doing there.

'You've been groaning in your sleep,' he said. 'I must have hurt you badly. Let me have a look.'

'My head feels giddy,' said Aroma, 'and I've got a sweet, sickly taste in my throat. Have a look on the floor.'

Bao-yu shone his lamp on the floor. Beside the bed, where she had spat, there was a mouthful of bright red blood. He was horrified.

'Oh, help!'

Aroma looked too, and felt the grip of fear on her heart.

The outcome will be told in the following chapter.

CHAPTER 31

A torn fan is the price of silver laughter
And a lost kylin is the clue to a happy marriage

A cold fear came over Aroma when she saw the fresh blood on the floor. She had often heard people say that if you spat blood when you were young, you would die early, or at the very least be an invalid all your life; and remembering this now, she felt all her bright, ambitious hopes for the future turn into dust and ashes. Tears of misery ran down her cheeks. The sight of them made Bao-yu, too, distressed.

'What is it?' he asked her.

'It's nothing.' She forced herself to smile. 'I'm all right.'

Bao-yu was all for calling one of the maids and getting her to heat some rice wine, so that Aroma could be given hot wine and Hainan kid's-blood pills; but Aroma, smiling through her tears, caught at his hand to restrain him.

'It's all right for *you* to make a fuss,' she said; 'but if you go involving the others, they are sure to accuse me of putting on airs. And besides, it will do neither of us any good to draw attention to ourselves – especially when so far no one seems to have noticed anything. The sensible thing would be for you to send one of the boys round tomorrow to Dr Wang's and get me some medicine to take. I shall probably be all right again after a few doses, without a single soul knowing anything about it. Surely that's best, isn't it?'

Bao-yu knew that she was right and abandoned his intention of rousing the others. Instead he poured her a cup of tea from a pot on the table and gave it to her to rinse her mouth with. Aroma was uneasy about being waited on by her master; but fearing that if she refused his services he would insist on disturbing everybody, she lay back and allowed him to fuss over her.

As soon as it was daylight, Bao-yu threw on his clothes and, without even waiting to wash or comb, went out of the Garden to his study in the front part of the mansion, whither he summoned the doctor Wang Ji-ren for detailed questioning. When this worthy had elicited the information that the hae-morrhage inquired about had been caused by a blow, he seemed less disposed to take a serious view of the case, merely naming some pills and giving perfunctory instructions for taking them internally and for applying them in solution as a poultice. Bao-yu made a note of these instructions and went back into the Garden to carry them out.

But that is no part of our story.

*

It was now the festival of the Double Fifth. Sprays of calamus and artemisia crowned the doorways and everyone wore tiger amulets fastened on their clothing at the back. At noon Lady Wang gave a little party at which Aunt Xue and Bao-chai were the guests.

Bao-yu, finding Bao-chai somewhat glacial in her manner and evidently unwilling to talk to him, knew that it must be because of his rudeness to her of the day before.

Lady Wang, observing Bao-yu's dejected appearance, attri-buted it to embarrassment about yesterday's episode with Golden and ignored him even more pointedly than Bao-chai.

Dai-yu, seeing how morose Bao-yu looked assumed that it was because Bao-chai was offended with him and, feeling resent-ful that he should care, at once became as morose as he was.

Xi-feng, having been told all about Bao-yu and Golden the night before by Lady Wang, could scarcely be her usual laugh-ing and joking self when she knew of her aunt's displeasure and, taking her cue from the latter, was if anything even more glacial than the others.

And Ying-chun, Tan-chun and Xi-chun, seeing everyone else so uncomfortable, soon began to feel just as uncomfort-able themselves.

The result was that after sitting for only a very short time, the party broke up.

Dai-yu had a natural aversion to gatherings, which she rationalized by saying that since the inevitable consequence of getting together was parting, and since parting made people feel lonely and feeling lonely made them unhappy, *ergo* it was better for them not to get together in the first place. In the same way she argued that since the flowers, which give us so much pleasure when they open, only cause us a lot of extra sadness when they die, it would be better if they didn't come out at all.

Bao-yu was just the opposite. He always wanted the party to go on for ever and flowers to be in perpetual bloom; and when at last the party did end and the flowers did wither – well, it was infinitely sad and distressing, but it couldn't be helped.

And so today, while everyone else left the party with feelings of gloom, Dai-yu alone was completely unaffected. Bao-yu, on the other hand, returned to his room in a mood of black despondency, sighing and muttering as he went.

Unfortunately it was the sharp-tongued Skybright who came forward to help him change his clothes. With provoking carelessness she dropped a fan while she was doing so and snapped the bone fan-sticks by accidentally treading on it.

'Clumsy!' said Bao-yu reproachfully. 'You won't be so careless with things when you have a household of your own.'

Skybright gave a sardonic sniff.

'You're getting quite a temper lately, Master Bao. Almost every time we move nowadays we get a nasty look from you. Yesterday even Aroma caught it. Today you're finding fault with me, so I suppose I can expect a few kicks too. Well, kick away. But I must say, I shouldn't have thought treading on a *fan* was such a very terrible thing to do. In the past any number of glass bowls and agate cups have got broken without your turning a hair. Why this fuss about a fan, then? If you're not satisfied with my service, you ought to dismiss me and get someone better. Easy come, easy go. No need for beating about the bush.'

By the time she had finished, Bao-yu was so angry that he was shaking all over.

'You'll *go* soon enough, don't you worry!' he said.

Aroma had heard all this from the adjoining room and now came hurrying in.

'Now what's all this about?' she said, addressing herself to Bao-yu. 'Didn't I tell you? As soon as I turn my back there's trouble.'

'If you knew that already,' said Skybright, 'it's a pity you couldn't have come in a bit sooner and saved me from provoking him. Of course, we all know that you're the only one who knows how to serve him properly. None of the rest of us knows how it's done. I suppose it's because you serve him so well that he gave you a kick in the ribs yesterday. Heaven knows what he's got in store for *me* for having served him so badly!'

Angry, and at the same time ashamed, Aroma was about to retort; but the sight of Bao-yu's face, now white with anger, made her restrain herself.

'Be a good girl – just go away and play for a bit. It's *we* who are in the wrong.'

Skybright naturally assumed that 'we' meant Aroma and Bao-yu. Her jealousy was further inflamed.

'What do you mean, "we"?' she said. 'You two make me feel ashamed for you, you really do – because you needn't think you deceive *me*. *I* know what goes on between you when you think no one is looking. But when all's said and done, in actual fact, when you come down to it, you're not even a "Miss" by *rights*. By *rights* you're no better than any of the rest of us. I don't know where you get this "we" from.'

Aroma blushed and blushed with shame, until her face had become a dusky red colour. Too late she realized her slip. By 'we' she had meant no more than 'you and I'; not 'Bao-yu and I' as Skybright imagined. But the pronoun had invited misunderstanding.

It was Bao-yu who retorted, however.

'I'll make her a "Miss" then; I'll make her my chamber-wife tomorrow, if that's all that's worrying you. You can spare your jealousy on *that* account.'

Aroma seized his hand impulsively.

'Don't argue with her, she's only a silly girl. In any case, you've put up with much worse than this in the past; why be so touchy today?'

Skybright gave a harsh little laugh.

'Oh, yes. *I*'m too stupid to talk to. *I*'m only a slave.'

'Are you arguing with me, Miss, or with Master Bao?' said Aroma. 'If it's me you've got it in for, you'd better address your remarks to me elsewhere. There's no cause to go quarrelling with me in front of Master Bao. But if it's Master Bao you want to quarrel with, then at least you might do it a bit more quietly and not let everyone else know about it. When I came in just now, it was for everyone's sake, so that we could have a bit of peace and quiet. I don't know why you had to turn on *me* and start picking on *my* shortcomings. It seems as if you can't make up your mind whether you're angry with me or with Master Bao. Slipping in a dig here and a dig there. I don't know what you think you're up to. Anyway, I shan't say any more; I'll just leave you here to get on with it.'

She walked out.

'There's no need for you to be so angry,' Bao-yu said to Skybright. 'I can guess what it is that's bothering you. I shall go and tell Her Ladyship that you're old enough to leave us now and ask her to send you away. That's what you really want, isn't it?'

'I don't want to go away. Why should I want to go away?' said Skybright with tears in her eyes – now more upset than ever. 'You're inventing this as a means of getting rid of me, aren't you, because I'm in your way? But you won't get away with it.'

'Look, I've never had to put up with scenes like *this* before,' said Bao-yu. 'What other reason *can* there be but that you want to leave? I really think I *had* better go and see Her Ladyship about this.'

He got up and began to go; but Aroma came in again and barred his way.

'Where are you off to?' she asked him smilingly.

'To see Her Ladyship.'

'Oh, that's silly,' said Aroma. 'I wonder you're not ashamed to. Even if Skybright really does want to leave, there will be plenty of time to tell Her Ladyship about it when everyone has cooled down a bit and you are feeling calm and collected. If you go rushing off in your present state, Her Ladyship will suspect something.'

'Her Ladyship won't suspect anything,' said Bao-yu. 'I shall tell her quite openly that Skybright has been agitating to leave.'

'When have I ever agitated to leave?' said Skybright, weeping now in earnest. 'Even if you're angry with me, you ought not to twist things round in order to get the better of me. But you go and tell her! I don't care if I have to beat my own brains out, I'm not going out of that door.'

'Now that's really strange,' said Bao-yu. 'You don't want to go, yet at the same time you won't keep quiet. It's no good; I really can't stand this quarrelling. I shall really *have* to see Her Ladyship about this and get it over with.'

This time he seemed quite determined to go.

Seeing that she was unable to hold him back, Aroma went down on her knees. Emerald, Ripple, Musk and the other maids, aware that a quarrel of more than usual magnitude was going on inside, were waiting together outside in breathless silence. When word reached them that Aroma was now on her knees interceding for Skybright, they came silently trooping in to kneel down behind her. Bao-yu raised Aroma to her feet, sighed, sat down on the edge of the bed, and told the other maids to get up.

'What do you want me to do?' he asked Aroma. 'My heart is destroyed inside me, but none of you knows or cares.'

Tears started from his eyes and rolled down his cheeks unheeded. Seeing his tears, Aroma too began to cry. Skybright, who stood crying beside them, was about to say something; but just at that moment Dai-yu walked in and she slipped outside.

Dai-yu beamed at the weeping pair:

'Crying on a holiday? What's all this about? Have you been quarrelling over the rice-cakes?'

Bao-yu and Aroma both burst out laughing.

'Well, if Cousin Bao won't tell me,' she went on, 'I'm sure that *you* will. Come!' she said, slapping Aroma familiarly on the shoulder. 'Tell sis all about it. It's obvious that the two of you have been having an argument. Tell me what it's all about and I'll make it up between you.'

'Oh, Miss!' Aroma gave her a push. 'Don't carry on so! I'm only a maid; you shouldn't say such things to me.'

'Only a maid?' said Dai-yu. 'I always think of you as my sister-in-law.'

'Don't you see that you're simply *encouraging* people to be nasty to her?' Bao-yu protested. 'Even as it is, people already gossip about her. How can she stand up to them if *you* come along and lend your weight to what they are saying?'

'You don't know what I feel, Miss,' said Aroma. 'If I only knew how to stop breathing, I'd gladly die.'

Dai-yu smiled.

'If you were to die, I don't know about anyone else, but I know that *I* should die of grief.'

'*I* should become a monk,' said Bao-yu.

'Try to be a bit more serious,' said Aroma. 'You and Miss Lin are both laughing at me.'

Dai-yu held up two fingers and looked at Bao-yu with a quizzical expression.

'That's twice you're going to become a monk. From now on I'm keeping the score.'

Bao-yu recognized the allusion to what he had said to her the day before. Fortunately he was able to pass it off with a laugh. Shortly after that, Dai-yu left them.

No sooner had Dai-yu gone than someone arrived with an invitation from Xue Pan. Bao-yu thought that this time he had better go. It turned out to be only a drinking-party, but Xue Pan refused to release him and kept him there until it was over. He returned home in the evening more than a little drunk.

As he came lurching into his courtyard, he saw that someone in quest of coolness had taken a bed outside and was lying down on it asleep. Assuming that it must be Aroma, he sat down on the edge of it and gave her a push.

'Is the pain any better?'

'Can't you leave me alone?' she said, rising up wrathfully.

He looked again and saw that it was not Aroma after all but Skybright. Taking her by the hand, he drew her down on the bed beside him.

'You're getting so self-willed,' he said laughingly. 'When you trod on that fan this morning, I only made a harmless little remark, but look how you flew up in the air about it! And then when Aroma, out of the kindness of her heart, tried to reason with you, look how you pitched into *her*! Seriously, now, don't you think it was all a bit uncalled-for?'

'I'm so *hot*,' said Skybright. 'Do you *have* to maul me about like this? Suppose someone were to see us? Anyway, it's not right for me to be sitting here.'

'If you know it's not right to be sitting here,' he said teasingly, 'what were you doing lying down?'

'Che-e-e!' Unable at once to reply, she gave a little laugh. Then she said:

'When you are not here it doesn't matter. It's *your* being here that makes it wrong. Anyway, let me get up now, because I want to have a bath. Aroma and Musk have had theirs already. I'll send *them* out to you.'

'I've just had rather a lot to drink and I could do with a bath myself,' said Bao-yu. 'As you haven't had yours yet, bring the water out here and we'll have a bath together.'

Skybright laughed and declined with a vigorous gesture of her hand.

'*Oh* no! I daren't start you off on that caper. I still remember that time you got Emerald to help you bath. You must have been two or three hours in there, so that we began to get quite worried. We didn't like to go in while you were there, but when we did go in to have a look afterwards, we found water all over the floor, pools of water round the legs of the bed, and even the mat on the bed had water splashed all over it. Heaven only knows what you'd been up to. We laughed about it for days afterwards. I haven't got time to fetch *that* amount of water. And in any case, you don't want to go taking baths with *me*. As a matter of fact it's cooler now, so I don't think I shall have a bath after all. Why don't you let me fetch you a bowl of water so that you can have a nice wash and comb your hair? Faithful just sent a lot of fruit round and we've got it soaking in iced water in the big glass bowl. I'll tell them to bring some out to you, shall I?'

'All right,' said Bao-yu. 'If you're not having a bath yourself, I'll just wash my hands; and you can get me some of that fruit to eat.'

Skybright smiled.

'You've already told me once today how clumsy I am. I can't even drop a fan without treading on it. So I'm much too clumsy to get your fruit for you. Suppose I were to break a plate. That would be terrible!'

'If you *want* to break it, by all means break it,' said Bao-yu. 'These things are there for our use. What we use them *for* is a matter of individual taste. For example, fans are made for fanning with; but if you prefer to tear them up because it gives you pleasure, there's no reason why you shouldn't. What you *mustn't* do is to use them as objects to vent your anger on. It's the same with plates and cups. Plates and cups are made to put food and drink in. But if you want to smash them on purpose because you like the noise, it's perfectly all right to do so. As long as you don't get into a passion and start taking it out on *things* – that is the golden rule.'

'All right then,' said Skybright with a mischievous smile. 'Give me your fan to tear. I love the sound of a fan being torn.'

Bao-yu held it out to her. She took it eagerly and – *chah!* – promptly tore it in half. And again – *chah! chah! chah!* – she tore it several more times. Bao-yu, an appreciative onlooker, laughed and encouraged her.

'Well torn! Well torn! Now again – a really loud one!'

Just then Musk appeared. She stared at them indignantly.

'Don't do that!' she said. 'It's *wicked* to waste things like that.'

But Bao-yu leaped up to her, snatched the fan from her hand, and passed it to Skybright, who at once tore it into several pieces. The two of them, Bao-yu and Skybright, then burst into uproarious laughter.

'What do you think you're doing?' said Musk. 'That's *my fan* you've just ruined.'

'What's an old fan?' said Bao-yu. 'Open up the fan box and get yourself another.'

'If that's your attitude,' said Musk, 'we might as well carry out the whole boxful and let her tear away to her heart's content.'

'All right. Go and get it,' said Bao-yu.

'And be born a beggar in my next life?' said Musk. 'No thank you! She hasn't broken her arm. Let her go and get it herself.'

Skybright stretched back on the bed, smiling complacently.

'I'm rather tired just now. I think I shall tear some more tomorrow.'

Bao-yu laughed.

'The ancients used to say that for one smile of a beautiful woman a thousand taels are well spent. For a few old fans it's cheap at the price!'

He called to Aroma, who had just finished changing into clean clothes, to come outside and join them. Little Melilot came and cleared away the broken bits of fan, and everyone sat for a while and enjoyed the cool.

But our narrative supplies no further details of that evening.

*

About noon next day, while Lady Wang, Bao-chai, Dai-yu and the girls were sitting in Grandmother Jia's room, someone came in to announce that 'Miss Shi' had arrived. Shortly afterwards Shi Xiang-yun appeared in the courtyard, attended by a bevy of matrons and maids. Bao-chai, Dai-yu and the rest hurried out to the foot of the steps to welcome her.

For young girls like the cousins a reunion after a mere month's separation is an occasion for touching demonstrations of affection. After these initial transports, when they were all indoors and the greetings, introductions and salutations had been completed, Grandmother Jia suggested that, as the

weather was so hot, Xiang-yun should remove her outer garments. Xiang-yun rose to her feet with alacrity and divested
herself of one or two layers. Lady Wang was amused.

'Gracious, child! What a lot you have on! I don't think
I've ever seen anyone wearing so much.'

'It's my Aunt Shi who makes me wear it all,' said Xiang-
yun. 'You wouldn't catch me wearing this stuff if I didn't
have to.'

'You don't know our Xiang-yun, Aunt,' Bao-chai interposed. 'She's really happiest in boy's clothes. That time she
was here in the third or fourth month last year, I remember
one day she dressed up in one of Bao-yu's gowns and put a
pair of his boots on and one of his belts round her waist. At
first glance she looked exactly like Cousin Bao. It was only
the ear-rings that gave her away. When she stood behind that
chair over there, Grandmother was completely taken in. She
said, "Bao-yu, come over here! You'll get the dust from that
hanging lamp in your eyes if you're not careful." But Xiang-
yun just smiled and didn't move. It was only when everyone
couldn't hold it in any longer and started laughing that Grandmother realized who it was and joined in the laugh. She told
her that she made a very good-looking boy.'

'That's nothing,' said Dai-yu. 'What about that time last
year when she came to stay for a couple of days with us in the
first month and it snowed? Grandma and Auntie Wang had
just got back from somewhere – I think it was from visiting
the ancestors' portraits – and she saw Grandma's new scarlet
felt rain-cape lying there and put it on when no one was looking. Of course, it was much too big and much too long for
her, so she hitched it up and tied it round her waist with a
sash and went out like that into the back courtyard to help the
maids build a snowman. And then she slipped over in it and
got covered all over with mud – '

The others all laughed at the recollection.

Bao-chai asked Xiang-yun's nurse, Mrs Zhou, whether
Xiang-yun was still as tomboyish as ever. Nurse Zhou laughed
but said nothing.

'I don't mind her being tomboyish,' said Ying-chun, 'but

I do wish she wasn't such a chatterbox. You wouldn't believe it – even when she's in bed at night it still goes on. Jabber-jabber, jabber-jabber. Then she laughs. Then she talks a bit more. Then she laughs again. And you never heard such a lot of rubbish in your life. I don't know where she gets it all from.'

'Well, perhaps she'll have got over that by now,' said Lady Wang. 'I hear that someone was round the other day to talk about a betrothal. Now that there's a future mother-in-law to think about, she can't be *quite* as tomboyish as she used to be.'

'Are you staying this time, or do you have to go back to-night?' asked Grandmother Jia.

'Your Old Ladyship hasn't seen all the clothes she's brought,' said Nurse Zhou. 'She'll be staying two days here at the very least.'

'Isn't Bao at home?' said Xiang-yun.

'Listen to her!' said Bao-chai. 'Cousin Bao is the only one she thinks about. He and she get on well together because they are both fond of mischief. You can see she hasn't really changed.'

'Perhaps now that you're getting older you had better stop using baby-names,' said Grandmother Jia, reminded by the talk of betrothal that her babies were rapidly turning into grown-ups.

Just then Bao-yu came in.

'Ah! Hallo, Yun! Why didn't you come when we sent for you the other day?'

'Grandmother has just this moment been saying that it is time you all stopped using baby-names,' said Lady Wang. 'I must say, this isn't a very good beginning.'

'Our cousin has got something nice to give you,' said Dai-yu to Xiang-yun.

'Oh? What is it?' said Xiang-yun.

'Don't believe her,' said Bao-yu. 'Goodness! It's no time since you were here last, but you seem to have grown taller already.'

Xiang-yun laughed.

'How's Aroma?'

'She's fine. Thank you for asking.'

'I've brought something for her,' said Xiang-yun. She produced a knotted-up silk handkerchief.

'What treasure have you got wrapped up in there?' said Bao-yu. 'The best present you could have brought Aroma would have been a couple of those cheap agate rings like the ones you sent us the other day.'

'What are these, then?'

With a triumphant smile she opened her little bundle and revealed four rings, each inset with the veined red agate they had so much admired on a previous occasion.

'What a girl!' said Dai-yu. 'These are exactly the same as the ones you sent us the other day by messenger. Why didn't you get him to bring these too and save yourself some trouble? I thought you must have got some wonderful rarity tied up in that handkerchief, seeing that you'd gone to all the trouble of bringing it here yourself – and all the time it was only a few more of *those*! You really are rather a silly.'

'Thilly yourthelf!' said Xiang-yun. 'The others can decide which of us is the silly one when I have explained my reason. If I send things for you and the girls, it's assumed that they are for you without the messenger even needing to say anything; but if I send things for any of the maids, I have to explain very carefully to the messenger which ones I mean. Now if the messenger is someone intelligent, that's all right; but if it's someone not so bright who has difficulty in remembering names, they'll probably make such a mess of it that they'll get not only the maids' presents mixed up, but yours as well. Then again, if the messenger is a woman, it's not so bad; but the other day it was one of the boys – and you know how hopeless *they* are over girls' names. So you see, I thought it would be simpler if I delivered the maids' ones myself. There!' – she laid the rings down one after another on the table – 'One for Aroma; one for Faithful; one for Golden; and one for Patience. Can you imagine one of the boys getting those four names right?'

The others laughed.

'Clever! Clever!' they said.

'You're always so eloquent,' said Bao-yu. 'No one else gets a chance.'

'If she weren't so eloquent, she wouldn't be worthy of the gold kylin,' said Dai-yu huffily, rising from her seat and walking off as she spoke.

Fortunately no one heard her but Bao-chai, who made a laughing grimace, and Bao-yu, who immediately regretted having once more spoken out of turn, but who, suddenly catching sight of Bao-chai's expression, could not help laughing himself. Seeing him laugh, Bao-chai at once rose from her seat and hurried off to joke with Dai-yu.

'When you've finished your tea and rested a bit,' said Grandmother Jia to Xiang-yun, 'you can go and see your married cousins. After that, you can amuse yourself in the Garden with the girls. It's nice and cool there.'

Xiang-yun thanked her grandmother. She wrapped up three of the rings again, and after sitting a little longer, went off, attended by her nannies and maids, to call on Wang Xi-feng. After chatting a while with her, she went into the Garden and called on Li Wan. Then, after sitting a short while with Li Wan, she went off in the direction of Green Delights in quest of Aroma. Before doing so, however, she turned to dismiss her escort.

'You needn't stay with me any longer,' she said. 'You can go off now and visit your relations. I'll just keep Fishy to wait on me.'

The others thanked her and went off to look for various kith and kin, leaving Xiang-yun alone with Kingfisher.

'Why aren't these water-lilies out yet?' said Kingfisher.

'It isn't time for them yet,' said Xiang-yun.

'Look, they're going to be "double-decker" ones, like the ones in our lily-pond at home,' said Kingfisher.

'Our ones are better,' said Xiang-yun.

'They've got a pomegranate-tree here which has four or five lots of flowers growing one above the other on each branch,' said Kingfisher. 'That's a double-double-double-decker. I wonder what makes them grow like that.'

'Plants are the same as people,' said Xiang-yun. 'The healthier their constitution is, the better they grow.'

'I don't believe that,' said Kingfisher with a toss of her head. 'If that were so, why don't we see people walking around with one head growing on top of the other?'

Xiang-yun was unable to avoid laughing at the girl's simplicity.

'I've told you before, you talk too much,' she said. 'Let's see: how can one answer a question like that? Everything in the world is moulded by the forces of Yin and Yang. That means that, besides the normal, the abnormal, the peculiar, the freakish – in fact all the thousands and thousands of different variations we find in things – are caused by different combinations of Yin and Yang. Even if something appears that is so rare that no one has ever seen it before, the principle is still the same.'

'So according to what you say,' said Kingfisher, 'all the things that have ever existed, from the time the world began right up to the present moment, have just been a lot of Yins and Yangs.'

'No, stupid!' said Xiang-yun. 'The more you say, the sillier you get. "Just a lot of Yins and Yangs" indeed! In any case, strictly speaking Yin and Yang are not two things but one and the same thing. By the time the Yang has become exhausted, it *is* Yin; and by the time the Yin has become exhausted, it *is* Yang. It isn't a case of one of them coming to an end and then the other one growing out of nothing.'

'That's too deep for me,' said Kingfisher. 'What sort of thing is a Yin-yang, I'd like to know? No one's ever seen one. You just answer that, Miss. What does a Yin-yang look like?'

'Yin-yang is a sort of *force*,' said Xiang-yun. 'It's the force in things that gives them their distinctive forms. For example, the sky is Yang and the earth is Yin; water is Yin and fire is Yang; the sun is Yang and the moon is Yin.'

'Ah yes! *Now* I understand,' said Kingfisher happily. 'That's why astrologers call the sun the "Yang star" and the moon the "Yin star".'

'Holy name!' said Xiang-yun. 'She understands.'

'That's not so difficult,' said Kingfisher. 'But what about things like mosquitoes and fleas and midges and plants and flowers and bricks and tiles? Surely you are not going to say that they are all Yin-yang too?'

'Certainly they are!' said Xiang-yun. 'Take the leaf of a tree, for example. That's divided into Yin and Yang. The side facing upwards towards the sky is Yang; the underside, facing towards the ground, is Yin.'

Kingfisher nodded.

'I see. Yes. I can understand that. But take these fans we are holding. Surely *they* don't have Yin and Yang?'

'Yes they do. The front of the fan is Yang; the back of the fan is Yin.'

Kingfisher nodded, satisfied. She tried to think of some other object to ask about, but being for the moment unable to, she began looking around her for inspiration. As she did so, her eye chanced to light on the gold kylin fastened in the intricate loopings of her mistress's girdle.

'Well, Miss,' she said, pointing triumphantly to the kylin, 'you're not going to say that *that*'s got Yin and Yang?'

'Certainly. In the case of birds and beasts the males are Yang and the females are Yin.'

'Is this a daddy one or a mummy one?' said Kingfisher.

'"A daddy one or a mummy one"! Silly girl!'

'All right, then,' said Kingfisher. 'But why is it that everything else has Yin and Yang but we haven't?'

'Get along with you, naughty girl! What subject will you get on to next?'

'Why? Why can't you tell me?' said Kingfisher. 'Anyway, I know; so there's no need for you to be so nasty to me.'

Xiang-yun suppressed a giggle.

'You're Yang and I'm Yin,' said Kingfisher.

Xiang-yun held her handkerchief to her mouth and laughed.

'Well, that's right, isn't it?' said Kingfisher. 'What are you laughing at?'

'Yes, yes,' said Xiang-yun. 'That's quite right.'

'That's what they always say,' said Kingfisher: 'the master

is Yang and the servant is Yin. Even I can understand that principle.'

'I'm sure you can,' said Xiang-yun. 'Very good.'

While they were talking, a glittering golden object at the foot of the rose pergola caught Xiang-yun's eye. She pointed it out to Kingfisher.

'Go and see what it is.'

Kingfisher bounded over and picked it up.

'Ah ha!' she said, examining the object in her hand. 'Now we shall be able to see whether it's Yin or Yang.'

She took hold of the kylin fastened to Xiang-yun's girdle and held it up to look at it more closely. Xiang-yun wanted to see what it was that she held in her hand, but Kingfisher wouldn't let her.

'It's *my* treasure,' she said with a laugh. 'I won't let you see it, Miss. Funny, though. I wonder where it came from. I've never seen anyone here wearing it.'

'Come on! Let me look,' said Xiang-yun.

'There you are, Miss!' Kingfisher opened her hand.

Xiang-yun looked. It was a beautiful, shining gold kylin, both larger and more ornate than the one she was wearing. Reaching out and taking it from Kingfisher, she held it on the palm of her hand and contemplated it for some moments in silence.

Whatever reverie the contemplation inspired was broken by the sudden arrival of Bao-yu.

'What are you doing, standing out here in the blazing sun?' he asked her. 'Why don't you go and see Aroma?'

'We were on our way,' said Xiang-yun, hurriedly concealing the gold kylin.

The three of them entered the courtyard of Green Delights together.

Aroma had gone outside to take the air and was leaning on the verandah railings at the foot of the front door steps. As soon as she caught sight of Xiang-yun, she hurried down into the courtyard to welcome her, and taking her by the hand, led her into the house, animatedly exchanging news with her as they went.

'You should have come sooner,' said Bao-yu when they

were indoors and Aroma had made Xiang-yun take a seat. 'I've got something nice for you here and I've been waiting for you to come so that I could give it to you.'

He had been hunting through his pockets as he said this. Not finding what he was searching for, he exclaimed in surprise.

'Aiyo!' He turned to Aroma. 'Have you put it away somewhere?'

'Put what away?'

'That little kylin I got the other day.'

'You've been carrying it around with you everywhere,' said Aroma. 'Why ask *me* about it?'

Bao-yu clapped his hands together in vexation.

'Oh, I've lost it! Wherever am I going to look for it?'

He got up to begin searching.

Xiang-yun now realized that it must have been Bao-yu who dropped the kylin she had only a few minutes earlier discovered outside.

'Since when have *you* had a kylin?' she asked him.

'Oh, several days now,' said Bao-yu. 'What a shame! I'll never get another one like that. And the trouble is, I don't know when I can have lost it. Oh dear! How stupid of me!'

'It's only an ornament you're getting so upset about,' said Xiang-yun. 'What a good job it wasn't something more serious!'

She opened her hand:

'Look! Is that it?'

Bao-yu looked and saw, with extravagant delight, that it was.

The remainder of this episode will be told in the following chapter.

CHAPTER 32

*Bao-yu demonstrates confusion of mind by making his
declaration to the wrong person
And Golden shows an unconquerable spirit by ending her
humiliation in death*

OUR last chapter told of Bao-yu's delight at seeing the gold
kylin again. He reached out eagerly and took it from Xiang-
yun's hand.

'Fancy *your* finding it!' he said. 'How did you come to pick
it up?'

'It's a good job it was only this you lost,' she said. 'One of
these days it will be your seal of office – and then it won't be
quite so funny.'

'Oh, losing one's seal of office is nothing,' said Bao-yu.
'Losing a thing like this is much more serious.'

Aroma meanwhile was pouring tea.

'I heard your good news the other day,' she said, handing
Xiang-yun a cup. 'Congratulations!'

Xiang-yun bent low over the cup to hide her blushes and
made no reply.

'Why so bashful, Miss?' said Aroma. 'Have you forgotten
the things you used to tell me at night all those years ago,
when we used to sleep together in the little closet-bed at Her
Old Ladyship's? You weren't very bashful then. What makes
you so bashful with me now, all of a sudden?'

Xiang-yun's face became even redder. She gave a forced
little laugh.

'Who's talking? That was a time when you and I were very
close to each other. Then I had to go back home when my
uncle's first wife died and you were given Cousin Bao to look
after, and I don't know why, but whenever I came back here
after that, you seemed somehow changed towards me.'

It was now Aroma's turn to blush and protest.

'When you first came to live here it was "Pearl dear this"

and "Pearl dear that" all the time. You were always coaxing me to do things for you – do your hair, wash your face, or I don't know what. But now that's all changed. Now you're the young lady, aren't you? You can't act the young lady with me and expect me to stay on the same familiar terms as before.'

'Holy name!' said Xiang-yun, now genuinely indignant. 'That's *tho* unfair. I wish I may die if I ever "acted the young lady" with you, as you put it. I come here in this frightful heat, and the very first person I want to see when I get here is you. Ask Fishy if you don't believe me. *She* can tell you. At home I'm *always* going on about you.'

Aroma and Bao-yu both laughed.

'Don't take it to heart so, it was only a joke. You shouldn't be so excitable.'

'Don't, whatever you do, admit that what *you* said was wounding,' said Xiang-yun. 'Say I'm "excitable" and put *me* in the wrong!'

While she said this, she was undoing the knotted silk handkerchief and extracting one of the three rings from it. She handed it to Aroma. Aroma was greatly touched.

'I've got one like this already,' she said. 'It was given to me when you sent those ones the other day to the young ladies. But fancy your bringing this one here specially! Now I *know* you haven't forgotten me. It's little things like this that show you what a person really is. The ring itself isn't worth much, I know. It's the thought behind it.'

'Who gave you the one you've already got?' said Xiang-yun.

'Miss Bao,' said Aroma.

'Ah,' said Xiang-yun, 'Miss Bao. And I was thinking it must have been Miss Lin. Often when I'm at home I think to myself that of all my cousins Bao-chai is the one I like best. It's a pity we couldn't have been born of the same mother. With her for an elder sister it wouldn't matter so much being an orphan.'

Her eyelids reddened as she said this and she seemed to be on the verge of tears.

'Now, now, now!' said Bao-yu. 'Don't say things like that.'

'And why not?' said Xiang-yun. 'Oh, I know your trouble.

You're afraid that Cousin Lin might hear and get angry with me again for praising Cousin Bao. That's what's worrying you, isn't it?'

Aroma giggled.

'Oh Miss Yun! You're just as outspoken as you used to be.'

'Well, I've said that you lot are difficult to talk to,' said Bao-yu, 'and I was certainly right!'

'Don't make me sick,' said Xiang-yun. 'You say what you like to us. It's with your Cousin Lin that you have to be so careful.'

'Never mind about that,' said Aroma. 'Joking apart, now: I want to ask you a favour.'

'What is it?' said Xiang-yun.

'I've got a pair of slipper-tops here that I've already cut the openwork pattern in, but as I haven't been very well this last day or two, I haven't been able to sew them on to the backing material. Do you think you'd have time to do them for me?'

'That's rather a strange request,' said Xiang-yun. 'Quite apart from all the clever maids this household employs you have your own full-time tailors and embroiderers. Why ask *me* to do your sewing? You could give it to anyone here you liked. They could hardly refuse you.'

'You can't be serious,' said Aroma. 'None of the sewing in this room is allowed to go outside. Surely you knew that?'

Xiang-yun inferred from this that the slippers in question were for Bao-yu.

'Oh well,' she said, 'in that case I suppose I'd better do them for you. On one condition, though: I'll do them if they are for *you* to wear, but if they are for anyone else, I'm afraid I can't.'

'Get along with you!' said Aroma. 'Ask you to make slippers for *me*? I wouldn't have the nerve. No, I'll be honest with you, they're not for me. Never mind who they're for. Just tell yourself that I'm the one you'll be doing the favour.'

'It isn't *that*,' said Xiang-yun. 'In the past I've done lots of things for you. Surely you must *know* what makes me unwilling now?'

'I'm sorry, I don't,' said Aroma.

'What about the person who got in a temper the other day when that fan-case I made for you was compared with hers and cut it up with a pair of scissors? I heard all about that, so don't start protesting. If you expect me to do sewing for you· after *that*, you're just treating me as your drudge.'

'I didn't know at the time it was you who made it,' Bao-yu put in hurriedly.

'He really didn't,' said Aroma. 'I pretended there was some-one outside we'd just discovered who could do very fine and original needlework. I told him I'd got them to do that fan-case for him as a sample. He believed what I said and went around showing it to everyone. Unfortunately while he was doing this he upset you know who and she took a pair of scissors and cut it in pieces. Afterwards he was very anxious to have some more work done by the same person, so I had to tell him who it really was. He was very upset when he heard that it was you.'

'I still think this is a very strange request,' said Xiang-yun. 'If Miss Lin can cut things up, she can sew them for him, too. Why not ask *her* to do them for you?'

'Oh, *she* wouldn't want to do them,' said Aroma. 'And even if she did, Her Old Ladyship wouldn't let her, for fear of her tiring herself. The doctors say she needs rest and quiet. I wouldn't want to trouble *her* with them. Last year she took practically the whole year embroidering one little purse, and this last six months I don't think she's picked up a needle.'

Their conversation was interrupted by a servant with a message:

'Mr Jia of Rich Street is here. The Master says will Master Bao receive him, please?'

Recognizing the 'Mr Jia' of the message as Jia Yu-cun, Bao-yu was more than a little vexed. While Aroma hurried off for his going-out clothes, he sat pulling his boots on and grumbling.

'He's got Father to talk to, surely that's enough for him? Why does he always have to see me?'

Xiang-yun laughed at his disgruntlement:

'I'm sure you're very good at entertaining people,' she said. 'That's why Sir Zheng asks you to see him.'

'That message didn't come from Father,' said Bao-yu. 'He'll have made it up himself.'

' "When the host is refined, the callers are frequent," ' said Xiang-yun. 'There must be something about you that has impressed him, otherwise he wouldn't want to see you.'

'I make no claim to being refined, thanks all the same,' said Bao-yu. 'I'm as common as dirt. And furthermore I have no wish to mix with people of his sort.'

'You're incorrigible,' said Xiang-yun. 'Now that you're older, you ought to be mixing with these officials and administrators as much as you can. Even if you don't want to take the Civil Service examinations and become an administrator yourself, you can learn a lot from talking to these people about the way the Empire is governed and the people who govern it that will stand you in good stead later on, when you come to manage your own affairs and take your place in society. You might even pick up one or two decent, respectable friends that way. You'll certainly never get anywhere if you spend all your time with us girls.'

Bao-yu found such talk highly displeasing.

'I think perhaps you'd better go and sit in someone else's room,' he said. 'I wouldn't want a *decent, respectable* young lady like you to get contaminated.'

'Don't try reasoning with him, Miss,' Aroma put in hurriedly. 'Last time Miss Bao tried it, he was just as rude to her. No consideration for her feelings whatever. He just said "Hai!", picked up his heels, and walked out of the room, leaving her still half-way through her sentence. Poor Miss Bao! She was so embarrassed she turned bright red. She didn't know *what* to say. A good job it was her, though, and not Miss Lin. If it had been Miss Lin, there'd have been weeping and carrying on and I don't know what. I really admire the way Miss Bao behaved on that occasion. She just stood there a while collecting herself and then walked quietly out of the room. Myself, I was quite upset, thinking she must be offended. But not a bit of it. Next time she came round, it was just as if nothing had happened. A real little lady, Miss Bao – and generous-hearted, too. And yet the funny thing is that his lordship seems to have fallen out with her, whereas Miss Lin, who is always getting on her high horse and ignoring him, has him running round and apologizing to her all the time.'

'Have you ever heard Miss Lin talking that sort of stupid rubbish?' said Bao-yu. 'I'd long since have fallen out with *her* if she did.'

Aroma and Xiang-yun shook their heads pityingly.

'So that's "stupid rubbish", is it?' they said, laughing.

*

Dai-yu rightly surmised that now Xiang-yun had arrived, Bao-yu would lose no time in telling her about his newly-acquired kylin.

Now Dai-yu had observed that in the romances which Bao-yu smuggled in to her and of which she was nowadays an avid consumer, it was always some trinket or small object of clothing or jewellery – a pair of lovebirds, a male and female phoenix, a jade ring, a gold buckle, a silken handkerchief, an embroidered belt or what not – that brought the heroes and heroines together. And since the fate and future happiness of those fortunate beings seemed to depend wholly on the instrumentality of such trifling objects, it was natural for her to suppose that Bao-yu's acquisition of the gold kylin would become the occasion of a dramatic rupture with *her* and the beginning of an association with Xiang-yun in which he and Xiang-yun would do together all those delightful things that she had read about in the romances.

It was with such apprehensions that she made her way stealthily towards Green Delights, her intention being to observe how the two of them were behaving and shape her own actions accordingly. Imagine her surprise when, just as she was about to enter, she heard Xiang-yun lecturing Bao-yu on his social obligations and Bao-yu telling Xiang-yun that 'Cousin Lin never talked that sort of rubbish' and that if she did he would have 'fallen out with her long ago'. Mingled emotions of happiness, alarm, sorrow and regret assailed her.

Happiness:

Because after all (she thought) I wasn't mistaken in my judgement of you. I always thought of you as a true friend, and I was right.

Alarm:

Because if you praise me so unreservedly in front of other people, your warmth and affection are sure, sooner or later, to excite suspicion and be misunderstood.

Regret:

Because if you are my true friend, then I am yours and the two of us are a perfect match. But in that case why did there have to be all this talk of 'the gold and the jade'? Alternatively, if there had to be all this talk of gold and jade, why weren't we the two to have them? Why did there have to be a Bao-chai with her golden locket?

Sorrow:

Because though there are things of burning importance to be said, without a father or a mother I have no one to say them for me. And besides, I feel so muzzy lately and I know that my illness is gradually gaining a hold on me. (The doctors say that the weakness and anaemia I suffer from may be the beginnings of a consumption.) So even if I *am* your true-love, I fear I may not be able to wait for you. And even though you are mine, you can do nothing to alter my fate.

At that point in her reflections she began to weep; and feeling in no fit state to be seen, she turned away from the door and began to make her way back again.

Bao-yu had finished his hasty dressing and now came out of the house. He saw Dai-yu slowly walking on ahead of him and, judging by her appearance from behind, wiping her eyes. He hurried forward to catch up with her.

'Where are you off to, coz? Are you crying again? Who has upset you this time?'

Dai-yu turned and saw that it was Bao-yu.

'I'm perfectly all right,' she said, forcing a smile. 'What would I be crying for?'

'Look at you! The tears are still wet on your face. How can you tell such fibs?'

Impulsively he stretched out his hand to wipe them. Dai-yu recoiled several paces:

'You'll get your head chopped off!' she said. 'You really *must* keep your hands to yourself.'

'I'm sorry. My feelings got the better of me. I'm afraid I wasn't thinking about my head.'

'No, I forgot,' said Dai-yu. 'Losing your head is nothing, is it? It's losing your kylin – the famous *gold* kylin – that is really serious!'

Her words immediately put Bao-yu in a passion. He came up to her and held his face close to hers.

'Do you say these things to put a curse on me? or is it merely to make me angry that you say them?'

Remembering their recent quarrel, Dai-yu regretted her careless reintroduction of its theme and hastened to make amends:

'Now don't get excited. I shouldn't have said that – oh come now, it really isn't *that* important! Look at you! The veins are standing out on your forehead and your face is all covered with sweat.'

She moved forward and wiped the perspiration from his brow. For some moments he stood there motionless, staring at her. Then he said:

'*Don't worry!*'

Hearing this, Dai-yu herself was silent for some moments.

'Why *should* I worry?' she said eventually. 'I don't understand you. Would you mind telling me what you are talking about?'

Bao-yu sighed.

'Do you really not understand? Can I really have been all this time mistaken in my feelings towards you? If you don't even know your *own* mind, it's small wonder that you're always getting angry on *my* account.'

'I really don't understand what you mean about not worrying,' said Dai-yu.

Bao-yu sighed again and shook his head.

'My dear coz, don't think you can fool me. If you don't

understand what I've just said, then not only have *my* feelings towards *you* been all along mistaken, but all that *you* have ever felt for *me* has been wasted, too. It's because you worry so much that you've made yourself ill. If only you could take things a bit easier, your illness wouldn't go on getting more and more serious all the time.'

Dai-yu was thunderstruck. He had read her mind – had seen inside her more clearly than if she had plucked out her entrails and held them out for his inspection. And now there were a thousand things that she wanted to tell him; yet though she was dying to speak, she was unable to utter a single syllable and stood there like a simpleton, gazing at him in silence.

Bao-yu, too, had a thousand things to say, but he, too, stood mutely gazing at her, not knowing where to begin.

After the two of them had stared at each other for some considerable time in silence, Dai-yu heaved a deep sigh. The tears gushed from her eyes and she turned and walked away. Bao-yu hurried after her and caught at her dress.

'Coz dear, stop a moment! Just let me say one word.'

As she wiped her eyes with one hand, Dai-yu pushed him away from her with the other.

'There's nothing to say. I already know what you want to tell me.'

She said this without turning back her head, and having said it, passed swiftly on her way. Bao-yu remained where he was standing, gazing after her in silent stupefaction.

Now Bao-yu had left the apartment in such haste that he had forgotten to take his fan with him. Fearing that he would be very hot without it, Aroma hurried outside to give it to him, but when she noticed him standing some way ahead of her talking to Dai-yu, she halted. After a little while she saw Dai-yu walk away and Bao-yu continue standing motionless where he was. She chose this moment to go up and speak to him.

'You've gone out without your fan,' she said. 'It's a good job I noticed. Here you are. I ran out to give it to you.'

Bao-yu, still in a muse, saw Aroma there talking to him, yet without clearly perceiving who it was. With the same glazed look in his eyes, he began to speak.

'Dearest coz! I've never before dared to tell you what I felt for you. Now at last I'm going to pluck up courage and tell you, and after that I don't care what becomes of me. Because of you I, too, have made myself ill – only I haven't dared tell anyone about it and have had to bear it all in silence. And the day that your illness is cured, I do believe that mine, too, will get better. Night and day, coz, sleeping and dreaming, you are never out of my mind.'

Aroma listened to this declaration aghast.

'Holy saints preserve us!' she exclaimed. 'He'll be the death of me.'

She gave him a shake.

'What are you talking about? Are you bewitched? You'd better hurry.'

Bao-yu seemed suddenly to waken from his trance and recognized the person he had been speaking to as Aroma. His face turned a deep red with embarrassment and he snatched the fan from her and fled.

*

After he had gone, Aroma began thinking about the words he had just said and realized that they must have been intended for Dai-yu. She reflected with some alarm that if things between them were as his words seemed to indicate, there was every likelihood of an ugly scandal developing, and wondered how she could arrange matters to prevent it. Preoccupied with these reflections, she stood as motionless and unseeing as her master had done a few moments before. Bao-chai found her in this state on her way back from the house.

'What are you brooding on, out in the burning sun?' she asked her, laughing.

Aroma laughed back.

'There were two little sparrows here having a fight. They were so funny, I had to stand and watch them.'

'Where was Cousin Bao rushing off to just now, all dressed

up for going out?' said Bao-chai. 'I was going to call out and ask him, but he is getting so crotchety lately that I thought I had better not.'

'The Master sent for him,' said Aroma.

'Oh dear!' said Bao-chai. 'I wonder why he should send for him in heat like this? I hope he hasn't thought of something to be angry about and called him over to be punished.'

'No, it isn't that,' said Aroma. 'I think it's to receive a visitor.'

'It must be a very tiresome visitor,' said Bao-chai, 'to go around bothering people on a boiling day like this instead of staying at home and trying to keep cool.'

'You can say that again!' said Aroma.

'What's young Xiang-yun been doing at your place?' said Bao-chai, changing the subject.

'We were having a chat,' said Aroma, 'and after that she had a look at some slipper-tops that I've got ready pasted and have asked her to sew for me.'

'You're an intelligent young woman,' said Bao-chai, having first looked to right and left of her to make sure that no one else was about, 'I should have thought you'd have sense enough to leave her a few moments in peace. I've been watching our Yun lately, and from what I've observed of her and various stray remarks I've heard, I get the impression that back at home she can barely call her soul her own. I know for a fact that they are too mean to pay for professional seamstresses and that nearly all the sewing has to be done by the women of the household, and I'm pretty sure that's why, whenever she's found herself alone with me on these last few visits, she's told me how tired she gets at home. When I press her for details, her eyes fill with tears and she answers evasively, as though she'd like to tell me but daren't. It must be very hard for her, losing both her parents when she was so young. It quite wrings my heart to see her so exploited.'

Aroma smote her hands together as understanding dawned.

'Yes, I *see*. I see now why she was so slow with those ten butterfly bows I asked her to sew for me last month. It was ages before she sent them, and even then there was a message to say that she'd only been able to do them roughly. She told me I'd better use them on something else. "If you want nice, even ones," she said, "you'll have to wait until next time I come to stay with you." Now I can see why. She didn't like to refuse when I asked her, but I suppose she had to sit up till midnight doing them, poor thing. Oh, how stupid of me! I'd never have asked her if I'd realized.'

'Last time she was here, she told me that it's quite normal for her to sit up sewing until midnight,' said Bao-chai; 'and if her aunt or the other women catch her doing the slightest bit of work for anyone else, they are angry with her.'

'It's all the fault of that pig-headed young master of mine,' said Aroma. 'He refuses to let any of his sewing be done by the seamstresses outside. Every bit of work, large or small, has to be done in his room – and I just can't manage it all on my own.'

Bao-chai laughed.

'Why do you take any notice of him? Why not simply give it to the seamstresses without telling him?'

'He's not so easy to fool,' said Aroma. 'He can tell the difference. I'm afraid there's nothing for it. I shall just have to work through it all gradually on my own.'

'Now just a minute!' said Bao-chai. 'We'll think of a way round this. Suppose *I* were to do some of it for you?'

'Would you really?' said Aroma. 'I'd be so grateful if you would. I'll come over with some this evening then.'

She had barely finished saying this when an old woman came rushing up to them in a state of great agitation.

'Isn't it dreadful? Miss Golden has drowned herself in the well.'

'Which Golden?' said Aroma, startled.

'Which Golden?' said the old woman. 'There aren't two Goldens that I know of. Golden from Her Ladyship's room, of course, that was dismissed the day before yesterday. She'd been crying and carrying on at home ever since, but nobody paid much attention to her. Then suddenly, when they went to look for her, she wasn't there, and just now someone going to fetch water from the well by the south-east corner found a body in it and rushed inside for help, and when they fished it out, they found that it was Golden. They did all they could to revive her, but it was too late. She was dead.'

'How strange!' said Bao-chai.

Aroma shook her head wonderingly and a tear or two stole down her cheek. She and Golden had been like sisters to each other.

Bao-chai hurried off to Lady Wang's to offer her sympathy. Aroma went back to Green Delights.

*

When Bao-chai arrived at Lady Wang's apartment she found the whole place hushed and still and Lady Wang sitting in the inner room on her own, crying. Deeming it an unsuitable moment to raise the subject of her visit, Bao-chai sat down beside her in silence.

'Where have you just come from?' Lady Wang asked her.

'The Garden.'

'The Garden,' Lady Wang echoed. 'Did you by any chance see your cousin Bao-yu there?'

'I saw him going out just now wearing his outdoor clothes, but I don't know where he was going to.'

Lady Wang nodded and gave a sigh.

'I don't know if you've heard. Something very strange has happened. Golden has drowned herself in a well.'

'That *is* strange,' said Bao-chai. 'Why ever did she do that?'

'The day before yesterday she broke something of mine,' said Lady Wang, 'and in a moment of anger I struck her a couple of times and sent her back to her mother's. I had only been meaning to leave her there a day or two to punish her. After that I would have had her back again. I never dreamed that she would be so angry with me as to drown herself. Now that she has, I feel that it is all my fault.'

'It's only natural that a kind person like you should see it in that way,' said Bao-chai, 'but in my opinion Golden would never have drowned herself in anger. It's much more likely that she was playing about beside the well and slipped in accidentally. While she was in service her movements were restricted and it would be natural for her to go running around everywhere during her first day or two outside. There's no earthly reason why she should have felt angry enough with you to drown herself. If she did, all I can say is that she was a stupid person and not worth feeling sorry for!'

Lady Wang sighed and shook her head doubtfully.

'Well, it may be as you say, but I still feel very uneasy in my mind.'

'I'm sure you have no cause, Aunt,' said Bao-chai, 'but if you feel *very* much distressed, I suggest that you simply give her family a little extra for the funeral. In that way you will more than fulfil any moral obligation you may have towards her as a mistress.'

'I have just given her mother fifty taels,' said Lady Wang. 'I wanted to give her two new outfits as well from one of the girls' wardrobes, but it just so happens that at the moment none of them apart from your Cousin Lin has got anything new that would do. Your Cousin Lin has got two sets that we had made for her next birthday, but she is such a sensitive child and has had so much sickness and misfortune in her life that I'm afraid she would almost certainly feel superstitious about the clothes made for her birthday being used for dressing a corpse with, so I've had to ask the tailors to make up a couple in a hurry. Of course, if it were any other maid, I should have given the mother a few taels and that would have been the end of the matter. But though Golden was only a servant, she had been with me so long that she had become almost like a daughter to me.'

She began to cry again as she said this.

'There's no need to hurry the tailors about this,' said Bao-chai. 'I've got two new outfits that I recently finished making for myself. Why not let her mother have *them* and save them the trouble? Golden once or twice wore old dresses of mine in the past, so I know they will fit her.'

'That's very kind of you, but aren't you superstitious?' said Lady Wang.

Bao-chai laughed.

'Don't worry about *that*, Aunt. That sort of thing has never bothered me.'

At that she rose and went off to fetch them. Lady Wang hurriedly ordered two of the servants to go after her.

When Bao-chai returned with the clothes, she found Bao-yu sitting beside his mother in tears. Lady Wang was evidently in the midst of rebuking him about something, but as soon as she caught sight of Bao-chai, she closed her mouth and fell silent. From the scene before her eyes and the word or two she had overheard, Bao-chai was able to form a pretty good idea of what had been happening. She handed the clothes over to Lady Wang and Lady Wang summoned Golden's mother to come and fetch them.

What happened after that will be told in the following chapter.

CHAPTER 33

*An envious younger brother puts in a malicious word or two
And a scapegrace elder brother receives a terrible chastisement*

OUR story last told how Golden's mother was summoned to
take away the clothing that Bao-chai had brought for Golden's
laying-out. When she arrived, Lady Wang called her inside,
and after making her an additional present of some jewellery,
advised her to procure the services of some Buddhist monks
to recite a *sūtra* for the salvation of the dead girl's soul.
Golden's mother kotowed her thanks and departed with the
clothes and jewellery.

*

The news that Golden's disgrace had driven her to take her
own life had reached Bao-yu as he was returning from his
interview with Jia Yu-cun, and he was already in a state of
shock when he went in to see his mother, only to be subjected
by her to a string of accusations and reproaches, to which he
was unable to reply. He availed himself of the opportunity
presented by Bao-chai's arrival to slip quietly out again, and
wandered along, scarcely knowing where he was going, still
in a state of shock, hands clasped behind him, head down low,
and sighing as he went.

Without realizing it he was drifting towards the main reception hall, and was in fact just emerging from behind the
screen-wall that masked the gateway leading from the inner to
the outer part of the mansion, when he walked head-on into
someone coming from the opposite direction.

'Stand where you are!' said this person in a harsh voice.

Bao-yu looked up with a start and saw that it was his father.
He gave an involuntary gasp of fear and, dropping his hands
to his sides, hastily assumed a more deferential posture.

'Now,' said Jia Zheng, 'will you kindly explain the meaning
of these sighs and of this moping, hang-dog appearance? You

took your time coming when Yu-cun called for you just now, and I gather that when you did eventually vouchsafe your presence, he found you dull and listless and without a lively word to say for yourself. And look at you now – sullenness and secret depravity written all over your face! What are these sighings and groanings supposed to indicate? What have *you* got to be discontented or displeased about? Come, sir! What is the meaning of this?'

Bao-yu was normally ready enough with his tongue, but on this occasion grief for Golden so occupied his mind (at that moment he would very willingly have changed places with her) that though he heard the words addressed to him by his father, he failed to take in their meaning and merely stared back at him stupidly.

Seeing him too hypnotized by fear – or so it appeared – to answer with his usual promptness, Jia Zheng, who had not been angry to start with, was now well on the way to becoming so; but the irate comment he was about to make was checked when a servant from the outer gate announced that a representative of 'His Highness the Prince of Zhong-shun' had arrived.

Jia Zheng was puzzled.

'The Prince of Zhong-shun?' he thought. 'I have never had any dealings with the Prince of Zhong-shun. I wonder why *he* should suddenly send someone to see me . . .?'

He told the man to invite the prince's messenger to sit in the hall, while he himself hurried inside and changed into court dress. On entering the hall to receive his visitor, he found that it was the Prince of Zhong-shun's chamberlain who had come to see him. After an exchange of bows and verbal salutations, the two men sat down and tea was served. The chamberlain cut short the customary civilities by coming straight to the point.

'It would have been temerity on my part to have intruded on the leisure of an illustrious scholar in the privacy of his home, but in fact it is not for the purpose of paying a social call that I am here, but on orders from His Highness. His Highness has a small request to make of you. If you will be so good as to oblige him, not only will His Highness be extremely grateful himself, but I and my colleagues will also be very much beholden to you.'

Jia Zheng was totally at a loss to imagine what the purpose of the man's visit might be; nevertheless he rose to his feet out of respect for the prince and smiled politely.

'You have orders from His Highness for me? I shall be happy to perform them if you will have the goodness to instruct me.'

'I don't think any *performing* will be necessary,' said the chamberlain drily. 'All we want from you is a few words. A young actor called Bijou – a female impersonator – has gone missing from the palace. He hasn't been back now for four or five days; and though we have looked everywhere we can think of, we can't make out where he can have got to. However, in the course of the very extensive inquiries we have made both inside and outside the city, eight out of ten of the people we have spoken to say that he has recently been very thick with the young gentleman who was born with the jade in his mouth. Well, obviously we couldn't come inside here and search as we would have done if this had been anyone else's house, so we had to go back and report the matter to His Highness; and His Highness says that though he could view the loss of a hundred ordinary actors with equanimity, this Bijou is so skilled in anticipating his wishes and so essential to his peace of mind that it would be utterly impossible for him to dispense with his services. I have therefore come here to request you to ask your son if he will be good enough to let Bijou come back again. By doing so he will not only earn the undying gratitude of the Prince, but will also save me and my colleagues a great deal of tiring and disagreeable searching.'

The chamberlain concluded with a sweeping bow.

Surprised and angered by what he had heard, Jia Zheng immediately sent for Bao-yu, who presently came hurrying in, ignorant of what the reason for his summons might be.

'Miserable scum!' said Jia Zheng. 'It is not enough, apparently, that you should neglect your studies when you are

at home. It seems that you must needs go perpetrating enor-
mities outside. This Bijou I have been hearing about is under the
patronage of His Royal Highness the Prince of Zhong-shun.
How could you have the unspeakable effrontery to commit an
act of enticement on his person – involving *me*, incidentally,
in the consequences of your wrong-doing?'

The question made Bao-yu start.

'I honestly know nothing about this,' he said. 'I don't even
know who or what "Bijou" is, let alone what you mean by
"enticement".'

Jia Zheng was about to exclaim, but the chamberlain fore-
stalled him.

'There is really no point in concealment, young gentleman,'
he said coldly. 'Even if you are not hiding him here, we are
sure that you know where he is. In either case you had much
better say straight out and save us a lot of trouble. I'd be
greatly obliged if you would.'

'I really don't know,' said Bao-yu. 'You must have been
misinformed.'

The chamberlain gave a sardonic laugh.

'I have, of course, got evidence for what I am saying and
I'm afraid you are doing yourself little good by forcing me to
mention it in front of your father. You say you don't know
who Bijou is. Very well. Then will you kindly explain how his
red cummerbund came to find its way around your waist?'

Bao-yu stared at him open-mouthed, too stunned to reply.

'If he knows even a private thing like that,' he thought,
'there's little likelihood of my being able to hoodwink him
about anything else. I'd better get rid of him as quickly as
possible, before he can say any more.'

'Since you have managed to find out so much about him,'
he said, finding his tongue at last, 'I'm surprised that so important a thing as buying a house should have escaped you.
From what I've heard, he recently acquired a little villa and an
acre or so of land at Fort Redwood, seven miles east of the
walls. I suppose he could be there.'

The chamberlain smiled.

'If you say so, then no doubt that is where we shall find

him. I shall go and look there immediately. If I do find him there, you will hear no more from me; if not, I shall be back again for further instructions.'

So saying, he hurriedly took his leave.

Jia Zheng, his eyes glaring and his mouth contorted with rage, went after the chamberlain to see him out. He turned briefly towards Bao-yu as he was leaving the hall.

'You stay where you are. I shall deal with you when I get back.'

As he was on his way in again after seeing the chamberlain off the premises, Jia Huan with two or three pages at his heels came stampeding across the courtyard.

'Hit that boy!' Jia Zheng shouted, outraged. But Jia Huan, reduced to a quivering jelly of fear by the sight of his father, had already jolted to a halt and was standing with bowed head in front of him.

'And what is the meaning of this?' said Jia Zheng. 'What has become of the people who are supposed to look after you? Why do they allow you to gallop around in this extraordinary fashion?' His voice rose to a shout: 'Where are the people responsible for taking this boy to school?'

Jia Huan saw in his father's anger an opportunity of exercising his malice.

'I didn't mean to run, Father, but just as I was going by the well back there I saw the body of a maid who had drowned herself – all swollen up with water, and her head all swollen. It was *horrible*. I just couldn't help myself.'

Jia Zheng heard him with incredulous horror.

'*What* are you saying? *Who* has drowned herself? Such a thing has never before happened in our family. Our family has always been lenient and considerate in its treatment of inferiors. It is one of our traditions. I suppose it is because I have been too neglectful of household matters during these last few years. Those in charge have felt encouraged to abuse their authority, until finally an appalling thing like this can happen – an innocent young life cut off by violence. What a terrible disgrace to our ancestors if this should get about!' He turned and shouted a command.

'Fetch Jia Lian and Lai Da!'

'Sir!' chorused the pages, and were on the point of doing so when Jia Huan impulsively stepped forward, threw himself on his knees and clung to his father's skirts.

'Don't be angry with me, Father, but apart from the servants in Lady Wang's room, no one else knows anything about this. I heard my mother say —'

He broke off and glanced around behind him. Jia Zheng understood and signalled with his eyes to the pages, who obediently withdrew some distance back to either side of the courtyard. Jia Huan continued in a voice lowered almost to a whisper.

'My mother told me that the day before yesterday, in Lady Wang's room, my brother Bao-yu tried to rape one of Her Ladyship's maids called Golden, and when she wouldn't let him, he gave her a beating; and Golden was so upset that she threw herself in the well and was drowned —'

Jia Zheng, whose face had now turned to a ghastly gold-leaf colour, interrupted him with a dreadful cry.

'Fetch Bao-yu!'

He began to stride towards his study, shouting to all and sundry as he went.

'If anyone tries to stop me *this* time, I shall make over my house and property and my post at the Ministry and everything else I have to him and Bao-yu. I absolutely refuse to be responsible for the boy any longer. I shall cut off my few remaining hairs (those that worry and wretchedness have left me) and look for some clean and decent spot to end my days in. Perhaps in that way I shall escape the charge of having disgraced my ancestors by rearing this unnatural monster as my son.'

When they saw the state he was in, the literary gentlemen and senior menservants who were waiting for him in the study, guessed that Bao-yu must be the cause of it and, looking at each other with various grimaces, biting their thumbs or sticking their tongues out, hastily retreated from the room. Jia Zheng entered it alone and sat down, stiffly upright, in a chair. He was breathing heavily and his face was bathed in tears. Presently, when he had regained his breath, he barked out a rapid series of commands:

'Bring Bao-yu here. Get a heavy bamboo. Get some rope to tie him with. Close the courtyard gates. If anyone tries to take word through inside, kill him!'

'Sir! – Sir! – Sir!' the terrified pages chorused in unison at each of his commands, and some of them went off to look for Bao-yu.

Jia Zheng's ominous 'Stay where you are' as he went out with the chamberlain had warned Bao-yu that something dire was imminent – though just how much more dire as a result of Jia Huan's malicious intervention he could not have foreseen – and as he stood where his father had left him, he twisted and turned himself about, anxiously looking for some passer-by who could take a message through to the womenfolk inside. But no one came. Even the omnipresent Tealeaf was on this occasion nowhere to be seen. Then suddenly, in answer to his prayers, an old woman appeared – a darling, precious treasure of an old woman (or so she seemed at that moment) – and he dashed forward and clung to her beseechingly.

'Quickly!' he said. 'Go and tell them that Sir Zheng is going to beat me. Quickly! Quickly! Go and tell. GO AND TELL.'

Partly because agitation had made him incoherent and partly because, as ill luck would have it, the old woman was deaf, almost everything he said had escaped her – except for the 'Go and tell', which she misheard as 'in the well'. She smiled at him reassuringly.

'Let her jump in the well then, young master. Don't you worry your pretty head about it!'

Realizing that he had deafness, too, to contend with, he now became quite frantic.

'GO AND TELL MY PAGES.'

'Her wages?' the old woman asked in some surprise. 'Bless you, of course they paid her wages! Her Ladyship gave a whole lot of money towards the funeral as well. And clothes. Paid her wages, indeed!'

Bao-yu stamped his feet in a frenzy of impatience. He was still wondering despairingly how to make her understand when Jia Zheng's pages arrived and forced him to go with them to the study.

Jia Zheng turned a pair of wild and bloodshot eyes on him as he entered. Forgetting the 'riotous and dissipated conduct abroad leading to the unseemly bestowal of impudicities on a theatrical performer' and the 'neglect of proper pursuits and studies at home culminating in the attempted violation of a parent's maidservant' and all the other high-sounding charges he had been preparing to hurl against him, he shouted two brief orders to the pages.

'Gag his mouth. Beat him to death.'

The pages were too frightened not to comply. Two held Bao-yu face downwards on a bench while a third lifted up the flattened bamboo sweep and began to strike him with it across the hams. After about a dozen blows Jia Zheng, not satisfied that his executioner was hitting hard enough, kicked him impatiently aside, wrested the bamboo from his grasp, and, gritting his teeth, brought it down with the utmost savagery on the places that had already been beaten.

At this point the literary gentlemen, sensing that Bao-yu was in serious danger of life and limb, came in again to remonstrate; but Jia Zheng refused to hear them.

'Ask him what he has done and then tell me if you think I should spare him,' he said. 'It is the encouragement of people like you that has corrupted him; and now, when things have come to this pass, you intercede for him. I suppose you would like me to wait until he commits parricide, or worse. Would you still intercede for him then?'

They could see from this reply that he was beside himself. Wasting no further time on words, they quickly withdrew and looked for someone to take a message through inside.

Lady Wang did not stop to tell Grandmother Jia when she received it. She snatched up an outer garment, pulled it about her, and, supported by a single maid, rushed off, not caring what menfolk might see her, to the outer study, bursting into it with such suddenness that the literary gentlemen and other males present were unable to avoid her.

Her entry provoked Jia Zheng to fresh transports of fury.

Faster and harder fell the bamboo on the prostrate form of Bao-yu, which by now appeared to be unconscious, for when the boys holding it down relaxed their hold and fled from their Mistress's presence, it had long since ceased even to twitch. Even so Jia Zheng would have continued beating it had not Lady Wang clasped the bamboo to her bosom and prevented him.

'Enough!' said Jia Zheng. 'Today you are determined, all of you, to drive me insane.'

'No doubt Bao-yu deserved to be beaten,' said Lady Wang tearfully, 'but it is bad for you to get over-excited. Besides, you ought to have some consideration for Lady Jia. She is not at all well in this frightful heat. It may not seem to you of much consequence to kill Bao-yu, but think what the effect would be on *her*.'

'Don't try that sort of talk with me!' said Jia Zheng bitterly. 'Merely by fathering a monster like this I have proved myself an unfilial son; yet whenever in the past I have tried to discipline him, the rest of you have all conspired against me to protect him. Now that I have the opportunity at last, I may as well finish off what I have begun and put him down, like the vermin he is, before he can do any more damage.'

So saying, he took up a rope and would have put his threat into execution, had not Lady Wang held her arms around him to prevent it.

'Of course you should discipline your son,' she said, weeping, 'but you have a wife too, Sir Zheng, don't forget. I am nearly fifty now and this wretched boy is the only son I have. If you insist on making an example of him, I dare not do much to dissuade you. But to kill him outright – that is deliberately to make me childless. Better strangle me first, if you are going to strangle him. Let the two of us die together. At least I shall have some support then in the world to come, if all support in this world is to be denied me!'

With these words she threw herself upon Bao-yu's body and, lifting up her voice, began weeping with noisy abandon. Jia Zheng, who had heard her with a sigh, sank into a chair and himself broke down in a fit of weeping.

Presently Lady Wang began to examine the body she was clasping. Bao-yu's face was ashen, his breathing was scarcely perceptible, and the trousers of thin green silk which clothed the lower part of his body were so soaked with blood that their colour was no longer recognizable. Feverishly she unfastened his waistband and drew them back. Everywhere, from the upper part of his buttocks down to his calves, was either raw and bloody or purplish black with bruises. Not an inch of sound flesh was to be seen. The sight made her cry out involuntarily.

'Oh my son! My unfortunate son!'

Once more she broke down into uncontrollable weeping.

Her own words reminded her of the son she had already lost, and now, with added bitterness, she began to call out his name.

'Oh, Zhu! Zhu! If only you had lived, I shouldn't have minded losing a *hundred* other sons!'

By this time news of Lady Wang's *démarche* had circulated to the other members of the inner mansion and Li Wan, Xi-feng, Ying-chun, Tan-chun and Xi-chun had come to join her. The invocation of her dead husband's name, painful to all of them, was altogether too much for Li Wan, who broke into loud sobs on hearing it. Jia Zheng himself was deeply affected, and tears as round as pumpkins rolled down both his cheeks. It was beginning to look as if they might all go on weeping there indefinitely, since no one would make a move; but just then there was a cry of 'Her Old Ladyship —!' from one of the maids, interrupted by a quavering voice outside the window.

'Kill me first! You may as well kill both of us while you are about it!'

As much distressed by his mother's words as he was alarmed by her arrival, Jia Zheng hurried out to meet her. She was leaning on the shoulder of a little maid, her old head swaying from side to side with the effort of running, and panting as she ran.

Jia Zheng bowed down before her and his face assumed the semblance of a smile.

'Surely, Mother, in such hot weather as this there is no need for you to come here? If you have any instructions, you should call for me and let *me* come to *you*.'

Grandmother Jia had stopped when she heard this voice and now stood panting for some moments while she regained her breath. When she spoke, her voice had an unnatural shrillness in it.

'Oh! Are you speaking to *me*? – Yes, as a matter of fact I *have* got "instructions", as you put it; but as unfortunately I've never had a good son who cares for me, there's no one I can give them to.'

Wounded in his most sensitive spot, Jia Zheng fell on his knees before her. The voice in which he replied to her was broken with tears.

'How can I bear it, Mother, if you speak to me like that? What I did to the boy I did for the honour of the family.'

Grandmother Jia spat contemptuously.

'A single harsh word from me and you start whining that you can't bear it. How do you think Bao-yu could bear your cruel rod? And you say you've been punishing him for the honour of the family, but you just tell me this: did your own father ever punish *you* in such a way? – I think not.'

She was weeping now herself.

'Don't upset yourself, Mother,' said Jia Zheng, with the same forced smile. 'I acted too hastily. From now on I'll never beat him again, if that's what you wish.'

'Hoity-toity, keep your temper!' said Grandmother Jia. 'He's your son. If you want to beat him, that's up to you. If we women are in your way, we'll leave you alone to get on with it.' She turned to her attendants. 'Call my carriage. Your Mistress and I and Bao-yu are going back to Nanking. We shall be leaving immediately.'

The servants made a show of compliance.

'No need for you to cry,' she said, turning to Lady Wang. 'You love Bao-yu now that he's young, but when he's grown up and become an important official, he'll like enough forget that you're his mother. Much better force yourself not to love him now and save yourself some anguish later on.'

Jia Zheng threw himself forward on his face.

'Don't say that, Mother! Don't reject your own son!'

'On the contrary,' said Grandmother Jia, 'it is *you* who have rejected *me*. But don't worry. When I have gone back to Nanking, there will be no one here to stop you. You can beat away to your heart's content.' She turned to the servants.

'Come on, hurry up with that packing! And get the carriage and horses ready so that we can be on our way.'

Jia Zheng's kotows were by now describing the whole quarter-circle from perpendicular to ground. But the old lady walked on inside, ignoring him.

From the sight that met her eyes she could tell that this had been no ordinary beating. It filled her with anguish for the sufferer and fresh anger for the man who had inflicted it, and for a long time she clung to the inert form and wept, only gradually calming down under the combined coaxing of Lady Wang, Xi-feng and Li Wan.

At this point several of the maids and womenservants came forward and attempted to raise Bao-yu to his feet.

'Idiots!' said Xi-feng. 'Haven't you got eyes in your heads? Can't you *see* that he's in no fit state to walk? Go and get that wicker summer-bed from inside and carry him in on that.'

The servants rushed out and presently reappeared carrying a long, narrow couch of woven rattan between them, on to which they lifted Bao-yu. Then, with Grandmother Jia, Lady Wang and the rest of the womenfolk leading the way, they carried him to Grandmother Jia's apartment and set him down inside it.

Jia Zheng, conscious that his mother's wrath against him had not abated and unwilling to leave things where they stood, had followed the little procession inside. His eyes travelled from Bao-yu, who, he now saw, really *had* been beaten very badly, to Lady Wang. She was sobbing bitterly, interspersing her sobs with cries of 'My child!' and 'My son!'. Presently she broke off and began railing at the object of her sorrow: 'Why couldn't you have died instead of Zhu? Zhu wouldn't have made his father angry the way you do and I should have been spared this constant anxiety. What is to become of me if *you* go away and leave me, too?' Then, with a cry of 'Poor, worthless boy!', she fell once more to weeping. When Jia Zheng heard this, his own heart was softened and he began to wish that he had not beaten the boy quite so savagely. He tried to find words of comfort for his old mother, but she answered him tearfully.

'A father *ought* to punish his son if he's done wrong, but not like *that*! – Why don't you go now? Won't you be content until you've seen the boy die under your own eyes?'

Jia Zheng, with flustered deference, withdrew.

By now Aunt Xue, Bao-chai, Caltrop, Aroma and Shi Xiang-yun were there too. Aroma was deeply distressed, but could not show the extent of her feelings in the presence of so many others. Indeed, Bao-yu was so ringed around with people fanning him or forcing water through his lips that there was nothing she could have done for him if she had tried. Feeling somewhat superfluous, she left the apartment and went out to the inner gate, where she asked the pages to look for Tealeaf, so that she could find out what had happened.

'Why did the Master suddenly beat him like that?' she asked Tealeaf when he arrived. 'He hadn't been doing anything. And why couldn't you have warned us in time?'

Tealeaf was indignant.

'I couldn't help it, I wasn't *there*. He was half-way through beating him before I even got to hear about it. I did my best to find out the reason, though. It seems that there were two things the Master was upset about: one was to do with Bijou and the other was to do with Golden.'

'How did the Master get to know about them?' said Aroma.

'Well, the Bijou business he probably knew about indirectly through Mr Xue,' said Tealeaf. 'Mr Xue had been feeling very jealous, and it looks as though he may have put someone else up to telling the Master about it out of spite. And Golden he probably heard about from Master Huan – leastways, that's what the Master's own people told me.'

The two reasons Tealeaf had given corresponded well enough with Aroma's own observations, and she was more than half inclined to believe them. Fairly confident, therefore, that she now knew the cause of what had happened, she returned once more to the apartment. The ministrations of those surrounding Bao-yu had by now restored him to full consciousness, and Grandmother Jia was instructing the servants to carry him back to his own room. There was an answering cry and something of a scramble as many willing hands lifted up the cane bed. Then, preceded as before by Grandmother Jia, Lady Wang and the rest, they carried him through into the Garden and back to Green Delights, where they finally got him on to his own bed. After a good deal more bustle they gradually all drifted away and Aroma at last had Bao-yu alone to herself.

But in order to know what happened then, you must refer to the following chapter.

CHAPTER 34

A wordless message meets with silent understanding
And a groundless imputation leads to undeserved rebukes

WHEN she saw that Grandmother Jia, Lady Wang and the rest had all gone, Aroma went and sat down at Bao-yu's bedside and asked him, with tears in her eyes, the reason why he had been beaten so severely.

Bao-yu sighed.

'Oh, the usual things. Need you ask? I wish you'd take a look down below, though, and tell me if anything's broken. It's hurting so dreadfully down there.'

Very gently Aroma inserted her fingers into the top of his trousers and began to draw them off. She had barely started when he gritted his teeth and let out a cry, and she had to stop immediately. This happened three or four times before she finally succeeded in getting them off. The sight revealed made her grit her own teeth.

'Mother of mine!' she gasped, 'he must have hit you savagely. If only you'd listened to me a bit in the past, it would never have come to *this*. Why, you might have been crippled for life. It doesn't bear thinking of.'

Just then Bao-chai's arrival was announced by one of the maids. Since putting his trousers on again was out of the question, Aroma snatched up a lightweight coverlet and hurriedly threw it over him. Bao-chai came in carrying a large tablet of some sort of solid medicine which she instructed Aroma to pound up in wine and apply to Bao-yu's injuries in the evening.

'This is a decongestant,' she said, handing it to her. 'It will take away the inflammation by dispersing the bad blood in his bruises. After that, he should heal quite quickly.'

She turned to Bao-yu.

'Are you feeling any better now?'

Bao-yu thanked her. Yes, he said, he was feeling a little

better, and invited her to sit down beside him. Bao-chai was relieved to see him with his eyes open and talking again. She shook her head sadly.

'If you had listened to what one said, this would never have happened. Everyone is so upset now. It isn't only Grandmother and Lady Wang, you know. Even – '

She checked herself abruptly, regretting that she had allowed her feelings to run away with her, and lowered her head, blushing. Bao-yu had sensed hidden depths of feeling in the passionate earnestness of her tone, and when she suddenly faltered and turned red, there was something so touching about the pretty air of confusion with which she dropped her head and played with the ends of her girdle, that his spirits soared and his pain was momentarily forgotten.

'What have I undergone but a few whacks of the bamboo?' he thought, '– yet already they are so sad and concerned about me! What dear, adorable, sweet, noble girls they are! Heaven knows how they would grieve for me if I were actually to die! It would be almost worth dying, just to find out. The loss of a life's ambitions would be a small price to pay, and I should be a peevish, ungrateful ghost if I did not feel proud and happy when such darling creatures were grieving for me.'

He was roused from this reverie by the sound of Bao-chai's voice asking Aroma what it was that had moved his father to such violent anger against him. Aroma's low reply, in which she merely repeated what Tealeaf had told her, was his first inkling of the part that Jia Huan had played in his misfortune. Her mention of Xue Pan's involvement, however, made him apprehensive that Bao-chai might feel embarrassed, and he hastily interrupted Aroma to prevent her from saying more.

'Old Xue would never do a thing like that,' he said. 'It's silly to make these wild assertions.'

Bao-chai knew that it was out of respect for her feelings that he was silencing Aroma, and she wondered at his considerateness.

'What delicacy of feeling!' she thought, '– after so terrible a beating and in spite of all the pain, to be still able to worry about the possibility of someone else's being offended! If only you could apply some of that thoughtfulness to the more important things of life, my friend, you would make my Uncle so happy; and then perhaps these awful things would never happen. And when all's said and done, this sensibility on my behalf is rather wasted. Do you *really* think I know my own brother so little that I am unaware of his unruly nature? Nothing has ever been allowed to stand in the way of Pan's desires. Look at the terrible trouble he made for you that time over Qin Zhong. That was a long time ago, and I am sure he has got much worse since then.'

Those were her thoughts, but what she said was:

'There's really no need to look around for someone to blame. If you ask me, the mere fact that Cousin Bao has been willing to keep such company was in itself quite enough to make Uncle angry. And though my brother can be very tactless and may well have let something out about Cousin Bao in the course of conversation, I'm sure it wouldn't have been deliberate trouble-making on his part. In the first place, it is, after all, true, what he is supposed to have said: Cousin Bao *has* been going around with that actor. And in the second place, my brother simply hasn't got it in him to be discreet. You have lived all your life with sensitive, considerate people like Cousin Bao, my dear Aroma. You have never had to deal with a crude, forthright person like my brother – someone who says whatever comes into his head with complete disregard for the consequences.'

When Bao-yu cut short her remarks about Xue Pan, Aroma had realized at once that she was being tactless and inwardly prayed that Bao-chai had not taken exception to them. To her, therefore, these words of Bao-chai's were a source of tongue-tied embarrassment. Bao-yu, on the other hand, could see in them only the refusal of a frank and generous nature to admit deviousness in others and a sensibility capable of matching and responding to his own. As a consequence his spirits soared yet higher. He was about to say something, but Bao-chai rose to her feet and anticipated him.

'I'll come and see you again tomorrow. You must rest now and give yourself a chance to get well. I've given Aroma something to make a lotion with. Get her to put it on for you in the evening. I can guarantee that it will hasten your recovery.'

She was moving towards the door as she said this. When she was outside, Aroma hurried after her to see her off and to thank her for her trouble.

'As soon as he's better,' she said, 'Master Bao will come over and thank you himself, Miss.'

'It's nothing at all,' said Bao-chai, turning back to her with a smile. 'Do tell him to rest properly, though, and not to brood. And if there's anything at all he wants, just quietly come round to my place for it. Don't go bothering Lady Jia or Lady Wang or any of the others, in case my uncle gets to hear of it. It probably wouldn't matter at the time, but it might do later on, next time there is any trouble.'

With that she left, and Aroma turned back into the courtyard, her heart full of gratitude for Bao-chai's kindness. Re-entering Bao-yu's room, she found him lying back quietly, plunged in thought. From the look of it, he was already half asleep. Tiptoeing out again, she went off to wash her hair.

But it was difficult for Bao-yu to lie quietly for very long. The pain in his buttocks was like the stabbing and pricking of knives and needles and there was a burning sensation in them as if he were being grilled over a fire, so that the slightest movement made him cry out. Already it was growing late. Aroma appeared to have gone away, but two or three maids were still in attendance. As there was nothing that they could do for him, he told them that they might go off and prepare themselves for the night, provided that they remained within call. The maids accordingly withdrew, leaving him on his own.

He had dozed off. The shadowy form of Jiang Yu-han had come in to tell him of his capture by the Prince of Zhong-shun's men, followed, shortly after, by Golden, who gave him a tearful account of how she had drowned herself. In his half-dreaming, half-awake state he was having the greatest difficulty in attending to what they were saying, when suddenly he felt someone pushing him and became dimly aware of a sound of weeping in his ear. He gave a start. Fully awake now, he opened his eyes. It was Lin Dai-yu. Suspecting this, too, to be a dream, he raised his head to look. A pair of eyes swollen like peaches met his own, and a face that was glistening with tears. It was Dai-yu all right, no doubt about that. He would have looked longer, but the strain of raising himself was causing such excruciating pain in his nether parts, that he fell back again with a groan. The groan was followed by a sigh.

'Now what have *you* come for?' he said. 'The sun's not long set and the ground must still be very hot underfoot. You could still get a heat-stroke at this time of day, and that would be a fine how-do-you-do. Actually, in spite of the beating, I don't feel very much pain. This fuss I make is put on to fool the others. I'm hoping they'll spread the word around outside how badly I've been hurt, so that Father gets to hear of it. It's all shamming, really. You mustn't be taken in by it.'

Dai-yu's sobbing had by this time ceased to be audible; but somehow her strangled, silent weeping was infinitely more pathetic than the most clamorous grief. At that moment volumes would have been inadequate to contain the things she wanted to say to him; yet all she could get out, after struggling for some time with her choking sobs, was:

'I suppose you'll change now.'

Bao-yu gave a long sigh.

'Don't worry, I shan't change. People like that are worth dying for. I wouldn't change if he killed me.'

The words were scarcely out of his mouth when they heard someone outside in the courtyard saying:

'Mrs Lian has come.'

Dai-yu had no wish to see Xi-feng, and rose to her feet hurriedly.

Bao-yu seized hold of her hand.

'Now that's funny. Why should you start being afraid of *her* all of a sudden?'

She stamped with impatience.

'Look at the state my eyes are in!' she said. 'I don't want them all making fun of me again.'

At that Bao-yu released her hand and she bounded round to the back of the bed, slipping into the rear courtyard just as Xi-feng was entering the room from the front.

'A bit better now?' said Xi-feng. 'Is there anything you feel like eating yet? If there is, tell them to come round to my place and get it.'

As soon as Xi-feng had gone, Bao-yu was visited by Aunt Xue, and shortly after that by someone whom his grandmother had sent to see how he was getting on. At lighting-up time, after taking a few mouthfuls of soup, he settled down into a fitful sleep.

Just then a new group of visitors arrived, consisting of Zhou Rui's wife, Wu Xin-deng's wife, Zheng Hao-shi's wife, and those other members of the mansion's female staff who had had most to do with Bao-yu in the past and who, having heard of his beating, were anxious to see how he was. Aroma came out smiling on to the verandah to welcome them.

'You're just too late to see him, ladies,' she told them in a low voice. 'He's just this minute dropped off.'

She ushered them into the outer room, invited them to be seated, and served them with tea. After sitting there very quietly for several minutes, they got up to take their leave, requesting Aroma as they did so that she would inform Bao-yu when he waked that they had been round to ask about him. Aroma promised to do so and showed them out. Just as she was about to go in again, an old woman arrived from Lady Wang's to say that 'Her Ladyship would like to see one of Master Bao's people.' After reflecting for a moment, Aroma turned to the house and called softly to Skybright, Musk and Ripple inside.

'Her Ladyship wants to see someone, so I'm going over. Stay indoors and keep an eye on things while I'm away. I shan't be long.'

Then she followed the old woman out of the Garden and round to Lady Wang's apartment in the central courtyard. She found Lady Wang sitting on a cane summer-bed and fanning herself with a palm-leaf fan. She appeared not entirely pleased when she saw that it was Aroma.

'You could have sent one of the others,' she said. 'There was no need for *you* to come and leave him unattended.'

Aroma smiled reassuringly.

'Master Bao has just settled down for the night, Madam. If he *should* want anything, the others are nowadays quite capable of looking after him on their own. Your Ladyship has no need to worry. I thought I had better come myself and not send one of the others, in case Your Ladyship had something important to tell us. I was afraid that if I sent one of the others, they might not understand what you wanted.'

'I have nothing in particular to tell you,' said Lady Wang. 'I merely wanted to ask about my son. How is the pain now?'

'Much better since I put on some of the lotion that Miss Bao brought for him,' said Aroma. 'It was so bad before that he couldn't lie still, but now he's sleeping quite soundly, so you can tell it must be better than it was.'

'Has he had anything to eat yet?' said Lady Wang.

'He had a few sips of some soup Her Old Ladyship sent,' said Aroma, 'but that's all he would take. He kept complaining that he felt dry. He wanted me to give him plum bitters to drink, but of course that's an astringent, and I thought to myself that as he'd just had a beating and not been allowed to cry out during it, a lot of hot blood and hot poison must have been driven inwards and still be collected round his heart, and if he were to drink some of that stuff, it might stir them up and bring on a serious illness, so I talked him out of it. After a lot of persuading, I got him to take some rose syrup instead, that I mixed up in water for him; but after only half a cup of it he said it tasted sickly and he couldn't get it down.'

'Oh dear, I wish you'd told me sooner,' said Lady Wang. 'We were sent some bottles of flavouring the other day that I could have let you have. As a matter of fact I *was* going to send him some of them, but then I thought that if I did they would probably only get wasted, so I didn't. If he can't manage the rose syrup, I can easily give you a few of them to take back with you. You need only mix a teaspoonful of essence in a cupful of water. The flavours are quite delicious.'

She called Suncloud to her. 'Fetch me a few of those bottles of flavouring essence that were sent us the other day.'

'Two will be enough,' said Aroma, 'otherwise it will only get wasted. If we run out, I can always come back for more later.'

Suncloud was gone for a considerable time. Eventually she returned with two little glass bottles, each about three inches high, which she handed to Aroma. They had screw-on silver tops and yellow labels. One of them was labelled 'Essence of Cassia Flower' and the other one 'Essence of Roses'.

'What tiny little bottles!' said Aroma. 'They can't hold very much. I suppose the stuff inside them must be very precious.'

'It was made specially for the Emperor,' said Lady Wang. 'That's what the yellow labels mean. Haven't you seen labels like that before? Mind you look after them and don't let the stuff in them get wasted.'

Aroma promised to be careful and began to go.

'Just a minute!' said Lady Wang. 'I've thought of something else that I wanted to ask you.'

Aroma returned. Lady Wang first glanced about her to make sure that no one else was in the room, then she said:

'I think I heard someone say that Bao-yu's beating today was because of something that Huan had said to Sir Zheng. I suppose *you* don't happen to have heard anything about that?'

'No. I haven't heard anything about *that*,' said Aroma. 'What *I* heard was that it was because Master Bao had been going around with one of Prince Somebody-or-other's players and the Master was told about it by someone who called.'

Lady Wang nodded her head mysteriously.

'Yes, that was one of the reasons. But there was another reason as well.'

'I really know nothing about any other reason, Your Ladyship,' said Aroma. She dropped her head and hesitated a moment before going on. 'I wonder if I might be rather bold and say something very outspoken to Your Ladyship? Really and truly —' She faltered.

'Please go on.'

'I will if Your Ladyship will promise not to be angry with me.'

'That's all right,' said Lady Wang. 'Just tell me what you have to say.'

'Well, really and truly,' said Aroma, 'Master Bao *needed* punishing. If the Master didn't keep an eye on him, there's no knowing *what* he mightn't get up to.'

'My child,' said Lady Wang with a warmth rarely seen in her, 'those are exactly my own sentiments. How clever of you to have understood! Of course, I know perfectly well that Bao-yu is in need of discipline; and anyone who saw how strict I used to be with Mr Zhu would realize that I am capable of exercising it. But I have my reasons. A woman of fifty cannot expect to bear any more children and Bao-yu is now the only son I have. He is not a very strong boy; and his Grannie dotes on him. I daren't *risk* being strict. I daren't risk losing another son. I daren't risk angering Her Old Ladyship and upsetting the whole household. I do once in a while have it out with him: but though I have argued and pleaded and wept, it doesn't do any good. He *seems* all right at the time, but he'll be just the same again a short while afterwards and I always know that I have failed to reach him. I am afraid he *has* to suffer before he can learn – but suppose it's too much for him? – suppose he doesn't get over *this* beating? What will become of *me*?'

She began to cry.

Seeing her mistress so distressed, Aroma herself was affected and began to cry too.

'I can understand Your Ladyship being so upset,' she said, 'when he's your own son. Even we servants that have been with him for a few years get worried about him. The most that *we* can ever hope for is to do our duty and get by without too much trouble – but even *that* won't be possible if he goes on the way he has been doing. I'm always telling him to change his ways. Every day – every hour – I tell him. But it's no use; he won't listen. Of course, if these people *will* make so much fuss of him, you can hardly blame him for going round with them – though it does make our job more difficult. But now that Your Ladyship has spoken like this, it puts me in mind of

something that's been worrying me which I should like to
have asked Your Ladyship's advice about, only I was afraid
you might take it amiss, and then not only should I have
spoken to no purpose, but I should leave myself without even
a grave to lie in . . .'

It was evident to Lady Wang that what she was struggling
to get out was a matter of some consequence.

'What is it you want to tell me, my child?' she said kindly.
'I've heard a lot of people praising you recently, and I confess
that I assumed it must be because you took special pains in
serving Bao-yu or in making yourself agreeable to other
people – little things of that sort. But I see that I was wrong.
These are not at all little things that you have been talking
about. What you have said so far makes very good sense and
entirely accords with my own opinion of the matter. So if you
have anything to tell me, I should like to hear it. But I must
ask you not to discuss it with anyone else.'

'All I really wanted to ask,' said Aroma, 'was if Your Ladyship could advise me how later on we can somehow or other
contrive to get Master Bao moved back outside the Garden.'

Lady Wang looked startled and clutched Aroma's hand in
some alarm.

'I hope Bao-yu hasn't been doing something dreadful with
one of the girls?'

'Oh no, Your Ladyship, please don't suspect that!' said
Aroma hurriedly. 'That wasn't my meaning at all. It's just that
– if you'll allow me to say so – Master Bao and the young
ladies are beginning to grow up now, and though they are all
cousins, there *is* the difference of sex between them, which
makes it very awkward sometimes when they are all living
together, especially in the case of Miss Lin and Miss Bao, who
aren't even of the same clan. One can't help feeling uneasy.
Even to outsiders it looks like a very strange sort of family.
They say "where nothing happens, imagination is busiest",
and I'm sure lots of unaccountable misfortunes begin when
some innocent little thing we did unthinkingly gets misconstrued in someone else's imagination and reported as
something terrible. We just have to be on our guard against

that sort of thing happening – especially when Master Bao has such a peculiar character, as Your Ladyship knows, and spends all his time with girls. He only has to make the tiniest slip in an unguarded moment, and whether he really did anything or not, with so many people about – and some of them no better than they should be – there is sure to be scandal. For you know what some of these people are like, Your Ladyship. If they feel well-disposed towards you, they'll make you out to be a saint; but if they're not, then Heaven help you! If Master Bao lives to be spoken well of, we can count ourselves lucky; but the way things are, it only needs someone to breathe a word of scandal and – I say nothing of what will happen to us servants – it's of no consequence if *we*'re all chopped up for mincemeat – but what's more important, Master Bao's reputation will be destroyed for life and all the care and worry Your Ladyship and Sir Zheng have had on his account will have been wasted. I know Your Ladyship is very busy and can't be expected to think of everything, and I probably shouldn't have thought of this myself, but once I *had* thought of it, it seemed to me that it would be wrong of me not to tell Your Ladyship, and it's been preying on my mind ever since. The only reason I haven't mentioned it before is because I was afraid Your Ladyship might be angry with me.'

What Aroma had just been saying about misconstructions and scandals so exactly fitted what had in fact happened in the case of Golden that for a moment Lady Wang was quite taken aback. But on reflection she felt nothing but love and gratitude for this humble servant-girl who had shown so much solicitude on her behalf.

'It is very perceptive of you, my dear, to have thought it all out so carefully,' she said. 'I have, of course, thought about this matter myself, but other things have put it from my mind, and what you have just said has reminded me. It is most thoughtful of you. You are a very, very good girl – Well, you may go now. I think I now know what to do. There is just one thing before you go, though. Now that you have spoken to me like this, I am going to place Bao-yu entirely in your hands. Be very careful with him, won't you? Remember that anything you do for him you will be doing also for me. You will find that I am not ungrateful.'

Aroma stood for a moment with bowed head, weighing the import of these words. Then she said:

'I will do what Your Ladyship has asked me to the utmost of my ability.'

She left the apartment slowly and made her way back to Green Delights, pondering as she went. When she arrived, Bao-yu had just woken up, so she told him about the flavourings. He was pleased and made her mix some for him straight away. It was quite delicious. He kept thinking about Dai-yu and wanted to send someone over to see her, but he was afraid that Aroma would disapprove, so, as a means of getting her out of the way, he sent her over to Bao-chai's place to borrow a book. As soon as she had gone, he summoned Skybright.

'I want you to go to Miss Lin's for me,' he said. 'Just see what she's doing, and if she asks about me, tell her I'm all right.'

'I can't go rushing in there bald-headed without a reason,' said Skybright. 'You'd better give me *some* kind of a message, just to give me an excuse for going there.'

'I have none to give,' said Bao-yu.

'Well, give me something to take, then,' said Skybright, 'or think of something I can ask her for. Otherwise it will look so silly.'

Bao-yu thought for a bit and then, reaching out and picking up two of his old handkerchiefs, he tossed them towards her with a smile.

'All right. Tell her I said you were to give her these.'

'That's an odd sort of present!' said Skybright. 'What's she going to do with a pair of your old handkerchiefs? Most likely she'll think you're making fun of her and get upset again.'

'No she won't,' said Bao-yu. 'She'll understand.'

Skybright deemed it pointless to argue, so she picked up the handkerchiefs and went off to the Naiad's House. Little Delicate, who was hanging some towels out to dry on the verandah railings, saw her enter the courtyard and attempted to wave her away.

'She's gone to bed.'

Skybright ignored her and went on inside. The lamps had not been lit and the room was in almost total darkness. The voice of Dai-yu, lying awake in bed, spoke to her out of the shadows.

'Who is it?'

'Skybright.'

'What do you want?'

'Master Bao has sent me with some handkerchiefs, Miss.'

Dai-yu seemed to hesitate. She found the gift puzzling and was wondering what it could mean.

'I suppose they must be very good ones,' she said. 'Probably someone gave them to him. Tell him to keep them and give them to somebody else. I have no use for them just now myself.'

Skybright laughed.

'They're not new ones, Miss. They're two of his old, every-day ones.'

This was even more puzzling. Dai-yu thought very hard for some moments. Then suddenly, in a flash, she understood.

'Put them down. You may go now.'

Skybright did as she was bid and withdrew. All the way back to Green Delights she tried to make sense of what had happened, but it continued to mystify her.

Meanwhile the message that eluded Skybright had thrown Dai-yu into a turmoil of conflicting emotions.

'I feel so happy,' she thought, 'that in the midst of his own affliction he has been able to grasp the cause of all *my* trouble.

'And yet at the same time I am sad,' she thought; 'because how do I know that my trouble will end in the way I want it to?

'Actually, I feel rather amused,' she thought. 'Fancy his sending a pair of old handkerchiefs like that! Suppose I hadn't understood what he was getting at?

'But I feel alarmed that he should be sending presents to me in secret.

'Oh, and I feel so ashamed when I think how I am forever

crying and quarrelling,' she thought, 'and all the time he has understood! . . .'

And her thoughts carried her this way and that, until the ferment of excitement within her cried out to be expressed. Careless of what the maids might think, she called for a lamp, sat herself down at her desk, ground some ink, softened her brush, and proceeded to compose the following quatrains, using the handkerchiefs themselves to write on:

1

Seeing my idle tears, you ask me why
These foolish drops fall from my teeming eye:
Then know, your gift, being by the merfolk made,
In merman's currency must be repaid.

2

Jewelled drops by day in secret sorrow shed
Or, in the night-time, in my wakeful bed,
Lest sleeve or pillow they should spot or stain,
Shall on these gifts shower down their salty rain.

3

Yet silk preserves but ill the Naiad's tears:
Each salty trace of them fast disappears.
Only the speckled bamboo stems that grow
Outside the window still her tear-marks show.

She had only half-filled the second handkerchief and was preparing to write another quatrain, when she became aware that her whole body was burning hot all over and her cheeks were afire. Going over to the dressing-table, she removed the brocade cover from the mirror and peered into it.

'Hmn! "Brighter than the peach-flower's hue",' she murmured complacently to the flushed face that stared out at her from the glass, and, little imagining that what she had been witnessing was the first symptom of a serious illness, went back to bed, her mind full of handkerchiefs.

*

From Dai-yu and her handkerchiefs let us return to Aroma, who, it will be remembered, had been sent off to Bao-chai's for a book. When she got there, she found that Bao-chai was not in the Garden, having gone round to her mother's place outside. Not liking to return empty-handed, she waited for Bao-chai to return. It was already the beginning of the first watch when she did so.

Knowing her brother as she did, Bao-chai had already, even before hearing anything to that effect, suspected that he was in some way responsible for Bao-yu's misfortune. What Aroma had earlier on told her had therefore been no more than confirmation of an already existing suspicion. Yet Aroma had only been echoing what Tealeaf had told *her*; and what Tealeaf had told her was pure guesswork without a shred of evidence to support it. Thus what started in everyone's mind as a suspicion, repetition very soon compounded into a certainty. Yet the ironical fact was that he who by his past behaviour had so richly merited the reputation which had caused them to suspect him was totally innocent on the one occasion when everyone was most unshakeably convinced of his guilt.

The object of this misunderstanding had on this particular evening returned home having had a good deal to drink outside. He greeted his mother and then, observing that his sister, too, was sitting there, addressed a few desultory remarks to her. Suddenly he seemed to remember something.

'I hear young Bao-yu's been in trouble,' he said. 'What was it about?'

This was too much for Aunt Xue, who had been seething inwardly and now broke out in a fury.

'Shameless villain! How can you have the face to ask such a question? You know very well it was all your doing.'

Xue Pan stared at her in astonishment.

'What do you mean, "all my doing"?'

'Don't act the injured innocent with me!' said his mother. 'Everyone knows it was you who told.'

'Oh, and I suppose if everyone said I'd killed somebody, you'd believe that too!'

'Even your sister knows it was you. I suppose you're not going to call *her* a liar?'

Bao-chai hurriedly intervened.

'Don't shout so, both of you! If you'd be a bit more calm and collected, you might have some chance of getting at the truth.' She turned to Xue Pan: 'Anyway, whether it *was* you or *wasn't* you, the damage is done now. There doesn't seem much point in raking it over or making an issue of it. My advice to you is to keep out of mischief from now on and stop interfering in other people's affairs. When you spend day after day fooling around outside, sooner or later something is *bound* to happen; and you are such a thoughtless creature, that when it does, people naturally suspect that you are the one to blame, even if you aren't. I know *I* do!'

Xue Pan, for all his faults, was a forthright, outspoken sort of fellow, unused to such ostrich-like avoidance of the issue. Bao-chai's strictures about 'fooling around' and his mother's insistence that he had brought about Bao-yu's beating by means of a deliberate indiscretion had exasperated him beyond endurance. He jumped about excitedly, protesting with the most solemn and desperate oaths that he was innocent.

'I'd like to find the comedian who's been making up these stories about me,' he shouted, turning in anger upon the domestics. 'I'll smash his rotten face in if I do. Of course, I know what this is all about: you all want to show how concerned you are for poor, darling Bao-yu, so you've decided to do it at my expense. What is he, anyway? a Deva King? Every time his dad gives him a few whacks on the bum, the whole household is in a state of uproar about it for days on end. I remember that time Uncle Zheng beat him for doing something he shouldn't have and old Lady Jia decided that Cousin Zhen was at the bottom of it. She had the poor so-and-so hauled up in front of her and there was hell to pay. Now, this time, you want to drag *me* into it. All right then: I don't care. A life for a life. I'll go in there and kill the little blighter – then you can all do what you like to me.'

In the midst of this bawling he had picked up a door-bar and was evidently going off to execute his threat; but his distraught mother clung to him and prevented him from going.

'You stupid creature!' she said. 'Who do you think you're

going to hit with that? If you're going to hit anyone, you'd better begin with me!'

Xue Pan's exasperation had now reached such a pitch that his eyes stood out in his head like a pair of copper bells.

'This is rich!' he shouted. 'You won't let me go and finish him off, yet you won't stop provoking me by making up all these lies. Every day that fellow stays alive means one more day of nagging and lies for *me* to put up with. We'd much better die, the pair of us, and make an end of it!'

'Have a little self-control!' said Bao-chai, joining in her mother's efforts to restrain him. 'Can't you see how upset poor Mamma is? You ought to be trying to calm her, not making things worse with this uproar.'

'Oh yes! *you* can say that now,' said Xue Pan, 'but it was you who started all this by telling her about me, wasn't it?'

'It's all very well to blame me for telling Mamma,' said Bao-chai. 'Why don't you blame yourself for being so care-less, you great blabber-mouth?'

'Me careless?' said Xue Pan. 'What about the way Bao-yu stirs up trouble for himself then? Let me just give you an example. Let me tell you what happened between him and Bijou the other day. I'd met Bijou ten times, near enough, and never had so much as a kind word out of him, yet Bao-yu, that didn't even know him by sight, meets him for the first time the other day, and before you know where you are, he's given him his sash! I hope you're not going to say that *that* got about because of me?'

His mother and sister were indignant.

'That's a *fine* example, isn't it? It's precisely because of that that he was beaten. Now we *know* it must have been you who told.'

'This is enough to drive a fellow mad!' said Xue Pan. 'It's not so much the lies you keep telling about me. What really gets my goat is the almighty fuss you make about this fellow Bao-yu.'

'Almighty fuss?' said Bao-chai. 'You've just been waving a door-bar at us, and you say that *we* have been making a fuss?'

Xue Pan could see that Bao-chai had reason on her side and that she was much harder to argue with than his mother. He was therefore eager to find something that would stop her mouth, so that he could say what he wanted to without contradiction. This, coupled with the fact that he was by now far too angry to weigh the seriousness of what he was saying, was responsible for the unpardonable innuendo that followed.

'All right, sis,' he said, 'you don't need to quarrel with me. I know what your trouble is. Mamma told me long ago that Mr Right would be someone with a jade to match your locket, so naturally, now you've seen that blasted thing that Bao-yu wears round his neck, you do all you can to stick up for him.'

Anger at first made Bao-chai speechless; then, clinging to Aunt Xue, she burst into tears.

'Mamma, listen to what Pan is saying to me!'

Realizing, when he saw his sister's tears, that he had gone too far, Xue Pan retired sulkily to his own room and went to bed. Bao-chai was left bursting with injury and outrage which she dared not express for fear of further upsetting her mother. She was obliged to bid the latter a tearful goodnight and go back to her own room in the Garden, where she spent the rest of the night weeping.

She was up early next morning. Too dispirited to make a proper toilet, she stopped only to tidy herself a little before setting off for her mother's. On the way she met, of all people, Dai-yu, standing on her own beneath a flowering tree.

'Where are you going?' said Dai-yu.

'To my mother's.' She answered without stopping.

Dai-yu noticed how dispirited she looked and saw that her eyes were swollen as if she had been weeping.

'Don't make yourself ill, coz,' she called out, almost gleefully, to the retreating back. 'Even a cistern-full of tears won't heal the smart of a beating!'

The nature of Bao-chai's reply will be revealed in the following chapter.

CHAPTER 35

Sulky Silver tastes some lotus-leaf soup
And Golden Oriole knots a flower-patterned fringe

BAO-CHAI heard Dai-yu's sarcasm quite clearly, but her mind was too taken up with her own family affairs to pay much attention, and she continued on her way without looking back.

As Dai-yu gazed towards the House of Green Delights, which was at some distance from the flowering tree in whose shade she was standing, she presently observed Li Wan, Ying-chun, Tan-chun and Xi-chun, attended by numerous maids, going into the gate of its courtyard. Then, as she continued to watch, she saw them one by one come out again and go their separate ways. It struck her that Xi-feng had not been with them, and she wondered why.

'It's not like her not to visit him,' she thought. 'Even if she's otherwise engaged, you'd expect her to find some means of getting over and doing her little turn, if only to keep in with Grandma and Auntie Wang. There must be some very pressing reason to keep *her* away.'

She lowered her head to reflect. Raising it again and looking once more in the direction of Green Delights, she observed a colourful throng of females just about to enter, and when she looked a little harder, she could make out Wang Xi-feng with Grandmother Jia leaning on her arm. Lady Wang and Lady Xing walked behind them, followed by Aunt Zhou and a large bevy of maids and womenservants. As the last of these disappeared inside the gate, Dai-yu nodded wistfully, thinking how good it must be to have a family, and soon her face was once more wet with tears. Presently she saw Aunt Xue and Bao-chai arrive. Not long after she had watched them enter the gate, Nightingale suddenly walked up behind her.

'Come and have your medicine, Miss,' she said. 'It's cool enough to drink now.'

'What's the matter with you?' said Dai-yu. 'Always fussing! What does it matter to you whether I take my medicine or not?'

Nightingale laughed good-humouredly.

'Your cough's only just beginning to get better, and already you want to stop taking your medicine! It may be the fifth month and the weather may be hot, but all the same, you still need to be careful. Come on, you've been standing quite long enough in this early morning damp. You ought to come in now and rest a bit.'

Now that Nightingale's words had recalled her attention to herself, Dai-yu became aware that her legs were in fact rather tired. For a moment or two she appeared rather bewildered, then, taking Nightingale's arm, she slowly made her way back to the Naiad's House.

As they entered the courtyard, the chequered shadows of the bamboos and the dew-pearled moss reminded her of two lines she had read in *The Western Chamber*:

> A place remote, where footsteps seldom pass,
> And dew still glistens on the untrodden grass.

'It's all very well,' she thought, as she reflected on the heroine of that play, 'Ying-ying may have been unfortunate, but at least she had a widowed mother and a little brother. I have no one.'

She was about to shed tears once more; but just then her parrot, which had been perched aloft under the verandah eaves, seeing that his mistress had returned, flew down with a sudden squawk that made her jump.

'*Wicked* Polly!' she said. 'You've shaken dust all over my head!'

The parrot flew on to its perch.

'Snowgoose!' it called. 'Raise the blind! Miss Lin is back!'

Dai-yu stooped in front of it and tapped its perch.

'Did they remember your food and water, Polly?'

The parrot heaved a long sigh, uncannily like the ones that Dai-yu was wont to utter, and recited, in its parroty voice:

> 'Let others laugh flower-burial to see:
> Another year who will be burying me?'

Dai-yu and Nightingale both burst out laughing.

'It's what you're always reciting yourself, Miss,' said Nightingale. 'Fancy Polly being able to remember it!'

Dai-yu made her take the perch down and hang it up outside the round 'moon-window' of her study.

Going indoors she sat down by the moon-window to take her medicine. Light reflected from the bamboos outside passed through the gauze of the window to make a green gloom within, lending a cold, aquarian look to the floor and the surfaces of the furniture. To keep her spirits up in these somewhat cheerless surroundings she spoke teasingly to the parrot hanging on the other side of the gauze until he jumped and squawked on his perch, after which she taught him a few snatches of her favourite poems.

At this point our narrative leaves her and returns to Bao-chai.

*

When Bao-chai arrived at her mother's apartment that morning, she found her mother still doing her hair. Aunt Xue greeted her daughter with a smile of surprise.

'You're very early this morning, my dear.'

'I wanted to know how you were, Mamma. Did he come in again and give any more trouble after I had left you last night?'

She sat down beside her mother and, in spite of herself, began to cry.

Aunt Xue, seeing her daughter's tears, could not forbear shedding a few herself, though she did her best to comfort her.

'There, there, my child! Don't be upset! I'll deal with that wicked brother of yours, you see if I don't. I don't want anything to happen to my girlie, do I? If anything were to happen to *her*, I should have *no* one to turn to.'

Xue Pan, who had overheard, came running into the room at this point. Clasping his hands together, he pumped them up and down, at the same time making sweeping bows to right and left of him, in token of his contrition.

'Forgive me, sis,' he said. 'I'd had too much to drink last

night. I met a friend on my way home. It was already quite late when I bumped into him, and I still hadn't sobered up properly when I got back here. I don't know myself what it was I said, but I know I must have talked a lot of silly nonsense. I'm not surprised you were angry with me.'

The clumsiness of his apology rapidly turned Bao-chai's weeping into laughter. Lifting her face up from the handkerchief in which it had been buried, she made a little grimace of derision.

'There's no need for you to put on this act,' she said. 'I understand what your real motive is perfectly well. You don't like having us womenfolk around you and you are looking for a means of getting rid of us, so that you can have the place here to yourself.'

Xue Pan laughed deprecatingly.

'I don't know where you got *that* idea from, sis,' he said. 'It's very unlike *you* to make a snide remark like that.'

'*Snide remark?*' said Aunt Xue indignantly. 'If that's a "snide remark", I don't know what sort of remarks you were making to your sister last night. I think you must have taken leave of your senses!'

'Now Mamma, don't be angry,' said Xue Pan, 'and don't you be upset, sis. Suppose I were to tell you that from now on I'm going to give up drinking with the others altogether, eh? What would you say to that?'

'I'd say that you had come to your senses at last,' said Bao-chai.

'And *I*'d say that the Heavenly Dragon had laid an egg,' said Aunt Xue, 'if you really had the will-power to do it.'

'All right then,' said Xue Pan. 'If you ever hear that I've been drinking with those others again, sis, you can spit at me – and you can call me a beast and a – and a – *worthless louse*! Dammit, it's too bad that the two of you should be worried all the time because of me! It's bad enough that I should make *you* angry, Mamma; but to have poor little sis, too, worrying her heart out – oh, I really *am* a louse! I ought to be extra good to you, Mamma, now that Father's dead, and extra kind to sis; but instead I make my own dear Mother angry and little sis upset. I'm not a beast, I'm *worse* than a beast!'

And the great booby began to cry.

At this Aunt Xue, who had not been crying when he started, was herself becoming upset, and Bao-chai was obliged to intervene with a brisk cheerfulness that she was very far from feeling.

'Haven't you caused enough trouble already without making Mamma cry again?'

'Who says I've been making Mamma cry?' said Xue Pan, restraining his tears and grinning back at her. 'All right then, all right. Let's drop the whole subject and say no more about it. We'll have Caltrop in and get her to pour you a nice cup of tea.'

'I don't want any tea, thank you,' said Bao-chai. 'As soon as Mamma has washed, I shall be going back into the Garden with her.'

'Let me look at that locket of yours,' said Xue Pan. 'I think it needs dipping again.'

'Whatever for?' said Bao-chai. 'The gilding's as bright as new.'

'Isn't it time you had a few more clothes?' said Xue Pan. 'Let me know what colours and what sort of patterns you want.'

'I wouldn't know what to do with them,' said Bao-chai. 'I haven't yet worn all the things I've got.'

Shortly after this exchange Aunt Xue re-emerged from changing her clothes and, taking Bao-chai by the hand, went through into the Garden with her, leaving Xue Pan to go off on his own.

Once in the Garden, Aunt Xue and Bao-chai made their way straight to Green Delights. From the large number of maids and older women they found when they got there waiting outside on the verandah or in the ante-room inside, they knew that Grandmother Jia and the other ladies must have arrived there before them. They exchanged greetings with the latter on entering, after which they went over to the couch on which

Bao-yu lay, to inquire if he was feeling any better. Seeing Aunt Xue, he attempted to raise himself a little.

'Thank you,' he said, 'I *am* a little better. But what a lot of trouble I am causing! I feel ashamed that you should have come over just to see me.'

Aunt Xue made him lie down again.

'If there's anything you want,' she said, 'do please let me know.'

'I certainly shall,' he said, 'if I can think of anything.'

'Is there anything you fancy to eat?' said Lady Wang. 'We can order it for you when we go back presently.'

'I can't think of anything,' said Bao-yu, 'unless – I did quite like that soup we had once with the little lotus-leaves and lotus-pods in it.'

Xi-feng, who was standing by listening, gave a crow of laughter.

'Listen to that, now! What *low* tastes the boy has! – Whatever makes you want to eat *that* leathery old stuff?'

'Have it made, have it made!' said Grandmother Jia vehemently. 'Let the boy have it by all means.'

'Don't be in such a hurry, Grannie!' said Xi-feng laughing. 'I'm trying to think who's got the moulds that they need for making the little shapes with.'

She turned and ordered one of the old women in attendance to go and ask the chief cook; but though the old woman was a long time gone, she came back empty-handed.

'Cook says the four moulds for the soup-shapes were handed in some time ago on your instructions.'

Xi-feng thought for a bit.

'Yes, I remember now: I *did* get them back from her. But I can't remember who I gave them to. I should think the likeliest place for them to be is the tea-room.'

She sent someone to the tea-room stewardess; but she hadn't got them either. In the end they turned out to be with the plate stewardess, who looked after the gold and silver. Aunt Xue was the first to examine them when they arrived.

There were four moulds fitted into a single box. They were made of silver, a foot or so long and about an inch wide.

Along the face of each mould were rows of very finely-cut
dies, each about the size of a bean, thirty or forty on each
mould. On one of the moulds the dies were in the shape of
chrysanthemums, on another of plum-flowers, on the third of
lotus pods and leaves, and on the remaining one of caltrops.
Aunt Xue turned to Grandmother Jia and Lady Wang with
amusement.

'You people really do think of *everything*! All these patterns
for a bowl of soup! If you hadn't told me, I should never have
guessed what these things were for.'

Xi-feng answered her before either of the older ladies could
reply.

'You wouldn't know about these anyway, Aunt. It's something they thought up last year for Her Grace's visit. They cut
shapes with these things out of some special dough – I'm not
sure exactly what it's made of – and put them in a clear soup.
There's supposed to be a suggestion of autumn lotuses in the
flavour, but it doesn't taste very much really. It's certainly not
the sort of thing you'd want to eat very often. In fact, I think
the only time we ever had it was when they made some for the
visit. I'm surprised he can still remember.'

She handed the moulds to an attendant woman-servant.

'Tell the kitchen to take as many chickens and other ingredients as they'll need to make ten bowlfuls with. Say it's
wanted immediately.'

'Why so much?' said Lady Wang.

'I have my reason,' said Xi-feng. 'This isn't the sort of
thing one eats every day, and now that Cousin Bao has mentioned it, it seems silly to make it just for him and not let you
and Grandma and Auntie Xue taste it as well. So while we are
about it, we might just as well do enough of it for everyone.'
She smiled mischievously. 'I might even have a taste of it
myself.'

Grandmother Jia laughed.

'Little monkey! We spoil you! Spending public money on
private entertainment, that's what this is!'

The others all laughed. Xi-feng, quite unconcerned, joined
in.

'That's no problem,' she said. 'I'm sure I can afford a little treat like this.' She turned to the waiting woman: 'Tell the kitchen to use plenty of everything and charge it all up to my account.'

The woman murmured a reply and went off to see about the order.

Bao-chai had been following these exchanges with amusement.

'Cousin Feng may be very artful,' she said, 'but I don't believe that in all the years I've been here I have ever seen her get the better of Lady Jia.'

'I'm an old woman, my dear,' said Grandmother Jia. 'What use would I have for artfulness at my time of life? Mind you, when I was the age that Feng is now, I could have taught her a thing or two. Still, though she may not be as sharp as I was then, she doesn't do so badly! A deal better than your Aunt Wang here, that's certain. *She* can't talk to save her life, poor soul, no more than a woman of wood! *She* could never get round me the way your Cousin Feng does. Fengie has the gift of a good tongue, my dear. That's why your old grannie is so fond of her.'

Bao-yu laughed.

'From what you say, Grandma, it sounds as if the good talkers are the only ones you can be fond of.'

'Oh no,' said Grandmother Jia. 'The silent ones have their merits, just as the good talkers have theirs. Good talkers can be very tiresome at times – and *then* I prefer the silent ones.'

'That's all right then,' said Bao-yu. 'I was going to say: my sister-in-law certainly isn't much of a talker, yet I'm sure you are as fond of her as you are of Feng. If being a good talker were the only thing that mattered, I should have thought that Cousin Feng and Cousin Lin would be the only two in the family you would really care about.'

'Well now, if we're going to start comparing,' said Grandmother Jia, '– I hope your Aunt Xue won't think I am only saying this because she is here, but really and truly I do think that of all the girls in this family her Bao-chai is the one that I like the best.'

Aunt Xue laughingly demurred.

'You mustn't say that. I'm sure you can't really mean it.'

'No, no, I'm sure she does,' Lady Wang hurriedly interposed. 'I've often heard Mother speak well of Bao-chai when you weren't around.'

Bao-yu's contribution to the conversation had been made with the intention of encouraging Grandmother Jia to say something nice about Dai-yu. It came to him as a surprise when she started praising Bao-chai instead. He looked at Bao-chai and grinned; but she turned quickly away and began talking to Aroma.

Just then a servant came to say that lunch over at the mansion was ready, and Grandmother Jia rose to go. Having first exhorted Bao-yu to 'hurry up and get better' and then admonished his maids, she began to move out of the room – not without a polite attempt to make Aunt Xue go out ahead of her – leaning on Xi-feng's arm.

'Is that soup ready yet?' she inquired when they were out of the room. Then, turning to Aunt Xue, she asked her if there was anything she particularly fancied for her lunch.

'Mind you let me know if there is,' she said. 'I have the power to make Fengie treat us to it.'

Aunt Xue laughed.

'You shouldn't tease the poor girl! She's always getting nice things for you. But you're not much of an eater at the best of times.'

'Don't you believe it, Aunt!' said Xi-feng. 'Grannie knows how to tuck in. She'd have eaten *me* by now if she weren't afraid that she'd find me a bit too vinegary.'

This set them all off laughing. Even Bao-yu, in the inner room, had to join in, though it hurt him to do so. Aroma, standing beside him, was helpless with mirth.

'Mrs Lian really is a caution!'

Bao-yu took her hand and drew her down beside him.

'Come!' he said. 'You must be tired. You've been on your feet for hours.'

'Hey, you've forgotten!' said Aroma. 'While Miss Bao's

still in the courtyard, you ought to ask her if she'll let Oriole come over to do that knotting for you.'

'Yes,' said Bao-yu. 'I'm glad you reminded me.' He raised his head and shouted towards the window.

'Cousin Bao! If you can spare her, after you've had your lunch, would you mind sending Oriole here to do some knotting for me?'

'Yes, certainly,' said Bao-chai, turning back to reply. 'I'll send her over presently.'

Grandmother Jia and the others had stopped to listen. Not having heard properly, the old lady asked what it was. Bao-chai explained.

'Oh *do*, my dear!' said Grandmother Jia. '*Do* let him have her to do the knotting! If you need someone in her place, I have plenty of free hands in my apartment. Just pick whichever of my maids you like to wait on you.'

Aunt Xue and Bao-chai were amused.

'Let her go to him by all means,' said Aunt Xue, 'but there certainly won't be any need of a stand-in. She has little enough to do but get up to mischief as it is.'

They had been walking on as they talked and presently came upon Xiang-yun, Patience and Caltrop picking balsams beside an artificial 'mountain' of rock. Seeing Grandmother Jia and the rest coming, they left off their flower-gathering and came forward to join them.

Soon the little party emerged from the Garden. Fearing that Grandmother Jia might be fatigued, Lady Wang proposed that she should stop on the way back and sit down for a while in *her* apartment. The old lady's feet were indeed beginning to trouble her and she nodded in consent. Lady Wang sent a maid on ahead to prepare for her arrival.

Aunt Zhao was prudently avoiding Lady Wang for the time being by feigning sick, so of the two concubines it was only Aunt Zhou who came out with the old women-servants and maids of the apartment to welcome Grandmother Jia, holding up the door-blind for her to enter and arranging the pillows and back-rest for her on the kang.

Moving up to it on Xi-feng's arm, the old lady installed herself on the right-hand side at the back with Aunt Xue in the guest's position beside her. Bao-chai and Xiang-yun sat nearer the edge of the kang on either side. Lady Wang served Grandmother Jia with tea, holding the cup ceremoniously in both her hands, and Li Wan in like manner offered tea to Aunt Xue.

'Let the younger women wait on us,' said Grandmother Jia to Lady Wang. 'You sit down over there so that we can talk to you.'

Lady Wang obediently took a seat on a stool-chair beside the kang. She instructed Xi-feng to be her deputy.

'You can tell them to serve Grandmother's lunch in here,' she said to Xi-feng. 'You had better get them to add a dish or two.'

Having said that she would, Xi-feng went outside and instructed a servant to take word round to Grandmother Jia's apartment. The old women there passed on the message in their turn, and soon a reinforcement of maids were hurrying on their way to Lady Wang's.

Lady Wang next gave instructions that the rest of the girls should be invited; but after a long wait only Tan-chun and Xi-chun turned up. Ying-chun was unwell and did not feel like eating. Dai-yu abstained so frequently – eating perhaps no more than five meals in every ten – that her absence on this occasion was scarcely noticed.

Soon lunch arrived and the servants brought up a low table and set it down on the kang. Xi-feng stood on the floor below, a bundle of ivory chopsticks wrapped up in a tea-towel in her hand.

'Now, Grannie and Auntie,' she said, 'I hope you are going to do as you're told and not stand on ceremony!'

Grandmother Jia looked at Aunt Xue and smiled.

'Shall we do as she says and stay put?'

'Yes, certainly,' said Aunt Xue, smiling back, whereupon Xi-feng proceeded to lay for them where they sat: two pairs of chopsticks on the far side for Grandmother Jia and Aunt Xue, one pair at either end for Bao-chai and Xiang-yun. Lady Wang and Li Wan stood on the floor below and supervised the serving of the dishes, while Xi-feng called for a set of clean things for one more person and went, chopsticks in hand, from dish to dish, making a selection from them for Bao-yu.

A few minutes later the lotus-leaf soup arrived and was presented to Grandmother Jia for her inspection. Lady Wang, glancing quickly round her, noticed Silver standing near at hand and ordered her to carry a bowl of it to Bao-yu together with the other things that Xi-feng had just put out for him; but Xi-feng objected that there was too much for one person to carry. Just then Oriole and Providence chanced to enter, and Bao-chai, knowing that they had already had their lunch, suggested that Oriole should help with the carrying.

'Master Bao has been asking if you could go over there to do some knotting for him,' she told Oriole. 'You might as well go with her and do it now.'

'Yes, Miss,' said Oriole, and went off with Silver, carrying her share of the bowls.

'They're terribly hot,' she said, when they were alone together. 'How are we going to carry them so far?'

'Don't worry!' said Silver, 'I know just the answer.'

She made one of the old women fetch a covered lacquer carrying-box. The bowls of soup, rice and so forth fitted into it easily. She told the old woman to follow them. She and Oriole then sauntered along empty-handed in the direction of Green Delights, while the old woman trotted along behind them carrying everything. When they reached the gate of the courtyard, Silver took the box from her and the two girls went on into the house alone.

They found Aroma, Musk and Ripple in the inner room, enjoying a joke with Bao-yu. The three of them got up, still laughing, when they saw Silver and Oriole enter, and Aroma, supposing that they had come from their respective apartments, remarked, as she relieved Silver of the box, on the coincidence of their arriving simultaneously. Having handed over the box, Silver plumped herself down on a stool-chair; but Oriole was less bold; and even when Aroma offered her a foot-stool to sit on, she still refused to be seated.

Bao-yu was naturally very pleased to see Oriole; but the sight of Silver, reminding him, with a pang of mingled shame

and sorrow, of her sister Golden, impelled him to ignore
Oriole and concentrate his attention on the other girl. Aroma
noticed this neglect and was afraid that Oriole might be
offended. Partly for this reason and partly because Oriole
looked so uncomfortable standing up, but was evidently determined not to sit down in Bao-yu's presence, she took her by
the hand and drew her into the adjoining room for a cup of
tea and a chat.

Meanwhile in the inner room Musk and Ripple had laid out
the bowls and chopsticks and were waiting in readiness to
serve Bao-yu his lunch; but Bao-yu was still occupied with
Silver and seemed in no hurry to begin.

'How is your mother?' he asked her.

The girl sat silent, with a sullen, angry look on her face.
When, with a muttered 'all right', she did at last answer him,
she averted her eyes and would not look at him. Bao-yu was
very much put out, but did his best to be pleasant.

'Who told *you* to bring this for me?'

'Her Ladyship and Mrs Lian. Who do you think?'

Bao-yu could see the misery in her face and knew that it was
because of Golden that she looked like that. He wished he
could humble himself before her, but the presence of the other
maids inhibited him. He had to think of some way of getting
rid of them. Having succeeded at last in doing so, he began, as
soon as they were out of the room, to exercise all his charm
upon Silver. At first she tried to ignore the questions with
which he plied her; but he was so patient and persistent, meeting her unyielding stiffness with such warmth and gentleness,
that in the end her heart misgave her and a faintly pleased
expression began to steal over her face. Bao-yu judged the
time ripe to entreat her smilingly for his lunch.

'Fetch me that soup will you, there's a dear. I'd like to try
it now.'

'I can't feed other people,' said Silver. 'I never could.
You'll have to wait till the others come back.'

'I'm not asking you to feed me,' said Bao-yu. 'I'm just
asking you to get it for me because I can't walk. Once you've
done that you can go back and tell them you've finished your

errand and get on with your own lunch. I don't want to keep you from your food: you're probably starving. However, if you don't even feel up to passing me a bowl of soup, I'll just have to put up with the pain and get it myself.'

He tried to rise from his bed, but the effort cost him a cry of pain. Unable to hold out any longer when she saw the state he was in, Silver jumped to her feet.

'All right. Lie down, lie down!' she said. ' "Past sin, present suffering." You've got *your* retribution without having to wait for it, so you needn't expect me to feel sorry for you!'

She broke into a sudden peal of laughter and fetched him the soup.

'Silver dear,' said Bao-yu, 'if you still feel angry with me, get it over with now. Try to look pleasanter when you are with Their Ladyships. You mustn't look angry all the time when you are with *them*, or you'll be getting yourself into trouble.'

'Go on, get on with your soup!' said Silver. 'Keep the sugary stuff for other people. *I* know all about it!'

Bao-yu drank a couple of mouthfuls of the soup at her insistence, but artfully pretended not to like it.

'It doesn't taste nice.'

'Doesn't *taste* nice?' said Silver with an expression of extreme disgust. 'Holy Name! if *that* doesn't taste nice, I'd like to know what does!'

'It's got no flavour,' said Bao-yu. 'Taste it yourself, if you don't believe me.'

Silver – to prove him wrong – indignantly raised the spoon to her lips and tasted.

Bao-yu laughed.

'Ah, *now* it'll taste all right!'

Silver realized that he had deliberately tricked her into drinking from the same bowl.

'You wouldn't drink it a moment ago,' she said, 'so now you shan't have any even if you say you want it.'

And though Bao-yu laughingly begged and pleaded, she refused to let him have it back and called in the other maids to give him the rest of his meal. No sooner had they come in, however, than it was announced that 'two old nannies from Mr Fu's' had arrived 'to call on Master Bao'.

Bao-yu knew that the 'Mr Fu' referred to must be one Fu Shi, an Assistant Sub-Prefect who had started life as one of Jia Zheng's protégés and made his way up in the world largely by trading on Jia Zheng's reputation. Jia Zheng thought highly of him, regarding him as the brightest of the various young fellows he had patronized, and Fu Shi for his part was assiduous in sending messages and compliments to the mansion in order to keep up the connection.

Now if there were two sorts of people Bao-yu could not at any price abide they were stupid old women and pushing young men. It may therefore seem strange that these two old nannies sent by the egregious Fu Shi should have been accorded instant admission to his sickroom. The reason was that Bao-yu had heard that Fu Shi had a younger sister called Fu Qiu-fang, who, though

a virgin-pearl, still chambered from men's sight,

was commonly said to be both beautiful and talented. Bao-yu had not actually seen her; but he had formed a picture of her in his imagination and worshipped her from afar. And since to have refused entry to the two old women would have been in his eyes tantamount to offering Qiu-fang an affront, he at once gave orders for them to be admitted.

Qiu-fang was, as a matter of fact, a girl of passable good looks and more than average intelligence. Her brother had entertained hopes of trading on these assets in order to ally himself matrimonially with some powerful or aristocratic family – an ambition which had hitherto led him to look frowningly on lesser offers, with the result that, at the relatively great age of twenty-two, Qiu-fang remained unbetrothed. For the fact of the matter was that the powerful and aristocratic families with whom he sought alliance looked on Fu Shi as an impoverished pen-pusher deficient in both breeding and refinement and showed not the slightest inclination to want his sister as a daughter-in-law. However, Fu Shi went on cultivating his intimacy with the Jia family and was still not without hopes of realizing his ambition in that direction.

It so happened that the two old nannies sent to see Bao-yu on this occasion were exceptionally ignorant old women. Hearing that they were to be admitted, they came into the room, delivered themselves of the sentence or two it took to inquire after his health, and thereafter lapsed into a stupid silence.

With the arrival of strangers, Silver had been obliged to drop the bantering tone she had begun to adopt with Bao-yu and stood, holding the soup-bowl in both her hands, listening in silence. It was left to Bao-yu to make what conversation he could with the women as he continued to eat his lunch. While so engaged, he reached out a hand for the soup, and Silver reciprocated mechanically; but as both of them had their eyes on the visitors, their uncoordinated movements resulted in a brief collision. The bowl was upset and hot soup spilled over Bao-yu's hand. Silver, startled, though herself unhurt, gave a nervous laugh.

'Now look what you've done!'

The other maids rushed forward to retrieve the bowl. Bao-yu, insensitive to his own pain, inquired anxiously after Silver.

'Where did you scald yourself? Does it hurt?'

Silver and the rest all laughed.

'*You*'re the one who's been scalded,' said Silver. 'Why ask *me*?'

Only then did Bao-yu become conscious that his own hand had been burned. The maids hurriedly mopped up. Not wishing to continue his meal after this, he washed his hands, drank some tea, and spoke a little longer with the old women, who then took their leave and were seen through the Garden as far as the bridge by Skybright and some of the other maids.

When they found themselves alone, the two old women began discussing the visit with each other as they went along.

'Well, I've heard people say that this Bao-yu is like a bad fruit – good to look at but rotten inside,' said one of them, 'and I must say I'm not surprised. He certainly does seem a bit simple. Fancy scalding his own hand and then asking someone else where it hurt! He *must* be a simpleton! Heh! heh! heh!'

'He really and truly *is* a bit simple,' said the other one. 'A number of them told me about it when I came here last. Once when he was out in the pouring rain and himself as wet as a drowned chicken, he says to someone, "It's raining," he says, "run inside and get out of the rain." What a laugh! Heh! heh! heh! And he often cries or laughs when no one else is by. They say that when he sees a swallow he talks to the swallow, and when he sees a fish in the river he talks to the fish, and when he sees the stars or the moon, he sighs and groans and mutters away to himself like a crazy thing. And he's as soft as a baby. Even the little maids can do what they like with him. If he's in the mood for saving, he'll make a fuss over a piece of thread; but other times they can smash things worth a fortune and he won't mind a bit.'

Still talking, they passed out of the gate of the Garden, at which point our narrative leaves them.

*

Back at Green Delights, Aroma, seeing that the others had now gone, led Oriole into Bao-yu's room to ask what it was that he wanted done. Bao-yu gave Oriole a smile.

'I'm sorry, I was busy talking just now,' he said. 'I'm afraid I neglected you. The reason I've dragged you here is because I want you to do some knotting for me.'

'What's it for?' said Oriole.

'Never mind that,' said Bao-yu airily. 'Do me some of every kind.'

Oriole clapped her hands and laughed.

'Goodness me! That would take me about ten years!'

'My dear young lady,' said Bao-yu pleasantly, 'you have all the time in the world at your disposal. I'm sure you could manage in less time than that.'

'Not in one sitting, at all events,' said Aroma. 'Better choose two or three of the main types and let her do one of each.'

'If you're talking about *types*,' said Oriole, 'there are really only three: fan-tassels, rosary-nets and net-and-tassel fringes for sashes.'

'All right,' said Bao-yu, 'a sash-fringe.'

'What colour's the sash?' said Oriole.

'Crimson.'

'Black or navy-blue would go well with crimson,' said Oriole. 'With anything lighter the crimson would be too overpowering.'

'What goes with viridian?' said Bao-yu.

'Peach pink.'

'Mm. That sounds very colourful, certainly. What about something colourful but a bit more on the quiet side?'

'What about leek-green and greenish-yellow?' said Oriole. 'That's a very tasteful combination.'

'All right, you make me those three then: one black, one peach-pink and one leek-green.'

'What pattern do you want for the netting?' said Oriole.

'What patterns are there?' said Bao-yu.

'There's stick-pattern, ladder-pattern, diamond, double diamond, linked rings, flower-pattern, willow-leaf . . .'

'What was the pattern of that netting you did the other day for Tan-chun?'

'Ah, that was a flower-pattern with filled-in centres.'

'I'd like it in that pattern.'

Aroma had meanwhile left them to fetch the silks. As she came back with them, an old woman called through the window to say that her lunch was ready.

'Off with you then,' said Bao-yu, 'and come back as soon as you have finished.'

'How can I possibly leave with a guest here in the room?' said Aroma.

'Don't be ridiculous!' said Oriole. 'You go and have your lunch.'

Aroma smiled at that and tripped off, leaving the two of them alone together, except for two very junior maids who were to remain at hand in case they were wanted.

Bao-yu lay and watched Oriole knotting, chatting to her in a desultory way as he watched.

'How old are you?' he asked her.

Oriole replied without raising her head from her work.

'Fourteen.'

'What's your surname?'

'Huang.'

'Huang? That means "yellow". It goes well with your name. They say "yellow oriole", don't they? – "yellow oriole", "golden oriole".'

'My name *was* "Golden Oriole" originally,' said Oriole, 'but Miss Bao found it too much of a mouthful, so she called me just "Oriole" for short, and now everyone else does.'

'Miss Bao must be very fond of you,' said Bao-yu. 'I expect later on when she gets married she'll want to take you with her.'

Oriole pulled a face and laughed.

'I've often said to Aroma,' Bao-yu went on, 'whoever gets you and your mistress will be a lucky man.'

'She's a *good* person, is our Miss Bao,' said Oriole, 'much more than you realize. There are things about her you don't find in many people in this world – more important things than good looks – though she's good-looking too, of course.'

Oriole's mellifluous, lilting voice and the simple, artless way in which she talked and laughed had powerfully affected Bao-yu. It increased his pleasure to hear her speaking in this way now about her mistress.

'What things?' he asked her eagerly. 'Tell me about them.'

'If I do,' said Oriole, 'you mustn't let her know that I told you.'

'Of course not.'

They were interrupted at this point by a voice from the outer room.

'You're very quiet in there!'

As the two of them simultaneously turned to look, it was Bao-chai herself who stepped into the room. Bao-yu at once invited her to take a seat. When she had done so, she inquired what Oriole was making and leaned forward to inspect it. The first of the three sash-ends was already half completed.

'What do you want to make a thing like that for?' she asked. 'Why don't you make him a necklet to wear with his jade?'

Bao-yu clapped his hands delightedly. He had intended to ask Oriole to do this for him in the first place, but had forgotten.

'Clever coz! What a good thing you mentioned it! I'd quite forgotten. But what would be the right colour for it?'

'Let's see,' said Bao-chai. 'The brighter colours definitely wouldn't do. Crimson would clash. Yellow wouldn't be a sufficient contrast. Black would be too heavy. I'll tell you what. If you were to take a gold thread and a very fine black bugle-thread and twist them together – *that* would look nice.'

Bao-yu was delighted with the suggestion, and shouted several times for Aroma to fetch the gold thread. She came in while he was still shouting for her, carrying two plates of food and looking puzzled.

'I can't understand it,' she said. 'Someone's just brought me these from Her Ladyship.'

'Oh, I expect they had more than they wanted there, so she's sent you this to share with the others,' said Bao-yu.

'No,' said Aroma. 'They said it was for me personally; but I'm not to go over and kotow for it. I don't know what to make of it.'

Bao-chai laughed.

'If it's for you to eat, I should go ahead and eat it! Never mind the whys and wherefores!'

'But it's never happened before,' said Aroma. 'I feel so embarrassed.'

Bao-chai's lips puckered up mockingly.

'Embarrassed? Before very long you're going to have much more than *this* to feel embarrassed about!'

Aroma sensed something behind this remark. She knew Bao-chai too well to suppose that any such remark of hers would be made triflingly. Remembering what Lady Wang had

seemed to hint at in her interview of the previous day, she
dropped the subject.

'I'll have these now then,' she said, holding the dishes out
for Bao-yu to inspect, 'and as soon as I've washed, I shall
bring you your gold thread.'

With that she hurried out again.

When she returned later, after having lunched and washed
her hands, bringing the gold thread for Oriole's knotting,
Bao-chai was no longer there, since she had been called away
by Xue Pan's messenger.

Bao-yu once more lay back and watched Oriole knotting;
but soon they were interrupted once more, this time by a
couple of maids from Lady Xing's. They brought two sorts of
fruit and a message for him from their mistress.

'Her Ladyship says are you able to walk? She says if you
are, she'd like you to come over some time and amuse yourself. She says tell him I'm thinking of him.'

'Tell her,' Bao-yu replied politely, 'that as soon as I *can*
walk, I shall certainly be round to pay my respects. Tell her
that the pain is a little better than it was and that she is not to
worry.'

Asking the two girls to be seated, he called Ripple to him
and asked her to take half of the fruit they had brought and
offer it to Dai-yu; but just as she was about to go, Dai-yu
could be heard talking in the courtyard. He told Ripple to
hurry outside and invite her in.

For further details, please consult the following chapter.

CHAPTER 36

*Bao-chai visits Green Delights and hears strange words from
a sleeper
Bao-yu visits Pear-tree Court and learns hard facts from
a performer*

WHEN Grandmother Jia got back to her own apartment after
lunching with Lady Wang, she was naturally very pleased to
have seen Bao-yu making such rapid progress; but her
pleasure soon gave way to worry when she began wondering
what would happen when he was well enough for Jia Zheng
to start asking for him again. To guard against that contin-
gency she had Jia Zheng's Head Boy brought before her to
receive instructions direct from her own mouth.

'In future,' she told him, 'whenever the Master is entertaining guests or seeing anybody and asks for Bao-yu, you are to
say, straight away, without needing to see me about it, first of
all that Master Bao was very seriously injured by his beating
and will need several months' complete rest before he can walk
properly; and secondly that he has just made an offering to his
star-guardian because of an unlucky conjunction in his horo-
scope and isn't allowed to see outsiders or go outside the
inner gate until the beginning of the eighth month.'

She called Nannie Li and Aroma to her as soon as the Head
Boy had gone and instructed them to tell Bao-yu this, so that
no worries should retard the progress of his recovery.

Bao-yu had always hated meeting or making conversation
with senior males of the scholar-official class and detested all
occasions which involved dressing up, such as visits of con-
gratulation and condolence and the various other formal exchanges to which members of that class devote so great a part
of their time. His grandmother's dispensation was therefore
particularly gratifying to him, and he used it as an excuse for
cutting himself off from all contact with visiting relations and
friends. He even pleased himself about whether or not he

made the customary morning and evening duty-calls on the senior members of the household. Each day was spent playing or resting in the Garden, and during the whole of the day, except for the brief period in the early morning when he went outside to visit his mother and grandmother, he was the willing captive of his maids and did for them whatever little services it pleased them to command. In such enjoyable indolence several weeks slipped agreeably by. From time to time, as opportunity presented itself, someone like Bao-chai would attempt to remonstrate with him; but her remonstrances would be indignantly rejected.

'Why should a pure, sweet girl like you want to go imitating that ghastly crew of thievish, place-hunting *career worms*,' he would say, 'bothering her head about "fame" and "reputation" and all that sort of rubbish? All these notions you are parroting were dreamed up by meddlesome old men in days gone by for the express purpose of leading astray the whiskered idiots who came after them. I really think it's too bad that I should have to live in an age when the minds of nice, sensible *girls* are contaminated by such idiocies. It's a rank abuse of the intellectual gifts that you were born with!'

Hearing him talk so wildly, the remonstrators concluded that he was slightly mad, and eventually gave up trying to be serious with him. The exception was Dai-yu, who, ever since they were little children together, had never once spoken to him about the need to 'get on in the world' or 'make a name for oneself'. This was one of the reasons why he so much respected her.

*

But to return to our narrative.

Some time after Golden's death, Xi-feng began receiving presents and courtesy calls from various senior members of the domestic staff. Though she could not for the moment guess what lay behind these flattering attentions, her suspicions were aroused, and one day, in the course of which she had once more received presents from these people, she laughingly questioned Patience on the subject when they were alone together in the evening.

'I'm surprised you haven't guessed *that*!' said Patience a little scornfully. 'I think, if you were to look into it, you'd find that all of these people had daughters working for Her Ladyship. There are four senior maids on Her Ladyship's establishment who each get one tael a month, the rest only get a few hundred cash each; and now that Golden's dead, one of the tael-a-month places is vacant. I expect these people are trying to get it for their own daughters.'

'Of course!' said Xi-feng, much amused. 'Of course! I'm sure you are right. Well, I do think it rather greedy of them. They earn quite good money as it is, they don't have any really hard work to do, *and* they've got daughters to bring them in a little extra income. I think for them to want to get this plum for themselves *as well* is really a bit too much. I wouldn't have thought they could afford to keep sending me presents like this. Still, that's their concern! If they want to go on giving me presents, I shall go on taking them. But I shall still do what I was going to do anyway. It won't make any difference to me.'

In pursuance of this policy she kept the servants waiting for a decision and watched the presents accumulate; then, when no more seemed to be forthcoming, she availed herself of the first opportunity to raise the matter with Lady Wang. This occurred one day about noon when Aunt Xue, Bao-chai and Dai-yu were in Lady Wang's apartment sharing a water-melon with her. Xi-feng tackled Lady Wang while they sat eating the melon.

'You've been short of a maid, Aunt, since Silver's sister died,' said Xi-feng. 'Have you anyone in mind to replace her with? You might let us know if you have, so that we know what to do with next month's allowance.'

Lady Wang thought for a bit.

'Do I *have* to have four maids or five maids or whatever it is?' she asked. 'It seems to me that if the maids I've got are adequate, I might as well do without the other one.'

Xi-feng smiled.

'In principle, of course, you are right, Aunt; but we *have* got fixed rules about these things, and when some people at the bottom of the scale are making a great fuss about keeping their number *up*, it wouldn't do to have you cutting yours *down*. In any case, the saving would only be one tael a month: it would hardly be worth making.'

Lady Wang again reflected for some moments.

'Very well,' she said at last, 'you can go on paying the allowance as before, but you needn't find me another maid. Silver shall have it. Her sister gave me a lot of service before she was so unfortunate, poor child. I don't think it would be excessive to give Silver a double allowance, for her sister's sake.'

After promising to see that this was done, Xi-feng turned smilingly to Silver and congratulated her. Silver hurried forward and kotowed in gratitude to Lady Wang.

'That reminds me,' said Lady Wang: 'what allowance do Aunt Zhao and Aunt Zhou get each month?'

'The fixed amount is two taels each a month,' said Xi-feng, but Aunt Zhao gets an additional two taels for Huan, so she really gets four taels. Then on top of that they each get two strings of cash a month for their maids.'

'Do they get the full amount every month?' said Lady Wang.

Xi-feng was somewhat taken aback.

'Of course. Why not?' she replied, a trifle sharply.

'It's just that I thought I heard someone the other day complaining that they were a string of cash short,' said Lady Wang. 'I wonder how that could have happened?'

Xi-feng smiled disarmingly.

'The allowance for Aunt Zhao's and Aunt Zhou's maids *used* to be one string each a month, but last year Accounts reduced it by a half to five hundred cash. Aunt Zhao and Aunt Zhou are allowed two maids each, so that means they now get one string a month less than they used to. This is something completely outside my control. I'd be only too happy to pay them more if I could, but the cut was made by Accounts, and all I can do is to hand out what I am given. It's not *my* decision. In fact, I've raised the matter once or twice with them and told them they ought to go back to the original payment, but all they'll say is that that's what's been decided and nothing can be done about it. Actually, now that *I* do the paying, people do at least get their allowances on time. In the old days, when Accounts made the payments direct, we were *always* having trouble. Never a month went by without someone getting into debt because they hadn't been paid on time.'

Another silence followed in which Lady Wang was evidently thinking.

'How many of Lady Jia's maids get one tael a month?' she asked eventually.

'Seven – well, eight really, if you count Aroma.'

'Yes, I see,' said Lady Wang. 'Bao-yu wouldn't have any tael-a-month maids of his own, of course. Aroma still counts as one of Lady Jia's maids.'

'Oh yes. Aroma is still Grandma's maid,' said Xi-feng. 'Grandma lets Bao-yu employ her, but her pay still comes out of Grandma's allowance. It would be quite out of the question to cut her pay simply because she's working for Bao-yu. If you wanted to do that, you'd first have to find another maid for Grandma. And even then, of course, if you wanted her to be paid as a member of Bao-yu's establishment, to make it fair you'd really need to give Huan another maid, too. Incidentally, the fact that Bao-yu's senior maids like Skybright and Musk get a string of cash a month and the juniors like Melilot five hundred is due to Grandma's own personal instructions; so I don't think anyone is really in a position to make a fuss about *that*.'

Aunt Xue laughed.

'Listening to Feng is like listening to a load of walnuts being emptied out of a cart – all those facts and figures! And everything accounted for – everything just and fair!'

'I trust none of the facts and figures were *wrong*, Aunt,' said Xi-feng.

'No, no, nothing wrong with the facts and figures,' said Aunt Xue pleasantly. 'It's just that you would save yourself some energy by taking them a little more slowly.'

Xi-feng seemed about to laugh, but checked herself to hear what her other aunt had to say. Lady Wang, however, deliberated for some little while longer before making her pronouncement.

'Find someone to wait on Lady Jia in place of Aroma,' she said eventually, 'and stop paying Aroma out of Lady Jia's allowance. Instead you can pay her two taels and a string of cash a month out of my personal allowance of twenty taels. And in future, whatever arrangements are made about Aunt Zhao's and Aunt Zhou's allowances, I want you to pay Aroma at exactly the same rate – only whatever it is, it's all to come out of my personal allowance. I don't want Accounts getting mixed up in this.'

Having promised to carry out these instructions, Xi-feng turned to Aunt Xue and nudged her playfully.

'There you are! What did I tell you? It's turned out exactly as I said.'

'And so it should,' said Aunt Xue warmly. 'It should have been done long ago. She's a lovely girl – and it isn't only her looks I'm referring to, either. She has such a generous, open way of doing things, and she is so polite and friendly to talk to. There's a strong little will there, though – plenty of determination underneath it all. Oh, I think she's a real treasure.'

'She is a dear, good child,' said Lady Wang. 'I don't think the rest of you realize just how good she is. Ten times better than my Bao-yu, that's quite certain. If Bao-yu can keep her with him always, he'll be a very lucky boy.'

'If you think that, Aunt,' said Xi-feng, 'why not have her plucked and painted and make her his chamber-wife openly?'

'No, it wouldn't do,' said Lady Wang. 'First of all he is too young; secondly Sir Zheng would never agree to it; and in the third place, even if we allow a certain amount of freedom between them, as long as he still thinks of her as his maid, there is some chance that he will listen to what she says, but once we make her his chamber-wife, she will feel less free to tell him what she thinks of him when he is being silly. No, I think for the moment at any rate we should leave it a little vague. We can make a more definite arrangement in two or three years' time.'

After pausing long enough to ascertain that Lady Wang had

nothing more to say, Xi-feng turned and went. A group of
stewards' wives were waiting for her under the eaves in the
narrow alley-way at the back to report to her on various
household matters. They smiled at her as she emerged, and
one of them chaffed her about the length of her visit.

'You've been a long time today, Madam. What can you
have been talking about to keep you so long? I hope you
haven't overheated yourself with so much talking!'

Xi-feng stood in the doorway in a very unladylike attitude,
one foot on the threshold, rolling her sleeves back and smiling
at no one in particular.

'There's a nice little draught out here. I think I'll stand here
for a bit and cool off.'

She turned to the women.

'Did you say I've been a long time? It's hardly surprising.
Today Her Ladyship has been asking about just about everything that's happened here during the past two hundred years.'
Her voice lost its jocular tone and became suddenly harsher.
'From now on if I ever feel like doing something really spiteful, I shall do it. Let her complain to Her Ladyship if she has a
mind to, I don't care. Stupid woman! Stupid, chicken-witted,
evil-tongued, snivelling, misbegotten *bitch*! She ought to wake
up. One of these days they'll make a clean sweep and take the
whole lot away – *then* she'll have something to shout about!
Complain about *me*, would she, because her maid's allowance
has been cut? Who the Holy Name does she think she is?
She's only a bit of bought goods herself. What's the likes of
her doing with maids to wait on her any way?'

Leaving the stewardesses to make what they would of this
explosion, she strode off to look for someone suitable to take
a message in to Grandmother Jia.

At which point we leave her.

*

After Aunt Xue and the two girls had finished their water-
melon, they sat talking for a few minutes longer with Lady
Wang before leaving, Aunt Xue to return to her own apartment, Bao-chai and Dai-yu to go back into the Garden. Bao-

chai invited Dai-yu to accompany her to the Lotus Pavilion to
pay a call on Xi-chun, but Dai-yu said she was going to have a
bath, and presently parted company with Bao-chai, leaving her
to continue on her way there alone. Bao-chai's route took her
past the House of Green Delights, and as she drew near it, she
thought she would call in to chat for a while with Bao-yu and
help him to dispel the sleepiness of the early afternoon.

The courtyard was silent as she entered it. Not a bird's
cheep was to be heard. Even the storks were asleep, hunched
up in the shadow of the plantains. Keeping to the relative coolness of the covered walk, she made her way round to the
house. In the outer room maids were lying about in all
directions asleep. Slipping behind the tall mirror and through
the elaborately carved partition, she passed into the inner room
where Bao-yu lay inside his protective summer 'cabinet' of
net. He, too, was fast asleep. Aroma sat at his bedside sewing,
a white horse-hair fly-whisk with a handle of white rhinoceros-
horn at her side. Bao-chai entered the 'cabinet' and laughed
softly at Aroma.

'Aren't you being rather over-cautious?' she whispered.
'What's the fly-whisk for? Surely no flies or mosquitoes can
get in *here*?'

Aroma looked up, startled, hurriedly put down her sewing,
and rose to her feet.

'Oh, it's Miss Bao! I wasn't expecting you,' she whispered.
'You gave me quite a shock – no, we don't get any flies or
mosquitoes in here, but there's a little tiny insect that finds its
way through the holes in the netting. They're so small, you
don't notice them; but when you're asleep they can give you
a nasty bite – a bit like an ant-bite.'

'That's not surprising,' said Bao-chai. 'You've got water
behind you here, you see; you've also got a lot of sweet-
smelling flowers outside; and indoors is perfumed as well.
This kind of insect breeds in the insides of flowers and is
attracted towards anything fragrant. That's why you get them
inside the house.'

While she was speaking, her eye fell on the sewing that
Aroma had just put down. It was a pinafore of the kind

children wear, with bib and apron in one. It was of white satin lined with red silk, and the pattern Aroma was embroidering on it was one of mandarin ducks disporting themselves in a background of lotuses. The ducks were in rainbow colours, and the lotuses had red flowers and green leaves.

'Goodness, how beautiful!' she exclaimed. 'Who's it for? It must be someone very special, to deserve work as fine as this.'

Aroma turned her head and shot her lips out in the direction of the figure sleeping on the bed.

'*Him?* He's too big to wear that sort of thing, surely?'

'He wouldn't wear them to start with. That's why I try to make them so nicely – so that when he sees them he can't resist putting them on. I try to get him to wear them in this hot weather, so that if he uncovers himself in his sleep, there's no risk of his getting chilled. If you think there's a lot of work in this one, you ought to see the one he's wearing!'

'I wonder you can have the patience,' said Bao-chai.

'I've done such a lot of work on it today,' said Aroma, 'my neck is quite stiff from bending over.' She smiled at Bao-chai entreatingly: 'Do us a favour, Miss: sit here a bit in my place, will you, while I go off and stretch my legs? I'll be back directly.'

Saying this, she slipped quietly out, not waiting for a reply.

So intent was Bao-chai on the embroidery that she sank down almost without realizing what she was doing into the place that Aroma had just vacated. It really *was* a most beautiful piece of work; in fact, she found it irresistible, and taking up the needle, began sewing it where Aroma had left off.

Meanwhile Dai-yu, on her way back to have a bath, had run into Xiang-yun and agreed to the latter's proposal that they should together call on Aroma to congratulate her on her promotion. They arrived in the courtyard of Green Delights to find everything plunged in silence. Xiang-yun went round to the side to see if Aroma was in any of the maids' rooms. Dai-yu went up to the main building and peeped through the gauze window into Bao-yu's bedroom. She saw Bao-yu, clothed in little else but a thin, rose-coloured shirt, sprawled out asleep on the bed and Bao-chai sitting beside him sewing, with a fly-whisk in readiness at her side.

For some moments she goggled incredulously at this touching domestic scene, then, fearful of disturbing it, she tore herself away to stifle her mounting giggles. When she had somewhat subdued them, she beckoned to Xiang-yun to come over and look. Wondering what extraordinary spectacle could have put her in such a state, Xiang-yun hurried over for a peep. She, too, found the scene inside a comical one and would have burst out laughing; but in her case it was the consideration that Bao-chai had always been so kind to her that caused her to control her mirth. And knowing how merciless Dai-yu could be with her witticisms, she took her by the hand and dragged her away, explaining as she did so that she had just remembered that Aroma had said something about going at noon to wash some clothes in the lake.

'I'm sure that's where she will be,' she said to Dai-yu. 'Let's go and look for her there.'

Dai-yu was not in the least deceived, and showed as much by her sardonic laugh. But she followed her nonetheless.

Bao-chai meanwhile continued her sewing undisturbed. She had just completed her second, or maybe it was her third petal, when Bao-yu, who appeared to be dreaming, cried out angrily in his sleep.

'Why should I believe what those old monks and Taoists say? I don't believe in the marriage of gold and jade. I believe in the marriage of stone and flower.'

The words astounded her. She had still not recovered from the shock of hearing them when Aroma returned.

'What, isn't he awake yet?'

Bao-chai shook her head.

'I just now ran into Miss Lin and Miss Shi,' said Aroma. 'I suppose they didn't come in *here*, did they?'

'Not that I know of,' said Bao-chai. She glanced up at Aroma with a sly smile: 'Did they tell you anything?'

Aroma coloured.

'Oh, a lot of nonsense – as usual! They were only joking, though.'

'They *weren't* joking,' said Bao-chai, '– not this time. I was going to tell you myself, but you went rushing off before I had a chance to.'

Just at that moment a maid arrived from Xi-feng summoning Aroma to go and see her.

'There you are!' said Bao-chai. 'That'll be what she wants to see you about.'

Aroma had to arouse two of the sleeping maids to take her place in the inner room; then she and Bao-chai left Green Delights together. They parted company outside, and Aroma went off to Xi-feng's place on her own. When she got there she was, as Bao-chai had predicted, formally acquainted with the new arrangements concerning her pay and status that had just been made for her by Lady Wang. She was told that she should go over to Lady Wang's to kotow her thanks, but that there was no need for her to see Grandmother Jia.

She found this interview with Xi-feng acutely embarrassing. By the time she got back from Lady Wang's, Bao-yu was already awake. She answered him evasively when he asked her where she had been and waited for the silence and darkness of the night to tell him of her unofficial promotion to his bed. Bao-yu was delighted.

'I hope there'll be no more talk of leaving me *now*!' he said, smiling broadly at her. 'Do you remember the time when you got back from visiting your family and tried to frighten me with all that talk about your brother wanting to buy you out of service and how there was no future for you here and no point in your staying permanently, and all those other heartless, unkind things you said? I'd like to see anyone trying to take you away from me now!'

'Huh!' Aroma sniffed scornfully. 'That's not at all the way it is. I belong to Her Ladyship now. *Now* if I want to leave you, I don't have to talk to *you* about it at all. All I have to do is have a word with Her Ladyship, and off I go!'

Bao-yu laughed.

'Suppose I *were* at fault and you told Her Ladyship and asked her to let you go; don't you think you'd feel just a tiny bit uncomfortable afterwards when it got about that you had left me because I wasn't good enough for you?'

'Why ever should I?' said Aroma. 'Of course, I wouldn't go if it meant marrying a thief or a murderer. There's always another way out. I could always take my own life. We all have to die some time or other; it's just a question of when. All you've got to do is stop breathing, that's all. After that you hear nothing, see nothing – it's all over!'

'Stop it, now! Stop it!' said Bao-yu, covering her mouth with his hand. 'You don't have to say things like that.'

All too familiar with the peculiarities of this master who condemned flattering 'auspicious' talk as false and hollow, but was upset and morose if you told him the truth, Aroma regretted her blunder in having too openly spoken her mind. Smilingly she turned the conversation on to topics which experience taught her were agreeable to him: the beauties of Nature, the beauties of girls, *girls*. But somehow from there the conversation imperceptibly found its way round to the subject of girls *dying*. Suddenly realizing this, Aroma – it was she who was talking at the time – broke off in alarm. Bao-yu, who up to that point had been listening to her enthralled, laughed at her sudden silence.

'We all have to die, as you said yourself just now. The problem is how to die well. Those whiskered idiots who take quite literally the old saw that "a scholar dies protesting and a soldier dies fighting" and get themselves killed off on the assumption that those are the only two ways in which a man of spirit can die gloriously, would do better to die in their beds. For when you come to think of it, the only real occasion for protesting is when one's ruler is misguided, and the only real occasion for fighting is when one's country is at war. If the scholar is so greedy for martyrdom that he throws away his life at the earliest opportunity, what is to become of the poor misguided ruler in the absence of good advisers? And if the soldier so hankers for a hero's death that he gets himself killed off in the first encounter, what is to become of his country without soldiers to fight its battles –?'

'But surely,' Aroma interrupted, 'those famous men in the olden days laid their lives down because they *had* to?'

'Nonsense!' said Bao-yu. 'The soldiers among them lacked generalship; as a consequence, they had nothing but their physical courage to rely on. They threw their lives away out of sheer incompetence. Do you call that dying because they had to? And the scholars were even worse. On the strength of having read a couple of books and got up a text or two by heart, they began to cry stinking fish as soon as they found the smallest thing at Court not as they thought it should be, in the hope of winning themselves an imperishable reputation for honesty; then, if the Court didn't immediately change its policy, they would work themselves into a passion and promptly get themselves killed. You won't, surely, say that *they* died because they had to? What you have to remember is that Emperors hold their power from Heaven, and it's unthinkable that Heaven should lay the huge responsibility of empire on any but the worthiest shoulders. So you can see that all those death-with-honour characters you have so high an opinion of were thinking only of their own personal fame and glory. They weren't really thinking of their loyal duty to their sovereign at all.

'Now *my* idea of a glorious death would be to die now, while you are all around me; then your tears could combine to make a great river that my corpse could float away on, far, far away to some remote place that no bird has ever flown to, and gently decompose there until the wind had picked my bones clean, and after that never, never to be reborn again as a human being – that would be a really *good* death.'

'I'm sleepy,' said Aroma, unwilling to reply, for she had observed that his mad fit was on him again. And Bao-yu at once closed his eyes and fell fast asleep.

By next morning the subject appeared to have been quite forgotten.

*

A day arrived when Bao-yu seemed to have exhausted the Garden's possibilities, and its charms were beginning to weary him. *The Return of the Soul* was very much on his mind at this time. He had read it through twice without in any way abating his appetite for more. Having recently been told that the best singer among the twelve little actresses of Pear Tree Court was the soubrette called Charmante, he resolved, for a change of scene, to go over there and look her up, so that he could ask her to sing him some of the arias from it.

The only girls he recognized when he arrived there were Trésor and Topaze, who greeted him with smiles and invited him to be seated. When he asked where Charmante was, the girls all answered him in chorus:

'In her room.'

Bao-yu at once went to the room indicated. Charmante was in there on her own. She was lying stretched out on her bed, but made no attempt to get up when she saw him enter. Nothing daunted, he sat himself down beside her and, in the familiar way he habitually adopted with girls, smilingly requested her to sing the section from the *Return* that begins with the words

In these quiet courts the floating gossamer . . .

But Charmante did not respond in the expected manner. She rose up quickly and drew away from him when he sat down beside her; and in answer to his request to sing, she informed him, with a cold, unsmiling expression, that she was 'not in voice'.

'I strained my voice the other day at a command performance for Her Grace,' she said. 'I am still resting it.'

She was sitting opposite him as she said this, so that he had a full view of her face. He remembered now, as he studied it, where he had seen that face before. *She* was the girl he had seen scratching QIANGs on the ground that day under the rose pergola.

And now here she was behaving as if his very presence was distasteful to her. Never in his life before had he experienced such instant rejection. Reduced to mumbling incoherence by his embarrassment, he coloured, and – since there was obviously no point in staying – left the room.

Surprised to see him come out again so soon, the others asked him the reason. Trésor laughed when he told her what had happened.

'Wait until Mr Qiang gets back,' she said. 'If *he* asks her to, she'll sing for you.'

Bao-yu did not know quite what to make of this.

'Qiang?' he said. 'Where is he, anyway?'

'He went out only a few minutes ago,' said Trésor. 'I expect Charmante said she wanted something and he's gone out to try and get it for her.'

Bao-yu seemed to find this of enormous interest and decided to stay a little longer and see what happened. Sure enough, Jia Qiang presently returned from his expedition. He was carrying a bird-cage with a bird inside. The cage had a miniature stage fastened to the top of it. Jia Qiang was on his way inside to look for Charmante, obviously feeling very pleased with himself, when he caught sight of Bao-yu and halted.

'What's that bird you've got there?' Bao-yu asked him.

'It's a whitecap,' said Jia Qiang, smiling proudly. 'It can hold a flag in its beak and do a little turn on the stage.'

'How much did you pay for it?'

'One tael and sixteen pennyweights of silver.'

He invited Bao-yu to be seated while he went into Charmante's room to show off his purchase; but Bao-yu, whose desire to hear Charmante sing was now quite forgotten in his eagerness to find out exactly how things lay between her and Jia Qiang, joined the girls as they clustered round the doorway to watch.

'Look! Look what I've brought for you,' said Jia Qiang, full of smiles.

'What is it?'

Charmante had been lying down again, but sat up when he entered.

'I've got a little bird to keep you company, to stop you getting so depressed. You watch! I'll make him perform for you.'

He took a few grains from his pocket and coaxed the bird out on to the stage, where it picked up a diminutive mask and flag and hopped and pirouetted about like an actor playing the

warrior's part in a play. The girls all laughed delightedly and
said it was 'sweet'. All except Charmante. She merely gave a
scornful 'huh!' or two and lay back on the bed again in disgust.

Jia Qiang smiled – almost beseechingly.

'How do you like it?'

'You and your family!' said Charmante bitterly. 'It isn't
enough to take decent girls from their homes and shut them
up in this prison to learn beastly opera all day. Now you have
to bring a *bird* along to do it as well. I suppose it's to keep me
reminded of my misery. And you have the audacity to ask me
"do I like it?"!'

Her words appeared to make Jia Qiang quite frantic, for he
uttered a string of the most violent and passionate oaths in
reply.

'I'm a stupid fool and I should have known better,' he said.
'I spent all that money on the thing because I thought it
might cheer you up. It never occurred to me that you might
take it like this. Well, let the thing go then! It's an "act of
merit" to free living creatures, so at least you'll get *some* good
from it. Either it will help you in the next life or free you from
sickness in this one.'

With that he released the bird, which promptly flew away,
and stamped on the cage until it was smashed to pieces.

'Maybe birds aren't as important as human beings,' said
Charmante, 'but they have mothers and fathers just the same.
Can't you see how cruel it is to take them away from their
nests and make them perform for people's amusement? I
coughed up two mouthfuls of blood today. Her Ladyship sent
someone to look for you. She wanted you to get me a doctor
so that we could find out what to do, but instead of a doctor
you bring *this* thing back with you, to make a mock of me. It's
just my luck to fall ill when I've got no one to care for me or
take any notice.'

She began to cry.

'But I asked the doctor about you yesterday evening and he
said it wasn't serious,' Jia Qiang protested. 'He said you were
to take a couple of doses of that medicine and he'd come and

look at you again in two days' time. I'd no idea that you'd been spitting blood. Well, I'd better go and get him straight away.'

He began to go, but Charmante called him back.

'Stay where you are! Don't go rushing off in this burning heat. You're only going to fetch him because you're in a temper, anyway. I wouldn't see him now if he came!'

Hearing her say this, Jia Qiang halted.

Bao-yu had been watching this scene with open-mouthed fascination. At last he understood the real meaning of all those QIANGS. There was obviously no place for him here, so he slipped away. Jia Qiang was so absorbed in his concern for Charmante that he did not even notice him go and it was left to the little actresses to see him out.

It was a reflective, self-critical Bao-yu who made his way back to Green Delights, so bemused that he scarcely noticed where he was going. When he arrived, Dai-yu and Aroma were sitting in conversation together. He looked at Aroma and sighed heavily.

'What I told you the other night was wrong,' he said. 'I'm not surprised that Father tells me I have a "small capacity but a great self-conceit". I mean, that stuff about all of you making a river of tears for me when I die: I realize now that it's not possible. I realize now that we each have our own allotted share of tears and must be content with what we've got.'

Aroma was surprised to hear him bring this up again. She had assumed that what he said that night was in jest and must long since have been forgotten. She laughed.

'You know, sometimes I think you really *are* a bit touched!'

Bao-yu was silent.

From the curious way in which he was behaving Dai-yu could see that something had got into him, but judged it not her business to inquire what. To change the subject she asked him about something of a more practical nature.

'When I was with your Mother just now she told me that it is Mrs Xue's birthday tomorrow. She told me to ask you whether you intend going or not. When you've decided, she'd like you to send someone round and let her know.'

'Well, I didn't go last time, when it was Uncle She's birth-day,' said Bao-yu. 'It will be a bit awkward if I go this time and run into someone from Uncle She's. I think I'd better stop going to birthdays altogether. In any case, it's terribly hot, and I should have to dress up for it. And I don't think Auntie would really *mind* if I didn't go.'

'That's no way to talk!' said Aroma. 'There's no compari-son whatever between Sir She and your Aunt Xue. You're no distance away from her, for a start. And she *is* your Mother's sister. I'm sure if you didn't go she'd wonder what was the matter. If you're afraid of the heat, why don't you go first thing in the morning, when it's still cool? All you need do is make your kotow and drink a cup of tea, and then you can come back again. Surely that would be more civil?'

'Of course you must go!' said Dai-yu, before he had time to reply. 'Surely you owe a visit to the person who saved you from the mosquitoes?'

'What mosquitoes?' said Bao-yu, mystified. 'What are you talking about?'

Aroma proceeded to tell him how Bao-chai had sat at his bedside with a fly-whisk beside her while he slept.

'How frightful!' Bao-yu was most upset. 'However did I come to be asleep when *she* was there? And I'd got hardly anything on. How disgusting of me!'

After that there was no further question, of course. He would *definitely* be going over for his Aunt Xue's birthday on the morrow.

While the three of them were talking, Xiang-yun came in wearing her going-out clothes and looking very dressed-up. Her uncle the Marquis's people had arrived to fetch her, and she had come to say good-bye. Bao-yu and Dai-yu both rose and invited her to be seated, but she could not stay, so the two of them accompanied her through to the front.

Xiang-yun was struggling to hold back her tears, for she dared not show her distress openly in front of her uncle's people. The arrival a few moments later of her dear Bao-chai, who had hurried over specially to see her off, made going back seem even more unbearable. Fortunately Bao-chai, always more perceptive than the others, realized that things would become even more difficult for Xiang-yun if the servants who had come to collect her were to tell her aunt when they got back that she had made a fuss, so she did all she could to hasten her departure.

The two girls and Bao-yu saw Xiang-yun as far as the inner gate. Bao-yu would have gone further, but Xiang-yun restrained him. Nevertheless, when she had gone a little way towards her carriage, she changed her mind and, turning back, called him to her so that she could whisper a parting request in his ear.

'Remind Her Old Ladyship of me from time to time, will you, in case she forgets? Then perhaps she'll send someone to invite me over again.'

Bao-yu gave vigorous assurances that he would do this for her, then, when they had seen her get into her carriage, they all turned and went in again.

As to what followed, that must be looked for in the following chapter.

CHAPTER 37

*A happy inspiration prompts Tan-chun to found the
Crab-flower Club
And an ingenious arrangement enables Bao-chai to settle the
chrysanthemum poem titles*

THIS year Jia Zheng was appointed Commissioner for Education in one of the provinces, with instructions to leave for his tour of duty on the twentieth of the eighth month. When the day for his departure arrived, he took leave of his ancestors in the family shrine, kotowed to his mother, and was seen on his way as far as the hostelry of the 'Tearful Parting' (the first post-halt on his journey) by Bao-yu and other junior male members of the clan.

Jia Zheng's doings after his departure are not recorded in this history; we merely observe that the departure left Bao-yu free to play and idle in the Garden to his heart's content without the least fear of restraint or reprisal.

> The days in idleness passed by
> To swell the tale of wasted years

On the day of which we write Bao-yu was feeling very bored. He had returned from perfunctory morning calls on his mother and grandmother and had just finished changing back into his everyday clothes, when Tan-chun's maid Ebony arrived carrying a carefully-folded letter from her mistress.

'I'm glad you've come,' said Bao-yu, as she handed him the letter. 'I'd been meaning to see your mistress this morning, but I forgot. How is she? Is she any better?'

'She's quite better, thank you,' said Ebony. 'She's stopped taking her medicine today. It was only a slight chill that she was suffering from.'

Bao-yu unfolded the elegant patterned notepaper and glanced at the contents:

Dear Brother,

Some nights ago, when the moon came out in a sky freshly clear after the rain, the garden seemed veritably awash with moonlight, and sleep in the face of so rare a spectacle was unthinkable. Thrice the clepsydra had been turned, and still I lingered beneath the tall paulownias, reluctant to go in. But in the end the treacherous night air betrayed me, and by morning I was lamentably indisposed.

How kind of you to have visited me in my sickroom! and how exquisitely thoughtful to have sent your maid-servant shortly afterwards with solicitous inquiries and with those delicious lychees and the calligraphy by Yan Zhen-qing!

While I have been lying here quietly on my own, I have been thinking how in the olden days even men whose lives were spent amidst the hurly-burly of public affairs would keep some quiet retreat for themselves with its tiny corner of mountain and trickle of running water; and how they would seek, by whatever arts and blandishments they knew of, to assemble there a little group of kindred spirits to share in their enjoyment of it; and how, on the basis of such leisure-time associations, rhymers' guilds and poetry clubs were then founded, so that the fleeting inspirations of an idle hour might often be perpetuated in imperishable masterpieces of verse.

Now although I am no poet myself, I am privileged to live 'midst rocks and streams' and in the company of such gifted practitioners of the poetic art as Xue and Lin; and it seems to me a great pity that the romantic courts and pavilions of our Garden should not echo with the jocund carousal of assembled bards, and its flowering groves and blossoming banksides not become places of wine and song. Why should the founding of poetry clubs be the sole prerogative of the whiskered male, and female versificators allowed a voice in the tunable concert of the muses only when some enlightened patriarch sees fit to invite them?

Will you come, then, and rhyme with us? The pathway to my door is swept to receive you and your arrival is eagerly awaited by

Your affectionate Sister,
Tan-chun

When Bao-yu had finished reading, he clapped his hands delightedly.

'Dear Tan-chun! Bless her poetic soul! I must go and discuss this with her straight away.'

He strode off immediately, with Ebony following at his heels. But he had got no further than Drenched Blossoms Pavilion when he saw one of the old nannies on duty at the back gate of the Garden hurrying from the opposite direction with a note in her hand. She came up to him when she saw who he was and handed him the note.

'From Mr Yun, sir. He's waiting at the back gate. He sends his compliments and says would I please give you this.'

Bao-yu opened it and read.

Dear Father,

I have the Honour to present my Humble Duty and hope this finds you as it leaves me in the Best of health, ever since you did me the great Kindness to recognize me as your Son I have been looking for some means of showing my appreciation of your great kindness but so far no opportunity has presented itself, to date. However, thanks to your esteemed Advice I have got to know several Nurserymen also a number of famous gardens and now through this contacts I have come across a very rare Variety of autumn crab flower (Pure White) only very little to be had, but using every means possible I have got two pots of it I hope you will think of me as a real Son and not refuse to keep them for your enjoyment. However, owing to the present Hot Weather I did not like to call in Person as the Young Ladies are outside in the Garden a lot owing to the heat, and not wishing to give Inconvenience

I remain,
Honoured Father,
Your Dutiful and Affc⁺ᵉ Son,
Jia Yun

Bao-yu laughed when he had finished reading it.

'Is he alone?' he asked the old woman, 'or is there someone with him?'

'He's got a couple of young chaps with him carrying potted plants.'

'I see. Well go back and thank him for me. Tell him it's very kind of him and I very much appreciate it. And have the pots taken to my room.'

When he had given these instructions, he continued with Ebony on his way to Autumn Studio. He arrived to find that

Bao-chai, Dai-yu, Ying-chun and Xi-chun had all got there before him. They laughed excitedly when they saw him enter.

'Here comes another one!'

'I hadn't realized that I was so popular!' said Tan-chun. 'I wrote to you all more or less on the spur of the moment. It was no more than a tentative suggestion. I had no idea it would meet with this instant response from everybody.'

'It's a pity you didn't think of it earlier,' said Bao-yu. 'We ought to have started a club long ago.'

'Well *I* don't think it's a pity,' said Dai-yu. 'Do, by all means, have a poetry club if you're all so keen to, only count *me* out of it, please. I don't feel up to it.'

Ying-chun laughed.

'If you're not, then what about the rest of us?'

'This is no time for false modesty,' said Bao-yu. 'Here is a serious proposition and one which we are obviously all enthusiastic about. What we need are some ideas that we can all discuss. Come on, Chai! Let's hear what you have got to say first, then perhaps we can hear from Cousin Lin.'

'What's the hurry?' said Bao-chai. 'We're not even all here yet.'

Just as she was saying that, Li Wan arrived. She smiled at them all as she entered.

'My! What a poetic lot we are! If you are going to have a poetry club, may I propose myself for president? The idea of having one did in fact occur to me earlier in the year, but I thought that as I can't write poetry myself, a proposal coming from me might seem a bit presumptuous, and I did nothing about it. Now that my poetical sister-in-law has had the same idea, I should like to do what I can to help her get it started.'

'If we are definitely going to have a poetry club,' said Dai-yu, 'then as members of the club we are all equals and fellow-poets. We can't go on calling ourselves "cousin" and "sister-in-law" all the time.'

'I quite agree,' said Li Wan. 'We ought to choose pen-names to sign our poems with, then we can use them for addressing each other by as well. I shall call myself "Farmer Sweet-rice". I don't suppose anyone else will want that title.'

'I shall call myself "Autumn Studio",' said Tan-chun.

'That's pretty unoriginal!' said Bao-yu. 'Can't you do any better than that? You've got all those paulownias and plantain-trees around your place: can't you make a name out of *them*?'

'All right,' said Tan-chun. 'I'm very fond of my plantains. I shall call myself "Under the Plantains".'

'That's *very* original,' said the others admiringly. But Dai-yu laughed.

'Come on, everybody!' she said. 'Pop her in the stew-pot! We'll have a nice piece of venison with our wine.'

As no one could understand this recondite joke, Dai-yu undertook to explain it for them.

"Under the plantains" is where the woodcutter in the old Taoist parable hid the deer he had killed; so the allusion means "a deer". In calling herself by that pen-name, Cousin Tan is therefore offering herself to her fellow-members as venison for them to feast on in their carousals.'

'Oh, all right, Miss Clever!' said Tan-chun. '"Plantain Lover", then. You wait! I'll be even with you yet. I've got just the name for her,' she told the others. 'When the Emperor Shun died, his two queens are supposed to have gone along the banks of the river Xiang looking for him. According to the legend, the two queens turned into river goddesses and their tears became the spots you find on the bamboos that grow along the banks of the river. That's why there's a kind of bamboo called "Naiad's Tears". Well now, Cousin Dai lives in the Naiad's House, and she cries so much that I shouldn't be at all surprised if one of these days the bamboos in her courtyard all turned out to have spots on them; so I think the best pen-name for her would be "River Queen".'

The others, applauding, agreed that this was *exactly* the right name for Dai-yu. Dai-yu herself hung her head and said nothing.

'I've thought of one for Bao-chai,' said Li Wan. 'Not regal, like Dai-yu's, but aristocratic, at any rate. What do you all think of "Lady All-spice"?'

'I think the title becomes her very well,' said Tan-chun.

'What about me?' said Bao-yu. 'Isn't anyone going to think of a name for me?'

'Oh, *you*!' said Bao-chai. 'The obvious one for you is "Busybody" – because you are always so busy doing nothing.'

'Why not stick to your old pen-name, "Lord of the Flowers"?' said Li Wan.

'Do you *have* to embarrass me by reminding me of my youthful indiscretions?' said Bao-yu.

'No, let *me* choose your name,' said Bao-chai. 'Actually I've already thought of one. It sounds a bit common, perhaps, but I think it suits you. You are a very *lucky* person, living in such luxurious and beautiful surroundings and you enjoy an exceptional amount of leisure – in fact, I can't think of anyone who combines quite so much luck with quite so much leisure – so I suggest "Lucky Lounger" as the most suitable pen-name for you.'

Bao-yu laughed good-humouredly.

'You are flattering me! – I think you'd better all call me by whatever name each of you fancies.'

'No, that won't do,' said Dai-yu. 'As you live in the House of Green Delights, why don't we simply call you "Green Boy"?'

'Yes,' said the others. 'Good.'

'Now, what names are we going to have for Cousin Ying and Cousin Xi?' said Li Wan.

'Neither of us is much good at poetry,' said Ying-chun. 'There doesn't seem much point in having any.'

'No, I think you *ought* to have pen-names,' said Tan-chun.

'As Ying-chun lives on Amaryllis Eyot, she could be "Amaryllis Islander", and as Xi-chun lives by the Lotus Pavilion, she could be "Lotus Dweller",' said Bao-chai. 'That would seem to be the simplest solution.'

'Yes,' said Li Wan. 'Those names will do very nicely. Now, I'm the eldest here, so I'm going to propose some conditions that I'd like you all to agree to. I don't think you'll have much difficulty in doing so when you've heard what they are. The first one is that as three out of the seven of us founding this club – that's to say Cousin Ying, Cousin Xi and myself – are no good at writing poetry, I propose that the rest of you should let us off versifying and allow us to act as your officers instead.'

'"*Cousin* Ying"? "*Cousin* Xi"?' said Tan-chun. 'What's the good of inventing all these new names if you're not going to use them? I think that from now on there ought to be a penalty for not using them.'

'First things first,' said Li Wan. 'Let's get the club properly founded, and we can talk about penalties later on. I suggest that the club should hold its meetings at my place, because I've got the most room. I can't write poetry myself, but if you don't object to having so illiterate a person as your host, I'm sure that as time goes by I shall grow more poetical and re- fined under your influence.

'My next condition is that you should make me your presi- dent. And as I shan't be able to manage all the official business on my own, I should like to be allowed to co-opt two vice- presidents. I therefore nominate Amaryllis Islander and Lotus Dweller as my assistants, one to set the themes and rhymes in our competitions and the other to act as invigilator and copyist.

'And lastly, although we three officers don't *have* to do any versifying, we should not be precluded from trying our hand at it if we want to. So if there is ever a fairly simple subject with easy rhymes and we feel like joining in, we should be allowed to do so. The rest of you, of course, have no option.

'Well, those are my conditions. If you agree to them, I'll be glad to help you found the club. If not, I don't think there would really be much point in my tagging along.'

The proposed arrangement was highly agreeable to Ying- chun and Xi-chun, neither of whom had much enthusiasm for writing poetry – least of all in competition with experts like Bao-chai and Dai-yu – and they assented readily. The rest, when they saw how willingly Ying-chun and Xi-chun acquiesced, felt that they could scarcely object themselves and added their assent – though Tan-chun did remark, somewhat ruefully, that it seemed a little hard, when she was the one who had thought of the idea in the first place, that she should now have these other three sitting in judgement over her.

'Right,' said Bao-yu. 'That's all settled. Let's all move over to Sweet-rice Village, then.'

'You're always in such a hurry!' said Li Wan. 'Today's meeting is just a preliminary discussion. Now you will have to wait for me to issue an invitation.'

'Before we do anything else,' said Bao-chai, 'we had better decide how often we are going to meet.'

'Not too often, I hope,' said Tan-chun, 'otherwise it will no longer be a pleasure. I suggest not more than two or three times a month.'

'Twice a month will be quite enough,' said Bao-chai. 'Once we've decided which two days to meet on, we should undertake *always* to turn up on those two days, wet or fine. At the same time, we should be allowed to arrange additional meetings outside the fixed dates as and when the fancy takes any of us to do so. If we leave it that much flexible, it will be more enjoyable.'

The others agreed that this was a good proposal and should be adopted.

'The poetry club was originally my idea,' said Tan-chun. 'I hope you will at least allow me the pleasure of being your hostess at its first meeting.'

'All right,' said Li Wan. 'We'll have a meeting tomorrow and you shall entertain us.'

'Why wait until tomorrow?' said Tan-chun. 'There's no time like the present. *You* choose a title for us, Amaryllis Islander can set the rhymes, and Lotus Dweller can supervise us while we compose our poems.'

'If you ask me,' said Ying-chun, 'I think that rather than always have the same two people to choose the titles and set the rhymes, it would be better to draw lots.'

'As I was on my way here just now,' said Li Wan, 'I saw them carrying in two pots of white crab-blossom. It was so pretty. Couldn't you have white crab-blossom for your subject?'

'We haven't all seen it yet,' said Ying-chun. 'How are they going to write poems about it if they haven't seen it?'

'We all know what white crab-blossom looks like,' said Bao-chai. 'I don't see why we necessarily have to look at it in order to be able to write a poem about it. The ancients used a poetic theme as a vehicle for whatever feelings they happened to want to express at that particular moment. If they'd waited until they'd *seen* the objects they were supposed to be writing about, the poems would never have got written!'

'Very well, then, I'll set your rhymes,' said Ying-chun.

She took a book of verse off the shelf, opened it at random, and held it up for the others to see.

'There you are: an octet in Regulated Verse. That's the form.'

She closed the book again and turned to a little maid who was leaning in the doorway looking on.

'Give us a word,' she said. 'Any word.'

'Door,' said the girl.

'That means the first line must end with "door",' said Ying-chun. She turned again to the girl: 'Another one.'

'Pot,' said the girl.

'Right, "pot",' said Ying-chun, and going over to a little nest of drawers in which rhyme-cards were kept, she pulled out one of them and asked the maid to select two cards from it at random. These turned out to be the cards for 'not' and 'spot'.

'Now,' she said to the girl, 'pick any card out of any drawer. Just one.'

The girl pulled out another drawer and picked out the card for 'day'.

'All right,' said Ying-chun. 'That means that your first line must end in "door", your second in "pot", your fourth in "not", your sixth in "spot", and the rhyming couplet in the seventh and eighth lines must end in "day".'

Tan-chun's maid Scribe laid out four identical sets of brushes and paper for the competitors, who all, except Dai-yu, now began, with quiet concentration, to consider what they were going to write. Dai-yu wandered around outside, playing with the bark of the paulownia trees, admiring the signs of autumn in the garden, occasionally joking with the maids, and in general not giving the slightest indication that she was engaged in the throes of composition. Ying-chun told one of the maids to light a stick of Sweet Dreams – a kind of incense which is only about three inches long and has a very thick wick so that it burns down fairly rapidly – and told the competitors that they had to complete their poems by the time the incense had burned itself out, otherwise they would be penalized.

Tan-chun soon had a poem ready. Taking up a brush, she wrote it out and, after going over it and making a few corrections, handed it in to Ying-chun. Then she turned to Bao-chai.

'How are *you* doing, Lady All-spice? Have *you* thought of a poem yet?'

'Well – yes, I've thought of *something*,' said Bao-chai, 'but I'm not very happy about it.'

Bao-yu, meanwhile, was pacing up and down, hands clasped behind his back, in the loggia outside. Hearing this exchange, he paused to address Dai-yu.

'Do you hear that?' he said. 'The other two have nearly finished.'

'Kindly mind your own business, would you?' said Dai-yu.

Bao-yu glanced inside and saw that Bao-chai was busy writing her poem down.

'Lord!' he said. 'There's only an inch left.' He turned to Dai-yu again: 'The incense has nearly burned out. What are you still squatting over there on the damp grass for?'

Dai-yu ignored him.

'Oh well,' said Bao-yu. 'I haven't got time to worry about you. I'll have to start writing my own now, whether it's any good or not.'

He went in then, and sat down at the table to write.

'I'm going to start reading the poems now,' said Li Wan. 'Anyone who hasn't handed in by the time I've finished reading will have to pay a fine.'

'Farmer Sweet-rice may not be much good at *writing* poetry,' said Bao-yu, 'but she is jolly good at *reading* it. She's a very fair critic. I'm sure we shall all be willing to accept her judgement.'

The others nodded in agreement. Li Wan picked up Tan-chun's draft and the others crowded round to read it with her:

> A wintry sunset gilds the vine-wreathed door
> Where stands, mossed by old rains, the flower-pot.
> Its snowy blooms, as snow impermanent,
> Are pure as pure white jade that alters not.
> O fragrant frailty, that so fears the wind!
> Most radiant whiteness! Full moon without spot!
> White flower-sprite, shake your silken wings! Away!
> And join with me to hymn the dying day![1]

All complimented Tan-chun on her poem when they had finished reading it. Then they looked at Bao-chai's:

> Guard the sweet scent behind closed courtyard door,
> And with prompt waterings dew the mossy pot!
> The carmine hue their summer sisters wore
> These snowy autumn blossoms envy not –
> For beauty in plain whiteness best appears,
> And only in white jade is found no spot.
> Chaste, lovely flowers! Silent, they seem to pray
> To autumn's White God at the close of day.

Li Wan smiled.

'That has the All-spice touch all right!'

Next they looked at Bao-yu's poem.

> White Autumn's sister stands beside the door;
> Like summer snow her blossoms fill the pot –
> A Yang-fei rising naked from the bath,
> With a cool, chaste allure that she had not.
> The dawn wind could not dry those pearly tears
> With which night's rain each floweret's eye did spot.
> Pensive and grave, her blossoms gently sway,
> While a sad flute laments the dying day.

When they had finished reading, Bao-yu said he liked Tan-chun's poem best of the three, but Li Wan insisted that Bao-chai's was superior. It had 'more character' she said. She was

1. See Appendix I, p. 583.

about to press Dai-yu for her contribution when Dai-yu sauntered in of her own volition.

'Oh! have you all finished?'

She picked up a brush and proceeded, writing rapidly and without a pause, to set down the poem that was already completed in her mind. She wrote on the first sheet of paper that came to hand and, having finished, threw it nonchalantly across the table for the others to inspect.

> Beside the half-raised blind, the half-closed door,
> Crushed ice for earth and white jade for the pot,

They had got no further than the first couplet, when Bao-yu broke out into praises.

'Clever! How do you get these ideas?'

> Three parts of whiteness from the pear-tree stolen,
> One part from plum for scent (which pear has not) –

All of them were impressed by this second couplet.

'This *is* good. Original. It's quite different from the other three.'

> Moon-maidens stitched them with white silken thread,
> And virgins' tears the new-made flowers did spot,
> Which now, like bashful maids that no word say,
> Lean languid on the breeze at close of day.

'Yes, this is the best,' they said. 'This is the best of the four.'

'For elegance and originality, yes,' said Li Wan; 'but for character and depth I prefer Lady All-spice's.'

'I think that's a fair judgement,' said Tan-chun. 'I think River Queen's has to take second place.'

'At all events,' said Li Wan, 'Green Boy's is bottom. Do you accept that judgement, Green Boy?'

'Oh yes,' said Bao-yu. 'It's a perfectly fair one. Mine is just not a good poem. But' – he smiled hopefully – 'I think we ought to reconsider the placing of All-spice's and River Queen's contributions.'

'You agreed to abide by my decisions,' said Li Wan. 'I don't think the rest of you have any say in the matter. If anyone questions a decision of mine in future, he will have to pay a penalty.'

Bao-yu was obliged to let the matter drop.

'I propose that our two meetings should be on the second and sixteenth of each month,' said Li Wan. 'On those occasions *I* shall be responsible for choosing the subjects and the rhymes. If any of you ever feels like having an extra meeting in between those dates, there's nothing to stop you. In fact, there's nothing to stop you having a meeting every day, if you feel like it. But that's entirely up to you. On the second and sixteenth you *must* all come round to my place, and the meetings on those two days are my responsibility.'

'We really ought to have a name for the club,' said Bao-yu.

'We don't want anything banal,' said Tan-chun; 'on the other hand we don't want anything too weird and wonderful. As we started off with a poem about white crab-blossom, why don't we simply call ourselves "The Crab-flower Club"? That *might* have seemed a somewhat banal title other things being equal, but in our case it wouldn't be because it would commemorate our founding meeting.'

Tan-chun's proposal was followed by general discussion. After partaking of the liquid and other refreshment which she provided, the party then broke up, some returning to their own apartments in the Garden, some going on to Grandmother Jia's or Lady Wang's apartments outside. Our record leaves them at this point and does not specify.

*

Aroma had been present when Bao-yu received Tan-chun's letter and had seen him rush off excitedly with Ebony as soon as he had finished reading it, but without having any idea what the cause of his excitement might be. Shortly after he left, two of the old women from the back gate arrived carrying pots of white-flowering autumn crab. Aroma asked them who the flowers were from, and when the old women had explained, showed them where she wanted them put, after which she took them into the servants' quarters and made them sit down while she went off to Bao-yu's room to fetch some money. She weighed out twelve penny-weights of silver and made it into a little parcel, then, taking out an additional three hundred copper cash, hurried back to the old women.

'The silver is to pay the bearers with,' she told them as she handed them the money. 'The cash is for you to buy your-selves a drink with.'

The old women stood up, beaming all over their faces. How kind, how very kind, they said, they couldn't possibly take it. But as Aroma insisted, they allowed themselves to be persuaded.

'Are there any boys on duty outside the gate?' Aroma asked them.

'Oh yes, there are always four there,' said the old women, 'to do any errands you young ladies in the Garden happen to want done outside. If there's anything you want done, Miss, just let us know and we'll get them to do it for you.'

'It isn't for *me*,' said Aroma smiling. 'I wouldn't presume. It's Master Bao. He wants someone to go to the Marquis of Zhong-jing's place to deliver some things to Miss Shi. I thought that now you're here I might as well ask you if you wouldn't mind when you get back telling the boys on the gate to go out and order a cab for me. Only if they do, will you come to me for the fare, please. Don't go bothering them in the front about it.'

The old women departed, promising to do as she asked, while Aroma went back into the main apartment for a saucer to put some of the things on that she was planning to send to Xiang-yun. But when she looked on the dresser she found that the saucer shelf was completely empty. She glanced back to where Skybright, Ripple and Musk sat sewing together.

'What happened to that white onyx saucer that used to be here?' she asked them.

The girls looked at each other blankly, trying to remember. After some moments, Skybright's face broke into a smile.

'I remember. I took it to Miss Tan's with those lychees on. It's still there.'

'Whatever did you take *that* one for, when there are so many other things you could have used?'

'Well, yes, that's what *I* said. But the dark brown lychees and the white-and-browny onyx *did* go very well together. Even Miss Tan said how pretty they looked. She made me leave the dish there, where she could look at it. That's why I didn't bring it back with me. By the way, that pair of identical vases that used to be on the very top of the dresser isn't back yet, either.'

'You'll laugh if I tell you about *them*,' said Ripple. 'You know how Master Bao never does anything by halves. Well, the other day he had a sudden rush of dutiful feelings come over him. He'd just picked a couple of sprays of cassia and was going to put them in a vase, when suddenly he said, "Oh! these are the first cassia flowers I've picked this year. I mustn't keep them for my own enjoyment." So what does he do but fetch down those two vases, put the water in them and arrange the flowers in them himself, and go along with them (someone else carrying them, of course) to Her Old Ladyship and Her Ladyship to give them each a vase. Anyway, the beauty of it was that some of the effects of this rubbed off on the person carrying the vases – which it so happens was me. When Her Old Ladyship saw the flowers, she was so delighted you just can't imagine. "Oh, look!" she said. "What a *good* boy he is to me! He can't even see a flower without thinking of his old grannie! – And people grumble at me for being too fond of him!" Well, as I expect you know, Her Old Ladyship normally doesn't seem to have much use for me – I don't know what it is, but there's something about me she doesn't seem to like – but on this occasion she gave me a hundred cash. And she called me a "poor little thing". "Poor little thing!" she said. "She looks so sickly!" I can tell you, I never expected a piece of luck like that! I mean, a hundred cash is nothing, but the honour! – in front of all those people! Then when we got to Her Ladyship's, Her Ladyship was with Mrs Lian and Mrs Zhao going through her chests and looking out some of the things she used to wear when she was a girl to give to someone – I don't know who it was. Anyway, when

she saw us, she left off to admire the flowers. So of course Mrs
Lian has to make the most of it by putting in *her* pennyworth –
going on about how dutiful Master Bao is and how thoughtful
and how this that and the other – I can't remember a half of
what she said, there was a whole cartload of it – but whatever
it was it gave Her Ladyship a lot of face, hearing him praised
like that in front of everybody, and You Know Who not
being able to say a word against him, so of course *she* was very
pleased. And what do you think? She gave me *two dresses!*
Admittedly, we get new dresses every year, so in itself being
given two dresses may not seem so wonderful. But the *honour!*'

'Pooh!' said Skybright. 'Silly girl! *You* don't know much!
Those would be two dresses that she thought weren't good
enough to give to the other person. I can't see much honour
in *that!*'

'I don't care,' said Ripple. 'It was still very kind of Her
Ladyship, for all that.'

'If it had been me, I shouldn't have wanted them,' said
Skybright. 'What? take someone else's old left-overs? All of
us here are only maids; none of us is supposed to be any
higher than the rest, you know. Why should she give someone
else the best and give me the left-overs? No, I'm sorry. *I*
should have had to refuse, even if it meant offending her. I
couldn't take a thing like that lying down!'

'Which of us was it that she gave those other dresses to?'
said Ripple, curious. 'I've been home ill these last few days. I
must have been away when it happened. Be a sport, Skyey –
tell us who it was!'

'Why, if I tell you, will you give those two dresses back
again?'

'Of course not, silly! I'd just like to *know*,' said Ripple. 'I
don't care if it was Master Bao's little puppy-dog she gave
them to, I still think Her Ladyship meant to do me a kindness,
and as far as I'm concerned, that's all that matters.'

The other maids laughed.

'You'd better watch what you say! That's just who she *did*
give them to: Master Bao's little dog, Flower.'

'*Wicked* girls!' said 'Flowers' Aroma, laughing in spite of herself, 'taking my name in vain! Whenever you've got a few moments to spare you are making fun of me. There's not one of you that will come to a good end!'

'Oh, it was *you*,' said Ripple. 'I'm so sorry, I didn't realize. Oh, I do apologize.'

'All right, that's enough fooling for now,' said Aroma. 'The question is, which of you is going to get that saucer?'

'Better get the vases back too, while we're about it,' said Musk. 'The one in Her *Old* Ladyship's room should be safe enough, but I wouldn't be too sure about the one at Her Ladyship's. There are so many people in and out of that place – especially You Know Who and her lot. If they see anything from *our* room in there, they're sure to find some way of breaking it accidentally-on-purpose, if they get half a chance. Her Ladyship won't stop them. She never notices. We ought to get that one back, at least, as soon as we can.'

'You're right,' said Skybright, laying down her sewing. 'I'll go and get it now.'

'No, I'll go for that,' said Ripple. 'You go and get your saucer.'

'I'm going for the vase,' said Skybright. 'Why should *you* have all the windfalls? You others have all had a go. Now it's my turn.'

'You do exaggerate,' said Musk. 'It's only Ripple who's had the luck. And it was only because of the coincidence that Her Ladyship happened to be going through her dresses when she arrived. Do you suppose she'll be going through them again if you go there now?'

'Maybe not,' said Skybright, with a tinge of malice. 'On the other hand maybe she'll notice how conscientious I am and pay me two taels a month out of her allowance. You see' – she paused to add this on her way out of the room – '*I* know what goes on in here. There's no need for the play-acting.'

She ran off with a mocking laugh.

Ripple went, too, and fetched the onyx saucer from Tanchun's room, after which Aroma made ready the things that were to go to Xiang-yun, and called in old Mamma Song – one of the nannies attached to Green Delights – to give her instructions for their delivery.

'Get yourself smartened up and change into your best things,' she said. 'I want you to go out presently and take some things for me to Miss Shi's.'

'You can give them to me now, Miss – and any message that you want me to deliver,' said Mamma Song; 'then I can go off straight away, as soon as I've got myself ready.'

Aroma fetched two little boxes of lacquer and bamboo basketwork and taking the tops off them, put foxnuts and caltrops in one and a saucerful of chestnut fudge (made of chestnut purée steam-cooked with cassia-flavoured sugar) in the other.

'These are all our own things or *made* from our own things freshly gathered in the Garden that Master Bao is sending Miss Shi a taste of,' she said. 'Tell her the onyx saucer the fudge is on is the one she was admiring last time she was here and she is to keep it. This silk bag has got the sewing in that she asked me to do for her. Tell her the needlework's a bit on the rough side, but I'm sure she'll understand. And say Master Bao sends his regards. And of course *I* present my compliments. I think that's all.'

'Isn't there any message from Master Bao?' said Mamma Song. 'Perhaps you'd better ask him, Miss, just in case. We don't want him saying afterwards that we've forgotten something.'

'Didn't he go round just now to Miss Tan's place?' Aroma asked Ripple.

'Yes,' said Ripple. 'They're *all* round there. They were having a discussion about setting up a poetry club, whatever that might be, and they were writing poems, some of them.' She turned to Mamma Song. 'I shouldn't think he'd have anything to say. I should just push on, if I were you.'

Mamma Song took up the boxes and went off to get herself ready.

'When you are ready, go out by the *back* gate,' said Aroma

as she was leaving. 'You'll find some of the boys there and a cab waiting for you.'

Mamma Song then left. The details of her expedition are unrecorded.

*

Some time after this Bao-yu got back. The first thing he did on arrival was to go and look at the autumn crab-flowers. When he had finished admiring them, he went into the house and told Aroma all about the poetry club, after which Aroma told him how she had sent Mamma Song to Shi Xiang-yun's with a present of things from the Garden. Bao-yu smote his palms together in vexation.

'Oh, we forgot about *her*! I knew there was something we ought to have done and hadn't, but I couldn't think what it was. I'm glad you've reminded me. We must invite her over at once, of course. The poetry club will be nothing without her in it.'

'I don't think I'd be in such a hurry to, if I were you,' said Aroma. 'It's only an amusement, this poetry thing, and Miss Shi doesn't have the time for amusement that the rest of you do. It isn't as if she were her own mistress, you know. Even if you tell her about this and she wants to come, it doesn't follow that they'll let her. Suppose they don't. She'll only fret about it; and then all you'll have done will be to have made her feel miserable for nothing.'

'That's no problem,' said Bao-yu. 'I shall ask Her Old Ladyship to have her fetched.'

Just then Mamma Song got back, mission completed, bearing Xiang-yun's thanks to Aroma for the things.

'She asked me what Master Bao was doing,' said the nannie, 'so I told her that he and the young ladies were starting a poetry club or some such. She was very upset. "Oh!" she said, "are they writing poetry? I wish they'd have told me about it!"'

Bao-yu waited to hear no more. Dashing round to his grandmother's, he insisted that she should send instantly to have Xiang-yun fetched.

'It's too late *now*,' said Grandmother Jia. 'We'll send for her first thing tomorrow.'

Bao-yu had to be content with that, and went back to his room much downcast. He was round at Grandmother Jia's first thing next morning again, pestering; but it was not until the early afternoon that Xiang-yun eventually arrived and his equanimity was restored.

As soon as they were all together, Bao-yu began to tell Xiang-yun how the club had come to be founded and what they had done at its first meeting. He was about to show her the poems that they had written, but Li Wan prevented him.

'Don't let her see them yet,' she said. 'Just tell her the rhymes. As she missed our first meeting, her penalty shall be to make up another poem now, using the same rhymes that we did. If it's all right, we shall invite her to join the club straight away. If not, she must first entertain us all at our next meeting as a further penalty.'

'I like that!' said Xiang-yun, laughing. '*You* should be the ones to pay a penalty, for having forgotten to invite me. Well, show me the rhymes, then. I'm not much good at this sort of thing, but I don't mind making a fool of myself. As long as you'll let me join your club, I don't mind *what* I have to do – sweep the floor and light the incense for you, if you like!'

Delighted to see her so enthusiastic, and still reproaching themselves for having forgotten about her at their inaugural meeting, the rest of them made haste to give her the rhyme-words so that she could begin.

Xiang-yun was much too excited for careful composition. Having, even while they were all talking, concocted a number of verses in her head, she took up a brush and proceeded to write them down, without a single pause for correction, on the first piece of paper that came to hand.

'There you are!' she said, handing it to the others. 'I've written two poems using the rhymes you gave me. I don't know whether they're any good or not, but at least I have done what I was told!'

'We thought our four had just about scraped the barrel,' they told her. 'We couldn't have written *one* more poem on the subject, let alone two! Whatever can you have found to say in them? I bet they just repeat what we said in ours.'

But when they looked at the poems, this is what they read.

I

Of late a goddess came down to my door
And planted seeds of white jade in a pot,
From which a wondrous white Frost Maiden grew,
Who, loving cold, all other things loves not.
Last night a cloud passed by, whose autumn shower
Her cold, unweeping eyes with tears did spot;
Since when, the poet here takes up his stay,
To praise her loveliness by night and day.

2

Where flower-fringed steps approach the ivied door,
At the wall's foot or in a graceful pot –
What flowers do more sad autumn-thoughts inspire
Than these, whose pureness others rival not?
Wax tears their petals seem, by wind congealed,
Or filtered moonlight, flecked with many a spot.
Weep they because the shadows stole away
Their goddess-queen, who now makes dark night day?

The reading of these poems was punctuated at the end of each line with expressions of admiration and surprise, and when they had got to the end, all of them agreed that these two poems had made the exercise a worth-while one and fully justified their naming the new society 'The Crab-flower Club'.

'You must let me provide the refreshments tomorrow as my penalty,' said Xiang-yun. 'I hope you will all consent to be my guests.'

'Splendid!' they said; and proceeded to show her the poems they had written the day before, and to discuss them with her.

*

That evening Bao-chai, who had invited Xiang-yun to spend the night with her at Allspice Court, sat with her guest under the lamplight while the latter discussed themes for the morrow's meeting and plans for the projected entertainment. As it became increasingly apparent that her ideas on the subject were quite impracticable, Bao-chai presently interrupted the flow.

'The club has only just been founded and this will be its first entertainment,' she said. 'Although it's all only a game, you are setting a precedent, so you need to think about it rather carefully. If the entertainment is to be equally enjoyable for everyone, you don't want it to be too much of a burden on *you*; but on the other hand you don't want the others to feel that they are being given short commons. Now, you are not your own mistress, and the few strings of cash they give you a month at home are not even enough for your own needs. And if your Aunt got to hear that you were spending money on a frivolous thing like this, she would have still more to grumble about than usual. In any case, even if you spent all you'd got, it still wouldn't be enough to provide an entertainment for several people. So what are you going to do? You obviously can't send home for money. Are you going to ask them here for some?'

Xiang-yun, brought back to the realities of her situation, was very much dashed. While she hesitated, Bao-chai went on.

'Actually I've thought of a way out of this. An assistant in one of our pawnshops comes from a place where they have very good crabs. Now nearly everyone here from Lady Jia and Aunt Wang downwards is fond of crabs and only the other day Aunt Wang was saying that we ought to have a crab and cassia-viewing party for Lady Jia. It's only because she has been otherwise occupied that she hasn't done anything about it. Why not issue a general invitation, making no mention of the poetry club – we can write all the poems we want to after the rest of them have gone – and I shall ask my brother to let us have a few baskets of the biggest, fattest-looking crabs and tell him to get us a few jars of good wine and side-dishes for four or five tables from the shop? That should save a lot of trouble for you *and* make more of an occasion of it for everybody else.'

Xiang-yun felt deeply grateful to Bao-chai and praised her warmly for her thoughtfulness. Bao-chai smiled deprecatingly.

'Now you mustn't go imagining things and feel that you

are being treated like a poor relation! It's only because I am so
fond of you that I have ventured to make this proposal. If you
promise you won't take it amiss, I can get them to arrange it
for us straight away.'

'My dearest girl!' said Xiang-yun. 'Of *course* I shan't take it
amiss! How can you suggest such a thing? If you do so again,
I shall begin to think that you aren't really fond of me at all! I
may be a silly goose, but there *are some* things I understand!
Do you think that if I didn't look on you as my own true
sister I should ever have told you last time I was here about
all those tiresome things I have to put up with at home?'

Reassured, Bao-chai called in an old woman to take a message outside to her brother.

'Tell Mr Pan to get us a few baskets of crabs like the ones
we had the other day. It's for after lunch tomorrow. We're
having a cassia-viewing party in the Garden for Their Ladyships. Tell him *please* not to forget, because I've already invited
all the guests.'

The old woman went off to deliver her message. In due
course she reported back again – but these are details omitted
from our story.

Bao-chai resumed her conversation with Xiang-yun.

'About the theme for tomorrow's poems,' she said. 'We
don't want anything too outlandish. If you look at the works
of the great poets, you find that *they* didn't go in for the weird
and wonderful titles and "daring" rhymes that people nowadays are so fond of. Outlandish themes and daring rhymes do
not produce good poetry. They merely show up the poverty
of the writer's ideas. Certainly one wants to avoid clichés; but
one can easily go too far in the pursuit of novelty. The important thing is to have fresh ideas. If one has fresh ideas, one
does not need to worry about clichés: the words take care of
themselves. But what am I saying all this for? Spinning and
sewing is the proper occupation for girls like us. Any time we
have left over from that should be spent in reading a few pages
of some improving book – not on this sort of thing!'

'Yes,' said Xiang-yun, without much conviction; but
presently smiled as a new idea occurred to her.

'I've just thought of something. Yesterday's theme was "White Crab-blossom". The flower I'd like to write about is the chrysanthemum. Couldn't we have "Chrysanthemums" as our theme for tomorrow?'

'It is certainly a very seasonable one,' said Bao-chai. 'The trouble is that *so* many people have written about it before.'

'Yes,' said Xiang-yun, 'I suppose it *is* rather a hackneyed one.'

Bao-chai thought for a bit.

'Unless of course you somehow involved the *poet* in the theme,' she said. 'You could do that by making up verb-object or concrete-abstract titles in which "chrysanthemums" was the concrete noun or the object of the verb as the case might be. Then your poem would be both a celebration of chrysanthemums and at the same time a description of some action or situation. Such a treatment of the subject *has* been tried in the past, but it is a much less hackneyed one. The combining of narrative and lyrical elements in a single treatment makes for freshness and greater freedom.'

'It sounds a splendid idea,' said Xiang-yun. 'But what sort of verbs or abstract nouns had you in mind? Can you give me an example?'

Bao-chai thought for a bit.

'What about "The Dream of the Chrysanthemums"?'

'Yes, that's a good one,' said Xiang-yun. 'I've thought of one too. Couldn't we have "The Shadow of the Chrysanthemums"?'

'Ye-e-es,' said Bao-chai, doubtfully. 'The trouble is, it's been used before. Still, if we had a *lot* of titles we could probably slip it in. I've thought of another.'

'Well, come on then!' said Xiang-yun.

'What about "Questioning the Chrysanthemums"?'

Xiang-yun slapped the table appreciatively.

'That's a lovely one!' Presently she added: 'I've thought of another. What do you think of "Seeking the Chrysanthemums"?'

'That should be interesting,' said Bao-chai. 'Let's start

making a list. We'll write down up to ten titles and then see what we think of them.'

The two of them busied themselves for some minutes grinding ink and softening a brush. Xiang-yun then proceeded to write down the titles at Bao-chai's dictation. Soon they had ten. Xiang-yun read them over.

'Ten doesn't make a set,' she said. 'We need two more to make a round dozen, then we shall have just the right number for a little album.'

Bao-chai supplied two more without too much difficulty.

'If we're thinking in terms of a *sequence* of poems,' she said, 'we may as well, while we're about it, arrange these titles in some sort of order.'

'That's it!' said Xiang-yun. 'Then they will be all ready for making our "Chrysanthemum Album" with afterwards.'

'"Remembering the Chrysanthemums" should come first,' said Bao-chai.

'Now, let's see. When you remember them, you realize you haven't got any, so you go and look for some. So "Seeking the Chrysanthemums" will be the second title.

'Well, having found some, you will want to plant them; so "Planting the Chrysanthemums" will be the third title.

'After you've planted them and the flowers have come out, you'll want to stand and look at them; so the fourth title will be "Admiring the Chrysanthemums".

'You won't be able to have enough of them by just standing and admiring them, so you'll naturally want to pick some and arrange them in a vase so that you can enjoy them indoors. That means "Arranging the Chrysanthemums" for Number Five.

'But however much you enjoy them, you will feel that they somehow lack their full lustre without words to grace them, and so you will want to celebrate them in verse. That means "Celebrating the Chrysanthemums" will be the sixth title.

'Well now, let's suppose you've just finished writing some verses about them. You've got the ink ready-made and the brush is still in your hand and you feel like paying the chrysanthemums a further tribute. What should you do but paint them? That's Number Seven: "Painting the Chrysan-themums".

'Now in spite of these silent tributes, you still don't know the secret of the chrysanthemums' mysterious charm and you can't resist asking them. Which brings us to Number Eight: "Questioning the Chrysanthemums".

'And if the chrysanthemums could really reply, it would be so delightful that you would want to have them near you all the time – and how better than by "Wearing the Chrysanthe-mums"? That's Number Nine.

'That brings us to the end of the verb–object titles which involve the poet himself as the understood subject of the action. But there remain other kinds of treatment, in which we consider the flowers by themselves without postulating the presence of the poet. So we have "The Shadow of the Chrysanthemums" and "The Dream of the Chrysanthe-mums" as Numbers Ten and Eleven.

'And of course "The Death of the Chrysanthemums" at the end of the album to round off on a suitable note of melan-choly.

'There you are! All three months of autumn condensed into a single sequence of a dozen poems!'

Xiang-yun recopied the twelve titles in the order that Bao-chai had indicated, then, after running her eye rapidly over them, she asked Bao-chai what rhyme-scheme they should set.

'I have always disliked set rhymes,' said Bao-chai. 'If you have a good poem in the making, why shackle it with the constraints of an arbitrary rhyme-scheme? Let us leave set rhymes to vulgar pedants; all *we* need do is give out the titles and let the others choose their own rhyme-schemes for them-selves. After all, the object of the exercise is to give people enjoyment – the enjoyment gained by producing an occasional felicitous line. We aren't out to make things difficult for them.'

'I entirely agree,' said Xiang-yun. 'And I am sure that in this way we shall get better poems. There's just one thing, though: we have twelve titles now but only five people writing poems. Presumably we aren't going to ask each of them to produce a poem for every one of the titles?'

'Oh no, that would be *much* too difficult,' said Bao-chai. 'Make a fair copy of the list of titles, merely indicating that the poems are to be octets in Regulated Verse, put it up on the wall where everyone can see it, and then simply let them choose whichever titles they like. If anyone has the energy to do them all, they are welcome to try. If they can't manage more than one, let them do just one. Skill and speed are what we shall be looking for. As soon as all of the twelve titles have been covered, we shall call a halt, and anyone who goes on writing after that will be made to pay a penalty.'

Xiang-yun did not see that this last stipulation was necessary, but otherwise agreed with her, and the two girls, having satisfied themselves that their plans for the morrow were now complete, put out the light and composed themselves for sleep.

As to the outcome of their plans: that will be told in the following chapter.

CHAPTER 38

*River Queen triumphs in her treatment of chrysanthemum themes
And Lady Allspice is satirical on the subject of crabs*

THE last chapter concluded with Bao-chai and Xiang-yun
retiring for the night after their plans for the morrow had been
completed. This one begins next morning, when Xiang-yun
invited Grandmother Jia and the rest to a cassia-viewing party
in the Garden. Touched by her enthusiasm, the grown-ups
readily agreed to go.

'She is so excited, bless her!' said Grandmother Jia. 'We
ought to let her do this, even though she *is* our guest.'

And having promised, she was as good as her word, and
arrived in the Garden at noon, bringing Lady Wang, Wang
Xi-feng and Aunt Xue with her and a number of attendant
maids.

'Now where is it going to be?' she asked them.

'Wherever you like, Mother,' said Lady Wang dutifully.

'I think they've already prepared for us in the Lotus
Pavilion,' said Xi-feng. 'The blossom on the two cassia-trees
is particularly fine there this year, and there is that lovely clear,
emerald water. When you sit in the little centre pavilion, you
have water all round you, which gives you a wonderful feeling
of spaciousness. And looking at water is so restful for the
eyes.'

'Very well,' said Grandmother Jia, and began to lead the
way to the Lotus Pavilion.

The pavilion was built in the middle of the Garden's little
river at one of the places where it broadened into a wide, deep
pool. It had windows all round it and could be approached
either circuitously from one side by way of one of the two
many-angled covered piers leading to its left- and right-hand
verandahs, or more directly from the other by means of a
bamboo bridge leading to the centre of the verandah at the
back. It was towards this bamboo bridge that the party was

now making its way. As Grandmother Jia stepped on to it, Xi-feng hurried forward to support her.

'You can put your feet down as hard as you like, Grannie,' she said. 'Bamboo bridges always creak like this when you go over them. They are *meant* to.'

The Lotus Pavilion was in reality not one pavilion but two, for the main pavilion properly so called gave on to a smaller pavilion, referred to simply as 'the water pavilion' or 'the centre pavilion', which was in the very middle of the little lake.

When they were all inside the main pavilion, they noticed that two bamboo tables had been set out on the verandah. On one of them were ranged winecups, chopsticks and all things needful for serving wine, and on the other were teacups, tea-pots, tea-whisks, saucers, and various other tea-things. Beside the tea-table two or three maids were busy fanning a little tri-pod stove on which water for tea-making was being boiled, while at the other end of the verandah maids were fanning a stove on which water for warming the wine-kettles was being heated. Grandmother Jia was particularly impressed by the arrangements for tea-making and remarked with pleasure how *clean* everything looked – including the spot that had been chosen for the party.

'Cousin Bao-chai helped me get it ready,' said Xiang-yun.

'Well, I've always said she was a thoughtful child,' said Grandmother Jia. 'A lot of thought has certainly gone into these preparations.'

As she was speaking, her eye fell on a pair of boards that hung from two of the pillars. The couplet inscribed on them was in mother-o'-pearl inlay on a black lacquer background. She asked Xiang-yun to read it out to her. This is what it said:

> Lotus reflections shatter at the dip of a lazy oar-blade
> Lotus fragrances float up from the swirl round a bamboo
>   bridge-pile

After hearing the couplet, Grandmother Jia glanced up at the horizontal board which bore the name of the pavilion and was in characters large enough for her to read herself. She turned to Aunt Xue, who was standing beside her.

'When I was a girl, there was a pavilion like this one in our garden at home. It was called – let me see – "Above the Clouds" – because of the sky reflected in the water below, you see. When I was about the same age as these young people are now, I used to go with the others every day there to play. One day I slipped and fell down into the water. I nearly drowned. They had a terrible job getting me out. And even then I caught my head on one of the wooden pegs on the way up. I've still got a place big enough to put the tip of a finger in where it hit me. It's on the side here, just where the hair begins. Of course, at the time everyone thought it was all up with me. They were sure that after being all that time in the water I'd catch my death of cold. But I got over it.'

'If you hadn't,' said Xi-feng before anyone else could speak, 'what would have happened to all the good fortune you've enjoyed, Grannie? It's obvious you were meant to have it, otherwise why would you have been given that dent in your head? The guardian spirits must have put it there to store your good fortune in. Old Longevity has got a dent in his head, too; only *his* has got so much good fortune packed into it that it bulges out a bit.'

This comical allusion to the God of Longevity's enormous cranium set all of them laughing – including, of course, the old lady herself.

'Naughty monkey!' she said. 'Make fun of *me*, would you? I'd like to tear that wicked mouth of yours!'

'It's because I wanted to make you laugh, Grannie. Laughter makes the humours circulate. We're going to be eating crabs shortly, and I was afraid that the cold of the crab-meat might settle on your heart. If I can make you laugh and stir your humours up, you'll be able to eat as much crab as you like without taking any harm from it.'

'In that case I shall have to keep you with me all the time, so that I am *always* laughing,' said Grandmother Jia. 'I'll have to stop you going home at night.'

'It's because you indulge her so much that she is so cheeky, Mother,' said Lady Wang. 'By saying things like that to her you will make her even worse.'

'But I *like* her cheekiness!' said Grandmother Jia. 'After all, there's no harm in it. She knows what's what underneath it all, of course she does. I think it's nice that the young people should feel free to joke and laugh a bit when we are all on our own together. We don't want them behaving like a lot of stuffed dummies, surely?'

While she was saying this, they all passed into the smaller pavilion, where tea was served, after which Xi-feng came bustling in with winecups and chopsticks and began to lay. Grandmother Jia sat with Aunt Xue, Bao-chai, Dai-yu and Bao-yu at a centre table, and Xiang-yun, Lady Wang, Ying-chun, Tan-chun and Xi-chun at a table on the east side of the room. A little table was laid for Xi-feng and Li Wan on the west side of the doorway, but this was only for form's sake, since both of them remained on their feet in order to wait on the other two tables.

'We shan't want all the crabs at once,' said Xi-feng to the servants bringing them in. 'Ten will be enough to start with. The others can go back into the steamer.'

She called for some water, and after washing her hands, stood at the centre table facing Grandmother Jia and began shelling the crabs. She offered the first meat, as a courtesy, to Aunt Xue.

'No thank you,' said Aunt Xue. 'I don't need anyone to do it for me. I like doing it myself and getting crabby fingers. I think they taste better when you eat them with your fingers.'

Xi-feng gave the crab-meat she had prepared to Grandmother Jia. The second lot she offered to Bao-yu. Then she called for some 'really hot wine'. She also sent a little maid to fetch mung-bean flour scented with chrysanthemum leaves and cassia for cleaning the fingers with and removing the smell of crab.

Xiang-yun sat with the others at her own table for a while, but as soon as she had finished her first crab, got up to look after her guests. She also went outside and gave orders for a plate of crabs to be taken to Aunt Zhao and another to Aunt Zhou. At once Xi-feng came bearing down on her.

'*You*'re not used to this. You get on with your eating and

leave this to me! I'll have mine when the rest of you have finished.'

But Xiang-yun, refusing to be put off, ordered a long table to be laid on the verandah at the far side of the Lotus Pavilion and invited the maids Faithful, Amber, Sunset, Suncloud and Patience to come and sit at it.

Faithful glanced laughingly in Xi-feng's direction.

'I can't very well sit down and eat while Mrs Lian is waiting on everybody.'

'That's all right,' said Xi-feng. 'You all go and sit down. I'll take care of everything.'

At that Xiang-yun, too, went back to her seat.

Li Wan and Xi-feng now made a brief pretence of joining in the party, but Xi-feng was soon on her feet again ministering to the rest. After a few minutes she went out on to the verandah, where Faithful and the other maids were regaling themselves with great gusto. They rose to their feet when they saw her come.

'What have you come out here for, Mrs Lian?' said Faithful. 'Can't you leave us alone to enjoy ourselves for a bit?'

'Well, aren't you disagreeable!' said Xi-feng. 'Here am I doing all the work for you, but instead of thanks I get grumbled at! I was hoping you would offer me a drink.'

Faithful, laughing, quickly filled a winecup and held it to Xi-feng's lips. Tilting her head back, Xi-feng drained it at a gulp. Amber and Sunset followed suit, and two more cupfuls went down in the same way. Meanwhile Patience had been scooping out some 'yolk' – the delicious golden crab-spawn – which she now offered to her mistress. Xi-feng told her to put lots of ginger and vinegar on it, then, having quickly disposed of it, 'You can all sit down now and get on with your party,' she said. 'I'm going.'

'What a nerve!' said Faithful. 'Scrounging off us like that!'

'You'd better be careful what you say to me, my girl,' said Xi-feng with a smile. 'I suppose you realize that Mr Lian has taken a fancy to you and is going to ask Her Old Ladyship if he can have you for his Number Two?'

Faithful tutted and shook her head. It was easy to see that she was blushing.

'Huh!' she said. 'Fancy a *lady* saying a thing like that! I'm going to wipe my smelly fingers on your face, Mrs Lian, if it's the last thing I do.'

'No, no! Please! Forgive me!' said Xi-feng, as Faithful stood up to carry out her threat.

'Even if *she* does,' said Amber, laughing, 'I wouldn't be too sure that Patience will. Look at her, all of you! She hasn't eaten two crabs yet, but she's already finished a saucerful of vinegar!'

Patience, who had in her hand a crab richly endowed with 'yolk' that she had just finished shelling, held it up when she heard this jibe and advanced on Amber, intending to smear her face with it.

'You nasty, spiteful little creature!' she said, both laughing and indignant. 'I'll —'

But Amber dodged aside, and Patience, losing her balance, plastered the crab smack on to her mistress's cheek. Xi-feng, at that moment still preoccupied with Faithful, was taken completely by surprise. Her startled 'Aiyo!' was too much for the maids, who collapsed in uncontrollable laughter. Xi-feng presently joined in, though cursing Patience as she did so.

'Stupid cow! Are you too drunk to see straight? All over my face!'

Patience hurriedly wiped it off and fetched water for her to wash with.

'Holy Name!' said Faithful. 'That was a judgement, if ever there was one!'

Hearing the laughter outside, Grandmother Jia eagerly asked to know its cause.

'What is it? What have you seen that's so funny? Tell us, so that we can share the joke.'

Faithful shouted back, amidst laughter.

'Mrs Lian came over here and stole some of our crab. Patience didn't like it, so she smeared crab-yolk all over her mistress's face, and now the two of them are having a fight.'

Hoots of laughter from Grandmother Jia and Lady Wang.

'Poor Mrs Lian!' said Grandmother Jia. 'You ought to feel sorry for her. Couldn't you spare her a few of the legs or some of the underneath bits?'

There was renewed laughter from the maids. Faithful shouted back again.

'She can have all the crab's-legs on this table, and very welcome to them!'

Xi-feng, taking all in good part, finished washing her face and went back to help Grandmother Jia and the others at the centre table with their crabs.

Dai-yu dared not eat very much because of her delicate health, and after consuming a little of the claw-meat, excused herself from the table. Soon Grandmother Jia, too, had finished eating, and everyone washed their hands and broke off for a while to amuse themselves, some going off to admire the flowers, some to drop things in the water and watch the fish rise.

'It's rather windy for you here, Mother,' said Lady Wang, '– especially after you've just been eating crab. Perhaps you ought to go back to your own room now and rest. If you have enjoyed it, we could come again tomorrow.'

'Yes, perhaps you are right,' said Grandmother Jia. 'I hadn't been going to leave, because I could see how much they were all enjoying themselves and was afraid of spoiling the fun. But perhaps you and I ought to be getting along now.'

As she rose to leave, she turned to address Xiang-yun.

'Don't let your Cousin Bao-yu eat too much!'

'No, Grandma.'

She turned once more as she was leaving, this time including Bao-chai in her admonition.

'And don't you two eat too much, either. Crab is very good to eat, but it isn't very good *for* you. If you eat too much of it, it will give you stomach-ache.'

'Yes, Grandma.'

The two girls saw her out of the Garden. When they were back again, they gave orders for the tables to be cleared and a new set of places to be laid; but Bao-yu objected.

'No, don't lay again,' he said. 'We want to get on with the poetry. Put the big round table in the middle with all the food and drink on it so that we can help ourselves when we feel like it and sit where we like. That will be much nicer than having set places.'

Bao-chai agreed; but Xiang-yun reminded them that there were others besides themselves to be considered, and having first ordered a separate table to be laid and some good hot crabs to be selected, she invited Aroma, Nightingale, Chess, Scribe, Picture, Oriole and Ebony to come and sit at it. After that she had a couple of carpets spread out on the ground beneath the cassia-trees at the foot of the rockery and made the old nannies and junior maids sit down on them and eat and drink to their hearts' content, insisting that they need only get up to wait on them if they were specially called for. Then she took the list of poem-titles and pinned it to the inside wall of the pavilion.

'Very original!' the others commented when they had finished reading the titles, but went on to express the fear that they might find them difficult to write on.

Xiang-yun explained what they had decided about rhymes: *viz.* that there should be no set rhyme-scheme and everyone should be free to choose their own.

'Now that's what I call sensible!' said Bao-yu. 'I can't stand set rhymes.'

Dai-yu had a barrel-shaped porcelain tabouret moved up to the verandah's edge, and having selected a fishing-rod for herself, sat leaning on the railing, fishing.

Bao-chai sat for some time silently contemplating a spray of cassia she had picked, then, leaning over the railings and idly plucking off the flowerets, dropped them one by one into the water and watched the fish swim up from below and nibble at them with plopping noises as they floated on the surface.

Xiang-yun for the most part sat quietly musing, occasionally getting up to look after Aroma and the other maids at the table outside, or to make sure that the people sitting on the carpets were getting enough to eat and drink.

Tan-chun stood with Li Wan and Xi-chun in the shade of a weeping willow, watching the water-fowl.

Ying-chun sat apart from the rest beneath a flowering tree, stringing jasmine blossoms into a flower-chain with a needle and thread.

Bao-yu watched Dai-yu fishing for a bit, then went over and leaned on the railings and talked with Bao-chai for a bit, and finally, after watching Aroma and the other maids eating and drinking at their table, ended up by drinking with them himself while Aroma shelled a crab for him.

Presently Dai-yu put down her fishing-rod, went over to the central table, took up a silver 'self-service' wine-kettle whose surface was carved with a nielloed plum-flower pattern, and, having selected a little shallow, rose-quartz winecup, was just about to pour herself a drink, when a maid observed her and came hurrying up to do it for her.

'No, let me pour it myself,' said Dai-yu. 'That is half the fun. You get on with *your* party.'

So saying, she proceeded to half-fill the tiny receptacle with liquor from the silver kettle. But it proved to be yellow rice-wine, whereas what she wanted was spirits.

'I only ate a small amount of crab,' she said, 'but it has given me a slight heart-burn. What I really need is some very hot samshoo.'

'We have some,' said Bao-yu, and quickly ordered a kettle of special mimosa-flavoured samshoo to be heated for her. Dai-yu took only a sip of it before putting the winecup down again.

Presently Bao-chai strolled up and helped herself to the samshoo. She, too, put her cup down after taking only a tiny mouthful of it. Then she moistened a brush with ink, and going over to the list of titles, put a tick over the first one, 'Remembering the Chrysanthemums', and wrote the word 'Allspice' underneath it.

'*Please* leave Number Two for me, Chai,' said Bao-yu anxiously. 'I've already thought of four lines for it.'

Bao-chai laughed.

'I've had a hard enough job thinking of lines for this first one. You've nothing to worry about as far as I'm concerned.'

Dai-yu, without saying a word, quietly relieved Bao-chai of the brush, ticked first 'Questioning the Chrysanthemums' and then the eleventh title, 'The Dream of the Chrysanthemums', and wrote 'River' underneath each of them.

After her, Bao-yu took up the brush and ticked 'Seeking the Chrysanthemums'. He signed himself 'Green'.

Tan-chun now drifted over and looked at the list.

'Oh, hasn't anyone chosen "Wearing the Chrysanthemums" yet?' she said. 'Let *me* do that one.'

She turned, smilingly, to Bao-yu and pointed a warning finger at him.

'We've just made a new rule, by the way. No naked ladies this time, please. You have been warned!'

Xiang-yun strolled up while she was saying this and ticked Numbers Four and Five – 'Admiring the Chrysanthemums' and 'Arranging the Chrysanthemums' – in rapid succession. She signed herself 'Xiang' underneath them.

'You ought to have a pen-name like the rest of us,' said Tan-chun.

'There are various pavilions and studios at home, of course,' said Xiang-yun, 'but I don't *live* in any of them. It would be rather pointless to call myself after a building like the rest of you.'

'What about that water pavilion "Above the Clouds" that Lady Jia was telling us about?' said Bao-chai. 'You could call *that* yours. Even if it doesn't exist any more, you can pretend that it *would* have been yours. You should call yourself "Cloud Maiden".'

'Yes, yes,' said the others; and before Xiang-yun herself could do anything, Bao-yu had crossed out the 'Xiang' and substituted the word 'Cloud' beneath it.

In less time than it would take to eat a meal, poems had been completed for each of the twelve titles. The young poets then wrote out their poems and handed them in to Ying-chun, who copied them out, each with the full pen-name of its author, on to the finest Snow Wave notepaper.

Li Wan then read them all through, the others overlooking her.

Remembering the Chrysanthemums
by Lady Allspice

The autumn wind that through the knotgrass blows
Blurs the sad gazer's eye with unshed tears;
But autumn's guest, who last year graced this plot,
Only, as yet, in dreams of night appears.
The wild geese from the North are now returning;
The dhobi's thump at evening fills my ears.
Those golden flowers for which you see me pine
I'll meet once more at this year's Double Nine.

*

Seeking the Chrysanthemums
by Green Boy

The crisp day bids us go on an excursion –
Resistant to the wineshop door's temptation –
Some garden, where, before the frosts, was planted
The glory of autumn, being our destination:
Which after weary walk having found, we'll sing
An autumn song with unsubdued elation.
And you, gold flowers, if all the poet told
You understood, would not refuse his gold!

*

Planting the Chrysanthemums
by Green Boy

Brought from their nursery and, with loving hands,
Planted along the fence and by the door –
A shower last night their wilting leaves revived,
Opening the morning-buds all silver-hoar.
Sweet flowers! a thousand autumn songs I'll sing
To praise your beauty, and libations pour,
And water you, and ridge with earth around.
No dust on *my* wet well-path shall be found!

*

Admiring the Chrysanthemums
by Cloud Maiden

Transplanted treasures, dear to me as gold —
Both the pale clumps and those of darker hue!
Bare-headed by your wintry bed I sit
And, musing, hug my knees and sing to you.
None more than you the villain world disdains;
None understands your proud heart as I do.
The precious hours of autumn I'll not waste,
But bide with you and savour their full taste.

*

Arranging the Chrysanthemums
by Cloud Maiden

What greater pleasure than the lute to strum
Or sip wine by your delicate display?
To hold the garden's fragrance in one vase,
And see all autumn in a single spray?
On frosty nights I'll dream you back again,
Brave in your garden bed at close of day.
Since with your shy disdain I sympathize,
'Tis you, not summer's gaudy blooms I prize.

*

Celebrating the Chrysanthemums
by River Queen

Down garden walks, in search of inspiration,
A restless demon drives me all the time;
Then brush blooms into praises, and the mouth
Grows acrid-sweet, hymning those scents sublime.
Yet easier 'twere a world of grief to tell
Than to lock autumn's secret in one rhyme.
That miracle old Tao did once attain;
Since when a thousand bards have tried in vain.

*

Painting the Chrysanthemums
by Lady Allspice

The brush that praised them, eager for more tasks,
Would paint them now – for painting's no great cost
When cunning black-ink blots the flowers' leaves make,
And white the petals, silvered o'er with frost.
Fresh scents of autumn from the paper rise,
And shapes unmoving by the wind are tossed.
No need at Double Ninth live flowers to pluck:
These living seem, upon a fine screen stuck!

*

Questioning the Chrysanthemums
by River Queen

Since none else autumn's mystery can explain,
I come with murmured questions to your gate:
Who, world-disdainer, shares your hiding-place?
Of all the flowers why do yours bloom so late?
The garden silent lies in frosty dew;
The geese return; the cricket mourns his fate.
Let not speech from your silent world be banned:
Converse with me, since me you understand!

*

Wearing the Chrysanthemums
by Plantain Lover

Just to admire and not for our adornment
Were these reared and arranged with so much care;
Yet young Sir Fop, with whom flowers are a passion,
And drunk old Tao both dote on flowers to wear.
One's head-cloth reeks of autumn's acrid perfume;
Chill dew of autumn pearls the other's hair.
The vulgar crowd, which nothing understands,
Stops in the street and, jeering, claps its hands.

*

The Shadow of the Chrysanthemums
by Cloud Maiden

The autumn moonlight through the garden steals,
Filtered in patches variously bright.
Flowers by the house as silhouettes appear;
Flowers by the fence are flecked with coins of light.
In the flowers' wintry scent their souls reside,
Not in those frost-forms, than a dream more slight.
Even the gross vandal, squinting through drunken eyes,
Can, by their scents, the crushed flowers recognize.

*

The Dream of the Chrysanthemums
by River Queen

Light-headed in my autumn bed I lie
And seem to chase the moon across the sky.
Well, if immortal, I'll go seek old Tao,
Not imitate Zhuang's flittering butterfly!
Following the wild goose, into sleep I slid;
From which now, startled by the cricket's cry,
Midst cold and fog and dying leaves I wake,
With no one by to tell of my heart's ache.

*

The Death of the Chrysanthemums
by Plantain Lover

The feasting over and the first snow fallen,
The flowers frost-stricken lie or sideways lean,
Their perfume lingering, but their gold hue dimmed
And few poor, tattered leaves bereft of green.
Now under moonlit bench the cricket shrills,
And weary goose-files in the cold sky are seen.
Yet of your passing let me not complain:
Next autumn equinox we'll meet again!

*

Each poem was praised in turn, and the reading of the whole twelve concluded amidst cries of mutual admiration.

'Now just a moment!' said Li Wan, interrupting their encomiums. 'Let me first try to give you an impartial judgement. I think there were good lines in *all* of the poems, but comparing one with another, it seems to be that one is bound to place "Celebrating the Chrysanthemums" first, with "Questioning the Chrysanthemums" second and "The Dream of the Chrysanthemums" third. The titles themselves were original, and – particularly in their treatment of the subject – these are three highly original poems. So I think that today the first place must undoubtedly go to River Queen. After those first three I would place "Wearing the Chrysanthemums", "Admiring the Chrysanthemums", "Arranging the Chrysanthemums", "Painting the Chrysanthemums" and "Remembering the Chrysanthemums" in that order.'

Bao-yu clapped his hands delightedly.

'Absolutely right! A very fair judgement!'

'I'm afraid mine *aren't* really all that good,' said Dai-yu. 'They are a bit too contrived.'

'There's nothing wrong with a bit of contrivance,' said Li Wan. 'One doesn't want the structure of a poem to stand out too ruggedly.'

'I very much like that couplet of Cloud Maiden's,' said Dai-yu:

'On frosty nights I'll dream you back again,
Brave in your garden bed at close of day.

It's a technique that painters call "white-backing". That marvellous couplet that comes before it:

To hold the garden's fragrance in a vase,
And see all autumn in a single spray

already sums up all there is to be said on the subject of flower-arrangement. You feel that she's left herself nothing else to say. So what does she do? She goes back to the time before the flowers were arranged – before they were picked, even. That *going back* in her "frosty nights" couplet is a very subtle way of throwing the main theme into relief, just as the artist's white-backing sharpens the highlights on the other side of the painting.'

Li Wan smiled.

'That may be so; but your own "acrid-sweet" couplet is more than a match for it.'

'*I* think Lady Allspice dealt with her subject most effectively,' said Tan-chun. 'That couplet of hers:

> But autumn's guest, who last year graced this plot,
> Only as yet in dreams of night appears

seems to bring out the idea of *remembering* so vividly.'

'Well, your "head-cloth reeking of autumn's acrid perfume" and "chill dew of autumn pearling the hair" give a pretty vivid image of *wearing* chrysanthemums,' said Bao-chai with a laugh.

'And River Queen's "who shares your hiding place?" "why do you bloom so late?",' said Xiang-yun, smiling mischievously, 'make so thorough a job of *questioning* them, that one feels the poor things must have been quite tongue-tied!'

'For that matter,' said Li Wan, entering into the spirit of the thing, 'your persistent haunting of the chrysanthemums – "sitting bare-headed by their wintry bed" and "hugging your knees and singing to them" – makes one suspect that if the chrysanthemums *really* had consciousness, they might, in the end, have grown just a tiny bit tired of your company!'

The others all laughed.

'I seem to be bottom again,' said Bao-yu ruefully. 'Though I must say I should have thought that

> ... to go on an excursion –
> Some garden where ... was planted
> The glory of autumn being our destination

and so forth was a perfectly satisfactory exposition of "*seeking* the chrysanthemums"; and that

> A shower last night the wilting leaves revived,
> Opening the morning-buds all silver-hoar

dealt with the theme of *transplanting* chrysanthemums rather successfully. Heigh-ho! I suppose it's just that I couldn't produce anything quite as good as River Queen's "acrid-sweet" line, or Cloud Maiden's "bare-headed by your wintry bed", or Plantain Lover's "reeking head-cloth" or "few poor, tattered leaves", or Lady Allspice's "autumn guest in dreams of night appears".

'Well, never mind,' he went on, after a moment's reflection. 'Perhaps tomorrow or the day after, if I've got the time, I'll try to do all twelve of them again on my own.'

'Your poems were perfectly all right,' said Li Wan consolingly. 'It's simply – as you yourself have just said – that they didn't have anything *quite* as good as the lines you have mentioned.'

Discussion of the poems continued a little longer, after which they called for another lot of hot crabs and sat down at the large round table to eat them.

'Eating crab and admiring the cassia like this is itself a good theme for a poem,' said Bao-yu. 'I've already thought of one. Is anyone else game to have a try?'

He quickly washed his hands and taking up a brush, wrote down the poem he had thought of. The others then read what he had written:

> How delightful to sit and a crab's claw to chew
> In the cassia shade – with some ginger-sauce, too!
> Old Grim-chops wants wine, though he's got no inside,
> And he walks never forwards, but all to one side.
> The 'yolks' are so tasty, who cares if we're ill!
> Though our fingers we've washed, they are crab-scented still.
> 'O crabs,' Dong-po said (and his words I repeat)
> 'You have not lived in vain if you're so good to eat!'

'One could churn out *that* sort of poem by the dozen,' said Dai-yu.

'You've used up all your inspiration,' said Bao-yu; 'but instead of admitting that you can't write any more, you make rude remarks about my poem!'

Dai-yu made no reply, but tilted her head back, lifted up her eyes, and for some minutes could be observed muttering softly to herself; then, picking a brush up, she wrote out the following poem rapidly and without hesitation:

> In arms and in armour they met their sad fate.
> How tempting they look now, piled up on a plate!
> The white flesh is tasty, the pink flesh as well –
> Both the white in the claws and the pink in the shell;
> And we're glad he's an eight- not a four-legged beast
> When there's plenty of wine to enliven the feast.
> So with crab let us honour the Double Ninth Day,
> While chrysanthemums bloom 'neath the cassia's spray.

Bao-yu had read this and was just beginning to say how good he thought it was when Dai-yu impetuously tore it up and told one of the servants to take away the pieces and burn them.

'It's not as good as yours,' she said. 'It deserves to be burnt. Actually yours is very good – better even than the chrysanthemum ones. You ought to keep it to show people.'

'I've thought of one too,' said Bao-chai. 'It was rather a struggle, so I'm afraid it won't be very good; but I'll write it down anyway for a laugh.'

Then she wrote down *her* poem, and the others read it.

> With winecups in hand, as the autumn day ends,
> And with watering mouths, we await our small friends.
> A straightforward breed you are certainly not,
> And the goodness inside you has all gone to pot –

There were cries of admiration at this point.

'That's a very neat bit of invective!' said Bao-yu. 'I can see I shall have to burn *my* poem now!'

They read on.

> For your cold humours, ginger; to cut out your smell
> We've got wine and chrysanthemum petals as well.
> As you hiss in your pot, crabs, d'ye look back with pain
> On that calm moonlit cove and the fields of fat grain?

When they had finished reading, all agreed that this was the definitive poem on the subject of eating crabs.

'It's the sign of a real talent,' they said, 'to be able to see a deeper, allegorical meaning in a frivolous subject – though the social satire *is* a trifle on the harsh side!'

Just then Patience arrived back in the Garden.

But what then ensued will be told in the following chapter.

CHAPTER 39

*An inventive old countrywoman tells a story of somewhat
questionable veracity
And an impressionable young listener insists on getting to
the bottom of the matter*

PATIENCE, you will recall, had just returned to the party.

'What's happened to your mistress?' the others asked her.
'Why doesn't she come back and join us?'

'She hasn't got time,' said Patience, laughing. 'She's sent
me to ask if you've got any crabs left. She says she didn't get
a proper chance to eat any earlier on, and as she hasn't got
time to come here herself, would I ask you, if you've still
got any, to let me take a few back for her.'

'We've got plenty left,' said Xiang-yun, and gave orders
for ten of the largest to be put in a box for her to take.

'Pick as many as you can with the round "navels",' said
Patience to the old servant who was departing to do Xiang-
yun's bidding.

Li Wan tried to make Patience sit down with them, but she
refused.

'You *shall* sit down!' said Li Wan, eyeing her skittishly;
and taking her by the hand, she drew her down beside her and
held a cup of wine up to her lips so that she was forced to
drink. Patience gulped down a mouthful of it and then rose
again to go.

'I won't *let* you go!' said Li Wan. 'The only person you
ever take any notice of is that precious Feng of yours; you
think you don't need to obey me; but you shall.' She turned
to the old woman, now waiting in readiness with the box of
crabs, and told her to go on ahead with them and tell Xi-feng
that Patience was being detained. The old woman went away.

She returned a short while after, still carrying the box, with
a message.

'Mrs Lian says thank you very much, and she hopes you

didn't think her greedy for asking. She's put some caltrop-cakes and some chicken-fat rolls in the box, that have just been sent her by the elder Lady Wang. She thought you and the young ladies might like to try them.'

There was a further message for Patience:

'Mrs Lian says she thought she sent you to fetch something for her, not to stay here and amuse yourself. Anyway, she says, tell her not to drink too much.'

'Oh,' said Patience, laughing, 'and what will happen to me if I do?'

As if in defiance of her mistress's instructions, she fell to eating and drinking with great gusto. Li Wan meanwhile encircled her waist in an affectionate embrace.

'What a pity that so distinguished-looking a young woman should have been born to so humble a fate!' said Li Wan. 'It's *you* who should have been the mistress. You would have made such a good lady. No one who didn't know would ever take you for a maid.'

Patience, who had continued eating and drinking with Bao-chai and Xiang-yun while Li Wan was saying this, now turned round and looked at her with a giggle.

'Stop it, Mrs Zhu! You're tickling me!'

'Aiyo!' said Li Wan. 'What's this great hard thing here?'

'Keys,' said Patience.

'Keys?' said Li Wan. 'What has your mistress got so precious that you need to carry keys round all the time? Do you know what I tell people about you? I tell them: Just as you can't imagine a Tripitaka going off to India to fetch the scriptures without his white horse or a Liu Zhi-yuan conquering the Empire without a Spirit of the Melon Fields to give him his armour, so you can't imagine a Wang Xi-feng without a Patience alongside helping her. *You* are your mistress's master-key. What does she need to make you carry these things around with you for?'

Patience laughed embarrassedly.

'You are making fun of me, Mrs Zhu. I'm afraid you've had too much to drink.'

'No, it's true,' said Bao-chai. 'Whenever we start gossiping about personalities, we nearly always end up by agreeing what exceptional people you and the other chief maids are. And all exceptional in your own different ways, too – that's what's so interesting.'

'It's almost as though Nature had in each case designed the mistress and the maid to suit each other,' said Li Wan. 'Take Grandmother and Faithful, for example. Grandmother would be completely lost without Faithful. Who in the family from Lady Wang downwards would ever dare answer Grandmother back? Yet Faithful does. And what's more, Grandmother will listen to her. And look at all the things that Grandmother has. No one else could ever remember them the way that Faithful can. Just think how Grandmother would be plundered and cheated if Faithful weren't there to look after them. And on top of it all, she's a very fair person. She'll often put in a good word for someone. And though she has so much influence with Grandmother, she never, never uses it to do anyone else down.'

Xi-chun smiled.

'Yesterday when Grannie was talking about Faithful she said, "She's better than all you grandchildren!"'

'Faithful's a good sort,' said Patience. 'I don't consider myself in her class at all.'

'Mother's Suncloud is a good, honest soul,' said Bao-yu.

'She certainly is,' said Tan-chun. 'She's got a mind of her own, though. You know what a Holy Buddha Mother is: she doesn't notice a half of what goes on around her. But Suncloud does. And *she* is the one who always has to remind Mother about everything. She even knows about outside matters. When Father is at home, it's Suncloud who has to remind Mother about them when she forgets.'

'I don't know about Mother and Suncloud,' said Li Wan, 'but what about this young gentleman here?' She pointed to Bao-yu. 'Can you imagine the sort of state *he* would be in if he hadn't got his Aroma to look after him? And Feng too. Even though she's a regular Tyrant King, she still needs her

Patience in order to be so efficient, just as much as the real Tyrant King needed his two strong arms in order to be able to lift up those hundredweight tripods.'

'There were four of us when I first came here with Mrs Lian,' said Patience, 'but the others all either died or left. I'm the only one who's stayed with her all along.'

'You're lucky then,' said Li Wan. 'And Feng is lucky, too. When I first came here to Mr Zhu, I had several maids, too, but – I don't know why it was, for I'm sure you wouldn't call me a hard mistress – they were always dissatisfied. So when Mr Zhu died, I took advantage of their being still young to get rid of them all. If only I'd had a dependable girl like you that I could have kept on with me, I shouldn't feel quite so helpless now.'

Her eyes began to redden as she said this, and she seemed about to cry.

'Oh, come now!' said the others. 'There's no need to upset yourself. If you're going to be like this, we might just as well break up the party.'

They did in fact begin washing their hands then and presently decided to go off in a body to pay their duty calls on Grandmother Jia and Lady Wang. Meanwhile the old women and maids busied themselves with sweeping out the pavilion and stacking and washing up the cups and dishes.

Aroma left in the company of Patience. On the way back she asked Patience into Green Delights. She made her sit down and invited her to take tea, but Patience declined, saying that she would drop in another time, and rose to go. Aroma had something to ask her, however, and called after her as she was going.

'What's happened to this month's allowances?' she said. 'Even Her Old Ladyship's and Her Ladyship's people haven't had theirs yet.'

Patience spun round when she heard this and came back again.

'Don't ask me about that, please!' she said in a low, agitated voice, after first glancing round to make sure that no one else was present. 'Whatever it is, you'll only have another day or two to wait, I promise you.'

Aroma was amused to see her so agitated.

'Why, what's the matter? Why should you be in such a state about it?'

Patience dropped her voice even lower.

'Mrs Lian has already put the money for this month's allowances out at interest. She's waiting for the interest on some of her other loans to pay your allowances with. It's all right for me to tell *you* this, but whatever you do, don't let anyone else know about it!'

Aroma laughed.

'But she's not short of money, she's got plenty. What does she want to go giving herself all this extra worry for?'

'She's certainly not short of money,' said Patience. 'Just in the few years since she started doing this, the amount she has got out on loan must have grown to several hundred times the original premium. And she doesn't spend all of her own allowance, either. Whenever she's got nine or ten taels saved up out of it, she invests them too. Why, just her profits alone after she's deducted the allowances from the interest must be in the region of a thousand taels a year.'

'You and your mistress are a nice pair, I must say!' said Aroma. Keeping the rest of us short while you use our money to feather your own nests with!'

'That's most unfair!' said Patience indignantly. 'Any way, I'm sure you can't really be short of money.'

'Not myself, it's true,' said Aroma. 'In any case, I haven't got anything to spend it on. I was thinking more of my young gentleman. I like to keep some by me in case *he* ever needs any.'

'Look, if you're in urgent need of money, I've got a few taels put by myself that I can let you have,' said Patience. 'You can have them as an advance on this month's allowance, if you like.'

'I don't really need any at the moment,' said Aroma, 'but may I take you up on your offer if I ever do?'

'Of course,' said Patience, and left without further ceremony.

Outside the courtyard gate a maid from Xi-feng's was looking for her.

'The Mistress wants to see you about something.'

'What has she got so urgent that she has to keep pestering me like this?' said Patience. 'I've just had Mrs Zhu all over me to make me stay and talk to *her*. It's not as if I'd run away.'

'Better ask her yourself,' said the girl. 'It wasn't *my* idea to fetch you.'

'Cheeky devil!' said Patience, and continued on her way.

When she got there, however, it was not Xi-feng she found waiting for her, but the old countrywoman she had admitted on a previous occasion as a suppliant, Grannie Liu, with her little grandson Ban-er. They were sitting in the side room on the kang with Zhang Cai's wife and Zhou Rui's wife on either side of them, while maids were emptying sacks of jujubes, melons and other farm produce on the floor below. The company rose hurriedly to their feet as Patience entered. Grannie Liu, who recognized her from her last visit, scrambled down from the kang and greeted her at once as 'Miss Patience' without any of the previous time's confusion.

'The family all send their regards, Miss. They'd have come themselves long since to see you and pay their respects to their Aunt Lian, only they've been too busy with the farm-work. Anyways, they've had a good harvest this year, thanks be, and it's been a good year for the fruit and vegetables. This here that I've brought is the first pickings. We didn't like to sell them, because we wanted our first-fruits to go to Mrs Lian and the young ladies. We thought that mayhap eating the rarities of earth and sea every day of their lives they might sometimes tire of delicate food and fancy a bit of plain country stuff for a change. Anyway, there you are! It's a poor gift, but it's given with a warm heart!'

'It's very good of you to have brought it,' said Patience, and begged her to be seated, sitting down herself as she did so. She invited Zhou Rui's wife and Zhang Cai's wife to be seated as well, and ordered one of the junior maids to pour tea.

Mesdames Zhou and Zhang chaffed her on her appearance.

'You've got the spring in your face, Miss. Your eyes are all red.'

Patience laughed.

'I know. I don't drink normally, but today Mrs Zhu and the young ladies got hold of me and just forced it down me. I was *made* to drink, against my will. That's why my face is so red.'

'Well *I* don't know,' said Zhang Cai's wife. 'Here's me just dying for a drink, but nobody offers me one. Next time anyone invites you, Miss, you must take me with you.'

The others laughed.

'I saw those crabs this morning,' said Zhou Rui's wife. 'Great big things. There couldn't have been more than two or three to a catty. And I should think altogether there must have been seventy or eighty catties in those hampers. Even so,' she said reflectively, 'there probably wouldn't have been enough for all the staff to have some.'

'Lots of them didn't,' said Patience. 'It was only the top ones that got one or two crabs to themselves. The rest of them only got a taste – some of them not even that.'

'Good crabs like that are selling at a pennyweight a catty this year,' said Grannie Liu. 'If one catty is a pennyweight, fifty catties is two taels ten, and another thirty is one and ten; ten and two is twelve and twice ten is a tael, that's thirteen, and then there's the wine and the other dishes. It couldn't have cost less than twenty taels in all. Bless us and save us! that'd keep a farmer and his family for a year!'

'I take it you've already seen Mrs Lian,' said Patience.

'Yes,' said Grannie Liu. 'She told us to wait.'

She glanced through the open window as she said this and noticed that the day was drawing on towards evening.

'It's getting dark earlier these days,' she said. 'We'd better be on our way. We don't want to find the city gates shut, or we shall be in a proper pickle.'

'Just wait while I slip over and find out what the Mistress is up to,' said Zhou Rui's wife. She left the room and was

gone for some considerable time. When she eventually returned, she was full of smiles.

'It's Grannie's lucky day,' she said. 'She's struck lucky with
both of them.'

'How do you mean?' said Patience.

'Well,' said Zhou Rui's wife, 'Mrs Lian was with Her Old
Ladyship when I got there, so I went up to her and told her
on the side that Grannie wanted to go now to make sure of
getting to the gates in time. "Oh," she said, "she came such
a long way with all that stuff. If it's getting late, she'd better
spend the night here and leave tomorrow morning." Well,
that was one piece of luck; but that's nothing to what followed, because Her Old Ladyship had overheard this and
asked her who this "Grannie Liu" was, and when Mrs Lian
told her, she said, "Oh, I've been just longing for someone
with a bit of age and experience to talk to! Bring her here!
Introduce her to *me*!" Now that really *was* a stroke of luck!'

She urged Grannie Liu to leave her place on the kang and
go over to the other apartment; but the old countrywoman
was seized with a sudden attack of shyness.

'Look at me! Dear soul, I'm in no fit state to see her now!
Tell her I've already left!'

'Go on, you go and see her!' said Patience. 'It'll be all
right. Our old lady is always very nice to poor or elderly
people She's not the least bit pretentious or stuck-up like
some I could mention. If you're nervous about meeting high-
ups, Mrs Zhou and I will go with you to give you confidence.'

She proceeded, with Mrs Zhou's assistance, to conduct the
old woman to her interview.

When they saw Patience coming out of the courtyard, the
pages on duty at the gate stood up, and two of them came running up to her.

'Miss! Miss!'

'What's it this time?' said Patience.

'I've been waiting to catch you for hours, Miss,' said the
first of the boys. 'My ma's took ill and I've got to go and
fetch the doctor for her. Will it be all right if I take the night
off?'

'You're a nice lot!' said Patience. 'It's my belief that you've got it all worked out between you so that one of you gets a holiday every day. And instead of telling the Mistress proper-ly, as you're supposed to do, you come round to me with these sad stories and make *me* take the responsibility. When Stoppo did this the other day, the Master called for him while he was still away and *I* got into trouble by speaking up for him. The Master accused me of doing favours. And now *you* want to do the same thing.'

'His ma really is ill, Miss,' said Zhou Rui's wife. 'I'm sure it would be in order for you to let him go.'

'All right, then. But mind you're back first thing tomorrow,' Patience told the boy. 'Now you heard that, didn't you? First thing. Because I've got work for you to do. No lying in bed until you can feel the sun on your backside! And I want you to take a message to Brightie for me on the way. Tell him the Mistress says that if he hasn't handed in the rest of that interest by tomorrow, she won't ask him for it again, because she'll know that he's keeping it for himself.'

The boy promised to deliver the message and scampered off, delighted to be released.

By the time Patience and her charges arrived at Grand-mother Jia's apartment, all the young denizens of Prospect Garden had for some time been assembled there in attendance, so that as Grannie Liu entered the room, she was confronted by a bevy of unfamiliar young ladies, all resplendent in orna-ments of pearl and kingfisher, like a bed of beautiful flowers, none of which she could give a name to. In their midst a venerable old lady reclined on a couch. A young woman, pretty as a picture and dressed in silk and satin from top to toe, sat behind her, gently pounding her legs. Xi-feng, the only person there she could recognize, was standing to one side of her, evidently in the midst of telling her something amusing. Deducing that the old lady on the couch must be Grandmother Jia, Grannie Liu hurried up to her and made her an antique curtsey.

'Your servant, my lady!'

Grandmother Jia inclined herself politely from the couch

and asked Zhou Rui's wife to bring up a chair for her to sit on. Ban-er, bashful as ever, would not attempt a greeting.

'Now, old kinswoman,' said Grandmother Jia, 'and what would your age be?'

'Seventy-five this year,' said Grannie Liu.

Grandmother Jia turned round to the others present.

'That's several years older than me. Fancy still being so fit and lively! Heaven only knows what *I* shall be like at that age!'

Grannie Liu laughed.

'I was born for a hard life, d'ye see, just as Your Ladyship was born for a soft one. We couldn't all be like Your Ladyship, or there'd be no one to do the farming.'

'Are your eyes and teeth still good?' Grandmother Jia asked her.

'All bar a back tooth on the left-hand side that's getting a bit loose this year.'

'There! and I'm already a useless old woman,' said Grandmother Jia. 'Poor eyesight, poor hearing, memory going – I can't even remember the names of old kinsfolk like yourself any longer. I'm scared to meet them when they come visiting, for fear they might laugh at me. There's not much I can do nowadays except eat – what I can get my teeth into – and sleep. Apart from that, I share a joke or two with these young people when I need a bit of diversion, and that's about all.'

'Your Ladyship is lucky,' said Grannie Liu. '*I* couldn't have such a life if I wanted it.'

'Lucky? No!' said Grandmother Jia. 'I'm just an old crock!'

The others all laughed.

'Our Feng has been telling me that you've brought a lot of fruit and vegetables with you,' said Grandmother Jia. 'I've asked the servants to bring them over. I'm so looking forward to some nice, fresh farm vegetables. The stuff we buy outside isn't as tasty as your home-grown stuff, you know.'

'That's the countryman's idea of a treat,' said Grannie Liu. 'He can't afford meat and fish, so when he fancies a little luxury, he likes to eat his food fresh from the ground.'

'Now that you're one of the family,' said Grandmother Jia, 'I hope you will stay long enough to enjoy your visit. Don't go hurrying back again. Stay here a couple of days or so, if you can put up with us. We've got a garden too, you know, and we grow a certain amount of fruit in it. Tomorrow you must try some of *our* stuff – and you must take some back home with you when you go. It will seem more like a proper visit to relations if you stay a bit, instead of popping in and popping straight out again.'

Xi-feng could see that Grandmother Jia took pleasure in the old woman's company and added her own persuasion.

'It's probably not as roomy here as your farmyard, but I expect we'll manage to tuck you in somewhere. And you'll be able to tell our old lady all the village gossip.'

'Feng!' said Grandmother Jia, laughing in spite of herself. 'Don't make fun! She's a simple countrywoman. You can't expect her to stand up to your teasing in the way that we can.'

She gave orders for Ban-er to be given some sweetmeats. He was unwilling to eat in front of so many people, however, so she told them to give him some money instead, and to get some of the younger pages to take him outside to play.

After Grannie Liu had taken tea, she regaled Grandmother Jia with some anecdotes of village life, thus further endearing herself to her new acquaintance. She was still holding forth when Xi-feng, who had slipped out some time previously, sent someone round to invite her back for dinner. Grandmother Jia selected some food from her own dishes and sent them to Xi-feng's place for Grannie Liu to try in addition to what Xi-feng was giving her.

Xi-feng could see that Grandmother Jia had taken a fancy to the old woman, so after dinner she sent her back to Grandmother Jia's apartment. As soon as she arrived, Faithful ordered some of the older domestics to conduct her to a bath. She herself went off to fetch her a change of clothes. She selected two fairly modest items from her own wardrobe and sent them to the bathroom with instructions that Grannie Liu should change into them after her bath. Such goings-on were outside even the old grannie's extensive experience, but she took them all in good part, and having submitted to the ordeal of the bath, quickly dressed herself in the proffered clothes and went in to take her place once more beside the couch and resume her role of *raconteuse*. In this she was eminently successful, since Bao-yu and the girls, now seated on all sides around her, found her simple country talk much more fascinating than any of the fictions told by the blind ballad-singers who sometimes visited the house.

Indeed, there was more than an element of fiction in what she told them: for Grannie Liu, though born and bred in the country, was a shrewd old soul to whom the years had given a pretty good understanding of human weakness, and when she sensed the old lady's pleased excitement and the avid attention of her younger listeners, she did her best not to disappoint them by supplying from her own invention whatever memory and experience were inadequate to provide.

'We country-folk working out there on the land – year in, year out, rain or fine, spring, summer, autumn and winter – we never get any time off,' she told them. 'If we rest, it's only as you might say "napping in harness", like the old post-horse in the story. And many a strange happening do we see, out there on the land.

'Take what happened last winter, for instance. It had been snowing for several days without a stop and the snow was two or three feet thick on the ground, and this particular morning I rose up early, and while I was still indoors, I heard the sound of something stirring outside in the woodpile. I thought to myself, "That'll be someone stealing the firewood." So I put my eye to the hole in the shutter, and sure enough there was someone there; but it wasn't anyone from the village – '

'It was probably some traveller,' Grandmother Jia interrupted. 'He was feeling cold and helped himself to a bit to make a fire with, so that he could get warm.'

'Ah, but it *wasn't* a traveller,' said Grannie Liu. 'That was the strange thing about it. Now who do you think it was, my old soul? 'Twas a young woman, seventeen or eighteen years of age seemingly, pretty as a picture, and with no more on her

but a red dress and a white satin skirt, and the hair on her bare
head combed as sleek and shining as black lacquer paint –'

At that point her story was interrupted by a confused hubbub of voices outside. One of them could be heard above the
rest saying, 'It isn't serious. There's no point in frightening
Her Old Ladyship.'

'What is it?' the old lady asked in some alarm.

'A fire has broken out in the South Court stables,' said one
of the maids. 'It isn't serious, though. They've already got it
under control.'

Always the most timorous of mortals where fire was concerned, Grandmother Jia struggled to her feet, and supported
by the maids, led the others out onto the loggia to see what
was happening. Somewhere beyond the south-east corner of
the courtyard the glare of flames was still distinctly visible.
Terrified out of her wits, she began calling on the names of
the Buddha, and hurriedly sent someone to burn incense
before the image of the Fire God.

By now Lady Wang had arrived with the younger women,
and added her voice to the others' in assuring the old lady that
the fire was well under control and urging her to go indoors;
but Grandmother Jia insisted on staying outside until the last
of the flames had been extinguished.

As soon as they were all inside again, Bao-yu began questioning Grannie Liu about her interrupted story.

'Why was the girl out in all that snow stealing firewood?'
he asked her. 'She might have caught her death of cold.'

'For goodness' sake don't ask about *that*!' said Grandmother Jia. 'It was talking about firewood that started that
fire just now. Think of something else to talk about for goodness' sake!'

Though privately far from satisfied, Bao-yu was obliged to
let the matter rest while Grannie Liu turned her inventive
faculties in another direction.

'In a farmstead east of ours there was an old dame of more
than ninety who had fasted and prayed to the Buddha every
day of her life. At last the Blessed Guanyin was moved by her

prayers and appeared to her one night in a dream. "It was to
have been your fate to be cut off without an heir," the Blessed
Mother told her, "but because of your great piety, I have peti-
tioned the Jade Emperor to give you a grandson."

'Now this old dame had an only son, and the son, too, had
an only son who in spite of all their care had died when he was
only seventeen or eighteen, to their sore and bitter grief. But
after she had this dream a second grandson was born. He'd be
thirteen or fourteen now – a very handsome lad, with skin as
white as snow, and that sharp and clever you'd hardly credit
it. So you see there *are* gods and Buddhas watching over us,
whatever folk may say!'

The circumstances of this tale so perfectly accorded with
the idea they had privately formed of their own situation, that
both the senior ladies in her audience – Lady Wang no less
than Grandmother Jia – were quite captivated by it. But Bao-
yu, whose thoughts were still on the beautiful pilferer of firewood, looked glum and preoccupied. His sister Tan-chun
observed this and sought to distract him.

'We've got to make some sort of return for Cousin Shi's
party, Bao. Why don't we go back now and discuss when the
next poetry meeting is to be? We can have our party for Cousin
Shi at the same time, and Grandma will be able to come and
look at the chrysanthemums.'

'Grandma's already promised to give a return party for
Cousin Shi herself,' said Bao-yu, 'and we are all invited. We'd
better wait until that's over before putting on anything of our
own.'

'The longer we delay, the colder the weather will be,'
said Tan-chun. 'It won't be much fun for Grandma if it's too
cold.'

'But she loves parties when it's raining or snowing,' said
Bao-yu. 'Why don't we wait until the first snowfall and have
it then? Call it a snow-viewing party. Think how romantic:
chanting poems in the falling snow!'

'It would be more romantic still,' said Dai-yu drily, 'if
instead of chanting poems we had a big bundle of firewood

and took it in turns to tiptoe through the snow and pull out sticks from it.'

Bao-chai and the other girls all laughed, but Bao-yu stared at Dai-yu rather crossly and said nothing.

After the company had dispersed, Bao-yu finally managed to get Grannie Liu into a corner and question her in detail about the mysterious snow maiden. Grannie Liu's inventiveness was once more put to the test.

'On the embankment that runs along the north side of our land,' she said, 'there is a little shrine. The image inside it is not a god or a Buddha, though. There used at one time to be a gentleman living in our parts — '

She broke off at this point and appeared to be trying to remember a name.

'Never mind his name,' said Bao-yu. 'Don't try to remember it. Just tell me what happened.'

'This gentleman had no son, but he had an only daughter called – I think it was Ruo-yu. She could read books as well as any scholar, this Ruo-yu, and the gentleman loved her more than all the treasure in the world. But sad to say, she took sick and died when she was only seventeen years old — '

Bao-yu groaned and stamped his foot.

'So what happened then?'

'Because the gentleman loved her so dearly, he had this shrine built for her out in the fields and had a likeness of her made out of wood and clay to put inside it; and he arranged for someone to burn incense there and always keep a spark of fire going inside the burner. But as the years went by, both the gentleman and the people who used to tend the shrine for him all died, and now the shrine is falling into ruin and the statue has come to life and started haunting people.'

'No, no,' Bao-yu interrupted hurriedly, 'that wouldn't be the statue coming to life. People like that are never really dead, even after they have died.'

'Holy Name!' said Grannie Liu. 'Fancy that now! And me thinking all along it was the statue. Well, whatever it is, every so often it takes on human shape and goes wandering abroad troubling people. And that's what I saw when I looked out that time and saw someone taking our firewood. The people in our village are talking of breaking up the image and knocking the shrine down so as to put a stop to the haunting.'

'Good gracious! they mustn't do that!' said Bao-yu. 'That's a terrible sin, knocking a temple down!'

'Now I am glad you told me that,' said Grannie Liu gravely. 'When I get back, I shall do my best to stop them.'

'My grandmother and Lady Wang and in fact just about everyone in this family is terribly keen on good works,' said Bao-yu. 'There's nothing they like better than repairing temples and restoring things. Tomorrow I'll write out an appeal and collect some subscriptions for you. *You* can be the fund's Treasurer, and when we've got enough money together, *you* can supervise the restoration. And I'll get them to send you some money every month for incense. How would that be?'

'Statue or spirit or whatever she is,' said Grannie Liu, 'I shall certainly be grateful to her for the money.'

Bao-yu pressed her for the names of the nearest farms and villages and the exact location of the shrine in relation to them as well as the distance to it and the general direction in which it lay. Answering all these questions with whatever came first into her head, Grannie Liu supplied a set of fictitious directions which Bao-yu, believing them to be genuine, carefully committed to memory and carried back to his room, where he lay awake half the night planning what he would do for the beautiful wood-thief in the days ahead.

He went out of the Garden first thing next morning, and handing Tealeaf a few hundred cash, told him the directions for getting to the shrine as given him by Grannie Liu the night before, and instructed him to follow them, inspect the shrine, and report back on what he saw. He would await Tealeaf's report before deciding what to do next.

But once Tealeaf had gone he found the waiting very tedious, and as the day wore on and Tealeaf still failed to return, he became as fidgety as a worm on hot earth. He was

obliged to wait until sundown before Tealeaf finally came
back. When he did, however, he was looking extremely
pleased with himself.

'You managed to find it then?' Bao-yu asked him eagerly.

'Yes,' said Tealeaf, smiling broadly, 'but you couldn't have
heard the directions right. I had a terrible job finding it. The
place where it is and the way to it are nothing like you said.
That's why I took so long. I was all day looking for it. In the
end I found that there *is* a ruined temple in that area, but it's
not where you said: it's at the *east end* of the north embankment, on a corner.'

Bao-yu's face beamed with pleasure.

'Grannie Liu's a very old woman,' he said. 'It's quite possible that she misremembered when she gave me those directions. Anyway, tell me what you saw.'

'The temple was south-facing, like you said,' Tealeaf replied, '*and* it was in a very tumble-down condition. I'd been
searching nearly all day by then, so of course when I saw *that*,
I was very relieved and hurried straight inside. But oh lor!
when I looked at the image, I was so scared I hurried straight
out again – it was so *real*!'

Bao-yu laughed delightedly.

'Of course. If she's capable of coming to life, you'd expect
a certain liveliness in the statue.'

'*She*?' said Tealeaf. 'This was no she. It was an ugly great
Plague God with a blue face and red hair!'

'Useless dolt!' said Bao-yu angrily. 'You can't even do a
simple little errand like this for me.'

'That's most unfair,' said Tealeaf in a deeply aggrieved
tone of voice. 'You send me off on a wild-goose chase to look
for something you've read about in some book or other or
heard about in some old-wives' tale, and then when I can't
find it (because there's probably no such thing any way) you
start abusing me.'

Bao-yu saw that he had hurt his feelings, and hastened to
comfort him.

'There, there, don't be upset! Some time when you're not
too busy you shall have another look for it. If the old woman

is deceiving us, you naturally won't be able to find it. But if there really is such a place and you do, then *you* will have a share in the merit when it's restored. And of course, I shall give you a very big reward.'

While he was talking to Tealeaf, one of the pages from the inner gate came up and said that 'one of the young ladies from Her Old Ladyship's room' was at the gate asking for Master Bao.

Who it was and what she wanted will be revealed in the following chapter.

CHAPTER 40

*Lady Jia holds two feasts in one day in the Prospect Garden
And Faithful makes four calls on three dominoes in the
Painted Chamber*

HEARING that he was wanted, Bao-yu hurried to the gate of
the inner mansion. Amber was standing in front of the screen-
wall waiting for him.

'Hurry! You're holding everyone up. There's something
they want to talk to you about,' she said.

In fact, when he arrived at his grandmother's room, she and
his mother and the girls were already discussing it – 'it' being
the question of what arrangements they should make for the
return party for Shi Xiang-yun.

'I'll tell you what to do,' said Bao-yu. 'Since there won't be
any outsiders at this party, instead of having a fixed menu and
formally-laid tables, why not get them to do one or two of
everyone's favourite dishes, put them in those lacquer food-
boxes that have different compartments for the different
dishes, and serve them on little individual tables with a "self-
service" wine-kettle each, so that everyone can pour their
own wine? I'm sure that would be jollier than a formal party.'

Grandmother Jia was much taken with this proposal and at
once sent orders to the kitchen to do as he had suggested.

'Tell them that tomorrow we want them to choose some
of the things they know we like and put them in boxes – one
box for each of us. And tell them that we shall want *lunch*
served in the Garden tomorrow as well.'

The lamps had by now been lit. Of the night which followed
our record gives no account.

Rising early next morning, they were delighted to observe
that it was going to be a beautiful clear, autumn day. Li Wan
was among the earliest up, and at once began to supervise the
older women and maids in sweeping up fallen leaves, polishing chairs and tables, and getting ready the sets of teacups,

winecups and so forth that would be needed for the party. Xi-feng's maid Felicity, accompanied by Grannie Liu and little Ban-er, arrived while they were in the midst of this activity.

'You are very busy, Mrs Zhu,' said Grannie Liu.

Li Wan smiled.

'I *told* you you'd never get away! You kept saying yesterday that you had to go, but I knew they wouldn't let you.'

'It was Her Old Ladyship that kept me,' said Grannie Liu. 'She said she wanted me to enjoy meself for a day or two before I went back.'

Felicity produced several large keys.

'Mrs Lian says the little tables already in use may not be enough and we'd better open the upstairs storeroom and get some more out, just for today. She meant to come over herself and see to it, but she's with Her Ladyship at the moment and can't get away, so she says would you mind opening the store-room for her and getting some of the servants to carry them down?'

Li Wan sent Candida to the storeroom with the keys and told one of the old women to go to the inner gate and get some of the pages on duty there to help with the carrying. She herself went and stood in the courtyard behind Prospect Hall and watched from below while the Painted Chamber was opened up and the tables were one by one carried down from it. The team of maids, pages and old nannies worked together with such enthusiasm that soon more than twenty of the little tables had been manhandled downstairs into the courtyard.

'Gently now, gently!' said Li Wan as they were moving them. 'No need to go at it as if all the devils in hell were after you! You'll chip the edges off them if you're not careful.'

She turned to Grannie Liu.

'Wouldn't you like to go up and have a look?'

The old woman needed no second asking. Holding Ban-er tightly by the hand, she scrambled up the stairway and looked inside. The interior was stacked high with folding screens, tables, chairs, lanterns and furniture of every kind. Much of what she saw she could not identify, but the dull gleam of gold, the rich glow of coloured lacquers, and the artistry and sump-

tuousness of the objects drew many a pious ejaculation from
her before she descended. The door of the storeroom was then
locked and the remaining maids came down.

'I wonder how energetic Lady Jia will be feeling today,'
said Li Wan. 'Perhaps while you are about it you had better
get out the oars and punt-poles and paddles and some boat-
awnings as well, in case she decides to go on the water.'

'Yes'm,' said the maids, and proceeded to unlock the store-
room again and carry down the items specified. Li Wan meanwhile sent one of the pages to tell the boatwomen that they
were to pole a couple of punts out from the boathouse and
have them by in readiness.

While this activity was still in progress, Grandmother Jia
arrived at the head of a troupe of females. Li Wan hurried forward to greet her.

'You are very energetic this morning, Grandmother; I
didn't expect you in the Garden so soon. I was hoping that
you would still be doing your hair. I've picked some chrysanthemums for you to wear and I was just about to send them
round to you.'

Even as she was saying this, Casta arrived carrying a large
dish of peacock-green glaze shaped like a lotus-leaf, in which
chrysanthemum-flowers of many different colours were being
kept in moisture. Grandmother Jia chose a dark red one to
fasten in the side of her hair. As she turned her head to do so,
she caught sight of Grannie Liu and smiled at her in welcome.

'Come over here! You must have one too!'

Before she had finished, Xi-feng had already seized the old
woman by the hand and was dragging her over.

'Come on, let me dress you up properly!'

She began sticking the chrysanthemums into her hair, putting them in at every angle, and continued until all the flowers
in the dish had been used up. The effect was so ludicrous that
Grandmother Jia and the rest all burst out laughing. Grannie
Liu, not a whit perturbed, good-humouredly joined in the
laughter.

'I don't know what my poor old head can have done to
deserve so much honour,' she said.

'You ought to pull them out and throw them in her face,' said the others. 'She's made you look like an old vamp!'

'I may be getting on now,' said Grannie Liu, 'but I used to be a stylish young woman in my time. I loved to have a bit of powder for my cheek and a flower to wear in my hair. 'Tis no matter: now I shall be a stylish *old* 'un.'

During this exchange they had been moving towards Drenched Blossoms Pavilion. Maids went on ahead with a rolled-up patterned rug which they spread out on one of the bench-boards that ran along the inner sides of the balustrades. Seating herself on the rug with her back against the railings, Grandmother Jia invited Grannie Liu to sit down beside her and tell her what she thought of the Garden.

'Holy Name!' said Grannie Liu. 'You know, we country folk like to get a picture at the New Year that we can stick up on the wall. Every year just before New Year the farmers come into town to buy one. Many's the time of an evening when the day's work was done we've sat and looked at the picture on *our* wall and wished we could get inside it and walk around, never imagining that such beautiful places could really be. Yet now I look at this Garden here, and it's ten times better than any picture I ever saw. If only I could get someone to make a painting of it all, just the way it is, that I could take back to show the others, I do believe I should die content!'

Grandmother Jia smilingly pointed a finger in Xi-chun's direction.

'You see my little great-niece over there? *She* can paint. Shall we get *her* to do you a painting of it?'

Grannie Liu jumped up and going over to Xi-chun, took her impulsively by the hand.

'Dear Miss!' she said. 'To think that one so young and pretty should be so gifted and all! I do believe you must be one of the holy spirits born in a human shape!'

The simple earnestness with which this was uttered made the others all laugh. After resting a little longer, Grandmother Jia, who intended to show her guest as much of the Garden as possible, got up again and resumed the tour.

The first place they came to was the Naiad's House. The

green bamboos engulfed them as they entered the gate and brilliant green moss carpeted the ground beneath. Through the midst of the bamboos a raised cobbled path wound its way towards the house. Grannie Liu stepped aside to let Grandmother Jia and the rest walk on it while she herself walked on the ground below. Amber held a hand out to draw her up.

'Walk on the path, Grannie! You'll slip on the moss down there.'

'Don't you mind me, my dear!' said Grannie Liu. 'I'm used to it. You keep to the path, though, with the rest. You don't want to muddy those fancy shoes of yours.'

Unfortunately the necessity of looking up to talk to someone who was walking at a higher level had distracted her attention from the ground beneath, and even as she said this, her feet slipped on the treacherous moss, her legs flew out from under her, and she landed on her posterior with a thump. The girls clapped their hands delightedly. Grandmother Jia laughed too, though trying her hardest to sound cross.

'Little monsters!' she said. 'Don't just stand there laughing. Help her up!'

But Grannie Liu had already scrambled up unaided, and was laughing herself.

'It serves me right,' she said. 'I shouldn't have spoken so soon!'

'Are you sure you haven't hurt your back?' Grandmother Jia asked her. 'Let one of the maids massage it for you.'

'God bless my soul!' said Grannie Liu. 'I'm not *that* delicate! I don't suppose a day goes by but what I take a tumble or two. If I was to have meself massaged every time, it would never do!'

Nightingale was already waiting with the bamboo blind raised for them to enter. Grandmother Jia led her party through the doorway and sat down inside. Dai-yu waited on her in person, offering her tea in a covered cup which she carried on a little tray.

'We shan't be taking tea, niece,' said Lady Wang. 'Don't bother to pour for the rest of us.'

Hearing this, Dai-yu ordered one of the maids to fetch the

chair by the window that she normally sat on herself and bring
it up for her aunt to sit on. Grannie Liu noticed the inkstone
and brushes on the table in front of it and all the books on the
bookshelves and said that she supposed this must be 'the
young gentleman's study'.

Grandmother Jia smiled and pointed to Dai-yu.

'It belongs to her – my little grand-daughter.'

As though incredulous, Grannie Liu studied Dai-yu attentively for some moments in silence.

'It doesn't look at all like a young lady's room,' she said
finally. 'It looks to me like a very high-class young gentleman's
study.'

'Where *is* Bao-yu, by the way?' said Grandmother Jia.

'He's on the lake in one of the punts,' said the maids.

'Oh? Whose idea was it to get the punts out?' she asked.

'It was my idea,' said Li Wan hurriedly. 'It occurred to me
just now when we were getting things out of the storeroom
that you might perhaps feel like going on the water today.'

Grandmother Jia was about to make some comment when
Aunt Xue's arrival was announced and she rose up, together
with the rest of the company, to welcome her.

'Aren't you energetic today, Lady Jia!' said Aunt Xue
smilingly when all were seated once more. 'Here already!'

'We were just discussing what sort of fine to impose on late
arrivals,' said Grandmother Jia teasingly. 'We didn't have *you*
in mind, of course!'

A certain amount of good-humoured banter followed. In
the course of it Grandmother Jia chanced to notice that the
gauze in Dai-yu's windows was faded, and drew Lady Wang's
attention to it.

'This kind of gauze looks very well on a window when it's
new,' she said, 'but after a while it loses its greenness. Green
isn't a suitable colour for the windows here in any case. There
are no peach or apricot trees outside to make a contrast when
they are in flower, and there is already enough green in all
those bamboos. I seem to remember that we used to have four
or five different shades of window gauze somewhere or other.

You must look some out tomorrow for her and have this changed.'

'The other day when I had to open the silk-store,' said Xi-feng, 'I came across a lot of rose-coloured "cicada wing" gauze in a long wooden chest. It was a beautiful fresh colour and the material was beautifully soft and light. I don't think I've ever seen any quite like it before. I'd like to have taken a couple of lengths of it for facing quilts with. I'm sure it would make lovely quilts.'

'Pooh!' said Grandmother Jia scornfully. 'I thought you were supposed to be such an authority on materials – and you can't even name a gauze properly! You're not as clever as you thought, my girl! You'll have to watch your tongue a bit in future.'

Aunt Xue put in an extenuating word for her niece, while laughing with the rest at her discomfiture.

'However much of an authority she may be, I'm sure she would never presume to compete with *you*, Lady Jia. If she is wrong about the gauze, you must give her the benefit of your greater experience and put her right. I am sure the rest of us would like to know too.'

'As a matter of fact that gauze is a good deal older than any of you here,' said Grandmother Jia, 'so it is not very surprising that Feng mistook it for cicada wing. There *is* a certain resemblance, and cicada wing is what anyone would most likely take it to be who hadn't seen it before. The proper name for it, though, is "haze diaphene".'

'What a pretty name!' said Xi-feng. 'I must have seen several hundred different gauzes in my time, but I must confess I've never heard *that* name mentioned before.'

Grandmother Jia laughed.

'And what great age have *you* now reached, my dear, to be talking so freely about your vast experience? Haze diaphene used to come in four colours: "clear-sky blue", "russet green", "pine green" and "old rose". Hung up as bed-curtains or pasted in windows it looks from a distance like a coloured haze. That's why they called it "*haze* diaphene". The old rose kind is sometimes called "afterglow". You won't find fabric made as fine or as soft as that nowadays, not even among the gauzes made for the Imperial Household.'

'Never mind about Feng,' said Aunt Xue, '*I*'ve never heard about this kind of gauze before either.'

While they continued to talk about it, Xi-feng sent someone to fetch a piece from the storeroom.

'That's right, that's it!' said Grandmother Jia when it arrived. 'When we first had it, we used it only for covering windows with, but later on we began experimenting and found that it made very good quilts and bed-curtains as well. Get a few lengths of it out tomorrow. You can use the "old rose" kind to re-cover these windows with.'

Xi-feng promised to see to it. Meanwhile the others were examining the gauze and admiring its quality. Grannie Liu was particularly impressed, uttering a whole series of 'Holy Names' as she subjected it to close and careful scrutiny. 'I could never hope to get anything as good as this to make a *dress* with,' she said. 'It seems a terrible waste to use it on *windows*.'

'Actually it isn't much good for clothing,' said Grandmother Jia.

'What about this, then?' said Xi-feng, pulling out a flap of the quilted crimson gauze dress she was wearing underneath her jacket and holding it up for them to see.

'Yes, very fine,' said Grandmother Jia, examining it. 'Ah, yes, now there you are! *This* is a modern Imperial Household gauze; but you see it's still not as good as that one there.'

'Well, what do you make of that?' said Xi-feng. 'That one there is only an' 'Official Use" fabric, yet this one I'm wearing, which isn't as good quality, is "Imperial Household"!'

'Anyway, have another look tomorrow,' said Grandmother Jia. 'I think you'll find that besides the "old rose" pieces you saw in that chest, there's a lot of "clear-sky blue" somewhere as well. If there is, get it all out; give a length of it to our kinswoman here; I should like two lengths myself for a set of bed-hangings; and any left over can be matched with suitable lining-material and made up into waistcoats for the girls. There's no point in keeping it until it gets mildewed.'

Xi-feng, having first promised that she would do all these things, told the servant who had brought the sample to take it back to the storeroom.

'We're a bit cramped in here,' said Grandmother Jia. 'Let's move on to somewhere else now.'

'They say that "great families live in great houses",' said Grannie Liu, 'and truly, when I first went into Your Ladyship's apartment yesterday and saw those great chests and cupboards and tables and beds, the size of everything fairly took my breath away. That great wardrobe of yours is higher and wider than one of our rooms back home. I'm not surprised you keep a ladder in the back courtyard. When I first saw it, I thought to myself, "Now what can they need a ladder for? They don't ripen things on the roofs as we do, so it can't be for that." And then of course I realized: it must be for getting things out of the compartment on top of that wardrobe of yours, for you could never reach it else. And yet this place here, for all it's so much smaller, seems to me more perfect than your big one. The things here are all so pretty. I don't know what they are, some of them, but the more I look at them, the less I want to leave!'

'There are other pretty places besides this,' said Xi-feng. 'We're taking you to see them all.'

As they left the Naiad's House, they could make out, at some distance from where they stood, a number of people punting on the lake. Remarking that since the boats were already out they might just as well use them, Grandmother Jia conducted her little party in the general direction of Amaryllis Eyot and Flowery Harbour. Before they had reached the water's edge, however, a number of elderly women approached, each bearing one of those large summer food-boxes of the kind they make in Soochow, with tops and bottoms of varicoloured lacquer-work delicately patterned in needle-engraving of gold, and panels of gilded bamboo basket-work in their sides. Seeing them approach, Xi-feng asked Lady Wang where she wanted lunch to be laid.

'Ask Grandmother,' said Lady Wang. 'Wherever *she* wants it, of course.'

Grandmother Jia, who had been moving on, now turned back to tell them.

'Your Cousin Tan's would be a nice place to have it. You go on ahead and lay it there, and the rest of us will follow by boat.'

Xi-feng, accompanied by Li Wan, Tan-chun, Faithful and Amber, led the women with the lunch-boxes by a short cut to the Autumn Studio. They put out a couple of tables there in the Paulownia Room.

'We're often hearing how the gentlemen at their parties outside have a buffoon to provide them with their laughs,' said Faithful while they were getting ready. 'Today *we*'ve got a buffoon of our own – a female one.'

Li Wan, being a good, simple soul, did not understand what she meant; but Xi-feng knew immediately that she was referring to Grannie Liu and gleefully agreeing that they should have some laughs at the old woman's expense, at once began plotting something with Faithful.

'You two are *awful*!' Li Wan protested laughingly. 'Anyone would think you were a couple of mischievous children. And what will Lady Jia say?'

'Don't worry, Mrs Zhu!' said Faithful. 'You won't be involved in this one little bit. I promise to keep you out of it.'

Grandmother Jia now arrived with the others, the company sat down informally, and maids went round and served everyone with tea. When they had all finished their tea, Xi-feng came in carrying a bundle of silver-tipped and silver-ornamented ebony chopsticks wrapped in a West Ocean linen napkin, and proceeded to lay the places.

'Put that little yellow cedar-wood table next to my place so that Mrs Liu can sit by me,' said Grandmother Jia.

As the maids hastened to comply, Xi-feng tipped a wink at Faithful, who took the opportunity presented by this diversion to draw Grannie Liu aside and quietly brief her on the decorums to be observed by anyone eating with the family.

'It's part of the rules of this household,' she told the old woman in conclusion. 'If you don't do it properly, they will laugh at you.'

The places being now all laid, the company sat down to table, with the exception of Aunt Xue, who had eaten already and continued sitting where she was, drinking tea. Bao-yu, Xiang-yun, Dai-yu and Bao-chai sat at one of the two large tables with Grandmother Jia at their head, and Ying-chun, Tan-chun and Xi-chun sat at the other one, presided over by Lady Wang. Grannie Liu had a little table of her own next to Grandmother Jia.

Normally when Grandmother Jia took her meals it was the junior maids who stood with spittoons, fly-whisks and napkins in their hands behind the chairs. Faithful had long since graduated from such menial duties. On this occasion, however, she borrowed a fly-whisk from one of the younger girls and did some whisking herself. This was a signal for the other maids, who knew that something was afoot, to melt discreetly away, leaving the stage clear for Faithful. Fly-whisk in hand, Faithful took up a position on her own and darted a questioning glance at her victim.

'All right, Miss, don't worry!' said Grannie Liu, and having settled herself in her place, picked up her chopsticks. She found them extremely heavy and unwieldy. They were a pair of old-fashioned, square-handled ivory ones inlaid with gold, which Xi-feng and Faithful had planted on her in furtherance of their plan.

'What's this you've given me?' said Grannie Liu. 'A pair of tongs? These are heavier than one of our iron shovels. I shall never be able to manage with these.'

The others all laughed.

A woman-servant now entered carrying one of the luncheon-boxes and stood in the middle of the room holding it while a maid removed the lid. There were two dishes inside. Li Wan took out one of them and set it down on Grandmother Jia's table. The second, a bowl of pigeon's eggs (deliberately chosen for their mirth-provoking possibilities) was taken out by Xi-feng and set down in front of Grannie Liu.

'Please!' said Grandmother Jia, waving her chopsticks at the food as a polite indication that they should begin. At once Grannie Liu leaped to her feet and, in ringing tones, recited the following grace:

> 'My name it is Liu,
> I'm a trencherman true;
> I can eat a whole sow
> With her little pigs too.'

Having concluded, she puffed out both her cheeks and stared in front of her with an expression of great determination.

There was a moment of awestruck silence; then, as it dawned on them that they really had heard what they thought they had heard, the whole company, both masters and servants, burst out into roars of laughter.

Shi Xiang-yun, unable to contain herself, spat out a whole mouthful of rice.

Lin Dai-yu, made breathless by laughter, collapsed on the table, uttering weak 'Aiyos'.

Bao-yu rolled over, convulsed, on to his grandmother's bosom.

Grandmother Jia, exclaiming helplessly 'Oh, my heart!' 'Oh, my child!', clung tightly to her heaving grandson.

Lady Wang pointed an accusing finger at Xi-feng, but laughter had deprived her of speech.

Aunt Xue exploded a mouthful of tea over Tan-chun's skirt.

Tan-chun planted a bowlful of rice on the person of Ying-chun.

Xi-chun got up from the table and going over to her nurse, took her by the hand and asked her to massage her stomach.

The servants were all doubled up. Some had to go outside where they could squat down and laugh with abandon. Those who could control themselves sufficiently helped the casualties to mop up or change their clothes.

Only Xi-feng and Faithful remained straight-faced throughout this outburst, politely urging Grannie Liu to begin. Mani-

pulating the unwieldy chopsticks with considerable difficulty,
the old woman prepared to do so.

'Even your hens here are special,' she remarked. 'Such
pretty little eggs they lay! I must see if I can't get one of these
under me belt!'

Under the impact of these remarks the company's composure, which it had only just recovered, once more broke
down. Grandmother Jia, abandoning any attempt at self-
control, was now actually weeping with laughter. Amber, who
feared a seizure, pounded her energetically on the back.

'That wicked devil Feng is behind this,' said Grandmother
Jia. 'Don't believe a thing she tells you!'

'They cost a silver tael apiece,' said Xi-feng, as Grannie
Liu continued to praise the diminutive 'hen's' eggs. 'You
should eat them quickly, while they're still hot. They won't
be so nice when they're cold.'

Grannie Liu obediently held out her chopsticks and tried
to take hold of one, but the egg eluded her. After chasing it
several times round the inside of the bowl, she did at last suc-
ceed in getting a grip on it. But as she craned forward with
open mouth to reach it, it slipped through the chopsticks and
rolled on to the floor. At once she laid down the chopsticks,
and would have gone down on hands and knees to pick it up,
but before she could do so one of the servants had retrieved
it and carried it off for disposal.

'That's a tael of silver gone,' Grannie Liu said regretfully,
'and we didn't even hear the clink!'

The others had by now lost all interest in eating, absorbed
by the entertaining antics of their guest.

'Who got those chopsticks out?' said Grandmother Jia.
'They're not meant for occasions like this; they're for using
at formal banquets. Whoever it was, I expect it was that
wicked Feng who put them up to it. Take them away at once
and get her another pair!'

The servants had in point of fact had nothing to do with
the chryselephantine chopsticks, which had been smuggled in
at the last moment by Faithful and Xi-feng; nevertheless, on
hearing the order, they obediently came forward and replaced

them with a silver and ebony pair like those that had been provided for the rest.

'Out goes gold and in comes silver!' said Grannie Liu. 'But when all's said and done, our wooden ones at home are handier.'

'If there's any poison in what you are eating,' said Xi-feng, 'the silver will tell you by changing colour.'

'If this food is poisoned,' said Grannie Liu, 'then what we eat at home must be pure arsenic. Anyway, I intend to eat it all, come what may!'

Delighted to have found someone who, besides being so amusing, had so evident a relish for her food, Grandmother Jia insisted on making all her own portion over to Grannie Liu and ordered one of the older women to go round with a pair of chopsticks and a bowl and make a selection from all the dishes to give to little Ban-er.

Presently, when they had finished eating, Grandmother Jia and the others moved into Tan-chun's bedroom for a chat, while in the Paulownia Room the servants cleared away the remains of the meal and hastily relaid a table for Li Wan and Xi-feng. Grannie Liu, who had lingered behind, observed them sitting down at opposite sides of it to begin their meal. She was greatly impressed by this glimpse of the upper-class etiquette which requires young married women to eat on their own when the rest have finished.

'What I like best of all here,' she said, 'is your way of doing things. I'm not surprised they say that "good breeding is to be found in great houses".'

The compliment was sincerely meant, but Xi-feng understood it in a different sense.

'I do hope we haven't hurt your feelings,' she said. 'It was only a joke, you know.'

The words were scarcely out of her mouth when Faithful came hurrying in.

'Please don't be offended, Mrs Liu. I've come in to apologize.'

'Bless you, I'm not offended!' said Grannie Liu. 'We were only cheering up Her Ladyship, dear old soul. What should I be offended for? I knew when you told me to say those things it was only for a laugh. If I'd felt offended, I should never have said them.'

A chastened Faithful turned angrily on the other servants.

'Come on! why aren't you pouring Mrs Liu some tea?'

'That's all right,' said Grannie Liu hurriedly. 'I've had some already. I drank the tea that the young woman handed to me a while ago. You get on with your own lunch, Miss. Don't mind me!'

Xi-feng took Faithful by the hand.

'Yes, eat now with us. It'll keep you out of mischief.'

Faithful sat down and one of the old women laid another bowl for her and another pair of chopsticks. When the three young women had finished, Grannie Liu, who had been watching them, remarked on how little they had eaten.

'None of you here seems to eat more than a bite or two,' she said. 'It's a marvel to me you're not famished. No wonder you all look as if the wind could blow you over!'

'There *is* a lot left over today,' Faithful commented. 'Where are all the others?' she asked the old serving-woman.

'They're still here in waiting, Miss,' said the old woman. 'They're not off duty yet. We can give it to them, if you like, before they go.'

'They'll never finish all this lot,' said Faithful. 'Pick out a couple of bowlfuls and take them to Patience in Mrs Lian's room.'

'No need,' said Xi-feng. 'She's had her lunch already.'

'If she can't eat it herself, she can give it to the cat,' said Faithful.

The old woman put the contents of two of the dishes into a box and carried it off to give Patience.

'Where's Candida?' said Faithful.

'She's in there eating with the rest,' said Li Wan. 'What do you want her for?'

'It's all right,' said Faithful. 'Nothing.'

'Aroma isn't here,' said Xi-feng. 'Why don't you send *her* a couple of dishes?'

Faithful gave orders for this to be done. She inquired of the remaining old women whether the boxes for the drinking party were ready yet.

'I think they'll be a while yet,' said one of them.

'Hurry them up a bit, will you?' said Faithful, and the old woman went off to do her bidding.

The young women, accompanied by Grannie Liu, now went into Tan-chun's room, where Grandmother Jia and the others were chatting and laughing together.

This room, a three-frame apartment which Tan-chun, who loved spaciousness, had left undivided, had in the midst of it a large rosewood table with a Yunnanese marble top piled high with specimen-books of calligraphy and littered with several dozen miscellaneous ink-stones and a small forest of writing-brushes standing in brush-holders and brush-stands of every conceivable shape and size. On one side of the table was a bucket-sized 'pincushion' flower-vase of Ru ware stuck all over with snow-white pompom chrysanthemums. On the west wall of the room hung a 'Landscape in Mist and Rain' by Mi Fei, flanked by a pair of scrolls bearing a couplet written by the Tang calligrapher Yan Zhen-qing:

My heart has discovered true ease amidst the clouds and mists
   of the mountains;
My life has gained a fierce freedom from the rocks and torrents
   of the fells.

Against the wall beneath was a long, high table. On it, to-wards the left, stood a large Northern Song porcelain dish heaped with those ornamental citrus fruits they call 'Buddha's hands', whose brilliant yellow contrasted agreeably with the greenish blue of the glaze. To the right a white jade chime in the form of a two-headed fish hung in a varnished wooden frame to whose side a tiny hammer was attached. Ban-er, whom growing familiarity was making bolder, was with diffi-culty restrained from unfastening the hammer and striking the fish with it. He then said that he wanted one of the 'yellow things' to eat, and Tan-chun selected a Buddha's hand from the dish and gave it to him.

'There you are,' she said, 'but it's only to play with. It isn't good to eat.'

On the opposite side of the room was a large four-poster bed whose silk gauze hangings had a pattern of bright green plants and insects in reversible embroidery. Ban-er ran over to it and began identifying the insects:

'That's a cricket. That's a grasshopper . . .'

Grannie Liu dealt him a hefty slap:

'Little varmint! Who said you could go running around putting your dirty hands on everything? Just because you've been allowed in to have a look, it doesn't mean you have to start getting above yourself.'

The blow had been hard enough to make him cry, and it took the combined efforts of the others present to comfort him.

Meanwhile Grandmother Jia had been looking through the gauze-covered windows into the courtyard behind.

'Those paulownias by the verandah eaves are still very fine,' she remarked. 'It's a pity they've begun losing their leaves.'

A little gust of wind blew across the courtyard as she spoke, bearing on it a faint strain of music from outside.

'That must be a wedding,' she said. 'I didn't realize we were so near to the street here.'

'You could never hear the street from *here*, Mother,' said Lady Wang, laughing. 'Those are our twelve little actresses rehearsing.'

'If they're going to be playing anyway,' said Grandmother Jia, 'we may as well have them to play in here. It will be entertainment for *us* and it will make an outing of sorts for *them*.'

Xi-feng at once ordered the troupe to be summoned, and made hurried arrangements for a long table to be brought in, that the actresses could sit down to perform at, and covered with a red rug.

'Much better put them in Xi-chun's water pavilion,' said Grandmother Jia. 'The music will sound even better coming across the water. Later on when we take our wine we can sit in the downstairs of the Painted Chamber. It's nice and open there and close enough to the pavilion for listening to the music from.'

Everyone agreed that this would be a good idea.

Grandmother Jia now turned with a smile to Aunt Xue.

'I think we'd better be on our way now. These young people don't much like having visitors, you know. They are terrified of getting their rooms dirty. We mustn't be tactless and overstay our welcome. I think we'd better take another little turn in the boats now, and then it will be just about time to go and have our drinks.'

'How unfair!' said Tan-chun laughing. 'When I *ask* you or Mother or Aunt Xue to come here, you never do.'

'Oh, my little Tan is all right,' said Grandmother Jia. 'It's those two Yus who are so detestable. We shall go and brawl in *their* rooms later on when we are drunk!'

The others (including the detestable Yus) all laughed.

Emerging in a single group from the Autumn Studio, they arrived after a short walk at Duckweed Island, where their specially imported Soochow boatwomen were waiting with two elegantly decorated punts. Grandmother Jia, Lady Wang, Aunt Xue, Grannie Liu, Faithful and Silver were handed one by one aboard the first one. They were joined a little later by Li Wan, and finally by Xi-feng, who stood in the bows and said she was going to punt.

'Feng!' Grandmother Jia called nervously from inside the cabin. 'It's too dangerous to fool about. It isn't like the open river here, but it's still quite deep. Come in here with us!'

'It's all right, Grannie! Don't be nervous!' said Xi-feng, laughing, as she shoved off from the bank. But the punt, being somewhat overloaded, was hard to manage, so that by the time they were in midstream she was already in difficulties and had to hand the pole over to one of the boatwomen and sit down rather abruptly on her haunches.

When their elders were safely away, Bao-yu and the six girls got into the second punt and were poled along in the wake of the first one. The maids and older women proceeded in the same direction on foot along the shore.

'These raggedy-looking lotus-leaves everywhere are rather ugly,' said Bao-yu. 'I can't think why they haven't been cleared away.'

'Now when *could* they have been?' said Bao-chai. 'With parties being held here practically every day this autumn, the Garden has never been free long enough.'

'I can't abide the poems of Li Shang-yin,' said Dai-yu, 'but there is just one line of his that I am rather fond of:

Leaves but dead lotus-leaves for the rain to play on.

Trust you *not* to "leave the dead lotus-leaves"!'

'It *is* a good line, I agree,' said Bao-yu. 'We'll tell them that in future they are *not* to remove them.'

They were drifting into Flowery Harbour now, and the dank chill of its creeper-hung grotto seemed to penetrate their bones. Dead reeds and dying caltrop-leaves added to the autumnal melancholy of the scene. A clean, airy-looking building was visible at some distance beyond the bank above.

'Isn't that Bao-chai's place?' said Grandmother Jia.

On being told that it was, she asked the women to moor the boats there, and having disembarked, ascended from the landing-stage by a flight of cloud-shaped stone steps and proceeded, with the rest of the party, to the gateway of Allspice Court.

A delectable fragrance assailed their nostrils as they entered. Outside the house the leaves of the mysterious, unnamable creepers had turned an even intenser green in the colder weather, and where before there had been flowers, there now hung trusses of the most beautiful coral-red berries. Indoors, however, it was stark and bare. The only decoration in Bao-chai's room was a vase of the cheaper kind of Ding ware on the table, with a few chrysanthemums in it. Apart from the flowers there were only a few books and some tea-things on the table. The bed-hangings were of black gauze, and the quilts and covers were of the same forbidding plainness as the hangings.

'This child is really *too* self-effacing!' Grandmother Jia muttered, evidently shocked by what she saw. The tone in which she addressed Bao-chai was a somewhat reproachful one: 'If you haven't any things of your own, why ever didn't you ask your Aunt Wang for some? I'm afraid I never thought about it before. Of course. I realize now. You must have left all your stuff behind in Nanking.'

She at once ordered Faithful to supply Bao-chai with some ornaments, and then turned, with some asperity, on Xi-feng.

'Really, Feng! I do think it *rather* stingy of you! Couldn't you have spared your cousin a few *knick-knacks*?'

Lady Wang and Xi-feng both laughed.

'She said herself that she didn't want any. We *gave* her some things, but she sent them all back again.'

Aunt Xue corroborated this.

'She was just the same in Nanking, Lady Jia. She's never cared much for that sort of thing.'

Grandmother Jia shook her head.

'That will never do. It saves trouble, no doubt, to keep one's room so bare. But what would any of our relations think if they were to come here and see this? Besides, it isn't natural for a young girl to be so austere. If *girls* are to live so austerely, what sort of a stable ought an old woman like me to live in? Think of the descriptions of young ladies' boudoirs you find in plays and romances – such exquisite refinement of luxury! I'm not exactly suggesting that you should emulate *them* – but you shouldn't fall *too* far short, all the same. After all, when the things are there for the asking, it seems silly not to use them. Use them sparingly, by all means, if your tastes are on the austere side; but don't dispense with them altogether! I've always had rather a flair for decorating interiors. I don't exercise it much nowadays, because I'm too old; but I think the girls have inherited a little of it from me. The thing one always has to be on one's guard against is bad taste – which generally means no more than arranging good things in a bad way. I don't think any of my girls has bad taste. Now why don't you let me decorate this room for you? I promise you it shall look both dignified and austere. There are still a few things tucked away in my dowry that Bao-yu doesn't know about. (I wouldn't let *him* see them, or they'd have disappeared long ago!).'

She called Faithful to her and instructed her what to bring.

'I want you to fetch that *bonseki* and the little screen and the little tripod of smoky agate. Those three things arranged on the table here will be enough. There's also a set of white satin hangings hand-painted in black ink. I'd like you to get them too and put them up in place of these bed-curtains.'

'Yes, madam,' said Faithful. 'But these things are all stored in the attic over the east wing and I'm not sure which chests they're in, so it will take me quite a while to find them. Can't I leave it until tomorrow?'

'Tomorrow or the day after tomorrow is immaterial,' said Grandmother Jia, 'as long as it gets done.'

After sitting for a while longer in Bao-chai's room, they got up and again moved on to the covered area underneath the Painted Chamber. Élégante and the other little actresses came forward to make their curtseys and to inquire what pieces they should play.

'Choose a few of the ones you are most familiar with,' said Grandmother Jia, and the little actresses went off to the Lotus Pavilion. No further mention of them is made in this part of our narrative.

Supervised by Xi-feng, the servants had by now completed the seating arrangements for the drinking-party. Two wooden couches covered with woven grass mats and embroidered cushions had been placed side by side at the head. Each had a pair of carved lacquer tables in front of it. On one of each pair there was an incense set – a miniature metal vase, a miniature cassolette and a miniature tripod, all for burning different kinds of incense in – on the other was a large lacquer box. These two couches with a pair of tables each were for Grandmother Jia and Aunt Xue.

Of the places ranged below them only one, Lady Wang's, had a couch and two tables; all the rest had one table and a chair. On the east side, nearest to Grandmother Jia, sat Grannie Liu with Lady Wang below her; on the west side Xiang-yun had been laid first, nearest to Aunt Xue, then Bao-chai, then Dai-yu, then Ying-chun, then Tan-chun, then Xi-chun, with Bao-yu in the very last place of all. A table and chairs had been laid for Li Wan and Xi-feng between the inner and outer mosquito screens which protected those inside the room from the insects of the lake.

The little lacquer tables were of many different shapes – some four-lobed like a begonia leaf, some five-lobed like plum-flowers, some shaped like multi-petalled sunflowers, some like lotus leaves, some square, some round – and the lacquer boxes were designed to match the shapes of the tables. Everyone had his own nielloed silver 'self-service' wine kettle and a little polychrome cloisonné winecup.

'Well now,' said Grandmother Jia when they were all seated, 'let's have a cup or two to warm up on, and after that I think it would be more fun if we played a drinking game.'

'I am sure you know lots of good ones,' said Aunt Xue, 'but what about the rest of us? I am afraid this is just a trick to make us all drunk. We might just as well drink the extra cups now, since we're bound to lose anyway, and forget about the game!'

'Come, Mrs Xue, you're being excessively modest all of a sudden!' said Grandmother Jia. 'But perhaps you think I'm too *old* for this sort of thing?'

'No, no, no. And I'm *not* being modest, either,' said Aunt Xue, laughing. 'I am afraid of not being able to give the answers and making a fool of myself.'

'Even if we can't give the answers,' said Lady Wang, 'it only means drinking a few more cups of wine. And if we get drunk, we can go to bed. No one is going to laugh at *us*, I hope!'

Aunt Xue smiled and nodded.

'Very well, I shall do as I am told then. But I think Lady Jia ought to drink a cup first, as proposer of the game.'

'Of course,' said Grandmother Jia, and drained off a cup forthwith.

Xi-feng stepped forward into their midst to make a proposal:

'If you are going to play a drinking game, may I suggest that you have Faithful as your M.C.?'

The others, knowing that when Grandmother Jia played drinking games it was generally Faithful who helped her out, agreed readily to this proposal, whereupon Xi-feng went to fetch Faithful and drew her into their midst.

'If Faithful is going to be our M.C.,' said Lady Wang, 'we can't possibly have her standing up all the time.' She turned to one of the little maids behind her: 'Put a chair for her over there, will you, where Mrs Zhu and Mrs Lian are sitting.'

When the chair had been brought, Faithful, offering polite resistance, allowed herself to be propelled towards it, and having first apologized for the liberty of doing so, sat down. At once she established her authority by drinking a bumper-cup.

'Right,' she said. 'The rules of drinking are as strict as the rules of war. Now that you've made me your M.C., any of you who doesn't do exactly as I say, no matter who it is, has to pay a forfeit.'

'Agreed, agreed,' said the others. 'Hurry up and tell us what the game is.'

Before she could do so, Grannie Liu, waving her hand in protest, got up and began to go.

' 'Tisn't right to make sport of folks like this. I'm going home!'

'No, no, we can't have that!' said the others, laughing.

'Back to the chair with her!' Faithful shouted to the younger maids. They complied gleefully, seizing the old woman on either side and marching her back to her seat.

'Let me off this game!' she pleaded, as they forced her into it; but Faithful was adamant.

'Another word from you,' she said, 'and you'll be made to drink a whole kettleful as a punishment.'

Grannie Liu's protests then ceased.

'What I'm going to do,' said Faithful, 'is to call threesomes with the dominoes, starting from Her Old Ladyship, going round in an anti-clockwise direction, and ending up with Mrs

Liu. First I shall make a separate call for each of the three dominoes and after that I shall make a call for the whole threesome, so you'll get four calls each. Every time I call, you've got to answer with something that rhymes and that has some connection with the call. It can be something from a poem or song or ballad, or it can be a proverb or some well-known expression – anything you like as long as there is a connection and it rhymes.'

'Good!' said the others approvingly. 'That's a good game. Let's have a call then.'

'Right,' said Faithful. 'Here comes the first one.' She laid down a double six. 'On my left the bright blue sky.'[1]

'The Lord looks down from heaven on high,' said Grandmother Jia.

'Bravo!' said the others.

The second domino was a five-six.

'Five and six together meet,' said Faithful.

'By Six Bay Bridge the flowers smell sweet.'

'Leaves six and ace upon the right.'

'The red sun in the sky so bright,' said Grandmother Jia.

'Altogether that makes: "A shock-headed devil with hair like tow",' said Faithful.

'The devil shouts, "Zhong Kui, let me go!",' said Grandmother Jia.

Amidst laughter, and applause for the successful completion of her turn, she picked up and drained her winecup.

'Here comes the next one,' said Faithful, laying down a double five. 'On my left all the fives I find.'

'Plum-blossoms dancing in the wind,' said Aunt Xue.

'On my right all the fives again,' said Faithful.

'Plum-blossoms in the tenth month's rain,' said Aunt Xue.

'Between them, two and five make seven.'

'On Seventh Night the lovers meet in heaven.'

'Together that gives: "The Second Prince plays in the Five Holy Hills".'

'The immortals dwell far off from mortal ills.'

Again there was applause, and Aunt Xue drank her wine.

1. See Appendix II, p. 586.

'Next threesome coming up,' said Faithful. 'All the aces, one and one.'

'Two lamps for earth, the moon and sun,' said Xiang-yun.

'On my right once more aces all.'

'And flowers to earth in silence fall,' said Xiang-yun.

'Between them, ace again with four.'

'Apricot trees make the sun's red-petalled floor,' said Xiang-yun.

'Together that makes nine ripe cherries.'

'Winged thieves have stripped the Emperor's trees of berries,' said Xiang-yun, and drank her wine.

'A pair on the left then, three and three,' said Faithful.

'Swallows in pairs round the old roof-tree,' said Bao-chai.

'A pair of threes upon the right,' said Faithful.

'Green duckweed-trails on the water bright.'

'A three and six between them lie.'

'Three peaks upon the rim of sky,' said Bao-chai.

'Together that gives: "The lone boat tied with an iron chain",' said Faithful.

'The waves on every hand and the heart's pain,' said Bao-chai, and drank what remained in her winecup.

'Sky on the left, the good fresh air,' said Faithful, putting down a double six.

'Bright air and brilliant morn feed my despair,' said Dai-yu.

Bao-chai, recognizing the quotation, turned and stared; but Dai-yu was too intent on keeping her end up to have noticed.

'A four and a six, the Painted Screen,' said Faithful.

'No Reddie at the window seen,' said Dai-yu, desperately dredging up a line this time from *The Western Chamber* to meet the emergency.

'A two and a six, four twos make eight.'

'In twos walk backwards from the Hall of State,' said Dai-yu, on safer ground with a line from Du Fu.

'Together makes: "A basket for the flowers you pick",' said Faithful.

'A basket of peonies slung from his stick,' said Dai-yu concluded, and took a sip of her wine.

'Four and five, the Flowery Nine,' said Faithful.

'The flowering peach-tree drenched with rain,' said Ying-chun.

'Forfeit! Forfeit!' said the others, laughing. 'It doesn't rhyme; and besides, the words don't fit.'

Ying-chun laughed and sipped her wine. As a matter of fact her failure was intentional. Eager for more laughs, Xi-feng and Faithful had secretly intimated to the four remaining cousins that they should give the wrong answers on purpose, in order to come the more quickly to Grannie Liu. Accordingly Tan-chun, Xi-chun and Bao-yu, all deliberately fell down on their first calls as well, leaving only Lady Wang to dispose of, which Faithful accomplished by the simple expedient of supplying the answers for her herself. It was now Grannie Liu's turn.

'We often play a game like this ourselves back home when we get together of an evening,' said Grannie Liu, 'only the way we do it, it doesn't sound so pretty as this. Howsomever. I don't mind having a try.'

'It's easy, really,' said the others. 'Don't worry about what it sounds like. Just say what comes naturally.'

Faithful began to lay.

'A pair of fours on the left, the Man.'

Grannie Liu was a good long while puzzling over this. Finally she said.

'Is it a farmer?'

The others roared with laughter.

'That's all right,' said Grandmother Jia reassuringly. 'That answer will do very well.'

'You young people shouldn't laugh at me,' said Grannie Liu to the others. 'I'm a countrywoman born and I can't help my country talk.'

'Green three, red four, contrasting colours,' called Faithful.

'The fire burns up the caterpillars,' said Grannie Liu.

'Why, so it might,' said the others. 'Stick to your "country talk", Grannie, you're doing fine!'

'Red four on the right and the ace is red,' said Faithful.

'A turnip and a garlic-head.'

More laughter.

' "The Flower" those three together show,' said Faithful.

'This flower will to a pumpkin grow,' said the flower-bedecked ancient, gesturing with her hands to demonstrate the size of the imagined pumpkin.

The following chapter will show how the party progressed.

CHAPTER 41

*Jia Bao-yu tastes some superior tea at Green Bower Hermitage
And Grannie Liu samples the sleeping accommodation at
Green Delights*

'THIS flower will to a pumpkin grow.'

As Grannie Liu of the flower-studded hair said this, gesturing with her hands to suggest the size of the full-grown pumpkin, a shout of laughter rose from all those present.

She drank the 'pass' cup.

'To be truthful,' she said, aiming for another laugh, 'I'm but a clumsy body at the best of times, and having drunk so much, I'm scared of breaking this pretty cup you've given me. You should have given me a wooden one; then if I dropped it, it wouldn't matter.'

The others laughed; but Xi-feng pretended to take her seriously:

'If you really want a wooden cup to drink out of, I can find you one. But I'd better warn you. The wooden ones aren't like these porcelain ones; they come in sets of different sizes, and if we get them out for you, you'll have to drink out of every one in the set.'

Grannie Liu calculated.

'I was only joking,' she thought. 'I didn't think they'd *really* have any. When I've dined with the gentry back home, I've seen many a gold and silver cup in their houses, but never a wooden one. I expect these will be wooden bowls that the children use. It's a trick to make me drink a lot. Well, never mind. This stuff's not much more than sugared water anyway. It can do me no harm if I drink a bit extra.'

Having so reflected, she made reply:

'Very well. Let's see them first though.'

'Go to the inner room of the front apartment,' Xi-feng told Felicity, 'and fetch me that set of ten winecups on the bookcase – the ones carved out of bamboo root.'

But before Felicity could go on her errand, Faithful made a counter-proposal:

'I know that set of yours: they're not very big cups, and in any case, you promised her wooden ones and yours are only made of bamboo. Much better give her ten boxwood ones and make her drink out of *them*.'

'All right,' said Xi-feng. 'Better still.' So Faithful sent someone to fetch them.

The sight of these cups when they arrived both alarmed and delighted Grannie Liu. What alarmed her was their size. The largest was as big as a small hand-basin and even the smallest one was twice as big as the cup she held in her hand. What delighted her was the consummate artistry of the carving. On each of the ten cups, in smaller and smaller replicas, was the same landscape with little trees and human figures in it and even some lines of minute 'grass character' writing and a tiny carved representation of an artist's seal.

'I'll take the smallest one,' she said hurriedly.

'Oh no!' said Xi-feng, smiling. 'These cups have never been used before, because up to now we've never found anyone with a big enough capacity to drink from them. Now that you've asked for them and we've been to the trouble of getting them out for you, we must insist on your drinking from every one of them.'

'I couldn't,' said Grannie Liu in a panic. 'Please, Mrs Lian, don't make me!'

Grandmother Jia, Aunt Xue and Lady Wang all realized that a person of Grannie Liu's advanced years could not possibly be expected to imbibe so huge a quantity of liquor without the direst consequences, and laughingly pleaded for her.

'Come now, a joke is a joke. You mustn't make her drink too much. Let her just drink from the largest one.'

'Holy name!' said Grannie Liu. 'Can't I just drink from the smallest one, like I said? I can take the largest one home with me and drink it up by degrees.'

The others laughed. Faithful, obliged to relent, ordered one of the larger, but not the largest cup to be filled, and Grannie Liu, holding it in both her hands, began to drink.

'Drink it slowly, now,' Grandmother Jia and Aunt Xue counselled her. 'Don't make yourself choke.'

Aunt Xue told Xi-feng to offer the old woman something to eat with her bowlful.

'What would you like, Grannie?' said Xi-feng. 'Just name it and I'll feed you some.'

'*I* don't know the names of any of these dishes,' said Grannie Liu. 'Anything you like. They all taste good to me.'

'Give her some of the dried aubergine,' said Grandmother Jia.

Xi-feng collected some between her chopsticks and held it up to Grannie Liu's mouth.

'There. I expect at home you eat aubergines every day. Try some of ours and see what you think of it.'

'You're having me on,' said Grannie Liu, when she had eaten the proffered mouthful. 'No aubergine ever had a flavour like that. If it did, we'd give up growing other crops and grow nothing but aubergines!'

'It really is aubergine,' the others laughingly assured her. 'This time we're *not* having you on.'

'Really?' said Grannie Liu in some surprise. 'Well, I couldn't have had my mind on it properly while I was eating it. Give me a bit more, Mrs Lian, and this time I'll chew it more carefully.'

Xi-feng took up some more from the dish in her chopsticks and popped it into Grannie Liu's mouth. After prolonged, reflective mastication Grannie Liu agreed that there was indeed a slight hint of aubergine in the flavour.

'But I still say this isn't really like aubergine,' she said. 'Tell me the recipe, so that I can make it for myself.'

'It's simple,' said Xi-feng. 'You pick the aubergines in the fourth or fifth month when they're just ripe, skin them, remove the pulp and pips and cut into thread-fine strips which you dry in the sun. Then you take the stock from one whole fat boiling-fowl, put the dried aubergine-strips into a steamer and steam them over the chicken stock until it's nearly all boiled away. Then you take them out and dry them in the sun again. You do that, steaming and drying, steaming and drying by turns, altogether nine times. And it has to be dried until it's quite brittle. Then you store in a tightly-sealed jar, and when you want to eat some, you take out about a saucerful and mix it with fried slivers of chicken leg-meat before serving.'

Xi-feng's 'simple recipe' caused Grannie Liu to stick her tongue out and shake her head in wonderment.

'Lord Buddha!' she exclaimed. 'That's ten chicken gone into the making of it. No wonder it tastes so good!'

And having laughed a while over the recipe, she applied herself once more to the wine and slowly drank it down. She continued to toy with the cup after she had finished drinking, as though loth to put it down.

'I do believe you haven't had enough,' said Xi-feng. 'Have another cupful.'

'Gracious goodness, that would be the death of me!' said Grannie Liu. 'No, I was just admiring the carving on it. Beautiful. How could they do it so fine?'

'Now that you've finished drinking from it,' said Faithful, 'why not tell us what wood it's made of?'

'Ah now, that question doesn't surprise me,' said Grannie Liu. 'You young ladies living in the lap of luxury wouldn't know much about wood; but people like us that live all our lives with the woods for neighbours, that lie on wood when we're tired and sit on it when we're weary and even have to eat it sometimes in years of famine: seeing it and hearing it and talking about it every day of our lives, we naturally get to know its different qualities and can tell the genuine from the imitation. Well now, let me see.'

She turned the cup round a good while in her hands and contemplated it with great attention before pronouncing:

'A household like yours wouldn't have anything cheap in it,' she said, 'so anything wooden you've got would be made from a wood that's not very easy to come by. And this is a heavy wood, so it's definitely not willow. I should say, without much doubt, this is red pine.'

The loud laughter which greeted this pronouncement was interrupted by the arrival of an old woman who reported to Grandmother Jia that the young actresses were in the Lotus

Pavilion awaiting instructions. Were they to perform now, or should they go on waiting a little longer?

'Bless me! I had completely forgotten about them,' said Grandmother Jia. 'Yes, tell them to begin straight away.'

The old woman departed, and presently, in the cold, clear air of autumn, the ululation of flutes rising above a drone of pipes and organs came stealing through the trees and across the water, ravishing the hearts and minds of those who heard it.

Bao-yu, the first to be affected, seized his wine-kettle, poured himself a cupful of wine, and drained it in a single gulp. He then poured himself a second cup; but just as he was about to drink it, he noticed that his mother had evidently been affected in the same way, for she was just at that moment giving orders to a servant to fetch her a supply of freshly-heated wine. At once he crossed over to where she was sitting and held his cup to her mouth for her to drink from.

Soon the newly-heated wine arrived and Bao-yu went back to his seat. Lady Wang rose from hers and picked up the wine-kettle that had just been brought, intending to pour some for Grandmother Jia. This was a signal for the others present, including Aunt Xue, to rise from their seats as well; but Grandmother Jia hurriedly gave orders for Li Wan and Xi-feng to take over.

'Let your Aunt sit down, so that the others can be at their ease,' she said to Xi-feng, whereupon Lady Wang relinquished the wine-kettle and went back to her seat.

'We're having such fun today,' said Grandmother Jia when Xi-feng had poured for her. '*All* of you must drink!'

She raised her cup to Aunt Xue, then, reaching beyond her, to Xiang-yun and Bao-chai.

'Come on, you two! You must have a cup too. And your Cousin Lin – we're not letting *her* off. I know she can't drink very much, but today is an exception.'

She drained her cup, and Xiang-yun, Bao-chai and Dai-yu drank something from theirs.

Grannie Liu, meanwhile, who had seldom before heard such fine music and was more than a little drunk, was showing

her appreciation of it with vigorous movements of hands and
feet. Bao-yu, catching sight of her, slipped from his seat to
whisper in Dai-yu's ear.

'Look at the old grannie!'

'It reminds me of the passage in the *History Classic* about
the animals dancing to the music of Shun,' said Dai-yu. 'Only
in this case it's just one old cow!'

The other girls, overhearing this, all laughed.

After a little while the music stopped and Aunt Xue suggested that as everyone appeared to have had about as much to
drink as was good for them, perhaps it would be a good idea
to break up and walk around for a bit. At this Grandmother
Jia, who was herself beginning to feel like some exercise, rose
to her feet. The others rose too and followed her outside.

Anxious to keep Grannie Liu with her as a source of diversion, Grandmother Jia took her by the hand to walk with her
among the trees at the foot of the rockery. She spent a goodish
while circumambulating this area with her, explaining what
the various trees, rocks and flowers were called. Grannie Liu
listened very attentively.

'Seems that in the city it isn't only the folks that are grander,' she remarked. 'The creatures too seem to be grander
than what they are outside. Even the birds here are prettier,
and they can talk.'

'What birds?' they asked her, curious.

'I know the one on the golden perch on the verandah –
him with the green feathers and red beak – is a polly parrot,'
she said defensively, 'but that old black crow in the cage – he's
grown a thingummy on his head and learned to talk, as well.'

The 'crow' that she was referring to was a mynah. The
others laughed at her mistake.

A little after this some maids came up and invited them to
take a snack.

'After drinking all that wine, I don't feel hungry,' said
Grandmother Jia. 'Still, bring it here anyway, and those who
want to can help themselves.'

The maids went off and returned carrying two small tables.
A couple of food-boxes followed. Each, when its cover was

removed, was found to contain two different kinds of delicacy. In the first box there were two kinds of steamed things: marzipan cakes made of ground lotus-root and sugared cassia-flowers, and pine-nut and goose-fat rolls. The second box contained two sorts of fried things, one of them a heap of tiny *jiao-zi* only about one inch long

'What have they got inside them?' Grandmother Jia asked.

'Crab-meat,' said one of the old women who had brought the boxes.

Grandmother Jia frowned.

'I shouldn't think anyone would feel like eating that *now*,' she said. 'Much too rich.'

The other type of fried confection consisted of a wide variety of little pastry-shapes deep-fried in butter. These, too, met with the old lady's disapproval. She invited Aunt Xue to choose first. Aunt Xue selected one of the little cakes of lotus-root marzipan. Grandmother Jia chose a goose-fat and pine-nut roll, but after merely tasting it, handed the uneaten half to a maid.

Grannie Liu was fascinated by the delicately fashioned pastries. They had been looped or perforated or criss-crossed in every conceivable shape and the soft dough instantaneously hardened in boiling butter-fat. The one she had selected was shaped like a peony.

'The cleverest girl in our village couldn't make a paper cut-out as fine as that,' she said, holding it up for the others to see. 'It seems almost a shame to eat it. I'd like to wrap up a few of these and take them home with me to use as patterns!'

The others laughed.

'I'll give you a jarful to take back with you when you go,' said Grandmother Jia. 'Eat these ones now, while they're still hot.'

The others contented themselves with nibbling only one or two of whichever delicacies in the boxes took their fancy, but Grannie Liu and Ban-er, partly because of the novelty (neither of them having eaten such things before), and partly because the little pastry-shapes really were very pretty and, being heaped promiscuously together, tempted you to go on eating them to discover what new shapes were lying underneath, went on munching away until they had tried several of every shape, by which time about half the pile had vanished. Xi-feng had what was left on the four dishes heaped together onto two of them and put into a single box, and sent it over to the Lotus Pavilion for Élégante and the eleven other little actresses to eat.

Just then the nurse appeared carrying Xi-feng's little girl, who at once became the main focus of their attention. She was clutching a large grapefruit, but as soon as she caught sight of the Buddha's hand that Ban-er was holding, she decided that she wanted *that*, and let up a wail when the maids who were attempting to coax it from Ban-er could not procure it for her quickly enough. A resourceful cousin saved the situation by hurriedly taking the grapefruit and inducing Ban-er to make an exchange. Ban-er had by this time been playing with the Buddha's hand for quite a long while and had more or less exhausted its possibilities; moreover at the moment he had his hands full of fried pastry-shapes; and the grapefruit not only smelled good but, being round, made an excellent football. For these three reasons he concluded that it was an altogether more satisfactory fruit than the Buddha's hand and abandoned all interest in the latter.

*

When everyone had taken tea, Grandmother Jia, with the rest of the party following, conducted Grannie Liu to Green Bower Hermitage, where they were met at the gate by the nun Adamantina. Inside the courtyard the trees and shrubs had a thriving, well-cared-for look.

'Monks and nuns always have the best-kept gardens,' said Grandmother Jia, in smiling approval of what she saw. 'They have nothing else to do with their time.'

They were walking towards the meditation hall on the east side of the courtyard. As they seemed to hesitate in the outer foyer, Adamantina invited them to go on inside, but Grandmother Jia declined.

'No, we won't go inside just now. We've all recently taken

wine and meat, and as you've got the Bodhisattva in there, it would be sacrilege. We can sit out here, where we are. Bring us some of your nice tea. We'll just drink one cup and then go out again.'

Adamantina hurried off to make tea.

Having heard a good deal about her, Bao-yu studied her very attentively, when she arrived back presently with the tray. It was a little cinque-lobed lacquer tea-tray decorated with a gold-infilled engraving of a cloud dragon coiled round the character for 'longevity'. On it stood a little covered tea-cup of Cheng Hua enamelled porcelain. Holding the tray out respectfully in both her hands, she offered the cup to Grand-mother Jia.

'I don't drink Lu-an tea,' said Grandmother Jia.

'I know you don't,' said Adamantina with a smile. 'This is Old Man's Eyebrows.'

Grandmother Jia took the tea and inquired what sort of water it had been made with.

'Last year's rain-water,' said Adamantina.

After drinking half, Grandmother Jia handed the cup to Grannie Liu.

'Try it,' she said. 'See what *you* think of it.'

Grannie Liu gulped down the remaining half.

'Hmn. All right. A bit on the weak side, though. It would be better if it were brewed a little longer.'

Grandmother Jia and the rest seemed to derive much amuse-ment from these comments.

The others were now served tea in covered cups of 'sweet-white' eggshell china – all, that is, except Bao-chai and Dai-yu, whom Adamantina tugged by the sleeve as an indication that they should follow her inside. Bao-yu stealthily slipped out after them and saw Adamantina usher them into a side-room leading off the foyer. This was Adamantina's own room. Inside it Bao-chai seated herself on the couch and Dai-yu sat on Adamantina's meditation mat. Adamantina busied herself at the stove, fanning the charcoal until the water was boiling vigorously and brewing them a fresh pot of tea. Bao-yu stepped softly into the room and made his presence known to the two cousins.

'So *you* get the hostess's special brew?'

'Yes,' they said laughing. 'And it's no good your gate-crashing in here after us, because there's none for you.'

Just as Adamantina was about to fetch cups for the girls, an old lay-sister appeared at the door carrying the empties she had been collecting in the foyer.

'Don't bring that Cheng Hua cup in here,' said Adamantina. 'Leave it outside.'

Bao-yu understood immediately. It was because Grannie Liu had drunk from it. In Adamantina's eyes the cup was now contaminated. He watched her as she got cups out for the girls. One of them, a cup with a handle, had

THE PUMPKIN CUP

carved in *li-shu* characters on one side and

Wang Kai his Treasure

in little autograph characters on the back, followed by another column of tiny characters:

> Examined by Su Dong-po in the Inner Treasury
> Fourth month Yuan-feng era anno 5°

When she had poured tea into this cup she handed it to Bao-chai.

The other cup was shaped like a miniature begging-bowl and was inscribed with the words

THE HORN LINK GOBLET

in 'pearl-drop' seal script. Adamantina filled it and handed it to Dai-yu.

She poured tea for Bao-yu in the green jade mug that she normally drank from herself. Bao-yu commented jokingly on the choice:

'I thought you religious were supposed to treat all earthly creatures alike. How comes it that the other two get priceless heirlooms to drink out of but I only get a common old thing like this?'

'I have no wish to boast,' said Adamantina, 'but this "common old thing" as you call it may well be more valuable than anything you could find in your own household.'

'In the world's eyes, yes,' said Bao-yu. 'But "other countries, other ways", you know. When I enter your domain, I naturally adopt your standards and look on gold, jewels and jade as common, vulgar things.'

Adamantina glowed with pleasure. In place of the jade mug she hunted out a large drinking-bowl for him to drink out of. It was carved from a gnarled and ancient bamboo root in the likeness of a coiled-up dragon with horns like antlers.

'There, that's the only thing I've got left. Do you think you can drink so much?'

Delightedly he assured her that he could.

'Yes, I dare say you could too,' said Adamantina. 'But I'm not sure that I'm prepared to waste so much of my best tea on you. You know what they say: "One cup for a connoisseur, two for a rustic, and three for a thirsty mule". What sort of creature does that make you if you drink this bowlful?'

Bao-chai, Dai-yu and Bao-yu all three laughed at this. Adamantina poured the equivalent of about a cupful into the bamboo-root bowl. Savouring it carefully in little sips, Bao-yu found it of incomparable freshness and lightness and praised it enthusiastically.

'You realize, of course,' said Adamantina seriously, 'that it is only because of the other two that you are drinking this. If you had come here alone, I should not have given you any.'

Bao-yu laughed.

'I fully realize that, and I don't feel in the least indebted to you. I shall offer my thanks to *them*.'

Adamantina pondered this statement with unsmiling gravity.

'Yes. I think that would be sensible.'

'Is this tea made with last year's rain-water too?' Dai-yu asked her.

Adamantina looked scornful.

'Oh! can you *really* not tell the difference? I am quite disappointed in you. This is melted snow that I collected from the branches of winter-flowering plum-trees five years ago, when I was living at the Coiled Incense temple on Mt Xuan-mu. I managed to fill the whole of that demon-green glaze water-jar with it. For years I couldn't bring myself to start it; then this summer I opened it for the first time. Today is only the second time I have ever used any. I am *most* surprised that you cannot tell the difference. When did stored rain-water have such buoyant lightness? How could one *possibly* use it for a tea like this?'

Dai-yu was too well aware of Adamantina's eccentricity to attempt a reply; and since it felt awkward to sit there saying nothing, she signalled to Bao-chai that they should go. While the three of them were leaving, Bao-yu stopped to have a word with Adamantina.

'That cup that the old woman drank out of: of course, I realize that you can't possibly use it any more, but it seems a shame to throw it on one side. Couldn't you give it to the old woman? She's very poor, and if she sold it, she could probably live for quite a long while on the proceeds. What do you think?'

Adamantina reflected for some moments and then nodded.

'Yes, I suppose so. Fortunately I have never drunk out of that cup myself. If I *had*, I should have smashed it to pieces rather than give it to her. If you want her to have it, though, you must give it to her yourself. I will have no part in it. And you must take it away immediately.'

'But of course,' said Bao-yu. 'No one would expect you to *speak* to her. That would be an even greater pollution. Just give the cup to me and I shall see to the rest.'

Adamantina ordered the cup to be brought in and handed over to Bao-yu. As he took it, Bao-yu said:

'After we've gone, shall I get my boys to bring a few buckets of water from the lake and clean the floor for you?'

Adamantina smiled graciously.

'That would be very nice. But tell them to bring the water only as far as the gate. They can leave it there at the foot of the outer wall. Tell them not to come inside.'

'Of course,' said Bao-yu, putting the cup into his sleeve as they went into the foyer. He found a junior maid of Grandmother Jia's there and entrusted it to her.

'When Grannie Liu goes, see that she takes this cup with her, will you?'

By the time he had done this, Grandmother Jia was already outside in the courtyard expressing a desire to get back. Adamantina made no serious effort to detain her, and after seeing her guests out of the Hermitage, went in again and closed the gate after her.

*

Back at the scene of the party, Grandmother Jia, who was feeling somewhat exhausted, told Lady Wang and the girls to act as hostesses to Aunt Xue while she herself went off to Sweet-rice Village for a rest. Xi-feng ordered the servants to fetch a little bamboo carrying-chair, which Grandmother Jia got into. Two old women lifted it up, and then off they all went, Xi-feng and Li Wan one on either side of it and a little cohort of maids and older servants bringing up the rear.

As soon as Grandmother Jia had gone, Aunt Xue excused herself and left. Lady Wang, having dismissed the young actresses and given orders for the left-over food in the lacquer boxes to be distributed among the maids, also availed herself of the opportunity of taking a rest. Putting her feet up on the couch lately occupied by Grandmother Jia, she first caused the blinds to be let down, then, instructing one of the junior maids to massage her legs, and murmuring something about 'calling her if anyone came from Her Old Ladyship', she settled herself down for a nap.

Bao-yu and the girls watched the maids take the food-boxes out onto the rockery. Some sat there on the rocks for their picnic; others spread out over the grass below or sat under the trees or down at the water's edge. Although so dispersed, they managed to create a considerable hubbub.

After a little while Faithful arrived with instructions to show Grannie Liu some more of the Garden. The cousins, hoping for more laughs, went along with them.

A short walk took them to the monumental stone arch at
the entrance to the Reunion Palace.

'Goodness me!' said the old woman. 'You even have a
temple here!'

She fell down on her knees and kotowed, causing her young
companions to double up with laughter.

'Why do you laugh?' she said. 'Do you think I don't know
what the words say? We have quite a few temples where I
come from and they all have arches like this. The writing on
the arch is the name of the temple.'

'All right. What's the name of *this* temple then?' they asked
her.

Grannie Liu pointed upwards at the characters inscribed
overhead.

' "Temple of the Jade Emperor". That's what it says,
doesn't it?'

This produced an ecstasy of merriment in the young people.
No doubt they would have gone on teasing her, but just at
that moment there was an alarming rumble from her bowels
and she clutched the hand of one of the little maidservants
standing by and begged her for the favour of a couple of
sheets of paper, while with the other hand she began undoing
the buttons of her dress.

The others, still laughing, shouted at her to stop.

'No, no! Not here! Not here!'

They told one of the older women to escort her to a place
beyond the north-east corner of the precincts where there was
a privy. Having led Grannie Liu to within sight of it and
pointed it out to her, the old servant deemed this an excellent
opportunity of taking some time off, and went away, leaving
Grannie Liu to make her way back alone.

Now Grannie Liu had drunk quantities of yellow rice-wine,
which did not in fact agree with her; on top of that she had
eaten a lot of rich, fatty food; and as the food had made her
thirsty, she had concluded by drinking an excessive amount of
tea. The upset stomach which was the inevitable consequence
of so much indulgence kept her a wearisome long time in the
privy before her business there was completed.

When she at last emerged, the colder air outside drove the
wine fumes up into her head, increasing the dizziness, which
might be thought normal in a woman of her years who has
suddenly got up after squatting for a long time on her heels,
to such an extent that she was quite unable to make out the
route that she had come by. Everywhere she looked there
were buildings, rocks and trees. Unable to decide which of
them lay in the right direction, she made for the nearest paved
path and, with slow and deliberate steps, followed it to see
where it would take her.

It took her in time to the courtyard wall of a house, but she
could find no gate in it, and after wandering round a long
while looking for one, she came upon a bamboo trellis, which
she contemplated with some astonishment.

'Hmn. Bean-sticks. What are they doing here?'

The 'bean-sticks' resolved themselves into a rose-covered
pergola. After walking alongside it for a while, she came to a
round 'moon-gate', which she entered. Ahead of her was a
channel of crystal-clear water, five or six feet wide. Its banks
were reinforced with stone, and a large, flat slab of white stone
had been laid across it to make a bridge. After she had crossed
the bridge there was a raised cobbled path which, after a
couple of right-angled bends, brought her up to the door of
the house.

The first thing she saw on entering it was a young woman
smiling at her in welcome. Grannie Liu smiled back.

'I'm lost, miss. The young ladies have left me to find my
own way and I've wandered in here by mistake.'

Surprised that the girl did not reply, Grannie Liu stepped
forward to take her hand and – *bang!* – hit her head a most
painful thump on the wooden wall. The girl was a painting,
as she found on closer inspection.

'Strange!' she thought. 'How can they paint a picture so
that it sticks out like that?'

Grannie Liu was ignorant of the foreign mode of light-and-
shadow painting and was sorely puzzled to discover, on touching the picture, that it did not in fact 'stick out' but was flat

all over. Turning from it with a sigh and a shake of her head, she moved on to a little doorway in the wooden partition-wall, over which hung a green, flower-patterned portière. She raised the portière and went inside.

In the room she now entered everything, from the top of the surrounding walls, delicately incised with shapes of swords, vases, musical instruments, incense-burners and the like, to the lavish furnishing below, in which

> The weaver's glowing art combined
> With gleam of gold and orient pearl,

and thence down to the very floor of brilliantly patterned green glazed tiles beneath her feet, was such as to make even more dazzled the eyes of an already intoxicated old woman.

She looked for the way out – but where was it? To the left of her there was a bookcase, to the right a screen. She tried behind the screen. Ah, yes! There was the door. But there too, to her intense surprise, approaching her from the opposite direction and causing her a momentary palpitation of the heart, was another old woman, whom she took to be her old gossip from the village.

'What? are you here too?' she asked her. 'I suppose you were wondering what had become of me these last few days. Well, it was neighbourly to come and look for me. Which of the young women brought you in?'

She noticed, with much amusement, that her old neighbour's head was covered all over with flowers.

'Hoo! You'll catch it! Picking the flowers from their garden to put in your own hair. Well I never!'

The other merely grinned back at her and said nothing. Grannie Liu stretched out a hand to give her the touch of shame. The other old woman stretched her hand out too to stop her. After a brief, soundless skirmish, Grannie Liu managed to get her finger onto the other one's face. But no sooner had she done so than she recoiled in horror, for the cheek she touched was as cold and hard as a block of ice. Suddenly the truth dawned on her:

'I've heard of rich folks having what they call "dressing mirrors" in their houses. Mayhap I'm standing in front of one of them and it's myself I'm looking at.'

She stretched out her hand again to feel and closely examined the surface. Yes, no doubt of it: it was a mirror, let into the carved surface of the wooden partition. She laughed at her own error.

'Yes, but how do I get out of here?' she thought, as she continued to finger the mirror's carved surround.

Suddenly there was a loud *clunk!* which so frightened the old woman that for some moments she rolled her eyes in terror. The mirror *was* in fact a kind of door. It had a West Ocean mechanism by which it could be opened or closed, and Grannie Liu, in feeling around it, had accidentally touched the spring which had made the mirror slide back into the panelling, revealing the doorway underneath.

Pleasantly surprised, she passed through the doorway into a room whose main feature was a rich and elegantly patterned bed. Now Grannie Liu was seven or eight parts drunk and thoroughly worn out from all her walking. Seeing a bed in front of her, she sat down on it gratefully, to rest her feet. But though she intended no more than a few moments' rest, as soon as she had sat down, her weariness overcame her. Her head went down and her feet went up as though she was no longer in possession of them; a darkness closed over her eyes, and she sank back on the bed, fast asleep.

Outside in the Garden meanwhile, the cousins were beginning to wonder what had become of her, and Ban-er, missing his grandmother, became panicky and began to cry.

'Perhaps she's fallen into the privy,' one of the young people suggested cheerfully. 'We'd better send someone to have a look.'

Two old women were sent to the privy to investigate. When they reported back that she was not there, the others were at a loss to think where she could have got to. It was Aroma who hit on the correct hypothesis.

'She must have missed the way back because she was drunk. If she followed the path in the wrong direction, it will have taken her to our back courtyard. Now if she went through the pergola and then on into the house through the back door, she'll probably have been seen by one of the maids. If she *didn't* go in through the pergola but went on walking in a south-westerly direction, Heaven only knows where she'll end up! I think I'd better go and have a look.

She hurried back to Green Delights, intending to ask the junior maids if they had seen her; but the place was deserted; they had all sneaked off elsewhere to play. Entering the main building by way of the front door, she made her way through the complicated carved partition. A thunderous snoring could be heard coming from the bedroom at the back. She hurried through. As she entered the bedroom, a heavy stink, compounded of farts and wine-fumes, assailed her nostrils. Her eyes travelled to the bed, from which the sounds were coming, and saw Grannie Liu, spreadeagled on her back and fast asleep.

As soon as she had overcome her shock, she rushed up to the bed and shook her relentlessly until she woke. Grannie Liu opened her eyes wide and saw Aroma standing over her.

'Oh, miss!' She scrambled hurriedly to her feet. 'Oh, I am sorry! Anyway – praise be! – I haven't dirtied the bed.'

She felt it nervously, to make sure.

Aroma, mortally afraid that someone would overhear and Bao-yu get to know of what had happened, gestured to her violently not to speak. Hurriedly she threw three or four whole handfuls of Hundred Blend aromatic onto the incense burner that stood always smouldering beside the bed and replaced its cover.

'At least it's a mercy she wasn't sick,' she thought to herself.

Speaking to her in an urgent whisper, she nevertheless contrived to smile at her reassuringly:

'It's all right. I'll look after this. Just follow me.'

Grannie Liu nodded gratefully and followed her to the junior maids' quarters outside, where Aroma made her sit down.

'If they ask what happened, just say that you passed out and had a little nap on the rockery.'

Grannie Liu willingly agreed, and Aroma gave her some tea. By the end of the second cup she had sobered up completely and was able to converse.

'Which of the young ladies does the bedroom belong to?' she asked Aroma. 'It's the most beautiful I ever saw. I thought I was in paradise.'

Aroma gave a wry little smile.

'It's – actually it's Master Bao's bedroom.'

Grannie Liu fell silent, horrified by the enormity of her trespass. Seeing that she had now recovered, Aroma led her out through the front courtyard and back to where the others were waiting.

'I found her asleep on the grass,' she said when she saw them, 'so I've brought her back for you.'

The others seemed satisfied with this explanation, for no further mention was made of it.

Shortly after this Grandmother Jia woke up and dinner was laid for her in Sweet-rice Village; but she felt too exhausted to eat anything, and getting into the bamboo carrying-chair again, had herself carried back to her own apartment to rest. When she was back, she told Xi-feng and the rest of the young folk who had escorted her to go and have their dinner, and the cousins went back into the Garden.

Ensuing events will be dealt with in the following chapter.

CHAPTER 42

Lady Allspice wins over a suspicious nature with some
well-intentioned advice
And River Queen enhances her reputation as a wit with
some amusing sarcasms

The last chapter showed how Grandmother Jia, escorted by
all the others, returned from Sweet-rice Village to her own
apartment. As soon as she arrived, she insisted that the young
people should go off and have their dinner. The young people
accordingly went back into the Garden, and when they had
eaten, the party finally broke up.

Returning from the Garden with little Ban-er, Grannie Liu
first called on Xi-feng to announce her intention of leaving for
home early next morning.

'We've only been here two or three days,' she said, 'but in
these two or three days we've seen and heard and eaten and
drunk more things than we ever dreamed of. I'm truly grateful to you and Her Old Ladyship and the young gentlewomen
and the young ladies working in the different apartments for
treating an old countrywoman with so much kindness. I don't
know what I can do in return. All I can think of is to buy
some sticks of best incense when I get back so that I can offer
some every day to the Lord Buddha and pray him to give you
long life. Leastways it would show my gratitude.'

'It's a bit early yet for rejoicing,' said Xi-feng drily. 'Thanks
to you, Her Old Ladyship seems to have caught a chill and is
at this very moment lying on her back complaining how bad
she feels; and my little girl has caught a cold, too, and is lying
in there with a fever.'

Grannie Liu murmured sympathetically.

'Her Old Ladyship's feeling her age, poor soul,' she said.
'And she isn't used to the exercise.'

'I've never seen her more lively than she was today,' said
Xi-feng. 'Generally when she goes into the Garden, she'll

visit just one or two places, sit there for a little while, and then come back again. But today, because *you* were there and she wanted to show you everything, she must have covered the greater part of the Garden. It was also because of you that I wasn't on hand when Lady Wang gave my little girl that piece of cake. I'm sure it was eating out in the cold that has made her feverish.'

'I suppose your little lass doesn't go into the Garden very much,' said Grannie Liu. 'Not like *our* young ones, off to play in the grave-garths almost as soon as they can walk. She may have caught a cold from the wind as you say. On the other hand, children of her age, being pure of body, often have the second sight. It *could* have been brought on by seeing a spirit. If I was you, I'd have a look in the Almanac, just in case. You never know, the child might have been pixified.'

Wondering why she had not thought of this herself, Xi-feng at once ordered Patience to fetch down the *Jade Casket*. Sunshine was summoned to look up the relevant passage and read it out to them. This, after some preliminary hunting, he proceeded to do:

EIGHTH MONTH, TWENTY-FIFTH DAY: Sicknesses occurring on this day have a south-easterly origin. *Possible causes* Encounter with spirit of hanged person or flower spirit. *Recommended action* Maximum benefit may be obtained by procuring voluntary departure of spirit. To do this, take forty pieces of coloured paper 'spirit money' and walk forty paces in a south-easterly direction offering one of the pieces at every step.

'There you are!' said Xi-feng. 'That *must* be it. The Garden is just where you'd *expect* to run into a flower spirit. I wouldn't be a bit surprised if that doesn't account for Her Old Ladyship's trouble as well.'

She sent someone forthwith to obtain two lots of spirit money and got two of the servants to carry out the exorcism, one on Grandmother Jia's behalf and the other on behalf of her little girl. As soon as it was over, she and Grannie Liu went in to see how Baby was getting on. They found her sleeping peacefully.

'There!' said Xi-feng delightedly. 'It takes an old, experienced person like yourself to know these things. Perhaps you could also tell me why she's such a sickly little girl. She's always going down with something or other.'

'There's nothing unusual about that,' said Grannie Liu. 'Children of well-to-do folks are brought up so delicate, their bodies can't stand any hardship. And for another thing, when young folks are cherished too much, it overloads their luck. It might be better for her if in future you tried not to make quite so much of her.'

'You may be right,' said Xi-feng without much conviction. 'It's just occurred to me: as we haven't named the child yet, I wonder if you'd like to name her *for* us? For one thing, being named by someone so old will help her to live longer; and for another – I hope you won't mind my saying this, but you country people *do* have quite a lot of poverty and hardship to contend with – being named by a poor person like yourself may help to balance her luck.'

Grannie Liu thought for a bit.

'When was she born?'

'Ah, that's just the trouble,' said Xi-feng. 'She was born on Qiao-jie – the Seventh of the Seventh – a very unlucky date.'

'No matter,' said Grannie Liu. '*Call* her "Qiao-jie" then. That's what the doctors mean when they talk about "fighting poison with poison and fire with fire". You call her "Qiao-jie" like I say, and I guarantee that she'll live to a ripe old age. I prophesy for this child that when she's a big girl and the others are all going off to get married, she may for a time find that things are not going her way; but thanks to this name, all her misfortunes will turn into blessings, and what at first looked like bad luck will turn out to be good luck in the end.'

Xi-feng was of course delighted with these 'auspicious words' and thanked her warmly.

'May it turn out for her as you say!'

She summoned Patience.

'We're going to be busy tomorrow and may not have the time then. As you've got nothing to do at the moment, why don't you get the things for Grannie together, so that everything will be ready for her to start first thing tomorrow?'

'Please don't go giving me a lot of things,' said Grannie Liu. 'I've already put you to so much inconvenience these last few days, I should feel even more uncomfortable carrying a lot of things back with me.'

'These are only very ordinary things,' said Xi-feng. 'Nothing special. Just a few things for you to take back with you and show off to the neighbours. Just so as to be able to say that you've been to town.'

'Come over here, Grannie, and have a look,' said Patience.

Grannie Liu followed her into the next room. A full half of the kang was occupied by her piled-up presents. Patience picked them up one by one and explained them to her.

'This sky-blue material is the gauze you said you wanted. The pale-blue gauze in a closer weave is a present from the Mistress to line it with. These are two lengths of wild-silk pongee. You can use it to make either a dress or a skirt with; it would do equally well for either. In this wrapping here there are two lengths of silk for making up into a New Year outfit. This is a box of various kinds of cakes and pastries made in the Imperial kitchens. There are some kinds that you've already eaten and some that you haven't. You want to put them out on plates when you're having someone to tea: you'll find they're a bit better than the ones you can buy in the shops. These two sacks are the ones you brought the vegetables in when you came. This one has got two bushels of pink "Emperor" rice in it. It makes a really delicious congee. This one has got fruit and nuts and other things from the Garden in it. And this packet here has got eight taels of silver in it. Everything up to here is from the Mistress. Now these two packets here have each got fifty taels of silver in them – a hundred taels in all. They're a present from Her Ladyship, for starting a little business or buying some land with when you get back, so that you can be self-sufficient in future and not have to keep falling back on your friends. The two jackets' – here Patience smiled somewhat embarrassedly – 'the two jackets and the two skirts and the four head-scarves and the packet of embroidery

silks are a present from me. The clothes have only been worn
a very little but they aren't new: so if you decide to throw them
back at me, I shan't complain.'

Grannie Liu had been exclaiming rapturously as each item
was shown to her and must have uttered several dozen 'Holy
Names' by the time Patience came to her own gift.

'Throw them back at you, Miss?' she said warmly, touched
by the maid's kindness and humility. 'How can you say such a
thing? Fine clothes like these? I shouldn't know where to buy
them if I had the money! You make me feel ashamed. I don't
like to take them off you; yet if I don't, you will think me ungrateful.'

'Get away with you!' said Patience. 'That sort of talk is for
strangers, and you are one of us. If I didn't think of you so,
I'd never have dared make the offer. You just take them and
stop worrying. In any case, there's something I want from you
in return. Next New Year, bring us some of your home-dried
mixed vegetables: pigweed and cowpeas and kidney beans and
dried aubergines and dried gourd-shavings. Everyone here
loves them. You just bring us some of them. We don't want
anything else from you, mind, so don't go wondering what
else to bring. Just bring some of them, and we'll be quits.'

Grannie Liu thanked her warmly and promised to remember the dried vegetables.

'Now off to bed with you!' said Patience. '*I'll* look after
this lot for you. You can leave it here tonight, and tomorrow
we'll send the boys out for a cab and get them to load it for
you. So you've got nothing to worry about.'

Overwhelmed by so much kindness, Grannie Liu went back
into the other room to take her leave of Xi-feng, and after
thanking her many times over, went off to Grandmother Jia's
apartment to spend the night.

She was up betimes next morning and would like to have
said good-bye to Grandmother Jia as soon as she had completed her toilet, and made an early start; but the family fore-
stalled her. Knowing that the old lady was indisposed, they
had trooped in first thing to inquire how she was and had
already sent outside for a doctor. The latter's arrival at the

mansion was shortly after announced by an old woman-
servant, whereupon the old women in attendance on Grandmother Jia urged her to conceal herself behind the curtains of
the summer-bed. But Grandmother Jia refused to budge.

'I'm old, too, woman – old enough to be his mother, I
shouldn't wonder. What have I got to fear from him at my
age? I'm not going behind any curtains. Let him examine me
where I am.'

Seeing that she was resolved to stay, the old women brought
up a little table and put a small pillow on it for her to rest her
arm on. These preparations completed, they gave orders for
the doctor to be admitted.

Dr Wang was shortly to be observed crossing the courtyard
below, conducted by Cousin Zhen, Jia Lian and Jia Rong.
Modestly declining to walk up the central ramp, he followed
Cousin Zhen up the right-hand side steps onto the terrace,
where two old women, one on either side of the doorway,
were holding up the door-blind in readiness. Bao-yu came forward to welcome the doctor as the two old women were
conducting him through the outer room, and led him, still
accompanied by the other gentlemen, to his grandmother inside.

The old lady was sitting up very stiffly on a couch. She was
wearing a black crepe jacket lined with pearly-haired baby
lamb's skin. Four little maids, their hair still done up in
childish 'horns', stood two on either side of her, holding fly-
whisks and spittoons, and five or six old serving-women were
fanned out in a sort of bodyguard behind her. Vaguely discernible glimpses of brightly-coloured dresses and golden
hair-ornaments betrayed the presence of numerous younger
women behind the green muslin curtains at the back. Not
daring to raise his head in so much female company, Dr Wang
advanced and saluted his patient. Observing that he was
dressed in the uniform of a mandarin of the sixth rank, Grandmother Jia deduced that he must be a Court Physician, and
in returning his salutation was careful to address him with the
'Worshipful' to which his appointment entitled him.

'And what is the Worshipful's name?' she asked Cousin
Zhen.

'Wang.'

'When I was a young woman, the President of the Imperial College of Physicians was a Wang,' said Grandmother Jia. 'Wang Jun-xiao. Famous for his diagnoses.'

The doctor bowed.

'He was my great-uncle,' he said, smiling demurely, but still not daring to raise his head.

Grandmother Jia laughed.

'That makes you a friend of the family.'

She stretched out an arm and slowly arranged it for him on the pillow. The old women brought up a large stool which they set down in front of her table and slightly to one side. Dr Wang knelt on it, squatting on his heel with one haunch so that he was half-sitting on the edge of the stool, and in that polite but uncomfortable posture proceeded at great length to take the old lady's pulses, first in one arm and then in the other. After that he made another bow and retired, eyes still on the floor, as they had been throughout the consultation.

'Thank you,' said Grandmother Jia as he was leaving. 'See him out, will you, Zhen? And see that he gets some tea.'

Murmuring a reply, Cousin Zhen himself withdrew, followed by Jia Lian and Jia Rong, and conducted Dr Wang back to one of the gentlemen's rooms in the front part of the mansion.

'There's nothing seriously wrong with Lady Jia,' said Dr Wang when they were seated. 'She has a slight chill. There is no need for her to take any medicine. A light, simple diet for a day or two and see that she keeps warm. That should be enough. I'll write out a prescription that you can have made up if she feels like taking something. If not, I should just forget about it.'

He drank his tea and wrote out the prescription. Just as he was about to leave, the nurse came hurrying in with Xi-feng's little girl in her arms.

'Doctor, have a look at us too, will you?'

The doctor went over, took one of the child's hands and supported it on his own left hand while he felt her pulse. Then he felt her forehead and inspected her tongue.

'I'm afraid the young lady is not going to be very pleased with my advice,' he said with a smile. 'A good, cleansing hunger is what she needs. Let her miss a couple of meals. No need for a prescription. I shall send you some pills that you can dissolve in hot ginger-water and give her to drink at bed-time. That should help do the trick.'

With that he took his leave once more and departed.

Cousin Zhen and the other two went back to Grandmother Jia's apartment with the prescription and reported what the doctor had said. Then they laid the prescription on the table and withdrew.

Lady Wang, Li Wan, Xi-feng, Bao-chai and the rest came out from behind the curtain as soon as the doctor had gone. Lady Wang sat with Grandmother Jia for a while before re-turning to her own apartment.

The coast was now at last clear for Grannie Liu to come forward and take her leave.

'You must come again when you have the time,' said Grand-mother Jia. She ordered Faithful to see her off. 'I can't see you off myself,' she said. 'I'm not feeling too well today.'

Grannie Liu, having thanked her and said good-bye, fol-lowed Faithful out of the room and into a room at the side of the courtyard. Faithful pointed to a large bundle on the kang:

'These are dresses given to Her Old Ladyship by various people over the years as birthday or festival presents, but as she refuses to wear any clothes made by outsiders, they've none of them ever been worn. It's a shame to keep them, really. She told me yesterday to pick out a few for you to take back with you, either to give away as presents or to wear yourself about the house. In this box here you'll find those pastries you wanted. This parcel has got the medicines in you were talking about the other day: the Red Flower Poison-Dis-pellers, the Old Gold Anti-Fever Pastilles, the Blood Renew-ing Elixir Pills and the Easy Birth Pills. You'll find each kind wrapped up separately inside its own prescription. These two little silk purses are to wear.' Faithful undid the draw-strings and extracted from each purse a golden 'Heart's Desire' medallion with a device showing an ingot, a writing-brush and a sceptre. She smiled at Grannie Liu mischievously:

'You give *me* these and keep the purses.'

Grannie Liu, surprised and delighted (as she showed by her many pious ejaculations) to be receiving these further presents in addition to what Patience had shown her the night before, seemed eager to accede to this request.

'Yes, yes, Miss. You keep them by all means.'

Faithful, who had not intended to be taken seriously, replaced the medallions in their purses and did them up again.

'I was only pulling your leg. I've got lots of these things already. Keep them to give the children at New Year.'

While she was speaking, a little maid came in carrying a Cheng Hua enamelled porcelain cup, which she handed to Grannie Liu.

'Master Bao said I was to give you this.'

'Well!' said Grannie Liu as she took the cup from her. 'Now what do you make of that? Reckon it must be something I did for him in a past life.'

'Those clothes I gave you to change into the other day when you had your bath were mine,' said Faithful. 'If you don't mind taking them off me, I've got some more like them that I'd like to make you a present of.'

As Grannie Liu made no objection, Faithful got out several more sets of clothing and wrapped them up for her.

Grannie Liu wanted to go into the Garden to thank Bao-yu and the girls and say good-bye to them; she also wanted to take her leave of Lady Wang; but Faithful prevented her.

'It isn't necessary. In any case, they won't be seeing anyone at this hour. I can thank them for you when I see them later. Well, good-bye then. Come again when you can.'

She ordered an old servant-woman to fetch two pages from the inner gate to help Grannie Liu out with her things. The old servant undertook to do this and also went with Grannie Liu to collect the things from Xi-feng's apartment. When they had got them all together, she fetched the boys from the outside corner gate who carried them out to the street for her and loaded them into a waiting cab. Grannie Liu and Ban-er then got in themselves and set off without more ado on their journey back home.

At this point they pass also out of our narrative, which turns now to other matters.

*

After they had eaten their lunch, Bao-chai and the rest of the young people called once more on Grandmother Jia, to see how she was progressing. On their way back, as they reached that point in the Garden where their paths separated, Bao-chai called Dai-yu over to her.

'Frowner, come with me. There's something I want to talk to you about.'

Dai-yu followed her to Allspice Court. When they were inside her room, Bao-chai sat down.

'Well?' she said to Dai-yu. 'Aren't you going to kneel down? I am about to interrogate you.'

Dai-yu was mystified.

'Poor Bao-chai!' she said, laughing. 'The girl's gone off her head. Interrogate me about what?'

'My dear, well-bred young lady!' said Bao-chai. 'My dear, sheltered young innocent! *What* were those things I heard you saying yesterday? Come now, the truth!'

Dai-yu, still mystified, continued to laugh. She was beginning to feel somewhat uneasy, though she would not admit it.

'What awful thing am I supposed to have said? I expect you're making it up, but you may as well tell me.'

'Still acting the innocent?' said Bao-chai. 'What were those things you said yesterday when we were playing that drinking game? I *couldn't* think where you could have got them from.'

Dai-yu cast her mind back and remembered, blushing, that the day before, when stumped for an answer, she had got through her turn by citing passages from *The Return of the Soul* and *The Western Chamber*. She hugged Bao-chai imploringly.

'Dear coz! I really don't know. I just said them without thinking. If you tell me not to, I promise not to say them again.'

'*I* really don't know either,' said Bao-chai. 'I just thought they sounded rather interesting. I thought perhaps you might be able to tell me what they were.'

'Dear coz! Please don't tell anyone about this. I promise not to repeat such things again.'

Moved by the scarlet, shame-filled face and pitifully entreating voice, Bao-chai relented and did not pursue her questioning. Having first drawn her down into a seat and handed her some tea, she began, very gently, to address her in the following manner:

'What do you take me for? I'm just as bad. At seven or eight I used to be a real little terror. Ours was reckoned to be rather a literary family. My grandfather was a bibliophile, so the house we lived in was full of books. We were a big family in those days. All my boy cousins and girl cousins on my father's side lived with us in the same house. All of us younger people hated serious books but liked reading poetry and plays. The boys had got lots and lots of plays: *The Western Chamber*, *The Lute-player*, *A Hundred Yuan Plays* – just about everything you could think of. *They* used to read them behind *our* backs, and we girls used to read them behind theirs. Eventually the grown-ups got to know about it and then there were beatings and lectures and burning of books – and that was the end of that.

'So, you see, in the case of us girls it would probably be better for us if we never learned to read in the first place. Even boys, if they gain no understanding from their reading, would do better not to read at all; and if that is true of boys, it certainly holds good for girls like you and me. The little poetry-writing and calligraphy we indulge in is not really our proper business. Come to that, it isn't a boy's proper business either. A boy's proper business is to read books in order to gain an understanding of things, so that when he grows up he can play his part in governing the country.

'Not that one hears of that happening much nowadays. Nowadays their reading seems to make them even worse than they were to start with. And unfortunately it isn't merely a case of their being led astray by what they read. The books,

too, are spoiled, by the false interpretations they put upon
them. They would do better to leave books alone and take up
business or agriculture. At least they wouldn't do so much
damage.

'As for girls like you and me: spinning and sewing are *our*
proper business. What do we need to be able to read for?
But since we *can* read, let us confine ourselves to good, improving books; let us avoid like the plague those pernicious
works of fiction, which so undermine the character that in the
end it is past reclaiming.'

This lengthy homily had so chastened Dai-yu that she sat
with head bowed low over her teacup and, though her heart
consented, could only manage a weak little 'yes' by way of
reply.

At that moment Candida came into the room:

'Mrs Zhu says will you please come over to discuss an
important matter with her? Miss Ying and Miss Tan and Miss
Xi and Miss Shi and Master Bao are there already, waiting for
you.'

'I wonder what it is this time,' said Bao-chai.

'We shall soon find out if we go,' said Dai-yu.

So off she went, and Bao-chai with her, to Sweet-rice Village. They found everyone else there, as Candida had said. Li
Wan greeted them with a smile.

'We've only just got our poetry club started, and already
someone is trying to wriggle out of it. It's Xi-chun. She's asking for a year's leave of absence.'

'I can guess why that is,' said Dai-yu. 'It's because of what
Grandmother said about painting the Garden. She's decided
to use that as an excuse.'

'I don't think you should blame Grandmother,' said Tan-
chun. 'It's what Grannie Liu said that started it.'

'Grannie Liu, yes, that's right,' Dai-yu hurriedly corrected
herself. 'Whose "grannie" is she anyway, I'd like to know?
"Old Mother Locust" we ought to call her, not "Grannie
Liu".'

This set them all laughing.

'If one wants to hear the demotic at its most forceful,' said

Bao-chai, 'one has to listen to Cousin Feng. Fortunately for us she can't read, so her jokes are somewhat lacking in finesse and the language she uses can never rise above the level at which it is commonly spoken. The secret of Frowner's sarcastic tongue is that she uses the method adopted by Confucius when he edited the *Spring and Autumn Annals*, that is to say, she extracts the essentials from vulgar speech and polishes and refines them, so that when she uses them to illustrate a point, each word or phrase is given its maximum possible effectiveness. The mere name "Old Mother Locust", for example, is sufficient to evoke the whole scene of yesterday's party and everything that happened at it. What's more, she is able to do this sort of thing almost without thinking.'

The others, still laughing, assured Bao-chai that she excelled as a commentator no less than Dai-yu and Xi-feng, in their different ways, as wits.

'The reason I asked you all here is because I wanted your advice on how long we *ought* to give her,' said Li Wan. '*I* said a month, but *she* says that's much too short. What do *you* all think?'

'Logically a year wouldn't be at all too long,' said Dai-yu. 'If it took a whole year to *build* the Garden, she would naturally require about two years in which to *paint* it. First she's got to grind her ink, then she's got to soften her brushes, then she's got to fix the paper, then she's got to find her colours, and then – '

The others realized that this was a joke at Xi-chun's expense.

'Yes?' they said, playing up to her. 'What then?'

Dai-yu, unable to maintain a straight face, was beginning to giggle.

' – and then proceed in like manner, by gradual degrees, to paint it.'

Prolonged hilarity and clapping of hands.

' "In like manner, by gradual degrees",' said Bao-chai. 'I like that. The telling phrase at the end. The trouble with all those jokes we were laughing at yesterday is that they were funny enough at the time, but on recollection they seem rather stupid. Dai-yu's jokes on the other hand, though the words at first appear colourless, are richly humorous to remember. They certainly make *me* laugh a lot.'

'You shouldn't flatter her, Cousin Chai,' said Xi-chun plaintively. 'It encourages her to show off. It's because you complimented her on her joke about Grannie Liu that she's started making fun of *me*.'

'Tell me now,' said Dai-yu, taking Xi-chun's hand in her own, 'is it to be a picture of the Garden alone, or are *we* to be in it as well?'

'It was originally to have been of the Garden alone,' said Xi-chun, 'but afterwards Grandmother said that that would make it look too much like an architect's drawing and told me to put in some people. She said what we wanted was something like one of those paintings of "Scholars Enjoying Themselves in a Landscape". The trouble is, I don't know how to do buildings in the Elaborate style, and I'm no good at human figures; but as I was too scared to refuse, I've got myself into a mess.'

'Human figures are no problem,' said Dai-yu. 'It's the insect-painting that's going to give you the trouble.'

'Now you're talking nonsense,' said Li Wan. 'What need will there be of insects in a painting of the Garden? A few animals and birds dotted here and there maybe, but no insects, surely?'

'If she has no other insects in it, she's *got* to have Old Mother Locust,' said Dai-yu. 'Without her the painting would be incomplete.'

The others all laughed. Dai-yu continued, laughing so much herself that she had to clutch her chest with both hands:

'You must hurry up and get on with the painting. I've already thought of a title to inscribe on it when it's finished. You must call it "*With Locust to the Chew*".'

The others threw back their heads and roared. Their laughter ended abruptly, however, when a loud crash caused them to look anxiously around them to see what had fallen.

It turned out to have been Xiang-yun's chair. It had been a somewhat rickety one to start with, and in laughing she had thrown herself back against it so violently that the two joints

connecting the chairback with the seat had sprung, causing
her to sink backwards and sideways, still sitting in the disin-
tegrating chair. Fortunately she was saved by the room's
wooden partition from falling onto the floor. The undignified
spectacle of her descent provoked fresh shouts of mirth
which only gradually subsided when Bao-yu hurried over and
helped her to her feet.

As he passed Dai-yu he signalled to her with his eyes.
Understanding that something must be wrong with her appearance, she slipped into Li Wan's bedroom and took the
cover off the mirror to have a look. It was the hair above her
brows that was coming loose. She pulled out the drawer in
Li Wan's dressing-box, took out two little vanity-brushes,
primmed her hair at the mirror, then, hurriedly replacing
everything, went back into the outer room, where the others
were still laughing. She pointed a finger accusingly at Li Wan.

'So this is your idea of "supervision in needlework and
moral instruction" – inviting us over here for jokes and horseplay!'

'Did you hear that, all of you?' said Li Wan. 'This is the
ringleader who sets everyone else laughing and misbehaving,
yet she has the effrontery to blame *me* for starting it all! Oh, I
could — ! Well, all I can say is that I hope when you marry you
have a real Tartar for a mother-in-law and lots of nasty
sisters-in-law with tongues as sharp as yours. It will serve you
right!'

Dai-yu, blushing, clung to Bao-chai's hand.

'Let's give her a year's leave, shall we?'

'Let me suggest what I think is a fair compromise and see
what the rest of you think of it,' said Bao-chai. 'It's true that
Lotus Dweller can paint, but "painting" in her case means no
more than an occasional sketch in the Impressionistic style.
Now of course, you couldn't paint this Garden in the first
place if you didn't have *impressions* of it; but the trouble is that
the Garden itself was designed rather like a painting, with
every rock, every tree, every building in it carefully and precisely placed in order to produce a particular scenic effect; and
if you tried to get your impressions of all of these different

scenes onto paper exactly as they are, they simply wouldn't make a picture. The shape of the paper imposes its own perspectives. You have to make them into a composition. You have to decide which to bring into the foreground and which to push into the background, which to leave out altogether and which to show only in glimpses. When you've done that, you can make your rough draft. And even then, it's only when you've studied the draft for a long time and corrected it until you're satisfied that you can go ahead with your transfer.

'One of your difficulties is going to be the ruler-work. With all those buildings you're going to *have* to do the straight lines with a ruler, and in ruler-work if you're not very careful it's easy to make the most terrible mistakes – railings that slant to one side, leaning pillars, windows on the skew or steps drawn out of line. Sometimes careless ruling can produce even more grotesque results, like a table squashed into a wall or a flower-pot apparently resting on the side of a curtain. Any one of these things is enough to make a painting look ridiculous.

'Putting in the human figures is going to be another problem. First of all you have to be very careful that you have got them in the right perspective. Then again, in painting figures the clothes and the position of the hands and feet are of great importance. A careless slip of the brush can mean a monstrously swollen hand or a crippled leg. Compared with these, little mishaps like the colour of the face running into the hair are of minor importance.

'In my opinion this painting *is* going to be very, very difficult. And since a year is thought to be too long and a month too short, the compromise I suggest is that she should be allowed half a year to do it in, but that Cousin Bao should be appointed to help her. My reason is not that I think he knows more about painting than she does and can tell her how to do it – I am sure that if he tried, it would only make matters worse – but because whenever there is anything she doesn't know about or has difficulty in putting in, he will be able to take the painting to one or another of his men friends outside who know about these matters and ask for their advice.'

Bao-yu was enthusiastic.

'That's a splendid idea. Zhan Guang can do Elaborate style buildings and Cheng Ri-xing is very good at women. I'll go and have a word with them now.'

'Didn't I tell you you ought to be called "Busybody"?' said Bao-chai. 'Just because I've mentioned the possibility, you don't have to go rushing off straight away. Wait until we've finished discussing what needs to be done, *then* you can go and see them. The question now is, what is she going to do this painting on?'

'We've got some Snow Wave paper still,' said Bao-yu. 'It comes in large enough pieces and it holds the ink well.'

'Oh, you're just hopeless!' said Bao-chai. 'Snow Wave is a good, ink-receptive paper for doing calligraphy or Impressionist style paintings on, and it will stand up to the wrinkle-and-wipe work in a Southern School landscape; but it is quite unsuitable for a painting like this one involving detailed colouring and layer upon layer of graded washes. You'd merely ruin the picture and waste the paper.

'Now I'll tell you what to do. Before they started on the construction of this Garden, they made a very detailed drawing of the layout. It was only an artist's impression, but the measurements shown on it were all accurate. Why don't you ask Lady Wang for that drawing and then ask Cousin Feng to give you a piece of heavyweight pongee of the same dimensions? Cousin Bao can get Uncle Zheng's gentlemen to size it for you, and they can make you a draft by adapting the architect's drawing and putting in the human figures. He could even get them to touch in some of the blue-and-green background for you and indicate where the outlines will need reinforcing with milk gold or milk silver.

'Meanwhile *you* must get hold of a portable stove that you can use for melting and extracting your glue on and for heating the water to wash your brushes with. You'll also need a long distemperer's table, and a blanket to cover it, for resting your painting on. And I don't suppose your present supply of paint-saucers and brushes is likely to be adequate. You'd better start from scratch and get yourself a completely new outfit.'

'I haven't got *any* equipment to speak of,' said Xi-chun. 'I just use my ordinary writing-brushes when I want to paint. As for colours: red ochre, Canton indigo, gamboge and safflower red are the only four I've got. Apart from that, all I have is a couple of colouring brushes.'

'Why ever didn't you tell me before?' said Bao-chai. 'I've still got lots of these things. The only thing is, if I give them to you before you actually need them, they will only be lying around doing nothing in *your* room the same as they now are in *mine*. On second thoughts I think I'll hang on to them for the time being. We can say that I am keeping them for you. But I can let you have any of them you want as soon as the need arises. I'd rather you used my stuff for painting fans with and that sort of thing, though. It would be a waste to use it on this great big painting of the Garden. What I'll do for you now is to make out a list of materials you can ask Lady Jia for. You may not know about some of these things, so perhaps it would be a good idea if Cousin Bao were to take them down at my dictation.'

Bao-yu had brush and ink already prepared. He had been intending in any case to take notes, in order to have his own record of what she said, and had merely to pick up his brush and wait for her to begin.

Here is the list she dictated:

large size raft brushes	4
No. 2 size raft brushes	4
No. 3 size raft brushes	4
large wash layers	4
medium wash layers	4
small wash layers	4
large Southern crab's claws	10
small Southern crab's claws	10
whisker brushes	10
large colouring brushes	20
small colouring brushes	20
face liners	10
willow-slip brushes	20
arrow-shaped cinnabar	4 oz.

Southern red ochre	4 oz.
orpiment	4 oz.
azurite	4 oz.
malachite	4 oz.
brush-stick gamboge	4 oz.
Canton indigo	8 oz.
oyster-shell white	4 boxes
safflower red	10 sheets
red powder-gold	200 leaves
gold foil	200 leaves
quality Canton glue	4 oz.
clear alum	4 oz.

'That doesn't allow for the alum and glue that will be needed for the sizing,' said Bao-chai. 'You can leave that to the menfolk.

'By the time these colours have been washed and ground and emulsified and graded, you should have enough there to last you a lifetime – messing about and practice-work included.'

She continued with her list:

superfine silk strainers	4
coarse silk strainers	2
strainer-brushes	4
mortars, various sizes	4
coarse bowls	20
5-in. saucers	10
3-in. porcelain ditto	20
portable stoves	2
casseroles, various sizes	4
new porcelain water-jars	2
new water-buckets	4
1-ft white linen bags	4
light charcoal	20 catties
willow-wood charcoal	1 catty
3-drawer chest of drawers	1
gauze, close-woven	1 ell
raw ginger	2 oz.
soy sauce	½ catty

' – a cooking-pot and a frying-slice,' Dai-yu added hurriedly.

'What are *they* for?' said Bao-chai.

'To use with the ginger and soy sauce,' said Dai-yu. 'Then she'll be able to cook the colours and eat them.'

The others laughed, including Bao-chai herself.

'Frowner! Frowner!' she said. 'What do *you* know about it? If you didn't first season the new saucers by rubbing ginger-juice and sauce on the bottom and burning them in, they would crack when you put them on the heat.'

The others assured Dai-yu that this was so. Dai-yu, meanwhile, was reading through the list.

'Just look!' she said, laying a hand on Tan-chun's arm and speaking to her in an undertone. 'All those water-jars and chests of drawers and things to paint a picture! I think she must have got confused at this point and started making a list for her trousseau.'

This set Tan-chun off into a fit of the giggles. 'Pinch her lips, Chai!' she said. 'You should hear what she's been saying about you.'

'I don't need to,' said Bao-chai. 'One doesn't expect ivory from a dog's mouth!'

Bearing down on Dai-yu as she said this, she forced her back, laughing and protesting, upon the kang and made as if she would pinch her face.

'Oh, please coz, forgive me!' Dai-yu pleaded. 'Little Frowner is younger than you and doesn't know any better. You should teach me how to be good. If *you* won't be nice to me, who else can I turn to?'

The others, not knowing what lay behind these words, were greatly amused.

'*Do* forgive her!' they said, laughing. 'How pitifully she pleads! Even *we* are melted.'

But Bao-chai knew she was referring to their recent confrontation on the subject of forbidden books, and feeling rather embarrassed to have this dragged up in the midst of a playful tussle, hurriedly released her. Dai-yu rose to her feet laughing.

'That's my good coz. If it had been *me*, I should never have let *you* off!'

Bao-chai pointed her finger at Dai-yu and smiled at her indulgently.

'I'm not surprised that Lady Jia is so fond of you or that the others find you so amusing. I can't help being fond of you too, little coz. Come here and let me do your hair for you.'

Dai-yu turned her head obediently while Bao-chai refastened her back hair. Bao-yu, watching from where he sat, thought how much better it looked for Bao-chai's attention, and wished that he had not told Dai-yu earlier to tidy the hair above her brows, for then Bao-chai could have done that for her too. His agreeable musings on the subject were interrupted by Bao-chai's voice:

'Have you finished writing the list? Perhaps *you*'d better be the one to see Lady Jia about it. If they've got those things here already, so much the better. If not, you'll have to get some money to buy them with. In that case I might be able to advise you on where to go for them.'

Bao-yu folded up the list and stowed it away inside his jacket. They continued to sit a while longer, chatting about this and that.

After dinner they went to call on Grandmother Jia to see how she was. She had been suffering from nothing more serious than a slight chill aggravated by fatigue, and by the evening, after a day's cosseting and two doses of the mild sudorific prescribed by Dr Wang, she was almost better.

If you want to know what the next day held in store, you will have to read the following chapter.

CHAPTER 43

*An old woman's whim is the occasion of a birthday collection
And a young man's remorse finds solace in a simple ceremony*

Our story recommences in Lady Wang's apartment next day. On the previous evening's visit she had found Grandmother Jia almost completely recovered after only two doses of the medicine prescribed for her that same morning by the doctor. Satisfied that it was only a mild chill, contracted during her day in Prospect Garden, and not anything more serious that the old lady had been suffering from, and deeming it unnecessary to make an early call again this morning, Lady Wang summoned Wang Xi-feng to her own apartment to discuss the getting together of some things to send to her husband, Jia Zheng. A summons from Grandmother Jia arrived nevertheless, and Lady Wang hurried over, taking Xi-feng with her, to see what was the matter.

'Are you still feeling better today, Mother?' she asked her when they arrived.

'I'm quite recovered now, thank you,' said Grandmother Jia. 'I've had a sip or two of the pheasant stew you sent me. It was very tasty. I ate some of the meat in it and enjoyed it very much.'

'You have Feng to thank for that,' said Lady Wang with a smile. 'See how dutiful she is to you! It shows that your kindness is not wasted on her.'

Grandmother Jia returned the smile and nodded affably.

'It was good of her to think of me. If there's any of the meat still left, I'd rather like a few pieces of it fried. It has a pleasant, salty tang that goes well with the rice-gruel I am taking. The stew is very nice, but stew and gruel don't go very well together.'

Xi-feng at once sent orders to the main kitchen to have the pheasant-meat prepared.

'Well, it wasn't really my diet that I wanted to talk about,' said Grandmother Jia. 'The reason I've sent for you is because the second of the ninth month is Feng's birthday. In previous years, though I've always *meant* to do something about it, something or other has always cropped up which has prevented me from celebrating it properly. As we're all of us here together this year and it doesn't look as if there are likely to be any distractions, I propose that we should get together and make a day of it.'

'I was thinking just the same thing,' said Lady Wang. 'Since you feel in such good spirits, Mother, why not settle now what we should do?'

'Well now, this is what I have been thinking,' said Grandmother Jia. 'In other years, no matter whose birthday it's been, we've each of us given our individual presents. Now that's *so* dull – and what's more, l think it's a rather unsociable way of celebrating a birthday. l've thought of a new way which will be much more sociable and also lots of fun.'

'Whatever it is, I'm sure that's what we ought to do,' said Lady Wang.

'I think we ought to imitate what they do in poorer families,' said Grandmother Jia. 'Everyone subscribes something towards a common pool, then, when it's all been collected, you spend it all on some treat or other, depending on how much you have. What do you think of the idea?'

'It sounds a very good one,' said Lady Wang. 'But how do we go about collecting the subscriptions?'

At this Grandmother Jia became still more animated. Let Aunt Xue and Lady Xing be invited without delay, she told them. Let Bao-yu and the girls be sent for. And You-shi from the other mansion. And why not Lai Da's wife and some of the more respected older members of the female staff? Infected by her enthusiasm, the maids and older women-servants went scurrying off in all directions to summon or invite.

In less time than it would take to eat a meal, all those invited, young and old, mistress and servant, had been assembled, and the room was packed. Aunt Xue and Grandmother Jia sat on their own facing the multitude, Lady Xing and Lady Wang on chairs at the opposite side of the room beside the door. Bao-chai, Dai-yu, Xiang-yun and the Three Springs sat in a row at the back of the kang behind Grandmother Jia and Aunt Xue. Bao-yu half reclined in his grandmother's lap. All the rest stood, shoulder to shoulder, on the floor below.

As soon as she saw that they were all assembled, Grandmother Jia gave orders for stools to be brought so that Lai Da's mother and various other of the more aged and respected servants present might sit down. It was customary in the Jia household to treat the older generation of servants – those who had served the parents of the present masters – with even greater respect than the younger generation of masters, so that in this instance it was not thought at all surprising that You-shi, Xi-feng and Li Wan should remain standing while old Mrs Lai and three or four other old nannies (though not without first apologizing for the liberty) seated themselves on the stools.

Grandmother Jia now smilingly announced the proposal that she had already outlined to Lady Wang. All present, it need hardly be said, were willing to fall in with it – some because they were on good terms with Xi-feng and were genuinely happy to give her pleasure, some because they were afraid of her and welcomed this as an opportunity of getting themselves into her good books, and all because in any case they could afford to do so. Accordingly, as soon as Grandmother Jia had finished speaking, they all enthusiastically and with one voice agreed.

Grandmother Jia opened the list with her own subscription:
'I'll give twenty taels.'

'I'll follow Lady Jia,' said Aunt Xue. 'Twenty taels.'

Lady Xing and Lady Wang called next:
'We obviously can't put ourselves on a level with Lady Jia. Sixteen taels.'

You-shi and Li Wan, decreasing their call by a like amount, came next:
'Twelve taels.'

'We can't have *you* paying out that sort of money,' Grandmother Jia said to Li Wan, ' – a young widow with no means of her own. I'll pay yours for you.'

'Now don't get carried away, Grandma!' said Xi-feng. 'You ought to do your sums first before you start interfering. Don't forget you've already got two of the young folk, Bao-yu and Cousin Lin, to pay for besides your own contribution. It's all very well promising to pay these additional twelve taels for Li Wan in the heat of the moment, but later on you'll be wishing you hadn't. You'll probably end up by saying that it was all because of that wretched Feng that you had to pay out so much money and think of some trick for getting it back from me three or four times over. *I* know. Don't tell me I'm imagining this.'

This made everyone laugh.

'All right,' said Grandmother Jia, laughing herself. 'Then what do you propose?'

'Well now, it isn't even my birthday yet, but already I'm feeling uncomfortable because so much is being done for me,' said Xi-feng. 'It seems unlucky – so many people being put to so much expense on my account while I don't pay a penny myself. I'd feel a lot easier if you'd let *me* pay this contribution for Li Wan; then, when the day comes, I shall be able to eat and drink as much as I like without any fear of spoiling my luck.'

Grandmother Jia hesitated, but consented when Lady Xing and Lady Wang both insisted that this was the best solution.

'I've got another suggestion to make,' said Xi-feng. 'Your own contribution is twenty taels, Grandma, and on top of that you're going to be paying contributions for Bao-chai and Cousin Lin. It's true that Aunt Xue will be paying Cousin Chai's contribution on top of *her* twenty taels, but that doesn't seem quite so unfair. What *does* seem unfair to me is that Mother and Aunt Wang should be paying only sixteen taels each for themselves, yet paying no extras at all for any of the young people. I think you're getting the worst of this arrangement, Grannie.'

'See what a good girl my Feng is to me!' said Grandmother Jia delightedly. 'You're quite right, my dear. If you hadn't mentioned it, I should have let them get away with it – as usual!'

'All you need do, Grannie, is to make the two young people *their* responsibility. Let each pay for one of them.'

'That's fair,' said Grandmother Jia. 'Yes, that's what I'll do.'

Lai Da's old mother rose up from her stool in mock indignation.

'But this is rank mutiny! It makes me feel really angry on Their Ladyships' behalf. What, side with Her Old Ladyship against your husband's mother and your own father's sister? That's a arrant breach of the laws o' consanguinity!'

This sally was greeted with a burst of laughter from Grandmother Jia and all the others present. Old Mrs Lai remained standing until it had subsided and then made her own offer.

'If Mrs Zhu and Mrs Lian are each contributing twelve taels, I suppose we'd better go a step lower?'

'Oh no, that won't do at all!' said Grandmother Jia. 'You may be a step below them in rank, but you're all wealthy women. I know you've got lots more money than they have. You can't give *more*, of course, but at least you should give as much.'

The old women, led by Mrs Lai, willingly agreed.

'The girls' contribution will be only for form's sake, anyway,' said Grandmother Jia in reference to the row of figures sitting silently behind her on the kang. 'I should think about the equivalent of a month's allowance would be the right amount.'

She turned to Faithful.

'Come on, now! We're not leaving *you* out! Go and get some of the other girls together and decide how much *you* are going to give.'

Faithful slipped out and presently returned with Patience, Aroma, Suncloud and one or two other of the senior maids. Some said they would give one tael, others two. Grandmother Jia noticed that Patience was one of them.

'Surely you'll be doing something for your mistress at home?' she said. 'You don't need to contribute to this fund as well.'

'Yes, ma'am, I *shall* be doing something at home,' said

Patience, 'but that's private. This is a public thing, so I shall contribute to this along with the rest.'

Grandmother Jia smiled at her graciously and commended her public spirit.

'Well,' said Xi-feng genially, 'now just about everyone seems to have been roped in except Aunt Zhou and Aunt Zhao. Wouldn't it be a politeness to ask them if they would like to contribute as well? They might take it as a slight if we left them out.'

'Of course,' said Grandmother Jia. 'Whatever made me forget about *them*? They probably won't be free to come over, though. One of the maids had better go and ask them.'

One of the maids had gone off on this mission almost before she had finished speaking. She returned, after a long interval, to say that the concubines would contribute two taels each.

'Good!' said Grandmother Jia. 'Now take a brush and ink, someone, and calculate how much we shall have altogether.'

In the interval thus created, You-shi addressed Xi-feng in a scornful whisper.

'What a mean, grasping young woman you are! Your aunt and your mother-in-law and all these other people forking out for your birthday, yet you still have to go squeezing more out of two poor, dried-up old gourds like Zhou and Zhao!'

Xi-feng laughed silently.

'Don't talk nonsense!' she whispered back. 'I'll settle accounts with you presently, when we get out of here. Anyway, what do you mean, "poor"? Whenever they've *got* any money they only pass it straight on to other people. We might just as well intercept it before it gets into the hands of their creditors and get a bit of pleasure out of it!'

By the time this whispered exchange was over, the calculations had been completed and it was announced that the amounts promised totalled a round sum of one hundred and fifty taels with a few taels left over.

'That's more than we could possibly spend on plays and wine in one day,' said Grandmother Jia.

'As we're not inviting anyone from outside,' said You-shi, 'it won't be a very *big* party, either. There should be enough for two or three days. The big saving, of course, is that now you've got your own troupe of players, you can have first-class entertainment for nothing.'

'Feng shall have whatever troupe she prefers,' said Grand-mother Jia. 'That's for *her* to decide.'

'We've heard our own troupe so often,' said Xi-feng. 'I think we should spend a bit of money and get in a troupe from outside.'

'Well, I propose to leave all the arrangements for this in the hands of Cousin Zhen's wife,' said Grandmother Jia, 'then Feng will have nothing at all to worry about – except how to get the greatest possible enjoyment out of her birthday!'

You-shi agreed to be organizer, after which she and the others stayed chatting for a few minutes with Grandmother Jia. Then, realizing that the old lady's stock of energy was exhausted, they gradually dispersed.

After the three younger women had seen Lady Xing and Lady Wang a part of their way home, You-shi accompanied Xi-feng to the latter's apartment to discuss with her what arrangements she should make for the party.

'Don't ask *me*,' said Xi-feng when You-shi questioned her. 'You want to study Grandmother and just do whatever seems to please *her*.'

'You really are the limit, you know,' said You-shi. 'Fortune's darling! I thought just now that I was being called over about something serious, but it turned out to be just for *this*! And then, if you please, quite apart from being asked to pay out money, I am to have all the worry of arranging everything for you as well. What are you going to do in return for all this, to show me your gratitude?'

'What am I going to do in return?' said Xi-feng. 'You must be joking. *I* didn't call you over. If you're afraid of the trouble, you'd better go back to Grandmother and tell her to give the job to somebody else.'

'Just look at her!' said You-shi. 'Really full of yourself today, aren't you? I should hold it in a bit, if I were you, my dear, or it might start running over!'

The two of them conversed for some minutes longer before finally separating.

*

When the first contributions arrived at Ning-guo House next morning, You-shi had only just got up and was about to begin her toilet. She asked who had brought the money, and on being informed that it was Lin Zhi-xiao's wife, sent the maid back to fetch her in from the servants' quarters, where she was waiting. When she arrived, You-shi asked for a stool to be brought so that the old woman could sit and talk to her while she continued with her toilet.

'How many of the contributions have you got in this packet?' You-shi asked her.

'These are the ones from us servants,' said Lin Zhi-xiao's wife. 'As they were all ready, I thought I might as well bring them over straight away. The contributions from Her Old Ladyship and the other ladies are still to come.'

Just then one of the maids came in to announce another arrival:

'The subscriptions from Mrs Xue and Lady Xing have arrived, ma'am.'

'*Subscriptions!*' said You-shi scornfully. 'How eagerly you fasten on the ridiculous word! It was only a passing fancy of Her Old Ladyship's yesterday that we should imitate what they do in poorer households. She used the word then as a joke; but now, I suppose, we shall have every witless maid solemnly talking about "subscriptions" all the time! – Well, go and get the money and bring it in then. And see that whoever it is has some tea before they go.'

The girl went out and returned with the two packets of money that the messenger had brought, one from Aunt Xue, including a contribution for Bao-chai, and one, including Dai-yu's contribution, from Lady Xing.

'Who does that leave now?' said You-shi.

'That leaves Her Old Ladyship, Her Ladyship, the young ladies and the maids,' said Lin Zhi-xiao's wife.

'What about Mrs Zhu's?' said You-shi.

'Mrs Lian will be paying out the money for all the others,' said Lin Zhi-xiao's wife, 'so you'll be able to get Mrs Zhu's from her too when you see her about the rest.'

You-shi, having completed her toilet, now called for her carriage. As soon as it was ready, she drove round to the Rong-guo mansion and went straight in to see Xi-feng. She found her with the money already packeted and on the point of bringing it round to her.

'Is it *all* here?' You-shi asked her.

'All there,' said Xi-feng gaily. 'Hurry up and take it away. I don't want to be responsible for it if it gets lost.'

'I don't think I altogether trust you,' said You-shi, returning her smile. 'I think I'd like to check it first in your presence.'

She opened up the packet and counted the money contained in it. The contribution for Li Wan appeared to be missing.

'I *thought* you were up to something,' she said. 'Why isn't the money for Wan here?'

Xi-feng smiled disarmingly.

'Isn't what you've already got there enough? Surely *her* little bit isn't going to make all that much difference? Why not wait and see what you need? If you find you haven't got enough, I'll give the money for Wan to you later.'

'I'm not letting you get away with this,' said You-shi, ' – playing the Lady Bountiful yesterday in front of all those others and then going back on it now, when the two of us are alone together. I shall have to go and ask Lady Jia for the money.'

'You're a hard woman!' said Xi-feng. 'One of these days when I have *you* at a disadvantage, you mustn't complain if you find me just as much of a stickler.'

'Threats?' said You-shi. 'I think *you* are the one who should feel afraid. Do you think if it weren't for the things you have done for me in the past I would let you off now? Here, Patience!' – She took Patience's contribution from the pile and held it out to her – 'Take this back. If later on I find that I need it, I'll make it good with my own money.'

Patience immediately understood what she was getting at and answered in the same vein.

'No, Mrs Zhen, *you* keep it. If you find you have any left over, you can give it back to me afterwards.'

'Take it,' said You-shi. 'Is your mistress the only one who's allowed to break the rules? Mayn't I do favours too, if I want to?'

Patience was obliged to take the money from her.

'Seeing your mistress so tight-fisted,' said You-shi, 'I often wonder what she's going to do with all this money she saves. Take it with her in her coffin?'

With that parting shot she went off to see Grandmother Jia. After greeting the old lady and exchanging a few generalities, she went into Faithful's room for a more serious discussion of arrangements for the birthday party. The 'discussion' consisted quite simply in finding out what would give Grandmother Jia most pleasure and deciding that that was what they should do. When all had been settled between them and You-shi was rising to go, she took out the two taels that Faithful had contributed and handed them back to her.

'Here you are. We shan't be needing this.'

From Grandmother Jia's apartment she went over to have a few words with Lady Wang. When Lady Wang presently left her to go into her Buddhist chapel, You-shi took advantage of her absence to return Suncloud's contribution; then, since Xi-feng was safely out of the way, she offered Aunt Zhou and Aunt Zhao their contributions as well. But the concubines were too scared to take them.

'Go on!' said You-shi encouragingly. 'I know how hard-up you are. You can't afford to give away money like this. If Feng finds out, I shall take full responsibility myself.'

They took the money then, voluble in their gratitude.

*

In a twinkling the second of the ninth was upon them. The denizens of the Garden had been informed that You-shi was planning an impressive variety of entertainment: not only the

customary plays, but also juggling, acrobatics, story-telling by
blind ballad-singers – in short, everything one could possibly
think of that might contribute to the success of the occasion
and the pleasure of the participants.

Li Wan reminded the cousins that the second of the month
was also one of the regular meeting-days of the poetry club.
Xi-chun was, of course, excused.

'But why hasn't Bao-yu turned up?' she asked. 'I suppose
he's so intent on enjoying the fun that he has forgotten his
former enthusiasm for these more civilized amusements! – Go
and see what he's doing,' she said to one of the maids, 'and
tell him to come here immediately.'

The maid was a long time gone.

'Miss Aroma says he went out first thing this morning,' she
reported when she eventually returned.

The others were incredulous.

'That's ridiculous. How could he possibly have gone out?
The girl must have got the message wrong.'

They sent Ebony over to ask again; but Ebony only confirmed what the first maid had said.

'Yes, he really has gone out. It seems that one of his friends
has died and he's had to go out to condole.'

'That's absolutely absurd,' said Tan-chun. 'Whatever the
reason, he can't possibly have gone out *today*. Fetch Aroma
here and I'll speak to her myself.'

As if anticipating a summons, Aroma herself walked in
while she was saying this. Li Wan tackled her at once.

'There's absolutely no justification for his going out today,
whatever the reason,' she said. 'In the first place it's Mrs Lian's
birthday and Her Old Ladyship was particularly anxious that
we should all join in celebrating it this year: it's monstrous
that he should go off on his own like this when everyone else
from both houses is here for the celebration. And in the second
place this is the first regular meeting of our poetry club and he
hasn't even asked leave to stay away.'

Aroma sighed miserably.

'Last night he told me that he had some important business
to attend to first thing this morning. He said he had to go to

the Prince of Bei-jing's palace, but that he would be back
again as soon as possible. I *told* him not to go, but he insisted.
When he got up first thing this morning, he asked for a suit
of mourning to wear. It looks as if some important person in
the Prince of Bei-jing's household must have died.'

'If that's really so,' said Li Wan, 'then he *ought* to have gone.
But then, on the other hand, he ought to have got back by
now.'

After a brief discussion the cousins decided to proceed
without him and to punish him in some way when he returned.
Before they could begin, however, a summons arrived from
Grandmother Jia to join her in the mansion. As soon as they
had done so, Aroma reported Bao-yu's absence. The old lady
was displeased and sent someone to fetch him back.

Bao-yu, evidently with some secret business on his mind,
had spoken the day before to Tealeaf about this excursion.

'I have to go out first thing tomorrow,' he told him. 'I
want you to be waiting for me outside the back gate with two
horses ready saddled. No one else is to accompany me but you.
Tell Li Gui that I am going to the Prince of Bei-jing's, and
that he must stop anyone going out to look for me. He can
tell them that the Prince is detaining me and that I shall come
back as soon as I can get away.'

Though somewhat mystified by these orders, Tealeaf felt he
had no choice but to follow them out, and before dawn next
morning was waiting with two horses ready saddled outside
the rear gate of the Garden. As soon as it was light, Bao-yu,
dressed in heavy mourning, emerged from the postern, leaped
onto one of the waiting horses, and crouching down over the
reins, set off at a brisk trot down the street – all without uttering a single word.

Tealeaf leaped onto the second horse, gave it the whip, and
did his best to catch up with Bao-yu, at the same time shouting
after him to inquire where they were going.

'Where does this road lead to?' Bao-yu asked him.

'This is the main road to the North Gate,' said Tealeaf.
'Outside the city it's pretty deserted in that direction. You
won't find much to amuse you there.'

'Good,' said Bao-yu. 'The more deserted the better.'

And by applying the whip he made his horse shoot on ahead, and presently, after a couple of turns, had left the city gate behind him.

Tealeaf, more mystified than ever, followed him as closely as he could. When they had galloped without stopping for two or three miles, in the course of which the signs of human habitation had gradually grown more and more sparse, Bao-yu finally reined to a halt and turned back to ask Tealeaf if there was anywhere where they could purchase some incense.

'I dare say we could find *somewhere*,' said Tealeaf without much conviction. 'It depends what kind of incense you want.'

Bao-yu reflected for some moments.

'Honeybush, sandal and lakawood,' he said. 'It has to be those three.'

'I doubt if you'll be able to get *them*,' said Tealeaf, smiling at the naïveté of one who could expect to make such purchases in such a place. But when he saw that Bao-yu was genuinely distressed, he added: 'What's it for? I've noticed that you often carry powdered incense in that sachet you wear. Why not see if you've got any in that?'

Bao-yu, glad to be reminded, extracted the silk purse that he wore suspended from his neck underneath the front fold of his gown, felt inside it with his fingers, and was delighted to find that there was still a pinch or two of powdered agalloch in the bottom.

'Seems a bit lacking in respect to use this though,' he thought.

'Still, it's more respectful to use something I've carried all the way here myself than it would be to use something I'd just bought in a shop.'

Having decided that the powdered incense would do, he asked Tealeaf where he could get hold of an incense-burner and some fire.

'Now those we *can't* get,' said Tealeaf. 'Where *could* we, out here in the middle of the wilds? If you knew you were going to need them, why didn't you tell me beforehand, and we could have brought them with us?'

'Stupid idiot!' said Bao-yu. 'Do you honestly think we could have ridden out at this break-neck pace if we'd been carrying an incense-burner full of hot coals with us?'

Tealeaf, after some moments of reflection, smiled uncertainly:

'I know what we *could* do, Master, though I don't know what you'll think of the idea. There's little enough hope of our getting the things you've just asked for round here, and the chances are that even if we could, you'd only start thinking of something else you needed that was even harder to get. Now if we were to go on for about another two thirds of a mile in this direction, we should come to the Temple of the Water Spirit — '

Bao-yu pricked up his ears.

'The Temple of the Water Spirit? Is that near here? Good. That will do even better. Let's go there then.'

With a touch of the whip he was away once more, still talking to Tealeaf over his shoulder as he rode ahead.

'The nun at the Water Spirit is one of our regular callers. If I see *her* when we get there and tell her we want to use one of her burners, she's sure to let us.'

'Even if this wasn't one of the temples we subscribe to,' said Tealeaf, 'I'm sure they wouldn't dare refuse if you asked them. But why is it that today you are so willing to go to the Temple of the Water Spirit when normally you can scarcely abide to hear it mentioned?'

'The reason I normally feel that way about it,' said Bao-yu, 'is because I hate the silly, senseless way in which vulgar people offer worship and build temples to gods they know nothing about. Ignorant old men and women with too much money to spend hear the name of some god or other – they've no idea who it is, but the mere fact that they've heard it from the lips of some ballad-singer or story-teller seems to them incontrovertible proof of the god's existence – and go founding temples in which these fictitious deities can be worshipped.

'Take this Temple of the Water Spirit. The reason it's called that is because the divinity worshipped in it is supposed to be the goddess of the river Luo. Now in point of fact no Goddess of the Luo ever existed. She was an invention of the poet Cao Zhi. But that didn't stop a lot of people making an image of her and worshipping it.

'The only reason I feel differently about this temple today is because the *idea* of a water-goddess just happens to fit in with the thing that is at the moment uppermost in my mind; so I'm glad to make use of it *for my own purpose.*'

By this time they had reached the gate of the temple. The old nun who kept it, hardly less surprised to hear of Bao-yu's arrival than she would have been if she had been told that a dragon had just fallen, alive and kicking, out of the sky, hurried out to greet him, and ordered the old temple-servant who did duty as a porter to take care of the horses.

Bao-yu went on inside. Instead of bowing down before the image, however, he stood and contemplated it appraisingly. Though the goddess was only a thing of wood and plaster and paint, the sculptor who made her had succeeded in capturing some of the spirit of Cao Zhi's famous description. To Bao-yu's gazing eyes she did indeed appear as the poet portrayed her:

> Fluttering like the wing-beats of a startled swan,
> Swaying with the lissome curves of a water-dragon . . .

Cao Zhi's beautiful images came crowding into his mind:

> Like a lotus flower emerging from the green water,
> Like the morning sun rising above the mist-bank . . .

And as he gazed and remembered, the tears coursed down his cheeks.

The old nun now appeared with some tea. While he sipped it, Bao-yu took the opportunity of asking her if he might borrow an incense-burner. At this she disappeared once more, to reappear, after considerable delay, carrying not only a burner but also a whole portion of incense and a set of garishly-printed 'picture-offerings'. Refusing all but the burner, Bao-yu made Tealeaf carry it outside into the rear courtyard of the temple, where he set about choosing a suitably clean spot on which to make his offering. Nowhere would do, however, until Tealeaf suggested placing the burner on the stone platform of the well. To this suggestion Bao-yu assented with a nod, and when Tealeaf had set down the burner and retired to a respectful distance, he took out his pinch of agalloch and dropped it on the burning charcoal; then, with tears in his eyes, he knelt down and made, not a kotow, but the sort of half-obeisance one makes to the spirit of a junior or a servant.

Having concluded his little ceremony, Bao-yu got up and ordered Tealeaf to take the burner back into the temple. But Tealeaf, though saying that he would, did nothing of the kind. Instead he threw himself on his knees, kotowed several times, and began praying aloud in the direction of the well:

'O spirit, in all the years I have served Master Bao this is the first time he has ever kept anything from me. But though I don't know who you are, O spirit, and don't like to ask, one thing I *do* know, and that is that you are sure to be some wondrously beautiful, clever, refined young female. And since Master Bao isn't able to tell you out loud what he wants of you, I, Tealeaf, am praying to you on his behalf.

'I beseech you, if you still have feelings as you used to when you were on earth, watch over my master from time to time, O spirit. I know you belong to a different world now, but being as it's for a special friend of yours that I'm asking this, please do it if you can, spirit, for old time's sake.

'And please use what influence you can to see that Master Bao is reborn in his next life as a girl, so that he can spend all his time with you; and don't let him be reborn as one of those horrible Whiskered Males he is always on about.'

At this point he knocked his head several more times on the ground. Bao-yu, who had been listening, could no longer hold back his laughter. Observing that Tealeaf had raised himself once more on all fours and appeared to be about to go on, he kicked him and told him to get up.

'Stop this nonsense! If anyone hears you, I shall become a laughing-stock.'

Tealeaf scrambled to his feet, picked up the burner and followed Bao-yu inside.

'I've already spoken to the nun about getting you some food,' he told Bao-yu as they were going in together. 'I told her you hadn't eaten yet. You ought to get something inside you. I realize that you came out here because there's a big party and lots of racket at home today and you wanted somewhere peaceful where you could do this. But I think just staying out here in the quiet all day is showing all the respect you need to this person you've just made the offering to. You don't need to fast all day as well. That's out of the question.'

'That seems reasonable,' said Bao-yu. 'As I'm missing the party all the time that I'm here, I am in a way abstaining already; so I suppose there can be no harm in my taking a bit of vegetarian stuff.'

'I'm glad to hear you say so,' said Tealeaf. 'Of course, there is another way of looking at it. Your going off like this is sure to cause others at home to worry. Now if no one at home was likely to worry, there'd be no harm in our not going back until evening. But since they *are* going to worry, I really think you ought to be getting back soon. For one thing it will set Their Ladyships' minds at rest, and for another, it will, in the long run, be more respectful to this person you've just made the offering to. Because if you go home, even if you drink and watch plays, it won't be because you want to, but out of duty to Their Ladyships. Whereas if you stay out here thinking only about the spirit and not caring how worried you make Their Ladyships, you'll in fact be making the spirit herself uneasy to think of all the anxiety that's being caused on her behalf. Think it over, Master Bao, and see if you don't agree with me.'

'I can see what's on your mind without much difficulty,' said Bao-yu, laughing. 'You're afraid that as *you* are the only one who came out here with me, *you* will bear all the blame for this outing when we get back. That's the real reason why I'm being treated to all this high-minded advice, isn't it? Well, don't worry! It was all along my intention to go back to the party when I had made the offering. *I* never said anything about staying out here all day. I've discharged my vow. If I hurry home now so that the others aren't too worried, it seems to me that my obligations to the dead and the living will *both* be met.'

Tealeaf expressed his relief. Still talking, they made their way to the old nun's parlour, or 'hall of meditation', where they found she had set out a very presentable (though, of course, vegetarian) repast for them. After briefly sampling it, the two of them mounted and set off again along the road by which they had come – Bao-yu at such a pace that Tealeaf was obliged to call out after him to slacken it.

'Go easy on that horse, Master Bao! He hasn't been ridden very much; you need to keep a pretty tight rein on him.'

Soon they had entered the city gate, and not long afterwards might have been seen slipping into the back gate of the Garden. Bao-yu hurried straight to Green Delights, which he found deserted except for a few old nannies left behind as caretakers.

'Holy name!' they said, their old faces lighting up with pleasure when they saw who it was. 'You've come at last! You've had Miss Aroma nigh out of her mind with worry. They're sitting at table in the front now, Master. Better hurry up and join them.'

Bao-yu quickly took off his mourning clothes and went off to look for something more colourful to change into.

'Where *is* the party?' he asked the old women as soon as he had dressed.

'In the new reception room.'

He hurried, by the shortest route, towards the faint sounds of fluting and singing that could soon be heard coming from the so-called 'new' reception hall that the old women had referred to. As he approached the gallery through which he must pass to reach it, he came upon Silver, sitting under the eaves of the covered way and crying. She left off hurriedly when she saw him coming.

'Here comes the phoenix at last!' she said sarcastically. 'Hurry up and go inside. If you stay away much longer, there'll be a riot!'

Bao-yu smiled at her sympathetically.

'Guess where I've been.'

She ignored his question and turned away from him to wipe her eyes. He hurried on, dejected because of his inability to comfort her. When he entered the hall where the others were assembled and went up to greet his grandmother and his mother, it really *was* as if a phoenix had appeared. Hurriedly he made his birthday kotow to Xi-feng.

'What do you mean by going off on your own like that?' Grandmother Jia grumbled. 'I never heard of such a thing. If this happens again, I shall tell your father when he comes back and get him to give you another beating.'

Bao-yu's pages came in next for her censure.

'Why do they listen to him – rushing off like that whenever he tells them to? They should tell *us* first. Where *have* you been, anyway?' she asked him. 'Have you had anything to eat? Has anything happened to give you a fright?'

'The Prince of Bei-jing's favourite concubine died yesterday,' said Bao-yu. 'I went to condole with him. He was in such a state when I got there that I didn't like to leave immediately. That's why I've been so long.'

'If you sneak out again without first telling us,' said Grandmother Jia, 'I really *shall* tell your Pa to beat you.'

Though Bao-yu promised to obey, she still wanted to have his pages whipped; but the others all begged for a reprieve: 'Don't take it to heart, Grandmother! He's already said he won't do it again. And anyway, he's back now, so we can forget our worries and concentrate on enjoying ourselves.'

Grandmother Jia had in fact been extremely worried and her anxiety had made her vengeful. Now that Bao-yu was back and she was no longer worried, her vengeful feelings evaporated and the subject of beatings was quickly dropped. Her concern now was lest Bao-yu should have been unduly distressed by his visit, or have failed to eat enough while he was away, or have been involved in some accident on the way there or back. While she continued to fuss over him, Aroma took her place at his side to wait upon him, and the rest of the company resumed the play-watching which his arrival had interrupted.

The play being performed on this occasion was *The Wooden Hairpin*. Grandmother Jia and the other ladies found it greatly affecting, shedding copious tears in the course of it and sighing or cursing in the appropriate places.

The events that ensued will be told in the following chapter.

CHAPTER 44

*Xi-feng's jealousy is the object of an unexpected provocation
And Patience's toilet is a source of unexpected delight*

BAO-YU having now taken his place amongst the girls, they
and the rest of the company were once more able to give their
undivided attention to the players.

The play being performed on this occasion was, as we noted
at the end of the previous chapter, *The Wooden Hairpin,* and it
chanced that they had reached that section of it popularly referred to as 'The Husband's Offering', in which the hero
Wang Shi-peng, believing that his wife has drowned herself,
goes with his aged mother to the river Ou-jiang to make
offerings to her soul. At this point Dai-yu, who was able to
guess what the real purpose of Bao-yu's early-morning
excursion had been, turned to Bao-chai and remarked, in a
voice loud enough for Bao-yu to overhear, that she thought
Wang Shi-peng a 'very silly sort of fellow'.

'He could have made his offering anywhere. Why was it
necessary for him to go rushing off to the riverside to make
it? They say that "objects aid recall": well, since all the water
in the world comes ultimately from a single source, a bowlful
of it scooped up anywhere should have sufficed. His feelings
could have been just as effectively relieved by weeping over a
bowlful of water as by rushing off to the banks of the river.'

Bao-chai made no reply. Bao-yu, who had certainly heard
her, turned away and called for hot wine to drink Xi-feng's
health with.

Grandmother Jia was determined that this should be a day
like no other and that Xi-feng should derive the greatest possible enjoyment from it. Not feeling sufficiently energetic to
sit with the rest, however, she had retired to the inner room
with Aunt Xue, reclining on a couch there in a position from
which it was still possible to watch the players. A small
selection from the dishes which had covered the two tables

laid for her outside had been set down within easy reach where she could pick at them while conversing with Aunt Xue. The remainder she had made over to the maids and older women on duty who had not been catered for, bidding them take their banquet outside on to the verandah where they could sit down and enjoy themselves without restraint.

Lady Wang and Lady Xing also sat in this inner room, not on the kang, where Grandmother Jia's couch had been placed, but at a high-topped table on the floor below. The young people sat at a number of tables in the outer room. From time to time Grandmother Jia would give orders to You-shi to make sure that Xi-feng was enjoying herself.

'Make her sit at the head. Why isn't she sitting at the head? It's up to you to act as hostess on my behalf,' she told You-shi. 'The poor child is run off her feet all the rest of the year. Today I want her to be made a fuss of.'

You-shi went off to do her bidding, but shortly afterwards returned, a smile on her face, to announce that Xi-feng was being difficult.

'She says she's not used to sitting at the head. She says it makes her uncomfortable. And she refuses to drink anything.'

'If *you* can't make her, I shall have to come out and deal with her myself,' said Grandmother Jia, laughing.

This brought Xi-feng herself running up. She spoke to Grandmother Jia from behind You-shi's shoulder.

'Don't believe her, Grannie. I've had lots and lots to drink.'

'Now look here,' said Grandmother Jia to You-shi, 'I want you to march this young woman back to her seat and *force* her to sit down in it. Then I want every one of you here to drink with her in turn. If she still refuses, I really and truly shall come out and deal with her myself.'

You-shi hauled Xi-feng out again, called for larger cups to be brought, and poured her out some wine.

'There you are, my darling! In token of my appreciation of the noble way in which you have served Lady Jia and Lady Wang and me during the past year, please accept this cup of wine that I have poured out for you with my own fair hand!'

'If you are really serious about wanting to show me your

appreciation,' said Xi-feng, 'you ought to offer it to me kneel-ing down.'

'Just listen to that!' said You-shi. 'I'll tell you something, my girl: you just don't realize how lucky you are. For all you know, things may never be as good as this for you again. If I were you, I'd have a good booze-up while you can. Come on, *two* cups!'

You-shi was so insistent that in the end Xi-feng had to drink two whole cupfuls from the larger cups. After that the cousins came up one by one to drink with her, which meant that she had to take at least a sip or two with each of them. Then old Mrs Lai, observing with what high spirits Grand-mother Jia was watching these antics, determined to join in the fun too, and came over, with the other old nannies, to drink Xi-feng's health along with all the rest. Because of the seniority of this group, it would have been difficult for Xi-feng to refuse them, so with each of them too she had to take a couple of sips. But when Faithful and the maids came trooping up, it was more than flesh and blood could bear and she begged to be excused.

'Really, my dears, I couldn't. Let me put it off until to-morrow.'

Faithful pretended to take umbrage.

'I call that most insulting! Even Her Ladyship treats me with more consideration. I used to think that I counted for something round here, but now, after being put in my place in front of all these others, I can see that I did wrong to come. Well, if you won't drink, I'm going!'

She turned away and began marching out, but Xi-feng ran after and detained her.

'No, please! I'll drink.'

She fetched the wine herself, filled a cup to the brim with it, and drank it down to the last drop, up-ending it afterwards to show that it was dry. At that Faithful laughed and went away content.

As soon as she had resumed her seat, Xi-feng knew that she had drunk too much. Her heart was pounding in her throat and she felt an overwhelming desire to go back home and lie down. But the leader of the jugglers was bearing down on her.

'Give this man his money,' she said, turning to You-shi. 'I have to go home to wash.'

You-shi nodded, and Xi-feng, choosing a moment when no one was looking, slipped outside and made her way along the outside of the hall under the shadow of the eaves. Patience, who had seen her go and was concerned about her, hurried after and gave her some support.

As they approached the passage-way which led from Grandmother Jia's rear courtyard to the gallery in the midst of the little enclosure surrounded by walls and buildings which had once been the scene of Jia Rui's night-long sufferings, they recognized one of the junior maids from their own apartment standing there, who, as soon as she caught sight of them, turned tail and ran. Xi-feng at once became suspicious and called out after her. The little maid at first pretended not to hear, but when the shouting behind her continued, could no longer keep up the pretence and had to turn about and face them.

Xi-feng's suspicions were now thoroughly aroused. Advancing into the gallery and calling the maid back into it, she first made Patience close the partitions, so that they were completely cut off from the outside, then, seating herself on the gallery's stone plinth and ordering the maid to kneel down in front of her, she told Patience in a fierce, loud voice to fetch two pages from the inner gate with a rope and whips to 'flog to a jelly' this abominable creature who had so little regard for the presence of her mistress. The wretched girl, already half-dead with fright, now wept for terror and knocked her head repeatedly on the ground, entreating Xi-feng for mercy.

'I'm not a ghost,' said Xi-feng. 'You're supposed to stand still and wait when you see me coming. What do you mean by running away from me like that?'

'I didn't see you at first, ma'am,' said the little girl tearfully. 'I was running because I'd just remembered that there was no one at home to look after things.'

'If there's no one at home, you had no business to go out in the first place,' said Xi-feng. 'And even if you didn't see me, you must have heard me calling you. Patience and I shouted to you at the tops of our voices ten or a dozen times, but you only ran the faster. We weren't all that far away from you, either, and you certainly aren't deaf. How dare you lie to me!'

She raised her hand and dealt the girl a slap on the cheek that made her reel, quickly followed by a second slap on the other cheek. An angry red patch swelled up instantly on either side of the girl's face.

'Don't, madam. You'll hurt your hand,' Patience pleaded.

'Hit her for me, then,' said Xi-feng, 'and ask her why she ran away. If she still won't talk, tear her lips!'

At first the maid tried sticking to her story, but when she heard that Xi-feng was going to heat an iron red-hot and burn her mouth with it, she broke down and tearfully confessed that Jia Lian was at home and had stationed her in the passage-way to look out for her mistress and give him warning of her coming; but as Xi-feng had left the party so much earlier than expected, she had been taken unawares.

This seemed to Xi-feng to have the ring of truth about it.

'*Why* did he ask you to look out for me?' she asked. 'Surely I'm allowed to go back to my own room? There must have been a reason. Tell me. If you do, from now on I shall love you and be your friend. But if you don't, I shall take a knife and cut your flesh with it!'

To reinforce her threat, she plucked a formidable hairpin from her hair and jabbed it violently in the neighbourhood of the girl's mouth, causing her to dodge this way and that from it in terror.

'I'll tell, madam, I'll tell. Only please don't let him know that it was me that told you,' she wept and implored.

Patience begged Xi-feng not to hurt the girl, at the same time urging the girl to make a clean breast of what she had to say. The story then came out.

'Mr Lian came in a while ago and had a bit of a nap. When he woke up, he sent someone to see what you were doing. They brought word back that your birthday party had only just started and you wouldn't be back for ages, so he opened the chest and took out two pieces of silver and two hairpins and two lengths of satin and told me to go and give them in secret to Bao Er's missus and tell her to come over. So then she came over to our room and Mr Lian made me go and wait in the passage here and look out for you. And that's really all I know.'

Xi-feng was by now shaking all over with anger. She pulled herself to her feet notwithstanding and strode off swiftly towards the house. As she approached the gateway of the courtyard, another little maid popped her head out but quickly drew it in again and ran when she saw that it was Xi-feng. When Xi-feng called to her by name, however, this maid, being more quick-witted than the other one, neither went on retreating nor stood still, but simply turned about and came running up to Xi-feng outside, an obsequious little smile upon her face.

'Oh madam, I was just going over to tell you when I saw you coming here yourself.'

'Tell me what?' said Xi-feng.

The girl then proceeded to relate voluntarily what the other girl had just told under duress.

Xi-feng spat contemptuously.

'You've left it a bit late, haven't you – waiting until you see me and then trying to act the innocent?'

She raised her hand and struck the girl a blow that sent her staggering, then, tiptoeing across the courtyard, applied her ear to the window to hear what was going on inside.

The first thing she heard was a laugh and a woman's voice.

'The best thing that could happen to you,' it was saying, 'would be if that hell-cat wife of yours was to die.'

'Suppose she did,' Jia Lian's voice said in answer, 'and I married another one who turned out to be just as bad?'

'If she *was* to die,' said the first voice, 'you ought to make Patience your Number One. I'm sure she'd be better than this one.'

'Patience won't let me come near her nowadays,' said Jia Lian. 'She has a lot to put up with, the same as me, that she doesn't dare talk about. I don't know, I reckon I must have been born under a hen-pecked husbands' star!'

Xi-feng heard this shaking with fury. The couple's praise of

Patience made her at once suspect that Patience had been complaining about her behind her back. The fumes of wine mounted up inside her, clouding her judgement. Without pausing to reflect, she turned and struck Patience twice before kicking open the door and striding into the room. There, without more ado, she proceeded to seize hold of Bao Er's wife and belabour her, breaking off only to block the doorway with her body in case Jia Lian might think of escaping.

'Filthy whore!' she shouted. 'Stealing a husband isn't enough for you, it seems. You have to murder his wife as well!' She turned to Patience: 'Go on, Patience, your place is over there with them – with that whoremaster of yours and his other whore! You're all three in this together. *You* hate me just as much as they do under that smarmy outside of yours!'

This was followed by several blows.

Poor Patience, overwhelmed by so much injustice, had only Bao Er's wife on whom she could vent her feelings.

'If you *have* to do these shameful things,' she said, 'you might at least leave me out of it.' And she began to pummel the woman in her turn.

Now Jia Lian had had a good deal to drink that day, and because of the euphoric state he was in, had taken insufficient precautions against surprise. Xi-feng's unexpected arrival had therefore left him completely at a loss. But Patience's outburst was another matter. The wine he had drunk rekindled his forgotten valour; and whereas the anger and shame he felt at seeing Xi-feng beat Bao Er's wife had rendered him speechless, the sight of Patience doing the same thing so roused his valiancy that he shouted at her and gave her a kick.

'Little whore! You want to join in too, do you?'

Patience, whose gentle nature was easily overawed, at once left off, tearfully protesting that it was cruel of them to speak about her in such a way behind her back.

Xi-feng, furious that Patience should be afraid of Jia Lian, rushed over and began striking her again, insisting that she should go on beating Bao Er's wife and take no notice of him. Finding herself thus attacked on both sides simultaneously by the pair of them, Patience became so desperate that she dashed from the room, vowing that she would find a knife and kill herself, and would undoubtedly have done herself an injury if the maids and nannies from outside had not seized her and gradually talked her out of it.

Xi-feng's reaction when Patience dashed off threatening suicide was to ram her head into Jia Lian's chest and shout hysterically.

'You're all in league against me, and now you're trying to frighten me because I overheard you. I don't care. Kill me! Strangle me!'

Jia Lian, in a fury, snatched a sword down from the wall and drew it from its scabbard.

'There's no need for any of you to talk about suicide. I'm desperate too. I'll kill the lot of you and swing for it. That'll make a clean end of the business!'

Just as the rumpus was at its height, You-shi arrived with a crowd of others.

'What on earth is happening? A moment ago everyone was enjoying themselves, and now here you all are shouting at each other!'

With the arrival of this audience Jia Lian pretended to be even drunker than he really was, striking a fiercely threatening attitude and behaving as if he was seriously intending to kill Xi-feng with his sword. Xi-feng, on the other hand, dropped tne shrewishness she had up to then been showing as soon as she saw them come and, breaking quickly away, ran weeping to Grandmother Jia.

The play had already ended when Xi-feng burst in upon the aged matriarch and flung herself trembling upon her bosom.

'Save me, Grannie, save me! Mr Lian is going to kill me!'

'*What?*' cried Grandmother Jia, Lady Xing and Lady Wang in startled simultaneity.

'When I went home just now to change my clothes,' Xi-feng tearfully related, 'I was surprised to hear Mr Lian indoors talking to somebody. I was scared to go in straight away, thinking it must be a guest, so I listened for a while outside the window. Then I found that it wasn't a guest that he was with but Bao Er's wife, and they were saying what a tyrant I was and planning to poison me so that he could marry Patience. I became very angry then; but I didn't want to make a scene with *him*. I struck Patience a couple of times. All I did to *him* was ask him why he should want to kill me, but he was so much put out by that that he tried to murder me on the spot.'

Grandmother Jia, believing this farrago to be true, was naturally appalled.

'How dreadful! Bring the wretch here at once!'

But before the words were out of her mouth, Jia Lian himself came running in, sword in hand, with a crowd pursuing at his heels.

Grandmother Jia had always treated Jia Lian and Xi-feng with indulgence, and on this occasion Jia Lian seemed to think that he could presume on this to riot in her presence with impunity, totally disregarding the fact that his mother and aunt were there as well. This deliberate flouting of their authority by a licensed favourite greatly incensed the two ladies. They seized hold of him with angry scoldings, one on either side.

'Disgusting creature! Have you no sense of decency left whatever? Can't you see that Grandmother is here?'

'It's because Grandmother spoils her so much that she has become the way she is,' said Jia Lian, leering at them through bloodshot eyes.

Lady Xing, having at last succeeded in wresting the sword from his grasp, shouted at him fiercely.

'Get out of here at once!'

But Jia Lian remained where he was and went on talking and talking in the same leering, disgusting manner, like a little boy who expects his naughtiness to be admired. Grandmother Jia, in a voice which shook with anger, uttered the only threat that she knew would shift him.

'I realize that *we* count for nothing with you. Fetch his father, some one, and see if he'll go then.'

At that Jia Lian finally shambled out. Sulkily avoiding the conjugal apartment, he took himself off to his study outside.

After he had gone, Lady Xing and Lady Wang turned on Xi-feng and began scolding her; but Grandmother Jia did

what she could to comfort her by dismissing the incident as
unimportant.

'Young men of his age are like hungry pussy-cats, my dear.
There's simply no way of holding them. This sort of thing has
always happened in big families like ours – certainly ever since
I can remember. It's all my fault, anyway. I shouldn't have
made you drink so much wine. It's all turned to vinegar inside
you.'

This made everyone laugh.

'Don't worry,' she went on. 'I'll see that he apologizes to
you tomorrow. Just for tonight, though, so as not to put him
too much out of countenance, I think you had better stay away
from him.'

Her voice became harsher when she remembered Patience.

'Little wretch! I always thought she seemed such a nice
girl. To think that underneath it all she should have been so
wicked!'

You-shi laughed.

'There's nothing wrong with Patience. She just happened to
be the person nearest at hand for Feng to work off her spleen
on. When Feng and Lian are angry with one another, they
both take it out on Patience. The poor girl is terribly unjustly
treated. Don't *you* go taking sides against her as well!'

'Oh well, that's all right,' said Grandmother Jia. 'I must
say, she never struck *me* as a wily seductress. In that case, of
course, I'm sorry for the poor child – bearing the brunt of it
all when she is the innocent party.'

She called Amber to her.

'Amber, I want you to take a message to Patience for me.
Tell her – and I want you to make it quite clear that the message comes from me personally – that I know she has been
unjustly treated and I shall make her mistress apologize to her
tomorrow. Only tell her not to make a fuss about it today,
because it is her mistress's birthday.'

*

Patience was at this time in Prospect Garden, whither she had
been carried off at the earliest opportunity by Li Wan and

where, as soon as they were indoors, she had collapsed in a sobbing heap, resisting all attempts at lifting her. Bao-chai tried reasoning with her.

'Come, Patience, you are an intelligent girl. Think how well your mistress treats you normally. Just because she's got a bit drunk today and taken it out on you – why, it shows how close you are to each other! You wouldn't want her to take it out on anyone *else*, would you? Everyone else is laughing at her for being such a drunken silly. If you alone insist on taking it so tragically, it will begin to look as if your reputation for good sense was undeserved.'

Just then Amber came in with the message from Grandmother Jia, and Patience, conscious of the aura of prestige it gave her, began gradually to perk up a bit. She remained in the Garden, however, and made no attempt to return to her mistress.

After she had sat with Patience and rested for a while, Li Wan, together with Bao-chai and the rest of the girls, went back to see Grandmother Jia and Xi-feng, whereupon Bao-yu invited Patience over to Green Delights. Aroma gave her an enthusiastic welcome.

'I'd like to have asked you here in the first place, but I saw that Mrs Zhu and the young ladies were taking care of you, so I didn't like to interfere.'

Patience's face was smiling as she thanked her, but fell again almost immediately.

'I can't understand it, I really can't. I'd done absolutely nothing to deserve such treatment.'

'Oh, it was a passing fit of anger,' said Aroma. 'I don't suppose Mrs Lian knew what she was doing. Look how well she treats you normally.'

'I wasn't thinking so much of Mrs Lian,' said Patience. 'It's what that hateful woman said. Why should she want to amuse herself at my expense? And then for that stupid master of mine to go and beat me –!'

Once more the sense of injustice overcame her and she could not restrain her tears.

'Don't be upset, Patience!' said Bao-yu consolingly. 'I offer you an apology on their behalf.'

Patience laughed.

'It has nothing to do with you.'

'We're all cousins,' said Bao-yu. 'What one of us does concerns all the others. If they have done you an injury, it's up to me to apologize.'

He turned his attention to her appearance.

'What a pity! You've made your new dress all damp. Aroma's dresses are in here. Why don't you change into one of hers, then you can spray some samshoo on this one and iron it? You'll need to do your hair again as well.'

He called to the junior maids to fetch water for washing and heat a flat-iron.

Up to this moment Patience had known only by hearsay of the remarkable understanding shown by Bao-yu in his dealings with girls. He had deliberately kept away from her in the past, knowing her to be Xi-feng's confidante and (he supposed) Jia Lian's cherished concubine. It had indeed been a source of frequent regret to him that he had been unable to show her how much he admired her. Seeing him like this for the first time, Patience reflected on the truth of what she had heard.

'He really has thought of everything,' she told herself, as she watched Aroma open up a large chest – specially for her – and select two scarcely-worn garments from it for her to change into. Then, since the water had already arrived, she took off her own dress and skirt and quickly washed her face. Bao-yu, who stood by smiling while she washed, now urged her to put on some make-up.

'If you don't, it will look as if you are sulking,' he said. 'After all, it *is* Feng's birthday, and Grandma *did* specially send someone to cheer you up.'

Inwardly acknowledging the reasonableness of this advice, Patience looked round her for some powder, but could not see any, whereupon Bao-yu darted over to the dressing-table and removed the lid from a box of Early Ming blue-and-white porcelain in which reposed the head of a white day-lily with five compact, stick-like buds on either side of the stem. Pinching off one of these novel powder-containers, he handed it to Patience.

'There you are. This isn't ceruse, it's a powder made by crushing the seeds of garden-jalap and mixing them with perfume.'

Patience emptied the contents of the tiny phial on to her palm. All the qualities required by the most expert perfumers were there: lightness, whiteness with just the faintest tinge of rosiness, and fragrance. It spread smoothly and cleanly on the skin, imparting to it a soft bloom that was quite unlike the harsh and somewhat livid whiteness associated with lead-based powders.

Then the rouge, too, was different – not in the usual sheets or tissues, but a tiny white-jade box filled with a crimson substance that looked like comfiture of roses.

'This is made from safflower, the same as ordinary rouge,' Bao-yu explained to her, 'only the stuff they sell in the shops is impure and its colour is inferior. This is made by squeezing the juice from the best quality safflower, carefully extracting all the impurities, mixing it with rose-water, and then further purifying it by distillation. It's so concentrated that you need only a dab of it on the end of a hairpin to do your lips with and still have enough left over to dilute with water in the palms of your hands for using on your cheeks.'

Following his directions, Patience found that her complexion had acquired a radiant freshness that she had never seen in it before. At the same time her whole face seemed to be bathed in the most delectable perfume.

Using a pair of bamboo scissors, Bao-yu now cut the twin blossoms from the stem of an autumn-flowering orchid that was growing in a pot and stuck them in Patience's hair.

At that very moment a maid arrived summoning her back to Li Wan's place and she had to leave him in a hurry.

Never before had Bao-yu been able to have Patience actually with him so that he could do things for her. She was such a superior sort of girl, so handsome, so intelligent, so

different from the average run of common, insensitive
creatures. His previous inability to serve her had been a source
of deep regret.

Today was – or would have been if she had lived – Golden's
birthday, and for this reason he had been feeling miserable
since early morning. The row which had broken out later in
the day between Xi-feng and Jia Lian had proved a godsend.
It had at last given him an opportunity of showing Patience
something of what he felt for her. This was an unlooked-for
happiness he might otherwise have waited a lifetime for in
vain. He stretched himself out on his bed in a pleasurable glow
of satisfaction.

These pleasant feelings were soon marred by the reflection
that a coarse sensualist like Jia Lian who never considered
anything but his own pleasure would certainly know nothing
about the scientific preparation of cosmetics. He thought of
Patience serving that precious couple, alone in the world
without parents or brothers and sisters to defend her, somehow contriving to steer an even course between Jia Lian's
boorishness on the one hand and Xi-feng's vindictiveness on
the other, yet today, in spite of all her efforts, falling a victim
to their cruelty. Truly her lot was an unhappy one – more unhappy even than Dai-yu's!

At this point in his reflections he became so upset that he
began to shed tears, not bothering on this occasion to restrain
them, because Aroma was not there to disapprove. Getting up
from his bed, he went over to inspect Patience's dress. The
samshoo that had been sprayed on it was now nearly dry. He
picked up the iron, ironed the dress for her, and neatly folded
it. Then he noticed that she had left her handkerchief behind.
As it was still marked with tear-stains, he washed it out in the
water she had used for her face and hung it up to dry. Feeling
a strange sensation in which sadness and happiness com-
mingled, he mused for some minutes in silence before going
over to Sweet-rice Village to join the others. He remained
there a long while talking. The lamps had already been lit
when he returned.

*

As Patience spent that night at Li Wan's place and Xi-feng slept with Grandmother Jia, Jia Lian returned to his room in the evening to find it gloomy and deserted. Not caring to call for anyone, however, he managed for himself as best he could and spent the night there alone. On waking next morning he felt nothing but revulsion and remorse when he remembered what had happened. His mother, Lady Xing, still worrying about the drunken exhibition he had made of himself the day before, came hurrying over first thing to urge him to go with her to see Grandmother Jia. This, despite the most acute feelings of shame and embarrassment, he now had to do.

'Well?' the old lady asked him, when he knelt before her.

'I had too much to drink yesterday, Grandmother, and I'm afraid I broke in on you and made a scene. I've come here now to apologize.'

Grandmother Jia snorted.

'Disgusting wretch! If you *must* go filling yourself with liquor, why can't you lie down quietly and sleep it off like a good, sensible creature? Fancy knocking your own wife about! Feng can normally hold her own against anyone – she's a regular little Tyrant King as a rule – but yesterday you'd reduced the poor child to a state of terror. Suppose I hadn't been here to protect her and you really had done her an injury, what would you have had to say for yourself then, I wonder?'

Though smarting under the ludicrous injustice of what she had just said, Jia Lian knew that he was in no position to argue, and humbly acknowledged his guilt.

'I should have thought that a couple of beauties like Feng and Patience would have been enough for you,' she went on. 'Why you should need to be forever sniffing after other skirts and bringing all this disgusting rag-tag and bob-tail back to your own room, I just do not understand. Fancy beating your own wife and your chamber-wife for a creature like that! And you a gentleman and member of a distinguished family! You ought to be thoroughly ashamed of yourself. If you have any consideration for my feelings at all, you'll get up off the floor now – because you are forgiven as far as *I* am concerned – and you'll apologize handsomely to that poor wife of yours and take her back home with you. Otherwise you can just take yourself off, for I shan't accept your kotow!'

Jia Lian turned and looked at Xi-feng, standing at his grandmother's side. She was wearing none of her finery today, her eyes were swollen with weeping, and her face, pinched and yellow without its make-up, was pathetic and somehow more appealing than usual.

'I suppose I'd *better* apologize,' he thought. 'It will help to patch things up between us; and it will please the old lady.'

Having so resolved, he looked up at Grandmother Jia with a smile.

'If that's what you want, Grandmother, I daren't disobey you. But it's going to make her even more wilful than before.'

'Nonsense!' said Grandmother Jia, though not ill-humouredly. 'I know for a fact that she is a model of wifely behaviour. I am sure she would be quite incapable of deliberately giving offence. If she *does* ever give you any trouble, I shall see to it myself that she submits to your authority.'

Jia Lian got to his feet then, and clasping his hands in front of him, made a low bow to his wife.

'It was all my fault, Mrs Lian. Please forgive me.'

This was said in so droll a manner that everyone burst out laughing.

'Now you're not to be angry any more, Feng,' said Grandmother Jia, 'or *I* shall be angry with *you*!'

She ordered someone to fetch Patience, and told Jia Lian and Xi-feng that she would now expect them to make it up with *her*.

When Jia Lian saw Patience, he was even more ready to pocket his pride for her than he had been for Xi-feng.

There's no wife like a chamber-wife

as the saying goes, and before anyone else could say a word, he had bounded up to her and began apologizing.

'You were very badly treated yesterday, Patience. It was all

my fault. It was because of me that Mrs Lian was so beastly to
you. Apart from offering you my own apology, I'd like to
apologize on her behalf as well.'

He clasped his hands again and bowed, once more provoking Grandmother Jia to laughter. This time Xi-feng laughed,
too.

Grandmother Jia told Xi-feng that it was now her turn; but
before she could do anything, Patience rushed up to her, threw
herself at her feet and kotowed.

'I made you angry on your birthday, madam. I shall never
forgive myself.'

Xi-feng was already feeling remorseful that in her previous
day's drunkenness she had so far forgotten herself as to
humiliate Patience, in spite of all they had always meant to
each other, because of a mere chance-heard remark. Seeing her
now so generous and so lacking in resentment, she was both
ashamed and deeply touched. There were tears on her cheeks
as she bent down and raised the girl to her feet.

'In all the years I've served you,' said Patience, 'you've
never laid so much as a finger on me before. I bear you no
grudge for striking me yesterday, madam. It was all that
wicked woman's doing. I don't blame you in the least for
losing your temper.'

She, too, was crying while she said this.

'See the three of them back to their room now,' said
Grandmother Jia to her women. 'And if you hear another
word about this, let me know straight away who said it. I don't
care who it is, I shall take a stick to them myself!'

The three of them now kotowed to Grandmother Jia, to
Lady Xing and to Lady Wang; then the old nannies, bidden
once more to escort them, stepped forward with cries of
obedience and conducted them back to their room.

As soon as the three of them were alone together, Xi-feng
started on Jia Lian.

'Am I really such a hell-cat? Are you really so terribly hen-
pecked? When that woman wished me dead, you agreed with
her. Surely I can't be *all* that bad? Surely I must have *some*

good days, even if it's only one in a thousand? You've made
it seem as if I'm worse even than that worthless whore. How
can I have the face to go on living now?'

She began to cry again.

'Aren't you satisfied *yet*?' said Jia Lian. 'Just think a bit:
who was most to blame yesterday? Yet today *I* was the one
who had to kneel down in front of everyone and apologize.
You've come out of this pretty well. So what are you yam-
mering at me now for? Do you want me to kneel down *again*?
Here? It doesn't do to be *too* greedy, you know.'

Xi-feng, unable to think of a reply to this, fell silent.
Patience giggled.

'There, it's all over!' said Jia Lian, laughing himself. 'It's
no good. I just can't help myself.'

Just then a woman came to the door to report.

'Bao Er's wife has hanged herself.'

Jia Lian and Xi-feng were both profoundly shocked; but
the look of fear on Xi-feng's face was of only momentary
duration.

'Well,' she said harshly, 'what of it? Why make such a fuss
about it?'

Shortly after this Lin Zhi-xiao's wife came in and spoke to
Xi-feng on the side.

'Bao Er's wife has hanged herself. Her family are talking
about taking it to court.'

Xi-feng laughed scornfully.

'Good! I was thinking of doing the same thing myself.'

'I've just been trying to talk them out of it,' said Lin Zhi-
xiao's wife. 'I tried frightening them a bit to start with, then
I promised them some money if they would drop it. They
seemed to be willing.'

'*I*'ve got no money to give them,' said Xi-feng, 'and I
wouldn't give it to them if I had. Let them go ahead and sue.
I don't want you to talk them out of it, *or* to try frightening
them out of it either. Just let them go ahead and sue. If they
lose their case, I shall bring a suit against them for *ex morte*
blackmail!'

As she stood there in some perplexity to know what to do, Lin Zhi-xiao's wife noticed that Jia Lian was signalling to her with his eyes. She understood his meaning and went off to wait for him outside.

Jia Lian followed soon after.

'I'm just going out to have a look — see what's going on,' he said on his way out.

'You're not to give them any money!' Xi-feng shouted after him.

Jia Lian went straight off to discuss the matter with Lin Zhi-xiao himself. As a result of their discussion, someone was sent to haggle with the family and promise whatever seemed necessary, and the family eventually agreed to keep quiet in return for a payment of two hundred taels 'towards funeral expenses'. Terrified that they might change their minds, Jia Lian sent someone to talk to the local magistrate and invited the police inspector and two or three of the constables in to 'help with the funeral'. Seeing the way things were, the family now dared not pursue the matter any further even if they wanted to, and were obliged to digest in silence whatever they might feel of grief or anger.

Jia Lian told Lin Zhi-xiao to account for the two hundred taels by adding a bit here and a bit there on to various items in the Current Expenses account. He also slipped Bao Er some money of his own and consoled him with a promise that he would pick a good wife for him at the earliest opportunity to replace the one he had just lost. Flattered by all the attention he was receiving and grateful for the money, Bao Er was only too willing to do as he was told and continued to serve Jia Lian with no less devotion than before. But that is no part of our story.

Whatever internal uneasiness Xi-feng may have felt about these developments, outwardly she affected complete indifference. Finding herself alone with Patience when Jia Lian had gone, she smilingly inquired after her injuries.

'I was terribly drunk yesterday,' she said. 'I hope you won't hold it against me, what I did then. Where did I hit you? Let me have a look.'

'You didn't hit me very hard,' said Patience.

Just at that moment they were interrupted by an announcement from outside.

'Mrs Zhu and the young ladies are here.'

If you want to know what they had come for, you will have to read the following chapter.

CHAPTER 45

*Sisterly understanding finds expression in words of
sisterly frankness
And autumnal pluviousness is celebrated in verses of
autumnal melancholy*

As we were saying at the end of the last chapter, Xi-feng had just begun expressing her concern for Patience when Li Wan and the cousins walked in. She broke off and invited them to be seated, and Patience went round and served them all with tea.

'What a crowd!' said Xi-feng. 'Anyone would think I'd sent out an invitation for something!'

'There are two things we wanted to see you about,' said Tan-chun. 'One is my affair; the other concerns Xi-chun but also includes instructions from Grandmother.'

'They must be very important things for a turn-out like this,' said Xi-feng.

'We started a poetry club recently,' said Tan-chun, 'and the very first time we had a regular meeting, somebody didn't turn up. As the rest of us are too soft to apply the rules ourselves, we want to invite you, as someone we could trust to apply them for us with iron impartiality, to be our Disciplinary Officer. That's the first thing. The second thing concerns this painting of the Garden that Xi-chun has been asked to do. There are all sorts of things she'll need for it that she hasn't got. We spoke to Grandmother about it and she said that there might still be some things that would do in the downstairs store-room at the back. She said we ought to have a look, and if there are, we can use *them*. Otherwise, anything we haven't got ourselves we should send outside for and buy.'

'I know nothing about poetry,' said Xi-feng. 'I couldn't compose a poem to save my life. I could come along to eat and drink with you if you like.'

'You wouldn't have to compose poems,' said Tan-chun.

'That's not what we want you for. All you have to do is keep
an eye on the rest of us, and if you find anyone slacking or
playing truant, decide how they ought to be punished.'

'Don't try to fool me,' said Xi-feng. 'I've already guessed.
It's not iron impartiality you're after, it's financial backing. If
you've got a club, you're sure to have some arrangement for
taking it in turns to pay the bill, and as you're short of money,
you've thought of this as a means of roping me in so that you
can get some out of *me*. That's the real reason for your invitation, isn't it?'

The others laughed.

'Too bad! You've guessed.'

'You're like the original Crystal Man, Feng,' said Li Wan.

'A heart of crystal in a body of glass.

You can see through everything!'

'Fancy!' said Xi-feng, mockingly. 'The respected elder
sister-in-law! The one who's put in charge of these young
ladies to guide their studies and teach them needlework and
good manners! You encourage them to start a poetry club,
but as soon as the question of money arises (and incidentally,
how much money is involved? – it can't surely be very much),
you're not interested: it has nothing to do with you! Now,
you have a monthly allowance of ten taels. Excluding Grandmother and Aunt Wang – and they are, after all, ladies of rank
and title – that's twice as much as any of the rest of us gets. Yet
Grandma and Auntie go on about how poor you are: "poor
young widow!" "no means of her own!" Oh yes, and because you've got a son, you get another ten taels a month on
top of that, which actually makes you equal with Grandma
and Auntie Wang. *And* you've got your land in the Garden,
the best plot there. It's down in the tithe-book for the highest
tithing. And you haven't got a big establishment. I doubt
there are ten of you there altogether, counting you and Lan
and all the servants, so your outgoings can't come to very
much. And in any case your food and clothing is all found out
of common funds. If one were to add it all up together, I
think your real income must be somewhere in the region of

four or five hundred taels a year. Even if you were to spend one or two hundred a year out of that on amusements for the girls like this poetry thing, it wouldn't be for many years. Another year or two from now and they'll all be getting married. And it's not as if you were saving up for their dowries, either. That's hardly likely to be *your* responsibility. No, you're frightened of spending that money of yours, that's why you've set these girls on to me. I'm supposed to go along like an innocent and eat and drink myself silly so that next day *I* can be made to foot the bill. That's your little game, isn't it?'

'Listen to her, all of you!' said Li Wan, laughing. 'I make a single, inoffensive remark to her, and in return I get this *cart-load* of ill-bred abuse! Really, Feng, what a mercenary creature you are! You're just like one of those muddy-legged wretches who stand haggling in the market-place with a little abacus up one sleeve to do their calculations on. It's a good job you were born a girl and brought up in an educated, upper-class family and that you married into a family of the same sort. If you'd been born a boy and your family had been poor and un-educated people, I dread to think what sort of a calculating monster you would have grown up into! Everyone in the world has to become the object of your calculations. Yester-day it was Patience's turn. It's a wonder you have arms to strike her with, for I'm sure it was a dog's stomach you poured all that wine into. None but a dog would have turned on Patience the way you did. I tell you, I was so angry, I felt like coming straight over and giving you a piece of my mind. Then I thought it over for a bit and decided not to. After all, it was your birthday, and as we know, "every dog must have his day". Also I was afraid that if I made a fuss I might upset Grandmother. And because I didn't have it out with you yesterday, I was still feeling angry about it when I came here to see you just now. Yet *you* have the gall to start on *me* – you who aren't worthy to pick up Patience's shoes! You ought to change places, you two. I'm sure Patience would make the better mistress.'

It made the girls laugh to hear Li Wan speaking with such unaccustomed heat.

'Oh, now I understand!' said Xi-feng, joining in their laughter. 'It wasn't about poetry or painting that you came to see me: it was revenge for Patience you were after. I didn't realize that she had so powerful a protector. Now that I do, I shall never dare to strike her again – not if all the devils in hell are tugging at my elbow! Here, Patience! *Miss* Patience! Let me apologize to you in front of Mrs Zhu and the young ladies. I "did evil in my cups". Please forgive me.'

The others laughed.

'There you are!' said Li Wan to Patience. 'I told you I'd stick up for you, didn't I?'

'It's all very well for you ladies to joke about it,' said Patience, 'but you make me feel very uncomfortable.'

'You've no cause to feel uncomfortable,' said Li Wan. '*I'll* look after you. You just get that key and tell your mistress to unlock the store-room and find those things for us.'

'My dear good Wan, *please* take these girls back to the Garden,' said Xi-feng. 'I've got the rice accounts to go over; I've got to see Lady Xing about something (I don't know what, but she's just sent over to say that she wants me); and I've got the New Year's clothes to see about. I have to find out what everyone wants and get the orders placed —'

'I don't care in the least about these things,' said Li Wan airily. 'You just settle my business first so that I can go back home and rest and not have these girls pestering me any more.'

'Give me a little *time!*' said Xi-feng pleadingly. 'You're so considerate towards me as a rule; I don't know why I'm so out of favour with you today. I suppose it must be because of Patience. Often in the past you've said to me, "Now I know how busy you are, Feng, but your health is important: you ought to find means somehow or other of taking a rest." That's what you would normally say in a situation like this; but today you seem more intent on driving me into an early grave! Incidentally, you may not think it matters very much if the arrangements for *other* people's winter clothing get put off, but what about the clothing for the girls? Strictly speaking that's *your* responsibility. Don't you think Grandmother would feel that you were taking non-interference just a *little* far if she discovered that the girls were going without winter clothes simply for want of a word from you? You know, of course, that I would rather get into trouble myself than involve *you* in trouble . . .'

'Listen to her, all of you,' said Li Wan. 'Marvellous, isn't it? I'd like to get hold of that clever tongue of yours, Feng, and – ! Just tell me this one thing, then: *are* you going to keep an eye on our poetry club for us or *aren't* you?'

'What a question!' said Xi-feng. 'If I refused to join your club and spend my money in it, I should be declaring myself in open rebellion against the Prospect Garden Residents' Association, and heaven help me then! – my life wouldn't be worth living! I shall be round first thing tomorrow to report for duty, and the first thing I shall do will be to pay down fifty taels to be spent as and when you wish on the club's entertainment. I can't write poetry – or anything else, for that matter – and I'm a very common, ignorant sort of person to be joining a poetry club; and as for taking on this disciplinary business: well, whether I do or whether I don't, I don't suppose there'll be much danger of your expelling me once you've seen the colour of my money.'

The others laughed.

'I'll open the store-room presently,' she continued, 'and I'll get them to put out anything that looks as if it might be of use for you to have a look at. If you can use it, keep it. Anything you're still short of after that, I'll tell them to buy for you outside. I can get the pongee cut for you straight away. The architect's drawing isn't at Lady Wang's, by the way; it's at Cousin Zhen's place. I'm telling you this to save you a wasted journey. I can get it for you, if you like; then I can have it taken with the pongee to Sir Zheng's gentlemen and ask them to do the sizing for you.'

Li Wan nodded approvingly.

'That would be very kind. If you'll really do all that for us, we shall have nothing more to say. Come on then, everybody! Let's go home and see what happens. If she *doesn't* send the stuff, we can come back and deal with her later.'

She began to leave the room as she said this, the cousins following in her wake.

'I know of only one person who could have stirred all this up,' said Xi-feng as they were going, 'and that's Bao-yu.'

The mention of his name stopped Li Wan in her tracks. She came back into the room.

'I'd completely forgotten: it was Bao-yu that I came about in the first place. He was the one who failed to turn up at our first meeting. *We*'re all too soft to know what to do with him. How do *you* think we ought to punish him?'

Xi-feng thought for a bit.

'The only thing I can suggest is that you should make him go round to each of your apartments in turn and sweep the floors for you.'

'Yes, yes,' said the others, laughing. 'The very thing!'

They were just about to leave for the second time when Lai Da's mother, old Mrs Lai, came in, leaning on the shoulder of a little maid. Xi-feng and the rest rose to greet her. They begged her to be seated and offered her their congratulations. The old woman sat down on the edge of the kang and smiled round at them with pleasure.

'The way I see it, since you are our employers, *our* good fortune is really *yours*. If it weren't for your family, how would the likes of us ever have come by a piece of good fortune like this in the first place? Yesterday when you sent young Sun-shine round with those presents, my grandson "kotowed upwards" in the doorway to show his gratitude.'

'When will he be leaving to take up his post?' said Li Wan.

Old Mrs Lai sighed, as though the thought made her melancholy.

'Oh, I don't concern myself with their affairs. I just let them get on with it. When he came round to me to kotow the other day, I didn't have a good word for him. I said to him, "Young man, don't tell me you're a mandarin now, because it's just plain ridiculous. Thirty years it is since you were born," I said, "and all that time, in actual fact, you've been a bondservant. Yet through the kindness of our Masters you were set apart from the moment you came out of your mother's womb.

Thanks to the Masters and your parents," I said, "you were
taught to read and write like a gentleman's son and fussed over
by a parcel of maids and nannies and wet-nurses as if you was
some sort of young phoenix. I doubt you know how the word
'bondservant' is written. You've known nothing but soft
living since you were born," I said. "You don't know the
bitterness your father and your grandfather had to go through.
You don't appreciate the generations of hardship that went
into the making of a fine gentleman like you. And the money
they spent on you," I said, "nursing you through all the fevers
and calamities of youth (for you were a sickly, ailing child): it
would have been enough to have made you anew out of silver!
Then, when you were twenty, the Master, out of the kindness
of his heart, undertook to buy you a place in the Service, so
that your future would be assured. Think how many freeborn
members of the clan go hungry," I said, "yet he did this for
you, that was born a slave. Such great fortune should make
you fearful. And now, after ten years of fooling around, you've
talked the Master – by what jiggery-pokery I do not know –
into getting you selected for a posting. A district magistrate
may not be very high in the scale," I said, "but the mandarin
who goes to a district to be its magistrate is supposed to be the
father and mother of all the people who live there. So mind
you don't go getting above yourself," I said. "Do all in your
power to show that you are worthy of the trust. And always
let the Master see how much you appreciate what he has done
for you. Otherwise Heaven will surely cast you off.'
    Li Wan and Xi-feng both laughed.
    'You worry too much, Mrs Lai,' said Xi-feng. 'He's all
right. It's true we don't see much of him nowadays. He used
to come in once in a while, but these last few years all we've
seen of him has been his visiting-card at New Years and
birthdays. He did come in the other day, however, to kotow to
Her Old Ladyship and Lady Wang. We saw him in Her Old
Ladyship's courtyard, dressed in his new uniform. He looked
very imposing. A little bit fatter than he used to be. You
ought to be happy now that he's a mandarin, not making
yourself miserable with all this worrying about him. Even if

he *doesn't* behave himself, I should leave his parents to do the worrying. All *you* have to do now is sit back and enjoy yourself. If ever you're at a loose end, you can always jump in your chair and have yourself carried round here for a game of cards and a chat with Her Old Ladyship. I'm sure no one here would dream of making you feel uncomfortable. After all, you've got upstairs and downstairs and halls and reception-rooms back home just the same as we have. You're as good as any lady in the land now, you know. I'm sure you will be respected as such.'

Mrs Lai hurriedly rose to her feet as Patience came up to pour tea for her.

'You shouldn't do that, miss. You should let one of the younger ones do it. 'Tain't right you should pour for me.'

Sitting down again she continued to hold forth between sips.

'You don't know that boy, Mrs Lian. He's like all young people: you have to be strict with them all the time. Even then if you're not careful they'll somehow find a way to raise the devil and grieve their parents' hearts. This young chap of ours now: those that know him realize it's just the mischief coming out, but those who don't are liable to think that he's taking advantage of the fact that he's got more money and influence than other people to throw his weight about; and that reflects badly on the Master's reputation as well. Oh, I get so angry about it sometimes, I don't know what to do with myself. I have to call his Dad in and give him a good talking-to and then I feels a bit better. I hope you won't mind my saying this' – she pointed a finger at Bao-yu – 'but I wouldn't have thought that *your* father was strict enough with *you*. Look at the way Her Old Ladyship was out in front the moment he started when he gave you that beating a while ago. You should have seen the way your grandfather used to lay into *him* when *he* was a lad. And your father wasn't the scapegrace that you are, either. Then there was your father's elder brother, Master She. Now he *was* mischievous – though even so, he didn't turn the whole household upsy-downsy the way you seem to. *He* was *always* getting beaten. Oh, and the way your Cousin

Zhen's grandfather over at the Ning-guo used to lay into *his* son! Oh, he had a fiery temper! Once it was up – well, you'd never have thought it was his son he was beating. Looked more like he was torturing a bandit. From what I've seen and heard, I should imagine that the way your Cousin Zhen at the Ning-guo disciplines *his* son is in his grandfather's tradition. Only trouble is, he's a bit too erratic. Can't control himself, that's his trouble. I don't blame the young ones for not respecting him. If you're sensible, young man, you'll be glad to hear me say this; otherwise, though you may be too polite to say so, I expect you'll think I'm an interfering old woman.'

Just then Lai Da's wife came in, followed almost immediately by the wives of Zhou Rui and Zhang Cai. The latter two had come to report to Xi-feng on various domestic matters. Xi-feng smilingly inquired of Lai Da's wife whether she had come to collect her mother-in-law.

'Well, no, madam, not exactly,' said Lai Da's wife. 'I really came to find out whether you and the young ladies will be favouring us with your presence or not.'

'Oh, how silly of me!' said old Mrs Lai when she heard this. 'Here have I been talking a load of stale old sesame and all the time forgetting the one thing I came here to ask you about! On account of our young chap's posting, all our friends and relations want to get together and celebrate, so we thought we'd better have a reception. Well, the way I saw it, if we only held it for one day, it would mean inviting some people and leaving out others, and that wouldn't seem right. So I thought about it for a bit, and I thought to myself, well, it's thanks to the Masters that this great honour has come our way, so we must do what we can to show our appreciation. Even if it means spending every penny we've got, we ought to be glad to do it. So I told the boy's father to arrange a reception for three days running. On the first day we'll have some tables and a stage in our little bit of garden at the back to entertain Her Old Ladyship and Their Ladyships and your good selves and the young ladies, and some more tables and a stage with another lot of players in the reception room at the front where we can entertain the gentlemen. The second day will be a reception for relations and friends of the family, and the third day will be for colleagues on the staffs of the two mansions. I do hope you will honour us with a visit. It will be the high-light of our celebrations.'

Li Wan and Xi-feng asked her when the reception would be, assuring her that they fully intended to come.

'I'm sure Lady Jia would love to come too,' they said, 'but I wouldn't bank on her being able to.'

'The date we've chosen is the fourteenth,' said Lai Da's wife hurriedly, before her mother-in-law had a chance to get under way again. 'We do hope you'll come, for Mother's sake.'

'I can't answer for the others,' said Xi-feng amiably, 'but *I* shall definitely be coming. I'd better warn you, though: I haven't got any present to bring, and you mustn't expect me to offer largesse – I wouldn't know how to go about it. You mustn't laugh if I just eat up and go.'

'Get along with you, madam!' said Lai Da's wife, laughing. 'If you feel like bringing a largesse, twenty or thirty thousand taels would do very nicely!'

Old Mrs Lai laughed.

'I been to see Her Old Ladyship already and she says she'll come. Reckon I ought to feel pretty pleased with myself.'

After further exhortations to attend the party and various other admonishments, the old woman was at last getting up to go when her eye chanced to fall on Zhou Rui's wife and she seemed to remember something.

'There's something else I wanted to ask you about, Mrs Lian. What's all this about Zhou's boy being dismissed? What did he do wrong?'

'Ah yes, I've been meaning to speak to your daughter-in-law about it,' said Xi-feng, 'but there were so many other things to think about that they drove it from my mind. Lai, dear,' – she turned to Lai Da's wife – 'when you get back, will you tell your husband that neither of our households will be employing Zhou Rui's son any longer and that he is to send him packing?'

Lai Da's wife could only agree, but the unhappy mother fell on her knees in supplication.

'What did he do?' old Mrs Lai repeated. 'Tell me what he did, and I'll be judge for you.'

'Yesterday on my birthday,' said Xi-feng, 'before the rest of us had even started drinking, he was already drunk, and when my grandmother sent her women round with some presents, instead of going out and being nice to them, he sat where he was swearing at everybody and made no attempt to receive the presents or take them inside. Eventually the two women came in by themselves and he did at last go with a couple of the pages to take in what they had brought. But though the pages made no trouble, this young Zhou dropped the box he was carrying and scattered wheat-cakes all over the courtyard. After the women had gone, I sent Sunshine out to give him a talking-to, but it ended up with *him* shouting and swearing at Sunshine. Faced with a young hooligan like that who is so utterly and completely uncontrollable, I don't see that one has any choice but to dismiss him.'

'Is *that* all it was?' said Grannie Lai. 'And I was thinking it must have been something serious! Take my advice, Mrs Lian. If that boy's done wrong, beat him and curse him and tell him to mend his ways, but dismiss him? – no, that would never do. He's not like one of your house-born servants. The Zhous came with Her Ladyship from her old home when she was married. If you insist on dismissing him, it will look like an affront to Her Ladyship. Give him a few whacks to learn him and tell him not to do it again; but keep him on, whatever you do. If you won't do it for his ma's sake, do it for Her Ladyship's.'

Xi-feng turned to Lai Da's wife.

'Very well then. Let him be called for tomorrow and given forty strokes with the heavy bamboo. And tell him he's not to drink any more.'

Lai Da's wife said she would see that done. After that Zhou Rui's wife kotowed to Xi-feng in gratitude. She wanted to kotow to Mrs Lai as well, but the old woman reached forward and prevented her. The four women then left, and Li Wan and the girls went back into the Garden.

Towards evening Xi-feng sent someone to the store-room, as promised, to hunt out any old painting gear that had been stored there and take it round for Bao-chai and the others to look over. On doing so the girls found only about half the things they wanted, and made a list of the other half which they gave to Xi-feng to have bought. But these are matters about which it is not necessary to go into detail.

Suffice it to say that the freshly-sized pongee arrived back from outside in due course together with a rough draft of the projected painting, and that Bao-yu began to spend a part of each day at Xi-chun's place helping her. Tan-chun, Li Wan, Ying-chun and Bao-chai developed the habit of dropping in to sit with them while they worked, partly to watch the painting and partly because it made a convenient rendezvous.

Reminded by the first nip in the air that the hours of dark-ness were gradually lengthening, Bao-chai went round for a long consultation with her mother from which she came away with quantities of extra sewing to occupy herself with in the evenings; but since, when making her morning and evening calls on Lady Wang and Grandmother Jia, she would often, if they seemed desirous of her company, spend a considerable while sitting and talking with them, and since she was also in the habit of dropping in from time to time to gossip with one or another of her cousins in the Garden, she had very little leisure for sewing in the daytime and as a consequence was invariably plying her needle under the lamp until eleven or twelve o'clock at night.

*

As for Dai-yu, twice every year, following the spring and autumn equinoxes, she suffered from a recurrence of her old sickness. This autumn the repeated junketings occasioned by Grandmother Jia's enthusiastic excursions into the Garden had drained her of energy. Recently she had begun coughing again; and as this year it seemed to be considerably worse than usual, she had stopped going out altogether and stayed at home nursing herself in her room. Sometimes when she was feeling depressed she would long for a visit from one of the girls and the distraction of someone to talk to. But when Bao-chai or one of the others did in fact look in to ask how she was, she would grow fidgety after only a few sentences had been exchanged between them and begin to wish that they would go. The others realized that it was being ill that made her like this; and knowing from past experience how hyper-sensitive she was, they were never sharp with her, even if she was somewhat remiss as a hostess and often lacking in courtesy.

Once when Bao-chai called in to see her, the nature of her illness became the subject of their conversation.

'I suppose the doctors in attendance on this family aren't too bad as doctors go,' said Bao-chai, 'but the medicines they prescribe for you don't seem to make you any better. Don't you think it's time they called in someone really first-rate who could cure this sickness once and for all? Every year all through the spring and summer you have this trouble; yet you're not an old lady, and you're not a little girl any longer. You can't go on in this way indefinitely.'

'It's no good,' said Dai-yu. 'This illness will never go away completely. Look what I'm like ordinarily, even when I'm not ill.'

Bao-chai nodded.

'Exactly! You know the old saying: "He that eats shall live"? What you ordinarily eat, when you're not ill, doesn't seem to nourish you or build up your resistance. That's one of your troubles.'

Dai-yu sighed.

> 'Life and death are as Heaven decrees; and rank
> and riches are as Heaven bestows them.

These things are not in human power to command. I seem to be worse this year than I have been in previous years.'

She coughed several times while she was saying this.

'I was looking the other day at that prescription of yours,' said Bao-chai. 'I should have said myself that there was too much cinnamon and ginseng in it. I know they are supposed to build you up; but you don't want to go overheating your-self. If you ask me, I think the first, most important thing to do is to calm your liver and strengthen your stomach a bit. If you could reduce the inflamed, over-active state of your liver so that it was no longer harming the earthy humour of your spleen, your stomach would begin functioning normally again and then the food you ate could begin to nourish you properly. First thing every morning you ought to take an ounce of the best quality bird's nest and five drams of sugar-candy and heat them up in a silver skillet until they make a sort of syrup. If you were to take that regularly, it would do you more good than medicine. There's nothing like it for building you up if you have low vitality.'

Dai-yu sighed again.

'You're such a kind person,' she said, 'but I've got such a suspicious nature that in the past I always suspected that your kindness was a cloak for something and rejected it. It wasn't until the other day, when you told me off for reading for-bidden books and offered me all that good advice, that I ever felt really grateful to you. I realized then that I had all along been wrong about you – right from the very start. I suddenly realized: I'm fifteen this year and have no brothers or sisters: ever since my mother died there has been no one – literally no one – who has ever spoken to me in that sort of way. I'm not surprised Cousin Yun speaks so highly of you. I used to hate it when I heard her praise your kindness, but since experienc-ing it myself, I know what she means. If it had been *you* who'd said those things in the drinking game, *I* should have been quite merciless. I should never have kept quiet about it at the time and gently remonstrated about it later, when we were alone together, as you did. I knew from that that I had been wrong about you, and that you must really care for me. If my eyes hadn't been opened for me then, I should never be talking to you like this today.

'Now about this bird's nest syrup you want me to take. I know bird's nest is fairly easy to come by, but this illness of mine is something I suffer from every year because of my weak constitution. There's nothing particularly serious about it, it's just something that I always get. Yet already everyone's put to a huge amount of inconvenience because of it, fetching doctors, brewing medicines, buying ginseng for me and Saigon cinnamon. If I now come up with some fancy new idea like asking to have bird's nest syrup made for me every day, then even though Grandmother and Aunt Wang and Cousin Feng may not say anything, the old nannies and maids on the staff are sure to resent the extra work. Cousin Bao and Cousin Feng are Grandma's favourites, yet you should see the looks these people give *them* sometimes – and you should hear the things they say about them behind their backs! So you can imagine what they must be like about *me*. I'm not even a proper member of the family: I'm just a refugee, with no family of my own, living here as a hanger-on. That in itself is enough to make them resent me. It's difficult enough for me as it is, without deliberately thinking up new ways to make them hate me.'

'I'm just as much an outsider as you are,' said Bao-chai.

'There's no comparison between us,' said Dai-yu. 'You've got your mother and your brother for a start. You've got property and businesses. You've still got land and a home of your own back in Nanking. It's true that as marriage-relations they allow you to live here free of charge, but you provide everything for yourselves apart from the accommodation. You don't cost them a penny. And any time you feel like it, you can just get up and go. I've got nothing at all of my own, absolutely nothing. Yet everything they give me – food, clothing, pocket-money, even the flowers and trees in my garden – are the same as they give their own girls. Can you wonder that the servants are so resentful?'

'Your being here only means one more dowry for them to find,' said Bao-chai. 'Surely so small an extra expense as that is hardly going to bother them?'

Dai-yu coloured.

'I've been telling you my troubles because I thought you really cared, but you turn them into a joke.'

'Perhaps,' said Bao-chai, smiling. 'But it's true, all the same. However, don't you worry: as long as I'm here, I promise to

do my best to make it easier for you. If you will promise
always to let me know when anything is bothering you, I will
promise to deal with it if it is in my power to do so. I have a
brother, it's true; but you know as well as I do what *he*'s like.
It's really only in having a mother that I can count myself a bit
luckier than you. In other respects we have enough in common to think of ourselves as fellow-sufferers. If you can see
this – as with your intelligence I am sure you must – you have
no cause to go echoing Si-ma Niu's complaint: "All men have
brothers, only I have none." Now, you have suggested that
"the less trouble the better" ought to be your motto here, and
I take your point. I shall have a word with Mother next time
I see her about this. I'll be surprised if we haven't got some
bird's nest of our own at home. If we have, I shall tell them to
send you a few ounces, so that you can get your own maids to
prepare it for you every morning. That way will be handier for
you and will also avoid the risk of any alarms and excursions
with the staff.'

Dai-yu smiled at her gratefully.

'It may be only a little thing, but it is very kind indeed of
you to have thought of it.'

'Nonsense!' said Bao-chai. 'It's not worth speaking of. I'm
only afraid that by spending so much time with other people I
may have been neglecting you rather. Well, I'd better be going
now. I'm afraid I'm tiring you.'

'Come again this evening and talk to me for a bit,' said
Dai-yu.

Bao-chai promised to do so and departed.

And at this point she departs for a little while from our
narrative.

*

Left alone, Dai-yu ate a few mouthfuls of congee and then lay
down on her bed.

Towards sundown a change of weather came, bringing the
whisper and rustle of rain. It was the pulsing, steady rain of
autumn, so constant that you sometimes wonder if it has
stopped. The afternoon slid imperceptibly into a sombre

evening, blackened by lowering rainclouds and made yet more melancholy for Dai-yu by the persistent drip of the rain on her bamboos. Reflecting that Bao-chai would now be unable to come, she picked up a book at random to read beneath the lamp.

It was a volume of *The Lyric Miscellany* consisting largely of songs of sorrow and separation: 'The Autumn Bride', 'The Grief of Parting' and suchlike. Moved by what she read, she was inevitably drawn to give outlet to her feelings in composition and had soon completed a 'song of separation' of her own. As she had modelled it on Zhang Ruo-xu's famous poem 'Spring River: A Night of Flowers and Moonlight', she decided to call it 'Autumn Window: A Night of Wind and Rain'. This is how it went:

Autumn Window: A Night of Wind and Rain

The autumn flowers are dead, the leaves are sere;
Lamp-light comes soon, the nights grow long again.
Outside my window autumn's signs appear
More dismal in the wind and rustling rain.

The rustling rain came in such swift downpour
It startled me from autumn-dream-filled sleep.
Now, in a muse, unable to sleep more,
I watch the candle at my bedside weep.

The candle weeps down to its socket low,
And my heart weeps and desolation feels.
Yet the same wind in other courts must blow;
The sound of rain through other windows steals.

The wind's chill strikes through quilt and counterpane,
The rain drums like a mad clock in my ears,
All night, in whispering, monotone refrain,
Companion to my own swift-coursing tears.

The courtyard now with mist begins to fill,
The bamboo's drip persists without a pause.
When will the wind cease and the rain be still,
That with its weeping soaks my window's gauze?

Having read it over to herself out loud, she laid down the writing-brush and was about to go back to bed and settle down for the night when one of her maids announced the arrival of 'Master Bao'. Almost simultaneously with this announcement, Bao-yu himself burst in wearing a rain-cape and an enormous rain-hat of woven bamboo. Dai-yu laughed at the spectacle he presented.

'The Old Fisherman! Where have *you* just sprung from?'

'How are you today?' Bao-yu asked her anxiously. 'Have you had your medicine? How much have you managed to eat today?'

He was divesting himself of the rain-clothes while he asked these questions. When he had disposed of them, he picked up the lamp from the table and, shielding it with one hand to throw the light on her, scrutinized her face. He appeared to be satisfied with what he saw.

'You've got a better colour today.'

Now that he had taken off the rain-clothes, Dai-yu could see what he was wearing underneath. He had on a somewhat worn-looking tunic of red silk damask tied with a green sash at the waist, and trousers of sprigged green silk. The ends of his trousers were stuffed into socks extravagantly patterned with a design of flowers picked out in gold, and there were flowers and butterflies embroidered on his satin slippers.

'The top part of you seems to have been pretty well protected against the rain,' said Dai-yu, 'but what about the bottom part? Still, you appear to have kept your feet dry.'

'This is a complete outfit I've been wearing,' said Bao-yu. 'There is a pair of pear-wood pattens that go with it as well, but I left them outside on your verandah.'

Dai-yu looked again at the cape and rain-hat. Both were exquisitely made – quite unlike those that are sold in the market.

'What sort of straw is this cape made of?' she asked him. 'It's so fine. I can see now why you didn't look like a hedge-hog in it as people usually do in these things.'

'The whole outfit was given to me by the Prince of Bei-jing,' said Bao-yu. 'It's exactly like the one he wears himself at home when it rains. If you like it, I'll get you one the same. There's nothing so very special about it really. The hat's rather fun. The centre part is detachable. If you want to wear it in winter when it's snowing, you undo this little bamboo fastener and the whole top comes out, leaving you with just the brim. So when it snows, it can be worn by a woman just as well as by a man. I'll get you a hat like this to wear in winter when it snows.'

'I don't want one, thank you,' said Dai-yu laughing. 'If I were to wear one of those, I should look like one of those old fisherwomen you see in plays and paintings.'

Immediately after saying this she realized that she had virtually been offering herself as a fishwife to Bao-yu's old fisherman and wished the remark unsaid. She blushed with embarrassment and leaned forwards, racked with coughing, over the table. But Bao-yu appeared not to have noticed. What drew his attention was the poem he had just spotted which lay on the table beside her. He picked it up and read it. A murmur of praise which escaped involuntarily from his lips at once brought Dai-yu to her feet. She snatched the paper from him and burned it over the lamp. But Bao-yu only laughed.

'Too late! I've already memorized it.'

'I want to go to bed now,' said Dai-yu. 'Please go now. Come again tomorrow.'

Hearing her speak of bed, Bao-yu felt inside his tunic and pulled out a gold watch about the size of a walnut which he proceeded to inspect. The hand was pointing exactly midway between the sign of the Dog and the sign of the Pig: nine o'clock at night.

'Yes,' he said, stuffing the watch hurriedly back into his tunic. 'Time for bed. I've tired you long enough.'

He put on his cape and his rain-hat and went out, but was back again almost immediately.

'Is there anything you fancy to eat? Let me know if there is, and I'll tell Grandmother first thing tomorrow. It will be safer to tell me than trying to explain what you want to the old women.'

Dai-yu smiled.

'I'll think about it during the night and let you know first thing tomorrow. Listen: it's raining harder. You'd better go quickly. Have you got anyone with you?'

'Yes,' one of the old women standing outside on the verandah called in to her. 'We're waiting with our umbrellas up and we've got the lantern ready.'

'Lantern?' said Dai-yu. 'In this weather?'

'The rain makes no difference,' said Bao-yu. 'It's a horn lantern. They're not affected by rain.'

Dai-yu reached out and took down a lamp with a balloon-shaped glass shade from the top of her bookcase. She ordered one of the maids to light a little candle in it and offered it to Bao-yu.

'Take this. It's brighter than a horn one, and it's specially made for going out in the rain with.'

'I've got one like that myself,' said Bao-yu, 'but I didn't bring it because I was afraid they might trip over and break it.'

'Which is worse,' said Dai-yu, 'a broken lamp or a broken leg? You're not used to wearing pattens, so it's important to see where you're going. The others can carry the horn lantern in front of you, and you can carry this glass lamp, which is handier and brighter and specially made for going out in the rain with, yourself. There. You can send it back to me tomorrow. And if you *should* break it – well, it won't be the end of the world. What has made you of all people so parsimonious about *things* all of a sudden? You're as bad as the Persian with his pearl!'

Thus persuaded, Bao-yu took the lamp from her and set off, two old nannies with umbrellas and a horn lantern in front of him and two little maids with umbrellas bringing up the rear. He made one of the little maids hold the glass lamp Dai-yu had given him and leaned on her shoulder until they were back home.

The departure of Bao-yu and his party was immediately followed by the arrival of two old women from Allspice Court, also carrying lanterns and umbrellas, with a large packet of bird's nest and another packet containing little frosty star-shapes of dazzling white imported sugar.

'You'll find these a bit better than the stuff you can buy in the shops,' they told Dai-yu. 'Our young lady says this is to be getting on with and when you've finished it she'll send you some more.'

'That's very kind,' said Dai-yu. 'Won't you sit outside with the girls and let them give you some tea?'

'We won't, miss, thank you all the same,' they said. 'We've got other things to do.'

'Ah yes, you're busy,' said Dai-yu, smiling. 'I should have remembered. Now that it's getting colder and the nights are longer, I expect you will have started your card-school again. Nothing like a little gambling to pass the long night hours!'

The women laughed good-humouredly.

'I won't deceive you, miss,' said one of them, evidently the chief organizer. 'I've got a really nice little school going this year. There are always a few of us on night-duty, you see, and we don't like to risk falling asleep and missing our watch, so we find our little card-school the best answer. It keeps us awake and, as you say, miss, it helps to pass the time. Tonight it's my turn to be banker. The Garden gate has been closed now, so it's time we got started.'

Dai-yu laughed.

'Well, all I can say is that it's very nice of you to have taken time off when you could have been winning money, to go out in the rain and bring me these things.' She turned to one of her maids: 'Give them a few hundred cash so that they can buy some wine to warm themselves up with after the rain.'

The women thanked her delightedly, and having kotowed, hurried outside to collect the money, after which they put up their umbrellas again and departed.

Nightingale first put away the bird's nest and sugar and then, having moved the lamp over to the bedside and let down the blinds, helped Dai-yu into bed.

As she lay there alone, Dai-yu's thoughts turned to Bao-chai, at first with gratitude, because of her kindness, but afterwards a trifle enviously, because Bao-chai had a mother and brother and she had none. Then she began thinking about Bao-yu and herself: how they had been such good friends to start with, but how later on suspicion and misunderstanding had grown up between them. Then she listened to the insistent rustle of the rain on the bamboos and plantains outside her window. The coldness penetrated the curtains of her bed. Almost without noticing it she had begun to cry. It was nearly three in the morning before she was properly asleep.

We leave her now, to continue our story in the following chapter.

CHAPTER 46

An awkward person is given an awkward mission
And a faithful maid vows faithfulness unto death

It was not, we observed in the last chapter, until nearly three o'clock in the morning that Dai-yu finally dropped off to sleep. We leave her at this point in our narrative and return to Xi-feng, who, it will be remembered, had been summoned on business of an unspecified nature by Lady Xing.

When the others had left, Xi-feng hurriedly changed into her going-out apparel, got into her carriage, and drove round to the establishment next door.

The air of mystery surrounding this summons persisted after her arrival. Lady Xing dismissed the others who had been present and addressed her daughter-in-law conspiratorially.

'The reason I have sent for you is that Sir She has entrusted me with a matter of some delicacy which I hardly know how to go about and I thought I had better discuss it first with you. He has taken a fancy to Lady Jia's maid Faithful and wants her for his concubine; and he has given *me* the job of asking Lady Jia for her. As I see it, there is nothing very unusual in such a request, but I am rather afraid that Lady Jia may refuse and wondered if you had any bright ideas on how one ought to go about this business.'

Xi-feng put on what she hoped was a disarming smile.

'I don't think it's worth trying. I think it would be merely asking for trouble. Without Faithful, Grandma would be completely lost; she'd *never* consent to give her up. In any case, she's often remarked, in private conversation about Father, that she can't understand why at his age he continues to surround himself with young girls – "wasting their young lives" she calls it. She says it's not good for his health, and that he ought to save up his energies for his job and not fritter them away on "drinking all day with his fancy women". You wouldn't derive much pleasure from hearing this sort of thing said to your face, Mother, and I am very sure that Father wouldn't. Yet if you *insist* on approaching Grandma about this, I'm afraid that that's what will happen. It will be like poking a straw up a tiger's nostril. I hope you won't be offended, but I'm afraid *I* daren't approach her about this. I should only be demonstrating my own powerlessness to help and making a lot of unpleasantness for myself into the bargain. Father is inclined to be a bit ga-ga at times nowadays. It's up to you to talk him out of it, Mother. This sort of thing is all very well in a younger man, but in someone of Father's years, with children and grandchildren of his own, it is really too shaming!'

Lady Xing sniffed.

'Lots of men in well-to-do families like ours have *troops* of concubines. Why should it be so shameful only in our case? Anyway, I don't know what makes you think he'd listen to *me*, even if I *did* try to talk him out of it. And even if Lady Jia *is* so attached to Faithful, she may not find it all that easy to refuse when the person asking is an eldest son with a grey beard who has held a position in the Government. Incidentally, I only asked you over here for your opinion. I don't see why you should have to start reading me a lecture. There was never any question of asking *you* to approach Lady Jia *for* me: I shall naturally undertake that task myself. And as for complaining that I haven't tried talking Father out of this – obviously you have no conception of what his temper can be like. I *did* try to dissuade him, but he started hollering at me almost before the words were out of my mouth.'

Xi-feng knew that her mother-in-law was a weak and silly woman, always willing, for the sake of a quiet life, to fall in with her husband's wishes. Apart from pleasing her husband, her principal aim in life was to see how much she could squeeze out of the domestic economy and divert into her personal savings. Decisions both great and small she left to him; but all household monies passed through *her* hands, and she saw to it that they suffered a considerable diminution in the process. The reason she gave for this pillage was Jia She's extravagance.

'I have to economize,' she would say, 'to make up for what Sir She wastes.' Among the children and servants of the household there was not one whom she trusted or whose advice she would listen to. From the tone of what she had just heard, Xi-feng knew that her mother-in-law's obstinate streak had been aroused and that it would now be quite useless to reason with her. She therefore smiled even more disarmingly and promptly changed her tack.

'Of course. You are right, Mother. I haven't had enough experience to be able to judge these matters. But now I come to think of it, it's only natural that a mother should give what she treasures to her own son. Who else would Grandma give her favourite maid – or any other precious thing – to if not to Father? One shouldn't believe everything that people say about other people behind their backs. No, I can see that now. I have been too credulous. One has only to think how you and Father are with Lian. Many a time when Lian has done something he shouldn't have done, you and Father have spoken as if you could hardly wait to lay your hands on him, but when he eventually turned up, you have forgiven everything and ended up by giving him some treasured possession. I've no doubt that in this case it will turn out in exactly the same sort of way with Grandma and Father. As a matter of fact, Grandma is in rather a good mood today, so if you are going to ask her, it would probably be best to do so straight away. Let me go over first to keep her sweet for you. I'll find some excuse for leaving and taking the others with me when you arrive. That will give you a good opportunity for raising this matter. If she says yes, that will, of course, be splendid. But even if she doesn't, no great harm will have been done, because no one else will know about it.'

Hearing what she wanted to hear, Lady Xing's good humour returned and she proceeded to tell Xi-feng what she had already decided to do.

'Actually my idea is *not* to mention this to Lady Jia at first. I think I shall begin by having a quiet word with Faithful herself. Though she may be bashful, as long as she doesn't say anything against it when I've explained it all to her, I shall

know that as far as *she* is concerned it is all right. If I talk to
Lady Jia *then*, though *she* may be unwilling to part with her,
she won't be able to get over the fact that Faithful herself is
willing to leave. "There's no holding someone who has a
mind to go," as they say. I think there should be no difficulty.'

'Trust you for sound planning, Mother!' said Xi-feng.
'That way sounds fool-proof. After all, every one of these
girls is ambitious – they all want to improve their position and
get on in the world – and it's unthinkable that she should
throw away this chance of becoming almost a mistress in
order to remain a maid and end up marrying one of the
grooms.'

'Exactly!' said Lady Xing. 'That's exactly what I thought.
Any of these senior maids would give her ears for a chance
like this. Anyway, you go over now – only don't breathe a
word of this to anyone else! – and I'll follow later on, when
I've had my dinner.'

Xi-feng reflected.

'Faithful's no fool,' she thought. 'Whatever Mother says,
it's far from certain that she'll accept. Suppose I *do* go first and
Mother follows later. If Faithful says yes, all well and good;
but if she *doesn't*, Mother has such a suspicious nature that she's
sure to think it's because I've blabbed and been encouraging
the girl to play hard to get. It will be humiliating for her to
discover that *my* prediction was right, and that will make her
angry; and then she'll take it out on *me* – which won't be very
amusing. It would be better if we went over together; then,
whether Faithful accepts or not, no suspicion can possibly fall
on me.'

'Just now as I was on the point of coming over,' she said,
bringing these reflections to a rapid conclusion, 'two crates of
quails arrived from my aunt's. I told the servants to fry them,
intending to send them over later for your dinner. Then, on
my way in through your gate, I met some of the boys from
here with your carriage. They said it had something wrong
with it and they were taking it outside to be mended. Why not
make use of *my* carriage instead? We can go over together in
it now, and you can dine at my place afterwards on the quails.'

Finding this proposal acceptable, Lady Xing called in her maids to help her change; then, supported by her ever-solicitous daughter-in-law, she got into the latter's carriage and drove with her to the establishment next door. On their way Xi-feng pointed out that if they arrived at Grandmother Jia's place together, the old lady might notice her outdoor clothes and ask her where she had been.

'It would be better if you went in there alone, while I slip back to my own place to change,' she said. 'I'll join you later, as soon as I've got into my everyday clothes.'

Lady Xing thought that this sounded reasonable and went in on her own to see Grandmother Jia. After chatting with her for a few minutes about nothing in particular, she left on the pretext of visiting Lady Wang. This meant that she went out through the rear of the apartment, so that her way took her past Faithful's room and she was able to look in casually in passing to see if she was there.

Faithful was sitting in her room sewing, but stood up as Lady Xing entered.

'What's that you're embroidering?' Lady Xing asked her. 'Let me look.'

She took the embroidery from her hand and inspected it.

'You are getting very good,' she said, laying it down again, and proceeded to scrutinize the girl carefully, from head to foot.

Faithful had on an almost new lilac-coloured dress of silk damask over which she wore a dag-edged sleeveless black satin jacket. Her skirt was a pale eau de Nil. Lady Xing observed the slender waist and elegantly sloping shoulders, the oval face, the lustrous, raven-black hair, the slightly aquiline nose, the cheeks slightly spotted with a few tiny moles. Faithful grew embarrassed and apprehensive beneath this scrutiny.

'What brings Your Ladyship here at this hour?' she asked. 'You don't often come over in the afternoon.'

Lady Xing made a sign to the maids who had accompanied her to leave the room, then, seating herself in Faithful's place, she took the maid by the hand and smiled at her graciously.

'I've come to wish you joy, my dear.'

Hearing this, Faithful was able to guess, more or less, what her visitor had come about. She coloured and hung her head in silence while Lady Xing continued.

'You see, Sir She has no one nowadays he feels he can really rely on. He was thinking of buying someone; but you know, you can never trust those girls you get from the dealers. You don't know how clean they are, and often you don't find out what the snags are until it is too late. They seem all right when you buy them, but two or three days later you find them getting up to the most frightful antics. Well, then he thought he'd pick someone from among our house-born servants, but he just couldn't seem to find anyone good enough. Either they weren't good-looking enough, or their looks were all right but their characters wouldn't do, or whatever it was there was always *something* wrong with them. Anyway – to cut a long story short – after half a year's careful study, he has finally decided that *you* are the cream of the cream. In looks, in character, in behaviour he finds you perfect: gentle, reliable – in fact, all the things he is looking for in a girl. So he's decided to ask Lady Jia if he can have you for his concubine. Of course, *you* would get much better treatment than a newly bought girl from outside could expect. In your case we should put your hair back straight away and treat you as a proper chamber-wife. You would be 'Auntie' to the children and 'Mrs' to the maids. In fact, you would have practically the status of a mistress. Now I know you are an ambitious young woman. You know what they say: "True gold will find its price." In your case it's proved by the fact that Sir She has taken this fancy to you. Here is a chance of doing all those things you ever set your heart on doing. And if you have any enemies, you will be in a position now to make them look very silly. Now – come along with me and tell Her Old Ladyship all about it.'

She took Faithful's hand and made as if to go, but Faithful reddened and snatched her hand away. Lady Xing assumed that she did so from bashfulness.

'Come,' she said, 'there's no need to be bashful. You don't

have to say anything yourself if you don't want to. Just come with me and let me do the talking.'

But Faithful still hung her head and did not move.

'Surely,' said Lady Xing, when it became evident that Faithful was determined not to accompany her, 'surely you can't mean to *refuse* this offer? I must say, you'll be a very silly girl if you do. What, throw away the chance of becoming a lady in order to go on being a maid? If you do, then in two or three years' time when they marry you off, it will only be to one of the boys, you know. You'll still be a slave just the same. Whereas if you come to live with us – well, you know my nature: I'm not a difficult person to get on with; and Sir She always treats his girls very nicely. And after you've been with him for a year or two, if you can bear him a child, you'll be on the same level as me: everyone in the household will have to jump to it when you give them orders. If you throw away an opportunity like this, you'll certainly live to regret it.'

Faithful continued to hang her head and say nothing.

'You're such a lively person as a rule,' said Lady Xing. 'What's got hold of your tongue? Is there any particular thing about this arrangement that doesn't suit you? Please let me know if there is, and I promise that it shall be altered.'

But Faithful still said nothing.

'Oh, I know what it is,' said Lady Xing. 'I expect you've got parents and don't like to say anything until you've heard from *them*. Why yes, very right and proper. I shall get in touch with your parents and no doubt you will be hearing from them in due course. Then anything you want to say, you will be able to say to them.'

With that she left, and went round to Xi-feng's apartment.

Xi-feng had long since changed back into her ordinary clothes. As no one else was about, she had taken the opportunity of telling Patience about her interview with Lady Xing. Patience was amused, but shook her head doubtfully at Lady Xing's optimism.

'If you ask me, I think it's very uncertain. From the way she's always spoken in the past when we've been alone together, I should think she'll refuse. Anyway, we'll just have to wait and see.'

'Lady Xing is sure to come here afterwards to talk about what happened,' said Xi-feng. 'If Faithful has accepted, it will be all right; but if Faithful *hasn't* accepted, she's not going to be in a very good mood, and it would embarrass her to have *you* here while she was telling me about it. You'd better order them to prepare some of those quails and a few other dishes to go with them so that I can offer her dinner when she arrives; but after you've done that, you'd better take yourself off for a bit – and don't come back until you think she's gone.'

Patience gave Xi-feng's instructions to the cook and then went off to enjoy herself in the Garden.

* * *

When Lady Xing left, Faithful felt sure that she would go straight to Xi-feng's for consultation and that soon after that someone else would arrive and put the same question to her again. It seemed to her that the best way of avoiding this would be to decamp. She sought out Amber in order to give some cover to her exit.

'If Her Old Ladyship should ask for me, tell her that I'm not feeling well and couldn't eat any lunch today. Say I've gone to walk in the Garden for a bit and shall be back again shortly.'

Amber agreed to do this and Faithful went off to wander about in the Garden. While she was doing so, she came by coincidence upon Patience doing exactly the same thing.

Seeing no one else but the two of them around, Patience felt no compunction in revealing her newly acquired knowledge.

'Look who's here!' she called out teasingly. 'Mrs Faithful!'

Faithful blushed bright red.

'I suppose you're in the plot against me too. Well, never mind. I'll be having it out with your mistress presently.'

Patience could see that Faithful was really angry, and regretted her foolish jibe. Taking her by the hand, she led her to some rocks beneath a stand of maple-trees where they could sit down together, and proceeded to tell her all that Xi-feng had a few minutes earlier told *her*.

'Thank you,' said Faithful when she had finished. 'You and I at least are still friends. When I think of our set – how many were we? – Aroma, Amber, Candida, Nightingale, Suncloud, Silver, Musk, Ebony, Kingfisher – she left to go with Miss Shi – Charmer and Golden – they both died – Snowpink that was dismissed – you and me – there must have been a dozen of us altogether: when we were young we always told each other everything and shared everything together; but now that we are older, the others all seem to go their different ways and just aren't interested. Not me, though: *I* haven't changed. I'm just the same as I always was. I don't have any secrets from any of you. Now listen: I'm telling you this now for you to remember – only don't go passing it on to your Mrs Lian. It's not just a question of not wanting to be his concubine. I wouldn't go to Sir She, not if Lady Xing had died and he sent matchmakers and witnesses and asked me to be his proper wife!'

Patience was about to answer when there was a laugh from behind the rocks on which they were sitting and a voice called out.

'What's this shameless boasting I hear? It's enough to set one's teeth on edge!'

Startled, the two of them rose to their feet and went to look behind the rockery to find out who it was. Aroma emerged, laughing, as they did so.

'What's all this about? Tell me about it too.'

The three of them sat down on the rocks together and Patience retold all that she had just told Faithful.

'Well!' said Aroma when Patience had finished. 'I suppose it's not for someone in my place to say so, but what a *nasty* old man! Unless they're downright misshapen, just about no one is safe from him.'

'I can tell you a way out of this if you want to refuse,' said Patience.

'What?' said Faithful.

'Have a word with Her Old Ladyship and get her to tell him that she's already given you to Mr Lian. That'll cool his ardour.'

'You too now?' said Faithful angrily. 'You're a nice lot, I must say! It was your mistress who suggested that the other day. I *thought* we hadn't heard the last of that.'

'If you don't want *either* of them,' said Aroma, 'then if you ask me I think your best plan would be to get her to tell him that she's promised you to Master Bao. That would put him off *right* away!'

Both embarrassed and exasperated by these taunts, Faithful rounded on her tormentors with some heat.

'You're *rotten*, both of you, and I hope you both come to bad ends! I thought you were decent sorts who might try to comfort me in my trouble. But even if you don't care, you might at least refrain from treating it as a joke. I suppose you think you don't have to worry about *me* because your own futures are assured and each of you will end up as chamber-wife to the person of your choice. Well, as I see it, things in this world don't always turn out the way you want them to. I wouldn't be quite so cock-a-hoop if I were you. You might be in for some nasty shocks yourselves.'

The others saw that they had really rattled her and laughingly did their best to calm her down.

'Now, now, Faithful, don't take it so much to heart. We three have been like sisters ever since we were little girls. We were only teasing you a bit because there's no one else around. Tell us what plan you've decided on, so that we shan't be so worried about you.'

'Plan?' said Faithful. 'I've got no plan. I just shan't go to him and that'll be the end of it.'

Patience shook her head.

'I very much doubt if it will. You know what Sir She's temper is like. It's true that he can't touch you as long as you're with Her Old Ladyship; but you're not going to be with her all your life, are you? You'll have to leave in the end, and if you fall into his clutches *then*, you'll be in real trouble.'

Faithful smiled grimly.

'As long as Her Old Ladyship lives, I shall stay with Her Old Ladyship. And when all's said and done, even when the old dear goes to her rest, there are still the years of mourning. There would be no question of his taking a concubine with his mother just dead. And by the time the period of mourning is over – well, anything might have happened. I'll just have to wait and see. If I get really desperate, I can always shave my hair off and become a nun; or failing that, there's always suicide. *I* don't mind going through life without a man. Glad to keep myself clean.'

The other two tittered protestingly.

'The things you say, Faithful! Have you no shame?'

'There's not much room left for shame when things have come to *this* pass,' said Faithful. 'Anyway, if you don't believe me, just wait and see. Lady Xing said just now that she was going to see my parents about this. I wonder if she will. She'll have to go all the way to Nanking if she does!'

'Your parents are looking after the house in Nanking and can't be fetched,' said Patience, 'but they can be got in touch with eventually. And in any case, your elder brother and his wife are here. It's a pity you're a house-born servant and not on your own here like me and Aroma.'

'It makes no odds,' said Faithful. ' "You can take an ox to the water, but you can't make him drink." Just because I refuse him, he's not going to kill my parents!'

While she was talking, her sister-in-law appeared some distance from where they were sitting, walking in their direction.

'There you are!' said Aroma. 'They've evidently found that they can't get in touch with your parents, so they've already had a word with your sister-in-law.'

'That cow!' said Faithful. 'She's a regular camel-dealer, that one. She'd just *jump* at a thing like this!'

The 'cow' was already upon them, smiling all over her face.

'Ah, *here* you are, miss! I've looked for you everywhere. Come with me. I've got something to tell you.'

Patience and Aroma fussed round her, inviting her to sit with them on the rock.

'No, you young ladies sit down,' said the woman. 'I've got to have a word with our Faithful.'

'Is it really very urgent?' they asked her innocently. 'We've been playing "I spy". Can't it wait until we've finished guessing?'

'What is it?' said Faithful. 'Why not just tell me?'

'Come with me,' said her sister-in-law. 'I'll tell you over there. It's good news, anyway.'

'Oh, is it by any chance the thing Lady Xing was talking about?' said Faithful.

'There!' said her sister-in-law. 'You knew about it all the time! What were you having me on for? Now come on, hurry, and I'll tell you all the details. It's a wonderful, wonderful piece of news!'

Faithful stood up and spat hard and deliberately in her sister-in-law's face.

'Why don't you take your bloody trap out of here?' she shouted, pointing at her angrily. ' "Wonderful news" indeed! I suppose you've been studying the way families of maids who've become concubines can throw their weight about, so you just can't wait to push *me* into that fire. If I find favour, then of course you'll be the great lady and be able to put on airs and throw your weight about too. If I don't, if I'm a failure – oh, you'll just draw your tortoise-head back into your tortoise-shell and leave me to get on with it. Whether I live or die, it will be all the same to you.'

She began crying hysterically and had to be restrained and comforted by Patience and Aroma.

'Huh!' said her sister-in-law in an unsuccessful attempt to retrieve her ruffled dignity. 'Whether you're willing or not, you might at least be civil. Anyway, I don't see why you need drag other people into it. "One doesn't discuss short legs in front of a dwarf," they say. I make no comment on the nasty things you said about *me*, but what about these young ladies? *They*'ve done nothing to provoke you. This talk about concubines is not very nice for *them*.'

'*Oh* no!' said the two young ladies in question. 'She wasn't

referring to *us* when she said that. It's *you* who are dragging in
other people. What makes you think that either of us has been
chosen as a concubine? By whom? Even if we had been,
neither of us has any family in this household to throw their
weight about, so she can say what she likes on the subject:
there's no occasion for *us* to get worked up about it.'

'It's because I made her look silly,' said Faithful. 'She's
trying to cover up by setting you two against me. Fortunately
you are too intelligent to be taken in. I lost my temper just
now and I'm afraid I didn't choose my words very carefully.
She evidently thought she could take advantage of that.'

Faithful's sister-in-law was by now finding her situation so
disagreeable that she removed herself from it by walking away
in a huff. Faithful herself was still extremely angry and for
some time continued to hurl invectives at her retreating back;
but Patience and Aroma reasoned with her, and gradually she
began to calm down.

'Why were you hiding there just now?' Patience asked
Aroma when Faithful's composure had been restored. 'It's
funny that we didn't see you.'

'I'd been over to Miss Xi-chun's to see Master Bao,' said
Aroma, 'but I got there a moment too late. They said he had
just that minute left for home. I couldn't understand why in
that case I hadn't run into him on the way, so I thought perhaps he might have gone to Miss Lin's; but just as I was going
there to look for him, I met one of Miss Lin's people who said
that he *wasn't* with her, so I began wondering if he might have
gone out of the Garden altogether. Then just at that moment
you came along from the direction I was looking in, so I slipped
behind a tree and hid. When Faithful came, I slipped out from
behind my tree and hid behind this rock. I could see you both
sitting there talking, but your two pairs of eyes couldn't see
me.'

'And your *three* pairs of eyes couldn't see *me*!' said a mocking voice behind them.

The three girls jumped in surprise. When they turned to
look, it was Bao-yu himself who walked out from behind the
rock.

Aroma was the first to recover her voice.

'You led me a nice dance!' she said. 'Where have you been all this time?'

'As I came out of Xi-chun's place, I could see you coming towards me,' said Bao-yu. 'I knew it must be me you had come for, so I hid myself to give you a surprise. I watched you as you walked by with your head in the air. Then I watched you go into Xi-chun's courtyard. Then I saw you come out again. Then I saw you stop and ask someone something. It was terribly funny. I was hoping that you would eventually come by the place where I was hiding, so that I could pop out and make you jump. But then you started dodging around, and I could see that *you* were hiding from someone else and evidently planning to play the same trick on *them*. So I peeped out to see who it was and found that it was these two. Then I began gradually working my way round behind you, and when you stepped out and showed yourself, I slipped forward and hid in the place where *you* had been hiding.'

'We'd better go behind and have another look,' said Patience. 'We'll probably find two more people hidden back there!'

'No, I think there really are no more now,' said Bao-yu.

When she realized that Bao-yu must have heard everything that had been said, Faithful lay face downwards on the rock and pretended to be asleep. Bao-yu laughed at her and gave her a little prod.

'It's damp on that stone. Much better come indoors if you want to lie down.'

He tried to pull her up, at the same time inviting Patience to accompany them back home for some tea. When Patience and Aroma added their own coaxing to his, Faithful finally rose to her feet and the four of them went together to Green Delights.

Bao-yu had, indeed, heard everything from his hiding-place, and his concern for Faithful made him very unhappy. When they were back, he lay back silent on his bed worrying about it while the three girls laughed and chattered in the adjoining room.

*

When Lady Xing asked Xi-feng about Faithful's parents, she learned that her father's name was Jin Cai and that he and her mother lived as caretakers at the Jia family mansion in Nanking and seldom came up to the capital.

'But she has an elder brother Jin Wen-xiang, who is one of Grandmother's buyers,' said Xi-feng, 'and her sister-in-law is Grandmother's chief laundress.'

The laundress was duly summoned and Lady Xing carefully explained what was required of her. The woman was naturally delighted and went off in a great bustle of self-importance to look for Faithful, confident that she had only to state her mission for the matter to be successfully concluded. Ill prepared, therefore, for Faithful's acrimonious rebuff or the strictures of Patience and Aroma which followed it, she returned to Lady Xing to make her report in a state of angry mortification.

'It's no good, I'm afraid. She just swore at me.' Since Xi-feng was present, the woman dared not mention Patience. 'That Aroma was there, too, helping her. Some of the things she said to me – well, I wouldn't offend Your Ladyship's ears by repeating them. I think you and Sir She would be well advised to buy a girl elsewhere. That little fool Faithful evidently wasn't *meant* for such great fortune – nor we to share it, seemingly.'

'Whatever has this got to do with Aroma?' said Lady Xing. 'I wonder how she got to know about it.' She paused for a moment. 'Was there anyone else there?'

'Miss Patience was there,' said the woman.

'I wish you'd given her a box on the ears then and told her to come home,' Xi-feng put in hurriedly. 'She went off wandering somewhere or other as soon as I left the house and there wasn't a sign of her when I got back. If *she* was there, she'll have put in her pennyworth too, I suppose.'

'Well, she wasn't exactly *there*,' said the woman, 'she was quite a way off. I couldn't see her very clearly. Maybe it *wasn't* her. I could have been mistaken.'

'Go and find her at once,' Xi-feng said to the servants. 'Tell her I'm back and Lady Xing is here and she is to come home immediately.'

Felicity hurried forward to report:

'Miss Lin sent round three or four times to ask if Patience would go over to *her* place, so Patience went to see what she wanted. I went there to call her back when you came in just now, but Miss Lin said would I please tell you that she wants Patience a bit longer to do something for her.'

'She's *always* asking Patience to do things for her,' said Xi-feng, with pretended annoyance. 'I wonder what it is this time.'

Resourceless, now that her plan had misfired, Lady Xing returned home as soon as she had eaten dinner and in the evening informed Jia She of what had happened. After reflecting for some moments, Jia She ordered Jia Lian to be summoned immediately.

' Jin Cai and his wife aren't the only couple looking after our Nanking property,' he began as soon as Jia Lian arrived. 'Have him recalled immediately.'

'Last time we had a letter from Nanking,' said Jia Lian, 'it said that Jin Cai was in a delirium and they'd already issued the money to buy his coffin. He may well be dead by now; and even if he isn't, he's probably unconscious and wouldn't be much use to us back here. And his old woman is as deaf as a post.'

'Villain! Parricide!' Jia She shouted, in instant fury. 'Trust *you* to know that! Get out of my sight!'

Startled by his father's unaccountable anger, Jia Lian retreated in a hurry. Shortly after he had done so, Jin Wen-xiang was sent for.

Jia Lian, not daring either to go back home or to go in again to his father, stayed near at hand in his outer study, waiting to see what happened. After a while Jin Wen-xiang arrived, and Jia Lian watched him being conducted through the inner gate by the pages. After a lapse of time in which he could comfortably (had he been so minded) have eaten four or five meals, he saw Jin Wen-xiang come out again, but was still too scared to

make inquiries. He did not do so until he had allowed what he
thought was a safe interval to elapse after Jin Wen-xiang's departure, and was then informed that his father had gone to
bed. Only then did he dare to go back home; and it was not
until Xi-feng informed him that night that he understood what
it was all about.

*

That night Faithful was unable to sleep. Her brother came
next morning to ask Grandmother Jia if he could take his
sister back home for the day. His request was granted, and
Grandmother Jia ordered Faithful to get ready. Faithful did
not want to go, but overcame her reluctance because she did
not want the old lady to suspect that anything was amiss.

When they were home, her brother told her all that Jia She
had said, promising that if she accepted, her position would be
an honoured one: she would become 'Mrs Jin', and all the
household would look up to her. But no matter what he said,
Faithful set her face firmly against it all and obstinately continued to say 'no'. In the end her brother had no alternative
but to go back to Jia She and tell him that his sister was unwilling. Jia She was greatly incensed.

'Now look here,' he said, 'you go back and get your wife
to tell her this: Sir She says:

The moon ever loved a young man.

He knows all about that saying. No doubt she thinks him too
old for her and has set her heart on one of the younger ones –
Bao-yu, probably, or my son Lian. Tell her, if she has, the
sooner she abandons hope in *that* direction the better, because
if *I* can't have her, she may be very sure that no one else in this
family will dare to. That's one thing. And here's another. She
may think that because she's Lady Jia's favourite, she can look
forward to marrying outside one day and becoming someone's
regular wife. Well if so, just let her get this firmly into her
mind: whoever or wherever she marries, she needn't think she
will ever escape me. If she dies or is prepared to live all her
life an old maid, I might admit myself beaten; but otherwise,

never. So unless she proposes to choose one of those alternatives, she'd better hurry up and change her mind. It will be a great deal easier for her if she does.'

Each sentence of the above had been punctuated by a nervous 'Yessir' from Jin Wen-xiang. Jia She continued.

'Now don't think you can fool me over this in the hope of getting better terms. Tomorrow I shall send Lady Xing over to have a word with Faithful herself. If Faithful still refuses after your wife has spoken to her, then that is no fault of yours and I shan't hold it against you. But woe betide you if when Lady Xing talks to her she finds that she is willing!'

After a good many more 'Yessirs' Jin Wen-xiang withdrew and went back home. When he got back, he did not even wait to transmit Jia She's message through his wife, but went straight in and told it all to Faithful himself. It made Faithful so angry that for some time afterwards she was unable to speak. Finally, after some inward calculation, she answered him as follows.

'Even if I *am* willing, you'll have to take me back first, so that I can have a word about it with Her Old Ladyship.'

Supposing this to mean that she had changed her mind, her brother and his wife were overjoyed, and the latter at once undertook to go with her to see Grandmother Jia.

It so happened that when they arrived, Lady Wang, Aunt Xue, Li Wan, Xi-feng, Bao-yu and the girls, and some of the senior stewardesses from outside were all there with the old lady sharing a joke. Faithful led her sister-in-law through their midst, knelt down at her mistress's feet, and with tears streaming down her face, proceeded to tell her what Lady Xing had said to her the day before, what her sister-in-law had said to her in the Garden, and what her elder brother had told her that morning.

'When I refused, Sir She said it was because I fancied Master Bao, or else because I was saving myself to marry someone outside. He said that even if I were to fly to the world's end, I should never as long as I live escape out of his clutches: sooner or later he'd have his revenge. But I've made my mind up, and I'm telling Your Ladyship here, in front of all these witnesses. I don't care whether it's Master Bao or Prince Bao or the Emperor Bao, I don't ever want to marry *anyone*. Even if Your Ladyship herself were to try and force me to, I'd rather cut my own throat than marry. I'll serve Your Ladyship until you leave this world for the next one; and when that day comes, I shan't go back to my brother and his wife; I shall either take my own life or I shall cut my hair off and become a nun. And in case anyone should think I don't really mean this and am only saying it to get myself out of a corner, I call on heaven and earth and all the gods and the sun and moon to be my witness: if I don't honestly and sincerely mean every word I say, may I be struck with a quinsy this very moment and matter burst out of my mouth!'

She had hidden a pair of scissors up her sleeve before she came, and as she uttered this oath, she undid her hair with her left hand and began hacking away at it with the scissors in her right. The servants rushed forward to stop her, but before they could lay hands on her, she had already cut off a large hank. It was fortunate that her hair was so thick and strong. Observing with relief that she had not succeeded in cutting through all of it, the servants wound up what remained and refastened it on her head.

By the time Faithful had finished speaking, Grandmother Jia was trembling all over with rage.

'I have only this one girl left that I can rely on,' she said, speaking half to herself, 'and now they are plotting to take her away from me.'

As she looked at those standing around her, her eye fastened upon Lady Wang.

'You deceive me, all of you. *You* who are outwardly so dutiful: you are secretly plotting against me like all the rest. Whenever I have any good thing you come and ask me for it. All my best people you take away from me. Now I have only this one poor girl left to me; and because you see that I am nice to her, it infuriates you – you can't *bear* it! And now you've found this means of getting her away from me, so that you can have me at your mercy.'

Lady Wang had risen to her feet as soon as Grandmother

Jia addressed her, but dared not defend herself; Aunt Xue could not very well intervene when the object of these strictures was her elder sister; and Li Wan had hustled her young charges from the room at the first hint of impropriety when Faithful began her complaint.

Tan-chun, always one of the more thoughtful members of the family, realized that however unjust the accusation, Lady Wang was in no position to answer back. She realized that Aunt Xue could not speak up for her own sister or Bao-chai say anything when her mother was silent and that Li Wan, Xi-feng and Bao-yu were even more disqualified from coming to the rescue. This was exactly the sort of situation in which a young unmarried granddaughter could be useful. And since Ying-chun was too docile and Xi-chun too childish, Tan-chun herself, after listening for a while at the window, boldly stepped into the room and faced her grandmother with an intrepid smile.

'How can this matter have anything to do with Mother, Grandma? Can you think of *any* reason why a younger brother's wife should be consulted about her brother-in-law's private business?'

Grandmother Jia was at once all smiles.

'Of course not, my dear. I am a silly old woman! Mrs Xue, you must try not to laugh at me. Your sister is a most dutiful daughter-in-law: not like She's wife, who is so scared of her husband that she has no time for me – beyond what she does for form's sake. I have done your sister a very grave injustice.'

Aunt Xue murmured something in reply, afterwards adding, as a politeness:

'The younger son's wife is often the more favoured one. Perhaps you are biased, Lady Jia.'

'No,' said Grandmother Jia firmly, 'I am *not* biased. Bao-yu,' she said, turning to her grandson, 'why didn't you speak up when I falsely accused your mother? How could you stand by like that and watch her being treated unjustly?'

'How could I take Mother's side against Uncle and Aunt?' said Bao-yu. 'Obviously *someone* was to blame; but if it wasn't Mother, who was I to say that it was? I could hardly have said that it was *me*. Somehow I don't think you would have believed me!'

Grandmother Jia laughed.

'Yes, I suppose you are right. Go and kneel down to your mother, then, Bao-yu. Tell her that I'm getting old and that she is not to be upset by what I said to her. Ask her to forgive me for *your* sake.'

Bao-yu quickly went over and knelt before Lady Wang. But before he could relay his grandmother's message, his mother had laughingly prevented him.

'Get up at once and don't be ridiculous, Bao-yu! How can you possibly apologize for Grandma to *me*?'

Bao-yu hurriedly got up to his feet.

'What about *you*, Feng?' said Grandmother Jia. 'Why didn't *you* try to stop me?'

'I've been trying to restrain myself from blaming *you* for what's happened,' said Xi-feng. 'I don't know why *you* should pick on *me*.'

Grandmother Jia's laughter was echoed by the others present.

'Oh? Now this is interesting. I should like to know why you think *I*'m to blame for what has happened.'

'You shouldn't be so good at training your girls,' said Xi-feng. 'When you've brought up a beautiful young bulrush like Faithful, can you blame other people for wanting her? It's a good job I'm only your granddaughter-in-law. If I'd been your *grandson*, I should have asked you for her for myself a long time ago. I shouldn't have waited till now, *I* can tell you!'

'Oh,' said Grandmother Jia, laughing. 'So it's all *my* fault, is it?'

'Of *course* it's your fault,' said Xi-feng.

'In that case I won't try to keep her,' said Grandmother Jia. 'You can take her back with you.'

'Not just now,' said Xi-feng. 'In my next life, perhaps. If I'm a good girl in this life, I might be reborn as a man, and I can ask you for her then!'

'Go on, take her with you!' said Grandmother Jia. 'You

can give her to your Lian. See if that shameless father-in-law of yours still wants her *then*!'

'Lian doesn't deserve her,' said Xi-feng. 'All he's fit for is a couple of sad old dumplings like me and Patience!'

This set everyone laughing.

A maid came in to announce someone.

'Lady Xing, ma'am.'

Lady Wang hurried out to meet her.

What followed will be revealed in the next chapter.

CHAPTER 47

In pursuit of love the Oaf King takes a fearful beating
And from fear of reprisal the Reluctant Playboy makes a
hasty getaway

HEARING that Lady Xing had arrived, Lady Wang at once hurried out to meet her.

Lady Xing had come over to see if there had been any change in Faithful's attitude. She was ignorant of the fact that the secret was now out and that Grandmother Jia knew everything. The first she heard of it was when quietly informed by some of Grandmother Jia's women as she entered the old lady's courtyard. She would have liked to turn back, but by then it was already too late: she had already been seen and announced by the servants inside, and when her sister-in-law Lady Wang came out to meet her, she was obliged to go in with her and pay her respects to Grandmother Jia. Finding that her greetings were received by the old lady in stony silence, she was covered with shame and confusion.

By this time Xi-feng had slipped out on pretext of other business and Faithful had gone off to her own room to nurse her anger alone. Fearing that their presence might add to Lady Xing's embarrassment, Aunt Xue, Lady Wang and the rest also, one after another, withdrew. When she saw that she and Lady Xing were alone together, Grandmother Jia at last broke her silence.

'I hear you have been playing the matchmaker for your husband,' she said. 'I must congratulate you on your wifely virtue – though I must say, I think that in this case you are carrying wifeliness a little far. You have children and grandchildren of your own now: why should you be frightened of his temper still at *your* age? Yet they tell me that you positively encourage his excesses.'

Lady Xing blushed crimson with embarrassment.

'I have tried several times to dissuade him, without success. I am sure you must realize that I have acted against my will in this matter.'

'You did what you were told, all the same,' said Grandmother Jia sharply. 'Would you do what you were told if he asked you to kill someone? Just reflect for a moment. There is only your sister-in-law, poor, simple soul – she is always ailing from something or other – to worry about the responsibilities of this household. It's true that she has Lian's wife to help her, but *she* has so much to do that she hardly knows which way to turn – always "putting the rake down to pick up the broom". And *I* have to cut down on all *my* activities nowadays. So if there is ever anything that your sister-in-law and Feng have overlooked, Faithful is the only one left to make sure that my needs are attended to. She is a child who notices things. If she sees that I lack something, she will either ask for it herself or have a word with one of the other two and make sure that I get it. Think of all the hundreds and thousands of things there are to be done in this household. If I hadn't got Faithful, how could the other two *avoid* overlooking something once in a while? So what would you have me do *then*? Would you expect me to start worrying about all these things myself? Should I have to start calculating what I needed every day and go running off to the other two to ask them for it? Of all the girls I've ever had, Faithful is the only one left me now who is a bit older and more responsible than the rest – who understands my little ways and knows how I like things done. There's a genuine bond between us – for example, *she* would never take advantage of our relationship, as some girls would, to ask other people for clothes or money for herself. One consequence of this is that not only Feng and your sister-in-law, but everyone else in the household, from the highest down to the lowest, is able to trust her. It means that quite apart from the fact that *I* have someone I can rely on, Feng and your sister-in-law are saved a great deal of worry; because with a girl like that to look after me, *I* don't suffer when they occasionally forget something, and that keeps me in a good temper. If Faithful were to leave me now, who would you get for me to put in her place? And even if you could find such a jewel, she'd need to have a tongue in her head too. She'd be no use to me if she didn't have my Faithful's gift for expressing herself. As a matter of fact I've been thinking of sending someone round to your husband to tell him that if he would care to *buy* himself a girl, he'd be very welcome to do it with my money. I don't mind if it costs me eight thousand – *ten* thousand even – but if it's this girl of mine he wants, I'm afraid he can't have her. Tell him that if he wants to be a dutiful son, he'll be doing more for me by leaving me my Faithful, to serve me during the few years that yet remain, than if he were to come over and wait on me in person, morning, noon and night. It's turned out very conveniently, your coming over just now: you'll be able to take this message back to him yourself and I can be sure of its being properly delivered.'

She called for the servants.

'What's happened to everybody? We were just in the middle of a nice chat when suddenly everyone went away.'

The maids, with answering cries, went off to look for the others. Soon all had been reassembled except Aunt Xue, who showed some resistance to the summons.

'I've only just got back,' she said. 'What's the point of going out again?'

'Have a heart, Mrs Xue!' said the maid. 'Her Old Ladyship is in a passion. If *you* don't come, no one else will ever shift her out of it. If it's the walking that bothers you, I'll carry you there on my back!'

'Get along with you, little monkey!' said Aunt Xue, laughing. 'A few hard words won't hurt you.'

She went with the maid nevertheless. On her arrival she was cordially welcomed by Grandmother Jia.

'What shall we do?' said the old lady. 'Shall we play cards? Come and sit by me, Mrs Xue. You haven't had much practice. If the two of us sit together, there will be less chance of Feng confusing us.'

'Yes,' said Aunt Xue. 'You will have to keep an eye on my hand and help me out a bit. Is it to be just the four of us, or shall we have one or two more?'

'Just us four, surely?' said Lady Wang.

'No, let's have one more,' said Xi-feng. 'It will make it more interesting.'

'Go and call Faithful, someone,' said Grandmother Jia. 'She can sit below me. Mrs Xue's eyesight isn't too good. Faithful will be able to keep an eye on *both* our hands.'

Xi-feng laughed.

'I know you can read and write,' she said to Tan-chun. 'I suppose you haven't learned how to tell fortunes too, by any chance?'

'What a strange question!' said Tan-chun. 'You should be concentrating all your energies on winning some of Grandma's money, not thinking about having your fortune told.'

'I thought you might be able to tell me how much I'm going to *lose* today,' said Xi-feng. 'No question of *winning* anything. Look how Grandma's got me ambushed on every side before we've even started playing!'

Presently Faithful arrived and sat in the place below Grandmother Jia. Xi-feng sat below Faithful. A red blanket was spread over the table, the cards were shuffled, the players cut for deal, and the game began.

After they had been playing for some minutes, Faithful noticed that Grandmother Jia had a nearly full hand and only needed a Two of Coins to go out. She made a sign to Xi-feng, whose turn it was to discard. Xi-feng pretended to be in great doubt as to what she ought to play.

'I'm sure Aunt Xue is hanging on to the card I want. I'd better let her have *this* one, and then perhaps she'll part with it.'

'I'm sure *I* haven't got anything you want,' said Aunt Xue.

'I'd need to look at your hand before I believed that,' said Xi-feng.

'You're very welcome to,' said Aunt Xue. 'Come on, now! Put that card down and let's see what it is.'

Xi-feng laid the card down in front of Aunt Xue: Two of Coins.

'It's no good to me,' said Aunt Xue, 'but I've an idea your grandmother may be going out now.'

'Oh, *no*!' cried Xi-feng in mock dismay. 'It's a mistake. I didn't mean to discard that one.'

But Grandmother Jia, with a crow of triumph, had already thrown down her cards.

'You *dare* take that back! You shouldn't make mistakes!'

'I told you I needed a fortune-teller,' said Xi-feng. 'Well, *I* played the card, so I suppose I've no one but myself to blame.'

'I should think so too!' said Grandmother Jia. 'Give yourself a good hard slap on the face if you want to know where the fault lies!' She turned to Aunt Xue. 'You mustn't think I'm grasping, Mrs Xue. I don't play for the money; but I do so enjoy winning!'

'Of course,' said Aunt Xue. '*No* one would be so idiotic as to suppose that you played for the money.'

Hearing this, Xi-feng, who had meanwhile been counting out the money she had lost, abruptly stopped, and threaded the coins back onto the string.

'Right!' she said, speaking to the others present. 'That settles it! She doesn't play for the money, she just enjoys winning. Well I *am* mean and grasping, I'm afraid, and when I lose, I like to know how much. But if that's the way she feels, back it all goes again!'

When Grandmother Jia played cards it was her unvarying custom to let Faithful shuffle for her. She had been talking to Aunt Xue throughout Xi-feng's bit of by-play, but broke off when she became aware that Faithful had made no move.

'Come child,' she said. 'You're not too upset to shuffle for me, are you?'

Faithful took up the cards with a laugh.

'No, only Mrs Lian hasn't paid up yet.'

'Oh, hasn't she?' said Grandmother Jia. 'She'll be lucky if she gets away with *that*!' She called one of the junior maids to her. 'Take that string of cash from in front of Mrs Lian and bring it here.'

The little maid did as she was bid and laid the money on the table beside Grandmother Jia.

'*Please* let me have it back,' Xi-feng pleaded, ' – so that I can give you the right amount.'

'Feng really *is* rather mean,' said Aunt Xue jokingly. 'It's only a game, after all.'

Xi-feng stood up and, laying a hand on Aunt Xue's arm, pointed out to her the wooden chest in which Grandmother Jia kept her money.

'You see that, Aunt? I don't know *how* much of my money has at one time or another found its way in there. Before I've been playing half an hour, my money in the chest begins calling to my money on the table to come and join it. All I have to do now is wait until it's called it all in, then the game will be over and Grannie will be in a good temper again and *I* shall be able to go and get on with my work.'

By the time she had finished saying this, Grandmother Jia and all the others present were laughing. They were still laughing when Patience, fearing that her mistress might have insufficient money by her, came in bringing another string of cash.

'Don't put it down in front of *me*,' Xi-feng told her. 'Put it down beside Her Old Ladyship, so that all my money can go into the chest together. We don't want the money in the chest to have to go through the business of calling for it all over again.'

This made Grandmother Jia laugh so much that she scattered the cards she was holding all over the table.

'Tear her mouth!' she said to Faithful, giving her a playful push.

Patience laid the money down as she was bidden, and after laughing a while with the others, went out again. On her way out of the courtyard she ran into Jia Lian, who was just about to enter the gate.

'Where's Lady Xing?' he asked her. 'Sir She has sent me to look for her.'

'She's been standing in there with Her Old Ladyship for the last half hour,' said Patience. 'She hasn't dared to move yet, but I dare say she'll get away as soon as she can. Her Old Ladyship has been in quite a tizzy this morning, but thanks to the Mistress, who's been all this time humouring her, she's gradually beginning to calm down a bit.'

'Oh well, when I go in I shall say that I've come to find out if Her Old Ladyship is going to Lai Da's place on the four-teenth, so that I know whether or not to have the carriages ready,' said Jia Lian. 'I can mention that Lady Xing is wanted as an afterthought. And after that perhaps I shall stay on and chaff the old lady a bit for a few minutes. That should be all right, shouldn't it?'

'If you're asking my opinion, I think you'd do much better not to go in at all,' said Patience. '*Everyone*'s been in trouble with her today – even Her Ladyship and Bao-yu. If *you* go in now, you'll walk straight into it.'

'Oh, surely it's all over now, isn't it?' said Jia Lian. 'Surely she's not going to start all over again? It's nothing to do with *me*, in any case. And Sir She did ask me to go and fetch Mother myself. If he finds that I've sent someone else to do it, he's in such a bad temper already, that he'll probably use that as an excuse to take it out on *me*.'

He began to go in, and Patience, to whom this sounded reasonable enough, turned back and followed him in across the courtyard. Entering Grandmother Jia's outer door, Jia Lian crossed the reception room on tiptoe and peered into the inner room at the back. He could see his mother standing there.

Xi-feng, who had sharper eyes than the rest, spotted him at once and made a sign to him not to enter and another sign to Lady Xing indicating that she was wanted outside. Lady Xing could not simply walk out, so she filled a cup with some tea and set it down in front of Grandmother Jia. This caused the old lady to turn round; and as Jia Lian chanced at that very moment to be looking in at the doorway and was unable to withdraw his head in time, she caught a momentary glimpse of him before he disappeared.

'Who's that outside?' she said. 'It looked like one of the boys peeping in there just now.'

'Yes,' said Xi-feng, quickly rising to her feet and going over to the doorway, '*I* thought I saw someone's shadow there just now.'

Jia Lian walked smiling into the room.

'I've come to ask if you are going on the fourteenth, Grandma, so that I shall know whether to get the carriages ready or not.'

'In that case why didn't you come in straight away,' said Grandmother Jia, 'instead of lurking around outside?'

'I could see that you were playing cards,' said Jia Lian with a somewhat artificial smile. 'I didn't like to interrupt you. I was hoping to get my wife to come out so that I could ask *her*.'

'And what is there so extraordinarily urgent about this that you needed to ask her *now*?' said Grandmother Jia. 'If you'd waited until she got home, you could have asked her all you wanted to then. Why this extraordinary conscientiousness all of a sudden? Eavesdropping is what you were up to more likely, or spying for somebody else. Whatever it was, you gave me a nasty turn, creeping around in that sneaky, underhand way. Disgusting creature! Your wife will be with me a long time yet playing cards. Better get back to that Zhao Er woman while you have the chance and carry on where you left off with your plans for poisoning her!'

The others all laughed.

'It was *Bao* Er's wife, my old love, not *Zhao* Er's,' said Faithful, laughing.

'That's what I said, didn't I?' Grandmother Jia snapped. 'Well, "Zhao" or "Bao" or brown cow – how can *I* be expected to remember such things? The very mention of them makes me feel angry. There were three generations of the family above me when I came to this household as a young bride, and now there are three generations below me, and I've seen many shocking and many wicked and many peculiar things during the fifty-four years since first I came here, but this sort of thing is simply outside my experience. Now be off with you!'

Jia Lian bolted, not daring to say a word. Patience, who had been standing meanwhile outside the window, quietly mocked him as he came out:

'I told you so, but you wouldn't listen. You walked straight into the net, didn't you?'

Just at that moment Lady Xing came out.

'This is all Father's doing,' said Jia Lian. 'Now *we* have to face the consequences.'

'Unfilial wretch!' said Lady Xing. 'Some people would *die* for their fathers, but *you* – a few harmless words and you are already whining and complaining. What's the matter with you? You haven't been hurt yet – though I should look out, if I were you: Father's been pretty angry these last few days.'

'Come on, you must hurry back, Mother,' said Jia Lian. 'He sent me to fetch you a long time ago.'

He saw his mother out of the main part of the mansion and round to Jia She's quarters next door. Lady Xing then gave her husband, in briefest possible outline, a report of what had happened; and since it was now evident that nothing more could be done about Faithful, Jia She had to put up with his mortification as best he could. He did, however, from that day onwards, discontinue all duty calls on his mother on the pretext of being ill. Lady Xing and Jia Lian were sent to make the mandatory calls on her in his stead.

Meanwhile his agents scoured the market for likely girls. A suitable one was eventually purchased for the sum of five hundred taels – a seventeen-year-old girl called Carmine, who was duly installed in his room. But that is another part of our story.

The card-game continued until dinner-time, and it was not until after dinner that the company finally broke up.

Of the day or two which followed these events our story preserves no record.

*

The fourteenth came. Before it was yet daylight, Lai Da's wife came round once more to renew her invitation. Grandmother Jia responded enthusiastically and, taking Lady Wang, Aunt Xue and the young people along with her, spent a considerable part of the day in the Lai family's private garden.

Lai Da's garden was not, of course, to be compared with Prospect Garden; nevertheless it was spacious and well-made, and among its pools, rocks, trees and pavilions were to be found several features of striking interest or beauty.

The menfolk who were gathered in the reception hall at the front or 'outer' part of the establishment included Xue Pan, Cousin Zhen, Jia Lian, Jia Rong and a number of the more closely related members of the Jia clan outside the immediate family. Jia She was conspicuously absent. Young Lai had also invited some of his office-holding colleagues and a few young men of good family as congenial company for the Jias.

One of these last was a young gentleman called Liu Xiang-lian whom Xue Pan had met on some previous occasion and hankeringly remembered ever since. The discovery that he was a keen amateur actor – one, moreover, who specialized in romantic roles – had led Xue Pan to jump to the wrong conclusion and assume that he must share the same 'wind and moonlight' proclivities as himself. Eager to make his closer acquaintance but hitherto denied any opportunity of doing so, he was overjoyed at finding him among the company on this occasion and consequently in a state of excitement which rendered his behaviour extremely unpredictable.

Cousin Zhen had also heard of Liu Xiang-lian and admired him. Today, under pretext of being a little drunk, he had taken the liberty of asking him to perform for them, and Liu Xiang-lian, supported by the hired professional players, had obliged by appearing on the stage in two operatic numbers. When he rejoined the company, Xue Pan took the opportunity of moving over to his table and began plying him with all sorts of questions and insinuations.

Liu Xiang-lian was a young man of excellent family who, having lost both his parents in early youth, had failed to complete his education. He was of a dashing, impulsive nature, impatient of niceties. His chief pleasures were exercising with spear or sabre, drinking, and gambling; but he was not averse to gentler pastimes: he frequented the budding groves and could play on both the flute and the zither. Because he was so young and handsome, many who did not know him mistakenly supposed that, being an actor, he must have the usual actor's propensities. Lai Da's son Lai Shang-rong had been a good friend of his for years and it was only natural that he should invite him on this occasion to help him entertain his guests. Under these circumstances Liu Xiang-lian was prepared to put up with a certain amount of drunken horseplay; but Xue Pan was too much for him, and soon his attentions were becoming so distasteful that Xiang-lian resolved to leave at the earliest opportunity in order to escape from them. Before he could break away, however, Lai Shang-rong detained him.

'Bao-yu gave me a message for you just now. He said that though he saw you briefly when he arrived, with so many other people around, he didn't have a chance of talking to you properly. He's most anxious that you should stay on so that he can talk to you afterwards. If you are really set on going, wait while I call him out and you can have a word with him now. What you do after that is your own affair: I certainly shan't try to detain you.' He called a waiter to him: 'Look inside and get hold of one of the old women. Tell her to have a quiet word with Master Bao to say that he's wanted here outside.'

After about the time it would take to drink a cup of tea in, Bao-yu appeared.

'Here you are, Uncle Bao!' said Lai Shang-rong when he had joined them. 'I leave Xiang-lian in your hands. I've got to go and look after my guests now.'

With that he left them.

Taking Xiang-lian by the hand, Bao-yu led him into a study at the side of the hall where they sat down together.

'Have you visited Qin Zhong's grave recently?' said Bao-yu.

'Certainly I have,' said Xiang-lian. 'The other day I was out hawking with a few of the others and happened to notice that we were only half a mile or so away from it. It occurred to me that it might not have stood up to all that heavy rain we had in the summer, so I left the others and went off to have a look. As a matter of fact it *had* been washed away a bit; so the day after I got back I scraped a few hundred cash together, went back first thing next morning, hired a couple of labourers, and got it patched up again.'

'That explains it,' said Bao-yu. 'Last month, when the pods were beginning to form on the lotuses in Prospect Garden, I picked ten of them and sent Tealeaf to offer them at his grave. When he got back, I asked him if the rains had damaged it at all, and he told me that not only had it not been damaged, but that it was in even better condition than it had been the time before. I knew from that that some friend must have been there recently and restored it. I wish I weren't so cooped up all the time at home. I can *never* do anything I want to by myself. The slightest move I make is sure to be seen and reported, and either I'm physically prevented from going where I want to or else lectured at until I promise not to go. It's useless for me ever to say that I'm going to do anything, because I know that I shan't be allowed to. I can't even spend my own money in the way I want.'

'This thing at least is something you don't need to worry about,' said Xiang-lian, 'with me outside to look after it for you. Anyway, it's the thought that counts. It's enough to know that you would do it yourself if you could. I've already put aside the money for his anniversary on the first of next month. You know how broke I always am. I never have any savings because as soon as I've got any money I spend it all. Well, this time I thought I'd better not take any chances, so I put some by well in advance, so as not to have to stretch my hands out helplessly when the time comes.'

'I was going to send Tealeaf round to see you about that,' said Bao-yu, 'but you never seem to be at home; and you're such a rolling stone that no one ever knows where to look for you.'

'Don't bother to try,' said Xiang-lian. 'This is a matter in which each of us does what he can. Anyway, I shall be going away quite soon. It will probably be three or four years before I come back again.'

'Why?' said Bao-yu in some agitation.

'That's something you'll know soon enough when the time comes. I must be going now.'

'*Must* you?' said Bao-yu. 'I so seldom get a chance of seeing you. Can't we leave together in the evening?'

'I'm afraid it's that cousin of yours,' said Xiang-lian. 'The usual problem. If I stay any longer, there's sure to be some kind of trouble. I'd much better go now and avoid it.'

Bao-yu reflected for some moments.

'Yes, I suppose in that case you'd better. Only, if you really and truly *are* going away for a long time, do please let me know before you start. *Please* don't just slip away without telling me.'

His eyes brimmed over with tears.

'Of course I'll come and say good-bye to you,' said Xiang-lian. 'As long as you promise not to tell anyone.' He stood up to go. 'You go in again now. Don't try to see me out.'

He left the study and made his way to the main gate: but there, unfortunately, was the very person he was trying to avoid.

'Who's let my little Liu get away?' Xue Pan bawled.

Xiang-lian's eyes flashed angrily. In other circumstances he would have laid him out there and then with a single blow of his fist; but reflecting that to do so now would be interpreted by the others as drunken brawling and would moreover be embarrassing to his host, he restrained himself with some effort.

Xue Pan, in whose besotted eyes he appeared as a coveted treasure that was moving at last within his grasp, lurched towards him, smiling happily, and gripped him firmly by the arm.

'Where are you off to, little pal?'

'Just going out for a stroll,' said Xiang-lian. 'I'll be back again directly.'

'It won't be any more fun here without you,' said Xue Pan. 'Do stay a bit longer – just to show me that you care for me, eh? If it's business that's taking you away, don't worry, leave it to me! I don't care how important it is – whether it's a career you're after or making a pile – with me for a pal you'll have no more to worry about!'

Angered and revolted by his odious intimacy, Xiang-lian

quickly thought of a plan for disposing of him. Drawing him aside to a spot where they could not be overheard, he pretended to question his sincerity.

'Are you really so fond of me, or are you just pretending?'

Xue Pan was almost beside himself. His eyes became tiny slits of pleasure:

'How can you ask such a question, my dear? Pretending? May I die this instant if I am!'

'Good. This place here is not convenient. We'd better go in again now and sit with the others for a bit. Then I'll leave, and you can leave a bit after me and follow me back to my place. We'll make a night of it. I've got a couple of very nice little boys there who've never been "out" before; so you needn't bring anyone with you: all the service we'll need is there already.'

Xue Pan was by now so delighted that his drunkenness had already half left him.

'Do you mean this?'

'What a person!' said Xiang-lian. 'One opens one's heart to you and you don't trust them.'

'No, no, no,' said Xue Pan hurriedly. 'I trust you. I'm no fool. There's only one thing, though: I don't know where you live. If you leave before I do, where am I to look for you?'

'My place is outside the North Gate,' said Xiang-lian. 'Do you think you can tear yourself from home and spend a whole night outside the city?'

'What do I need a home for if I've got you?' said Xue Pan.

'All right,' said Xiang-lian. 'I'll wait for you on the bridge then, outside the North Gate. We'd better get back to the party now. Don't forget: wait a bit after I've gone before going yourself; then no one should suspect anything.'

'Yes,' said Xue Pan, 'yes.'

The two of them then went in again and resumed their places. Xue Pan found waiting difficult and kept his eyes constantly on Xiang-lian, watching for him to go. At the same time he began, in joyous anticipation of the pleasures in store, to drink with greater and greater abandon, not waiting for the wine to be offered, but stretching out rudely to left and right of him and plying himself from the wine-kettles of his neighbours. Soon he was very drunk indeed.

Xiang-lian now rose to go and succeeded in slipping out of the main gate unobserved. First he gave an order to his page Almond, who was waiting there:

'You go home now. I have some business outside the city to attend to. I'll be back later.'

Then he vaulted into the saddle and rode off until he came to the North Gate of the city. Passing through, he rode on till he came to the bridge, where he halted and took up his station to wait for Xue Pan's arrival.

After the time it would take to eat a meal, he caught sight of Xue Pan hurrying along in the distance. His mouth was open, his eyes were staring, and his head turned from side to side as he looked anxiously about him, for all the world like one of those little clapper-drums that children twirl upon a stick. So intent was he on scanning the remoter parts of the landscape that he failed to take note of what was nearer at hand and rode right past Xiang-lian without seeing him. Xiang-lian, who for all his loathing could not but laugh at this, gave his horse rein and followed after. Presently Xue Pan began to notice that he was getting into the open country and brought his horse round about. As he did so, he found himself almost face to face with Xiang-lian.

'I *knew* you wouldn't fail me,' he cried delightedly.

Xiang-lian smiled back.

'Let's go on a bit further – just in case anyone is tracking us.'

He trotted on ahead and Xue Pan followed, keeping as close to him as he could. Presently, having satisfied himself that the country ahead was quite deserted, Xiang-lian dismounted near the edge of a reed-filled dyke and tied his horse up to a tree.

'You get down too,' he called pleasantly to Xue Pan. 'Let's first swear an oath that if either of us is unfaithful to the other or betrays our secret to anyone, it shall happen to him as the oath shall say.'

'Yes,' said Xue Pan. 'Good idea!'

He dismounted eagerly, tied his horse to another tree, and straightway knelt down and began his oath:

'If ever, in the days to come, I prove unfaithful or betray this secret to another, may Heaven and Earth destroy –'

He got no further. At that point there was a great *thump*! and the sensation of being hit on the back of the neck by an object like a large iron hammer. Everything became suddenly black, except that the darkness was filled with a confusion of flying stars, and he collapsed forwards helplessly upon the ground.

Xiang-lian stepped up and surveyed him from above. Someone not used to taking punishment, he concluded. It would be unwise to use too much force on him. Turning him over, he performed, with a few deft flicks over Xue Pan's face, the operation which is described in the profession as 'opening up the fruitshop'.

At first Xue Pan struggled to get up, but Xiang-lian lashed out with his foot and sent him sprawling once more upon his back.

'You were willing, just as much as I was,' Xue Pan muttered plaintively. 'You had only to say so if you weren't. Why fool me into coming out here with you and then beat me up?'

He began cursing him obscenely.

'You blind iniquity!' said Liu Xiang-lian. 'You don't know who you're dealing with. You should be begging for mercy right now, not swearing at me. You're not worth killing, though. I'll just give you a little lesson.'

He picked up his horsewhip and turning Xue Pan on his face once more, proceeded to deal him thirty or forty cuts along the length of his body, from his shoulders down to his calves. Xue Pan was by now half sober, and finding the pain unbearable, began to roar.

'Look at you!' said Xiang-lian contemptuously. 'I should have thought you could take your medicine a bit better than that.'

He took him by the left leg and dragged him a few steps to where the reeds began, in the stagnant ooze of the dyke, so that he was coated from head to foot with the liquid mud.

'Now,' he said, 'do you know who I am?'

As Xue Pan merely lay in the mud whimpering and made no reply, he threw away his whip and gave him a few thumps with his fist. Xue Pan rolled about and bellowed:

'You've broken my ribs. I know you're straight. It was the others who told me you weren't. I shouldn't have listened to them.'

'Leave the others out of this,' said Xiang-lian. 'I'm talking about now.'

'Now?' said Xue Pan. 'Now I know you're straight. I know I was wrong. What more can I say?'

'You'll have to talk a bit prettier than that before I've finished with you,' said Xiang-lian.

'Old pal –' Xue Pan began, whimpering.

Xiang-lian dealt him another thump with his fist.

'Ow! Old chap –'

Two thumps this time.

'Ow! Ow! Sir, then. Please sir, forgive me for being so blind. From now on I shall honour you and fear you.'

'Now drink some of this water,' said Xiang-lian.

Xue Pan knitted his brows with disgust:

'But this water is really filthy. I couldn't get it down.'

Xiang-lian raised his fist threateningly.

'I'll drink,' said Xue Pan hurriedly. 'I'll drink.'

He bent down and drank a mouthful of the water at the base of the reeds; but before he could swallow it, there was a great retching noise and he vomited up all that he had recently eaten and drunk.

'Filthy pig!' said Xiang-lian. 'Now eat *that* up and I'll let you off.'

Xue Pan began kotowing to him.

'Please, for your soul's sake, earn a bit of merit: don't try to make me do that! I couldn't do that if you killed me.'

'This stench is poisoning me,' said Xiang-lian; and leaving Xue Pan, he unfastened his horse, led it off a few paces, vaulted into the saddle, and galloped away.

Observing with relief that Xiang-lian had really gone, Xue Pan, cursing his folly for having been so egregiously mistaken in his man, attempted to struggle to his feet; but every part of him was hurting so much that it was impossible for him to rise.

*

Meanwhile, back at the party, Cousin Zhen and the others, suddenly noticing that the two of them were missing, sought them for a while without success. Someone did say that they thought they might have gone out of the North Gate; but Xue Pan had told his pages not to follow him, and they were all in such dread of their master that none of them dared go out there to look. In the end Cousin Zhen became so uneasy that he sent Jia Rong with some of the boys to track them down.

Their trail led them through the North Gate and about two thirds of a mile along the road which crosses the bridge outside it. There, suddenly, they caught sight of Xue Pan's horse, tied up to one of the trees at the side of a reed-filled dyke.

'Good!' they said. 'Where the horse is, the rider must be.' And all of them went over to where the horse was standing.

As they did so, they heard someone groaning among the rushes; and there, when they went to look, was Xue Pan, his clothes torn, his face cut and swollen almost beyond recognition, and so besmirched with mud from head to foot that he had more the appearance of an old wallowing sow than of a human being.

Jia Rong had little difficulty in guessing what had happened. Slipping from his horse, he ordered the servants to help Xue Pan to his feet.

'Tireless in the pursuit of love, Uncle!' he said cheerfully, while they struggled to do his bidding. 'This time it's led you into the reeds of the marshes. I suppose the Dragon King must have taken a fancy to you and carried you off to be his son-in-law. To judge from appearances, I should say that you must have got caught up on his horn!'

Xue Pan wished that the earth would open and swallow up his shame.

As there was clearly no question of getting him onto his

horse, Jia Rong told one of the boys to hurry back to the street outside the North Gate and hire a carrying chair. When Xue Pan had been helped into this, they had him carried into the city, themselves accompanying him on horseback. Jia Rong mischievously proposed that they should take him back to the Lais' house to rejoin the party: but Xue Pan entreated so piteously and begged him so earnestly not to tell anyone of his plight, that Jia Rong relented and allowed him to go back home alone.

Jia Rong himself returned to the party to report back to his father. From his account of the state Xue Pan had been in when they found him Cousin Zhen deduced that he must have been beaten up by Liu Xiang-lian but appeared remarkably unconcerned, for he merely laughed and observed that 'he could do with the lesson'. It is true that he went to inquire after him in the evening, when he got back home from the party; but Xue Pan was by that time nursing his injuries in bed and declined to see him on the grounds that he was feeling too ill.

When Grandmother Jia and her party had got back to their several apartments, Aunt Xue and Bao-chai found Caltrop with her eyes all swollen from weeping. On discovering the cause, they rushed in to look at Xue Pan. Fortunately he appeared to have no bones broken, but his face and body had taken a terrible battering. Torn between maternal anguish at his plight and anger at the folly which had occasioned it, Aunt Xue inveighed against Xue Pan and Xiang-lian by turns. She wanted to tell Lady Wang and get her to have Xiang-lian arrested, but was dissuaded from doing so by Bao-chai.

'It's not important enough for that, Mamma. The two of them had been drinking and fell out over their cups, that's all there was to it. Whenever that happens, it's always the drunker of the two who gets the worst of it. Besides, everyone knows what a lawless, ungovernable creature Pan is. It's only because you're his mother that you feel differently. If it's satisfaction you want, that can easily be arranged. Just wait a few days until Pan is better and can get about again. I'm sure Mr Zhen and Mr Lian and the other menfolk will be unwilling to pass over this in silence. Probably they will get up a little party and ask this person to it and make him apologize to Pan in front of everyone and admit that he was to blame. But if you insist on making an issue of it *now* and telling Aunt about it, you will make it appear that you are so blind to Pan's faults that you allow him to go around provoking other people, but that as soon as someone stands up to him, you fly up in arms and use our relations' influence to oppress them.'

Aunt Xue at once saw the force of this.

'You are quite right, my child. I was being silly.'

'Dear Mamma! But now you are being sensible. He doesn't fear you, and he won't listen to anyone else. He just goes on getting worse and worse. One or two good, sharp shocks like this might bring him to his senses.'

Meanwhile Xue Pan lay on the kang in his bedroom, cursing Xiang-lian by every name he could think of and calling on his boys to smash up his house, to beat him to death, to have the law on him. Aunt Xue shouted to them that they were to do no such thing. To Xue Pan she explained that Xiang-lian was in any case beyond the reach of his vengeance.

'Xiang-lian behaved very badly because he was drunk. When he came to himself afterwards he was very sorry; and now, because he is afraid of the consequences, he has fled the country.'

When Xue Pan heard that, he —

But you shall learn *that* (if you wish) in the following chapter.

CHAPTER 48

The Love Deluded One turns his thoughts to trade and travel
And the Poetry Enthusiast applies herself to making verses

XUE PAN gradually calmed down when his mother told him
that Xiang-lian had fled.

After four or five days the pain of his injuries had subsided,
but not the bumps and bruises; and as, while these still dis-
figured him, he was unwilling to meet any of his acquaintance,
he kept to his room on the pretext that he was still too ill to
go out.

The tenth month soon came. Several of the employees working in Xue Pan's shops in the capital wanted to go back home
for the annual settling of accounts and Xue Pan found himself
giving a farewell party for them in his room. Among those
present was one Zhang De-hui, the sixty-year-old manager of
his largest pawnshop. He had worked with the family since
he was a lad and now had a household of his own and an income
of two or three thousand taels. He was planning to leave with
the others but not return until half way through the following
year, as he explained to Xue Pan on this occasion.

'There's a great shortage of stationery and perfumed goods
just now,' he said. 'These things are sure to fetch high prices
next year. I'm proposing to send my eldest boy here after
New Year to look after the shop, so that *I* can travel back later.
I shall buy up supplies of stationery and sandalwood fans on
my way, aiming to get back here in time for the Double
Fifth. I reckon it should be possible to make several hundred
percent profit, even after the excise and all the other expenses
have been deducted.'

This gave Xue Pan an idea.

'I haven't felt like seeing anyone since that beating,'
he thought, 'and some excuse for getting away from everybody for a year or so is just what I've been looking for.
Obviously I can't go on staying indoors and pretending I'm

ill indefinitely. And for another thing, I haven't *done* very much with my life to date: I'm neither a scholar nor a soldier, and though I call myself a merchant, I've never handled a pair of scales or an abacus in my life, not to mention the fact that I know nothing about the places and peoples of the Empire or its roads and waterways. Why don't I get a bit of capital together and spend a year or so travelling around with Zhang De-hui? It won't matter much whether I make any money or not; the main thing is that it will get me away from my disgrace; and there is the added advantage that I shall be able to put in a bit of sight-seeing as well.'

Having so decided, he waited until the other guests had gone and then, making himself as agreeable as he knew how, informed Zhang De-hui of his decision and asked him to delay his departure by a few days so that he would have time to prepare.

That evening he told his mother.

Aunt Xue's initial reaction was one of pleasure, but this quickly gave way to misgivings. It was not that she attached much importance to the loss of a little capital; she was concerned about the scrapes he might get into away from home. And so she ended up by refusing.

'I think you'd better stay here with me. I should worry less. After all, you don't *need* to make this money. It isn't as if you haven't got enough to spend.'

But Xue Pan had made his mind up and was not to be put off.

'You're always telling me how inexperienced I am and how ignorant and how unwilling to learn; yet now that I'm making a real effort to turn over a new leaf by standing on my own feet at last and learning a bit about the business, you won't let me. What do you *want* me to do? I'm not a girl, to be shut up at home all the time: you'll have to let me out *some* time or other. Besides, Zhang De-hui is an old, experienced person and he's worked for our family all his life. If I'm with him, I don't see how anything *can* go wrong. Even if I did ever slip up, I'm sure he'd soon tell me off about it and put me right. And as he knows all there is to know about prices and so forth, I should naturally always consult him on business matters. You couldn't ask for better conditions; yet you won't let me go. Very well, I'll get ready in secret and leave without telling you. You'll see me when I come back next year, after making a fortune! I'll show you!'

With that he went off to bed in a huff.

Aunt Xue discussed the matter with Bao-chai after he had gone.

'It's good that he should want to occupy himself with something serious at last,' said Bao-chai. 'The trouble is, of course, that however fair-sounding his intentions may be *now*, once he's outside he may succumb to his old weaknesses again, and then it will be that much more difficult to control him. However, I suppose that is a risk one has to take. If he is really going to reform, then this experience may prove a life-long blessing. If he is *not*, I don't see that there is very much left that you can do. After all, there is only so much one *can* do for another person: the rest must be left to Heaven. Pan is a grown man now, Mamma. If you maintain that he is too ignorant of the world to be allowed out into it, you are not going to make him any less ignorant by keeping him shut up indoors. And since he is being so reasonable for once, I should make up your mind that you are going to lose eight or nine hundred taels and hand it over to him to see how he manages. After all, he will have someone from our own business helping him and they may well feel some compunction about cheating him; so it's by no means a foregone conclusion that he *will* lose it all. And for another thing, away from home there won't be those worthless companions of his to egg him on; nor, on the other hand, will he have anyone to fall back on if he gets into trouble. He will have to fend for himself: eat when he can and go hungry when he can't. And when it dawns on him that he is on his own and has no one he can lean on, he *may* begin to behave a bit better. Surely it's worth trying?'

Aunt Xue pondered her daughter's words for some minutes.

'I think you are probably right,' she said eventually. 'I

certainly don't mind using up some of our money on the experiment. If he can learn a bit of sense from it, it will have been money well spent.'

Having thus concluded their discussion, the two of them went to bed.

Next day Aunt Xue had Zhang De-hui invited round once more, and while he was being entertained by Xue Pan in the study, stationed herself in the loggia at the back and, addressing him through the window from this hidden vantage point, entrusted her boy, with many a fond and careful instruction, to his care. Zhang De-hui gave vigorous assurances of good intent, and having finished his meal, stood up and took his leave, stopping on his way out to add a few words to Xue Pan about arrangements for their departure:

'The almanac says the fourteenth is the best day for travelling. I should start packing and hiring mules straight away if I were you, Mr Xue, so that we can make a start first thing on the fourteenth.'

Xue Pan, delighted at the prospect of getting away so soon, hastened to relay this to his mother.

Assisted by Bao-chai, Caltrop and a couple of old nannies, Aunt Xue devoted the whole of the next few days to packing. She selected five male members of the domestic staff to accompany Xue Pan on his travels: the husband of his old wet-nurse, two experienced older servants who had been in service with his father, and two of the pages who normally waited on him. Three heavy carts were hired for the luggage and four travelling-mules. Xue Pan himself planned to ride on a mule from his own stables – a large, sturdy animal with an iron-grey coat. He also planned to take a saddle-horse of his own as an alternative mount. When all other preparations had been completed, Aunt Xue and Bao-chai devoted the remaining evenings to exhortation and admonishment of the prospective traveller.

On the thirteenth Xue Pan went to take leave of his Uncle Wang's family in the city, after which he went round the two mansions saying his good-byes to the Jias. There was some talk of Cousin Zhen and one or two of the others seeing him off next day for a parting cup on the road; but whether or not anything came of it our narrative does not disclose.

Early on the morning of the fourteenth Aunt Xue and Bao-chai accompanied him to the outer threshold of the inner gate and watched him with tearful eyes until they could see him no more.

*

When Aunt Xue moved from Nanking to the capital, she had brought only four or five couples with her in addition to the handful of old nannies and young unmarried maids of her immediate household. Now that five of the menfolk had gone off to accompany Xue Pan on his travels, only one or two male servants were left. The very day that Xue Pan started on his journey, Aunt Xue went into his study, had all the small furniture, blinds, curtains and other movables carried out and stored in her own apartment, and ordered the wives of the absent menservants to move in with her to sleep. She also ordered Caltrop to tidy up Xue Pan's sleeping quarters, lock the door, and move into her apartment with the rest.

'But Mamma,' Bao-chai protested, 'you've already got all those others to keep you company. Why not let Caltrop move in with me? It gets lonely in the Garden now that the nights are longer: another companion to sit with me in the evenings when I am sewing would be very welcome.'

'Of course,' said Aunt Xue. 'I was forgetting. I should have thought of it myself. I was telling Pan only the other day: Apricot is so young and scatter-brained and Oriole on her own really isn't enough for you. We really ought to buy you another girl.'

'Buying is all very well if you know what the girl is going to be like,' said Bao-chai; 'but if you make a bad choice, then not only have you wasted your money — that's a small consideration — but you have a very great deal of trouble on your hands. If we are going to buy a girl, it would be much better to take our time over the inquiries and not get one until we are quite sure about her background.'

She told Caltrop to get her bedding and toilet things together and ordered Advent and one of the old nannies to
carry them for her to Allspice Court. Then she and Caltrop
went into the Garden together.

'I was dying to ask the Mistress if she would let me move in
with you after Mr Xue had gone,' said Caltrop, 'but I was
afraid she might think I only wanted to get into the Garden
to play. How wonderful that you should have asked her *for*
me!'

'I knew you'd had your heart set on this Garden for some
time past,' said Bao-chai with a smile, 'but you haven't really
been free till now. Dashing in and out for a few minutes each
day wouldn't have given you time to enjoy it properly. That's
why I have waited for this opportunity before asking. Now
you will be able to settle in and spend a whole year here.
You get your wish, you see, and *I* gain a companion!'

'*Dear* Miss!' said Caltrop. 'Now that there is the time and
the opportunity, will you teach me how to write poetry,
please?'

Bao-chai laughed.

'You're like the famous general: "one conquest breeds
appetite for another". I advise you to take things more gently.
Today is your first day in the Garden. If I were you, I should
go out of that corner gate and, beginning with Lady Jia's,
call in at all the different apartments and pay your respects to
everybody. You needn't go out of your way to tell them that
you have moved into the Garden; but if the subject should
happen to arise, tell them that I have brought you in as
my companion. After that, when you get back into the
Garden, you ought to go round and call on all the young
ladies.'

Caltrop was just going off to do as Bao-chai advised, when
Patience came hurrying in. She was in a state of some agitation, which she smilingly masked, however, in response
to Caltrop's eager greetings.

'I'm bringing her in here to live with me as my companion,'
Bao-chai explained. 'I was just about to report the matter
to your mistress.'

'You don't need to do *that*, Miss!' said Patience. 'Whatever next?'

'On the contrary,' said Bao-chai. 'It's the correct thing to do. "Every inn has its landlord and every temple its priest," as they say. Even though it is not a very important matter, I think I should report it, if only so that the women on night-watch may know that there are two more girls – her and Advent – living in the Garden now, and make no difficulties about letting them in and out. Anyway, if you will tell your mistress when you get back, I won't bother to send anyone about it myself.'

Patience promised that she would.

'Now you're here,' she said to Caltrop, 'you ought to go and introduce yourself to your new neighbours.'

'I was just sending her off to do that when you came,' said Bao-chai.

'Well, you can leave *us* out,' Patience told Caltrop. 'Mr Lian is ill at home in bed.'

Caltrop murmured a reply and went off to make her calls, beginning with Grandmother Jia.

As soon as she had gone, Patience seized Bao-chai's hand and asked her, in a low and urgent voice, whether she had heard 'their' news.

'No,' said Bao-chai. 'I've been so busy these last few days helping to get Pan off that I haven't heard *anyone*'s news. I haven't even seen any of the girls during the past day or two.'

'Sir She has beaten Mr Lian so badly that he can hardly move. Do you mean to say you haven't even heard *that*?'

'I heard something to that effect,' said Bao-chai, 'but I didn't know whether to believe it or not. I'd been thinking of going to ask your mistress about it when you came in just now. What did he beat him for?'

'It was that toad Jia Yu-cun's doing,' said Patience bitterly. 'Horrible man! It was a bad day for this family when they got to know him. I don't know *how* much trouble he hasn't stirred up in the few years since first he came here. Last spring Sir She saw some antique fans somewhere which so impressed him that when he got home and looked at his own collection

he decided that they were all no good and at once sent everyone scouring around for some more. Now there was a certain
poor, unlucky devil they call "Stony" – that's a nickname, of
course: I don't know what his real name is – so hard up that
he never had enough to eat but who, it so happened, was the
owner of a collection of twenty antique fans that he guarded
very closely, not even allowing them to be taken out of his
door. Mr Lian had a terrible job even getting to see this man.
In the end he did though, and eventually, after a great deal of
persuasion, managed to get himself invited into the house to
have a look at the fans. Mr Lian said he was only allowed a
glimpse of them even then, but he said you could see at once
that they were the kind of fans that simply can't be had
anywhere today. The fansticks were made of very special
kinds of bamboo – naiad's tears, black bamboo, fawnskin and
jadewood – and the paintings on them were all by old masters.
When he told Sir She about them, Sir She said at once that
come what may he must have them and that Stony could
name his price. But Stony didn't want a price – not if they
offered him a thousand taels a fan, he said. He said he would
rather die of hunger and cold than sell them. There was
nothing Sir She could do about that, of course, except swear
all the time at Mr Lian for being "incompetent". But I ask
you, Miss: Mr Lian had already promised five hundred taels
cash down and still old Stony had refused, so what more was
there he could do? The matter might have rested there if that
black-hearted villain Jia Yu-cun hadn't got to hear about it.
He soon thought of a way. He made out that Stony owed the
government some money, had him hauled off to the yamen,
and when he got there, told him they would have to distrain
on his property to pay off the debt. Then he sent his officers
round to Stony's house, seized the fans, valued them at a
government price, and sent them to Sir She as a present.
Poor old Stony! I don't know whether he's alive now or dead.
What I *do* know is that when Sir She was telling Mr Lian
how he had come by the fans at last, Mr Lian couldn't help
remarking that he didn't see anything very "competent"
about ruining a man and stripping him of all he possessed for

so trifling a reason. That made Sir She very angry, because of course he assumed that Mr Lian was really getting at *him*. That was the main reason for the beating; but then there were a number of smaller things a few days later – I don't even remember now what they were. *They* seem to have brought things to a head, because he suddenly went for him. He didn't pull him down and beat him with a flat-stick or a cudgel in the normal way either: he just picked up the first thing that came to hand – I don't know what it was – and started hitting him with it where he stood. He cut his face open in two places. We heard that Mrs Xue has got some kind of lotion for injuries of this sort and I wondered if you'd mind letting me have a tablet.'

Bao-chai at once sent Oriole for the tablets and told her to bring two of them.

'I won't go and see your mistress now, under the circumstances,' she said, when she handed them to Patience. 'Give her my regards, though, won't you?'

Patience thanked her and left.

*

Our story returns now to Caltrop. After dinner, by which time she had finished making her calls, while Bao-chai went to join Bao-yu and the others in Grandmother Jia's apartment, Caltrop went off on her own to visit the Naiad's House.

Dai-yu was by this time well on the way to recovery. She seemed so delighted to hear that Caltrop had moved into the Garden, that Caltrop felt emboldened to make her a request:

'Now that I'm here and have got more time to spare, do you think you could teach me to write poetry? It would be such a piece of luck for me if you would.'

'You can make your kotow and become my pupil if you like,' said Dai-yu goodnaturedly. 'I'm no expert myself, but I dare say I could teach you the rudiments.'

'Would you really?' said Caltrop. 'Then I'll be your disciple. But you must promise not to get impatient with me.'

'There's nothing in it really,' said Dai-yu. 'There's really hardly anything to learn. In Regulated Verse there are always four couplets: the "opening couplet", the "developing couplet", the "turning couplet" and the "concluding couplet". In the two middle couplets, the "developing" and "turning" ones, you have to have tone-contrast and parallelism. That's to say, in each of those couplets the even tones of one line have to contrast with oblique tones in the other, and *vice versa*, and the substantives and non-substantives have to balance each other – though if you've got a really good, original line, it doesn't matter all that much even if the tone-contrast and parallelism are wrong.'

'Ah, that explains it!' said Caltrop, pleased. 'I've got an old poetry-book that I look at once in a while when I can find the time, and I long ago noticed that in some of the poems the tone-contrast is very strict, while in others it's not. Someone told me the rhyme:

> For one, three and five
> You need not strive;
> But two, four and six
> You must firmly fix.

and at first that seemed to explain the exceptions. But then I found that in *some* old poems even the second, fourth and sixth syllables seemed to have the wrong tones, and I've been puzzling about it ever since. Now, from what you've just said, it sounds as if these rules really aren't important after all – that the most important thing is that the language should be original.'

'You've hit it exactly!' said Dai-yu. 'As a matter of fact even the *language* isn't of primary importance. The *really* important things are the ideas that lie behind it. If the ideas behind it are genuine, there's no need to embellish the language for the poem to be a good one. That's what they mean when they talk about "not letting the words harm the meaning".'

'I love that couplet by Lu You,' said Caltrop:

> 'Behind snug curtained doors the incense lingers;
> In well-worn concave patch the ground ink settles.

That's genuine, isn't it? So vivid.'

'Good gracious! You mustn't go reading *that* sort of stuff!' said Dai-yu. 'It's only because of your lack of experience that you can think shallow stuff like that any good. Once you get stuck into *that* rut, you'll never get out of it. You do as I tell you. I've got the *Collected Works* of Wang Wei here. You take a hundred of Wang Wei's pentasyllabic poems in Regulated Verse and read and re-read them, carefully pondering what you read, until you are thoroughly familiar with them all. After that read a hundred or two of Du Fu's Regulated Verse heptasyllabics and a hundred or two of Li Bo's heptasyllabic quatrains; then, with a firm foundation of those three poets inside you, if you go on to look at some of the earlier poets like Tao Yuan-ming, Xie Ling-yun, Ruan Ji, Yu Xin and Bao Zhao, with your quickness and intelligence you should have no difficulty in turning yourself into a fully-fledged bard within less than a twelvemonth.'

'In that case,' said Caltrop excitedly, '*dear* Miss Lin, would you please lend me that book you mentioned, so that I can take it back with me and study it before I go to bed?'

Dai-yu told Nightingale to fetch down the volume of Regular Pentasyllabics from the *Collected Works* of Wang Wei.

'Read the ones I've marked with red circles,' she said, handing the book to Caltrop. 'They are my own selection. Just work your way through them gradually, taking each one as it comes. If you have any difficulties, you can either ask Miss Bao about them or else get *me* to explain them to you next time you see me.'

Caltrop carried the book back with her to Allspice Court, and sitting down under the lamp, began reading the poems, oblivious to all around her. Bao-chai made several attempts at making her go to bed, but in the end, impressed by such total absorption, gave up and left her alone.

*

Next morning, just as Dai-yu had completed her toilet, a smiling Caltrop walked in, holding out the volume of Wang Wei and asking to exchange it for a volume of Du Fu's heptasyllabics.

'How many of them do you think you can remember?'
Dai-yu asked her.

'I've been through all the ones marked with red circles,'
said Caltrop.

'And do you think you have learnt anything from them?'

'I *think* so,' said Caltrop. 'Though I can't be sure. Perhaps
you can tell me.'

'Certainly,' said Dai-yu. 'Discussion is what I was hoping
for. It is the only way of making progress. Tell me what you
think they have taught you.'

'Well,' said Caltrop, 'as I see it, poetry is very good at
saying things which you can't exactly explain but which leave
a very vivid impression in your mind; also it often says things
which at first seem illogical but are quite logical and natural
when you stop to think about them.'

'That sounds very perceptive,' said Dai-yu. 'What about
giving an example or two of what you mean?'

'Take that third couplet from his poem "On the Frontier",'
said Caltrop:

> 'Over a lone fire the straight smoke hangs;
> In the long river the round sun sets.

Now how can smoke really be "straight"? And why "the
round sun"? Of *course* the sun is round! Yet when you close the
book and start thinking about those lines, the scene they describe is so vivid that it's almost as though you had been
there. And if you ask yourself what other two words he could
have used instead of "straight" and "round", you realize that
there aren't any. Then again, in a couplet from another of
his poems:

> When the sun sets, the water whitens;
> When the tide rises, all the world is green.

"Whitens" and "green" at first seem like nonsense; but when
you start thinking about it, you realize that he *had* to use those
two words in order to describe the scene exactly as it was.
When you read those lines out loud, the flavour of them

is so concentrated that it's as though you had an olive weighing several thousand catties inside your mouth! And there's another couplet of his:

> Down by the ford the late sun lingers;
> Over the village a smoke-thread climbs.

"Lingers" and "climbs": so simple, but so clever! I remember that year we came up to the capital we moored the boat one evening towards dusk in a very lonely stretch of country with only a few trees on the bank and a few houses far away in the distance from which the blue smoke of peasants cooking their evening meal was rising high, high into the clouds. When I read this couplet last night, it suddenly took me back to that very spot.'

Bao-yu and Tan-chun had come in while she was talking and quietly sat down to listen. Bao-yu was impressed.

'To judge by what you've just said, you don't need to read any more poetry. The Emperor Jian-wen once remarked that "appreciation needs not to seek far afield". From your discussion of that last couplet, I should say that you have already reached the *samādhi*!'

'Actually, although you won't know this yet,' said Dai-yu, 'that "smoke-thread climbs" line you admire so much is based on a line written by an earlier poet. If I show it to you, I think you will agree that it is even more austerely effective than Wang Wei's line.'

She took down a copy of Tao Yuan-ming's *Works*, hunted out the couplet she had in mind, and handed it to her to look at:

> Half-lost in haze the distant haunts of men,
> Whose dawdling smoke the unseen hamlet marks.

Caltrop read it and nodded approvingly:

'Yes, I see. He got the idea for "climbs" from the "dawdling" of this earlier line.'

Bao-yu laughed delightedly.

'Perfect! You must end your discussion there. If you go on any longer, you'll begin unlearning what you've already discovered. You can start writing poetry yourself now, straight away. It's sure to be good.'

'I can see I shall soon be writing an invitation asking you to join our poetry club,' said Tan-chun smilingly.

'Don't make fun of me, Miss Tan,' said Caltrop. 'Writing poetry is something I've always wanted to do, and now I've got the chance, I'm learning for the fun of it. I don't expect I shall ever be any good.'

'Good heavens! *we* only write for the fun of it ourselves,' said Tan-chun. 'You surely don't imagine that what we write is good poetry? If we set ourselves up to be real poets, people outside this Garden who got to hear of it would laugh so loud that their teeth would drop out!'

'That's what Mencius calls "throwing yourself away",' said Bao-yu. 'You shouldn't do that. The other day, when I was discussing Xi-chun's painting with some of Father's gentlemen, they told me they had heard about our poetry club and asked if they could see some of our poems, so I wrote a few out for them from memory. I assure you, they were genuinely impressed. In fact, they have calligraphed them for blocks to have them printed.'

'Is this really true?' Tan-chun and Dai-yu asked incredulously.

'If anyone's telling lies, it must be the parrot,' said Bao-yu. The two girls were aghast.

'You really are the limit! Quite apart from the fact that the poems aren't good enough, you have no business to go showing our stuff to people outside.'

'What's the harm?' said Bao-yu. 'If those famous poems written by poetesses in days gone by had never been taken outside the women's quarters, we shouldn't know about them today.'

Just then Xi-chun's maid Picture arrived and called Bao-yu away to her mistress. Caltrop pressed Dai-yu to lend her the volume of Du Fu; she also begged Dai-yu and Tan-chun to set her a subject for a poem.

'Let me try my hand at writing one myself,' she said, 'and you can correct it for me.'

'Last night there was a very fine moon,' said Dai-yu. 'I've been thinking of writing a poem about it myself, but haven't yet got round to it. Why don't you write a poem about the moon? You can use "sky" and "light" as your rhymes; but I won't set the other rhyme-words for you, you can use whichever ones you like.'

Clutching the volume of poems, Caltrop returned in great glee and at once began thinking about her composition. After working out the first line or two, she could not resist peeping at the Du Fu and reading a couple of poems. And in this way she continued, alternately reading and composing by fits and starts, too excited to think about eating or drinking or to sit still in the same place for two or three minutes together.

'Why give yourself so much trouble when you don't have to?' Bao-chai asked her. 'It's all that Frowner's fault. I shall have to go and have it out with her. You are inclined to be a dreamer at the best of times, but now you are becoming a real *case*!'

'*Please*, Miss Bao!' said Caltrop. 'You are putting me off.'

She was writing while she said this. Soon she had completed the draft of a poem and handed it to Bao-chai to look at. Bao-chai read it and laughed.

'No, this is no good. This isn't the way to write poetry. Still, don't be disheartened. I should take it to her just the same and see what she says.'

Caltrop followed her advice and went off to look for Dai-yu. Dai-yu took the poem and looked at it. This is what Caltrop had written:

> A chilly radiance bright, a fair round shape,
> The cold white moon hangs in the middle sky.
> The poet for inspiration seeks her oft;
> The homesick traveller from her turns his eye.
> Like a jade mirror hanging on azure wall,
> Like disc of jade suspended from on high.
> No need for lamps on such a glorious night,
> When every beam and post is bathed in light.

Dai-yu smiled.

'You've certainly got some ideas there, but the words you've expressed them in somehow don't hang together properly. It's because you haven't read enough poetry yet. It looks to me as if you've got rather stuck with this poem. If I were you, I'd abandon it altogether and begin another one. Let yourself go a bit more this time.'

Caltrop returned in silence. This time she did not even go indoors but remained outside among the trees at the water's edge – to the considerable mystification of those who passed by and saw her – sitting on a rock meditating, or squatting on her heels in order to scratch characters on the ground.

Li Wan, Bao-chai, Tan-chun and Bao-yu, hearing of this interesting sight, stood on a little hillock some distance away from her and watched with amusement. Bao-chai insisted that Caltrop had gone mad.

'You should have heard her last night. She was muttering away to herself until four or five in the morning. And she can't have slept for more than half an hour, for as soon as it was daylight, I could hear her getting up again. She rushed through her toilet and then rushed off to see Frowner. Presently she came back again, and after mooning around for half the day, she produced a poem; and as *that* was no good, I assume she is now trying to write another one.'

' "The genius of the place brings out the excellence of the person",' said Bao-yu, misquoting slightly. 'The lord above doesn't give us our talents for nothing. We always used to say what a pity it was that a person of her qualities should lack refinement – but look at her now! It proves there is some justice in the world.'

'If only *you* had her powers of concentration,' said Bao-chai, 'you might study to some purpose.'

Bao-yu did not reply.

Just then a very pleased-looking Caltrop was to be seen hurrying off in the direction of the Naiad's House.

'Let's go after her and see if it's any better this time,' said Tan-chun.

When the three of them arrived, Dai-yu had the poem in her hand and was already discussing it.

'What's it like?' they asked her.

'Well, for a beginner, of course, it's very good,' said Dai-yu; 'but it isn't really right yet. It's too laboured. She'll have to try again.'

The others asked if they might have a look. This is what they read:

> Silver or water on the casement cold?
> See its round source in yon clear midnight sky.
> Blanched ghostly white, plum-blossoms spread their scent,
> And dew on willow-slips begins to dry.
> Is it white powder on the paving spilled?
> Or grains of frost that on the railings lie?
> I wake to find no other soul in sight
> But that still face which through the blind sheds light.

'It's not much like a poem about the moon,' said Bao-chai, 'but if you altered the title to "Moon*light*", it would fit rather well. Look at these lines: each of them is not about the moon, it's about moonlight. Well, *all* poetry is only a lot of nonsense! I should leave it for a few days, Caltrop, if I were you. There's no hurry.'

But Caltrop, though she had truly believed that this second poem was a minor masterpiece and was extremely dashed by its rejection, was most unwilling to give up. She wanted to begin thinking about her next poem straight away; and as she found the talk and laughter of the cousins distracting, she went out to where the bamboos began, at the foot of the terrace. There she gave herself up to cogitation of such fierce intensity that she became totally oblivious to all sights and sounds around her, and when Tan-chun jokingly called to her through the window to 'call it a day', she merely looked up with a somewhat dazed expression and replied that ' "day" didn't rhyme: the rhyme-word she was using was "sky" '. The others, hearing this, all burst out laughing.

'The girl's got poetry mania!' said Bao-chai. 'This is all Frowner's doing.'

'Nonsense!' said Dai-yu. 'The Sage tells us that we should be "tireless in teaching others". She came and asked me for help. How could I possibly refuse her?'

'Let's take her to Xi-chun's place and get her to look at the painting,' said Li Wan. 'Perhaps it will take her mind off poetry for a bit.'

She went outside, the others following, and taking Caltrop by the hand, led her to the Spring In Winter room of Lotus Pavilion, where they found Xi-chun, fatigued by her labours, lying on the couch taking an afternoon nap. The painting was on the wall, masked by a covering of gauze. The cousins woke up Xi-chun and removed the cover from the painting. Barely three-tenths of it had been completed. Several female figures were to be seen scattered about here and there in the landscape.

'Look,' they said, pointing them out to Caltrop, 'anyone who can write poetry gets put into the picture. You must hurry up and learn, so that she can put you in too!'

After chatting and joking for a while, they broke up and went off to their several apartments.

Caltrop could think of nothing else but her poem. In the evening she sat by the lamp thinking about it, and it was after midnight when she went to bed. Even in bed she lay with her eyes wide open, continuing to think about it; and it was not until three or four in the morning that she gradually dropped off to sleep.

At daybreak Bao-chai woke up and listened: Caltrop appeared to be fast asleep.

'She was tossing about all night,' thought Bao-chai. 'I wonder if she managed to finish her poem. I won't call her now; she must be exhausted.'

Just then she heard Caltrop laugh and call out in her sleep:

'Ha! Got it! Let her try saying that *this* one isn't any good!'

Bao-chai was both touched and amused.

'*What* have you got?' she asked, quickly waking her. 'This poetry business is becoming positively unnatural! I don't know about learning how to write poetry: what you'll likelier get, if you go on much longer in this fashion, is a serious illness!'

The intensity of Caltrop's application had, in fact, induced a concentration of the vital fluids which, finding no outlet during the daytime, had resulted in her being able to produce a whole eight-line poem in her sleep. She wrote it down as soon as she had combed and washed, and then went out to look for the others.

At Drenched Blossoms, in the little pavilion on the bridge, she came upon Li Wan and the cousins on the way back from their morning duty-call on Lady Wang. Bao-chai was just telling them how Caltrop had composed a poem while she was dreaming and how she had cried out in her sleep, and the others were laughing as they listened. When they looked up and saw Caltrop herself approaching them, they eagerly asked her if they might see her poem.

For further details, please see the following chapter.

CHAPTER 49

Red flowers bloom brighter in dazzling snow
And venison reeks strangely on rosebud lips

WHEN Caltrop saw the cousins talking and laughing about
her, she came forward, smiling herself, and handed the poem
she was carrying to Dai-yu.

'See what you think of *this* one,' she said. 'If this one is all
right, I shall go on learning; if it's still no good, I shall just
have to give up the whole idea.'

The others clustered round Dai-yu to look. This is what
they read:

> Ethereal splendour no cloud can blot out!
> Chaste lovely presence of the cold night sky!
> From a white world the washer's dull thud sounds,
> Till in the last watch cocks begin to cry,
> While, by a fisherman's sad flute entranced,
> A lady leans out from her casement high;
> And you, White Goddess, lulled in sweet delight,
> Wish every night could be a fifteenth night.

There were exclamations from all of them when they had
finished reading it.

'But this is not just "all right",' they said, 'this is a good
and highly original poem. It shows the truth of the proverb:
"Nothing is too difficult for one who has a mind to do it."
We shall definitely be inviting you now to join our poetry
club.'

Caltrop, supposing that they were only saying this to
humour her, could not quite believe them and continued to
press Dai-yu and Bao-chai for the truth.

Just at that moment a number of maids and old serving-
women came hurrying towards them in a state of great excitement:

'Mrs Zhu! Young ladies! Come and meet your relations! A

whole lot of young ladies and other people we've never seen before have just arrived.'

Li Wan laughed.

'What are you talking about? *Whose* relations have just arrived?'

'There are two young cousins of yours, Mrs Zhu,' they said, 'and there's a young lady who says she's Miss Bao's cousin, and a young gentleman that's cousin to Mr Xue. *We*'re on our way now to fetch Mrs Xue. Why don't you and the young ladies go on ahead and meet them?'

They hurried off to complete their mission.

'It sounds as if my cousin Xue Ke and his sister must have come,' said Bao-chai. '*Can* it be them, though?'

'And it sounds as if my Aunt Li must have decided to bring her two daughters to the capital,' said Li Wan. 'But how strange that they should have arrived together!'

When she and the cousins entered Lady Wang's main reception room, they found it packed with people. Apart from the ones whom the servants had mentioned, they found Lady Xing's brother's wife with her daughter Xing Xiu-yan. The three of them, Lady Xing's brother and his wife and daughter, had come up to the capital to put themselves under the protection of Lady Xing. By a coincidence Xi-feng's brother Wang Ren was starting out for the capital just as they were planning to set out themselves, so, on the strength of the marriage connection (Wang Ren being the brother of Lady Xing's daughter-in-law), they had elected to travel in his company.

While stopping at one of the canal ports half-way along their route, they had made the acquaintance of Li Wan's widowed aunt and her two daughters, Li Wen and Li Qi, also on their way to the capital, and when it emerged that all of them were marriage-relations of the Jia family, these three, too, had joined the party. A little after this, Xue Pan's cousin Xue Ke had decided to bring his sister Bao-qin to the capital to attend to the formalities of her betrothal. Some years previously her father, while temporarily residing in the capital, had promised her to the son of a certain Academician Mei, but had died before the betrothal could be made formal. Hearing that his aunt's kinsman Wang Ren was also on his way to the capital, Xue Ke and his sister had pushed on ahead to join him. Thus it was that today all these people presented themselves simultaneously at the Rong mansion looking for their various relations.

When at last the introductions and courtesies were over, it became clear that Grandmother Jia and Lady Wang were delighted with the new arrivals.

'I *knew* something nice was going to happen from the way the lampwick was behaving last night,' said Grandmother Jia. 'It kept flaring up and then forming into little balls at the top. You see, I was right!'

A general exchange of family talk ensued, and the handing over by the visitors of the presents they had brought with them. After that Grandmother Jia invited them all to take lunch with her, with wine to celebrate.

Xi-feng, it goes without saying, was now busier than ever. Li Wan and Bao-chai, who had a great deal of catching up on family news to do, were also kept busy exchanging information with their relations about all the things that had happened during the years since they last met. Dai-yu, observing them, at first shared in their happiness, but when she began to reflect on the contrast with her own solitary and orphaned state, she was obliged to go away in order to hide her tears. Bao-yu, well aware of the reason for her sudden disappearance, went after her, and with a good deal of coaxing, succeeded at last in comforting her.

As soon as Dai-yu had dried her tears, Bao-yu hurried back to Green Delights to tell Aroma, Musk and Skybright about the visitors.

'You ought to go and have a look,' he told them. 'This nephew of my Aunt Xue's is *completely* different from Cousin Pan. From his looks and behaviour you'd think he was Bao-chai's brother. He's certainly more like her than Pan is. And as for the sister – you're always saying what a beauty Cousin Chai is, but wait till you've seen *her*! And then there are my sister-in-law's two cousins – well, words just fail me! Heavenly lord, what a store of beauty you must have at your disposal to be able to produce such paragons! I've been like the frog living at the bottom of the well who thought the world was a little round pool of water. Up to now I've always believed that the girls in this household were without equals anywhere; but now, even without my needing to go outside, here they come, each one more beautiful than the last! Today has been an education for me. Don't tell me there are any *more* like this: the shock would be too great!'

He laughed excitedly. Aroma saw that he was in one of his crazy moods and refused to go and look. But Skybright and the others were more curious and at once hurried over for a peep. They returned soon after, full of smiles, to report on what they had seen.

'*Do* go and look!' they urged Aroma. 'There's Lady Xing's niece and this cousin of Miss Bao's and Mrs Zhu's two cousins: it's not often you get a chance to see four such beautiful bul-rushes together!'

Scarcely had these words been uttered when a smiling Tan-chun came in looking for Bao-yu.

'Our poetry club is in luck,' she said, finding him indoors with the maids. 'Think of all those new members!'

'Yes,' said Bao-yu. 'What a happy inspiration of yours it was to start it! It's almost as though providence had sent these people here to make it prosper. But are you sure they can all write poetry?'

'I've already asked them,' said Tan-chun. 'They are too modest to say outright, of course, but from what I can judge I'm pretty sure that either they all can, or even if they can't, would learn very quickly. Look how quick Caltrop has been.'

'Which of the four do you think is the prettiest, Miss?' said Skybright. '*I* say Miss Bao's cousin.'

'Yes, I think I agree,' said Tan-chun. 'I think even Bao-chai is not quite as beautiful as her.'

Aroma had been listening to all this with growing curiosity.

'This is certainly news to *me*!' she said. 'I shouldn't have thought it possible to find *anyone* more beautiful than Miss Bao. I must go and have a look.'

'Grandmother was completely captivated as soon as she set

eyes on her,' said Tan-chun. 'She's already insisted that Mother should become her godmother, and it's decided that Grandmother shall bring her up as her own grandchild.'

'*Really?*' Bao-yu seemed delighted.

'When have I ever told you a lie?' said Tan-chun. There was a glint of mischief in her eye: 'Now that she's got such a beautiful granddaughter, she'll probably lose interest in her darling grandson.'

'That doesn't matter,' said Bao-yu unconcernedly. 'She *ought* to give preference to girls. That's as it should be. By the way, it's the sixteenth today. It's the day for our poetry club meeting.'

'Cousin Lin has only recently got up, and Ying-chun is ill again,' said Tan-chun. 'We're not really in any shape for a meeting at the moment.'

'Ying-chun doesn't care much about writing poetry anyway,' said Bao-yu. 'Surely we can manage without *her*?'

'Yes, but I think we ought to wait a few days, even so,' said Tan-chun. 'Why don't we wait until we've got to know the newcomers a bit better and then invite them to join us? I shouldn't think sister-in-law or Cousin Chai can either of them be much in the mood for writing poetry at the moment. And Xiang-yun isn't here. And Frowner has only just recovered. No one is really up to it yet. We ought to wait until Yun arrives and the new lot have settled in; then, when Frowner is completely better and sister-in-law and Cousin Chai are a bit less preoccupied and Caltrop has made some more progress, we can invite everyone to a plenary session. What you and I ought to do now is go round to Grandma's and see what arrangements are being made about these people's accommodation. We know that Chai's cousin is staying here, because Grandma has adopted her; but we don't know yet about the others. If there are no plans for them to stay here, we must ask Grandma to invite them. If possible we should get her to let them live in the Garden. It would be fun to have some more neighbours.'

Bao-yu grew quite radiant at the thought.

'How clever you are, Tan!' he told his sister admiringly.

'I'm such a stupid ass. I get so carried away that I don't think about the important things like you do.'

Brother and sister then went together to Grandmother Jia's apartment, where they found the old lady in wonderful high spirits following Lady Wang's recognition of Xue Bao-quin as her god-daughter. She considered that this entitled her to treat the girl as her grandchild, which she had begun doing by insisting that she spend the nights with *her* in her apartment and not in the Garden with Bao-chai. Xue Ke would naturally stay with his aunt and occupy the study that Xue Pan had vacated.

'This niece of yours surely doesn't need to go back to her parents yet?' Grandmother Jia said to Lady Xing. 'Let her stay in the Garden for a few days and enjoy herself.'

Lady Xing's brother and sister-in-law had been living in extremely straitened circumstances, and now that they had come up to the capital, were relying on her to provide them with accommodation and financial assistance. She was naturally only too delighted to have one less person to her charge, and promptly handed Xiu-yan over to Xi-feng to dispose of.

Bearing in mind the varied, somewhat peculiar, temperaments of the Garden's inhabitants, Xi-feng doubted the wisdom of putting Xiu-yan in with one of the others; on the other hand she foresaw disadvantages in opening up a separate establishment for her. In the end she put her in with Ying-chun, reflecting that if the girl *did* experience any difficulties in living with Ying-chun, then even if Lady Xing got to hear of it, she, Xi-feng, could not be held responsible, since Ying-chun was Lady Xing's own half-daughter.

From this time onwards, not counting the time she spent at home with her parents, Xiu-yan received, for every whole month that she lived with Ying-chun in Prospect Garden, an allowance from Xi-feng of exactly the same amount as the monthly allowance that was paid to Ying-chun herself.

To Xi-feng's dispassionate eye it soon became apparent that in both temperament and behaviour Xiu-yan was quite unlike Lady Xing and her parents – that she was in fact an extremely sweet and lovable person. Sorry that so gentle a soul should be so poor and unfortunate, Xi-feng treated her with a tact and considerateness that she did not always show the others. Lady Xing, on the other hand, seemed scarcely aware of her niece's existence.

Grandmother Jia and Lady Wang esteemed Li Wan as a good and virtuous young woman who, having lost her husband at an early age, bore widowhood with fortitude and restraint. Now that this widowed aunt had arrived, they refused to hear of her taking lodgings outside, and though the good lady made many polite efforts to decline, insisted that she and her two daughters, Li Wen and Li Qi, should move into Sweet-rice Village and stay there with Li Wan at the family's expense.

No sooner had the new arrivals begun settling in than news came that Grandmother Jia's nephew Shi Ding, the Marquis of Zhong-jing, was being transferred to an important position in one of the outer provinces and would shortly be leaving for his new post, taking his family with him. Grandmother Jia could not bear the idea of a permanent separation from her great-niece, and so it was agreed that Xiang-yun, too, should move into residence with the Jias. It was Grandmother Jia's original intention that Xi-feng should set up a separate establishment for her in the Garden; but as Xiang-yun herself rigorously opposed this idea and insisted on living with her beloved Bao-chai, she was allowed to have her way.

The Garden's society was now larger and livelier than it had ever been before. With Li Wan as its doyenne it numbered – if you counted Xi-feng as an honorary member – thirteen people: Li Wan, Ying-chun, Tan-chun, Xi-chun, Bao-chai, Dai-yu, Xiang-yun, Li Wen, Li Qi, Bao-qin, Xing Xiu-yan, Bao-yu and Xi-feng. Apart from the two young married women, the rest were all fifteen, sixteen or seventeen years old. Most of them were in fact born in the same year, several of them in the same month or even on the same day. Not only Grandmother Jia and Lady Wang and the servants, even the young people themselves had difficulty in remembering who was senior to whom, and soon gave up trying, and abandoned any attempt at observing the usual formalities of address.

Caltrop could now think of nothing else all day long but writing poetry. Up to now she had refrained from importuning Bao-chai too persistently for advice, but with the arrival of an unwearying talker like Shi Xiang-yun upon the scene she was in her element. Xiang-yun was only too willing to accede to her requests for instruction, and morning, noon and night the two of them were to be found together, always in animated discussion.

'You two are deafening me with your perpetual chatter,' Bao-chai complained. 'Imagine how ridiculous and unmaidenly it would seem to a man of letters if he heard that *girls* were treating poetry as a serious occupation! Caltrop on her own was bad enough, but with a chatterbox like you on top of it, Yun, I'm finding it a bit too much. Everywhere I go it's "the profundity of Du Fu", or "Wei Ying-wu of Soochow's limpidity", or "the somewhat meretricious charm of Wen Ting-yun", or "Li Shang-yin's obscurity". Still, there are two important *living* poets I've so far heard no mention of.'

'Oh?' said Xiang-yun, all agog. 'Which two?'

'I've heard no mention of Crazy Caltrop's prodigious pertinacity or the linguipotent loquacity of Shi Xiang-yun,' said Bao-chai.

The other two burst out laughing.

At that moment Bao-qin arrived. She was wearing a magnificent rain-cape that glittered as she moved with gold and greenish lights. Bao-chai asked her where she had got it from.

'Lady Jia gave me it,' said Bao-qin. 'She looked it out for me because it was beginning to sleet.'

Caltrop examined it curiously.

'No wonder it looks so beautiful: this is woven out of peacock's down.'

'That's not peacock's down,' said Xiang-yun. 'It's made from mallard's head-feathers.' She smiled at Bao-qin teasingly: 'One can see how fond of you she must be. She's fond of Bao-yu, but she's never let him wear *this*.'

Bao-chai laughed:

'To each a different fortune meted –

that's certainly a true saying. I never dreamt that she would be coming here – much less that when she did, Lady Jia would immediately fall for her like this!'

'Apart from the time you spend with Her Old Ladyship,' Xiang-yun advised Bao-qin, 'I should stick to the Garden as much as possible if I were you. In these two places you can eat and drink and play anywhere you please. But be careful of Lady Wang's place. If *she*'s in when you go there, then you can sit and talk with her as long as you like; but if she's not, it's best not to go inside. There are a lot of nasty people in there who like to do us harm.'

This highly indiscreet warning was uttered so matter-of-factly that Bao-chai, Bao-qin, Caltrop and Oriole were compelled to laugh.

'I won't say you are thoughtless,' said Bao-chai, 'because you obviously mean well; but you really are a bit too outspoken. You and Qin ought to be sisters, since you are so concerned about her.'

Xiang-yun looked at Bao-qin appraisingly.

'She is the only one of us who *could* wear this cape,' she said. 'Anyone else would look wrong in it.'

Just then Amber walked in with a message from Grandmother Jia:

'Her Old Ladyship says please Miss Bao don't be too strict with Miss Qin; she's still only little and should be allowed to have her own way. And she says if there's anything Miss Qin wants, she shouldn't be afraid to ask for it.'

Bao-chai stood up politely to acknowledge the message. Afterwards she nudged Bao-qin playfully.

'*I* don't know! Some people have all the luck. You'd better leave us, hadn't you, before we start maltreating you? It beats me. What have *you* got that *I* haven't got?'

She was still teasing Bao-qin when Bao-yu and Dai-yu arrived.

'You say that in jest, Chai,' said Xiang-yun, noting their entry, 'but I know someone who really thinks that way.'

'If anyone's really upset, it must be him,' said Amber, pointing her finger at Bao-yu.

Xiang-yun laughed at her simple-mindedness:

'No, he's not that sort of person.'

'Then if it's not *him* you mean, it must be *her*,' said Amber, pointing now at Dai-yu.

Xiang-yun fell silent. This time it was Bao-chai who spoke:

'Wrong again. She feels the same way about my cousin as I do. In fact, I believe if anything she's even fonder of her; so how *could* she be upset? Don't be taken in by Miss Shi's nonsense, my dear Amber. When did you ever hear Miss Shi say anything serious?'

From past experience Bao-yu – who still knew nothing of Dai-yu and Bao-chai's recent rapprochement – was too familiar with Dai-yu's jealous disposition not to feel apprehensive that Grandmother Jia's new partiality for Bao-qin might upset her. He was puzzled, therefore, by Bao-chai's rejoinder, and even more puzzled when he studied the expression on Dai-yu's face and found that, far from showing any trace of the resentment he would have expected, it exactly tallied with what Bao-chai had said.

'Those two used not to be like this,' he thought. 'Yet to judge from appearances, they are ten times friendlier towards each other now than they are towards anyone else.'

Shortly after this he heard Dai-yu calling Bao-qin 'dear' and fussing over her as if she were Bao-qin's elder sister.

Bao-qin was a young, warm-hearted creature; she was, moreover, highly intelligent and had been taught her letters from an early age. By the time she had been a couple of days in the Jia household, she had already formed some impression of its members. Finding that her cousins were quite different from the vapid, giggling creatures to be found in the women's quarters of so many houses, she was soon on friendly terms with all of them and was careful not to show off; but in Dai-yu she recognized a superior intelligence, and consequently felt even more affection and respect for her than she did for any of the others. Hence the intimacy which Bao-yu had just witnessed. He studied the pair of them curiously and marvelled in silence.

Shortly after this, when Bao-chai and Bao-qin had gone off to Aunt Xue's place and Xiang-yun had gone to see Grandmother Jia and Dai-yu had gone back to her own room to rest, Bao-Yu went after Dai-yu to question her.

'I've read *The Western Chamber*,' he said, 'and understood it well enough to have offended you on more than one occasion by quoting it at you; yet there's one line in it I still don't understand. Do you think, if I told you it, you could explain it to me?'

Dai-yu realized that something must lie behind this request, nevertheless she smilingly promised that she would do her best.

'It comes in the section called "Ying-ying's Reply",' said Bao-yu:

'Since when did Meng Guang accept Liang Hong's tray?

The question seems rather an apposite one. Those two little words "since when" particularly intrigue me. Kindly expound them for me, will you? *Since when* did Meng Guang accept Liang Hong's tray?'

Dai-yu could not but be amused by the droll way in which he had gone about making his inquiry.

'That's a good question,' she said. 'It was a good question when Reddie asked it in the play, and it's a good question when *you* ask it now.'

'There was a time, not so long past, when you might have been deeply offended by it,' said Bao-yu, 'yet now you say nothing.'

'It's because now I know she's a very good person,' said Dai-yu. 'Before I used to think she was two-faced.'

She proceeded to tell him, at some length, about the motherly talking-to Bao-chai had given her after her lapses in the drinking-game and about the gift of bird's nest and sugar and the long talk Bao-chai had had with her when she was ill.

'I see,' said Bao-yu. 'I needn't have been so puzzled then.
It seems that the question

Since when did Meng Guang accept Liang Hong's tray?

could have been answered with another line from the same act
of the same play. It was since you spoke

Like a child whose unbridled tongue knows no concealment!'

Dai-yu went on to talk about Bao-qin, whom she evidently
looked on as a younger sister. Alas, this only reminded her that
she had no *real* sister of her own and she began to cry. Bao-yu
would have none of this.

'Now come on, Dai! You're *making* yourself upset. Look at
you! You're thinner than ever this year. It's because you won't
take care of yourself. You positively *look* for ways of making
yourself miserable. It's almost as though you felt you hadn't
spent the day properly unless you'd had at least one good cry
in it!'

'No,' said Dai-yu as she wiped her eyes. 'I feel very low
these days, but I don't think I cry as much as I used to.'

'I'm sure you *do*,' said Bao-yu. 'It's just that it's become so
much a habit with you that you no longer know whether
you're crying or not. I'm sure you cry just as much as you
always did.'

Just then one of the maids from his room arrived carrying
his scarlet felt rain-cape.

'Mrs Zhu has just sent someone round with a message for
you, Master Bao,' said the maid. 'She says it's starting to
snow now and she wants to discuss with you about inviting
people for the poetry meeting.'

She had barely finished speaking when Li Wan's emissary
arrived to deliver the same message to Dai-yu. Bao-yu suggested that they should go to Sweet-rice Village together and
waited while she put on a pair of little red-leather boots which
had a gilded cloud-pattern cut into their surface, a pelisse
of heavy, dark-red bombasine lined with white fox-fur, a

complicated woven belt made out of silvery-green shot silk,
and a snow-hat. The two of them then set off together through
the snow.

They arrived to find that nearly all the others were there
already, mostly in red felt or camlet snow-cloaks. The exceptions were Li Wan, who wore a simple greatcoat of plain
woollen material buttoned down the front, Xue Bao-chai in
a pelisse of ivy-green whorl-patterned brocade trimmed with
some sort of exotic lamb's-wool, and Xing Xiu-yan, who had
no protection against the snow of any kind beyond the everyday clothes she was wearing.

Presently Xiang-yun arrived. She was wearing an enormous
fur coat that Grandmother Jia had given her. The outside was
made up of sables' heads and the inside lined with long-haired
black squirrel. On her head was a dark-red camlet 'Princess'
hood lined with yellow figured velvet, whose cut-out cloud
shapes were bordered with gold, and round her neck, muffling
her up to the nose, was a large sable tippet.

'Look, Monkey!' said Dai-yu, laughing at this furry appari-
tion. 'Trust Yun to turn the need for wearing snow-clothes
into an excuse for dressing up! She looks just like a Tartar
groom!'

'You haven't seen what I am wearing underneath yet,'
said Xiang-yun, and opened out the fur coat to show
them.

She had on a short, narrow-sleeved, ermine-lined tunic
jacket of russet green, edge-fastened down the centre front,
purfled at neck and cuffs with a triple band of braiding in
contrasting colours, and patterned all over with dragon-
roundels embroidered in gold thread and coloured silks.
Under this she was wearing a short riding-skirt of pale-red
satin damask lined with white fox belly-fur. A court girdle of
different-coloured silks braided into butterfly knots and ending
in long silken tassels was tied tightly round her waist. Her
boots were of deerskin. The whole ensemble greatly enhanced
the somewhat masculine appearance of her figure with its
graceful, athletic bearing.

The others laughed:

'She loves dressing up as a boy. Actually she looks even more fetching in boy's clothes than she does as a girl.'

'Let's get down to business,' said Xiang-yun. 'What *I* want to know is, who's paying for the entertainment this time?'

'Well, this is what *I* thought,' said Li Wan. 'We've already passed the date for our regular meeting, and we don't want to wait until the next one comes round, because it's too far ahead. As it's snowing, I thought it would be rather nice if we clubbed together for a little snow-party in honour of the newcomers and used it as an occasion for doing some poetry-making as well. What do the rest of you think?'

'I think that's exactly what we should do,' said Bao-yu. 'The only thing is, it's a bit late for a party today, but if we wait until tomorrow, the snow may have stopped by then and it won't be so much fun.'

'It's very unlikely to,' said the others. 'And even if it has stopped by tomorrow morning, it will surely be snowing still tonight, so it should be well worth looking at in the morning.'

'This place here is all right, of course,' said Li Wan, 'but I thought that for this occasion it would be nicer if we met in Snowy Rushes Retreat. I've already told them to light the stove there and get the underground heating system started. I don't think Grandma would much like the idea of our sitting round the stove making verses, so, as it's only a very *little* party, I propose that we don't tell her about it. As long as we let Feng know, it should be sufficient. As regards contributions: if each of you will bring one tael to me here, it ought to be enough. Not you five,' she pointed to Caltrop, Bao-qin, Li Wen, Li Qi and Xiu-yan – 'And Ying-chun and Xi-chun won't be contributing either. Ying-chun is ill and Xi-chun is on leave of absence. That leaves only Bao-chai, Dai-yu, Xiang-yun and Dai-yu. If you four will contribute one tael each, I will undertake to contribute five or six taels myself. Together that should be ample.'

Bao-chai and the other three promised to bring her their

contributions later and went on to ask what titles and rhymes should be set for the poetry-making.

'I've already decided that,' said Li Wan. 'Let it be a surprise for you when you come.'

Arrangements for the party having now been settled, the cousins chatted together for a while longer before going off in a body to visit Grandmother Jia.

That concludes the narrative for that day.

*

At first light next morning Bao-yu, who in excited anticipation of the day ahead had barely slept all night, crawled from the covers and lifted up a corner of the bed-curtain to inspect the weather. Although the doors and windows were still fastened, there was an ominous brightness about the latter which led him to conclude – inwardly groaning with disappointment – that the snow must have cleared and the sun be shining. Jumping out of bed, he opened one of the inner casements and looked through the glass. It was not the sun after all, he found, but the white gleam of snow. It had been snowing all night; there was a good foot of snow on the ground and it was still coming down in great, soft flakes, like the flock from a torn-up quilt.

Overjoyed to find that he had been wrong, he at once began shouting for his maids, and as soon as he had finished washing and dressed himself in an aubergine-coloured gown lined with fox, a jacket with a sealskin shoulder-cape, and a belt round his waist for warmth, he donned his elegant rain-hat and cape (the Prince of Bei-jing's present that Dai-yu had so much admired), stepped into his pear-wood pattens, and set off for Snowy Rushes Retreat.

Once outside the courtyard gate, the Garden stretched out on every hand in uniform whiteness, uninterrupted except for the dark green of a pine-tree or the lighter green of some bamboos here and there in the distance. He felt as if he was standing in the middle of a great glittering crystal bowl. Proceeding on his way, he had just turned a spur in the miniature mountain whose foot he was skirting, when his senses were suddenly ravished by a delicate cold fragrance. On looking around him, he found it to be coming from the dozen or so trees of winter-flowering red plum growing inside the walls of Green Bower Hermitage where the nun Adamantina lived. The brilliance of their carmine hue against the white background and the bravura of their blossoming amidst the snow so enchanted him that he stopped for some minutes to admire them.

As he moved on again, he saw someone carrying a green oiled-silk umbrella crossing over Wasp Waist Bridge. It was one of Li Wan's servants on her way to invite Xi-feng to the party.

Arriving at Snowy Rushes Retreat, he found several women-servants outside, sweeping a pathway up to the door.

Snowy Rushes Retreat was built at the water's margin in the shelter of a little hill. It had a thatched roof and adobe walls and a post-and-bar fence round it and bamboo-barred windows, just like a farmhouse or a peasant's cottage. By merely opening a casement and leaning out, it was possible to fish in the lake from its rear windows. Reeds and rushes grew all around it. A meandering pathway through them led to the bamboo bridge by which Lotus Pavilion could be approached from the back.

When the snow-sweepers caught sight of Bao-yu in his rain-hat and cape, they paused from their labours and laughed.

'We were just saying a moment ago that all we need now is an old fisherman, and here he comes! You're too impatient, Master: the young ladies won't be coming until they've eaten.'

Hearing that, there was nothing for Bao-yu to do but go back again.

Looking out from Drenched Blossoms Pavilion while he was crossing over the bridge, he caught sight of his sister Tan-chun emerging from Autumn Studio. She was wearing a dark-red camlet cloak and Guanyin hood and leaning on the arm of a little maid. A woman-servant walked behind her carrying a green oiled-silk umbrella. Realizing that she must

be on her way to see Grandmother Jia, Bao-yu waited by the
pavilion for her to catch up with him and accompanied her
out of the Garden.

When they arrived, Bao-qin was still at her toilet in the
inner room. The other cousins joined them shortly after. Bao-
yu kept telling everyone how hungry he felt and grumbling
because the servants were so long in serving. When the food
at last arrived, the first dish to be put on the table was unborn
lamb stewed in milk.

'That's a health-food,' said Grandmother Jia. 'It's for
old folk like me. I'm afraid you young people couldn't eat it.
It's a creature that's never seen the light. There's some fresh
venison today, though. Why don't you wait and have some
of that?'

The others agreed to wait, but Bao-yu professed himself
unable to hold out, and helping himself to a bowl of plain
boiled rice, poured a little tea over it and shovelled it straight
from the bowl into his mouth with one or two collops of
pickled pheasant-meat to help it down.

'I know you've got something on today,' said Grandmother
Jia. 'That's why you've no time to eat properly.' She turned
to the servants. 'Save some of the venison for them to eat
in the evening.'

'There's plenty more,' said Xi-feng. 'I've already spoken to
them about it.'

Xiang-yun had a brief consultation on the subject with
Bao-yu:

'If they've got fresh venison, why don't we ask for a piece
and cook it ourselves in the Garden? That would be fun.'

Bao-yu eagerly took up her suggestion and begged a piece
from Xi-feng. He got one of the women to take it into the
Garden for them.

Presently, when they had all left Grandmother Jia's place
and reassembled in Snowy Rushes Retreat and were waiting to
hear what themes and rhymes Li Wan had decided on, they
noticed that Xiang-yun and Bao-yu were missing.

'Those two should never be allowed together,' said Dai-yu.
'As soon as ever they get together there is some kind of

mischief afoot. No doubt the reason they've gone off this time is because they have designs on that deer's meat.'

Just then Li Wan's aunt, Mrs Li, came in, drawn by the noise and numbers to see what was happening.

'That boy with the jade and the girl with the gold kylin,' she said to Li Wan anxiously, 'they both seem such clean, well-bred children, and they *look* as if they had enough to eat, yet just now the two of them were discussing how to eat a piece of raw venison. They seemed to be quite serious about it, too. *Can* one eat venison raw? I find it hard to believe that it can be very good for you.'

'Shocking!' exclaimed the others. 'Better go out and stop them.'

'Yun is at the bottom of this,' said Dai-yu. 'Mark my words!'

Li Wan hurried off to find the culprits.

'If you are proposing to eat raw meat,' she said when she had found them, 'I shall have to send you back to Grandma's to do it there. You can take a whole deer and stuff yourselves sick on it as long as it's not my responsibility. Come on, now! Come back and make verses with the rest of us. Out in all this snow – it's *much* too cold!'

'You're absolutely mistaken,' said Bao-yu, laughing. 'We're planning to roast it.'

'Oh *well*,' said Li Wan, 'that's different.'

Some old women arrived just then, carrying an iron stove, some metal skewers and a grill.

'Now be careful about cutting that meat,' said Li Wan. 'If you cut your fingers, you'll have nobody to blame but yourselves!'

Having uttered that warning, she went indoors again.

Not long after she had gone in, Patience came by on her way to the Retreat. Xi-feng had sent her, in response to Li Wan's invitation, to explain that she was unable to join them because she was busy seeing to the various annual payments that fall due at this time of year. Xiang-yun stopped her to exchange greetings, and having once stopped her, was unwilling to let her go again. Patience was by nature a fun-loving

girl and she knew that Xi-feng would generally let her do as
she liked. Considering the idea of cooking outdoors a great
lark, she entered into the spirit of the thing, and taking off her
bracelets, joined the other two round the brazier and asked
for three of the cut-up pieces of venison to roast.

Bao-chai and Dai-yu had seen this kind of thing before
and were not particularly interested, but it was a novelty to
Mrs Li and Bao-qin and the newcomers, and they were greatly
intrigued.

'What a lovely smell!' said Tan-chun, when she and Li Wan
had finished discussing the theme for the verse-making.
'You can smell it from here. I'm going outside to have some.'

She went out to join the three around the brazier. Li Wan
followed her.

'Everyone's ready and waiting,' said Li Wan. 'Haven't
you two finished eating yet?'

'I need wine to inspire my verse,' said Xiang-yun, speaking
with a mouth full of venison, 'and eating roast venison gives
me a thirst for wine. So if I didn't eat this venison, I shouldn't
be able to write any poetry for you.'

She caught sight of Bao-qin, in the beautiful drake's
head cloak that Caltrop had thought was made of peacock's
feathers, hanging back somewhat from the rest and smiling
wistfully.

'Thoppy!' she called out to her. 'Come and try thome!'

'Too dirty!' said Bao-qin.

'Go and try some,' Bao-chai urged her. 'It's very good.
The only reason your Cousin Lin isn't having any is because
she's delicate and can't digest it. If it weren't for that, she
would love to have some herself.'

Hearing this, Bao-qin went over and nibbled a bit, and
finding it good, began to tuck in with as much gusto as the
rest.

Presently a little maid arrived from Xi-feng summoning
Patience to return; but Patience told the girl to go back
without her and tell her mistress that she was being detained
by Miss Shi. Shortly after the maid's departure Xi-feng herself arrived, with a rain-cape over her shoulders.

'This looks good,' she said jovially. 'You might have told me!'

With that she joined the other five in their alfresco feast round the brazier.

'You look like a party of down-and-outs,' said Dai-yu. 'Oh dear, oh dear! Poor Snowy Rushes Retreat, polluted by Butcher Yun and her reeking carnivores! I weep for you!'

'What do *you* know about it?' said Xiang-yun scornfully. ' "True wits make elegant whate'er they touch." Yours is a false purity. *Odious* purity! Now we may reek and raven; but presently you will see us with the pure spirit of poetry in our breasts and the most delicate, silken phrases on our lips!'

'You'd better see to it that the verses you make *are* good ones,' said Bao-chai, laughing, 'otherwise we shall make you expiate the pollution by plucking the venison from your insides and stuffing you with snowy rushes!'

They had now made an end of eating, and washed their hands. In putting on her bracelets again, Patience noticed that one of them was missing; but though she and the others looked all around them, they were unable to find it. They were still puzzling over its disappearance when Xi-feng smilingly put an end to the search:

'*I* know where the bracelet's gone. You others go in and get on with your poetry.'

'There's no need to look for it any longer,' she told Patience. 'You will have to go home without it; but I promise that within three days from now you shall have it back again.'

'What are your poems to be about this time?' she asked the cousins. 'Grandma says that as it's getting near the end of the year, we shall soon be needing some First Month lantern riddles.'

'Ah yes, of course!' they said. 'We'd quite forgotten. We'd better make some good ones up in advance to have ready for the festival.'

During this exchange they had been trooping into the room in the Retreat which had the under-floor heating. Wine-cups and prepared dishes had been laid there in readiness by the servants. A paper stuck to the wall announced the theme, form and rhyme for the forthcoming poetry contest. Bao-yu and Xiang-yun, who had not yet seen it, quickly went over to look. This is what it said:

> *Theme*: The Snow
> *Form*: Linked Pentameters
> *Rhyme*: Eyes

No order of composition had been indicated.

'I'm not much good at poetry myself,' said Li Wan, 'so I shall merely start you off by giving you the first three lines. After that, whoever is the first to think of a good following line can carry on.'

'I think we ought to have a fixed order,' said Bao-chai.

As to whether or not her advice was taken, that will be made clear in the following chapter.

CHAPTER 50

Linked verses in Snowy Rushes Retreat
And lantern riddles in the Spring In Winter Room

'I THINK we ought to have a fixed order,' said Bao-chai. 'Just let me write the names down and we can decide what it is to be by lot.'

When she had written down their names and torn up the paper, the slips were drawn and she copied them down in the order in which they came out. Li Wan, by coincidence, retained the first place.

'If *this* is what you are doing,' said Xi-feng, 'I may as well contribute a line of my own to start you off with.'

'Yes, yes,' said the others. 'Please do!'

Bao-chai added the name 'Feng' to the list, above that of 'Farmer Sweet-rice', while Li Wan explained what the subject was and what sort of line it had to be. Xi-feng listened attentively and thought for some moments before speaking.

'You mustn't laugh if this sounds a bit unpolished,' she said at last, 'but at least I think it's the right length. Mind you, I've no idea how it could go on.'

'Never mind how unpolished it is,' they said. 'Just tell us what it is; then you can leave, if you want to, and get on with your own work.'

'Well, when it snows, there's always a north wind,' said Xi-feng, 'and last night I could hear the north wind blowing all night long; so I've made a line up about that:

Last night the north wind blew the whole night through.

There you are – take it or leave it!'

The others looked at each other in pleased surprise.

'Even if the language of this line *is* a bit unpolished and you *can't* see what's going to follow it, it's exactly the kind of line that a skilled poet would begin with. Not only is the line good in itself, but it leaves so many possibilities open to the person who follows. Put that down for our first line then, Sweet-rice, and *you* can finish the couplet.'

Before they proceeded any further, however, Xi-feng, Mrs Li and Patience drank two cups of wine with them, after which they left. As soon as they had gone, Li Wan wrote out the line that Xi-feng had given them, adding a line of her own to make it into a couplet and a third line after that to make the beginning of a second couplet. Thereafter, as each of them in turn completed the couplet started by the previous person and then added the first line of another couplet, she continued to write down the lines at their dictation.

XI-FENG:
Last night the north wind blew the whole night through –
LI WAN:
Today outside my door the snow still flies.
On mud and dirt its pure white flakes fall down –
CALTROP:
And powdered jade the whole earth beautifies.
Flakes on the dead plants weave a winter dress –
TAN-CHUN:
And on dry grasses gemlike crystallize.
Now will the farmer's brew a good price fetch –
LI QI:
His full barn to a good year testifies.
The ash-filled gauge shows winter's solstice near –
LI WEN:
And the Wain turns as Yang revivifies.
Snow robs the cold hills of their emerald hue –
XIU-YAN:
And frost the river's motion petrifies.
Snow settles thickly on sparse willow boughs –
XIANG-YUN:
But on dead plantain-leaves less easy lies.
Now perfumed coals in precious braziers burn –
BAO-QIN:
And heavy furs the girls' slim shapes disguise.
Firelight the mirror by the window catches –
DAI-YU:
And burning nard the chamber purifies.
Still sobbing through the night the mournful wind –

BAO-YU:

Each sleeper's dreams with sadness sanctifies.
Somewhere a melancholy flute is playing –

BAO-CHAI:

Whose sad notes with the wind's plaint harmonize.
With groans the Earth Turtle sideways shifts his load –

At this point Li Wan laid down her brush and rose to her feet.

'I think I'll just slip out and see about getting some more wine heated. Someone else can take my place.'

Bao-chai took up the writing-brush and called on Bao-qin to complete the couplet; but before she could do so, Xiang-yun had leapt to her feet with two lines of her own:

XIANG-YUN:

As dragons brawl, the cloud-wrack liquefies.
A lone boat from the lonely shore puts out –

Nothing daunted, Bao-qin completed *that* couplet instead:

BAO-QIN:

While from the bridge a horseman waves good-byes.
Now warm clothes to the frontier are dispatched –

Xiang-yun would yield to no one; and her invention was so much quicker than anyone else's, that they were content to let her break the order, and watched with amusement as she returned now, exulting, to the attack:

XIANG-YUN:

And wives to distant dear ones send supplies.
On still untrodden ways masked pitfalls threaten –

'That's a good line!' said Bao-chai admiringly as she wrote down what Xiang-yun had recited; and she followed with two lines of her own:

BAO-CHAI:

In snowbound woods a bough's creak terrifies.
The wind-blown snow around the traveller whirls –

Dai-yu hurriedly followed:

DAI-YU:

And clouds of powdery snow at each step rise.
Steamed taros makes a good snow-party fare –

She nudged Bao-yu to follow; but Bao-yu was so absorbed in watching the contest that seemed to be developing between Xiang-yun on the one hand and Bao-qin, Bao-chai and Dai-yu on the other, that he was failing to think up lines of his own to follow their half-couplets with. He did the best he could, however, in response to Dai-yu's nudge:

BAO-YU:
The guests on 'scattered salt' themes improvise.
Now is the woodman's axe no longer heard –

'Clear off, you – you're no good!' said Xiang-yun, laughing. 'All you're doing is getting in other people's way!'
Her pausing to say this gave Bao-qin an opportunity of cutting in:

BAO-QIN:
Yet still his rod the straw-clad fisher plies.
Mountains like sleeping elephants appear –

Xiang-yun hurried back into the fray:

XIANG-YUN:
A snake-like path the climber's skill defies.
After long cold the trees strange frost-fruits bear –

This evoked admiring murmurs from Bao-chai and the rest. Tan-chun managed to get in a contribution at this point:

TAN-CHUN:
Which, bold in beauty, winter's blasts despise.
The hushed yard startles to a cold chough's chatter –

Xiang-yun was ready at once with two lines to follow, but as she was feeling thirsty, she first stopped to gulp down some tea. In doing so, she lost her turn to Xiu-yan:

XIU-YAN:
An old owl wakes the vale with mournful cries.
The driving flakes make angles disappear –

Xiang-yun put down her teacup in a hurry, before more ground could be lost:

XIANG-YUN:
  But dimples on the water's face incise.
  In the clear morn how radiant gleams the snow! —

Dai-yu followed:

DAI-YU:
  How ghostly, as the too short daylight dies!
  Its cold the Chengs' disciples could withstand —

Xiang-yun laughed excitedly as she hurried to complete the couplet:

XIANG-YUN:
  Its promise can a king's cares exorcise.
  Who'd lie abed all stiff with cold indoors —

Bao-qin laughed, too, as she followed:

BAO-QIN:
  When friends invite to red-cheeked exercize?
  Who o'er the land the merfolk's silk unrolls? —

Xiang-yun quickly capped this:

XIANG-YUN:
  Who the white weft from Heaven's loom unties?

But before she could begin another couplet, Dai-yu slipped in a line of her own:

DAI-YU:
  Tall tiled pavilions cold and empty stand —

Xiang-yun capped it:

XIANG-YUN:
  Snug thatch more favour finds in poor men's eyes.

Bao-qin, concluding that this was now a free-for-all, cut in with the next half-couplet:

BAO-QIN:
  Ice lumps we thaw and boil to make our tea —

Xiang-yun, having evidently thought of something amusing, began to giggle:

XIANG-YUN:
  The fuel being damp, they greatly tantalize.

Dai-yu began to giggle too:

DAI-YU:
  The Zen recluse with non-broom sweeps the ground –

The infection of giggles had now reached Bao-qin:

BAO-QIN:
  His stringless lute-play still more mystifies.

Xiang-yun was by now so doubled up with laughter that
the others could not make out the words of her next line.
'*What?*' they asked her. '*What* was that you said?'
Xiang-yun had to repeat it:

XIANG-YUN:
  On the stone tower a stork unwatchful sleeps –

Dai-yu was laughing so much that she had to clutch pain-
fully at her chest and the words she recited came out in a
laughing shout:

DAI-YU:
  On the warm mat a cat contented sighs.

All the lines that followed were uttered in rapid succession
and to the accompaniment of much laughter.

BAO-QIN:
  In moonlit caves the silvery water laps –
XIANG-YUN:
  And red flags flutter against sunset skies.
DAI-YU:
  Soaked winter plums make the breath fresh and sweet –

'That's a good line,' said Bao-chai. She capped it herself:

BAO-CHAI:
  And melted snow the wine-fumes neutralize.
BAO-QIN:
  The stiffened aigrette gradually thaws –
XIANG-YUN:
  The snow-soaked silken girdle slowly dries.

DAI-YU:
The wind has dropped, but snow still wetly falls –

Bao-qin capped this, laughing:

BAO-QIN:
And frequent drips the passer-by baptize.

Xiang-yun had collapsed, weak with laughing, upon Bao-chai's shoulder. The others had long since given up trying to participate and become mere laughing spectators of the three-cornered contest between Xiang-yun, Dai-yu and Bao-qin. Dai-yu urged Xiang-yun to go on.

'Don't tell me you've run out of inspiration! Surely your famous gift of the gab is still good for a few more lines?'

Bao-chai prodded Xiang-yun, who was now laughing helplessly upon her lap.

'See if you can exhaust the rhyme, Yun. If you can do that, I shall be *really* impressed.'

'This isn't verse-making,' said Xiang-yun, raising her head from Bao-chai's lap, 'it's more like a duel to the death!'

'Well, whose fault is that?' they asked her, laughing.

Tan-chun, having decided that she would be unlikely to make any further contributions herself, had some time before this taken over the task of amanuensis from Bao-chai. She now pointed out that the poem needed finishing off. Li Wan, who had just arrived back, took the paper from her and embarked on a suitable finishing couplet:

LI WAN:
Our verses shall this happy day record –

Her cousin Li Qi completed it:

LI QI:
And a wise Emperor loyally eulogize.

'Now that's enough,' said Li Wan. 'We still haven't exhausted the rhyme, but if we go on any longer, we shall be tying ourselves up in knots trying to use words that aren't really suitable.'

They now went over the whole poem from beginning to end and discussed it all in detail. It appeared that Xiang-yun had contributed far more lines than anyone else. The others laughed.

'It's because of all that venison you ate!'

'If we consider quality rather than quantity,' said Li Wan, 'I think all the contributions are of about equal merit. Except Bao-yu's, of course. *He* goes to the bottom of the list, as usual.'

'I can't do Linked Verses, anyway,' said Bao-yu. 'You have to make allowances for me.'

'That's all very well,' said Li Wan, smiling, 'but we can't make allowances for you at every single meeting. One time you're in trouble because we have fixed rhymes, another time you fail to turn up altogether, and this time you tell us you "can't do Linked Verses". I think this time there really has to be a penalty. I noticed just now that the red plum in Green Bower Hermitage is very fine. I'd like to have broken off a branch to put in a vase, but I find Adamantina such a difficult person that I prefer not to have anything to do with her. The first part of your punishment shall be to get us a branch of that red plum and put it in a vase here where all of us can admire it.'

'What a delightful penalty!' said the others. 'How civilized!'

Bao-yu, too, was delighted with the penalty, but just as he was setting off to perform it, Xiang-yun and Dai-yu simultaneously rose to their feet and detained him.

'It's very, very cold outside. Have a cup of hot wine before you go.'

Xiang-yun already had the wine-kettle in her hand. Dai-yu found an extra large cup for her to pour the wine in.

'There!' said Xiang-yun, filling it up to the brim. 'If you come back empty-handed now, after drinking our wine, we shall double the rest of your penalty when you get back!'

Bao-yu quickly drank down the proffered cup of freshly heated wine and walked out into the snow. Li Wan wanted to send a servant out after him, but Dai-yu intervened.

'I wouldn't, if I were you. If he has anyone else with him, he won't be able to get any.'

Knowing Adamantina, Li Wan reflected that this was probably true and nodded. She sent the maids to fetch a large *mei-
ping* vase with wide shoulders and a very narrow neck to put
the plum-blossom in when it arrived.

'When he comes back, we must compose some red plum
poems,' she said.

'I can do one now,' said Bao-qin.

'*Oh* no!' said Bao-chai. 'We're not letting *you* do any more.
You've already hogged enough turns for today. It's no fun for
the others if they are left with nothing to do. No, it's Bao-yu's
penalty we've got to think about. He said just now that he
can't do Linked Verses. When he comes back we ought to
make him do some other kind of verses for us by himself.'

'Good idea!' said Dai-yu. 'And I've got another idea.
Several people didn't get sufficient opportunity in the Linked
Verses of showing what they can do. I propose that those who
contributed least in the Linked Verses should be given the red
plum poems to do.'

'Yes, I agree,' said Bao-chai. 'Cousin Xing, Cousin Wen
and Cousin Qi were practically crowded out altogether – and
they are, after all, our guests. Qin and Yun and you, Frowner,
hogged nearly all the turns. This time the rest of us ought to
keep out of it and let Cousin Xing and Cousin Wen and
Cousin Qi have the floor to themselves.'

'Qi isn't very good at making verses,' said Li Wan. 'I think
you'd better give *her* place to your cousin Bao-qin.'

This was scarcely what Bao-chai had intended, but she felt
herself in no position to dissent.

'Why don't we use the words "red plum flower" as
rhymes?' she suggested. 'Each of the three can do an octet on
"Red Plum Flower", but Cousin Xing can use "red" for her
rhyme, Cousin Wen can use "plum" for hers, and Qin can use
"flower".'

'We seem to be letting off Bao-yu,' said Li Wan. 'I can't
agree to that.'

'Give him a separate theme,' Xiang-yun suggested.

'What theme shall we give him?' the others asked.

'What about "On Visiting the Nun Adamantina with a

Request for Red Plum Blossom"?' said Xiang-yun. 'That might be interesting.'

'Oh *yes*!' said the others. 'That would do splendidly.'

At that very moment the object of their discussion walked in, smiling triumphantly, with a flowering plum-branch in his hand. The maids at once relieved him of it and put it in the waiting vase, while the cousins crowded round them to admire it.

'I hope you enjoy it, all of you,' said Bao-yu. 'It took me enough trouble to get!'

Tan-chun handed him a cup of hot wine to revive him; but first the maids removed his cape and rain-hat and shook the snow off them.

Maids from several different apartments now began arriving with extra clothing for their mistresses. Bao-yu's Aroma sent him an old surtout lined with fox's belly-fur. Li Wan made the servants fill three dishes, one with extra large steamed taros, the other two with blood-oranges, yellow Canton oranges and olives, to take back to her.

Xiang-yun now told Bao-yu the title of the poem they wanted him to compose and urged him to begin thinking about it.

'I will,' said Bao-yu; 'but there's just one thing I would ask of you all: please let me use my own rhymes; *please* don't make me do it to set rhymes.'

'All right,' said the girls. 'Use whatever rhymes you like.'

They had been admiring the plum-blossom meanwhile. The vertical part of the branch – the part, that is, which was stuck into the neck of the vase – must have been less than two feet high; but growing at right-angles from the top of it was a side branch which rose and fell in a spreading cascade of blossom all of four feet long. Of the branchlets forming this flowery cascade

> some were like writhing serpents,
> some were like frozen worms;
> some were as straight and smooth as a writing-brush,
> some were as densely twigged as a tiny coppice.

As for the blossoms, they had

> A colour like the rosy lips of love
> And scent that made summer's scents seem uninviting.

While the others were studying the blossoming branch and praising its beauties, Xing Xiu-yan, Li Wen and Bao-qin were busy composing their poems about it and presently began writing them out for the others to inspect.

This is what the others were now able to read:

On a Branch of Red Plum Flower

I

Rhyming 'red'   By Xing Xiu-yan

> So brave, so gay they bloom in winter's cold,
> Before the fragrant peach and almond red;
> Like rosy clouds that clothe the springtime slopes
> Of Yu-ling, where my dream-soul oft has sped.
> Each little lamp in its green calyx lies
> Like drunken snow-sprite on a rainbow bed.
> Yet do these flowers, of hue so rich and rare,
> Reckless, in ice and snow their charms outspread.

II

Rhyming 'plum'   By Li Wen

> What richness blooms before my drunken eyes?
> 'Tis not the white I sing, but the red plum.
> See, its pale cheeks are streaked with blood-red tears,
> Even though its bitter heart with cold is numb.
> No flower this, but a fairy maid transformed
> And here transplanted from Elysium!
> In this bleak North it makes such brave display,
> I'll tell the bees that spring's already come.

III

Rhyming 'flower'   By Xue Bao-qin

> Like spendthrift youths in spring's new fashions dressed,
> Its bare thin branches burst in glorious flower.
> Snow no more falls, but a bright rosy cloud
> Tints hills and streams in one long sunset hour.

Through this red flood my dream-boat makes its way,
While flutes sound chill from many a maiden's bower.
Sure from no earthly stock this beauty came,
But trees immortal round the Fairy Tower.

They read these poems with smiles of pleasure. There were words of praise for all three of them; but Bao-qin's, they finally agreed, was the best of the three. Bao-yu, realizing that she was the youngest present, was greatly impressed. Dai-yu and Xiang-yun between them poured out a tiny cupful of wine and offered it to her in celebration of her victory.

'All three were *equally* good,' said Bao-chai deprecatingly. 'It was you two who in the past were always fooling *me* that *my* poems were the best. Now, it appears, you've found someone else to fool.'

'What about *you*?' Li Wan asked Bao-yu. 'Is *yours* ready yet?'

'I *did* have one ready,' said Bao-yu, 'but these three are so much better that reading them has made me nervous and put it completely out of my mind. You'll have to give me a bit longer while I think up another.'

Xiang-yun picked up one of a pair of large bronze chopsticks used as tongs for feeding the stove with and beat a preliminary tattoo with it on her metal hand-warmer.

'I'll drum for you,' she said. 'If you can't produce something each time the drumming stops, we'll double your penalty.'

'I think I've got something,' said Bao-yu.

Dai-yu picked up a writing-brush.

'I'll write it down for you while you recite it,' she said.

Xiang-yun struck up a tattoo.

'Right!' she said presently, as she stopped her drumming. 'End of first round.'

'Yes, I've got something,' said Bao-yu. 'Get ready to write.'

'Wine not yet broached nor verses yet composed – '

Dai-yu wrote down the words, shaking her head as she did so.

'That's a *very* indifferent beginning.'

'Come on!' said Xiang-yun. 'Hurry!'
Bao-yu continued:

'In quest of spring I sped to Elysium –

Dai-yu and Xiang-yun nodded.
'Hmn. Not bad.'
Bao-yu went on:

''Twas not the balm from Guanyin's vase I craved
Across that threshold, but her flowering plum – '

Dai-yu shook her head again as she wrote this down.
'That's a bit contrived, isn't it?'
Xiang-yun began another tattoo on the hand-warmer. When she finished, Bao-yu continued at once:

'A frozen worldling, for red flowers I begged;
The saint cut fragrant clouds and gave me some.
Pity my verse so angular and thin,
For convent snow has soaked it to the skin!'

As soon as Dai-yu had finished writing this down, Xiang-yun and the rest began a critical discussion of the whole poem. They were still in the midst of this when a little maid dashed in to announce that Grandmother Jia was approaching. Bao-yu and the girls hurried out, laughing and chattering, to welcome her.

'She must be feeling in good spirits,' they said, 'to come out in the snow like this.'

Grandmother Jia was still quite a way off when they saw her. She was sitting in a little bamboo carrying-chair and holding a green silk umbrella over herself. A large cape and squirrel-lined hood almost completely enveloped her. Faithful, Amber and three or four other maids, all carrying their own umbrellas, formed a little escort around the chair and its bearers. Li Wan and the others would have gone out into the snow to meet her, but Grandmother Jia called out to them to stay where they were.

'Wait there under cover. I'll come over to *you*.'

'I've given Feng and your Aunt Wang the slip,' she told

them, chuckling mischievously, when the chair had reached
them and they were helping her out of it. 'It's all right for *me*,
going out in all this snow, because I'm sitting in *this* thing; but
I didn't want them trudging along in the snow beside me, getting cold and miserable.'

Some of them relieved her of her snow-clothes while others
supported her on either side and conducted her into the room
where the heated kang was.

'What pretty plum-blossom!' she said as they entered it.
'You children certainly know how to enjoy yourselves. I feel
quite angry with you for not inviting me!'

Li Wan made the servants bring in a big wolfskin rug and
spread it out in the middle of the kang for Grandmother Jia
to sit on.

'Now you just all go on enjoying yourselves exactly as you
were before I came,' said the old lady when she had settled
herself on the rug. 'I daren't sleep after lunch at this time of
year, because the days are so short. I had a little game of
dominoes instead; then I started wondering what *you* were all
up to and thought I would come over and join you.'

Li Wan handed her a hand-warmer while Tan-chun fetched
a winecup and a pair of chopsticks, poured out a cup of warm
wine, and offered it to her with both her hands. Grandmother
Jia accepted it from her and sipped the wine.

'What have you got in that dish over there?' she asked
them.

'Pickled quails,' said one of the cousins, bringing the dish
over for her inspection.

'That will do very nicely,' said Grandmother Jia. 'Tear off
a little leg for me, will you?'

Li Wan called for water, and having first washed her hands,
performed the operation for her in person.

'Now I want you all to sit down again and go on talking,'
said Grandmother Jia. 'It does me good to hear you. – You
too,' she said to Li Wan. 'You're to sit down as well. I want
you to behave exactly as if I hadn't come. Otherwise I shall go
away again.'

At this the others resumed their former places – all except

Li Wan, who took the lowest place, farthest away from Grandmother Jia.

'What have you been doing to amuse yourselves?' the old lady asked them.

'We were making up poems,' they said.

'You ought to make up some lantern riddles,' said Grandmother Jia, 'then you'll be ready for the Lantern Festival when it comes.'

The others agreed to change over to riddle-making. For a while there was general conversation interspersed with jokes and laughter; but the old lady quickly became restless.

'This is rather a damp place here, isn't it?' she said. 'You don't want to sit here too long or you'll be catching colds. I think Xi-chun's room is warmer than this. Why don't we go and see how she's getting on with the painting – see if she'll be able to finish it in time for New Year?'

'New Year?' said the others, laughing. 'You'll be lucky if she finishes it by midsummer!'

'Good gracious, that won't do!' said Grandmother Jia. 'She's taking longer to paint this Garden than the workmen took to build it!'

Soon she was enthroned once more in the bamboo carrying-chair and the others tramped after her through the snow on their way to Lotus Pavilion. Passing by the pavilion itself, they entered an alley-way which had roofed gateways at either end. These had inscribed stone slabs built into them underneath the eaves on both the inward-facing and outward-facing sides. The gateway at the western end of the alley-way, which was the one they were entering, had

THROUGH THE CLOUDS

inscribed on its outer face and

ACROSS THE MOON

on its inner one. Half-way along the left-hand side of the alley-way they came to the main entrance to the courtyard of Xichun's Spring In Winter room, which was both her living-quarters and the place where she worked on the painting. The bearers turned into this and put the chair down just inside it for Grandmother Jia to get out. Xi-chun was already waiting there to welcome her and conducted them all through the covered way which ran round the sides of the courtyard from the gateway to her living quarters at the back. A framed board hanging underneath the eaves announced the name of the building:

SPRING IN WINTER.

Servants held up the red felt portière for them as they approached its doorway. They could feel the hot air fanning their cheeks as they entered it.

Grandmother Jia tackled Xi-chun as soon as they were inside, not even waiting to sit down.

'What's happened to the painting?'

'The glue gets tacky in this cold weather,' said Xi-chun. 'It stops the paint from going on properly. I've put the painting away because I was afraid it might get spoiled.'

Grandmother Jia brushed aside this excuse with a dismissive laugh.

'I want that painting ready by the end of the year. Don't be so lazy! Fetch it out at once and get on with it, my girl!'

Just then a smiling Xi-feng made her appearance. A purplish woollen gabardine was thrown loosely over her shoulders.

'You've led me a fine dance,' she grumbled, 'sneaking off on your own like this!'

The old lady was delighted to see her.

'I didn't want you all catching colds; that's why I told them not to let you know I was going out. I suppose I ought to have realized that that sharp little nose of yours would soon ferret me out again. You mustn't think you are being dutiful in tracking me down like this.'

'Being dutiful!' said Xi-feng. 'That's not at all the reason why I came out to look for you. Just now when I went round to your apartment I found it all deathly quiet, and it was quite clear from the maids' answers, when I tried to find out where you had gone, that they didn't want me to go into the Garden to look for you. That aroused my suspicions; and when a

moment later a couple of nuns appeared on the scene, my
suspicions were confirmed: I realized that they must have
come to make their annual collection for some charity or other
and that my dear, saintly Grannie, who no doubt has rather a
lot of subscriptions to pay out at this time of year, had gone
into hiding to avoid them. I asked the nuns, and sure enough
it was for your annual subscription that they had come. I paid
it for you myself. So now your creditors have gone, you can
come out of hiding. You ought to be getting back now in any
case. You've got some nice, tender pheasant for dinner and if
you leave it much longer it will spoil.'

All this was spoken, of course, to the accompaniment of
much laughter from the others. Before Grandmother Jia could
say anything in reply, Xi-feng had ordered the bearers to bring
up the bamboo carrying-chair and Grandmother Jia, in
laughing acquiescence, took Xi-feng's hand, got back into it,
and was at once lifted up and whisked away by the bearers.
The others followed after, chattering and laughing as they
went.

As they emerged from the east end of the alley-way into the
silvery snowscape of the Garden, they could see Bao-qin,
identifiable by the glossy green mallard-cape, standing a long
way off behind the shoulder of a little hill, waiting for the rest
of them to arrive. A maid, hugging a large vase with a
branch of red plum in it, was standing behind her.

'So *there* she is!' said the others. 'We *thought* there seemed
to be two of us missing. And she's got herself some plum-
blossom, as well.'

Grandmother Jia smiled proprietorially at the distant
figure.

'What does that remind you all of, seeing her there on that
snowy bank, wearing a cape like that and with the spray of
plum-blossom behind her?'

'Why,' they said, 'it's like that painting by Qiu Ying you
have hanging in your room: "The Beauty of the Snow".'

Grandmother Jia shook her head.

'No, the girl in that picture isn't wearing a cape like that –
and she isn't half as pretty as Qin, either.'

Just at that moment a third figure, previously invisible, stepped out from behind Bao-qin's back. Whoever it was was wearing a red felt snow-cape.

'Which of the girls is that?' said Grandmother Jia.

'There aren't any more girls; we're all here,' said the others laughing. 'That's Bao-yu.'

'My eyes are getting worse and worse,' said Grandmother Jia. Soon they had caught up with the three figures on the hill and she could see that it was indeed Bao-yu whom she had failed to recognize with Bao-qin and the maid.

'I've been over to Green Bower Hermitage again,' Bao-yu told the girls. 'Adamantina ended up by giving me a branch of plum-blossom for each of you. I've just been arranging to have them delivered to your rooms.'

The others thanked him for his kindness.

Talking as they went, they presently passed through the gate of the Garden and accompanied Grandmother Jia back to her apartment. After dinner, while they were still sitting there in conversation, Aunt Xue arrived.

'*What* a heavy fall of snow!' she said. 'I haven't been able to come over and see you all day long. You ought to go out and have a look at it, Lady Jia, if you are feeling low. It would do you good.'

'Who said I was feeling low?' said Grandmother Jia with some amusement. 'I've only just got back from visiting the children. I've been having a fine old time!'

'Oh?' said Aunt Xue. 'Yesterday evening I was intending to ask if my sister and I could have the use of the Garden today so that we might arrange a little snow-viewing party for you, but you'd already gone to bed, and Bao-chai said that you were feeling out of sorts, so I thought I'd better not bother you. If I'd known differently, I'd have come round this morning and invited you.'

'We're only just into the eleventh month,' said Grandmother Jia. 'There'll be plenty more snow yet and plenty more opportunities for taking advantage of your kind offer.'

'I do hope so,' said Aunt Xue. 'It's something I should very much like to do for you.'

'Isn't there a danger you might forget, Aunt?' said Xi-feng. 'Why not weigh out fifty taels now and leave them with me? Then next time it snows, I can get it all ready *for* you. That would save you the trouble of arranging it yourself and also avoid the danger of your forgetting.'

'In that case you and I might just as well split the money between us,' said Grandmother Jia. 'Next time it snows, all I have to do is say that I'm feeling out of sorts, and you won't have to do anything at all. That way Mrs Xue will have even less trouble, while you and I will each of us have twenty-five taels clear profit.'

Xi-feng clapped her hands delightedly.

'What a wonderful idea! Why didn't I think of it myself?'

The others laughed.

'Shameless hussy!' said Grandmother Jia, laughing with the rest. 'You're like the monkey on the pole: give you an inch and you take an ell. What you *ought* to have said is: "No, Aunt, you are our guest. Since you honour us by staying in our house, it is *we* who should be inviting *you*. We can't allow *you* to go spending money on *us*." That's what you ough to have said; not asked your poor aunt for fifty taels. Whoever heard of such a thing!'

'She's a canny old lady, this Grandma of ours,' Xi-feng explained to Aunt Xue. 'She watches you first to see if you'll weaken or not. If you'd weakened and coughed up the fifty taels, she'd have been quite willing to go halves with me and pocket twenty-five of them herself; but having gauged that you probably won't, she adopts a holier-than-thou attitude and makes an example of *me*, even though she was the one who suggested it. All right, all right. I'll pay for the whole party myself, and when Grandma arrives, I'll have fifty taels out of my own savings wrapped up all ready to give her as a present. That shall be my punishment for having opened my big mouth and occupied myself with other people's affairs.'

Bao-yu and the girls were by this time rolling about on the kang.

Presently, when the conversation got round to what a beautiful picture Bao-qin had made standing in the snow with the spray of plum-blossom behind her, Grandmother Jia began inquiring about her parentage and the exact day and hour of her birth. Aunt Xue guessed that she was considering her as a possible match for Bao-yu. She would have been glad enough to go along with this had not Bao-qin already been promised to the Meis; however, since Grandmother Jia had not asked her outright, she could do no more than hint at a prior attachment.

'She's been very unlucky, poor child. The year before last her father died quite suddenly. She used to go with him everywhere on his travels, so she has seen a great deal of the world for one so young. Her father was a great one for combining business with pleasure. He always took the family with him when he went away on business. They would spend perhaps a whole year in one province, seeing all the sights; then the next six months they might spend travelling around in another. At one time and another they must have covered well over half the provinces of the Empire in that way. While he was on one of his trips to the capital, he promised her to Academician Mei's boy, but unfortunately it was in the year after that that he died, so nothing could be done about it. And now her poor mother has gone down with a consumption . . .'

Xi-feng interrupted, sighing and stamping her foot in an exaggerated display of disappointment.

'Oh, what a *shame*! I was just going to offer my services as a match-maker, but it seems that she's already betrothed.'

'Who did you have in mind?' Grandmother Jia asked her.

'Never you mind!' said Xi-feng. 'I'm sure they would have made a very good pair; but since she's already got someone else, there doesn't seem any point in discussing it.'

Grandmother Jia knew very well whom Xi-feng had in mind, but hearing that Bao-qin was already spoken for, she dropped the subject and made no further mention of it.

The company talked for a while longer before breaking up; but of the rest of that day and the night which followed our narrative supplies no account.

*

Next day the snow had cleared. After lunch Grandmother Jia told Xi-chun that, cold or no cold, she must get on with the painting as quickly as possible.

'If you *really* can't get it finished by the end of the year,' she said, 'it doesn't matter. But what you *must* do is get Bao-qin with the maid and the branch of plum-blossom into it. I want you to do that straight away; and they are to be painted exactly as they looked when we saw them on that bank yesterday.'

Xi-chun said that she would, though miserably aware that she would find doing so extremely difficult. Later, when the others went round to her place to see how she was getting on, she was pondering gloomily over this latest problem. Li Wan somewhat heartlessly proposed that they should leave her to her own thoughts and carry on their conversation without her.

'When we got back from Grandmother's last night,' she said, 'Qi and Wen and I were unable to get to sleep, so we lay in bed making up riddles. I made up two using quotations from the *Four Books* and the other two each made up one.'

'Ah yes, that's what we *all* ought to be doing,' said the others. 'Tell us your four first and we'll try to guess the answers.'

'Guan-yin lacks a biography,' said Li Wan. 'The answer is a phrase from the *Four Books*.'

'Resting in the highest good,'

Xiang-yun promptly suggested.

'What's that got to do with "biography"?' said Bao-chai.

'Try again,' said Li Wan.

'I know,' said Dai-yu. 'Isn't it

... though good, yet having no memorial?'

'Ah yes, that must be it,' said the others.

'What is the green plant that grows in the water?' said Li Wan.

'That just *has* to be

'It is a fast-growing rush,'

said Xiang-yun. 'I don't see how that *could* be wrong.'

'Good for you!' said Li Wan. 'Now here is Wen's riddle:

Beside the rocks the water runs cold.

It's the name of an historical person.'

'That must be "Shan Tao",' said Tan-chun. 'His surname means "mountain" – that's the "rocks" – and "Tao" means "billows".'

'Right,' said Li Wan. 'Now Qi's riddle is just a single word:

Firefly

The answer is a single word, too.'

They all puzzled for a long time over this without being able to think of any answer. It was Bao-qin who finally came up with the solution.

'Yes, I see. It's rather involved. The answer is "flower" isn't it? – I mean the flower that grows.'

Li Qi acknowledged smilingly that this was correct.

'What has "flower" got to do with "firefly"?' the others asked her.

Bao-qin explained:

'In the Record of Rites it says

Corrupt grass by transmutation breedeth fireflies.

Now the character for "flower" is written with "grass" at the top and "change" – or, if you like, "transmutation" – underneath. So "corrupt grass by transmutation" – which, according to the Rites, produces fireflies – makes the character for "flower".'

The others laughingly acknowledged that the riddle was an ingenious one.

'All four of these riddles are very good,' said Bao-chai, 'but I don't think they are quite the sort of thing that Lady Jia had in mind. I think we ought to make up some about fairly easy, everyday objects, so that those of us who aren't quite so learned can enjoy them as well.'

Xiang-yun thought for a bit.

'I've got one,' she said presently. 'It's in the form of a "Ruby Lips" stanza:

'Far away
From the high fell
Where I used to dwell
Amidst men I play.
But for what gain?
My labour's vain;
My tale is hard to tell.'

No one was able to make out what this could be. After puzzling for a long time, they produced a number of different guesses. Someone thought it was 'a monk'; someone else thought it was 'a Taoist'; a third person suggested that it might be 'a marionette player'.

'You're all wrong,' said Bao-yu, who had been grinning silently to himself while the others guessed. 'I've thought of the answer. It's "a performing monkey".'

'That's it,' said Xiang-yun.

'We can understand the first part all right,' said the others; 'but what about the last line? What's that supposed to mean?'

'Have you ever seen a performing monkey that hadn't had its tail docked?' said Xiang-yun.

Groans and laughter.

'Trust Yun's to have a frightful pun in it – as if the riddle wasn't hard enough already!'

'Mrs Xue was telling us yesterday that you've travelled a lot and been to all sorts of interesting places,' Li Wan said to Bao-qin. 'With so much material you ought to be just the person for making up riddles – especially as you're so good at verse-making as well. Why don't *you* make up a few, and the rest of us will try to guess them?'

Bao-qin said nothing, but smiled and nodded, and at once went off into a corner to think.

Bao-chai had now composed a riddle, too, and recited it for them to try and guess while Bao-qin was doing her thinking.

'Tier upon compact tier of fragrant wood:
No craftsman's hand could carve one half so well.
A gale blows all about the temple's eaves,
Yet, though it shakes, no sound comes from my bell.'[1]

1. See Appendix III, p. 588.

While the others were still trying to guess the answer to this, Bao-yu recited one that he had just completed himself:

> ''Twixt heaven and earth amidst the clouds so high
> Bamboo gives warning to the passer-by.
> Eyes strain some feathered traveller to descry
> Who'll bear my answer back into the sky.'

Dai-yu also had one ready, and proceeded to recite it to them:

> 'See my little prancing steed!
> Of silken rein he has no need.
> Round the city wall he goes,
> Wreaking havoc on his foes.
> At his master's touch he moves
> With thunder of advancing hooves.
> In isles by tortoises supported
> His deeds are honourably reported.'

Tan-chun, too had composed a riddle, but as she was on the point of reciting it, Bao-qin came back from her corner to announce that she had finished.

'I've been visiting places of historical interest ever since I was little,' she said, 'so I really have seen quite a lot. What I've done now is to choose ten of them, mostly associated with some famous person or other, and make up a poem about each one. The verses themselves may sound rather like doggerel, but the point about them is that, as well as commemorating these famous places and people, each of them contains hidden references to some common object which you have to guess.'

'Ah, that sounds *very* ingenious!' they said. 'But why not write them down, so that we can take our time thinking about them?'

What happened next will be related in the following chapter.

CHAPTER 51

A clever cousin composes some ingenious riddles
And an unskilful physician prescribes a barbarous remedy

WHEN Bao-qin explained that the riddles she had composed
were in the form of quatrains, each containing a clue to some
well-known object, about famous places she had visited in the
course of her travels, the cousins were greatly impressed, and
waited with eagerness for her to copy them out. This is what
they read when she had finished doing so[1]:

Red Cliff

The river at Red Cliff was choked with the dead,
And the ships without crew carried naught but their names.
A clamour and shouting, a wind took the blaze,
And a host of brave souls rode aloft in the flames.

*

Hanoi

His column of brass bade the nations obey:
The noise of him spread through barbarian parts.
Brave Ma Yuan to conquest and empire was born:
He needed no Iron Flute to teach him those arts.

*

Mt Zhong-shan

Though ambition had never been part of your nature
And the call from retirement was none of your choosing,
You danced in the end at another's commandment,
So you can't be surprised if we find it amusing.

*

Huai-yin

The brave must beware of the vicious dog's bite:
The gift of a throne on your fate set the seal.

1. See Appendix III, p. 588.

Let us learn from your story the humble to prize,
And due gratitude show for the gift of a meal.

*

Guang-ling

Your crows and cicadas no more you shall hear
By the old Sui embankment back home in the South;
But the scandalous story of those wanton times
Wags in many an idle, unsavoury mouth.

*

Peach Leaf Ford

In the waters a scene of decay is reflected;
Long since from its bough did the last peach-leaf fall.
Your old Southern mansion has tumbled in ruins,
And only your likeness looks down from the wall.

*

Green Mound

The Amur's black flood for pure grief is arrested;
The frozen string twangs with a heartbroken sound;
And, deploring the harsh rule that ordered this exile,
A few crooked trees bow in shame to the ground.

*

Ma-wei

The sad, ravaged face seemed to shine in its sweat;
Then soon that sweet softness all vanished away.
Yet something remained, for the well-known perfume
In the clothing she wore lingers on to this day.

*

The Monastery at Pu-dong

Young Reddie was ever a light, empty creature,
Always to-ing and fro-ing in all kinds of weather.
Though her Mistress in ire hung her up from the ceiling,
Those two had already been walking together.

*

The Plum-tree Shrine

'Twill be by the willow and not by the plum.'
But who is it there will her likeness discover?
Let not her full moon make you think that Spring's coming,
For the cold parts her now till next year from her lover.

After reading these poems, the cousins all praised the remarkable ingenuity with which they had been constructed.
Only Bao-chai was critical.

'The first eight of these poems have historically verifiable
subjects, but what about the last two? I'm afraid I don't quite
understand what they are about. I think you ought to make up
another two to replace them with.'

'Don't be so stuffy, Chai!' said Dai-yu. 'Talk about "gluing
the bridges of the zither"! It's true that the subjects of those
last two poems can't be found in the history books, but how
can you say that you don't know what they are? Even if, as
well-bred young ladies, we may not read the books in which
they *are* to be found, we've all watched plenty of plays. Every
three-year-old child is familiar with these stories. It's sheer
hypocrisy to pretend that you've never heard of them.'

'Hear, hear!' said Tan-chun.

'In any case,' said Li Wan, 'she *has* actually been to the
places associated with the stories, even if the stories themselves are unhistorical. Stories pick up all kinds of circum-
stantial detail in the course of centuries of re-telling. Sooner or
later some know-all invariably equips them with a location in
order to fool more people into believing them. I remember on
my journey here when I first came up to the capital we visited
three or four different sites all claiming to be the burial-place
of Guan Yu. Now no one doubts that Guan Yu actually
existed or that he actually did the heroic things he is supposed
to have done; but he can't have been buried in more than one
grave. Obviously the tradition that he was buried in those
places was invented by people living long after Guan Yu's
death who loved and admired Guan Yu and all that he had
stood for and wanted to claim him for themselves. And if you
look in the *Geographical Gazetteer*, you'll find that it isn't only

Guan Yu who has graves in several different places: practically all the famous men who ever lived appear to have been buried in more than one place. And when it comes to sites which are famous because of people who never even existed, they are still more numerous. It may well be that the people those last two poems are about didn't exist; but though the stories about them are unhistorical, they are certainly well-known. You can hear them told by story-tellers; you can see them acted on the stage; you can even find references to them on the divination-sticks that people tell their fortunes with in temples. There can't be a man, woman or child who isn't familiar with them. And even if one knows them from the *books*, it can hardly be said that to have read a few lyrics from *The Western Chamber* or *The Soul's Return* is tantamount to reading pornography. No, I see no harm in these two poems. I think she should leave them as they are.'

This, coming from Li Wan, effectively silenced Bao-chai's objection.

Some time was now spent in trying to guess answers to the riddles concealed in these poems, but all of their guesses were wrong.

The days in winter are very short and in no time at all, it seemed, they were trooping back into the mansion for their dinner. While they were there, a message arrived for Lady Wang to say that Aroma's brother, Hua Zi-fang, had come and was waiting outside in the front.

'His mother is seriously ill and has been asking to see Aroma,' said the messenger. 'He asks if, as a special kindness, you will allow her to go home and see her.'

'We shouldn't dream of preventing a mother from seeing her daughter under such circumstances,' said Lady Wang. 'Of course she may go.'

She called for Xi-feng and, having explained the situation to her, left it to her to decide what arrangements should be made for Aroma's departure. Xi-feng promised to attend to the matter and hurried back to her own apartment to do so. She told Zhou Rui's wife to break the news to Aroma about her mother. She also gave detailed instructions for the visit.

'Get hold of another of the women in your group to go
with you as second chaperone. And take two of the junior
maids with you as well. And you'll want four of the grooms
from the front. Take responsible ones: not too young. Tell
them you'll need two carriages, one large and one small. You
two can sit in the larger one with Aroma, and the two maids
can go in the smaller one.'

Zhou Rui's wife was on the point of going off to execute
these orders, but Xi-feng had evidently not finished.

'Aroma's a girl who doesn't like fuss. You'd better tell her
that it's my wish that she should dress herself up in the very
best things she's got. Tell her to take a good big bundle of
extra clothes with her as well. The cloth it's wrapped in is to
be of the highest quality. Her hand-warmer is to be a good
one, too. And tell her that before she goes I want her to come
here so that I can have a look at her.'

Zhou Rui's wife went off to do her bidding. In due course
Aroma herself arrived, dressed up in all her finery. She was
accompanied by Zhou Rui's wife and the other woman and by
two little maids, one carrying her bundle and the other one her
hand-warmer. Xi-feng proceeded at once to inspect her, beginning at the top. Aroma's hair, liberally studded with pearled
and golden jewellery, was satisfactory; her clothing, it seemed,
less so. She had on an ermine-lined silk tapestry dress of
peach-pink satin, sprigged with a pattern of different sorts of
flowers, a leek-green padded skirt embroidered in couched
gold thread and coloured silks, and a black satin jacket lined
with squirrel.

'I see. These are all things that Her Ladyship gave you.
That's good. But the jacket is too plain. And it's not warm
enough for the time of year, either. You want something with
a heavier fur in it.'

'This is the only one she gave me,' said Aroma, 'and the
only other one I've got is lined with ermine. She promised me
one with a heavier fur in time for the New Year, but I haven't
been given it yet.'

'*I've* got one with a heavier fur which I haven't worn because the trimmings don't suit me,' said Xi-feng. 'I'd been

meaning to get it altered, but I could let you have it now if you like and you can give it back to me to have altered when Her Ladyship gets this other one made that she's promised you. We'll call it a loan.'

The servants laughed.

'You like to have your little joke, Mrs Lian. All the year round you're handing things out on the quiet that Her Ladyship has overlooked, yet you never ask her for anything back for them. Why so stingy all of a sudden about a little old jacket?'

'Her Ladyship can't be expected to remember *everything*,' said Xi-feng, 'and these are, after all, rather trifling matters. Of course, *someone* has to think about them, for the sake of appearances. Even if it leaves me a bit out of pocket, I've got to see that everyone is dressed decently. If that gets me a reputation for being generous – well, that's just one of the hardships I must learn to put up with! It would be much worse to have everyone going around looking like tramps. Think of the jokes I should hear about my housekeeping *then*!'

'There can't be many like you, Mrs Lian,' said the women admiringly, 'so considerate towards Her Ladyship and yet at the same time so thoughtful towards us servants. You really do think of everything.'

While they were praising her, Xi-feng was already ordering Patience to fetch the jacket she had mentioned. It had in fact arrived from the tailor's only a day or two previously. It was a very grand one, in slate-blue satin, with eight large, embroidery-like silk tapestry roundels woven into it, and with a lining of arctic fox. After giving Aroma the jacket, Xi-feng inspected her bundle. The carrying-cloth was of silk gauze in a nondescript black-and-white pattern, lined with strawberry-coloured silk. All she had got wrapped up in it were a couple of padded dresses, by no means new, and her other fur-lined jacket. Xi-feng told Patience to fetch a better carrying-cloth – one made of a good-quality foreign broadcloth and lined with turquoise-coloured silk – and a snow-cape to add to the contents of her bundle. Patience went off to get them. When she came back she was carrying not one snow-cape but two: one of them, in dark-red felt, showed signs of wear; the other, in dark-red camlet, seemed to be almost new.

Aroma protested.

'I can't possibly take both of these,' she said. 'Even one of these would seem a bit on the grand side for me.'

'Just pack the felt one,' said Patience. 'You can carry the other one on your arm and on your way out get someone to take it over to Miss Xing. Yesterday when we had that heavy snow there were ten or a dozen of them all wearing felt or camlet snow-capes. They made quite a picture in their red capes against the background of white snow. She was the only one there who hadn't got one. She looked all hunched-up with the cold, poor thing: I felt really sorry for her. Let *her* have the camlet one.'

'See how liberal she is with my possessions,' Xi-feng expostulated jokingly. 'Heavens, girl, I give enough away already without needing *you* to help me!'

'Like mistress, like maid,' said the woman who had spoken before. 'It's because you yourself are so considerate towards Her Ladyship and so kind to us servants that she feels free to behave in that way. If you were a mean, tight-fisted sort of person, she'd never dare.'

Xi-feng laughed.

'I suppose you could say that she understands me a bit – about thirty per cent perhaps!'

She turned back to Aroma to deliver her parting instructions.

'We must hope that your mother recovers, but if by any chance she *doesn't*, you will obviously have to stay on for a bit. Let me know, in that case, and I'll have your bedding sent on to you. Don't use their bedding or any of their toilet things.' She turned to Zhou Rui's wife. 'You know our rules, don't you? I don't need to go over them again.'

'Yes, ma'am,' said Zhou Rui's wife. 'All their people are to keep away from us while we are there, and if we stay they have to give us one or two inside rooms to ourselves.'

With that she accompanied Aroma outside and called to the pages to fetch lanterns, for it was already getting dark. The

little party then made its way to the carriages, and having disposed themselves inside them, were driven off to Hua Zi-
fang's house, where our story leaves them.

*

Back at the mansion Xi-feng summoned two of the nannies
from Green Delights.

'I doubt very much whether Aroma will be coming back for
a day or two,' she told them. 'You'd better tell whichever two
of the senior maids you think are most reliable to be on call at
night in Bao-yu's room while she is away. And keep an eye on
things yourselves. See that he doesn't get up to mischief.'

The two women went off, saying that they would attend to
the matter, and a little later came back to report on what they
had arranged.

'We've put Skybright and Musk on night-call in his room.
There are always four of us outside, of course. We take it in
turns to be on duty throughout the night.'

Xi-feng nodded.

'See that he goes to bed early and doesn't get up too late.'

The old women promised, and went back into the Garden.

Not long after this Zhou Rui's wife returned with the message that Xi-feng had been half expecting: Aroma's mother
had already breathed her last and Aroma would be unable to
come back. Xi-feng went off to report this news to Lady
Wang. She also sent someone into the Garden to collect
Aroma's bedding and toilet things. Bao-yu stood by and
supervised, while Skybright and Musk got them ready.

When Aroma's things had been despatched, the two girls
removed their hair ornaments and changed into their night-
clothes. Skybright showed no disposition, after changing, to
remove herself from the clothes-warmer over which she was
crouched.

'Now don't start acting the young lady,' said Musk. 'I
advise you to stir yourself a bit.'

'I'll stir myself soon enough when you are out of the way,'
said Skybright. 'As long as you are around, I might as well
take it easy.'

'Now come on, there's a good girl!' said busy Musk. '*I'll*
make his bed and *you* can put the cover over the dressing-
mirror and fasten the catch. You're taller than I am.'

She bustled off and began making up Bao-yu's bed.

'Hai!' said Skybright disgustedly. 'Just as I was beginning
to get warm!'

Bao-yu, who up to that moment had been sitting apart,
abstractedly wondering about Aroma's mother (he had still
not been told of her death), chanced suddenly to catch this
remark. At once he got up, went into the next room, and
attended to the dressing-mirror himself.

'Carry on warming yourself,' he said with a smile to Skybright as he came in again, 'I've done it for you.'

'I don't think I shall *ever* get warm,' said Skybright. 'And
I've just remembered: I haven't brought in the hot-water
bottle.'

'How thoughtful we are all of a sudden!' said Musk. 'He
never has a hot-water bottle. And *we* shan't need one tonight.
It'll be much warmer in here on the clothes-warmer than it is
on the kang in the other room.'

'You're not *both* going to sleep on the clothes-warmer, are
you?' said Bao-yu. 'I shall be scared, all on my own in the
closet-bed with nobody near me. I shan't be able to sleep.'

'Well, *I*'m sleeping on the clothes-warmer at all events,'
said Skybright. 'Let Musk sleep beside the closet-bed.'

The time was well after nine. Musk, who had by this time
let down the curtains, moved the lamp to its night-time
position, and lit the slow-burning incense, now helped Bao-yu
into bed and tucked him up. After that she and Skybright
themselves settled down for the night, Skybright on top of the
clothes-warmer and Musk outside the curtains which separated the alcove of the closet-bed from the rest of the room.

Some time in the middle watch of the night Bao-yu called
out for Aroma a couple of times in his sleep and, not getting
the customary response, woke up. Awake he remembered,
with some amusement, that Aroma was not there to answer.
The noise he made had woken Skybright, who called out from
where she lay to Musk.

'Musk! He's even woken me up, over here. Do you mean to say you really haven't heard anything, lying there right beside him? You must sleep like a corpse!'

Musk turned over and yawned.

'He was calling for Aroma; what's it got to do with me? – What do you want?' she asked Bao-yu.

'I want some tea,' he said.

Musk hopped out of bed to get him some. She was wearing only a quilted red silk tunic.

'You'll get cold,' said Bao-yu. 'Put my fur gown on.'

She picked up the winter dressing-gown that lay always ready beside him, in case he should need to get up during the night. It was lined with the orange-yellow chest fur of pine-martens and had a big fur collar. Slipping the gown over her shoulders, Musk first washed her hands in the basin, then she poured him a cup of hot water and held the spittoon for him to spit into when he had washed his mouth out. After that she took a teacup from the shelf where the tea-things were kept, rinsed it out with hot water, and filled it from a pot in a padded wicker case in which ready-brewed tea was kept warm for such emergencies. Having ministered to Bao-yu's wants, she rinsed her own mouth out with the hot water and poured half a cup of tea out for herself.

'Musk,' Skybright called out to her, 'give us a drop too, there's a dear!'

'What a nerve!'

'Go on!' said Skybright. 'Tomorrow night you can lie back all night long and let me wait on you.'

Musk held out the spittoon, as she had done for Bao-yu, while Skybright rinsed her mouth out, then fetched her half a cupful of tea.

'Don't go to sleep yet, you two,' she said, as soon as Skybright had been attended to. 'Keep talking while I go outside for a bit.'

'There's a ghost waiting for you out there,' said Skybright.

'There's no ghost out there, but there's a very fine moon,' said Bao-yu. 'Go ahead: we'll keep talking, don't worry!'

He coughed significantly.

Musk opened the door and lifted up the felt portière. There was, as Bao-yu had predicted, a beautiful moon outside. As soon as she had gone out, Skybright slipped down from the clothes-warmer and tip-toed after her, intending to give her a scare. Physically the hardiest of the maids and, as a rule, the one who was least afraid of the cold, she went as she was, with nothing but a short tunic to cover her. Bao-yu tried to dissuade her from going out.

'I wouldn't, if I were you. If you catch cold, it won't be quite so funny.'

But Skybright motioned impatiently to him to be quiet and crept out of the door.

The moonlight outside was like water. Suddenly she heard the wind. It was only a brief, faint gust, but the chill of it penetrated to the marrow of her bones and made her shudder.

'It's certainly true what they say about a warm body fearing the wind,' she reflected. 'This cold is really no joke.'

She was still determined to frighten Musk; but just as she was about to do so, Bao-yu called out in a loud voice from indoors.

'Careful Musk! Skybright's outside.'

Immediately Skybright ran in again.

'What an old woman you are!' she said. 'The shock wouldn't have killed her.'

'I wasn't thinking about that,' said Bao-yu. 'I was worried about your catching cold; and besides, if she'd called out when you startled her she might have woken somebody up, and you know what it would have been like then. They'd never have believed it was a practical joke, they'd have said, "Just look, Aroma only away for a single night and already the girls in his room are seeing things. Not one of them's to be trusted." Come on, come over here and tuck this quilt in for me.'

Skybright went over to arrange his bedding. While she was doing so, she stuck one of her hands inside the cover and held it against his skin.

'Your hand is *freezing*!' he said. 'I told you you'd get cold.'

He noticed how red her cheeks were and put out his hand to touch them. They were as cold as ice.

'Quick, you'd better get inside here and warm up,' he said.

Just as she did so, there was a loud bang and Musk rushed giggling into the room, slamming the door behind her.

'Whew, what a shock!' she said. 'I thought I saw someone crouching down in the shadows behind the rockery. Actually it was that long-tailed pheasant. I was just going to cry out, when it heard me coming and flew up into the light, so that I could see what it was. If I'd lost my head and started screaming, I might have woken everybody up.'

She said this while washing her hands. Presently she finished washing and laughed.

'Did you say Skybright had gone outside? I wonder why I didn't see her. I bet she went outside to scare me.'

'What's this lump here then?' said Bao-yu. 'She's down in here getting warm. She *did* go outside. If I hadn't called out when I did, she would have scared you.'

'She doesn't need *me* to scare her, silly little goose!' said Skybright, laughing, from inside the bedclothes. 'By the looks of it she's perfectly capable of scaring herself!'

She emerged from Bao-yu's bedding now and crossed the room to the clothes-warmer to get inside her own. Musk gazed at her incredulously as she did so.

'Is that all you were wearing when you went outside, that circus rider's outfit you've got on now?'

'That's all she was wearing,' said Bao-yu.

'You'll die before your time!' said Musk. 'What, standing around with only *that* on? It's enough to freeze the skin off you!'

She took the copper cover off the brazier and damped down the glowing charcoal by shovelling some ash on to it with the fire-shovel. Before replacing the cover, she threw on a couple of pieces of agalloch to sweeten the air. Then she went behind the screen and trimmed the lamp up. After that she too went back to bed.

The effect on Skybright of the sudden change of temperature was to make her sneeze. Bao-yu groaned.

'I told you so. You *have* caught a cold.'

'She was complaining that she didn't feel too good when we

got up this morning,' said Musk, 'and she hasn't eaten properly all day. Yet instead of looking after herself she has to go playing pranks on people outside. It will be her own silly fault if she *is* ill tomorrow.'

'Does your head feel hot?' Bao-yu asked Skybright.

Skybright coughed a few times.

'It's nothing,' she said. 'I'm not *that* delicate!'

Just then the chiming clock that hung on the partition in the outer room struck twice and they heard the old woman on night duty cough a couple of times and call out:

'Go to sleep, young ladies! There'll be plenty of time for talking in the morning.'

Bao-yu gave a subdued chuckle.

'Better not talk any more,' he said. 'We don't want *them* talking about *us*.'

After that the three of them settled down and went to sleep again.

When Skybright got up next morning, her nose was stuffed up, her voice was hoarse, and the slightest movement cost her an effort.

'We'd better keep this dark,' said Bao-yu. 'If my mother gets to hear of it, she's sure to insist on your going back home until you're better; and however nice it may be at your home, I'm sure it won't be so warm as here, so you'll be better off with us. I'll get a doctor in through the back gate to have a look at you on the quiet.'

'That's all very well,' said Skybright, 'but at least let Mrs Zhu know what you're doing. Otherwise, when the doctor comes, what are you going to say if they start asking questions?'

Bao-yu knew that she was right and instructed one of the old nannies to go to Li Wan with a message.

'Tell Mrs Zhu that Skybright has got a bit of a chill. Say it's nothing very serious, and with Aroma away we shall be even more short-handed if she goes back home to get better, so we'd like to get a doctor in quietly through the back gate to have a look at her and not tell Her Ladyship about it.'

The old nannie was gone for quite a long time. When she did return it was with the following answer.

'Mrs Zhu says all right, as long as she's better after one or two doses of medicine, otherwise she thinks it would really be better to send her home. She says there's so much danger of infection at this time of year. She's particularly worried that one of the young ladies might catch something.'

All this time Skybright had been lying in the closet-bed inside, coughing. She stopped coughing when she heard this message and called out angrily.

'Anyone would think I'd got the plague! I suppose I'd better go, if she's so scared that I might infect somebody. It would be just too terrible if any of you lot were to get a headache or a sore throat as long as you live!'

She actually began getting up as she said this, but Bao-yu rushed in and made her lie down again.

'Now don't start getting angry. She is, after all, responsible for the girls and she's probably terrified that Lady Wang might get to know about this and grumble at her. I'm sure that's the only reason she says this: to cover herself in case it's found out. You're inclined to be quick-tempered at the best of times. Now, with so much extra heat inside you, you are even more inflammable!'

At this point the doctor was announced and Bao-yu barely had time to conceal himself behind a bookcase as he entered the outer doorway, conducted by two or three old women from the gate. The maids had all fled as soon as the arrival of a male visitor was announced, leaving only three or four old nannies in charge of the apartment. The old nannies quickly let down the closet-bed's red embroidered curtains and Skybright stretched forth her hand through a join in them.

This hand held out for the doctor's inspection had nails two or three inches long on two of its fingers, stained with balsam juice to a delicate shade of pink. The doctor averted his eyes from this inflaming sight and would not proceed with the examination until one of the old nannies had covered it up with a handkerchief. When he had finished feeling the pulses, he got up, went into the outer room, and announced his diagnosis to the nannies.

'The young lady is suffering from inner congestion caused by exposure. In view of the severe weather we have been having we should probably not be far wrong in calling it a minor case of cold-fever or *grippe*. Fortunately your patient is a young lady and therefore probably fairly modest in her diet; and the exposure does not appear to have been a very serious one. What we have, then, is no more than a mild infection picked up by someone whose stamina is normally rather low. One or two doses of something to disperse the congestion should be sufficient to put her right.'

Having pronounced this diagnosis, he went off, conducted once more by the women who had brought him in.

Li Wan had sent warning of the doctor's arrival both to the servants on the gate and the maids in the various apartments, so that his passage through the Garden, both coming and going, was through an empty landscape in which not a single female was to be seen. After passing through the Garden gate, he sat down in the outer lodge which the pages occupied and wrote out his prescription.

'Don't go yet, sir,' said one of the old women when he had finished writing it. 'Our young master always likes to have his say about these matters. Like as not he'll have some question to ask you.'

The doctor looked startled.

'Did you say "master"? But surely that was a young lady I examined just now? The room was certainly a young lady's boudoir, and the consultation was made with the patient behind a curtain. Surely it cannot have been a young gentleman?'

The old woman laughed.

'I see now why the boys said we had a "new doctor" coming in today. You certainly don't know much about this family, sir! That *was* our young master's room you were in just now, but the person you examined was one of his maids – one of the senior ones. That was no young lady's room. If one of the young mistresses had been ill, you wouldn't have got into *her* room that easy – not on your first visit!'

She took the prescription from him and went back inside to show Bao-yu. Bao-yu glanced through it rapidly. 'Perilla', 'kikio root', 'wind-shield' and 'nepeta-seed' appeared among the drugs at the head of the list, and lower down he noticed 'thorny lime' and 'ephedra'. He was appalled.

'He's prescribing for her as if she were a man. However bad the congestion is, you can't expect a young girl to stand up to drugs like thorny lime and ephedra. Who sent for this man, anyway? You'd better get rid of him straight away and send for someone we know.'

'We weren't to know what his prescriptions would be like,' said the woman defensively. 'I suppose we could send one of the boys for Dr Wang. The only thing is, as we didn't tell the Office about this one, we shall have to pay him ourselves.'

'How much?' said Bao-yu.

'Well, you don't want to give too little,' said the old woman. 'I should think for a single visit a family like ours would give a tael.'

'How much do we give Dr Wang for a visit?' said Bao-yu.

'Ah, Dr Wang and Dr Zhang are our regular doctors. They aren't paid by the visit. They get a fixed yearly amount paid to them in quarterly instalments. But this is a new man who's only ever been here the once, so we have to pay him now.'

Bao-yu ordered Musk to fetch a tael for him, but Musk said that she didn't know where Aroma kept her money.

'I've seen her taking silver from the little pearl-inlaid cabinet,' said Bao-yu. 'I'll go along with you and have a look.'

The two of them went into the room that Aroma used as her store-room and opened the cabinet that Bao-yu had referred to. In the top compartment they found nothing but writing-brushes, ink-sticks, fans, incense-pastilles and a wide variety of scarves and sachets. In the lower compartment, however, they found several strings of cash, and there was a drawer in it in which they found a work-basket containing several pieces of silver and even a little balance for weighing it with. Musk picked up the balance.

'Which of these is the one tael mark?' she said.

'That's rich,' said Bao-yu, '*your* asking *me*! Anyone would think you were new here.'

Musk laughed. She was about to go outside and ask, but Bao-yu stopped her.

'Just pick out one of the larger pieces and give her that. There's no need to bother about the exact amount. We aren't shopkeepers.'

Putting the balance back into the basket, Musk picked up one of the pieces of silver and felt the weight of it on her palm.

'I should think this one is about a tael,' she said. 'Anyway, it's better to give too much than too little. A poor creature like that, used to scrimping and scraping himself, would say that it was meanness if we gave him too little. He'd never believe it was because we didn't know how to use a balance.'

The woman who had brought the prescription was standing in the doorway, following all this with amusement.

'That piece you've got in your hand is half of a five-tael ingot,' she said. 'It must weigh two taels at the very least. Since you haven't got any silver-shears, I should keep that piece if I were you and pick out a smaller one.'

But Musk had already closed the cabinet.

'Oh, I can't be bothered to look in there again. Just take it. Never mind the weight.'

'And tell Tealeaf to go and get Dr Wang,' said Bao-yu.

The old woman took the silver and went off to deal with the matter.

Tealeaf must have been quick, for Dr Wang arrived quite soon afterwards. The diagnosis he gave after taking Sky-bright's pulses was similar to the other man's, but there was no ephedra or thorny lime in his prescription: their place was taken by milder drugs such as angelica, bitter-peel and white peony root; and the quantities prescribed were smaller. Bao-yu was pleased.

'That's more like it!' he said. 'She certainly needs treating for congestion, but not in the savage way this other man was

proposing. I remember last year when I was suffering from the
same thing and Dr Wang came to look at me – in my case I
was badly constipated as well – he said that my constitution
wouldn't stand up to harsh decongestants like ephedra,
gypsum and thorny lime. Well, if *my* constitution won't stand
up to those drugs, I'm quite sure that yours or Skybright's
wouldn't. In comparison with you girls, I'm like one of those
old aspens that have stood for half a century or more in some
grave-garth in the countryside, while you are like those delicate crab-flowers that Yun brought round for me in the
autumn.'

'Aspens aren't the only trees you find growing in grave-
garths,' said Musk, smiling. 'What about pines and cypresses?
I hate aspens – great, stupid trees! It's not as if they had more
leaves than others, yet at the slightest breath of wind they start
making a racket. Why compare yourself to an aspen? How
common!'

'I wouldn't compare myself with a pine or a cypress,' said
Bao-yu. 'Confucius himself speaks highly of those two trees:

> "When the year is coldest, we see that pine and
> cypress are the last to fade."

That shows you how noble they are. I should need to be a very
conceited person to compare myself with *them*.'

While he was still discussing this with Musk and Skybright,
the old woman who had shown him the prescription arrived
back again with the drugs. Bao-yu told one of the maids to
find the silver medicine-skillet and brew them on the brazier
in his room.

'Now do be sensible!' said Skybright. 'Tell them to do it in
the tea-kitchen. You'll stink the place out with the smell of
boiling herbs if you do it in here.'

'But the smell of boiling herbs is the finest smell in the
world,' said Bao-yu, '– far superior to the perfume of any
flower. Even the Immortals are supposed to gather herbs and
cook them; and gathering herbs to make medicine with is the
favourite occupation of hermits and holy men. The smell of
medicine: that is the one aesthetic treat that has so far been

missing from this apartment; and now, today, we shall enjoy
it!'

And he insisted that they should prepare the medicine on
the spot. Then he told Musk to get some things ready to send
to Aroma and commissioned one of the old women to take
them to her. She was to see how Aroma was and urge her not
to endanger her health by excessive weeping. When all these
matters had been attended to, he went off to pay his morning
calls on Lady Wang and Grandmother Jia and to have his
lunch.

He found Xi-feng at Grandmother Jia's place discussing
mealtime arrangements with his mother and grandmother.

'Now that it's so cold and the days are so short,' she was
saying, 'wouldn't it be better if Li Wan and the young people
were to have their meals in the Garden, to avoid all this trek-
king to and fro? They can begin coming in for them again
when the weather is warmer and the days are not so short.'

'Oh, much better, surely?' said Lady Wang. 'Especially
when it's snowing or blowing, as it has been recently. It's so
bad for one to be exposed to the cold immediately after eating.
It's also not good to eat food after being out in the cold with
an empty stomach. The empty parts fill up with cold air and
then the food presses it down inside one. That big five-frame
room inside the back gate of the Garden would make an ideal
kitchen. We've already got all those women there who keep
watch in the Garden at night, so there are plenty of hands for
fetching and carrying. All we need are a couple of women
from the kitchens here to go over and do the cooking. There
are regular allowances for vegetables and so forth, so they can
either get the money from Accounts and do their own shop-
ping themselves, or, if they prefer, they can ask the Office to
get the stuff for them. And when we have anything special
here, like pheasant or roebuck, we can always arrange for a
share of it to be sent over to them.'

'I'd been thinking along these lines myself,' said Grandmother Jia, 'but I was afraid that opening another kitchen
might mean extra trouble for you and Feng.'

'No trouble at all,' said Xi-feng. 'It's simply a matter of

switching allowances – spending a bit less here and a bit more there. And even if it does put our expenses up a bit, we don't want the girls getting colds. Cousin Lin is particularly susceptible. Even Bao-yu is liable to suffer from the cold; and none of our girls is really strong.'

How Grandmother Jia replied will be shown in the following chapter.

CHAPTER 52

*Kind Patience conceals the theft of a Shrimp Whisker bracelet
And brave Skybright repairs the hole in a
Peacock Gold snowcape*

'QUITE SO,' said Grandmother Jia in answer to Xi-feng's advocacy of the separate kitchen. 'I would have mentioned it myself, but you have so many burdens already and I didn't want to add to them. I know, of course, that you wouldn't have complained, but you might easily have got the impression that I only care about the younger ones and have no consideration for you busy people who are responsible for running the household. However, now that you have suggested it yourself, I am naturally delighted.'

It chanced that besides Aunt Xue and Mrs Li, Lady Xing and You-shi were also present on this occasion, having come over some time previously to make their morning calls and not yet gone back again. Grandmother Jia availed herself of their presence to sing Xi-feng's praises.

'I wouldn't say this as a rule because I don't want to make her conceited, and in any case the younger ones might not agree with me: but tell me now – as older married women you have all had a good deal to do with her – have you ever met anyone quite as thoughtful as Feng?'

Aunt Xue, Mrs Li and You-shi agreed that people with Xi-feng's virtues were indeed extremely rare.

'Other young married women put on a show of liking their husband's relations for form's sake,' they observed, 'but she really does seem to care for the young people; and she is plainly devoted to *you*.'

Grandmother Jia nodded and sighed.

'*I'm* very fond of *her*, but I'm afraid she's a bit too sharp. It doesn't do to be too sharp.'

Xi-feng laughed.

'Now there you are quite wrong, Grannie. The saying is

that sharp-witted people don't live long. Everyone says that and everyone believes it, but you should be the last person to agree with them. Look how long-lived and lucky *you* are, and yet you are ten times more sharp-witted than me. By rights I should live twice as long as you, if there is any truth in the saying. I expect to live until I am at least a thousand. At all events I shan't die until I have seen *you* go to heaven!'

'It will be a very dull sort of world when all the rest are dead and only we two old harpies are left alive,' said Grandmother Jia.

The others laughed.

Remembering Skybright, Bao-yu left before the others and hurried back to his apartment to see how she was. The air in it reeked of medicine. Skybright, lying on the kang, her face a dusky red now with the fever, appeared to be completely on her own. He felt her forehead and found it burning to the touch. Quickly warming his hands over the stove, he slipped one of them inside the bedclothes and felt her body. That too was fiery hot.

'I should have thought Musk and Ripple might have stayed with you, if no one else,' he said disgustedly. 'I call that pretty heartless, leaving you on your own like this.'

'Ripple's not here because I made her go and have her lunch,' said Skybright. 'And Musk has only just this moment been called outside by Patience. They're whispering together in the front about something or other – probably about the fact that I didn't go home to get better.'

'Patience isn't that sort of person,' said Bao-yu. 'She wouldn't have known that you were ill in any case, so she wouldn't have come specially about *you*. Probably she came to talk to Musk about something else, but happening to find you ill, pretended she had come about you out of politeness. It's the sort of social fib that anyone might tell under the circumstances. Even if you *were* in trouble for not going home, it's got nothing to do with Patience; and as you have always been on good terms with her in the past, there's no earthly reason why she should want to make unpleasantness between you now by interfering in something that doesn't concern her.'

'I expect you're right,' said Skybright. 'But I don't understand why she should want to hide things from me.'

'I'll go and find out what they're talking about,' said Bao-yu. 'If I go out the back door and round the side, I shall be able to listen to them from outside the window.'

Going round to the front as he had said, he inclined his ear to the window and listened. He could hear Musk talking in a low voice to Patience inside:

'How did you come to get it back again?'

'It was when I was washing my hands in the Garden that day that I lost it,' he heard Patience reply. 'Mrs Lian made me keep quiet about it at the time, but as soon as we got back she sent word round to the nannies in the different apartments and told them to investigate. To tell the truth, we rather suspected Miss Xing's maid. We thought being so poor and not used to seeing things like that lying around she might have been tempted. We never dreamed that it would turn out to be one of *your* people.

'It was Trinket who stole it. She was seen by your Mamma Song. Fortunately, when Mamma Song came round with the bracelet to tell Mrs Lian, Mrs Lian was out, so I quickly took it from her and told her to keep quiet about it.

'I couldn't help thinking how considerate Bao-yu is to you girls and how proud of you all he is. It's only two years since that girl Honesty stole the jade and there are some I could mention who are still gloating about it, and now here's this girl stealing gold – not from him this time but from one of his neighbours, which is worse. I could just imagine the gloating there would be if *that* got around. It seemed so unjust that he, of all people, should be let down by his own girls in this way.

'Anyway, I told Mamma Song that she was under no circumstances to let Bao-yu know about this. "In fact," I said, "you'd better not tell anyone. Just behave as if nothing had happened." Of course, it wasn't only Bao-yu I was thinking about. I knew that Their Ladyships would be very angry if *they* got to hear of it and then it would be very unpleasant for Aroma and the rest of you.

'The story I told Mrs Lian when she got back was that I'd

been to see Mrs Zhu and picked the bracelet up on the way. I told her it must have slipped off into the grass that day while I was washing and got buried under the snow, which explains why nobody could find it. When the snow melted, there it was, shining in the sun for all to see. I think she believed me.

'The reason I'm telling *you* this is so that you should be on your guard about that girl. Keep an eye on her and don't send her on any errands. When Aroma gets back, have a word with *her* about it and see if you can't cook up some excuse for dismissing her.'

'Little wretch!' said Musk. 'It isn't as if she hasn't seen things like that before. How could she be so stupid?'

'It wasn't a particularly valuable bracelet,' said Patience. 'It's one that Mrs Lian gave me. It's what they call a "shrimp whisker" bracelet. I think the pearl on it might be quite valuable. That Skybright of yours is such a fire-brand that if I told *her* this, I'm sure she'd never be able to keep quiet about it. She'd blow up immediately and start hitting the girl or shouting at her, and then the whole thing would be out, in spite of all I had done to keep it dark. That's why I'm telling *you*. I thought *someone* ought to be warned, so that you can keep an eye on her.'

With these words Patience took her leave.

Bao-yu had listened to what she said with conflicting emotions: pleasure at discovering that Patience understood him so well; anger that Trinket should be a thief; regret that so intelligent a person should be capable of so ugly an action. Going back to Skybright, he relayed to her everything he had just heard except what Patience had said about Skybright herself, which he emended somewhat for her benefit.

'She said you're such a worrier that if you were to hear this now, while you are ill, it would make you worse. She's planning to tell you about it when you are better.'

Skybright's reaction was as fiery as Patience had foreseen it would be. Her eyebrows flew up and her eyes became round with anger. She wanted to summon Trinket immediately.

'Isn't it rather a poor return for Patience's considerateness immediately to start making an outcry about it?' said Bao-yu, restraining her. 'Why not accept what she has done in the spirit in which it was intended and get rid of Trinket later on?'

'That's all very well,' said Skybright, 'but I feel so angry. If I don't get it off my chest now, I shall burst.'

'What have you got to be angry about?' said Bao-yu, amused. 'You just concentrate on getting better.'

Skybright had already had one dose of her medicine. Towards evening she was given the second infusion. But although she perspired a bit during the night, it didn't really seem to do much good. She still had a temperature, her head still ached, her nose was still blocked, and she was still just as hoarse. In the morning Dr Wang came again, and after taking her pulses, made a few alterations in the prescription; but although the revised dosage brought down her temperature a little, her head still ached as before.

'Fetch the snuff,' Bao-yu commanded. 'If sniffing it can make her give a few good sneezes, it will clear her head.'

Musk went off to do his bidding and presently returned with a little oval box made of aventurine, edged and embellished with gold. Bao-yu took it from her and opened it. Inside the lid, in West Ocean enamel, was a picture of a naked, yellow-haired girl with wings of flesh. The box contained snuff of the very highest quality, which foreigners call *uncia*.

'Sniff some,' he told Skybright, who had taken the box and was gazing fascinatedly at the picture inside it. 'If you leave it open too long, it will lose its fragrance and then it won't be so good.'

Skybright took a little of the snuff with her finger-nail and sniffed it up her nose. Nothing happened, so she scooped up a really large amount and sniffed again. A tingling sensation passed through the root of her nose, right up inside her cranium and she began to sneeze: four, five, six times in succession. Immediately her eyes and nose began to stream. She shut the box hurriedly with a laugh.

'Goodness, how it burns! Give me some paper.'

At once one of the younger maids handed her a wad of tissue. Skybright used sheet after sheet of it to blow her nose on.

'How's that?' said Bao-yu.

'Much clearer,' she said. 'But I still have this headache in the front of my head.'

'Now that we've started using foreign medicine, we may as well go the whole hog,' said Bao-yu. 'I expect we'll have you better again in no time. Musk, go to Mrs Lian's and tell her I said please could she let me have some of that Western stuff she uses to make her headache plasters with. It's called *yi-fu-na*.'

Musk went off, returning after a goodish while with half a tablet. She hunted out a scrap of red satin and cut out two little circles each about the size of a finger-tip from it; then, having melted the *yi-fu-na* to an ointment-like consistency over the stove, she spread a little of it on each of them with a hairpin. Skybright stuck them on herself, one over each temple, with the aid of a hand-mirror. Musk laughed.

'You already looked like a banshee to start with, with your ill face and your hair all over the place. Now, with those two things on you, you really *do* look a sight! Funny: one hardly notices them on Mrs Lian. I suppose it's because she wears them so often. – By the way.' she said, turning to Bao-yu, 'Mrs Lian asked me to tell you that tomorrow is your Uncle Wang's birthday and Her Ladyship wants you to go. Tell me what clothes you'll be wearing tomorrow so that I can get them ready now and not have to rush around in the morning.'

'Oh, anything,' said Bao-yu. 'Whatever comes first to hand. Birthdays! It's nothing but birthdays from one year's end to the next.'

He got up and left the room, intending to go to Xi-chun's place to see how she was getting on with the painting; but as he came out of the courtyard gate, he saw Bao-qin's little maid Periwinkle hurrying across the pathway ahead of him and hurried forward to catch up with her.

'Where are you going?' he asked.

'To Miss Lin's,' said Periwinkle. 'Miss Xue and Miss Bao-qin are there already and I'm on my way to join them.'

Bao-yu changed his mind about going to see Xi-chun and accompanied Periwinkle to the Naiad's House. He found not only Bao-chai and Bao-qin there but Xing Xiu-yan as well. Dai-yu and her three visitors were sitting on the clothes-warmer gossiping, while Nightingale sat in the closet-bed alcove by the window, sewing. The girls laughed when they saw him enter.

'*Another* one? There's nowhere for you to sit.'

'What a charming picture!' said Bao-yu. '"A Bevy of Beauties Keeping Warm in Winter." I should have come earlier. Still, your room is so warm, I shall be perfectly all right on this chair.'

He sat on the chair that Dai-yu normally occupied. On this occasion it was covered with a squirrel-skin rug. A marble jardinière in the closet-bed alcove where Nightingale was sitting caught his eye. It was full of single-petalled 'water nymph' narcissi growing in clumps of four or five flowers from each bulb.

'What beautiful flowers!' he said. 'The warmth of the room makes their scent even richer. How is it I didn't notice them yesterday?'

'They were given to Qin by your Chief Steward Lai Da's wife,' said Dai-yu: 'two pots of narcissi and two of winter-sweet. Qin gave these ones to me and one of the two pots of winter-sweet to Cousin Yun. I didn't really want them, but as she was kind enough to offer them to me, I thought it would be churlish not to accept. If *you*'d like them, I'd be very happy to pass them on to you.'

'Thank you,' said Bao-yu, 'but I've got two pots of them already. Though mind you, they are not as good as these. In any case, if Cousin Qin gave them to you, you can't possibly go handing them over to somebody else.'

'There's hardly a minute of the day when I haven't got a medicine-skillet on the stove,' said Dai-yu. 'I seem practically to live on medicine nowadays. The smell of medicine is bad enough as it is, but this heavy flower-scent on top of it makes me feel quite faint. Besides, the smell of medicine spoils the smell of the flowers, which is a pity. Much better carry them off somewhere where they can regain their purity away from competing odours.'

'*I*'ve got a sick person in *my* room today,' said Bao-yu. '*My* room is full of medicine-smells too. How did you know?'

'What an extraordinary question!' said Dai-yu. 'I know nothing about it. How should *I* know what goes on in your room? I don't think you've been attending to a word I've been saying. You're like someone who comes in half-way through a story and disturbs the rest of the audience by asking questions.'

'At least we shan't want for a theme at our next poetry meeting,' said Bao-yu. '"Narcissus" and "winter-sweet" will make splendid subjects.'

'Oh no!' wailed Dai-yu, burying her face in her hands. 'What's the point of having poetry meetings? Another meeting only means another lot of penalties. It's so shaming.'

'I suppose that's meant for me,' said Bao-yu, 'since *I*'m the one who's always getting penalized. But if it doesn't bother *me*, I don't see what *you* have got to go burying your face in your hands about.'

'*I* shall call the next meeting,' said Bao-chai brightly. 'There will be four themes for poems in Regular Verse and four for poems in other metres and everyone will have to do all eight of them. The first will be a three-hundred-line poem in pentasyllabics exhausting the rhyme "first". It's subject will be "On the Diagram of the Supreme Ultimate".'

Bao-qin laughed.

'One can see that it isn't really poetry you're interested in but in making things difficult for others. It *could* be done, of course, if one really wanted to do it – it would simply be a question of selecting bits from the *Book of Changes* and torturing them into some sort of verse – but what would be the point?

'When I was eight I went with my father on one of his trips to buy foreign merchandise to one of the Western sea-ports and while we were there we saw a girl from the country of Ebenash. She was just like the foreign girls you see in paintings: long, yellow hair done into plaits, and her head was smothered in jewels: carnelians, cat's-eyes and emeralds. She was wearing a corselet of golden chain-mail and a dress of West

Ocean brocade and she had a Japanese sword at her side covered all over with jewels and gold. Actually she was *more* beautiful than the foreign girls you see in paintings. They said that she had a perfect understanding of our literature and could expound the *Five Classics* and write poems in Chinese. My father asked her through an interpreter if she would write something for us in Chinese characters and she wrote out one of her own poems for him.'

The cousins were enthralled and Bao-yu eagerly begged her to show them the poem.

'That's not possible,' said Bao-qin. 'I left it behind in Nanking.'

Bao-yu was very disappointed.

'Just my luck!' he said. 'And I was hoping to broaden my experience.'

'Don't be a tease!' said Dai-yu, giving Bao-qin a tug. '*You* didn't leave anything behind in Nanking. Look at all the luggage you brought with you! I think you're making it up. The others can believe you if they like, but *I* don't.'

Bao-qin blushed and hung her head. She made no reply, but a little, secret smile was faintly discernible in her features.

'How like you to say that, Frowner!' said Bao-chai. 'You really are too sharp.'

'Well, if she's brought it with her, she ought to let us have a look and satisfy our curiosity,' said Dai-yu.

'She's got such a great pile of stuff,' said Bao-chai, 'she simply hasn't had time to go through it all yet. How does she know which of all those trunks and boxes she put it in? Wait until she's had time to sort her things out: no doubt she will come across the poem and let you see it then.' She turned to Bao-qin. 'Or perhaps you can remember it? If so, why don't you recite it for us now?'

'It was in Regular Pentameter,' said Bao-qin. 'I can remember that. For a foreigner it was really quite a good poem.'

'Hold on!' said Bao-chai. 'If you are going to recite it, let me first send for Yun, so that she can hear it as well.'

She gave instructions to Periwinkle.

'Go back to my room and tell Miss Shi that we've got a

beautiful foreigner here who can write poems in Chinese. Tell
her that as she's so crazy about poetry, we thought she'd like
to meet her. And tell her to bring that other poetry maniac
with her when she comes.'

Periwinkle went off laughing to deliver the message.
Presently Xiang-yun's voice, loudly inquiring 'Where's this
beautiful foreigner?' could be heard outside, and a moment
later she and Caltrop walked into the room.

'Ere yet the shape was seen, the voice was heard'

said the others, laughing. When Xiang-yun and Caltrop were
seated, Bao-qin repeated for their benefit what she had just
been telling the others. Xiang-yun pressed her to recite the
poem, and this she now proceeded to do:

The Land of Ebenash

Last night I dreamt I dwelt in marble halls;
Tonight beside the watery waste I sing.
The island's cloud-cap drifts above the sea,
And mists about its mountain forests cling.
Our pasts and presents to the moon are one;
Our lives and loves beyond our reckoning.
Yet still my heart yearns for that distant South,
Where time is lost in one eternal spring.

'Fancy a foreigner being able to write that!' said the cousins
admiringly. 'It's better than we Chinese could do ourselves.'

While they were still enthusing over the poem, Musk
arrived to report that someone had just been round with a
message for Master Bao from Lady Wang.

'Her Ladyship says, when you go to your Uncle Wang's first
thing tomorrow, will you tell them that she's sorry she can't
go herself, but she's not feeling very well?'

Bao-yu stood up, out of respect for his mother, to reply. He
asked Bao-chai and Bao-qin if they would be going too. No,
said Bao-chai, they had sent a present yesterday, and that was
all they would be doing.

Conversation continued a little longer and then the company broke up. As Bao-yu politely insisted on the others going

out before him, he would have been the last to leave, but just as he was about to do so, Dai-yu called him back.

'Tell me,' she said, 'just how long *will* Aroma be away?'

'I don't know,' said Bao-yu, 'but she certainly won't come back until after the funeral.'

Dai-yu evidently had something on her mind that she wanted to say but was finding difficulty in expressing. Whatever it was, she must have abandoned it, for, after reflecting for a few moments in silence, all she said was:

'You'd better go.'

Bao-yu, too, had a feeling that there were a lot of things he ought to be asking her, but he could not for the moment recollect what any of them were. After trying unsuccessfully to remember, he left her with a cheerful 'See you tomorrow' and went down the steps outside, his head bent low as he continued ruminating. Just as he was about to set out across the forecourt, something occurred to him and he remounted the steps and went in again.

'The nights are getting so much longer now. How many times do you cough in the night? Do you wake up very often?'

'I'm much better at night than I was,' said Dai-yu. 'Last night I only coughed twice. But I still don't sleep very well. Last night I only slept between about two and four in the morning. After that I couldn't get back to sleep again.'

'Ah, I knew there was something important I wanted to ask you about,' said Bao-yu. 'I've just remembered what it was.' He drew closer to her ear and went on in a lower voice. 'You know that bird's nest that Cousin Bao sent you, —'

But before he could finish, Aunt Zhao called in to inquire if Dai-yu was feeling better. Dai-yu knew that she had dropped in on her way back from seeing Tan-chun, and that the kindness, if kindness it were, was of a somewhat tangential nature; nevertheless she begged her with eager politeness to be seated and thanked her warmly for the visit.

'How kind of you to think of me, Mrs Zhao – and to come here yourself in such bitter weather!'

She ordered tea to be poured for her visitor, simultaneously darting a look at Bao-yu which he rightly interpreted as an order to make himself scarce. It was in any case time for his dinner, so he went to his mother's place to have it. She made him go back early, bearing in mind that he must be up betimes next morning.

When he got back to his own room, Bao-yu found that Skybright had already taken her medicine. He judged it best to let her stay where she was in the closet-bed. He himself slept on the space outside the curtain which Musk had occupied the previous night. This time Musk slept on the clothes-warmer. He had it moved up beside the closet-bed before they went to bed, so that she could be near at hand during the night.

The night passed by without event.

*

Next day, before it was yet light, Skybright was calling on Musk to wake up.

'Come on, Musk! You ought to be awake by now. Haven't you slept enough yet? You go outside and tell the others to get his morning drink ready while I try waking him up.'

Musk hurriedly drew on a garment and got out of bed.

'We'd better *both* wake him and wait till he's dressed and the clothes-warmer has been carried back to its usual place before we let the others in,' she said. 'The old women have already said that he's not to sleep in the same room as you in case he catches your sickness. We shall never hear the end of it, if they find out that we've been sleeping all crowded up together like this.'

'Yes,' said Skybright. 'I was thinking that too.'

The two girls began calling Bao-yu. He must in fact have been awake already, for he got out of bed and began dressing immediately. Musk called in one of the junior maids to help her move the warmer back into place and fold up the bedding. Only when all traces of the previous night's sleeping arrangements had been effaced were Ripple and Emerald called in to assist Bao-yu with his toilet.

'It's very overcast again,' said Musk, when Bao-yu's toilet had been completed. 'It looks as if it will snow. You'd better put on your felt.'

Bao-yu nodded and changed the outer garment he had put on for a more substantial one. A junior maid came in carrying a little tea-tray on which was a covered cup containing a concoction of red dates and Fukien lotus-seeds. Bao-yu drank a few mouthfuls, took a piece of ginger from a saucerful of crystallized shapes held out to him by Musk and put it in his mouth to nibble, addressed a few brief admonitions to Sky-bright to look after herself while he was away, and went off to see his grandmother.

She had not yet risen when he arrived at her apartment, but the servants, knowing that he was going visiting and could not wait for her to get up, admitted him at once to her bedroom. He caught a glimpse of Bao-qin lying asleep behind her, her face turned inwards to the wall. The old lady observed that her grandson was wearing, over his formal dress of lychee-brown broadcloth, a dark-red felt cape embellished with roundels of gold thread and coloured silk embroidery. Its slate-blue satin border was fringed with tassels.

'Is it snowing?' she asked him.

'Not yet,' said Bao-yu, 'but it looks as if it will.'

Grandmother Jia turned to Faithful:

'Give him that peacock-feather cloak we were looking at yesterday.'

Faithful murmured a reply and went out of the room, returning presently with a magnificent snow-cape that gleamed and glittered with gold and green and bronzy-bluish lights. It was like Bao-qin's mallard-cape and yet somehow different.

'This is what they call "peacock gold",' said Grandmother Jia. 'It is made by the Russians. They twist the barbs of peacock-feathers into a kind of yarn and weave it from that. The other day I gave your cousin Bao-qin a cape like this made out of mallard feathers. Now I am giving this one to you.'

Bao-yu kotowed and put it on. Grandmother Jia smiled.

'Go and show your mother.'

Bao-yu obediently hurried off to do so. On his way out he came upon Faithful, standing beside the kang in the outer room. She affected to be rubbing her eyes in order not to have to look at him. She had avoided speaking to him ever since the frightful scene nearly two months earlier when she had vowed never to marry, and Bao-yu was continually being made uncomfortable by her avoidance of him. Seeing her once more preparing to ignore him, he went up to her with a friendly smile in the hope of breaking her silence.

'Faithful, see this! How do you think I look in it?'

But Faithful simply turned and fled, retreating into Grandmother Jia's bedroom. Obliged to give up, he continued on his way to Lady Wang's. After his mother had seen the cape, he went into the Garden to show himself off to Musk and Skybright. After that he returned to his grandmother's to report.

'I showed it to Mother. She said it seems almost a pity to wear it and I must be very, very careful not to spoil it.'

'That was the only one I had left,' said Grandmother Jia. 'If you do spoil it I haven't got another one to give you. And there would be no question of getting another one made for you – not in these parts.'

She put on her admonitions-for-the-departing-grandchild voice:

'Now don't drink too much. And leave early.'

'Yes, Grandma.'

Old women from his grandmother's apartment accompanied him as far as the reception hall of the outer mansion. Below the steps outside it his foster-brother Li Gui, together with Wang Rong, Zhang Ruo-jin, Zhao Yi-hua, Qian Sheng and Zhou Rui and the pages Tealeaf, Storky, Ploughboy and Sweeper, had been waiting a long time in readiness. The pages were carrying clothing-bundles and blankets, and two of the older men were holding a splendidly caparisoned horse by the bridle. The old women issued a few words of admonition to the men, the men, after acknowledging them with a few perfunctory cries, handed Bao-yu his whip and held the stirrup for him to mount, and Bao-yu, mindful of the precious cape, got up slowly into the saddle. The little party then began to advance, Li Gui and Wang Rong, one on either side, holding the bridle-rings, Qian Sheng and Zhou Rui walking ahead, and Zhang Ruo-jin and Zhao Yi-hua following closely behind.

'Zhou, Qian,' Bao-yu called out from the saddle to the two in front, 'let's go out of the side gate, otherwise it will mean going past my father's door and I shall have to get down.'

'Since Sir Zheng went away, his door's kept locked all the time,' said Zhou Rui, turning a grinning face back to his young master. 'You don't need to get down.'

'Even though it *is* locked, I still ought to get down,' said Bao-yu.

'Quite right, sir,' said Li Gui and Qian Sheng approvingly. 'If you was to get slack about dismounting and Mr Lai or Mr Lin was to see you, they'd be sure to have something to say about it. Even though they couldn't very well tell *you* off, like enough they'd blame us for not teaching you manners.'

By now Zhou Rui and Qian Sheng were moving towards the side entrance. While the point of etiquette was still being discussed, they ran head-on into Lai Da himself, of whom they had just been speaking. Bao-yu at once reined to a halt and made as if to dismount, but Lai Da hurried up and prevented him by clinging to his leg. Bao-yu thereupon stood up in the stirrups and, taking him by the hand, addressed him graciously for some moments before continuing on his way. He had barely done so when thirty or forty pages armed with dustpans and brushes came trooping into the courtyard. Immediately they caught sight of Bao-yu, they lined up in a row along the wall and stood with their arms at their sides while one of their number, evidently the leader, stepped forward and, dropping to one knee in the Manchu salute, wished Bao-yu a good morning. Bao-yu did not know the page's name, so he merely smiled and nodded. The whole troop remained motionless until the horse and its rider had passed by.

Bao-yu's little party now issued out of the side gate, where ten horses were ready waiting for them: one for Li Gui and each of his fellows and one for each of the pages. All sprang at once into the saddle and were off down the street like a puff of smoke.

At this point our story leaves them and turns to other matters.

*

Back at Green Delights Skybright, exasperated to find, after another dose of her medicine, that the sickness still showed no disposition to depart, was holding forth loudly against the whole generation of doctors.

'They're all cheats,' she said. 'They take your money, but none of the medicine they give you is any good.'

'Don't be so impatient,' said Musk soothingly. 'Getting better is always a lengthy business. You know what they say: "Sickness comes like an avalanche but goes like reeling silk". This stuff isn't the Elixir of Life. You can't expect it to cure you in a twinkling. You'll be all right if you take things easy for a few days. Getting yourself worked up will only give the sickness a tighter grip on you.'

Skybright's anger changed direction and vented itself now upon the junior maids.

'Where have you lot all sneaked off to?' she called out to them. 'Very bold, aren't you, now that you see me helpless? Just you wait till I'm better: I'll have the hide off every one of you.'

Her outcry produced a solitary response. A little girl called Steadfast came hurrying in and inquired, 'What is it, Miss?'

'What's happened to the others?' said Skybright. 'Are they all dead? Are you the only one left alive?'

While she was speaking, Trinket, too, came in – at a somewhat more ambling pace than the other girl.

'Look at this little creature, now!' said Skybright. 'Why couldn't *she* have come sooner? You'd have come running here fast enough if we'd been handing out monthly allowances or sharing out sweets, wouldn't you? *Then* you'd have been the first to arrive. Come closer. I'm not a tiger. I won't eat you.'

Trinket edged a few steps nearer. As she did so, Skybright suddenly raised herself from her lying position, snatched hold of her hand, and began jabbing at it violently with an enormous hairpin which she had been keeping concealed under her pillow.

'What do you want this little claw for?' she said. 'It's no good with a needle and thread. All it's good for is picking and stealing. Shifty eyes and light fingers! A little claw like this can only bring you disgrace. Much better *stab* it! – and *stab* it! – and *stab* it! so that it can't do any more thieving.'

Trinket was by now screaming with pain. Musk quickly dragged her away out of Skybright's clutches and forced Skybright to lie down again in bed.

'You've only just been sweating after the medicine,' she said. 'What's the matter with you? Do you want to die? If you'll just wait until you're better, you can punish her as much as you like. Don't start making a scene about it *now*!'

But Skybright insisted on calling in Mamma Song and dealing with the matter at once.

'Master Bao has told me to tell you that he finds Trinket lazy,' she said when Mamma Song arrived. 'She answers him back and doesn't do anything when he gives her orders, and even when Aroma tells her to do things she says rude things about her behind her back. Master Bao is most anxious that she should be dismissed immediately. He says he will speak to Her Ladyship about it himself when he sees her tomorrow.'

When Mamma Song heard this, she knew that the story of the bracelet must have leaked out.

'That's as may be,' she said. 'But oughtn't we to wait until Miss Aroma comes back and tell her first?'

'What I am giving you are Master Bao's own orders,' said Skybright. 'He was most particular that she should be dismissed immediately. I don't see that Miss Aroma – or Miss Sweetscents or Miss Smellypots, for that matter – has got anything to do with it. I know what I'm doing. Just do as I say. Go and get someone from her family to come here immediately and take her away.'

'You might just as well,' said Musk. 'She'll have to go

sooner or later. Let them take her away now and get it over with.'

So Mamma Song had to go off and summon the girl's mother from outside. When Trinket had finished getting her belongings together, her mother went in with her to see Musk and Skybright.

'Now what's all this about?' she said. 'If the girl's done wrong, why can't you just punish her for it? Why do you have to dismiss her? It doesn't leave us much face, does it, if she's dismissed?'

'You'll have to ask Bao-yu about that when he gets back,' said Skybright. 'It's nothing to do with us.'

The woman sneered.

'You know perfectly well that I wouldn't dare. He always does what you young ladies want him to in any case. Even if I saw him and he agreed that she could stay, there's no guaranteeing that she would if you young ladies weren't agreeable. Take what you said just now. I know he's not here at the moment, but even so. If *I* was to name his name as you did just now without a "master" or a "mister" to it, people would say I was a savage, but for you young ladies, seemingly, it's quite all right.'

Skybright became red with anger.

'I called him by his name, did I? Why don't you go and report me to Their Ladyships? Tell them that I'm a savage and get *me* dismissed.'

'I advise you to take that girl out of here and be on your way,' said Musk. 'If you have anything to say, you can say it later. You can't stand here wrangling about it *now*. When have you ever seen other people bandying words with us? Even Mrs Lai and Mrs Lin show a bit of restraint when they talk to us. And as for this business of saying "Bao-yu" instead of "Master Bao": everyone knows that it's Her Old Ladyship's particular wish that we *should*. Because he's not strong and she's afraid he might die young, she likes as many people as possible to use his name, to bring him luck. She even has it written in big characters and pasted up on walls outside to get people saying it. It would be funny if *we* couldn't use his name when every water-carrier and dung-carrier and beggar in town can do so. As a matter of fact only yesterday Mrs Lin got told off by Her Old Ladyship for calling him "Master Bao".

'And for another thing, we senior maids are constantly having to take messages to Her Old Ladyship and Her Ladyship about him, and when we do, we always say "Bao-yu", never "Master Bao". Why, I should think we must each of us use his name a couple of hundred times every day. You certainly chose the wrong thing to find fault with when you picked on *that* one! If you don't believe me, go round one of these days when you are free to Her Old Ladyship's or Her Ladyship's and you will hear us openly calling him "Bao-yu" to their faces. But of course, you don't have any important business that would bring you in contact with Their Ladyships, do you? All your time is spent doing odd-jobs outside. One could hardly expect you to know the way things are done in *here*.

'But I'm afraid we really can't have you standing around here any longer. If you stay much longer, I'm afraid even though *we* don't object someone else may come along and ask what you are doing here. If you want to appeal against the girl's dismissal, you should get her out of here first and take it up with Mrs Lin afterwards and *she* will speak to Master Bao about it. With all the hundreds of people there are in this household we can't have just anyone running in and out whenever they feel like it. We don't even know the names of half of them.'

By way of emphasizing her point, Musk ordered one of the junior maids to fetch a floor-cloth and begin wiping the floor. At this Trinket's mother, unable to find a reply and fearful of being caught staying too long, swept out angrily, taking her daughter with her. But Mamma Song was not letting them get away so easily.

'You certainly don't have much idea of manners, my good woman. After all the time she's been here, your daughter could at least make the young ladies a kotow before she goes. She may have no other parting gift to give them – I don't suppose they'd set much store by it if she had – but she might at least have the decency to make them a kotow. You can't both just up and go.'

Trinket was obliged to come in again and kotow to the two inside. She also went round to do the same for Ripple and Emerald, but they refused to look at her. After that she departed with her mother, the latter indicating as they went, by many a sniff and sigh, the hatred that she dared not express more openly.

A consequence of this latest exposure to the cold and of the accompanying emotional upset was that Skybright was now feeling bad again. At lighting-up time, after tossing about feverishly all day, she was just beginning to settle down at last when Bao-yu returned in a great fret and began stamping and groaning almost as soon as he entered the room. Musk asked him what the matter was.

'It's this cloak that Grandmother gave me this morning. She was so pleased about it, and now – I don't know how it happened – I've gone and got a burn in it behind the lapel. Fortunately it was fairly dark just now when I came back and neither Grandmother nor Mother noticed anything.'

He took it off for Musk to examine. It was only a little burn, about the size of a finger-print, but clearly visible.

'It must have been caused by a spark from your hand-warmer,' said Musk. 'It's nothing to worry about. We'll send someone out on the quiet with it immediately to find a good invisible mender and get it mended for you.'

She wrapped it up and called in one of the old nannies to take it out for them.

'Tell them it has to be ready by daylight tomorrow. And for heaven's sake don't let Her Old Ladyship or Her Ladyship find out about it!'

The woman was gone a very long time. When she at last returned, she was still carrying the bundle with the peacock cloak in it.

'I've tried everywhere – invisible menders, tailors, embroiderers, seamstresses – and none of them will touch it. They all say they don't know what the material is and don't want to be responsible.'

'Oh dear!' said Musk. 'What are we going to do now? Well, you just can't wear it tomorrow, that's all.'

'But I must,' said Bao-yu. 'Tomorrow is his actual birthday. Grandmother and Mother have both said I must. Today was only the first day of the celebrations, not his actual birthday. Isn't it just my luck to burn it the very first time I put it on?'

Skybright, who had listened to all this in silence, could contain herself no longer and sat up immediately in bed.

'Come on, let me have a look. If you weren't meant to wear it, you won't wear it. No good making all this fuss about it now.'

'There's something in that,' said Bao-yu laughing, and handed it to her. He brought the lamp over so that she could examine it more closely.

'This is made of "peacock gold",' said Skybright. 'If we could get hold of some of the thread and make a little darn with it, I think it would probably pass.'

'We've got peacock gold thread,' said Musk. 'The trouble is that apart from you there's no one else here who could do the darning.'

'I shall just have to make the effort and do it then, shan't I?' said Skybright.

'No, that's out of the question,' said Bao-yu. 'You've only just started getting better. You're not in a fit state to do sewing yet.'

'Oh, don't be such an old woman!' said Skybright. '*I* know what I'm capable of.'

So saying, she sat up again in bed, knotted up her loosely flowing hair, and drew a jacket on over her shoulders. Her body felt abnormally light and she was almost overcome with dizziness. It really did seem as if the effort would be too much for her; but knowing what a state Bao-yu would be in if the snow-cape was not repaired, she gritted her teeth, and fighting back the weakness that threatened to engulf her, told Musk to pinch the yarn and thread a needle for her while she herself took a length of it and held it against the material.

'It's not really a very good match,' she said, 'but I don't suppose it will show very much when it's been darned.'

'I'm sure it will do very nicely,' said Bao-yu. 'At all events, we're not going to be able to find a Russian tailor to do it for us!'

Skybright began by opening up the seam of the lining underneath the burnt patch so that she could insert a cup-sized darning mushroom from inside. Having stretched the material out over the mushroom, she scraped away the charred parts and the surrounding nap with a razor until the threads were clearly exposed, then, with her needle and thread, she worked first across in one direction and then at right-angles in the other until she had filled the hole with a criss-cross darn. Using this as a foundation, she now began to weave the thread in and out with her needle so as to imitate the surrounding pattern. This was the most difficult and exhausting part of the work. After each couple of stitches she had to stop and examine what she had done, and after every four or five she had to lean back on the pillow and rest. Meanwhile Bao-yu fussed around her unceasingly, one moment asking her if she would like a 'nice hot drink', another moment suggesting that she should rest, one moment fetching a squirrel-skin cloak to put over her shoulders, the next moment a pillow for her back, until she became quite frantic and had to entreat him to leave her alone.

'My dear little grandfather – *please* just go to bed! If you stay up any longer, you'll have rings under your eyes in the morning, and that will never do!'

Bao-yu could see that he was exasperating her and made a pretence of settling down in his bed; but he could not get to sleep. After he had been lying awake for some time, he heard the chiming clock strike four. Skybright had just completed the mending and was finishing off the job by carefully teasing the nap out with a little toothbrush.

'That's wonderful,' said Musk. 'If you didn't look at it carefully, you could never tell it was a darn.'

Bao-yu asked to see.

'It's perfect,' he said. 'It looks exactly the same as the rest.'

Skybright had been coughing a good deal during the final stages of her task and it had been all she could do to conclude it.

'Anyway, it's done,' she said. 'It doesn't really look right, but I can't do any more – Aiyo!'

With a cry of weariness she sank back, utterly exhausted, upon the bed.

If you wish to know the outcome, please read the chapter which follows.

CHAPTER 53

*Ning-guo House sacrifices to the ancestors on New Year's Eve
And Rong-guo House entertains the whole family on
Fifteenth Night*

SEEING that Skybright's repair of the peacock gold snow-cape had so utterly exhausted her, Bao-yu called in a junior maid to help massage her and for a while they pummelled her between them. After that they all went to bed; but in less than no time it seemed to be broad daylight and they had to get up again. Instead of going straight off to his uncle's, however, Bao-yu first sent someone to summon Dr Wang. The doctor arrived promptly and proceeded to take Skybright's pulses. He appeared to be disconcerted by what he found.

'Yesterday she seemed to be a little better,' he said, 'but this pulse today takes us right back to where we started from – empty, superficial, faint, constricted. Now why should that be? She must have been eating or drinking too much. Either that, or she has been worrying about something. The original attack was not a serious one; but failure to take care of oneself after perspiration has been induced *can* be very serious.'

He went outside and wrote another prescription, which was presently brought in to Bao-yu. Bao-yu noticed that the sudorifics and decongestants of the earlier prescription had been omitted and restorative drugs to increase the vitality and nourish the blood, such as lycoperdon, nipplewort and angelica, had been substituted. He gave instructions for the medicine to be made up immediately. He seemed distressed.

'This is dreadful. If anything should happen to you after this, I shall never forgive myself.'

Skybright, lying back on her pillow, hooted derisively at his concern:

'My dear young Master, just get on with your own affairs and don't worry about me. I'm not about to go into a decline, I assure you!'

Bao-yu was in any case obliged to go now; but having held out at his uncle's place until the afternoon, he managed to get back to her by pretending that he was feeling unwell.

Skybright was certainly quite ill. Fortunately she was normally an active, lively sort of girl, not given to moping and vapours; she had always been sensible – even abstemious – in her diet; and her constitution was a sound one. The Jias were great believers in the virtues of fasting. Masters and servants alike were put on a starvation diet at the slightest hint of a cough or cold, the physic and nursing they received being considered of only secondary importance to this, and Skybright had been fasting now for two or three days, ever since the influenza began. In addition to this, she had taken her medicine regularly and, except for the one night's lapse, had looked after herself reasonably well. Although the over-exertion set her back a few days, she was soon on the mend again. And as the new catering arrangements whereby the cousins now ate in their own apartments made ordering things much easier, Bao-yu was able to get all sorts of soups and broths made up to aid her recovery.

Omitting details of this convalescence, our story passes on to the return of Aroma, which occurred shortly after her mother's funeral. As soon as she got back, Musk told her all about Trinket and how Skybright had dismissed her first and reported the dismissal afterwards to Bao-yu. Aroma merely remarked that Skybright had been 'too hasty', but made no further comment.

Li Wan had herself now fallen a victim to the season's cold; Lady Xing was suffering from an inflammation of the eyes which necessitated Ying-chun's and Xiu-yan's attendance on her both mornings and evenings to dress them for her; Mrs Li had been invited to spend some days with a younger brother and gone off taking Li Wen and Li Qi with her; and Bao-yu was preoccupied with Aroma, who was still thinking constantly of her mother and liable at any moment to break down, as well as with Skybright, who had still not entirely recovered. So what with one thing and another, no one felt much in the mood for writing poetry and one or two of the club's fixture-days went by without a meeting.

It was now well into the twelfth month and Lady Wang and Xi-feng were busily preparing for the New Year. The season of appointments brought news that Wang Zi-teng had been promoted to the post of Inspector-General of Armies in the Nine Provinces and that Jia Yu-cun was to become Under Secretary to the President of the Board of War with occasional duties at Court. Over in the Ning mansion Cousin Zhen had opened up the Hall of the Ancestors and set his people to work sweeping it, setting the vessels out in readiness for the New Year sacrifices, and welcoming the spirits back into the ancestral tablets. He also had the main hall of the Ning-guo mansion swept in readiness for the annual ceremonial hanging of the ancestral portraits. Everyone in both mansions, both high and low, was in a fever of activity.

One morning in the course of these preparations, as You-shi, who had not long since risen, was, with the assistance of Jia Rong's new wife, getting the presents of newly made clothes ready for sending to Grandmother Jia, a maid came in bearing a trayful of New Year medallions.

'It's from Merry, ma'am. He says that loose silver you gave him the other day was of several different marks but the total weight was one hundred and fifty-three taels and thirteen pennyweights and he says they've managed to make two hundred and twenty medallions from it.'

She held out the tray for You-shi to inspect. On it there were medallions shaped like plum-flowers, crabflower-shaped medallions, medallions with 'heart's desire' rebus patterns of ingot, brush and sceptre, and others with patterns of auspicious flowers.

'Yes,' said You-shi, 'they seem to be all right. Tell him to take them inside immediately.'

The maid went off to do her bidding. Shortly after that Cousin Zhen came in to have his lunch and Jia Rong's wife hurried out to avoid him.

'Have we received the bounty money for the New Year

sacrifices yet?' Cousin Zhen asked You-shi when they were alone together.

'I sent Rong to draw it this morning,' said You-shi.

'It's not that we *rely* on the money exactly,' said Cousin Zhen, 'but it is after all the gift of the Emperor and I think we ought to draw it as soon as possible and get it across to Lady Jia so that it can be used to pay for the offerings. It's a double blessing when the gracious favour shown us by His Majesty can be passed on to the ancestors. However many thousands of our own we were to spend on them, it wouldn't do them nearly as much honour as these offerings subsidized by the Imperial bounty – not to mention the advantages that *we* enjoy as recipients of Imperial favour. And we have to remember that apart from the one or two great families like ours who don't really need this money, there are many, many families of poor hereditary officials who do actually depend on it for their ancestral sacrifices and who wouldn't be able to celebrate New Year properly without it. So you see it really was extra-ordinarily benevolent and far-seeing of the dynasty to institute this annual bounty.'

'Yes, indeed,' said You-shi.

'Master Rong is back,' a servant came in to report while the two of them were still talking.

'Tell him to come in,' said Cousin Zhen.

Jia Rong entered carrying a little yellow bag, not as one would normally carry a bag, but holding it in both hands at shoulder height.

'You've been a long time, haven't you?' said Cousin Zhen.

Jia Rong smiled nervously.

'This year they're not paying it at the Board of Rites any longer but at the treasury of the Imperial Victuallers; so having first gone to the Board of Rites, I had to go from there all the way to the Imperial Victuallers to draw the money. The people at the Imperial Victuallers' office all asked after you, by the way. They say they haven't seen you for a long time, but they often think about you.'

'It's not me they think about but my things,' said Cousin

Zhen with a dry smile. 'Either that, or they are hoping for an invitation to come round over the New Year.'

He was inspecting the yellow bag as he said this. It had a sealing-slip with the words

PERPETUAL BOUNTY

written on it in large characters. On the other side was the chop of the Department of Sacrifices of the Board of Rites and some columns of smaller characters:

Annual grant awarded in perpetuity to Jia Yan, Duke of Ning-guo, and Jia Yuan, Duke of Rong-guo, for New Year Sacrifices: goods to the value of ——— taels net Cash received by: Jia Rong, Captain, Imperial Body- guard, Inner Palace, on (*date*) Issuing officer for the year: (*name*)

This was followed by a cipher in red ink.

After inspecting the yellow bag, Cousin Zhen had his lunch; then, when he had washed his hands and rinsed his mouth out, he changed into formal hat and boots and, ordering Jia Rong to follow him with the bag, set off for the other mansion to report the arrival of the bounty-money, first to Grandmother Jia and Lady Wang and then to Jia She and Lady Xing next door. When they got back he took out the money and ordered the bag to be carried into the Hall of the Ancestors and burnt there in the great incense-burner in front of the ancestral tablets.

There were further orders now for Jia Rong:

'I want you to go and ask your Aunt Lian whether she's decided yet on which days she'll be entertaining in the New Year. If she has, get the office to make out a good, clear list of the dates, so that we don't have any duplicating this year. Last year several families got invitations from both of us for the same day, and of course, people being what they are, instead of realizing that it was a mistake, they assumed that we had deliberately worked it out between us as an economy.'

Jia Rong hurried off to see Xi-feng, returning presently

with the list of dates that his father had asked for. After running his eye over it, Cousin Zhen handed it to a servant.

'Give this to Lai Sheng. Tell him to avoid these dates when he sends out our New Year invitations.'

He and Jia Rong went on to inspect operations in the hall, where a number of pages were carrying in and arranging the large screens on which the portraits of the ancestors were to be hung, and cleaning and polishing the tables and the ritual vessels of gold and silver which were to be set up in front of them. While they were thus engaged, a page came in holding a red greetings-card and a schedule containing some sort of list.

'Bailiff Wu from Black Mountain village, sir. He's just arrived.'

'That old rascal?' said Cousin Zhen. 'He's been long enough getting here!'

Jia Rong took the greetings-card and schedule from the servant, and opening up the card, held it out for his father to read. Cousin Zhen folded his hands behind his back and bent over to read the inscription:

Wu Jin-xiao, Bailiff, presents his Humble Compliments
to the
Master and Mistress
and compliments to
The Young Gentlemen and Ladies
wishing you
Wealth, Health and Prosperity
Increase of Pay and Promotion
and
all your Heart's Desire in the
Coming Year

Cousin Zhen laughed.

'These country people have an original sense of style.'

'Never mind the style,' said Jia Rong, echoing his father's laughter with obsequious laughter of his own, 'just think of all the good luck he is wishing us!'

He opened up the schedule and held it out while Cousin
Zhen ran his eye down the list:

tufted deer		30
water deer		50
spotted deer		50
Siamese pigs		20
scalded pigs		20
wild boar		20
wild pigs		20
salted pigs		20
wild sheep		20
goats		20
scalded sheep		20
sheep, salted in fell		20
sturgeons		200
fish, various		200 catties
live chickens, ducks and geese	(each)	200
dried ditto	(each)	200
pheasants & hares	(each)	200 brace
bear's paws		20 pairs
deer's sinews		20 catties
sea-slugs		50 catties
deer's tongues		50
ox-tongues		10
dried mussels		20 catties
filberts, pine-nuts, peach-kernels, almonds	(each)	2 bags
crayfish		50 pairs
dried shrimps		200 catties
high quality selected Silver Frost charcoal		1000 catties
medium grade ditto		2000 catties
red charcoal		30,000 catties
red Emperor rice		5 bushels
green glutinous rice		60 bushels
white ditto		60 bushels
powder rice		60 bushels
millet, sorghum & other grains	(each)	60 bushels
general purpose rice		2500 bushels
dried vegetables		1 cartload

Item, total realized from sales of
    livestock and cereals   2500 taels silver
Item, Present for the young ladies and
    gentlemen (Pets)
          2 deer
          4 pair white rabbits
          4 pair black rabbits
          2 pair golden pheasants
          2 pair Foreign ducks

'Bring him in,' said Cousin Zhen when he had finished perusing the schedule.

Wu Jin-xiao promptly appeared. He knelt down in the courtyard below and had already kotowed and called out his greetings before Cousin Zhen could have him raised up and brought into the hall.

'You are still hale and hearty then?' Cousin Zhen asked him.

'Yes, sir, thank you sir,' said the old man, beaming. 'I still manage to get about.'

'Your sons must be quite big fellows by now,' said Cousin Zhen. 'Why don't you let them do the travelling for you?'

'To tell you the truth, sir, I'm so used to the journey, I'd miss it now if I wasn't to come. Shouldn't know what to do with myself. The boys would be only too glad to come if I'd let them, of course – see what it's like here "in the Emperor's shadow" as we say – but they're only youngsters yet: I'd be afeared of them having some mishap on the way. A few years longer and I shan't need to worry.'

'How many days have you been on the road?' said Cousin Zhen.

'Well, sir, as you know, there was a lot of snow this year: it must have been lying three or four foot thick in places. And that sudden thaw we had coming on top of it made the going very difficult. That must have put us back several days. It's taken a month and two days altogether. But I do assure you, sir, seeing that the time was running out and knowing how anxious you'd be, we made as much speed as we could.'

'I was wondering what could have made you so late,' said

Cousin Zhen. 'Well, I've been looking at this list of yours. I see you're holding out on me again this year, you old devil.'

Wu Jin-xiao advanced a couple of steps – springing, as it were, to his own defence:

'It's like this, sir. The harvests this year have been really terrible. From the third month to the eighth month it rained on and off all the time. I doubt we had six fine days in a row together. Then in the ninth month we had hail as big as tea-cups. For fifty miles around, the damage to crops and livestock – and houses and people as well, for that matter – was terrible. That's why I haven't brought you more this year. That's the honest truth, sir. You know I wouldn't lie to you.'

'I'd reckoned on your bringing me at least five thousand taels,' said Cousin Zhen, frowning. 'What am I supposed to do with an amount like this? We have only eight or nine farms now and of those eight or nine two have declared themselves disaster areas this year and aren't contributing anything. With you holding back on me too, I might as well give up celebrating New Year altogether.'

'Your lands have done better than some,' said Wu Jin-xiao. 'Take my cousin's place. That's only thirty mile from where I am, but my word, what a difference! My cousin manages eight farms for your relations at the other House. They've got several times as much land as you, but the vittles he's brought them this year are no more than this lot here, and their cash yield on sales is no more than two or three thousand. Now they really *have* got something to make a fuss about.'

'It's true,' said Cousin Zhen. 'We're not *too* badly off on this side. At least we haven't got any new major commitments outside our regular annual expenditure. For us it's a question of spending a bit more freely when we're flush and economizing a bit when things are tighter. And even in the case of these New Year expenses, I suppose I *could* cut down on them if I really had to. It would simply be a question of brazening it out. But with our Rong-guo cousins it's different. They've had all these new expenses during the past few years, none of which were optional, but no new source of income to set against them. Which means that for the past year or two they've had to start eating into their capital. If *you* folk can't help them to make up the deficit, who else is there they can turn to?'

'I know they've got a lot on their plate,' said Wu Jin-xiao with a knowing smile, 'but it can't *all* be outgoings, can it? There must be something coming in as well. Surely Her Grace and old Live-For-Ever must give them a hand-out once in a while?'

Cousin Zhen turned to Jia Rong with a laugh.

'You heard that? Rich, isn't it?'

Jia Rong tittered.

'What does a countryman like you living at the back of beyond know about such matters? You don't suppose Her Grace has handed them the keys of the Emperor's treasury, do you? She's not her own mistress, even if she wanted to. She does give presents, of course, but it's only on birthdays and feastdays and the like and never more than a few lengths of figured satin or some curios or knick-knacks. Even when she gives money, at the very most it will be a hundred gold. Now say a hundred gold is worth a thousand silver taels – it can't be much more than that – what possible good can a thousand taels do them, when during each of the past two years they've been forced to draw on their capital to the tune of several thousands a year? During the first of those two years they had the Visitation – including the building of that great garden. Just imagine what *that* must have cost them. Another two years like these last two with another Visitation thrown in and they'll be cleaned out!'

'These simple country souls see "the bright outside but not the dark within",' said Cousin Zhen. 'The situation our Rong-guo cousins are in is like the proverbial chime-hammer made of phellodendron wood: imposing to look at but bitter inside.'

'You can tell they really *are* hard-up,' said Jia Rong half-jokingly. 'The other day I heard Auntie Lian plotting with Faithful to steal some of Lady Jia's things to use as security for a loan.'

'No, I think that was merely our Feng being her usual artful self,' said Cousin Zhen, laughing. 'They're still not *that* poor.

I expect she has noticed how much they have been spending beyond their means and is planning some economy or other. What you overheard would simply have been her way of letting people know how hard-up they are and preparing them for some cuts. I've got a rough idea of how their finances stand at present and I assure you that they aren't quite as desperate as *that* yet.'

Concluding the conversation on this more reassuring note, Cousin Zhen gave Wu Jin-xiao into the charge of the servants with instructions that he was to be properly looked after and entertained. Our narrative does not follow the old man into the servants' quarters, however, but remains in the hall with Cousin Zhen.

Cousin Zhen had a portion of the things that Wu Jin-xiao had brought set aside to be used as offerings to the ancestors; he had another portion set aside for sending to Rong-guo House; and while Jia Rong attended to its delivery, he personally supervised the selection of a third portion which he intended to keep for his own use. What remained he had piled up in orderly heaps on the pavement beneath the hall terrace to be shared out among the junior members of the clan, who were forthwith invited to come and collect their shares.

At that point a large consignment of things arrived from the other mansion, most of them things to be used in the ancestral sacrifices, but some of them for Cousin Zhen himself. Having given orders for their disposal, Cousin Zhen went back to his supervision of the polishing and furniture-shifting in the hall. When that work was completed, he put on a lynx-skin coat and went out, still in his slippers, on to the terrace, where, having found himself a warm place under the eaves, he got the servants to spread out a wolfskin rug for him so that he could sit there and watch the young clansmen as they came to collect their shares. He noticed that Jia Qin was among them.

'What are *you* doing here?' he called out to him. 'Who told *you* to come?'

Jia Qin came over and stood in front of him, arms held submissively at his sides.

'I heard that you were having a family share-out, Uncle, so I came along without waiting to be called.'

'These things I'm giving away now are intended for those of your uncles and cousins who haven't got jobs or private incomes to support them,' said Cousin Zhen. 'During the years when you were unemployed yourself, I used to give *you* a share of the New Year things. But you aren't unemployed now: you've got that supervisor's job that my Rong-guo cousins gave you, looking after those young nuns in the family temple. Not only have you got a salary of your own, but you control all the nuns' allowances as well. Yet still you come here for my things. You are too greedy. And just look at you! No one would think from your appearance that you had money to spend and a responsible position. You used to have the excuse that you had no money, but what excuse have you got now? You look even more disreputable now than you did when you were unemployed!'

'I've got a big family to support,' said Jia Qin. 'I have a lot of expenses.'

'Humbug!' said Cousin Zhen. 'I know what you get up to in that temple of yours, don't think I don't! Once you set foot in that place, *you* are the master and nobody there can gainsay you. With money to spend and the rest of us a long way away in the city, you can do exactly as you like: invite the local riff-raff in every night to gamble with you and fill the place with your kept women and fancy boys. So having squandered all the money and reduced yourself to the disgraceful state I see you in now, you have the effrontery to try and get something out of *me*. All you are likely to get out of *me*, young man, is a good stout stick across the shoulders! And when this holiday is over, I shall make it my business to have a word with your Uncle Lian and see to it that he has you recalled.'

Jia Qin reddened, but dared not say anything.

A servant came up then to report:

'Someone with a present from the Prince of Bei-jing, sir. Two scrolls and a perfume-bag.'

Cousin Zhen turned to Jia Rong.

'Go and entertain him for me. Tell him I'm out.'

Jia Rong hurried off.

Cousin Zhen then dismissed Jia Qin, and having presided over the distribution until all the things had been taken, returned to his own apartment to have his dinner with You-shi.

Concerning the rest of that day and the night which followed our narrative is silent.

The day after that was even busier. But to give further details of these preparations would be tedious. Suffice it to say that by the twenty-ninth of the twelfth month they had been completed. In both mansions new door-gods had been pasted up on all the doors, the inscribed boards at the sides and over the tops of gateways had been repainted, and fresh 'good luck' slips – auspicious couplets written in the best calligraphy on strips of scarlet paper – had been pasted up at the sides of all the entrances. In the Ning-guo mansion the central doors of the main outer gate, of the ornamental gate, of the outer reception hall, of the pavilion-gate, of the inner reception hall, of the triple gate dividing the inner from the outer parts of the mansion, and of the inner ornamental gate were all thrown open, so that a way was opened up from the street right through into the family hall inside. Red lanterns on tall scarlet stands lined either side of this route. At dusk, when the candles in them were lit, they took on the appearance of two long, parallel serpents of light, undulating slightly where they ascended or descended the steps of terraces.

Next day, the last of the Old Year, Grandmother Jia and any of the Jia ladies who possessed patents of nobility attired themselves in the court dress appropriate to their rank and were borne in procession to the Palace, Grandmother Jia at the head in a palanquin carried by eight bearers, to make their kotows to the Imperial Concubine and felicitate her on the successful conclusion of the year. On their return from the banquet which she gave them, their chairs were set down outside the pavilion-gate of the Ning-guo mansion, where those of the younger Jia males who had not escorted them to the Palace were lined up on either side of the gateway waiting to receive them. When the ladies had all alighted, the young men conducted them on foot to the Jia family's Hall of the Ancestors.

Bao-qin had never been inside this part of the mansion before. She was being allowed in on this occasion by virtue of her recent adoption into the family and was anxious to take in every detail in order that she might retain as accurate an impression of it as possible.

The Jia family's Hall of the Ancestors was in a separate courtyard of its own in the west part of Ning-guo House, away from the more domestic parts of the mansion – a courtyard that was entered through an imposing five-frame gateway behind a black-lacquered wooden paling. An inscription in large characters hung over the central arch of the gate:

ANCESTRAL TEMPLE
OF THE
JIA FAMILY

with a column of smaller characters in the lower lefthand part of the board indicating that the calligrapher was a direct descendant in the sixty-somethingth generation of the Sage Confucius. A long couplet from the brush of the same calligrapher occupied the two vertical boards at the arch's sides:

With loyal blood poured out willingly upon the ground
   a myriad subjects pay tribute to their benevolent rulers

For famous deeds lauded resoundingly to the skies
   a hundred generations offer sacrifices to their heroic ancestors

Inside the gate a raised white marble walk shaded by an avenue of venerable pines and cypresses led up to a terrace on which ancient bronze tripods were ranged. Over the entrance to the temple's vestibule, whose penthouse-roof swept forwards from the main building's façade, hung a board framed in a carved and gilded border of nine interlacing dragons and inscribed in the Late Emperor's calligraphy with the following words:

HIS MINISTERS ARE AS SHINING STARS

The vertical inscriptions on either side were in the same Imperial hand:

Their achievements outshone the celestial luminaries
Their fame is reflected in the generations that come after them

The board over the entrance to the main hall of the temple was framed by two contending dragons and its inscription was of incised characters infilled in green. Both it and the matching couplet below it were in the calligraphy of the reigning sovereign:

HONOUR THE DEAD AND KEEP THEIR MEMORIAL

Their sons and grandsons enjoy the fruits of their blessedness
The common people recall Ning and Rong with kindness

Beyond the flickering brilliance of many lights and the glint and sheen of drapes and hangings Bao-qin could make out some of the spirit tablets of the ancestors, but not very clearly.

By ancient custom the menfolk were divided in ranks to left and right of the hall so that each generation was on a different side from the one which followed it, fathers and sons separated, grandfathers and grandsons together. Jia Jing presided over the sacrifice with Jia She acting as his assistant; Cousin Zhen held the drink-offering; Jia Lian and Jia Cong the silk-offering; Bao-yu carried the incense; Jia Chang and Jia Ling unrolled the kneeling-mat in front of the great incense-burner. Then the black-coated musicians struck up and the ceremony began: the threefold offering of the Cup, the standings, kneelings and prostrations, the burning of the silk-offering, the libation – every movement precisely in time to the solemn strains of the music. The music ceased at the same time as the ceremony, and the participants filed out and, grouping themselves round Grandmother Jia, conducted her to the main hall of the Ning-guo mansion where, under the richly-embroidered frieze which hung high in front of them, against a background of brilliantly-decorated screens, high above the smoking incense and flickering candles of the altar, the portraits of the ancestors hung, those of the ducal siblings, Ning-guo and Rong-guo, resplendent in dragon robes and jade-encrusted belts, in the centre and somewhat raised above the rest.

The men ranged themselves in ascending order of seniority in the space between the hall and the ornamental gate, so that the two most junior ones, Jia Xing and Jia Zhi, were just inside the gate and the two most senior ones, Jia Jing and Jia She, were at the top of the terrace steps and under the eaves of the hall. The womenfolk of the family were ranged inside the hall in corresponding ranks but in reverse order: that is to say, the most junior were nearest the threshold and the most senior furthest inside the hall, but whereas the senior male in a generation was at the east end of his row, the senior female in the same generation would be at the west end of hers, and *vice versa*. The male domestics of all ages were ranged in the courtyard on the further side of the ornamental gate.

The manner of making the offerings was as follows. Each 'course' was passed from hand to hand by the servants until it reached the ornamental gate. There it was received by Jia Xing and Jia Zhi and passed on from hand to hand until it reached Jia Jing at the top of the terrace steps. Jia Rong, as senior grandson of the senior branch of the family, was permitted, alone of all the males, to stand inside the threshold with the women. He received the dishes from his grandfather Jia Jing's hands and passed them to his wife, Hu-shi. Hu-shi passed them to the row ending in Xi-feng and You-shi, who passed them forwards to Lady Wang standing at the side of the altar. Lady Wang then put them into the hands of Grandmother Jia, who raised them up reverently towards the portraits before laying them down on the altar in front of her. Lady Xing stood to the west of the altar facing eastwards and helped her lay them down. When meat, vegetables, rice, soup, cakes, wine and tea had all been transmitted to the altar by this human chain and offered up there by Grandmother Jia and her two daughters-in-law, Jia Rong withdrew and took up his position next to Jia Qin in the courtyard below, at the head of the most junior generation of Jia family males.

Now came the most solemn part of the ceremony. As Grandmother Jia, clasping a little bundle of burning joss-sticks with both her hands, knelt down for the incense-offering, the entire congregation of men and women, rank upon rank of them, close-packed as flowers in a flower-bed, knelt down in perfect time with her and proceeded to go through the motions of the Great Obeisance. This was done with such silent concentration that, from five-frame hall and three-frame vestibule, from portico and terrace, terrace steps and courtyard, for some minutes nothing could be heard but the faint tinkling made by jade girdle-pendants and tiny golden bells and the soft scrape and scuffle of cloth-soled boots and shoes.

The ceremony over, Jia Jing, Jia She and the rest of the menfolk hurried back to the Rong-guo mansion so that they could be waiting there in readiness to make their kotows to Grandmother Jia on her return.

In You-shi's main reception-room, whither the ladies repaired now from the hall, the floor had been entirely covered with a great red carpet and a huge gold cloisonné incense-burner with a loach-lipped rim and three massive legs shaped like the trunks of elephants stood in the middle.

In the centre of the kang – also new-carpeted, but in scarlet – a dark-red back-rest had been placed with a design showing a couchant dragon coiled around the character for 'longevity'. Large bolsters of the same colour and with the same design on them had been placed as arm-rests at right-angles to it; for extra warmth a black fox-fur had been draped around the top of it, and there was a white fox-fur rug between the bolsters, for sitting on. When Grandmother Jia had been installed on this furry throne, several old great-aunts were invited to sit on fur rugs that had been spread out on the kang to left and right of it. Lady Xing, Lady Wang and other ladies of their generation were installed on fur rugs on a smaller kang in an alcove-room to the side of the main kang and discreetly separated from it by an openwork wooden screen. On the floor below, in two facing rows, were a dozen carved lacquer chairs, on which Bao-qin and the other cousins were invited to sit. They had chair-backs and seat-covers of squirrel, and large copper foot-warmers in place of footstools.

You-shi and her daughter-in-law Hu-shi now appeared with tea-trays in their hands, and while You-shi offered tea to Grandmother Jia, Hu-shi served the old aunties. After that You-shi passed into the alcove and served tea to Lady Xing and the other ladies on the smaller kang, and Hu-shi served the cousins sitting in chairs below. Xi-feng, Li Wan and a few other young married women of their generation, debarred from taking tea either with the elder ladies or with their young unmarried cousins, stood idly by, on the floor below the kang, 'in attendance'. Lady Xing and her group, as soon as they had finished drinking their tea, rose and moved over to where Grandmother Jia was sitting on the kang so that they too might be 'in attendance'.

After exchanging a few words with the other old ladies while she sipped her tea, Grandmother Jia gave orders for her palanquin to be made ready. At once Xi-feng climbed up on to the kang and began helping her to her feet.

'But we've already prepared dinner for you here,' said You-shi. 'You never stay with us for dinner on New Year's Eve. Won't you make an exception just this once? Surely my catering can't be all that inferior to Feng's?'

Xi-feng continued to help Grandmother Jia from the kang.

'Come on, Grannie, let's be getting home! Pay no attention to her!'

Grandmother Jia laughed.

'You're so busy with the sacrifices,' she said. 'You're worked off your feet as it is; I'm sure you don't want the bother of feeding me as well. Besides, in past years when I haven't stayed, you have sent the food over to me. Why don't you do that again this year? I don't feel like eating very much now; but if you send it over, I shall be able to save it up for tomorrow, and then I shall be able to eat more of it than I could now.'

This made everyone laugh.

'See that you get someone thoroughly dependable to sit up

and keep an eye on the candles tonight,' Grandmother Jia said by way of parting admonition. 'Where fire is concerned, one can't afford to take chances.'

You-shi, escorting her meanwhile from the room, assured her that she would do so.

At the pavilion-gate You-shi and the other ladies hid themselves behind the gate-screen from the eyes of the waiting menservants while Grandmother Jia got into her palanquin. Pages of the Ning-guo mansion went ahead of the bearers and, as they approached the outer gate, directed them through the centre of its three gateways. Lady Xing and Lady Wang followed in their less imposing conveyances, accompanied by You-shi, who was also going over to the other mansion.

Outside, while they were being borne in a westerly direction down the street, the ladies could see the achievements, insignia and musical instruments (bells, gongs, stone-chimes and drums hung in magnificently carved, painted and tasselled stands) of the Dukes of Ning-guo and Rong-guo, those of the Duke of Ning-guo along the eastern half of the street outside the south wall of the Ning-guo property, and those of his brother-duke outside the Rong-guo wall to its west.

As in the other mansion, the centre-gates throughout Rong-guo House were all thrown open so that a way was clear from the outer gate right through to the Hall of Exalted Felicity inside. But this time, instead of going through to the pavilion-gate and getting out there, they turned left after the outer reception hall and were carried to the main reception hall in Grandmother Jia's part of the mansion. The others assembled round the old lady as they got out of their sedans and followed her into the hall. Here, too, everything had been transformed: brilliantly embroidered screens and cushions specially brought out for the occasion and an incense-burner set down in the middle of the room from which emanated delicious odours of pine and cedar and Hundred Blend aromatic.

As soon as Grandmother Jia was seated, a venerable nannie came up to her to report that 'the old ladies had arrived to make their kotow' and she hurriedly got up again and advanced to welcome two or three elderly female relations who had just come into the hall. A good deal of polite tussling ensued, accompanied on both sides by laughter and protestations, as Grandmother Jia took the hands of each old lady in turn and, while the old ladies pretended that they were struggling to kneel, made a great show of struggling to prevent them – for although Grandmother Jia was their senior, they were in the same generation as her and too elderly to be allowed to kotow in earnest. They sat down for a while after that and took a cup of tea; then Grandmother Jia saw them out, but no farther than the inner ornamental gate.

When she had returned and was once more enthroned on the principal seat in the hall, Jia Jing and Jia She came forward with all the menfolk in the family in rows behind them to make their kotow.

'You all do so much for me during the year,' Grandmother Jia protested. 'Can't we forget about the kotow?'

But nobody heeded her. Rank upon rank of them, the males in one large group and the females in another, knelt down together and bowed their foreheads to the ground. After that folding chairs were brought and put down in a row to left and right of Grandmother Jia's seat and the next most senior members of the family sat down and received *their* kotows, and so on by order of seniority downwards, until all but the most junior members of the family had been kotowed to; but now even *their* turn arrived and they too were allowed to sit down as the domestics of both households, men-servants and women-servants, pages and maids, came in by order of their various ranks and duties and made *their* kotows to their employers.

After that the New Year's Eve wish-penny was distributed to servants and children – gold or silver medallions in little embroidered purses – and the New Year's love-feast was laid, tables on the east side of the hall for men and boys, tables on the west side for girls and women. There was herb-flavoured New Year's Eve wine and love-feast soup, there were lucky-cakes and wish-puddings; and when all had eaten and drunk, Grandmother Jia rose and went into an inner room to change

out of her court dress, which she had all this time been wearing. This was a signal for the others present to disperse.

As darkness came on, offerings of cakes and burning joss-
sticks were made in front of all the Buddha-shrines and in all
the little niches of the Kitchen God, who is welcomed back
this night from his annual trip aloft. In the main courtyard,
outside Lady Wang's apartment, an 'altar to heaven and
earth' was set up – a long table on which offerings of sticky
fried honey-sticks and fresh apples and steamed wheat-flour
cakes and other goodies had been built up, layer upon layer,
into a little pagoda of offerings in front of a large colour-print
representing the whole host of heaven (or as much of it as the
artist had been able to fit in). Great horn lanterns hung at
either side of the main entrance to Prospect Garden to
illuminate the gateway, and innumerable standard lamps lit up
its alley-ways and courtyards and walks. As for the inhabitants
of the mansion, all of them, both masters and servants,
seemed, in their dazzling holiday array, like walking flower-
gardens of brilliant embroidery and brocade. And all night
long a confused hubbub of talking and shouting and laughter
arose, punctuated by the continual, unceasing pops and bangs
of exploding firecrackers.

At four o'clock in the morning, as the drums of the fifth
watch were sounding, Grandmother Jia and the other ladies
once more got into their court dresses and were borne in procession to the Palace, this time to felicitate Yuan-chun on the
advent of the New Year. Liveried footmen walked ahead of
them carrying the full paraphernalia to which Grandmother
Jia's rank entitled her. Once more Yuan-chun feasted them;
once more, on their return from the Palace, they made offerings to the ancestors in their shrine in the Ning-guo mansion;
and once more, on returning to her own apartment in Rong-
guo House, Grandmother Jia received the prostrations of the
assembled family. As soon as that was over, she changed out
of her court clothes and declared that she was going to rest,
refusing to see any of the friends and relations who now began
arriving in great numbers to offer their New Year felicitations,

and spending her time either quietly conversing with Aunt Xue and Mrs Li or, as an occasional diversion, playing games of cards or Racing Go with Bao-yu and the girls.

But Lady Wang and Xi-feng, on both this and each of the seven or eight days which followed, were kept busy entertaining the guests whom the family had invited to drink their New Year wine. In both the reception hall and the courtyard outside it there were plays to watch and tables at which the unending stream of visitors could sit for a while and eat and drink while they watched them.

And no sooner was that lot of entertaining over than another lot had to be prepared for as the First Moon waxed greater and the Lantern Festival drew near. Again the Ning and Rong mansions were gay with lanterns and decorations. On the eleventh of the month Jia She entertained Grandmother Jia and the rest of the family and on the twelfth it was Cousin Zhen's turn to play host, while for several days running Lady Wang and Wang Xi-feng were most of the time out visiting one or other of the innumerable families from whom they had received invitations.

On the evening of the fifteenth Grandmother Jia had tables laid for a feast in her big 'new' reception hall – the scene of Xi-feng's fateful birthday-feast. A stage was set up for a troupe of child-actors which she had specially hired for this occasion, and both the stage and hall were hung all over with lanterns of every imaginable shape and colour. When her preparations were completed, she summoned all her children and grandchildren, nephews and nieces, great-nephews and great-nieces to a family feast.

As a matter of fact it is not strictly true that *all* of them were invited. Jia Jing was, for religious reasons, a total abstainer from meat and strong drink, so *he* was not invited. Obligations to the dead rather than to the living had brought him back for the holiday, and on the seventeenth, two days after this, as soon as the last of the ancestral sacrifices was over, he returned to his Taoist monastery outside the city and the briefly interrupted pursuit of immortality. Meanwhile, when not actually engaged in discharging ceremonial duties, he spent all the time on his own in a quiet, out-of-the-way corner of the mansion, in a state of incommunicado with the other members of the family.

And Jia She, although he was invited, excused himself as soon as he had received a party-gift from his mother. She knew that he felt uncomfortable in her presence and did not attempt to detain him. Back in his own quarters, surrounded by cronies and dependants, he could drink and admire the lanterns while beautiful young women played and sang for his delectation:

> Ears with pipes and songs beguiled,
> Eyes by silk skirts hypnotized.

— A different scene altogether from the one he had just left.

But let us return to the latter — to the reception hall in Grandmother Jia's rear courtyard, where a covered stage had been erected to accommodate the players.

Inside the hall some dozen or more tables had been laid facing outwards towards the stage. They were arranged in a fan shape, with the two central tables in the place of honour at the back and the rest of them raying out forwards to left and right of them. At the side of each table a smaller, ornamental table had been placed on which were arranged

1. a little three-piece incense set (a vase, a cassolette and a tripod, all made on a miniature scale out of metal) in which Hundred Blend aromatic — a gift from the Palace — was burning;

2. a porcelain dish, eight inches long, four or five inches wide and two or three inches deep, containing a miniature landscape made out of stones and mosses;

3. a small japanned tea-tray on which was one of Grandmother Jia's best china teacups and a little individual *mille fiori* teapot in which choicest tea was brewing;

4. a little table-screen of red silk gauze, embroidered with flowers and appropriate lines of 'grass character' verse,

framed in a delicately carved pierced-work sandalwood frame;*

5. a vase (each one a collector's piece and each different from the rest) containing the 'three friends of winter' or 'riches in a jade hall' or some other flower arrangement, mostly of fresh flowers that had been specially forced for the occasion.

The two tables in the place of honour at the back were occupied by Aunt Xue and Mrs Li. To their left, at the head of the row of tables radiating outwards towards the east side of the hall, there was a large, low wooden settle with a carved

* *Stone's Note to Reader:*

These screens were embroidered by a Soochow girl called Hui-niang, who, as member of a highly-cultivated Service family and an accomplished amateur painter and calligrapher, embroidered only occasionally for her own diversion and not as a means of making money. As the flowers embroidered on them were all copied from flower-paintings by famous masters, their design and colouring were far superior to the cruder, more garish productions of professional embroiderers; and the accompanying verses, all chosen with impeccable taste from a wide range of literary sources, were executed in black embroidery-silk with such consummate skill that every hook and squiggle, every variation in thickness of line, every join and break in the brush-written 'grass script' calligraphy was exactly reproduced, not mangled and deformed as in the stilted, wooden attempts at copying of the commercial embroiderer.

Since Hui-niang did not depend on her embroidery for a living, specimens of it, despite its great fame, have always been hard to come by. Even among the rich and great there are very few households which can boast a specimen. Such as do exist are referred to by collectors as 'Hui embroidery'. But what are sometimes sold as specimens of 'Hui embroidery' today invariably turn out to be imitations deliberately made to take in the inexpert buyer. The real Hui-niang died tragically at the age of eighteen, and there are in fact no genuine specimens of her work now to be had, since the few houses which possess a piece or two hold on to them tenaciously and refuse to part with them to would-be purchasers. Indeed, if a genuine specimen of Hui-niang's work *were* ever to come upon the market, its value would be incalculable. The Jia family originally possessed three, of which two had been presented as a gift to the Emperor only a year previously, leaving this set of sixteen little table-screens, to which Grandmother Jia was so much attached that she kept them always in her own apartment, unwilling that they should remain with the stock of objects commonly drawn on for the family's entertainment of guests, and only rarely, on occasions of her own devising, brought them out to be admired.   *Stone* pierced-work back of interlacing dragons, which had been put there for Grandmother Jia to lie on. It was furnished with a back-rest and bolsters and was large enough to have a fur rug spread out on it and still leave room at one end for a small, exquisitely gilded table of foreign make on which had been placed a teapot, a teacup, a spittoon, a napkin and, among various other small objects, an eyeglass-case. Grandmother Jia rested with her feet up on the settle and, after talking for a while with the company, took out the eyeglasses from their case and looked through them at the stage.

'I do hope you will forgive me for lying down like this in your presence,' she apologized to Aunt Xue and Mrs Li. 'It's very rude of me, I know, but I'm getting so rheumaticky in my old age.'

She made Amber get up on to the settle beside her and massage her legs by gently pounding them with a 'maiden's fist' – a sort of short-handled mallet with a padded leather head.

No feaster's table with cover and drapes had been put in front of the settle, only the little ornamental table with the table-screen and the incense set and vase of flowers. The very elegant, somewhat larger table of normal height which would have been hers if she had been sitting up with the rest had been placed somewhat to the left of the settle and laid with wine-cups, soup-spoons and chopsticks for four. It was occupied by Bao-qin, Xiang-yun, Dai-yu and Bao-yu. Although she could not sit with them, Grandmother Jia kept up a pretence that they were eating together: each dish as it arrived would be submitted to her inspection, and if she fancied it, would be placed on the little table at her elbow; then, when she had tasted it, it would be removed and set down in front of the four young people for them to finish.

After Grandmother Jia and her four grandchildren, the next along on the east side was Lady Xing; after her came Lady Wang, then You-shi, then Li Wan, then Xi-feng, and lastly Jia Rong's wife, Hu-shi. Along the west side Bao-chai came first, next to her mother, then Li Wen, then Li Qi, then Xiu-yan, then Ying-chun, then Tan-chun and then Xi-chun.

Red-tasselled glass lanterns hung in rows from the beams
overhead to left and right of the diners. In front of them, on
each of their tables, was an ingenious light consisting of a
flower-shaped candle attached to the base of a reflector in the
form of a vertical lotus leaf. These lotus leaves, though made
of metal, were so skilfully engraved and enamelled that they
looked almost real. They were attached to their metal stands
by means of a swivel, so that the beams of the candle could be
concentrated in any direction desired. When all the reflectors
were simultaneously directed towards the stage, the diners'
view of the players was wonderfully improved.

The wooden partitions with their window-lattices and doors
which normally separated the hall from the verandah had been
removed and great palace lanterns of glass, whose elaborately
carved wooden frames were hung with strings of crimson
tassels, were suspended at intervals in the space thus created.
More rows of lanterns – lanterns of every kind of material and
design – horn lanterns, glass lanterns, gauze lanterns, lanterns
of Yunnan glitter-glass, embroidered ones, painted ones, lanterns with cut-outs of paper or silk in them, hung in lines
under the verandah eaves, both inside and outside the archi-
traves, and from the eaves of the loggias on either side of the
courtyard.

The tables on the verandah were all occupied by males:
Cousin Zhen, Jia Lian, Jia Huan, Jia Cong, Jia Rong, Jia
Qin, Jia Yun, Jia Ling and Jia Chang.

Although Grandmother Jia had sent invitations by word of
mouth to every clansman and clanswoman residing in the city,
some of them were too elderly to stand up to the noise and
excitement of a party, some were unable to come because they
had no one to look after the house for them while they were
away, some had intended to come but were prevented from
doing so by illness, some stayed away from envy of their
richer clansmen or because they were ashamed of their own
poverty, others because they could not stand Xi-feng, and yet
others because they were so unused to company and in-
capacitated by shyness that they *dared* not come – in short,

although the clan was a numerous one, for one reason or another, of all those invited the only female guest who turned up was Lou-shi, mother of Bao-yu's former classmate, the intrepid little Jia Jun, who came bringing Jia Jun with her, and the only male ones were those who had found employment with the family under Xi-feng's auspices and were therefore obliged to put in an appearance: Jia Qin, Jia Yun, Jia Chang and Jia Ling. Yet even with the absence of so many who had been invited from outside, for a family party the company was a large one.

Presently, while they all sat watching the players, Lin Zhi-xiao's wife came into the hall leading six other women, each pair of whom were carrying between them a small kang-table covered with a red felt top on which was a bundle of strung cash: hundreds and hundreds of newly-minted copper coins, specially chosen for size and quality, fastened together by a single long cord of crimson silk. Under the direction of Lin Zhi-xiao's wife two of these tables were set down in front of Mrs Li and Aunt Xue and the third one beside Grandmother Jia's settle.

'Do it in the middle, where everyone can see,' said Grandmother Jia.

The women all knew what was expected of them. Setting the tables down in the centre of the hall, they simultaneously undid the ends of the crimson cords with which the money was fastened and began pulling them out so that the coins tumbled in heaps upon the tables.

The play being performed on this occasion was *The House in Ping-kang Lane*, and the actors had just come to the end of that section of it called 'Meeting in the Sickroom'. The hero Yu Shu-ye, having at last met the love of his life only to be called by stern duty from her side, had just left the stage in chagrin. At this point the child-actor playing the part of his little page Leopard Boy, observing what was going on in the hall, began to extemporize:

'*You* can go off in a huff if you like; but today is the fifteenth of the first month and old Lady Jia of Rong-guo House is holding a family party; so what *I* am going to do is to get on this horse and gallop there as quickly as I can and ask them for some sweeties!'

This caused Grandmother Jia and the rest of the audience to burst out laughing.

'That's a sharp little fellow,' said Aunt Xue. 'How sweet!'

'And he's barely nine,' said Xi-feng.

'Barely nine!' said Grandmother Jia. 'And being able to come out with it so pat!'

She nodded in the direction of the waiting women.

'Largesse!'

Three of the women had already provided themselves with small shallow baskets in readiness for this order. At the word of command they walked up to the little tables, shovelled up basketfuls of coins from the heaped-up money, and took them outside to the foot of the stage which Leopard Boy had just vacated.

'Largesse from Lady Jia, Mrs Xue and Mrs Li for Leopard Boy to buy himself some sweets with,' said one of the women.

The three of them then discharged the contents of their baskets upon the stage. The money landed with a mighty clatter and at once the whole stage was covered with shining pennies.

Cousin Zhen had ordered his own pages to have a large flat basket of money ready for his own largesse to the players.

But you will have to wait for the next volume, gentle reader, in order to find out whether they received it.

EXPLICIT SECUNDA PARS LAPIDIS HISTORIAE

APPENDIX I

Regulated Verse

REGULATED Verse, a form which was perfected in the eighth century and continued to be the most commonly used verse form until modern times, exploits the characteristic tonality of the Chinese language, using a very rigid formal structure in which tension is created by combining tonal contrast with verbal parallelism. Two metres only are allowed, the pentasyllabic (five syllables) and the heptasyllabic (seven syllables) and only one of them may be used in the same poem. For prosodic purposes the four tones of medieval Chinese are divided into two classes, level and oblique, and only level-tone words may be used as rhymes.

Except in a variation of the form called Linked Verse and in the Regulated Verse quatrain, which has slightly different rules, all Regulated Verse poems have eight lines (four couplets) and have the same rhyme throughout in alternate lines (ll.2, 4, 6 and 8), rhyme in the first line being optional (1, 2, 4, 6, 8). In the two central couplets (ll.3 and 4 and ll.5 and 6) there has to be verbal parallelism: that is to say, if you have 'brown cow' in the first line of the couplet, you must have some matching expression such as 'white horse' in the same position in the following line. This verbal parallelism sometimes extends to the first and, more rarely, to the last couplet as well. Tonal contrast has to be observed throughout the whole poem, in all four couplets. Several patterns of tonal contrast are possible. The following is one of the two patterns available for a Regulated Verse poem in pentasyllabics, using o to represent level and x to represent oblique tones. The underlined symbols represent the rhymes:

$$
\begin{array}{ccccc}
\text{x} & \text{x} & \text{o} & \text{o} & \text{x} \\
\text{o} & \text{o} & \text{x} & \text{x} & \underline{\text{o}} \\
\text{o} & \text{o} & \text{o} & \text{x} & \text{x} \\
\text{x} & \text{x} & \text{x} & \text{o} & \underline{\text{o}} \\
\text{x} & \text{x} & \text{o} & \text{o} & \text{x} \\
\text{o} & \text{o} & \text{x} & \text{x} & \underline{\text{o}} \\
\text{o} & \text{o} & \text{o} & \text{x} & \text{x} \\
\text{x} & \text{x} & \text{x} & \text{o} & \underline{\text{o}} \\
\end{array}
$$

(Lines 3–4: } verbal parallelism; Lines 5–6: } verbal parallelism)

In practice it is only the second, fourth and final syllables of each line that must conform to the pattern. In the great majority of

Regulated Verse poems there are four or five syllables occurring in the first or third place which do not conform, and wholly conforming poems are comparatively rare. Nevertheless the form is an extremely difficult one to master, and was made doubly so for Bao-yu and the girls by the fact that the tones and rhymes of the medieval poetic language to which the verses had to conform no longer corresponded with the tones and pronunciation of the language they spoke. Speakers of Southern Standard English may get some faint idea of what this must have been like if they try to imagine the difficulty of avoiding 'Cockney rhymes' in some English of the future which made no distinction in either pronunciation or spelling between 'caw' and 'core'.

The following, using noughts and crosses again to represent level and oblique tones and underlining to indicate the rhymes, is a transcription of Tan-chun's crab-flower poem in modern (i.e. Tan-chun's) pronunciation.

This is in heptasyllabic metre and the tonal pattern is somewhat more complicated than the one in the example just given. It will be seen that the rhymes, which would have been perfect rhymes to a Tang poet, are in two cases merely conventional rhymes for Tan-chun. The 'non-conforming' syllables are bracketed:

xie°   yang°   (han°)   cao×   dai×   chong°   <u>men°</u>
(tai°)   cui×   ying°   pu°   yu×   hou×   <u>pen°</u>

yu×   shi×   jing°   shen°   nan°   bi×   jie×
(xue×)   wei°   (ji°)   gu×   yi×   xiao°   <u>hun°</u>

fang°   xin°   yi×   dian×   jiao°   wu°   li×
qian×   ying×   san°   geng×   yue×   you×   <u>hen°</u>

mo×   dao°   gao°   xian°   neng°   yu×   hua×
duo°   qing°   ban×   wo×   yong×   huang°   <u>hun°</u>

A comparison of the above with any of my translations will show that I have been unable to reproduce the Chinese rhyme-scheme in its entirety. (The tonal pattern cannot, of course, be reproduced, because English is not, in the Chinese sense, a tonal language.) For facility of rhyming, Chinese is like Italian: it is possible to use the same rhyme – as is in fact done in chapter 50 – a score or more times in succession almost without trying, which is, of course, emphatically not the case in English. But though the rhyme-scheme I have adopted is a somewhat different one from the Chinese and my renderings may be accounted of little or no poetic value, at least they should give the reader some idea of the cross-word puzzle nature of the task which the young members of the poetry club had set themselves, and enable him to appreciate why several of them elsewhere in the novel express vehement dislike of what they call 'set rhymes'.

APPENDIX II

Threesomes with the Dominoes

THE Chinese 'tiles' of bone or ivory which I generally translate 'dominoes' were in appearance very similar to our dominoes, though the games played with them were more often the sort of games we play with cards. The same word, *pai*, is in fact used in Chinese for both the dominoes and the old-fashioned Chinese playing-cards. Dominoes are 'bone *pai*' and cards are 'paper *pai*', but the qualifying word is often omitted and in the text of the novel it is not always clear which of the two is intended.

Chinese dominoes differed from ours in having coloured spots – green and red – on a white ground. Aces and fours were red, the other numbers were green, except that double sixes were half and half. In both dice and dominoes there were conventional names for certain combinations: a double six was 'heaven' or 'the sky', a double ace 'earth', a double four 'man', a double five 'plum', a four and a six 'the embroidered screen'. Some of these conventional names are used by Faithful in her calls: for example, she calls 'the bright blue sky' for Grandmother Jia's double six and 'the Man' for Grannie Liu's double four. In other cases both she and the players replying modify the conventional usage or invent their own interpretations. Thus single – not just double – sixes are interpreted as 'sky', a single five becomes 'plum' (or simply 'flower'), a four, because of its four red spots, suggesting petals, may also become a flower, the single red spot of the ace suggests the sun or a cherry, the green double three suggests duckweed on water, and so on.

In the following diagrams the red spots are represented by white circles and the green spots by black ones.

Grandmother Jia

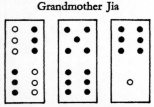

'A shock-headed devil'

Aunt Xue

'The Second Prince plays
in the Five Holy Hills'

Xiang-yun

Bao-chai

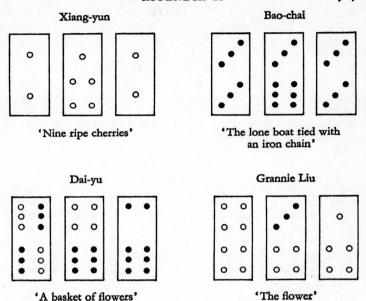

'Nine ripe cherries'

'The lone boat tied with
an iron chain'

Dai-yu

Grannie Liu

'A basket of flowers'

'The flower'

APPENDIX III

Unsolved Riddles

THE answer to Bao-chai's riddle (p. 510) is evidently 'a fir cone'. Temples sometimes had little bells fastened to their eaves. The cones hanging from the boughs are likened to soundless bells hanging from the 'eaves' of the tree.

I have assumed the answer to Bao-yu's riddle to be 'a pigeon flute' – a little bamboo whistle tied to a pigeon's leg so as to give off a musical note when the bird is in flight. Flocks of pigeons emitting this delightful music were still to be heard in the air above Peking's courtyards as recently as 1950.

The answer to Dai-yu's riddle is thought to be 'a revolving lantern' – a lantern with cut-out figures (in this case, presumably, galloping horses) which revolve when the candle inside it is lit, working on the same principle as our 'angel chimes'. Dai-yu's lantern appears to have a stationary frieze of islands supported on the backs of turtles (like the Isles of the Blest in Chinese mythology) above which the cardboard horses revolve.

Bao-qin's concealed riddles (chapter 51, p. 512 *seq.*) are much harder to find answers to, and the learned eighteenth and nineteenth century readers whose guesses are recorded are startlingly at variance with each other in the solutions they offer. In the notes which follow I usually mention only one of the available answers, for the simple reason that, as I have had to make each of the translations with one particular answer in mind, I have tended to produce versions to which the other solutions are no longer plausible alternatives.

RED CLIFF

Red Cliff, near the modern city of Wuchang on the R. Yangtze, was the scene of one of China's most famous battles when in A.D. 208 the adventurer Liu Bei, later to become founder of the kingdom of Shu in Szechwan, and Zhou Yu, general of the recently established kingdom of Wu whose capital was at Nanking, combined forces to defeat the armada of Cao Cao, who, acting as titular Chancellor of the puppet Han emperor, had recently consolidated his hold over the whole of northern China and was now attempting to extend his control south of the river.

This troubled period of China's history, dominated by the power-struggles of warlords and condottieri, is the theme of China's great prose epic, *The Romance of the Three Kingdoms*, which up until modern times supplied much of the stock-in-trade of the Chinese theatre.

In *The Romance of the Three Kingdoms* Cao Cao, historically one of the wisest and most beneficent rulers of his day, becomes a scheming villain. The heroes of the epic are Liu Bei and his sworn brothers Zhang Fei and Guan Yu. (Guan Yu was later deified as Guan-di, the God of War.) This trio, like the Three Musketeers who really were four, were joined by a fourth hero, Liu Bei's adviser Zhu-ge Liang, who in the epic becomes a sort of Merlin, able to read prophecies in the stars and summon up winds by magic. According to the epic it was Zhu-ge Liang who thought of the fire-ships which burned Cao Cao's troop transports (referred to in the poem) and who raised the wind which blew them onto their target.

The best available explanation of the riddle concealed in this poem is that of Gao E's contemporary, Xu Fengyi, who thought it was 'a *dharma*-boat'. What these objects were is explained in a little booklet called *An Account of the Most Notable Annual Festivals and Customs of the Imperial Capital* written by a contemporary of Cao Xueqin called Pan Rongbi and published in 1758. He tells us that on the Buddhist Festival of All Souls on the fifteenth of the seventh month it was the custom in Peking to construct boats as much as fifty or sixty feet long out of bamboo and paper to represent the Buddhist 'ship of salvation' (i.e. the teaching of the Lord Buddha), which were launched on the nearest available stretch of water and set on fire. Pan Rongbi does not say so, but it seems to me quite likely that the 'ship of souls' might have carried paper banners inscribed with names of the recently departed whose salvation was requested. This would explain the 'naught but their names' of the second line of this quatrain.

HANOI

Ma Yuan (14 B.C.–A.D. 49) was a Chinese empire-builder of the Later Han period whose most famous military exploit was to re-establish Chinese hegemony in Hanoi. He is also said to have erected a column of brass to mark the southern limit of Han dominion. I have to admit that the point of the 'Iron Flute' reference escapes me.

The likeliest answer to the riddle seems to be 'a brass trumpet'.

MT ZHONG-SHAN

The 'you' of this poem is Lei Cizong (A.D. 385–448), a would-be recluse who was repeatedly hauled out of retirement by a talent-spotting emperor and forced to become a professor. Mt Zhong-shan near Nanking is where, on the last of these occasions, the emperor constructed a special *ashram* to house him in.

The likeliest answer to the riddle seems to be 'a string puppet'.

HUAI-YIN

Han Xin (d. 196 B.C.), foremost among the great captains who helped Gao-zu to become founder of the Han dynasty, rose from very humble beginnings as an unemployed and often hungry young ne'er-do-well in Huai-yin. (Later in life he was to become Marquis of Huai-yin.) While a poor down-and-out he was on one occasion fed by an old washerwoman, whom he rewarded magnificently years later when he came into his own. This is the incident referred to in the second half of the quatrain.

Like most of Gao-zu's great generals, Han Xin ultimately fell a victim of Gao-zu's suspicious nature – though it was not Gao-zu himself but his savage empress, Lü-hou, who seized Han Xin by a trick and had him executed. Gao-zu's suspicions may be said to have dated from an incident in the fighting which preceded the establishment of the new dynasty, in which Han Xin, having just made himself master of the area of China called Qi, more or less insisted that Gao-zu, who was in difficulties at the time, should recognize him as King of Qi. This appears to be what the second line of the quatrain is referring to. The first line I think refers to the fact that Han Xin's final undoing came about when one of his servants, fearful that Han Xin was about to proceed against his brother, laid information against him to the empress. (Even the lowest cur, when cornered, will turn and bite you.)

One eighteenth-century scholar thought that the answer to the riddle concealed in this quatrain was 'a close-stool', which certainly fits line 2, and I suppose line 4 too. It makes the riddle seem a somewhat scatological one for a well-bred young lady to compose; though I am not at all sure that a contemporary Chinese would have found the idea of a young lady making jokes about excrement shocking. The best of the solutions proposed seems to me to be 'a hare'. It fits line 1 very well, and the fact that there was a famous remark made by Han Xin and preserved in the history books which has to do with a dog and a hare predisposes me to think that that is the answer. If it is, it is less easy to see in what ways the other lines are relevant, however. In the last resort I have to confess that this quatrain still baffles me.

GUANG-LING

Guang-ling was the starting-point of the magnificent willow-lined Grand Canal constructed for the scandalous emperor Yang-di of the Sui dynasty, who reigned from A.D. 605–16.

The best of the answers that have been suggested for the concealed riddle is 'a toothpick'.

PEACH LEAF FORD

The Peach Leaf Ford near Nanking was named after a favourite concubine of Wang Xian-zhi (A.D. 344–88), son of the celebrated 'grass script' calligrapher Wang Xi-zhi and himself a distinguished calligrapher and littérateur. There was a popular song which was supposed to have been made by Wang Xian-zhi in her honour, though its attribution to him is probably rather fanciful:

> Peach Leaf, o, my Peach Leaf dear,
> Cross the river and have no fear.
> To cross the river you need no oar,
> And here I am waiting upon the shore.

The answer to the riddle is thought to be 'a door-god'. Doorgods (mentioned in chapter 53) took the form of colour prints representing ferocious-looking warriors. They were sold in pairs around the time of the New Year and stuck up on the double doors of gateways to repel evil influences and prevent them from crossing the threshold. Like many other demon-repelling talismans, they were originally made of peach-wood, which was believed to be an effective prophylactic against the powers of darkness. The 'peach-wood' element often remained in the names of such objects long after peach-wood had been replaced by paper or some other material in their manufacture. Thus the slips stuck up at the sides of gateways in chapter 53 (p. 567) are referred to in the Chinese text as 'peach-wood charms' though in fact they were simply strips of scarlet paper.

GREEN MOUND

Green Mound, near Guisui in Suiyuan province, was reputedly the
grave of Lady Bright (Wang Zhaojun, *al.* Ming-fei), the unfortunate
court lady who in the 1st century B.C. was passed off as a Chinese
princess and sent north into the frozen steppes to become the con-
sort of the Hunnish king.

Green Mound is near the banks of the Black River, which, according to one version of the legend, Lady Bright jumped into rather
than continue her journey into a life of exile. It is a tributary of the
Hwang-ho near the most northerly part of its course. In translating it 'Amur' for reasons of poetical expediency I have used the
same licence as the medieval playwright who makes her jump into
the 'Black Dragon River' – which is, in fact, the Chinese name for
the Amur. Green Mound was supposed to be so called because
Lady Bright's grave was the only green place in the miles of surrounding desert.

Lady Bright is associated with the *pipa* (Japanese *biwa*), or
Chinese lute, which as a matter of historical fact may well have
found its way into China round about her time. Chinese painters
generally represent her clothed in furs and holding a *pipa* under one
arm. The twanging string of the second line of the quatrain is
presumably a lute-string. Chinese half-believed, or professed to
believe, that if the person playing a note on a stringed instrument
did so sufficiently sadly or passionately, the string was liable to
break.

The most favoured guess for the riddle is 'an inked string' – the
device which Chinese carpenters used for marking a straight line
on wood.

MA-WEI

Ma-wei was the site of the post-house where Lady Yang (Yang
Gui-fei), another unfortunate Chinese court lady, was strangled.
Lady Yang was the favourite of the Tang emperor Ming-huang
(*reg.* A.D. 712–56), whose infatuation with her is supposed to have
been one of the contributory causes of the An Lushan rebellion.
When the Chinese court fled from Changan on a July night in 756
to escape from the approaching rebels, the emperor's military
escort mutinied at Ma-wei about forty miles west of the city, killing
Lady Yang's cousin, the detested Prime Minister Yang Guozhong,

and insisting that Lady Yang herself should be delivered up to them. She was strangled by the Chief Eunuch and her dead body handed over for the mutinous soldiery to trample on, while the grieving emperor stood helplessly by. According to one tradition, when some years later the emperor – or ex-emperor as he now was – had her buried remains exhumed, everything had disappeared except for a perfume-sachet, which filled the whole grave with its scent. The ex-emperor had this sachet wrapped up in some of his favourite's clothes and reinterred. This is clearly the story that is referred to in the last line of the quatrain.

The most convincing of the various solutions proposed for the concealed riddle is 'scented soap', doubly appropriate because Ming-huang first became enamoured of Lady Yang when he saw her taking a bath. She is, in fact, the naked lady of Bao-yu's crab-flower poem in chapter 37 to which his girl cousins took such exception.

THE MONASTERY AT PU-DONG

This was the scene of the action taking place in that much-loved drama, already several times referred to in the pages of this novel, *The Western Chamber*. The story exists in several different forms, both fictional and dramatic, the best-known being the play by the thirteenth century dramatist Wang Shifu. This, in a heavily-edited seventeenth century version, is the *Western Chamber* so frequently referred to and quoted from in *The Story of the Stone*.

The play's plot, which derives from a short story by Yuan Zhen (A.D. 779–831), a friend and collaborator of the poet Bo Juyi (the 'Po Chü-i' familiar to Western readers through the translations of Arthur Waley), follows the love-affair of a poor young scholar, Zhang Jun-rui, who had taken up lodging in the monastery, and a high-born young lady, Cui Ying-ying, travelling with her widowed mother and her maid, the witty and vivacious Hong-niang ('Reddie'), who acts as the lovers' go-between. The third line of the quatrain refers to the rough treatment meted out to Reddie when the lovers' affair became known. The 'mistress' of that line is Ying-ying's widowed mother.

To my mind the most convincing guess for the concealed riddle is 'a red travelling-lantern'.

THE PLUM-TREE SHRINE

The subject of this quatrain is taken from another much-loved play, *The Return of the Soul* by Tang Xianzu (1550–1616)[1], in which the heroine, Li-niang, dreams of meeting a handsome young scholar called Liu ('willow') while sleeping under a plum-tree in a deserted garden and is so affected by her dream that she pines away and apparently dies. Before she dies she paints a portrait of herself and inscribes a poem on it, the last line of which is the first line of this quatrain. She is buried under the plum-tree beneath which she had had her dream, and her sorrowing father has a Taoist oratory – the Plum-tree Shrine – built near by where prayers may be said perpetually for her soul. Meanwhile Li-niang's dream-lover had himself been dreaming of Li-niang. He eventually finds his way to the shrine and its garden, where he discovers the portrait and inscribed verses (hence the second line of this quatrain), and later has Li-niang exhumed, whereupon she comes back to life and the lovers, after various further vicissitudes, become man and wife.

The subject of the concealed riddle appears to be 'a white silk fan'. Such fans were called 'full moon fans' (cf. line 3 of the quatrain). Like all fans, they would be discarded with the passing of the hot weather and not required again until the following year.

1. A very fine description of this play can be found in Dr H. C. Chang's *Chinese Literature: Popular Fiction and Drama*, Edinburgh 1973, pp. 268–72.

CHARACTERS IN VOL. 2

COUSIN BAO (1) *see* JIA BAO-YU
    (2) *see* XUE BAO-CHAI
COUSIN CHAI *see* XUE BAO-CHAI
COUSIN DAI *see* LIN DAI-YU
COUSIN FENG *see* WANG XI-FENG
COUSIN LIAN *see* JIA LIAN
COUSIN LIN *see* LIN DAI-YU
COUSIN PAN *see* XUE PAN
COUSIN QIN *see* XUE BAO-QIN
COUSIN SHI *see* SHI XIANG-YUN
COUSIN TAN *see* JIA TAN-CHUN
COUSIN WAN *see* LI WAN
COUSIN XI *see* JIA XI-CHUN
COUSIN XUE *see* XUE PAN
COUSIN YING *see* JIA YING-CHUN
COUSIN YUN *see* SHI XIANG-YUN
COUSIN ZHEN son of Jia Jing; acting head of the senior (Ning-guo) branch of the Jia family
CRIMSON maid of Bao-yu later employed by Xi-feng
DAI *see* LIN DAI-YU
DAI-YU *see* LIN DAI-YU
DELICATE junior maid of Dai-yu
DR WANG *see* WANG JI-REN
EBONY maid of Tan-chun
ÉLÉGANTE one of the Jia family's troupe of child actresses
EMERALD maid of Bao-yu
FAITHFUL principal maid of Grandmother Jia
'FARMER SWEETRICE' poetry club pseudonym of LI WAN
FELICITY maid attendant on Xi-feng
FENG *see* WANG XI-FENG
FENG ZI-YING family friend of the younger Jias
FU QIU-FANG sister of Fu Shi
FU SHI ambitious protégé of Jia Zheng
GOLDEN principal maid of Lady Wang
GRANDMOTHER JIA née SHI; widow of Bao-yu's paternal grand-father and head of the Rong-guo branch of the Jia family
GRANNIE LIU an old countrywoman patronized by Xi-feng and later by Grandmother Jia
'GREEN BOY' poetry club pseudonym of JIA BAO-YU
HU-SHI Jia Rong's second wife
HUA ZI-FANG Aroma's elder brother
HUAN *see* JIA HUAN

JIA BAO-YU incarnation of the Stone; the eldest surviving son of Jia Zheng and Lady Wang of Rong-guo House

JIA BIN obscure member of the Jia family in the same generation as Cousin Zhen and Jia Lian

JIA CHANG junior member of the clan given casual employment by the Rong-guo Jias

JIA CONG little son of one of Jia She's concubines

JIA HUAN Bao-yu's half-brother; the son of Jia Zheng and his concubine, 'Aunt' Zhao

JIA HUANG member of the Jia family in reduced circumstances belonging to the same generation as Cousin Zhen and Jia Lian

JIA JING father of Cousin Zhen and nominal head of the Ning-guo branch of the family living in retirement in a Taoist monastery outside the city

JIA JUN young schoolboy attending the Jia family school

JIA LAN Li Wan's little son

JIA LIAN son of Jia She and Lady Xing and husband of Wang Xi-feng

JIA LING⎱ junior members of the clan given casual employment by
JIA PING⎰ the Rong-guo Jias

JIA QIANG distant relation of the Ning-guo Jias patronized by Cousin Zhen and later given charge by the Rong-guo Jias of the family's troupe of actresses

JIA QIAO-JIE little daughter of Jia Lian and Wang Xi-feng

JIA QIN junior member of the clan employed by the Rong-guo Jias to look after the nuns from Prospect Garden in the family temple outside the city

JIA QIONG obscure member of the Jia family in the same generation as Cousin Zhen and Jia Lian

JIA RONG son of Cousin Zhen and You-shi

JIA SHE Jia Zheng's elder brother; father of Jia Lian and Ying-chun

JIA TAN-CHUN daughter of Jia Zheng and 'Aunt' Zhao; half-sister of Bao-yu and second of the 'Three Springs'

JIA XI-CHUN daughter of Jia Jing and younger sister of Cousin Zhen; youngest of the 'Three Springs'

JIA XING obscure junior member of the Jia clan occasionally present at family gatherings

JIA YING-CHUN daughter of Jia She by a concubine; eldest of the 'Three Springs'

JIA YU-CUN a careerist claiming relationship with the Jia family

JIA YUAN-CHUN daughter of Jia Zheng and Lady Wang and elder sister of Bao-yu; the Imperial Concubine

JIA YUN poor relation of the Rong-guo Jias employed by Xi-feng in Prospect Garden

JIA ZHENG Bao-yu's father; the younger of Grandmother Jia's two sons

JIA ZHI obscure junior member of the Jia clan occasionally present at family gatherings

JIA ZHU deceased elder brother of Bao-yu; husband of Li Wan and father of her little son Jia Lan.

JIANG YU-HAN a female impersonator patronized by the Prince of Zhong-shun

JIN WEN-XIANG Faithful's elder brother

KINGFISHER Shi Xiang-yun's maid

'LADY ALL-SPICE' poetry club pseudonym of XUE BAO-CHAI

LADY JIA see GRANDMOTHER JIA

LADY WANG wife of Jia Zheng and mother of Jia Zhu, Yuan-chun and Bao-yu

LADY XING wife of Jia She and mother of Jia Lian

LAI DA Chief Steward of the Rong-guo mansion

LAI SHANG-RONG Lai Da's son, educated and enabled to obtain advancement under the Jia family's patronage

LAI SHENG Chief Steward of the Ning-guo mansion

LANDSCAPE maid of Xi-chun

LI GUI Nannie Li's son; Bao-yu's foster-brother and chief groom

LI QI Li Wan's cousin; younger sister of Li Wen

LI WAN widow of Bao-yu's deceased elder brother, Jia Zhu, and mother of Jia Lan

LI WEN Li Wan's cousin; elder sister of Li Qi

LIN DAI-YU incarnation of the Crimson Pearl Flower; orphaned daughter of Lin Ru-hai and Jia Zheng's sister, Jia Min

LIN ZHI-XIAO
LIN ZHI-XIAO'S WIFE } domestics holding the highest position in the Rong household under the Chief Steward Lai Da

LIU XIANG-LIAN young man of independent means friendly with Lai Shang-rong and the younger Jias

'LOTUS DWELLER' poetry club pseudonym of JIA XI-CHUN

LOU-SHI Jia Jun's mother.

MACKEREL maid of Bao-yu

MAMMA SONG old servant attached to Bao-yu's apartment, mostly employed on errands

MARQUIS OF ZHONG-JING, THE see SHI DING

MASTER BAO see JIA BAO-YU

MASTER RONG see JIA RONG

MELILOT junior maid of Bao-yu
MERRY page in employment of Cousin Zhen and You-shi
MISS BAO *see* XUE BAO-CHAI
MISS LIN *see* LIN DAI-YU
MISS SHI *see* SHI XIANG-YUN
MISS XING *see* XING XIU-YAN
MR LIAN *see* JIA LIAN
MR QIANG *see* JIA QIANG
MR XIA *see* XIA BING-ZHONG
MR ZHEN *see* COUSIN ZHEN
MR ZHU *see* JIA ZHU
MRS BAI mother of Golden and Silver
MRS LAI aged mother of the Chief Steward, Lai Da
MRS LI Li Wan's widowed aunt; mother of Li Wen and Li Qi
MRS LIAN *see* WANG XI-FENG
MRS SONG *see* MAMMA SONG
MRS XUE *see* AUNT XUE
MRS ZHEN *see* YOU-SHI
MRS ZHU *see* LI WAN
MUSK maid of Bao-yu
NANNIE LI Bao-yu's former wet-nurse
NIGHTINGALE principal maid of Dai-yu
NUAGEUSE a sing-song girl
NURSE ZHOU Shi Xiang-yun's nurse
OLD MRS LAI *see* MRS LAI
OLDIE one of Bao-yu's pages
ORIOLE principal maid of Bao-chai
PARROT maid of Grandmother Jia
PATIENCE chief maid and confidante of Wang Xi-feng
PEARL maid of Grandmother Jia
PERIWINKLE Bao-qin's maid
PICTURE principal maid of Xi-chun
'PLANTAIN LOVER' poetry club pseudonym of JIA TAN-CHUN
PLOUGHBOY one of Bao-yu's pages
PRETTIKINS junior maid of Grandmother Jia
PRINCE OF BEI-JING, THE *see* SHUI RONG
PRINCE OF ZHONG-SHUN, THE an ageing pederast, patron of the
    female impersonator 'Bijou'
PROSPER   } maids of Aunt Xue
PROVIDENCE
QIAN SHENG groom in the employment of the Rong-guo mansion
QIAO-JIE *see* JIA QIAO-JIE

QIN ZHONG dead friend of Bao-yu; younger brother of Jia Rong's deceased first wife

RIPPLE maid of Bao-yu

'RIVER QUEEN' poetry club pseudonym of LIN DAI-YU

SCRIBE principal maid of Tan-chun

SHI DING Marquis of Zhong-jing; nephew of Grandmother Jia and uncle of Shi Xiang-yun

SHI XIANG-YUN orphaned great-niece of Grandmother Jia

SHUI RONG Prince of Bei-jing; princely connection of the Jias friendly with Bao-yu

SILVER maid of Lady Wang; Golden's younger sister

SIR SHE *see* JIA SHE

SIR ZHENG *see* JIA ZHENG

SKYBRIGHT maid of Bao-yu

SNOWGOOSE maid of Dai-yu

STEADFAST junior maid in Bao-yu's apartment

STOPPO one of Jia Lian's and Xi-feng's pages

STORKY one of Bao-yu's pages

SUNCLOUD ⎱
SUNSET   ⎰ maids of Lady Wang

SUNSHINE page employed by Wang Xi-feng for clerical duties

SWEEPER one of Bao-yu's pages

TAN *see* JIA TAN-CHUN

TAN-CHUN *see* JIA TAN-CHUN

TANGERINE maid of Ying-chun

TEALEAF Bao-yu's principal page

TOPAZE ⎱
TRÉSOR ⎰ girl-actresses in the Jia family troupe

TRINKET junior maid in Bao-yu's apartment

TWO-TIMES one of Bao-yu's pages

WANG BAN-ER little grandson of Grannie Liu

WANG REN Xi-feng's elder brother

WANG JI-REN doctor in regular attendance on the Rong-guo Jia family

WANG RONG groom in the employment of the Rong-guo mansion

WANG XI-FENG wife of Jia Lian and niece of Lady Wang, Aunt Xue and Wang Zi-teng

WANG ZI-TENG elder brother of Lady Wang and Aunt Xue

WU JIN-XIAO bailiff of the Ning-guo farms

WU XIN-DENG Clerk of Stores at the Rong-guo mansion

XI-CHUN *see* JIA XI-CHUN

XI-FENG *see* WANG XI-FENG

XIA BING-ZHONG eunuch Master of the Bedchamber in the Imperial Palace

XIANG-LIAN *see* LIU XIANG-LIAN

XIANG-YUN *see* SHI XIANG-YUN

XING XIU-YAN Lady Xing's niece; gifted daughter of improvident and sponging parents

XIU-YAN *see* XING XIU-YAN

XUE BAO-CHAI daughter of Aunt Xue

XUE BAO-QIN niece of Aunt Xue and younger sister of Xue Ke

XUE KE Xue Bao-qin's elder brother

XUE PAN the 'Oaf King'; son of Aunt Xue and elder brother of Bao-chai

YING-CHUN *see* JIA YING-CHUN

YOU-SHI wife of Cousin Zhen and mother of Jia Rong

YU-CUN *see* JIA YU-CUN

YUAN-CHUN *see* JIA YUAN-CHUN

YUN (1) *see* SHI XIANG-YUN

  (2) *see* JIA YUN

ZHANG CAI'S WIFE senior domestic employed in the Rong mansion

ZHANG DE-HUI manager of Xue Pan's largest pawnshop

ZHANG RUO-JIN ⎫ grooms in the employment of the Rong-guo
ZHAO YI-HUA ⎭ mansion

Genealogy of the Ning-guo and Rong-guo Houses of the Jia Clan

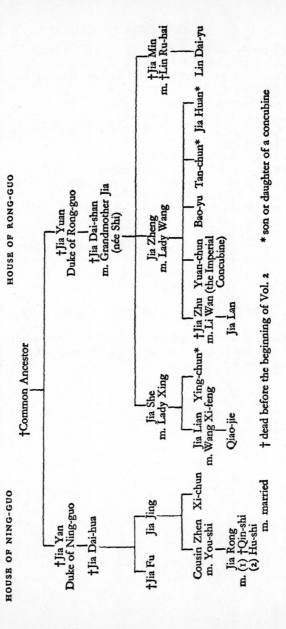

HOUSE OF NING-GUO

HOUSE OF RONG-GUO

†Common Ancestor

†Jia Yan
Duke of Ning-guo

†Jia Dai-hua

†Jia Fu   Jia Jing

Cousin Zhen   Xi-chun
m. You-shi

Jia Rong
m. (1) †Qin-shi
(2) Hu-shi

†Jia Yuan
Duke of Rong-guo

†Jia Dai-shan
m. Grandmother Jia
(née Shi)

Jia She
m. Lady Xing

Jia Lian   Ying-chun*
m. Wang Xi-feng

Qiao-jie

Jia Zheng
m. Lady Wang

†Jia Zhu   Yuan-chun
m. Li Wan   (the Imperial
            Concubine)

Jia Lan

Bao-yu   Tan-chun*   Jia Huan*

†Jia Min
m. †Lin Ru-hai

Lin Dai-yu

m. married   † dead before the beginning of Vol. 2   * son or daughter of a concubine

The Wang Family

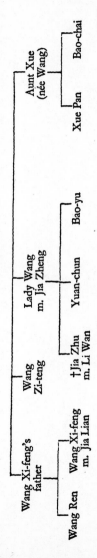

Shi Xiang-yun and the Jias

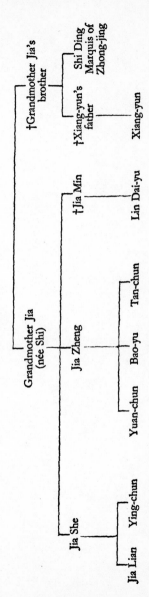